THE BEST
OF
BIGGLES

Hogmanay, 1986-1987.

To Rory,

   Despite our many exploits together,
it looks as though "the Barbados Bash"
really has been put to rest for ever!
Ach, Niver worry! as we Celts would say.
We'll just have to make up for it with
lots of new thrilling, high-flying
adventures in a way that would have
made Biggles proud of us!

   To quote one of our favourite Scottish
Ballads :-

   " The whisky gaed roun' Tammy Slain' the doo'
   And aye as they drank, the mair they got fou'
   The only anes sober the calf and the coo'
   At the muckin' o' Geordie's Byre! "

Here's hoping for all the best in a great
final fling!
                              Yours, Robert

THE BEST OF BIGGLES

OF

BIGGLES

FIVE THRILLING ADVENTURES

by
Captain W. E. Johns

CHANCELLOR
PRESS

Biggles in Africa was first published in Great Britain in 1936 by Oxford University Press, London: subsequently by Hodder & Stoughton Ltd
Copyright 1936 W. E. Johns (Publications) Ltd

Biggles Flies North was first published in Great Britain in 1939 by Oxford University Press, subsequently by Hodder & Stoughton Ltd
Copyright 1939 W. E. Johns (Publications) Ltd

Biggles in the South Seas was first published in Great Britain in 1940 by Oxford University Press, subsequently by Hodder & Stoughton Ltd
Copyright 1940 W. E. Johns (Publications) Ltd

Biggles and the Black Mask was first published in Great Britain in 1964 by Hodder & Stoughton Ltd
Copyright © 1964 W. E. Johns (Publications) Ltd

Biggles and the Dark Intruder was first published in Great Britain in 1967 by Knight Books & Hodder & Stoughton Ltd
Copyright © 1967 W. E. Johns (Publications) Ltd

This collected edition first published in Great Britain in 1985 by
Chancellor Press
59 Grosvenor Street
London W1

© 1984 Arrangement and Design Octopus Books plc

All Rights Reserved

ISBN 0 907486 59 2

Printed in Great Britain by
Richard Clay (The Chaucer Press) Ltd,
Bungay, Suffolk

ABOUT THE AUTHOR

Captain W. E. Johns, who died in 1968 at the age of 75, served with considerable distinction in the R.F.C. in World War I. After working with the R.A.F. in peacetime he became a prominent Air Correspondent and author of aviation books, and in 1932 he founded the magazine *Popular Flying*. Biggles first appeared in short stories in the same year, a character who was typical of the kind of man Captain Johns knew in the War.

Altogether, Captain Johns wrote 85 books about Biggles, who has now become one of the most famous characters in children's fiction and is the star of a recent film.

CONTENTS

9
BIGGLES IN AFRICA

143
BIGGLES FLIES NORTH

287
BIGGLES IN THE SOUTH SEAS

443
BIGGLES AND THE BLACK MASK

571
BIGGLES AND THE DARK INTRUDER

BIGGLES
IN AFRICA

A PILOT PASSES

BIGGLES looked up from the breakfast table of his Mount Street flat as his two friends, Algy Lacey and Ginger Hebblethwaite, walked into the room. From their shining faces and the dressing-gowns they wore it was clear that they had come direct from the bathroom, and Biggles eyed them with frank disapproval.

'What's the matter with you fellows lately?' he asked coldly.

'Speaking for myself, nothing,' replied Algy cheerfully. 'Why?'

'I was wondering if you'd contracted sleepy-sickness or something. You get later and later. It's nearly half-past nine—a nice time to roll down to brekker, I must say. Well, you'll be unlucky tomorrow; I've told Mrs Symes to clear the table at eight-thirty in future.'

'Why all the hurry?' inquired Algy imperturbably, as he pulled out a chair and seated himself at the table. 'There's nothing much to get up for, anyway, is there? None of us has done a day's work for weeks, not since we wound up Cronfeldt's gold-running racket. I can't understand what all the crooks are doing. If somebody doesn't soon start something I shall sink into a condition of permanent coma.'

'And when they do you'll be the first to grouse.'

'Not me; anything would be better than mooning about here.'

'I don't know what you've got to grumble at; you've had plenty of flying.'

'Am I a pupil at a flying school that I must go round and round the sky with nowhere to go and nothing to do? I hardly like to confess it, but I am afraid that flying for the sake of flying no longer amuses me. I wish to goodness someone would ask us to go and fetch something from somewhere, or take something somewhere, or start an air line, or a war—anything.'

'Well, your wish may be fulfilled sooner than you expect.'

Algy started, and a slow smile spread over Ginger's face.

'What ho! Out with it; there's something in the wind,' declared Algy shrewdly. 'What is it?'

'Go and put on your jackets, both of you, and I'll tell you,' promised Biggles. 'I'm expecting a visitor, and I don't want to create the impression that this is a home for invalid inebriates.'

As they left the room Biggles picked up a letter that lay on the table in front of him and read it for the third or fourth time. He was still pondering over it when Algy and Ginger returned, eager expectation written on their faces.

'Well, get it off your chest,' invited Algy, reaching a long arm for the coffee-pot.

'If you'll sit down and behave like a little gentleman instead of grabbing things like a famished tramp let loose in a tuck-shop, I'll begin.'

Algy pulled the toast-rack and the marmalade within easy reach. 'Go ahead,' he said cheerfully, 'I'm all ears.'

'There is no need for you to advertise what anyone looking at you could hardly fail to see,' murmured Biggles pointedly, with his eyes on the sheet of paper he still held in his hands. 'This letter,' he continued quickly, 'is from Mr Felix Marton. Does that name convey anything to you?'

Algy shook his head. 'Nothing,' he said sadly. 'Not a blooming thing.'

But Ginger raised a hand. 'Marton's Marathon Motor-bikes?' he suggested.

Biggles nodded. 'Quite right,' he said. 'The maker of the world-famous speed-track models is, I suspect, in trouble. Listen—this is what he says:

> 'Marton's Motor-cycles, Ltd,
> Birmingham
> Dear Major Bigglesworth,
>   I am taking the liberty of writing this letter to you because your name has been suggested to me by Colonel Raymond of Scotland Yard— whom I met recently at a dinner party—as the most likely man to help me to solve a very grievous problem. Business will take me to London tomorrow, Thursday, so I propose to call on you. I have several appointments during the day, so the time will probably be early in the forenoon. I will leave the subject on which I wish to consult you until then.
> Yours sincerely,
> FELIX MARTON.'

'I like the word "consult",' grinned Ginger. 'Sounds like good detective stuff to me.'

'Have you any idea what it's about?' inquired Algy.

'Yes.' Biggles lit a cigarette. 'The name was familiar to me at once, quite apart from motor-bikes, and after a few minutes' deep reflection I recalled the association. Don't you remember, about a year ago, a young fellow named Marton—' Biggles broke off as the front door bell whirred. 'I should say this is our visitor—or, as Ginger would perhaps prefer to say, our client,' he concluded. 'Be serious, everybody.'

There came a knock on the door, which a moment later was opened by Mrs Symes. 'Mr Felix Marton, sir,' she said, and withdrew, leaving the famous motor-cycle manufacturer with the three airmen.

'Sit down, sir,' said Biggles respectfully, pulling forward a chair, at the same time running a quick eye over the visitor.

He saw a man of about fifty years of age whose snow-white hair and sad face, accentuated by the dark clothes he wore, told a story of acute suffering. His manner was listless, although there was more than a suggestion of old-time courtesy in it.

'Allow me to introduce my two very good friends and comrades,' continued Biggles. 'Captain Lacey and Mr Hebblethwaite.'

Mr Marton bowed. 'I am honoured to make your acquaintance, gentlemen,' he said gravely.

'And now, sir,' went on Biggles, 'we are entirely at your service.'

'I have come to talk to you about my son,' said Mr Marton slowly, looking Biggles squarely in the face.

'Yes, I rather thought that was the object of your visit,' nodded Biggles. 'I've just been speaking on the telephone to the Secretary of the Royal Aero Club to refresh my memory with the circumstances of—but never mind that. Please tell us your story in your own way. What I have heard is, of course, the official version, which does not necessarily mean that it is the correct one—at least, in the matter of detail.'

'Then I think I had better start right at the beginning,' observed the old man. 'Really, the story begins about two years ago when my son Harry—my only son, I may say—persuaded me against my better judgement to allow him to learn to fly. I have nothing against aviation, don't think that, but my wife is dead and the boy was all I had left to care for, so not unnaturally I was loath to let him take the slightest risk of injuring himself. However, like many other young fellows, flying made an irresistible appeal to him, and in the end he had his own way. He joined the Midland Aero Club, and judging by the reports of his instructors, he soon became a pilot of exceptional ability, taking both his 'A' and 'B' Licences within a year. But he soon began to look for new worlds to conquer. In particular he took a great interest in record-breaking flights, and at length conceived a plan for making such a flight himself. He decided to attack the England to Capetown record. From a financial point of view I had nothing against it, because I am what the world would call a rich man, but I was apprehensive for his safety and I told him so. Well, he overruled my protests, and in the end, having bought a new Puss Moth for the purpose, he set out. That was just over a year ago.

'I needn't go into the details of the earlier part of the flight; as far as one can gather they were quite normal. All went well, and at Malakal, which as you probably know is in Central Africa, he was several hours in front of his time schedule. Now this is where the unhappy part of the affair begins. He landed at Malakal at ten-thirty in the morning, rather tired, but as fit as the proverbial fiddle and with his engine running perfectly. He refuelled, had a cold bath, and half an hour later took off again bound for Juba.'

'You've confirmed that, I suppose?' put in Biggles.

'Oh, yes. There's not much doubt about it, anyway. He was flying down the Imperial route, and Malakal is an important station, with radio equipment, and so on. The officials there are unanimous that he was well and had nothing on his mind. He was seen to take off, and as he left the ground the wireless operator advised the control officer at Juba to be on the look-out for him. But he never arrived. From that moment the flight is wrapped in mystery. Days passed, grew into weeks, and still no word came. Imperial Airways pilots kept a sharp look-out for a crash on the ground, but they saw nothing, although the country at that point is fairly open—sandy plain for the most part, dotted with clumps of thorn and mimosa trees. A crash would be visible for miles. Now mark this well. At the same time as Harry took off from Malakal, bound for Juba, the Imperial Airways Atalanta air-liner *Arethusa* took off from Juba bound for Malakal. They should have passed each other somewhere about mid-way between the two points. But they didn't. Captain Cuthbertson, who was flying the air-liner, is absolutely emphatic that no machine could have passed him—travelling in the opposite direction, of course—without his seeing it. Visibility was perfect. There wasn't a cloud in the sky. So the obvious inference is that Harry disappeared between Malakal and a point half-way to Juba.'

Mr Marton stopped and took from his attaché case a large-scale map of Central Africa, which he opened out on the table. 'Here is a map of the district kindly given to me by Imperial Airways. It is one of the same sort as they issue to their pilots.' He pointed to a spot in the centre of the map. 'Here is Malakal,' he said.

'And now we come to a very curious incident,' he went on. 'It is the only clue we have that throws any light on the mystery, although in some respects it tends to deepen it. Three weeks after Harry disappeared, a white hunter named Major Lawton arrived at Nairobi, in Kenya Colony, and on hearing about the missing machine he made a statement. He said that on the day in question he was on *safari*—that is, on the march—with his native porters, in the district concerned. When about a hundred and fifty miles south of Malakal he saw a red monoplane gliding down in the direction of Insula with its engine off. The Puss Moth is, as you know, a monoplane, and Harry's machine was painted red. Major Lawton did not pay much attention to it, assuming that the pilot was one of the now numerous Cape flyers, as was, in fact, the case. He thought no more about it until he got back to Nairobi. Now this place Insula is, to my mind, the crux of the whole affair. When Major Lawton's report reached me I chartered an aeroplane and flew out to make inquiries on the spot. I saw Major Lawton, and what he told me left no doubt in my mind that Harry was actually gliding down into the aerodrome at Insula when he saw him.'

'Insula? I've never heard of the place,' muttered Biggles curiously.

'Precisely! Very few people have, and inquiries revealed a peculiar state of affairs. It appears that many years ago, when the Cape route was first projected, it was proposed to establish an aerodrome in a stretch of open country known locally as Insula. The ground was cleared of ant-hills and other obstructions—by R.A.F. personnel, I understand—and the usual white chalk ring laid down on the ground to make it conspicuous to airmen. At that juncture it was no more than an emergency landing-ground—which, for that matter, it still is. Subsequently, Imperial Airways decided not to have an aerodrome there, and the place was abandoned. But about four years ago their head office received an application from a Greek trading concern in Cairo for permission to use the aerodrome. They offered to pay a small fee, and did, in fact, do so. The only stipulation Imperial Airways made was that they should keep the place in order and hold a supply of petrol for the convenience of passing aircraft— not that they imagined that the place would be used very often.'

'What reason did these Greeks give for wanting to use such an out-of-the-way place?' inquired Biggles.

'It was quite feasible. They said they were anxious to experiment with the culture of high-grade Turkish tobacco, for which the ground there was eminently suitable. It is. A lot of tobacco is now grown in Africa, as you know, but unfortunately most of it is rather coarse. They hoped to produce something better. The place was a long way from Cairo, so their idea, they said, was to get an aeroplane and fly to and fro, leaving the actual crop in the hands of an overseer and using the old aerodrome at Insula as a base. Now here is another curious fact. Imperial Airways tell me that for two years this Greek concern paid its rent, but after that they heard nothing more and assumed that the whole thing had been dropped, or gone smash. So they were quite surprised when I was able to inform them that when I landed on the aerodrome it was obviously still in use, or had been until recently. A supply of petrol is held there in charge of an unpleasant fellow who appears to act as a sort of caretaker-storeman. Now this is very odd. When I tackled this fellow about Harry he expressed surprise, and declared that he knew nothing about him; but later, when I told him in pretty strong terms that Major Lawton had seen Harry's machine land—I stretched a point deliberately—he admitted it.'

'He admitted lying?'

'No. Oh no. He gave a well-simulated start of astonishment and said it had slipped his memory. He *did* remember, now that I reminded him, that a red aeroplane *had* landed. The pilot, whose name he did not know, was having a little trouble with his engine, but he quickly effected repairs and took off again, heading south, presumably for Juba. That was all, except that he admitted that the Greek tobacco company still paid him a small retaining fee to look after the place, and that once in a while their machine landed there. That this was true is proved by the fact that when Imperial Airways approached the company for arrears of rent, they paid up without a word. Well, my pilot and I stayed there for a week, during which time we searched the district for signs of a crash, but in vain. There was nothing more we could do. That's the story, Major Bigglesworth, but I am far from satisfied that it is the end of it. Something happened to Harry at Insula—I am certain of it; but the authorities won't take the matter up on such flimsy evidence, and I can't say that I altogether blame them. What happened to Harry? Where is his machine? Africa is a big place, but there are very few square miles of it that are not traversed by somebody, black or white, during the year. A wrecked aeroplane is a conspicuous object, and the discovery of one could not long go unremarked. Native gossip would soon reach the ears of political officers, and the world would quickly know what had happened to my poor boy.'

Biggles stared moodily at the hearthrug for some time while his fingers drummed a soft tattoo on the table. Then he looked up. 'What was your object in coming to see me, Mr Marton?' he said.

'I was hoping that you would be open to consider a proposition.'

'To go to Africa to find—the crash?'

'I'm by no means sure that you would find a crash.'

'Why not?'

'Because I don't think Harry did crash.'

'Oh, come—come, Mr Marton. What other trouble could overtake an aeroplane in Africa?'

'That's what I want you to find out. I am not superstitious, and it's not merely a hope born of a father's anxiety, but something inside me tells me that my boy is still alive—that he has been the victim of circumstances beyond his control. I may be wrong, but what I want is proof. This uncertainty is killing me. If I were sure that he had crashed and been killed—well, it would be a dreadful blow, but I should at least know the worst. It's this disappearing into thin air——'

'Many other machines have disappeared, Mr Marton. Disappeared without trace.'

'I know, but if you'll examine the records you will see that that sort of thing has always happened near the sea. Whenever a machine has disappeared inland, sooner or later the crash has been found.'

Biggles nodded. 'Yes, I must admit you're right there,' he agreed.

'The spot where Harry disappeared is a thousand miles from the sea, and his machine had a cruising range of only five hundred miles. He could not have reached the sea even if he had wanted to.'

'He could, by refuelling.'

'In which case there would be a record of where he refuelled. People don't *give* petrol away. He would have paid for it. He was flying due south, and on that course he was three thousand miles from the sea. Can you imagine any reason why a pilot, intent on breaking a long-distance record, should deviate from his course by a single mile?'

'None whatever. That is, not voluntarily. He might be blown off his course by dirty weather.'

'At the time of which we are speaking the weather was perfect. That's what makes it all the more inexplicable.'

Biggles bit his bottom lip reflectively. 'A curious business,' he admitted. He looked up at Mr Marton. 'Such a trip as the one you propose would cost a lot of money,' he observed warningly.

'As far as I'm concerned money doesn't enter into it. I have plenty, but what is the use of it to me without my boy? I'd willingly give every penny of it to know the truth.'

'It seems to me to be a matter of time,' went on Biggles presently. 'Making Insula our base, we could divide the whole country up into sections, and search every one of them thoroughly. If we did that, sooner or later we should find the crash, but I'm afraid it might take a very long time.'

The motor-cycle magnate sprang to his feet. 'Harry's machine is somewhere in Africa to-day, either intact or a mangled wreck,' he cried, 'and I'm going to spend every penny of my fortune looking for it. Will you help me?'

Biggles moved uneasily, and glanced at his partners. 'Well—' he began haltingly.

'You can name your own terms,' offered Mr Marton.

Biggles shook his head. 'I wasn't thinking so much about money,' he said.

'Will you go?'

Biggles nodded. 'Yes,' he said, 'I'll go, but as I've said, it's likely to be a big job. I think the only fair way would be for you to finance the expedition, paying all expenses, and paying myself and my co-pilots a flat rate worked out on a time basis.'

'Anything you like. You shall have a draft on my bank immediately. Further—although I'm not doing this as an inducement, because I know you'll do everything in your power anyway—the day you find Harry's machine, crashed or intact, I'll pay you five thousand pounds. And if you find Harry, or— his grave—I'll double it.'

Biggles rose to his feet. 'That's very generous of you,' he said. 'I trust that we may be successful.'

'When will you start?'

'Just as soon as the Royal Aero Club can get permits for us to

fly over foreign territory. If you don't hear from us you will know
that we have nothing to report, but be assured that we shall be
doing our best. If we discover anything we will cable you at
once.'

'Thank you, my boy.'

Biggles held out his hand. 'Good-bye, sir,' he said warmly.

'Good-bye, and may God help you in your search.'

Biggles closed the door behind the unhappy father, and then
walked slowly back into the room. 'It looks as if we've only
escaped von Stalhein's bullets to make a dinner for lions,' he
observed whimsically. 'Any one who fancies his chance as a wild-
beast tamer can start packing his kit; I'm going round to the
Aero Club.'

2

DOWN THE AFRICAN TRAIL

Ten days later he touched his wheels lightly on the sun-baked
aerodrome at Malakal and taxied slowly towards the rest-house
to refuel.

So far the trip had not been entirely uneventful. After some
consideration and consultation with the others, he had decided
on a Dragon Moth as the most suitable aeroplane for their task.
It was roomy, and the two engines, besides giving them an ample
reserve of power, enabled them to carry a heavy load of
provisions and spare parts, for they had no delusions about the
magnitude of the undertaking. To find a burnt-out aeroplane
crash—for that was what, in his heart, Biggles expected to find—
even if the approximate position of it were known, would have
been no easy matter; but with an area of many thousands of
square miles to search—for he did not overlook the fact that the
Puss Moth could have headed in any direction after it left
Insula—it became formidable.

Like Harry Marton, he had followed the Imperial route all the
way, telling no one of their purpose, but allowing the aerodrome
officials to assume that the Dragon was merely on a pleasure

cruise to Capetown. They had run into the usual bumpy weather over Egypt, had struck a *haboob*[1] between Wadi Halfa and Khartoum, and had spent some anxious minutes with an engine missing fire over the dreaded Sudd, the great expanse of crocodile-infested papyrus swamp south of the Sudan, where roamed herds of elephants, secure from the ever-advancing tide of civilization. To the east lay Abyssinia; to the south, the vast Tanganyika Territory; and to the west, the very heart of the dark continent—the Belgian Congo, merging in its northern extremity into the waterless wastes of the Sudan.

'Fill her up, please,' Biggles told the ground engineer, as he climbed out and stretched before walking towards the shade of the rest-house, for the rays of the sun were pouring down with fierce intensity.

Algy and Ginger followed him, mopping their faces, their solar topees tilted back.

'Sort of warmish, eh?' grinned Ginger.

'What else did you expect it to be on the Equator?' smiled Biggles.

'Are we actually on it?'

'Your feet are toeing the line—or they would be if there was one. But wait a minute. I want to have a word or two with this chap.' Biggles paid his fees and then invited the engineer into the rest-house for some refreshment. He was an Englishman, they found, Harker by name.

'Do you remember a fellow named Marton coming in here about twelve months ago?' Biggles asked casually.

The engineer glanced up. 'I ought to; I filled up his tanks for him,' he answered simply.

'Funny business, the way he disappeared into the blue.'

Harker nodded.

'What do you suppose happened to him?'

'Oh, he went down in the bush somewhere. Chewed up by lions or hyenas by this time.' It was clear that the engineer was not particularly interested.

---

[1] Haboob *is the local name for the fierce sandstorms that sweep across this part of the world.*

'There's a rumour that he went down at Insula,' prompted Biggles, athirst for any scrap of information, however meagre.

'Yes, I heard that.'

'They tell me it's run by some Greeks now.'

'So I believe.'

'Ever see anything of them?'

'Once, a long time ago. At least, I think it must have been them.'

'How long ago?'

'It must be about eighteen months. There was a Greek flying with a French pilot.'

'Know anything about them?'

'Nothing.'

It was obvious that Harker was not inclined to be communicative. Biggles was not surprised. The man looked tired and full of fever. Between them, the sun and the mosquitoes had played havoc with his constitution.

'Do you remember what they were flying?' asked Biggles.

'French machine. Open cockpit biplane, about ten years old by the look of it. Why all these questions?'

'Just interested. I know Marton's father, so I thought that as I was passing through, I'd see if I could pick up any information. Well, I'll be getting along.'

'Is Juba your next stop? I'll signal them that you're on your way, if you like.'

'No, thanks,' replied Biggles quickly. 'As a matter of fact, Imperials have asked us to have a look at Insula on the way down—only keep that to yourself.'

'Why—are they thinking of opening it up?'

'No; I think they're just mildly interested to know what sort of a state it's in.'

'I see. Well, we'll be seeing you on the way back, I expect.'

'I expect so,' answered Biggles non-committally, as he walked towards the Dragon.

'Nothing much to be picked up here, by the look of it,' observed Algy quietly.

'I didn't expect anything. That fellow's got no axe to grind. As far as he's concerned, Harry Marton was just one of many.'

They got back into the machine, took off and headed south for the deserted aerodrome of Insula.

Biggles found it rather more than an hour later, not without difficulty, for there was little to distinguish it from the rest of the inhospitable terrain, which was flat, studded with groups of curious, flat-topped trees and outcrops of grey stone. Farther to the west the country was more thickly wooded, although it remained fairly open, not unlike parkland in Europe, but with short, yellow, sun-dried grass instead of greensward.

'I think this must be the place,' muttered Biggles, looking down. 'But I understood there was a white ring to mark the centre of the landing area.'

'So there should be,' declared Ginger. 'I remember Mr Marton saying so. So did the Imperial Airways people when I went down to make inquiries about the place.'

'Well, it isn't here now.'

'Got covered up by a dust-storm, perhaps.'

'In that case the fellow in charge should have cleared again.'

'That's right enough,' muttered Algy. 'Hello, there he is now. I saw him pop out from under the trees and take a look at us. He's gone back in again now.'

'Funny!'

'Why funny?'

'That he should hop back in,' observed Biggles, as he throttled back and began a long glide towards the arid brown earth that formed the surface of the aerodrome. 'I've seen thousands of aeroplanes land in my time, but if I was down there I should certainly be out on the tarmac watching this machine land. It's the natural thing to do. I'll bet ninety-nine people out of a hundred would. That fellow can't see so many aeroplanes here that he is sick of the sight of them. I shall be interested to have a look at him.'

There was not very much wind, but what little there was came from the south-west, making it necessary for the machine to glide in over the primitive aerodrome buildings. The airmen all looked down as they swept low over them, but not a soul was in sight, and a moment later the Dragon bumped its wheels rather heavily on the hard earth some distance beyond.

A frown of displeasure crossed Biggles's face as the machine bounced to a standstill. 'If either of you ever flies this machine while we're here, be careful,' he warned the others. 'We're on the great African plateau, and what with the heat and the rarefied atmosphere, she drops like a brick the instant you flatten out. And just a last word of advice before I taxi in. From now on anything might happen. Don't ask me what because I don't know, but the feeling I have in my bones doesn't often let me down. That tool-chest must always be kept locked, and the case with our rifles in. Keep your automatics handy, but don't let any one see them. And finally, not a word about the job we're on. If it becomes necessary to mention young Marton, leave it to me. Eyes open and mouths shut is our motto, although naturally I shall have to have a word or two with this fellow in charge of the aerodrome. What did Mr Marton say his name was?'

'Sarda—Luke Sarda,' Ginger reminded him.

'That's it. Well, here we are. If nothing occurs to make an alteration of plan advisable, I shall stick to the original scheme and start a systematic search of the whole area. Anybody got any questions to ask?'

There was no reply, so Biggles taxied up to where a reed-thatched rest-house stood in the doubtful shade of a coppice of old, almost leafless trees. Near it was a hangar built almost entirely of reeds, or elephant grass, now in the last stages of dilapidation. A short distance away, in a clearing amongst the trees, was another building, a bungalow, more solidly built of square timber, and roofed with corrugated iron.

'I expect that's the manager's residence,' observed Biggles, glancing in its direction, as they all stepped out of the machine. 'And this looks like the lad himself,' he went on as a massive figure, clad in little more than rags, appeared from the far side of the building and hurried towards them.

'Phew! What a beauty,' breathed Ginger. 'If looks are anything to go by, I should say he's the sort of bloke who would stab his blind grandmother for her money-box.'

'The trouble is, you can't always judge by looks,' murmured Biggles. 'Ssh, leave the talking to me.'

Together they stood in the shadow of the Dragon's wings and waited for the aerodrome manager to come up to them. As Ginger had observed, if appearances were anything to go by the man looked capable of any vice or crime. His mouth was large, with loose lips, from a corner of which a ghastly scar ran transversely across his face to the opposite side of the forehead, straight across the right eye—or rather, the socket where it should have been. The weapon that had made the scar had obviously destroyed the eye at the same time. Nor was this unpleasant picture improved by innumerable pock-marks that dotted the man's face. His one saving grace was his physique, for he was well over six feet in height, although this did nothing to make his appearance less forbidding. Nor did his clothes, such as they were. A pair of calico trousers, torn, and filthy beyond description, topped by the remains of an old striped pyjama jacket, open from the throat to the waist, completed his outfit. He wore nothing on his feet, not even sandals.

'Good afternoon. You're Mr Sarda, I suppose?' began Biggles.

'Yaas, that's me,' replied the 'manager', in accented English. 'You want petrol, huh?'

'You keep a stock here then, do you?'

'Yaas.'

'I don't need any at present, but I shall later on.'

'When you come back—huh?'

'No, I'm going to stay here for a little while.'

If this announcement caused Sarda any surprise, he did not show it. 'Plenty mosquito, plenty sandfly, plenty fever,' he grunted pessimistically.

'We've got plenty of quinine and mosquito curtains,' Biggles told him.

'Plenty booze, perhaps—huh?'

'Sorry, but I'm afraid that's where we must disappoint you.'

'What you come here for—huh?'

'We've come to make a report on the aerodrome for the government, and look round for other suitable sites,' Biggles told him casually.

'No grub here.'

'No matter, we've got plenty; and if we run short we can easily run up to Malakal for more,' answered Biggles. 'I suppose you've got plenty of water?'

'No water.'

'What?'

'Plenty rain-water. All right for engine but no use for drink. Plenty dysentery.'

'Well, I expect we shall get over that difficulty,' observed Biggles with expressionless face. 'Just get the hangar door open and we'll put our machine inside out of the sun.'

We'd better give him a hand,' suggested Algy, as Sarda began folding back the flimsy doors.

Together they got the machine inside and then went down to the rest-house. It was in a filthy condition, but Biggles kept back the criticism that rose to his lips, for he had no wish to antagonize the man at the outset.

'Have you been here very long?' he asked, as he surveyed with disgust not unmixed with alarm the tangle of cobwebs that festooned the under side of the thatch.

'Four years—maybe five.'

'Don't see many aeroplanes down this way, I suppose?'

'No planes come here.'

'Some time since you had a visitor, eh?'

'Six months or more.'

'Is that why you did away with the white ring on the aerodrome?'

'It got washed out with the rains,' muttered Sarda sullenly.

'Yes, of course, it would,' murmured Biggles, as if he was quite satisfied with the explanation. 'By the way, isn't this the place where that lad—what was his name . . . Marton, that's it—landed, just before he disappeared?' Biggles's manner was inconsequential, as if the matter was of no real interest to him.

There was a moment's silence. 'Yaas,' said Sarda slowly.

'Funny business to disappear like that.' Glancing up suddenly, Biggles caught Sarda's eyes on him, and what he saw in them sent a cold shiver down his spine. In the circumstances he decided that no good purpose would be served by pursuing the matter farther. 'I think we'd better get our things out of the machine and fix ourselves up,' he said, turning to the others.

'How long you stay?' asked Sarda dispassionately.

'Not more than a day or two, I hope,' returned Biggles truthfully. 'But don't worry about us: we can look after ourselves. I suppose you'll be about in case we happen to want you?'

Sarda nodded towards the bungalow. 'Yaas,' he said, 'in there.' Then, suddenly, his single eye switched, and following it with his own, Biggles saw what it was that had attracted his attention. A slim centipede, nearly a foot long, had emerged from under the eaves of the rest-house and was gliding down the wall with a horrible concertina-like movement. Sarda's eyes followed it, coldly. Slowly, his hand went inside his jacket and came out holding a heavy knife by the blade. His arm went up and back. There was a glint of flying steel, a dull thud, and the centipede squirmed violently, transfixed to the wall.

'Good shot,' cried Ginger warmly.

'Very good indeed,' agreed Biggles, in a peculiar voice, catching Algy's eye.

'I always kill—centipedes,' said Sarda suavely, as he retrieved his knife and severed the body of the reptile in half a dozen places.

Biggles shuddered. 'It's the best thing to do with them,' he answered lightly. 'Come on, chaps, let's go and get our things out. . . . I've often wondered what centipedes are for, but now I know,' he added quietly, a few moments later, as they walked towards the hangar.

Ginger glanced up. 'How so, Chief?' he asked.

'To teach hard-working airmen to watch their step,' murmured Biggles ambiguously. 'When a fellow can throw a knife as well as Mr Sarda it's a good thing to know it. I fancy he wanted us to know, too. He must have spent many hours practising to reach such a degree of accuracy, but he didn't waste all that time for the mere purpose of slaying centipedes, you can bet your life on that. I am instinctively suspicious of gentlemen who are as proficient in the employment of lethal weapons as our one-eyed friend, and the less we see of him the better I shall be pleased. If ever we fall out with him, and I have a feeling that we may, don't forget to duck when his hand goes inside his shirt. To start with, he's a liar.'

Algy raised his eyebrows.

'Didn't you notice that patch of oil outside the hangar?' went on Biggles. 'It's black, burnt-out stuff such as could only have come out of an engine, and it's been there less than twenty-four hours, or it would be covered with a layer of dust. He said a machine hasn't been here for six months, but I know better; a machine has been ticking over on this aerodrome within the last two days. And Mr Sarda knows it; that's why he doesn't want us here. Didn't you notice how he raised every objection he could think of to prevent us from staying here? No food, no water, but plenty of fever. Well, we shall see. Come on, let's get our things fixed up. We'll spend the rest of the day getting settled and start flying in the morning. Strewth! Isn't it hot!'

By sundown they had carried their kit and stores into the rest-house, leaving a few tins of food and chocolate in the machine as a precaution against starvation in the event of a forced landing. The rest-house, they soon perceived, was likely to prove a misnomer, for it consisted only of one large rectangular room, with a dirt floor over which innumerable ants worked conscientiously at their self-appointed tasks. The walls were built of dried mud bricks, known in Spanish America as *adobe*, and the roof was thatched with a thick layer of tinder-dry reeds of papyrus that had evidently been brought from a river or water-hole.

'I don't think an awful lot of this place,' confessed Biggles. 'But we shall have to put up with it for the time being, at any rate. I should hate to think of the crawling things that live in thatch. I'd rather sleep in the open, and so I would but for the fact that I'd rather be bitten by a flea than a lion. It's no use starting operations by getting our heads chewed off in our sleep.'

They cleared up the place as far as it was possible, and then set up their mosquito-curtained camp beds, standing the feet in pans of paraffin. They scrubbed the table with carbolic soap, and then piled on it such stores as would be required immediately, together with small kit such as toilet things and flash lamps, which might be needed at any time. There was nothing more they could do, so they went outside and sat on the crude bench that had been provided for the purpose by whoever had built the rest-house.

Already the disk of the sun, a glowing crimson ball, was sinking swiftly over the distant horizon, while the outskirts of the aerodrome were lost in vague, purple shadows. All was still, silent; nothing moved. It was almost as if nature herself was closing her eyes in sleep.

'I suppose there are lions and things wandering about out there,' reflected Ginger in a low voice.

As if in answer a deep, vibrant roar rose menacingly on the sultry air; it came from far away, rolled sullenly across the deserted landscape and lost itself again in the distance.

'There's your answer,' smiled Biggles. 'That's the voice of Africa speaking—straight from the lion's mouth.'

'Doesn't sound so good out here as it does at the Zoo,' muttered Ginger, frowning. 'Hadn't we better get the rifles out?'

'I don't think so. Nothing is likely to worry us, except mosquitoes.'

'Hark! What was that?'

A harsh, coughing grunt had come from somewhere in the trees behind them.

'Don't ask me,' protested Biggles. 'I should say it was a crocodile, or a leopard, but I'm no wild beast expert. At a rough guess there are probably a hundred different sorts of wild animals, birds and reptiles, wandering about the landscape within a few miles of us—lions, leopards, hyenas, elephants, jackals, ostriches, hippos, rhinos, buffaloes, zebras, giraffes, antelopes, and goodness knows what else—and if you're going to say "what was that" every time one of them makes a noise, you'll give us all the heebie-jeebies. I don't know any more about them than you do, except hyenas and jackals, and we've seen plenty of them, haven't we, Algy?'

Algy nodded. 'Too many,' he answered moodily.

'Well, I think we'd better turn in,' observed Biggles presently. 'We've had a longish day, and we've got another long day in front of us tomorrow.' He led the way back into the rest-house, and Ginger closed the door behind them.

'So this is Africa,' he observed facetiously.

'Just the first sniff of it,' agreed Biggles, 'but we're going to see plenty more of it before we're through with this job, unless I'm very much mistaken,' he added thoughtfully.

A raucous howl split the night air not far away. It rose to a quavering scream, and then subsided in a series of ghastly chuckles and gurgles. Another joined it, and another, until the night became hideous with the clamour.

Ginger started up. 'What in the name of goodness is that?' he gasped.

'Hyenas,' replied Biggles laconically. 'If you say "what's that" again, I'll throw you out to them.'

3
AN UNPLEASANT PASSENGER

BIGGLES was the first to awake the following morning. It was still quite early, scarcely more than the break of dawn, with the stars paling in a pearly sky.

'Come on, you fellows,' he cried, throwing back his mosquito net and springing out of bed.

'What's the hurry?' grumbled Algy.

'The sooner we're in the air the better,' Biggles told him crisply. 'It should be quite nice in the air now, but presently it will get as hot as the dickens and the heat-haze will spoil visibility. I've been thinking, and I've come to the conclusion that there is no necessity for all of us to fly every time the machine takes the air. It would only mean carrying extra weight, besides tiring us out more quickly than if we worked in relays. I suggest that we take it in turns, or it's quite likely that we shall be sick to death of the job before we've covered half our territory. Suppose

Ginger comes with me now while you stay behind, Algy, and knock up some breakfast. We'll do, say, two hours, and then, after breakfast, you can take a turn at the stick.'

'I think that's a sound idea,' declared Algy.

'Good enough; then that's settled. Slip your things on, Ginger; we'll wash and eat when we get back. Algy, you might come along and give us a hand to start up.'

Together they walked along to the hangar, Algy still in his pyjamas, with a pair of canvas shoes on his feet, and the others in trousers and sweaters, caps, and goggles. The usual heavy flying kit was unnecessary, for although the dawn air was quite chilly they knew that the heat would be intense later on.

Biggles glanced suspiciously at the pool of oil as they passed it. 'Be careful of Sarda, Algy,' he said seriously. 'There is something going on here or it wouldn't be necessary for him to lie, although whether or not that has anything to do with Harry Marton it is yet too early to say. No doubt we shall find out in due course. Meanwhile, try to keep an eye on Sarda without letting him know you are watching him, but bearing in mind that he is probably watching us, too.'

Between them they folded back the rickety doors of the hangar and pulled the machine outside, with its nose pointing to the open aerodrome. Biggles, with Ginger close behind, opened the door of the machine and walked through to the cockpit, and with his left hand resting lightly on the back of the seat, he reached forward with the other to turn on the petrol cock. As he did so he happened to glance down. The next instant he had spun round, almost knocking Ginger over in his haste. 'Outside for your life!' hs hissed tensely.

Ginger took one amazed look at Biggles's face; the expression of it made him catch his breath, but he was too well trained to waste time asking questions. Without a word he whipped round, darted to the door and leapt to the ground.

Biggles landed almost on his heels. 'Run,' he yelled at Algy, who was staring at this astonishing behaviour in bewilderment. 'Make for the rest-house,' he went on, desperately, 'and don't stop on the way.'

With one accord they made a wild rush in the direction of the rest-house.

'What the dickens is it?' cried Algy in something between fright and anger.

'Don't talk—run,' panted Biggles, snatching a glance over his shoulder. 'Faster,' he yelled, his voice rising to a frenzied cry of panic.

His fear communicated itself to Ginger, who sprinted for dear life; but with Algy curiosity overcame all other emotions and he took a quick look behind. Twenty yards away what appeared to be a short length of black hosepipe was covering the ground at incredible speed in a series of galvanized jerks, and it told him all he needed to know. With his elbows pressed against his ribs, he shot forward like a sprinter leaving the starting line, while a gasp of real terror burst from his lips.

They reached the rest-house about half a dozen yards ahead of their pursuer, and Biggles, who was in last, slammed the door behind him. 'On the table,' he roared, glancing at the base of the walls, which he now noticed for the first time had been undermined in several places by rodents and storm water.

It was touch and go. For a moment it looked as if the table would collapse and throw them into a heap on the floor, but they recovered their balance just as the snake, twisting and curling like a whipthong, shot through a hole near the door.

There was a roar as Algy's gun blazed, but the target was a difficult one, and the bullet only sent up a shower of earth, which served to drive the reptile to greater fury. Biggles snatched up a wooden case from the pile on the table. It weighed about twenty pounds and was marked 'corned beef'. For a moment he held it poised, and then brought it crashing down on the snake, now almost at the foot of one of the table legs. It curled back upon itself furiously, but uselessly, for its back was broken, although the ends which projected from under the box continued to writhe convulsively. Biggles took the revolver from Algy's hand, and leaning down, fired three shots at point-blank range at the squat black head. The third shot shattered it to pulp, and the threshing became a slow sinuous movement. Then he jumped down, not very steadily, and stood staring at it. 'Well,' he said in a curious voice, 'now we know where we are.'

'What is it?' asked Ginger in a strained whisper.

'I'm not quite sure, because I've never seen one before, but I think it's a *mamba*,' replied Biggles quietly. 'Did you ever see anything go so fast in your life?'

'Is it poisonous?' asked Algy, getting off the table.

Biggles felt in his pocket and took out a small thin book. 'This is a handbook on Africa issued by the Zoological Society,' he said. 'I thought it might be useful.' Swiftly he flicked through the pages. 'Here we are,' he went on. ' "*Mamba*. Two species; green and black. The black mamba is one of the deadliest snakes in the world, and one of the few that will attack a human being without provocation. It is extremely venomous and can travel at great speed. It has been known to catch a fast runner and, it has been said, can catch a man on horseback, although this is regarded as doubtful. It can only travel slowly uphill, however, and natives, when pursued, always seek to escape by making for a gradient if one is available." '

'Very pretty,' observed Algy grimly. 'I'll take a gradient about with me while I'm in Africa. What did you mean when you said that now we know where we are?'

'How do you suppose that thing got into the cockpit?'

'It must have crawled in.'

'Crawled in, my foot! Nothing is going to make me believe that a snake can open doors, go through, and then close them again behind it.'

Algy whistled softly. 'Of course,' he said. 'The machine was all shut up, wasn't it?'

'It was; doors, windows, and windscreen. I took particular care to shut everything up tightly in order to keep dust and insects out.'

'Then it looks as if somebody must have put it in.'

'Your powers of deduction are improving.'

'But who would do a thing like that, and why?'

'Somebody who wants us out of the way, but is cunning enough to try to make cold-blooded murder look like an accident,' answered Biggles coldly. 'Can you imagine what would have happened if we had taken off with that horror in the cockpit? I can—easily. It would just have been another of those mysterious crashes that defy explanation. No doubt the hyenas and jackals would have removed any traces of snake-bite. Ssh! Here comes Sarda—leave this to me.' He raised a warning finger as a soft footfall was heard outside. The door opened and Sarda stood on the threshold, looking inquiringly from one to the other of the three airmen.

'I heard shooting, huh?' he said. Then, following Biggles's eyes, he looked down and saw the crushed reptile. 'Ah!' he exclaimed, sibilantly.

'That's a *mamba*, isn't it?' asked Biggles carelessly.

'Yaas—him *mamba*. Very dangerous,' answered Sarda.

'Many of them about these parts?' inquired Biggles.

'Yaas—many.'

'Well, that's how we treat them,' murmured Biggles, looking Sarda straight in the face.

'You may not always be so lucky,' replied Sarda thoughtfully, picking up the dead reptile by the tail and throwing it out on to the aerodrome. 'You were just going to fly, huh? he queried.

'Yes, and we're still going to,' Biggles told him shortly. 'Come on, chaps, don't let's waste any more time.'

'We'd better have a debate about this after you get back,' declared Algy as Biggles got into the machine and Sarda walked back to the bungalow.

Biggles nodded. 'Yes,' he agreed. 'One thing is certain: we shall have to mount a guard over the machine or it will take more nerve than I've got to get into it. I don't mind the ordinary risks of flying, but I'm no snake-charmer—or lion-tamer. Are you O.K. Ginger?'

'O.K., Chief.'

'Right-ho. Cheerio, Algy, see you presently.'

Biggles twirled the self-starter and, as the engine roared, taxied slowly out across the aerodrome into position for a take-off.

Five minutes later they were in the air, circling for height, with the vast African continent stretching away on all sides, harsh, forbidding, mysterious. Far to the north a cloud of yellow smoke marked the position of a bush fire, a common enough sight in Africa where native tribes employ this method of driving game towards their traps. To the west, a range of mountains, their blue serrated peaks softened by distance, rose above a bank of heat-haze that was now beginning to form.

'I'm going to try the south first,' declared Biggles to Ginger, who was sitting beside him, gazing around with absorbed interest. 'It's almost certain that Marton started for Juba, whatever may have happened afterwards to make him change his course,' he concluded.

For an hour they flew on, watching the ground closely on each side for any signs of a crash, but in vain. Automatically they also kept a watchful eye open for prominent landmarks, and although they picked out one or two, salient features were few and far between. For the most part the landscape was wearisome in its monotony. Wild animals they saw in large numbers, giraffe, buffalo and deer, and occasionally a solitary lion. Once they saw a small herd of elephants standing flank deep in a lake by a forest of considerable dimensions.

'We'd better be getting back,' murmured Biggles at last, and suiting the action to the word brought the nose of the Dragon round until it was pointing to the north. 'I've learnt something, anyway,' he added as an afterthought.

'What's that?'

'The size of the task we've taken on. It's all very well to sit at home and look at maps, but when you get out here and see this'—he indicated the vast territory below with a wave of his left hand—'one begins to get an idea of what one is faced with. And I don't mind telling you that it gives me a sort of hopeless feeling.'

Ginger said nothing, possibly because he shared Biggles's pessimism. Nor did they speak again until the aerodrome came into sight and they were gliding down towards it.

'What the dickens does Algy think he's playing at?' asked Biggles, as he flattened out and landed.

Ginger peered forward through the windscreen and saw Algy

standing just inside the hangar making strange but definite
signals to them. 'I fancy he's got something to tell us,' he said
slowly. 'If I were you I'd taxi right up to the shed.'

This apparently was what Algy was trying to induce them to
do, for he remained in the shed, beckoning them on, without
making any attempt to meet them.

'Has the sun given you St Vitus's dance or something?'
inquired Biggles, opening the windscreen and looking down.

'No! Come on out; I've got something to tell you,' was the
impatient answer.

'Well, what is it?' asked Biggles a moment later, as he jumped
lightly to the ground.

'There's someone else in the bungalow besides Sarda.'

Biggles pursed his lips. 'How do you know?' he asked quickly.

'I heard Sarda talking to him. Shouting might almost be a
better word.'

'How long ago?'

'It's happened twice. Once, immediately after you had taken
off, and again just now. I may be wrong but I fancy he didn't
know I was in here. He thought we'd all gone off together.'

'What makes you think that?'

'Because as the machine took off he dashed out and looked up
at it; then, as soon as you were well away, he ran back without
even glancing in this direction and started shouting at somebody. I was so surprised that I stayed here in the hope of learning
something else, instead of letting him see me as he would have
done if I had gone back to the rest-house to make the coffee.'

'Very interesting. Is the other fellow still in there, do you
think?'

'I'm certain of it. I've kept my eyes on the place all the time.'

'Good! Ginger, watch the bungalow until further orders,'
commanded Biggles; and as Ginger jumped to obey he turned
again to Algy. 'By fair means or foul we've got to find out who it
is,' he declared.

'Why not go to the place openly?'

'Because I'm afraid that if there is anyone there he won't let us
in, and we couldn't force our way in without an open declaration

of war. Still, there may be no harm in trying. Come on, let's go.
Leave the talking to me.'

Side by side they walked down to the bungalow. Sarda must
have seen them coming, for he opened the door and stepped on to
the threshold as they reached it.

'Phew! It's warm,' muttered Biggles, truthfully enough. 'May
we come in?'

'Yaas. With pleasure. Why not?' was the prompt reply.

Biggles concealed his surprise at this invitation, and threw a
quick glance round the room into which the front door gave
access, but except for the fact that it was in a filthy condition
there was nothing unusual about it. Indeed, it was pretty much
as a stranger would expect to find it. 'Not a very big place to have
to spend your life in, is it?' he murmured sympathetically, with
his eyes on Sarda's face.

'Plenty big enough for me,' the aerodrome manager assured
him. 'Another big room here.' He opened a communicating door
and showed them an adjoining room which, in a primitive sort of
way, was furnished as a bedroom.

'These are all the rooms you have, aren't they?' asked Biggles,
making a quick mental calculation of the overall dimensions of
the place.

'All except the kitchen. Kitchen's over there.' Sarda pointed
to a small door on the opposite side of the living room.

Biggles strolled over and opened it. As Sarda had said, the
room into which it led was a small kitchen. But there was no one
in it.

'Well, well,' he said smiling, 'you're better off than we are in
the rest-house. What we really came down for was to ask you if
you'd care to have two or three tins of preserved fruit; we've got
quite a large stock.'

'Thanks,' answered Sarda with alacrity.

'Come across and collect them when you have time,' Biggles
told him, and with a cheerful wave of farewell, led the way back
to their quarters. Inside the rest-house Algy gave full rein to his
astonishment. 'Well, I'm dashed,' he muttered. 'If that doesn't
beat the band. I'd have bet my life someone was in there.'

'It's time you knew that betting is called a mug's game,' smiled Biggles.

'I had a good look round and there wasn't an inch of space unaccounted for,' said Ginger.

'Quite right,' agreed Biggles. 'Sarda is the only man in that house.'

'In which case he must have been talking to himself.'

'Not necessarily.'

Algy started. 'You mean that he *was* talking to somebody?'

Biggles nodded.

'Who?'

'Ah! That's what we've got to find out.'

'But where has the other fellow gone?'

'He was never there.'

'Are you trying to be funny?'

'Far from it. Mr Sarda was speaking to somebody, but the person with whom he was conversing might be anywhere in Africa.'

'You mean——!'

'He was talking on the telephone.'

'Great heavens! I never thought of that. But I didn't see a telephone.'

'Neither did I, but I saw the wire.'

'Here he comes now,' put in Ginger quickly.

Biggles made one of those quick decisions that had been responsible for much of his success in the past. 'Look, Ginger,' he said tersely, 'slip across to the hangar. As soon as you see Sarda come in here, nip down to the bungalow, find the telephone receiver by following the lead-in wire, and, if you can, pick it up and see if you can get on to anybody without giving yourself away. Jump to it; we might find it difficult to keep Sarda here for very long.'

Ginger went out as Sarda came in, and Biggles selected from the stores the tins of preserved fruit that he had promised him.

'Ah! Here you are,' he said. Then, as a thought struck him, he added, 'Have a drink?'

An unpleasant smile spread over Sarda's face. 'Yaas,' he said.

'I can't let you have much,' apologized Biggles, 'because we don't carry liquor in the ordinary sense of the word—just a bottle of brandy for medicinal purposes in case of accident; still, I don't suppose it will taste any the worse for that. Where the dickens did you put that bottle, Algy?' he went on, making a long business of finding it, and then polishing a glass carefully before pouring a small measure of the spirit into it. Anything to gain time.

'Did you find a new landing-ground this morning, huh?' asked Sarda, sipping with relish the brandy that Algy had passed over to him.

Biggles shook his head. 'No; I'm afraid it's going to be a big job,' he replied. 'I think it would be a better proposition if a little more money was spent on this place, which would mean better business for you, eh?'

Sarda looked doubtful.

'Insula wouldn't be a very popular place, of course, if you are going to allow *mambas* and things to crawl about people's machines,' went on Biggles good humouredly, with the object of putting to rest in Sarda's mind any idea that they suspected him of being concerned with the snake incident.

Sarda laughed boisterously. 'You bet,' he said ambiguously, putting down the now empty glass. 'You flying again to-day, huh?'

Biggles nodded. 'Yes, we shall make another flight presently,' he answered. Out of the corner of his eye he saw Ginger bolt out of the bungalow and run towards the hangar, so he knew there was no point in delaying Sarda any longer. 'Well, well, we'll be seeing you sometimes,' he smiled.

The aerodrome manager picked up the tins that Biggles had given him. 'Yaas,' he said again, noncommittally, and with a nod of thanks left them.

'That fellow's "yaas" gets monotonous,' muttered Algy after he had gone.

'It does rather, but no doubt his English vocabulary is a bit limited. But unless I'm mistaken, it will be when he starts saying "no" that the fun will begin. But here comes Ginger. My goodness, the lad's pale. He's discovered something, judging by the look on his face.'

Ginger burst into the rest-house, but stopped short just inside the door, staring at the others.

'Well?' asked Biggles shortly. 'Have you got cramp in your tongue?'

Ginger nodded. 'I have had,' he answered grimly. 'I found that 'phone: it's in a little box in the kitchen. I took it out, put it to my ear, and wound up the thing like a self-starter. After a minute a voice said "Hello", but it sounded a long way away. I said "Hello". Then a voice said, "You're English? For God's sake help me". I said "Who are you?" Then he told me his name.' Ginger stopped, unconsciously dramatic.

Biggles eyed him coldly. 'Keep going,' he said. 'What was the name?'

Ginger tossed his hat on to the table. 'Harry Marton,' he said simply.

4
SINISTER DEVELOPMENTS

THERE was a profound silence which lasted for some seconds after Ginger had made his momentous announcement.

Biggles was the first to speak. 'Well, well,' he said in a quiet voice, while a curious smile spread slowly over his face. It did not express humour so much as comical surprise. 'This is a development that I did *not* expect,' he added whimsically.

Algy merely continued to stare at Ginger as if he could not believe his ears. 'Well, it's something to know young Marton is still alive,' he observed presently in a tense voice. Biggles hoisted himself on to a corner of the table and rubbed his chin reflectively. 'What's going on here, I wonder?' he murmured. 'This has sort of taken the wind out of my sails with a vengeance. We shall have to readjust our ideas, that's certain. What earthly reason could anyone have for kidnapping a perfectly harmless lad like Harry Marton? If anyone can tell me the answer to that I should be very glad.'

'Maybe somebody wanted his machine,' suggested Ginger.

Biggles looked at him thoughtfully. 'There's something in that,' he said seriously. 'But why not get rid of him altogether instead of leaving him alive, perhaps to bear witness one day against the thief, or thieves? He is certain to get away if ever he gets a chance.'

'I think we may assume that the people who are holding him are not likely to give him a chance,' ventured Algy grimly. 'I should say myself that he had either seen something, or heard something, that he shouldn't have seen or heard, and that's why they've collared him.'

Biggles nodded. 'Well, it's not much use sitting here guessing; we'd better start and do something about it.'

'Are you going to let old man Marton know that the boy's alive?' inquired Algy.

'No, I don't think so,' replied Biggles, drumming on the table with his fingers. 'We don't know what's behind this, and if a spy lets the people we are up against know what we know now, we may be the means of causing the boy's death. It would be a ghastly thing to raise the old man's hopes only to dash them down again. I think we'd better keep our knowledge to ourselves for the present. Obviously the first thing we've got to do is to find out the direction in which that telephone of Sarda's leads, in order to get an idea of where the other end of it is. When we know that I fancy our troubles will begin in earnest.'

'Why take the risk? Why not let the authorities know the truth so that they can handle the affair? They've a better chance of clearing things up than we have.'

'And a better chance of putting the tin hat on the whole thing. One of the troubles of a service is that it can't move without people knowing. It would be fatal to let the world know that Harry Marton is alive, and we should have to reveal that fact before the authorities would help us. After that anything might happen, but Marton would disappear for ever and we should just look a trio of fools.'

'Well, what's our first move to be?' asked Ginger impatiently.

Biggles did not answer for a minute or two. 'I think the first thing should be to get on friendly terms with Sarda and allay any suspicions that we may have aroused in his mind. I only hope that Marton hasn't given the game away at his end of the line. It's a pity we don't know the direction of it or we could do a bit of exploring from up topsides. We don't know that yet, but I hope we shall soon find out. Meanwhile, I think it might be a good plan to pretend to leave the place for a time, in which case Sarda might make a move that would tell us something. I say "pretend" because I should remain concealed in the hangar to watch what happened after the machine was out of the way. You can take her off and cruise around, keeping out of earshot. You might spot something, but I don't think you will, because the other end of that telephone must be a long way away or it wouldn't be necessary to have a telephone at all. Come on, let's be going.'

Within a quarter of an hour the Dragon's engines were ticking over just in front of the hangar, a position from which only the front part of it was visible from the bungalow. Then, all wearing flying kit, they made a business of getting aboard; but when the machine took off Biggles was sitting on an empty oil drum at the back of the hangar.

Within five minutes of the machine leaving the ground Sarda emerged from the bungalow and walked towards the hangar in a manner that left no doubt but that he had a definite object in view. Biggles saw him coming and looked around quickly for a place of concealment. There was none, but a pile of old sacking lying in a corner—kept, so Sarda had told them, for covering engines when the wind was raising a dust—offered possibilities. Holding his breath, for the pile looked a likely home for crawling things of all sorts, Biggles lay down beside the sacks and pulled them over him. Almost at once he heard the soft pad of Sarda's footsteps. There was silence for a moment; then he heard them receding. After a cautious peep to make sure that the coast was clear, he lost no time in evacuating his undesirable nest, and shaking himself violently to dislodge the ants that were already indicating their disapproval at being disturbed, he dashed across to the flimsy wall and peered through a crack just in time to see Sarda go back into the bungalow. He waited, fully expecting to see him come out again, but that evidently was not the airport manager's intention.

Then began an interminable wait which caused Biggles to wish fervently that he had decided on some other plan, for what with the heat, which was almost unendurable, and the flies, which kept up a vicious and continuous attack on all exposed parts of his person, he was driven nearly to distraction. Torn between discarding his clothes on account of the heat, and muffling himself up in his flying kit as protection against the insects, he could only pace up and down, stopping every few seconds to glance at the bungalow. Leave the hangar he dare not for fear Sarda should see him, in which case the airport manager's suspicions would certainly be increased rather than allayed.

An hour and a half passed in this way, and just as Biggles had reached the point when he felt that whatever the cost might be he must rush out into the open or go mad, he heard a sound that set his blood tingling and caused his troubles to recede to insignificance. It was the sound of an aero engine, a single engine, ever increasing in volume, and before he had time to conjecture who the stranger might be a black-painted Puss Moth had swept low over the hangar and landed in the middle of the aerodrome. Swinging round almost in its own length, it then taxied tail up in the direction of the rest-house, towards which Sarda was now walking briskly.

From his hiding-place Biggles saw the door of the cabin open, and a short, stockily built man step out on to the baked earth; he beckoned impatiently to Sarda, who broke into a run and joined him near the door of the rest-house, where a swift altercation took place. It was only of short duration, but from it Biggles learned two things. The first was that the new-comer was a foreigner; and the second, that he was either Sarda's employer or superior officer. That he was not English was revealed clearly by the way he waved his hands when talking; and that Sarda was his employee was made obvious by the airport manager's servile manner. Indeed, his servility was not far short of abject fear. So much Biggles was able to surmise within a minute of time. That the stranger did not intend staying long was also suggested by the fact that he left his machine out in the broiling sun with the engine ticking over; so Biggles was disagreeably surprised when, instead of getting back into his machine at the end of the conversation, the Puss Moth pilot strode into the rest-house, closely followed by Sarda.

Biggles bit his lip, for this was something he had nor foreseen. In the rest-house were their belongings—papers and miscellaneous kit that were too bulky to be carried about in their pockets—and the last thing he wanted was their inspection by the lessees of Insula aerodrome. Even although it meant disclosing himself, he knew he must prevent that, for amongst his papers were letters from Mr Marton.

Swiftly, and without any attempt at concealment, he walked towards the rest-house. As he approached it the voices of the occupants, speaking in broken English, reached him clearly, and he slowed down to listen. 'Here it is,' the new-comer was saying. 'Do what I tell you and we shall have no more trouble. Nuzzing could be more simple.'

'But——' began Sarda, but the stranger interrupted him. 'Say no more,' he said shortly. 'Leave all ze rest to us; we make ze finish.'

Then fell a silence that Biggles could not understand, so he walked quickly to the open door and looked in. One glance was enough. The pilot, clad only in a thin sweater, shorts, shoes and stockings, was opening Biggles's log-book, which he had just taken from the kit-bag that lay open at his feet. Sarda, with a white envelope in his hand, was watching him closely. Neither of them saw Biggles standing in the doorway, and the announcement of his arrival was dramatic.

'Can I help you?' he said quietly.

At the words, both Sarda and the stranger leapt round as if a gun had been fired. Sarda's hand flew to his shirt and the stranger's went to his hip pocket. In that position they remained, while Biggles eyed them coldly. 'I said, can I help you?' he repeated.

A queer expression crossed the stranger's face, while Sarda simply stared at him as if waiting for a lead. Presently it came.

'Ha! Why zere you are,' cried the pilot effusively, removing his hand from his pocket. 'Zis fool 'ere'—he indicated Sarda—'told me you were in ze air.'

'I changed my mind,' answered Biggles calmly. 'Have you finished with my log-book? If so, I'll put it back.'

The other smiled apologetically. 'I vas just interest to know who come to zis part of ze world,' he explained with an expressive shrug of his shoulders.

'Well, I can tell you all about it,' replied Biggles suavely. 'Sorry I can't offer you a drink. My name is Bigglesworth.'

'Mine is . . . Leroux—Leon Leroux.'

Biggles knew from the momentary hesitation that the man was lying, but he did not let him see it. 'What are *you* doing in this part of the world, anyway?' he asked coolly.

'Oh, I fly for Stampoulos *et Cie*, of Cairo. They have tobacco plantations near.'

'Where?'

'Over zare.' The other waved his hand vaguely.

'You're French, aren't you?'

'Yes.'

'Prefer to fly a British machine, though, eh?'

'My firm buy ze aeroplane, not me,' answered the Frenchman quickly.

'That's a mistake,' smiled Biggles. 'I wouldn't work for a firm who didn't allow me to choose my equipment. But that's neither here nor there. If you leave your machine out in the sun much longer the dope will be blistered off it.'

The other walked towards the door. 'Yes,' he said, and then hesitated. 'You are ver interested in zis aerodrome, is it not?' he inquired, eyeing Biggles shrewdly.

'More or less. We've been asked to have a look round,' answered Biggles casually.

'It is a bad place. Ze fever——'

'Yes, I know,' interrupted Biggles smiling. 'I've heard all about it from Sarda. Still, we shan't be here long,' he added.

'No, you will not be here long,' agreed the other slowly, in an expressionless voice, as he walked towards his machine.

Biggles followed him out, wondering what he was really thinking, for the formal conversation had meant nothing, and he was well aware of it. His eyes ran quickly over the machine as Leroux got into his seat. Then he stepped back out of the slipstream as the engine roared, and waved his hand as the machine raced across the barren earth and into the air.

He turned to find Sarda watching him narrowly. 'I suppose Mr Leroux often comes here?' he observed, hoping to lead him into conversation.

But Sarda was not to be drawn. 'He my boss,' he said in a surly voice, and turning on his heel, walked quickly towards the bungalow.

Biggles retired to the rest-house and sat down to contemplate the situation. He was still sitting there deep in thought when, twenty minutes later, the Dragon landed and the others joined him.

'Well, have you discovered anything?' he asked.

Algy shook his head. 'Nothing,' he answered laconically. 'Have you?'

'Yes,' replied Biggles.

Algy started, and Ginger's eyes whipped round to his chief. 'What is it?' they both asked together.

'While you've been away a machine has landed here, a Puss Moth belonging to the Stampoulos Company—the people we're up against. The pilot, with whom I had a short conversation, told me his name was Leroux, but unless I am mistaken, he is Jean Lazarre, who lost his job with the Aeropostale people a few years ago for being drunk on duty. I've never seen him in the flesh, but I remember seeing his photo in the French paper *L'Aile*, when he was reckoned to be one of the best civil pilots in France. What happened to him afterwards I never heard, but he is here now, doing the sort of job one would expect a man of his sort to be on.'

'Anything else?' asked Algy.

Biggles lit a cigarette and put his heel on the match. 'Yes,' he said. 'As I told you, Leroux—we'd better call him that for the time being—is flying a Puss. It is painted black, but here and there where the paint has peeled off one can see another colour underneath; and that colour is——'

'Red,' muttered Ginger succinctly.

Biggles smiled. 'For one of such tender years your perspicacity approaches the abnormal,' he observed approvingly.

There was silence for a few moments. 'And what now?' asked Algy, opening a bottle of soda water.

'As you rightly remark, what now?' murmured Biggles. 'Things are moving fast—almost too fast. We shall skid if we aren't careful. I caught Leroux in here going through my log-book. He has given something to Sarda, something to do with us, I believe, but I don't know what it is. Leroux suspects that we are what we really are, that's certain, but how much he actually knows about us is more than I can say. I fancy Sarda told him over the telephone that the machine had gone off, so he took the opportunity of slipping over to have a word with him and give him some instructions. We've got to watch out.'

'Which way did Leroux go when he took off?'

'Due east.'

'Which means that his head-quarters are somewhere in that direction.'

'You may be right, but I fancy it is more likely to mean that the plantation—or whatever it is—lies to the west. That is, unless Leroux is a bigger fool than I take him to be. Even before he took off I made a mental note that he would choose a line of flight other than the one he is most concerned with.'

'What can we do to confirm it?'

'Nothing at present, but as soon as it is dark I propose to find out the direction in which our objective lies.'

'How?'

'By seeing which way the telephone wire goes. That's bound to go straight to it, because when it was set up there was surely no need to lay a false trail. So unless anyone has a better plan, what I suggest is this. As soon as it is dark I am going down to the back of the bungalow to find out where the telephone lead emerges, and then follow it for a distance—that is, assuming it is an overhead wire, as I expect it will be. You'd better come with me, Algy, to keep *cave*. Ginger will have to stay in the hangar while we're away to guard the machine. With Sarda prowling about I don't think it would be wise to leave it even for a moment. We don't want to get in it to-morrow and then find that a longeron has been sawn through, or a turnbuckle unscrewed.'

'No, you're right there,' declared Algy emphatically.

'Good! Then if that's settled a bite of lunch won't do us any harm.'

The remainder of the day passed slowly, though rather than waste time they employed themselves by refuelling the machine and giving it a top overhaul. But the heat and the flies were trying, and they were all glad when the sun sank behind the distant hills and darkness fell. There was no moon, but one by one the stars came out and glowed against a background of sky that was like purple velvet.

'Well, I think it's dark enough to be moving,' announced Biggles, when he was satisfied that it was safe to act. 'You know what you are to do, Ginger? Whatever happens, don't leave the machine. If Sarda starts monkeying around, stop him; we shan't be far away—not out of earshot, anyway.'

'Good enough, Chief,' answered Ginger firmly. 'Can I take one of the rifles?'

'You may, but be careful what you're up to. Don't shoot me or Algy if we happen to walk in unexpectedly.'

'I'll try not to,' promised Ginger, smiling. 'I don't mind Sarda, but the idea of things creeping about gives me the pins and needles down the back.'

'Never mind the pins and needles: you look after that machine,' Biggles told him as, with Algy by his side, he set off on a detour that would bring them to the rear of the bungalow, from the window of which a shaft of yellow light told them that Sarda was at home.

Neither of them was accustomed to night work in a country

where wild beasts roamed at large; it called for an entirely different form of mental strength from flying, and more than once they stopped and strained their eyes in the gloom when a slight sound suggested that they were not alone in the coppice. They saw nothing, however, but it took them a good deal longer to reach their objective than they had allowed for. Further, the business of finding the telephone lead in the darkness—for with the windows of the bungalow blindless, they dare not risk striking a match—was more difficult than they expected. In the end they found it, but by that time Biggles's watch told him that they had been away for nearly two hours.

'We shall have to move faster than this or we shall be out all night,' he breathed as, feeling along the wire with his hand, he followed it to an insulator on a tree some ten or twelve yards away from the house.

Thereafter there was no great difficulty in following the wire, but it was slow work. Once they nearly stampeded as a dark form sprang up just in front of them and dashed away into the darkness.

'We ought to have brought rifles with us,' growled Algy as he stood staring wildly in the direction in which the beast had disappeared. 'Automatics are about as much use as pea-shooters in this sort of place. What do you suppose that was?'

'I haven't the remotest idea,' answered Biggles irritably. 'It might have been anything except an elephant, and it wasn't big enough for that. Where's that confounded wire?'

It took them some minutes to find it again, but shortly afterwards it emerged from the coppice into the open plain where, supported at intervals by bamboo poles sunk into the ground, it went in a straight line for as far as they could see. The direction, as Biggles pointed out with a nudge at Algy, was due west.

They followed it for a little way, but the direction remained constant, and at last Biggles stopped. 'I don't think there is any point in following it farther,' he said. 'If we fly on a compass course due west, sooner or later we shall find what we're looking for.'

'Could we see the wire from the air, do you think, if we flew low?' asked Algy.

'I doubt it,' replied Biggles. 'That is, not unless we flew very low, which might be a bit risky in this sort of country. In the early morning, while the sun is at an angle, we might see the shadows of the poles on the ground, but in the middle of the day, with the sun slap overhead, there wouldn't be any shadows. Anyway, I don't think we need worry about that. If we fly west, and fly high, we shall be able to see at least fifty or sixty miles in all directions in this atmosphere, and—hark!'

Both Biggles and Algy sprang round as the silence was broken suddenly by an unmistakable noise. It was the soft, rhythmic purr of aero engines ticking over.

'Great heaven! That's the Dragon,' gasped Algy.

'I didn't think it was a buffalo,' rasped Biggles. 'What does that young fool think he's up to, I wonder?'

Even then it did not occur to either of them that the machine was preparing to take off.

'He'll fetch Sarda out to see what's going on, the young ass,' began Algy. He got no farther, but clutched Biggles's arm as, with a deafening roar, the engines broke into full song. For a moment or two the noise receded, then it increased again to ear-splitting force as it swept towards them. Staring up, they could just make out the dark silhouette of the machine as it raced low across the sky on a westerly course.

As the sound faded away Biggles pulled his paralysed faculties together. 'Come on,' he cried; and regardless of Sarda, wild beasts, or anything else, he sprinted for dear life towards the hangar.

Ducking under branches and jumping over obstacles, Algy followed until, panting and dishevelled, they dashed into the empty shed.

'Ginger,' cried Biggles sharply.

There was no reply.

With trembling fingers Biggles struck a match and looked around the floor, afraid of what he might find. His eyes fell on a rifle lying in the dust; it was one of their own, and he glanced at

Algy with a peculiar expression on his face. Then, as the match went out, he drew a deep breath. 'Well,' he said, in a hopeless sort of voice, 'that's that. I can't say I blame myself or anyone else; it's hard for anyone to make allowances for this sort of thing. We'd better go down to the rest-house and talk it over.'

In the gaping doorway of the hangar they met Sarda, lantern in hand.

'What is happening here?' he asked with studied politeness. 'Did I hear an aeroplane—huh?'

'Oh, no; it was just the breeze sighing through the trees,' sneered Biggles sarcastically. 'Come on, Algy.'

Without another word they set off towards the rest-house.

5
ALONE WITH A LION

GINGER had been by no means happy when he left the others to take up his position of guard over the Dragon. He was not exactly afraid, but the idea of remaining alone, in the dark, in a building that would not have kept out a determined sheep, in the heart of lion-infested country, gave him—to use his own expression—pins and needles down the back. Nevertheless, it did not occur to him to quibble at his allotted task.

On reaching the hangar his first act was to go into the machine and unlock the armament chest with the key he had obtained from Biggles. From it he selected an Express rifle and a clip of ammunition. Then he relocked the chest, put the key in his pocket, loaded the weapon, and with it resting across his knees, took up a position on an oil-drum at the rear of the building from which it was possible to command a view of the whole machine, the dark bulk of which he could just distinguish in the gloom.

For a time all was silent, but the minutes passed slowly. Once a lion roared in the far distance, and sound did nothing to make him feel happier. Later, strange noises began to occur; soft rustlings and unexplainable whispering sounds. What caused these he did not know, but as they were obviously animal and not human, he did not investigate. Once, too, he distinctly heard the faint swish of wings over his head, and looking up fearfully, with eyes now accustomed to the darkness, he could just make out the form of a huge bat that circled the hangar thrice before disappearing as mysteriously as it had arrived.

In such circumstances he had not the slightest fear of going to sleep, but in this he was mistaken, for as the night wore on, although he certainly did not sleep, he was by no means wide awake when a fresh sound brought every nerve in his body with a rush to the alert. Somewhere, not far away, a dry twig had snapped. Obviously, only a weight could have caused the twig to break, and he was well aware of it, although at the moment just what shape the weight in question took he had no means of knowing. He was not kept long in suspense. There came a soft footfall, a muttered word, and then a harsh, crackling noise. A wide slit of star-studded sky appeared, and he knew that one of the rush-plaited doors of the hangar had been opened. No longer was he in any doubt as to the character of the visitors. Animals might break twigs, but they did not open doors.

Leaving his seat, he crept stealthily as far back in the hangar as possible, both in order to prevent his face being seen and in the hope that he might see something of the visitors who, until then, had been just outside his field of view on account of the machine. He saw them at once. It was too dark for faces to be recognized, but by his outstanding physique he could see that one was Sarda; the other was a short, stoutish man whom he had never seen before.

Quietly and deliberately they opened the hangar doors wide, and then stood talking in whispers just inside.

Now Ginger was in what is commonly called a quandary. Should he challenge them, at the same time calling aloud for Biggles, or should he wait to see what they proposed to do? That was the problem with which he was faced. As he reasoned it out, he decided that if the men were on legitimate business, which admittedly seemed unlikely, his presence in the hangar and his actions would make it clear to them that something in the nature of a trap had been set. In any case, if he shouted for help, and the others came to his assistance, what could they say? What could they do? No doubt the intruders would soon find a feasible excuse for being there—anyway, Sarda, who, after all, as aerodrome manager had even more right there than he, Ginger, had. So he decided that the only thing he could do was to let them commit themselves by some act of sabotage, if such was their intention, before he disclosed his presence.

It was quite a sensible course to adopt, but he was utterly unprepared for what was to follow. Not when Sarda turned and walked away towards the bungalow did he suspect it; nor even when the stranger opened the door of the machine and got inside. When he heard the whirr of the self-starter the explanation struck him like a blow, but by that time the engines had come to life and the propellers were filling the hangar with a dust-laden whirlwind.

Now, only those who have stood immediately behind the revolving propellers of an aeroplane on a dusty aerodrome have any idea of just what the effect can be. Ginger was literally blinded—temporarily, of course. To open his eyes was a physical impossibility, so he could only grope his way to the machine. His questing hands found the tail, and worked their way along the fuselage until they came to the door. It was shut. By the time he got it open the machine was moving forward, slowly, but with swiftly increasing speed, and as the full desperation of the situation struck him he acted in a sort of frenzy of consternation. He dropped the rifle, for it only impeded him, and flung himself through the doorway. He was round in an instant, and although he was still unable to see, he managed to close the door behind him. Then he sank down and put his hands over his eyes, for the pain in them was intense.

It was two or three minutes before he could see reasonably well, and by that time the machine was in the air, banking steeply as the pilot turned. 'I suppose I ought to be thankful that I'm inside,' he thought, as he rose to his feet and blinked forwards towards the cockpit, where he could just see the vague outline of the pilot, clearly unaware of his presence, silhouetted against the glow of the luminous instrument board. Feeling in his pocket he took out his automatic. Then, with a sudden feeling of helplessness, he sat down again, for he perceived that although he held all the advantages of surprise attack—perhaps the most vital element in fighting of any sort—he was by no means master of the situation. To attempt to hold up Leroux—for such he assumed the pilot to be—at the point of a gun must be a palpable bluff, and the Frenchman, when confronted, could hardly fail to realize it. It would be no use telling him to go back and land. However much he, Ginger, might threaten, the man could ignore him with impunity, knowing perfectly well that he dare not use his weapon even if he was capable of shooting an unarmed man at point-blank range, for during the interval that must inevitably elapse while he was removing the body in order to get to the controls, the machine would fall out of control and crash. Added to this, there was always the risk of the body falling across the joystick and jamming it.

The more Ginger thought about it the more awkward the situation appeared. He had enough common sense to see that by revealing himself he automatically reduced by a considerable margin his chance of success in any plan he might formulate. So in the end he did nothing, but resolved to preserve his advantage of surprise until the machine was on the ground, when it could be employed with telling effect.

He had barely reached this decision when, to his astonishment, the roar of the engines died away and the nose of the machine tilted down, the pilot obviously making preparations to land. He could see him peering down while he held the Dragon in a steady spiral glide.

In something like a panic, he looked about for a hiding-place, for the dark interior of the cabin was not the ideal place to start proceedings. The luggage compartment in the rear was clearly indicated, and into it he bundled just as the wheels touched the ground in a landing that was by no means smooth. For a minute or two he remained where he was, hardly daring to breathe, ears strained for any sound that might indicate the pilot's movements. At first, after the machine had finished its run, he could hear him moving about, but then there was silence. Slowly, an inch at a time, with his automatic held at the ready, he opened the door. There was no sign of the pilot. With finger crooked round the trigger, he opened the door wider, but was still unable to see Leroux. With no sound in his ear but the beating of his heart, he crept out. The machine was empty. A short rush took him to the cockpit, but there was no one in it. Then the open cabin door told its own story. Leroux had left the machine.

Ginger must be forgiven for hesitating, for the situation was both unusual and nerve-testing. But he did not wait long. His first inclination was to get into the now vacated seat, push the throttle open and take off, and he strained his eyes through the windscreen to see what sort of country lay in front of him; but it was too dark to make out the details beyond the fact that the ground was covered with long, coarse grass with an isolated tree here and there. Whether he was facing an open runway, or whether the nose of the machine was pointing to the near edge of the landing-ground and the obstacles that would undoubtedly occur there, he could not tell, and anxious as he was to get away, he knew that to attempt to take off in such circumstances would be an act of madness. Where was Leroux? What on earth was he doing?

Swiftly he made his way to the cabin door and looked out. In the dim starlight he could just see that in all directions except one the ground was flat, a wilderness of dry earth and coarse grass; but behind the machine, some fifty to a hundred yards away beyond the tail, a sombre, blurred mass rose high into the night sky. From the ragged outline of the top he could just make out that it was either the edge of a forest or a clump of trees. But of Leroux there was neither sight nor sound. What the man was doing in such a place he could not imagine; nor did he care particularly, for his main idea still was to get the machine into the air and back to Insula with all possible speed. As near as he could judge they had been in the air about twenty minutes to half an hour, which meant that Insula was at least fifty miles away, but in what direction he could only guess. That did not worry him; once in the air he could cruise round in a wide circle until he saw a landmark he recognized, after which the location of the aerodrome would be a fairly simple matter.

His next move was a mistake. Later, and in the very near future, he realized it, but at the moment he was so taken up with the idea of getting away before Leroux returned that he proceeded with the plan to the exclusion of everything else. A hundred yards was all the distance needed to get the lightly loaded machine off the ground, and it was with the object of examining the surface that he jumped out and ran quickly for a little way in the direction in which the nose of the machine was pointing. He may have gone seventy or eighty yards; then he stopped, peering into the gloom. Satisfied that the course was clear, he was about to turn back to the machine when a low, choking grunt brought him round with a rush to the point whence it came, which was a few yards to the right. To his horror he saw a dark form rise slowly out of the grass. From the centre of it two orbs of green light glowed balefully.

Too late he realized what he had almost forgotten: that he was not on a European aerodrome but in untamed Africa. To say that he was petrified with fright is to express his sensations but mildly. He was not rooted to the ground, as the saying is, but he felt as if he was. At least, he was quite unable to move, although he wanted to run more than ever in his life before. Fortunately, he did not do so, or this story might have had a different ending. He just stood and stared, moistening his dry lips with his tongue. The creature, whatever it was—for he did not know for certain, although he supposed it to be a lion—did not move either, and thus they remained for several seconds.

At the end of that time he began to think more clearly, and remembering his automatic, he took it out and levelled it. At the precise moment that his finger was tightening on the trigger there came a sound that put a new complexion on the situation. It was the door of the Dragon being slammed. Simultaneously, the green orbs went out as abruptly as electric lights that have been switched off. The Dragon's engines roared. The noise threw him into a condition of hopeless despair such as he had never before experienced, but there was little time to dwell upon the calamity. With a bellow that shook the earth the engines roared full out, and an instant later he saw the black bulk of the machine rushing towards him. For a second he stood transfixed; then he flung himself flat as the machine swept past him not five yards away, the wing-tips actually passing over his recumbent body.

He was up in a moment, staring wild-eyed at the spot where the lion had been. It was no longer there. Quickly he looked round, but the beast had completely disappeared. Nevertheless, the relief he experienced at this discovery was more than a little squashed when he realized that he was alone on the veldt.

But was he? When he thought about it he was by no means sure, and he would have been far more comfortable in his mind had he been certain of it. What was to be done? He must think— think.

What would Biggles do in a case like this, he asked himself, but he could find no answer until a solitary tree about a hundred yards away caught his eye. To his distraught mind it was like an island to a shipwrecked mariner, and he started off towards it with more haste than dignity; but he had not taken a dozen paces when, happening to glance over his shoulder, his worst fears were realized. The lion was trotting along behind him. He stopped. The lion stopped.

He could see it clearly now, see the great tufted tail switching from side to side. The desire to run was almost uncontrollable, but the first shock of horror having worn off, he had the sense to realize the folly of it, for there is no creature on earth that can outdistance a lion over a hundred yards, which it can cover in three or four mighty springs.

Slowly, still watching the beast, he began to edge nearer to the tree, a move to which the lion instantly responded by uttering a low growl. It reminded him of what he had once read in a book, that all wild animals are afraid of the sound of the human voice. Forthwith he proceeded to put this to the test. The noise that emanated from his dry throat was by no means a triumphant shout; to him it sounded more like a plaintive howl, so the test was hardly a fair one. In any case it failed, for the lion took not the slightest notice of it, but stood its ground, regarding him with significant interest.

Ginger, in his despair, remembered something else, and he could have kicked himself for not thinking of it earlier. In his pocket was a box of matches. It was the work of a moment to find it and drop a lighted match into the dry grass. To his infinite relief a little tongue of flame licked hungrily round his shoes. There was no breeze to help it, but the grass was tinder dry, and crackled cheerfully as the flames began to spread in a little circle. It had the disadvantage of making it difficult to see clearly what lay outside the radius of light, but he could just make out the form of the lion backing slowly away, and he offered a prayer of thankfulness.

Following up his advantage, he walked to the outside of the circle of fire on the side nearest to the tree and repeated the performance. Thereafter the gaining of his goal became only a matter of time, although he had some anxious moments as he crossed small areas of bare earth, similar to those that occurred at Insula, which he knew were caused by the levelling of ant-hills.

He had rather a job to climb the lower part of the tree, for the trunk was bare of branches, but his fears lent him unsuspected strength, and he managed to find a secure perch in a fork fairly near the top, from which he regarded with disfavour the fires he had started; for while they were burning only in a desultory sort of way, the smoke hung about and made his eyes and throat smart unmercifully. However, on the whole he had little cause for complaint, he decided, as he settled down to review the state of affairs, trying to muster the facts into some sort of coherent order.

First of all there was Biggles and Algy. What would they be thinking? They would have heard the Dragon take off, of course, and rush to the spot. What would they do then? What could they do, stranded as they were at Insula, without transport and hopelessly cut off from civilization? And Leroux? Where had he taken the machine? Wherever it was, there seemed small chance of recovering it. Why had he done it? Obviously, either to leave them stranded or to curtail their activities; to prevent them from finding—what? In either case it was a cunning move; Ginger was forced to admit that. How had Leroux achieved it? How had he managed to take off in the Puss, yet return to the aerodrome so quickly on foot?—for it was certain that he had not landed in an aeroplane. That would have been impossible without its being heard. These were questions for which he could find no answer, and which time alone might explain.

Somehow or other he had got to get back to Insula, there was no doubt about that, for it was useless to expect Biggles or Algy to come to his assistance when they could have no idea of where he was. In which direction was Insula? It gave him a severe jolt when he was forced to admit to himself that he did not know, although if Biggles's theory had been correct when they had discussed why the Puss Moth had taken off towards the east, Insula ought to lie in an easterly direction. Biggles had contended that Leroux's easterly take-off had been only a blind—that his real destination lay to the west. Following that line of argument, the Dragon would have been on a westerly course when it landed, and if that were so, then Insula must now be to the east. But even if this assumption were correct, the thought of walking fifty or sixty miles across wild-beast-infested country without a rifle, and without food or water, appalled him; yet he could see no alternative if he was ever to get back.

At last, with his brain aching from the contemplation of so many vital problems, he leaned back with a sigh of weariness and prepared to wait for the dawn.

6
SARDA STRIKES

AFTER the first shock occasioned by the disappearance of the Dragon had passed off, Biggles's reasoning ability quickly returned to normal. Taking an electric torch, he went back with Algy to the hangar and made a thorough examination of the place, both inside and out, Algy assisting him in the search. They found nothing more, of course, for the simple reason that there was nothing more to be found, but Biggles was able to reconstruct the scene fairly accurately.

'Ginger was sitting over there on the oil drum when the business started,' he observed half to himself. 'Leroux then came in and went to the machine.'

Algy started. 'You think Leroux did it?'

'Who else? Ginger was hardly likely to take the machine off himself, and the chances against any other pilot but Leroux being in the district must be pretty remote. As I say, someone, who for the sake of argument we will assume was Leroux, got into the machine, or attempted to do something to it; whereupon Ginger came across to see what was going on. Leroux must have seen him and struck him down. He then put him into the machine and flew it away, leaving the rifle where it had fallen.'

'But why in the name of goodness should he take Ginger with him?'

'God knows. But he isn't here, is he?'

Algy shook his head. 'I'm sorry, old lad, but your theory strikes me as being a bit weak in places. I can't think that Leroux would lumber himself up with a prisoner.'

'I can't imagine Ginger getting in of his own free will. And what about young Marton? He's being held prisoner, isn't he?'

Algy nodded. 'That's true enough,' he admitted reflectively.

'Then as I see it the odds are that before the night is out Ginger will either find himself with, or in the same place as young Marton.'

'Don't overlook the possibility that Leroux might have killed him and taken the body away to cover up the crime.'

Biggles thought for a moment. 'I can't somehow think that's likely,' he observed. 'Had there been a struggle, Ginger would have cried out and we should have heard him. In the same way we should have heard a shot if Leroux had used a gun.'

'He might have used a knife.'

'In which case, surely there would be bloodstains.'

'Yes, I suppose there would.'

'I suppose it wasn't quite fair of us to leave him here alone; but without making any excuses I must confess that I did not think matters had reached the stage when these people—Stampoulos—Leroux—or whoever they are—would go to such lengths as this. Well, I don't think it's much use staying here; let's get back.'

Without speaking they walked over to the rest-house.

'I'm afraid it's going to be a bad business for Ginger,' muttered Biggles, with a worried frown, when they were inside. 'And for us, if it comes to that. Without transport our hands are absolutely tied. It would be out of the question for us to start walking about looking for him; we might spend the rest of our lives searching in a country of this size, even if it were possible to get about without supplies, which it isn't. It seems to me that the only thing left for us is to get to Malakal and cable home for another machine.'

'Get to Malakal—how?'

'Hoof it; there's no other way.'

'You don't think these people will make another move?'

'Why should they? They've effectually put us out of action, as no doubt they intended.'

'What about seizing Sarda and making him speak?'

'How would you propose to do that?'

'By beating the hide off his back if necessary. He's a dirty skunk.'

Biggles smiled grimly. 'I don't think he could tell us much even if he wanted to; I fancy he is in a very subordinate position,' he said. Then he started. 'By gosh! I tell you what we can do, though,' he whispered sibilantly. 'What about the telephone?'

'Yes, by James! We can at least tell these swine what we'll do to them if they don't send Ginger back.'

'I don't think we're in exactly the position to threaten,' Biggles reminded him gently.

'No, perhaps not. Never mind, let's go.'

'Wait a minute; not so fast. What do you suppose Sarda is going to say if we just stroll in and ask him if he minds us using his telephone?'

'Why ask? Let's stick a gun in his ribs and tell him.'

'Your impetuosity will one day be your downfall, I fear,' murmured Biggles sadly. 'Fixed as we are, I think it would be a wiser plan to keep what few cards we hold up our sleeves. I also think that we should be fools to start a rough house with our friend over there in the middle of the night; no doubt he could find his way about blindfolded, whereas we hardly know it.in broad daylight. No, we'll wait for morning and then say what we have to say. "When in doubt, sleep on it," is a very sound axiom. For the moment we'll get some sleep, although we'd better take it in turns; the idea of closing my eyes while I am within striking distance of that wall-eyed *baboo* becomes more repugnant every minute.'

The remainder of the night passed slowly, for although they tried to sleep, the knowledge of their desperate plight made it difficult, and they were both glad therefore when the sky grew grey with the approach of dawn, and the light enabled them to see about the preparation of a meal before proceeding to the prosecution of their plan.

Algy, whose job it was to make the coffee, strolled to the door and looked out while he was waiting for the pot to boil. He was back instantly, gripping Biggles's arm excitedly. 'Here's Sarda coming now,' he said tersely.

Biggles swung round. 'Sarda!'

'Yes.'

'What the dickens does he want at this hour, I wonder?'

'I don't know, but it looks as if he's carrying something.'

'All right; stand fast. Don't let him see we're antagonistic.'

A moment later Sarda appeared in the doorway. 'Goot morning,' he said cheerfully.

'Morning,' answered Biggles, smiling. 'What have you got there?'

Sarda was holding a large calabash in his hand. 'Milk,' he replied. 'I think perhaps you like milk with coffee, huh?'

Biggles stared. 'Milk!' he cried. 'Where did you get it?'

Sarda raised his eyebrows as if questioning Biggles's surprise. 'From my goat,' he explained.

'Of course,' nodded Biggles, who remembered seeing the animal tethered at the back of the bungalow. 'That's very kind of you,' he went on. 'A little fresh milk will be a treat.' If Sarda

was anxious to hold out the olive branch, it was up to them
to accept it, he thought. 'By the way,' he continued, 'I suppose
you know that our young friend went off last night on a joy-ride
and hasn't come back?'

'Yaas, I heard him go,' was the frank answer.

'If he's had to make a forced landing out on the veldt he'll be in
a mess,' Biggles told him. 'And without an aeroplane to look for
him, so are we. What do you think would be the quickest way of
getting in touch with Mr—what was his name?—Leroux. The
gentleman who landed here yesterday. He can't be very far
away, and he might be willing to help us.'

'Yaas, sure he'll help you,' declared Sarda emphatically. 'You
ring him up on my telephone.'

Algy, who had heated the milk and was pouring it over the
coffee in the cups, nearly dropped the lot in his agitation at this
very unexpected suggestion. Even Biggles was at a loss for words
for a second or two.

'Telephone!' he exclaimed. 'You didn't tell us you had a
telephone.'

'You never asked me,' returned Sarda simply.

'That's true enough,' Biggles had to admit. 'Where does it go
to?' he inquired quickly.

'To Karuli.'

'Where's that?'

'That's the tobacco plantation where my boss lives.'

'Why, that's fine,' declared Biggles. 'Sit down a minute while I
drink my coffee and I'll come back with you. I shan't be a
minute.'

Nothing more was said until Biggles drained his cup and then
stood up, reaching for his hat which lay on the table. Suddenly,
as if his legs were too weak to support him, he sat down again.
'Dash it!' he muttered, 'I feel queer. Must have got a touch of
fever.' He raised his hand to his forehead. 'Algy, do you mind
passing me the quinine?'

A moment later, as Algy made no reply, he raised his head
wearily and looked across at him. He was sitting on his bed,
swaying gently, while beads of perspiration rolled down his pale

face. 'Sorry,' he said slowly, as if with an effort, 'but I can't move.'

With a dreadful suspicion in his mind Biggles turned towards Sarda, although it required a tremendous effort of strength to do so. The airport manager was grinning broadly.

'You like my milk?' he sneered.

'You swine!' Biggles ground the words out through his teeth. He tried to reach to his pocket for the automatic he carried there, but the effort was too much for him and he sagged forward limply.

Calmly, and without haste, Sarda walked across to him, removed the gun from his pocket and tossed it on to the table, afterwards treating Algy in the same way. Then he walked to the door. 'I'll be back,' he said with an unpleasant leer.

'Algy—old son—I'm afraid—we're sunk,' whispered Biggles weakly. 'That skunk—has—poisoned us.'

Algy made no reply; he had rolled on to the floor and lay rigid. Only his eyes moved and showed that he was still conscious.

Biggles felt his strength ebbing fast. For a minute he fought against the action of the toxin as he had never fought before, but it was in vain. He made a stupendous effort to get to the table where the automatics lay, but it was beyond his strength, and he collapsed backwards across the low camp bed.

Lying thus, on the point of unconsciousness, he saw their poisoner reappear, and, in a dreamy, subconscious way, saw that he carried a can of petrol in his hand. Sarda unscrewed the cap and then proceeded to splash the contents of the can on the flimsy walls of the building. When it was empty he tossed it aside and took out a box of matches. With a match between his fingers he turned to Biggles. 'You think you're damn smart,' he sneered. 'But you ain't smart enough. Not likely.' He struck the match. 'Presently I'm going to make out report how English gents like fools made big camp fire in the rest-house and set the whole place afire. Got burnt to death. Good story—huh? And no one to say no. Only me here to see it so no one calls me a liar. Now I go outside and hark at you frizzling.' With that he struck the match and tossed it against the petrol-soaked wall. With a dull, terrifying roar a sheet of flame leapt upwards.

7

GINGER COMES HOME

FOR Ginger the long night passed slowly. He saw no more of the lion. One by one the fires he had started died down and went out, and in spite of his predicament the desire for sleep became almost irresistible: more than once he caught himself nodding. Yet sleep he dare not, for fear he fell off his perch and injured himself, for he had no means of tying himself to the branches between which he sat astride.

It was, therefore, with profound relief that he saw the stars begin to pale, and the faint flush of dawn steal upward from the eastern horizon. A shaft of light shot upwards, another, and another, and in spite of his position he found heart to admire the glory of the African sunrise.

He waited no longer. A searching scrutiny of the landscape revealed nothing more alarming than a small herd of giraffes peacefully grazing, their ungainly legs outstretched, a mile or two to the south, so he prepared to evacuate his haven of refuge. Before he did so, however, he glanced fearfully at the edge of the forest, still dark and forbidding, not more than a few hundred yards away. His eyes fell on something and he started, an expression of incredulity crossing his face. At the risk of falling, he leaned forward and stared as if he could not believe his eyes, for standing amongst the trees on the edge of the forest, close to a tumble-down shack, was an aeroplane. It was a Puss Moth, painted black.

A short, sharp scuffle, in which he left some of the skin of the palms of his hands on the rough bark of the tree, and he was on the ground, running towards his new hope of deliverance. He slowed down as he neared it, and advanced towards the hut cautiously, automatic at the ready. No sound came from inside, so very quietly he opened the door and peeped in. The hut was empty. That is to say, it contained no human occupant, although there were other things which at first made his eyes go round with wonder. Stacked on one side was a high pile of petrol-cans, which a swift investigation showed were full. There was also a spare propeller, two under-carriage wheels, some fabric, and tins of dope. On a shelf were some tins of bully beef, biscuits, and condensed milk. 'An emergency repair depot, eh?' he breathed, as he took in all these things with a sweeping glance. 'My goodness! This is a bigger thing than we thought, and no mistake.'

There was nothing else of interest, so he went out, closing the door behind him, and hurried towards the Puss. The tanks, he found, were more than half full, which was far more than he would need for the short run to Insula, so he did not stop to fill them up, for he was afraid that someone might arrive at any moment. Inside five minutes he had started the engine and had taxied out to the spot from which the Dragon had taken off. Watching carefully ahead for obstacles, he opened the throttle, and with fierce exultation in his heart, swept over the burnt patches of his fires into the air.

But his troubles were not yet over, for before many minutes had passed he detected a certain roughness in the engine, and a glance at the rev-counter confirmed what his ears had told him. The needle was flickering unpleasantly, and as he watched it he saw it sink slowly backwards. The trouble, whatever it was, was not very bad, but once trouble starts in an aero engine it usually develops quickly if it is allowed to run on, and this case was no exception, for although he throttled back to as near stalling point as he dare risk, the rev-counter dropped steadily, while the ever-rising thermometer warned him that if he went on much longer the whole thing might seize up.

'If I can only get back to the aerodrome I don't mind,' he thought desperately, as he throttled right back for a few seconds and dipped his nose in the hope of cooling the engine. But it was not to be. The noise grew steadily worse, and the vibration became alarming. He gave a grunt of satisfaction as his anxiously questing eyes picked out a dried-up waterhole that he had marked down on an earlier flight; it was not more than three or four miles from Insula, and looking ahead he could just see the small clump of trees that hid the bungalow.

At that moment there was a sharp explosion in the engine and a little cloud of black smoke swirled away aft. 'It's no use,' he told himself bitterly as he throttled right back and examined the ground swiftly for a landing-place, for he had very little altitude.

The country was still fairly open, sun-baked earth for the most part covered with the usual coarse grass, and here and there stunted trees, alone and in little groups. There were also an unpleasant number of high, conical mounds which he knew were ant-hills, and it was these that worried him most. However, he chose the most open place he could see within gliding distance, and with teeth clenched he side-slipped down to land, for the place he had chosen was almost immediately below him. The wheels touched, bumped, and bumped again, and then the whole machine quivered as it ran over the rough surface. He pressed on the rudder with his left foot as a low group of ant-hills appeared directly in his path; the machine swerved sickeningly, and for a moment he thought his under-carriage must collapse, but it stood up to the strain, and the machine came to rest in a little fold in the ground.

'Well, I'm down, anyway,' he muttered, expressing the relief that most pilots would have experienced in similar circumstances; and his relief was intensified by the knowledge that the machine was likely to prove their only link with civilization. He switched off the petrol and ignition and then jumped to the ground. There was nothing more he could do. He did not like the idea of leaving the machine out in the sun, but there was no help for it; all he could do was to hurry to the aerodrome and advise the others of how things stood. Between them they might be able to effect the necessary repairs and get the machine into the hangar at Insula before the sun reached its zenith. Accordingly, he took a last look round to make sure there were no wild animals about, and then set off at a steady trot in the direction of the aerodrome.

A trifle more than half an hour later, hot and dishevelled, he arrived at the aerodrome, and after a glance at the empty hangar and the bungalow, he turned his steps towards the rest-house. He was still several yards away when he was amazed to hear Sarda's voice speaking, although he could not catch the words. Wondering what was going on, he hurried forward just in time to catch Sarda's last sentence when he informed Biggles that he was going outside to 'hark at them frizzling'.

Ginger heard the *whoof* of the petrol as it flamed up, and then Sarda appeared in the doorway.

Considering that he was taken completely unawares, Sarda acted with commendable promptitude. His right hand flew to his shirt. Ginger's hand flashed to his pocket. Both weapons came out together. There was a flash of steel as the knife sped through the air. Simultaneously, Ginger's gun roared. A sharp stinging pain in the cheek made him jerk his head convulsively, but he recovered himself to see Sarda stumble, clutching at his chest. For a moment or two he swayed, coughing; then his legs seemed to collapse and he pitched forward on to his face.

In a kind of daze Ginger leapt over the fallen body and tore into the rest-house, trying to fight off with his arms the heat that seemed to be blistering his skin. He saw Biggles lying across his bed and Algy stretched out on the floor. At the same time he was also subconsciously aware of a snake that was threshing about on the table on to which it had evidently fallen from the blazing roof. Stooping, he seized Algy, who was the nearer, by the collar, and dragged him outside. Then he dashed back to Biggles. The heat was appalling, and his nostrils were filled with the stench of singeing hair and clothes. Seeming to move in a ghastly nightmare from which he could not awaken, he dragged his two unconscious comrades farther out on to the aerodrome, and then made a final sally into the flames for the kit-bags. He saw the rifle and the two automatics lying on the table, and paused for a moment to fling them through the doorway before snatching up the kit-bags and leaping clear. He would have liked to save some of their stores, but it was out of the question, so he ran towards Sarda, who was still lying near the doorway where he had fallen. But before he could reach him there was a rending, tearing crash, and the whole building collapsed in a cloud of flying sparks, burying Sarda under the debris. Another moment and Ginger, too, would have been caught in the blazing ruin; as it was, he only just managed to leap back in time.

He saw that the sky had turned a peculiar shade of purple, and wondered vaguely why. His face was still smarting and he raised his hand to it to see what was the matter. It felt wet and sticky, and unaccountably his legs began to tremble. 'I'm going to faint,' he thought, 'but I won't . . . I won't. Water . . . I must get water.'

Unsteadily he began to run towards the bungalow. The movement saved him and the crisis passed, and by the time he reached the building he felt better, although his actions still seemed to be unnatural and automatic. He found a pail of water in the kitchen and drank deeply, using his cupped hands. He also splashed some of the water over his face. Then he snatched up the bucket and ran back to where the others lay. They looked ghastly, and a dreadful fear that they were dead set him trembling again.

'Hi, Biggles,' he croaked, tipping some of the water over the white face. Then he treated Algy in the same way. But it was a good five minutes before he could get any response. Then Biggles moaned feebly and opened his eyes. Slowly, from vague wonderment, recognition crept into them.

'Hello,' he said with a foolish smile. 'Where the dickens have you sprung from?'

Ginger tried to speak, but the sky seemed to be going dark again. It was nearly black, and the sun a great white ball that bounced about on it. 'I—I——' he faltered, but he could get no farther. His knees crumpled under him and he flopped down like a coat falling from a peg.

8
SAVAGES

WHEN he opened his eyes again he was lying in the shade inside the hangar. Biggles, in his shirt sleeves, was dabbing his face with a wet rag, while Algy, still looking very groggy, was watching the proceedings.

'Feeling better?' grinned Biggles.

Ginger struggled into a sitting position, his hand going to his face at the same time. 'What's all this?' he asked as his fingers came in contact with a rough bandage that had been bound round his head.

'We had to tie your face up,' Biggles told him. 'Somehow or other you've managed to cut it pretty badly; it isn't deep, but you've bled quite a bit.'

'Sarda's knife did it,' announced Ginger briefly.

Biggles whistled. 'My gosh! You must have had a pretty close squeak.'

'Closish,' admitted Ginger.

'Where did Sarda go?'

'Go?'

'Yes, where is he now? There isn't a sign of him.'

Ginger scrambled to his feet, walked unsteadily to the door of the hangar and pointed to the smoking remains of the rest-house. 'He's under there,' he said quietly.

Biggles stared at him. 'How did it happen?' he asked.

'I shot him,' muttered Ginger. 'Not intentionally, though. We met at the door. He went for his knife and I pulled my gun, intending to tell him to put his hands up; but before I could speak he flung the knife at me and somehow or other the gun went off. I remember feeling the knife whizz past my cheek, and—well, I don't know quite what happened after that, except that I managed to drag you out and was just going to haul Sarda clear when the whole place collapsed on top of him.'

There was silence for a few moments.

'Well, no one can say that he hasn't got his desserts,' observed Biggles philosophically. 'If ever there was a cold-blooded murderer he was one. It may sound callous, but I'm no hypocrite, and I don't mind telling you that I feel happier with him out of the way. What with losing the Dragon and all our stores we are in a bad enough mess without him taking pot shots at us. And now, if you're feeling well enough to talk, you might tell us what happened in here last night. In fact, there are a lot of things I should like to hear, such as where you've been and how you got back here so providentially. Another five minutes and all you'd have found of us would have been cinders.'

Briefly, but omitting nothing of importance, Ginger described the events from the time Leroux made his entry into the hangar.

'The sooner we get out to that Puss the better,' declared Biggles, when he had finished. 'With it we've got a good chance to put up a show; without it we're sunk. How far away is it, do you think?'

'I should say about three miles.'

'That's three-quarters of an hour's walk. Do you feel fit enough to travel?'

'Me! I'm as right as rain,' answered Ginger. 'But what about you and Algy? Neither of you look in what one might call the pink of condition.'

'I think we're pretty well all right,' answered Biggles. 'At least, I am, except for a sort of stiffness in the joints. How about you, Algy?'

'Same as you,' replied Algy quickly. 'A bit stiff and a headache, that's all. I wonder what that dope was Sarda gave us.'

'Never mind about that; I'm glad it was only a drug and not poison. Let's muster up our things and get away. It seems reasonable to suppose that Leroux will soon be looking for his Puss, and we've got to get to it first. It's fairly clear now to see what happened. After he left here yesterday morning he didn't go back to Karuli, or whatever Sarda called his head-quarters, but dropped down at that secret landing-ground of his either because his engine was giving trouble or because he had resolved to steal our machine. I rather suspect it was on account of his engine, though, because, having given Sarda the dope to put us out of action—that was what was in he envelope he gave him, I expect—he could have come back here today without any risk. He may have been in a hurry to get to Karuli, and when his engine started to conk he decided to go down and come back for our machine.'

'It was a tidy step if he came on foot,' put in Ginger.

'Possibly he had a horse. I should say that that telephone of

Sarda's goes to the aerodrome where you found the Puss, or at least passes through it. Did you notice a receiver in the hut, Ginger?'

'No, I didn't, but I wasn't there many seconds and I might easily have overlooked it.'

'I was thinking that perhaps Leroux got into touch with his head-quarters at Karuli from there. No matter; he got back here somehow, as we know to our cost. But we'd better not stay here talking. Let's get some food and water from the bungalow and make a bee-line for the Puss. With three automatics and a rifle we ought to be able to give a good account of ourselves if anyone starts any rough stuff.'

'What are you going to do with the machine?' Algy asked Biggles, as they all walked to where their kit-bags still lay on the aerodrome.

'Put the engine right if we can and fly it back here. Then, after we've had a rest, we'll either go to Malakal and report what has happened, or else go and have a look for this plantation that we've heard so much about. I can't quite make up my mind which is the best course, but we'll talk more about that when we've got the machine. We'd better park these in the bungalow for the time being,' Biggles added, as they picked up their kit-bags. 'It's not much use trying to do anything about—that,' he concluded, nodding towards the still smouldering ruins of the rest-house. 'It will be hours before those ashes have cooled down.'

They hurried on to the bungalow, put their kit in the living-room, and after closing the doors and windows, they set off in the direction of the abandoned aeroplane.

'Suppose the telephone rings?' asked Ginger as they hurried along.

'I thought of that,' nodded Biggles. 'In fact, I seriously considered putting a call through, but decided that it would be better left alone. The silence will get the people at the other end guessing, whereas if we try to use it we might easily slip up, which would tell them that Sarda's scheme has misfired, and that we are in charge of the situation here. It's another thing we shall

have to think about when we get back. For the present, I shan't
have any peace until we've got that machine in safe custody.'

They had no difficulty in finding the Puss Moth, nor did they
encounter trouble of any sort on the way. For this they were all
thankful, for what with nervous reaction after what they had
been through, sheer weariness, and the heat of the sun, they were
in no case to meet adversity with their customary optimism.

'Well, here she is,' observed Biggles, as he opened the cabin
door. 'It's Harry Marton's machine, there's no doubt about
that. Look!' He pointed to the fabric under the exhaust pipe
where the black paint had been rather carelessly applied, with
the result that the original red dope showed through it as a dull
maroon tint. 'Did you form any opinion as to what was wrong
with the engine, Ginger?'

'Yes, I fancy it's faulty lubrication. She started by running
rough and got hot very quickly.'

'If it's nothing worse than that it shouldn't be a very big job,'
muttered Biggles, as he brought out the tool kit. 'Great Sam!
This sun is the dickens; mind how you handle that cowling—it's
nearly red-hot.'

None of them is likely to forget the next hour and a half. The
sun, as it approached its zenith, blazed down with relentless fury,
making all the metal parts of the machine so hot that the
handling of them was a matter of extreme discomfort. Flies and
stinging insects added to their misery. However, in the end they
found the cause of the trouble—a piece of cotton waste in an oil
lead—and thereafter it was only a question of time before the job
was done.

With a grunt of satisfaction Ginger screwed up the last engine-
cowling bolt, and then turned to where the others were collecting
the tools and replacing them in the kit. As he did so, a movement
some distance beyond caught his eye, and he looked up.

'Say, Chief, look what's coming,' he cried.

Both Biggles and Algy sprang up and followed the direction of
his eyes with their own.

Approaching them at a fast trot, in single file, and not more
than two hundred yards away, was a line of savage warriors. And

they were the real thing. Nude except for a short skirt of leopard skin and a garter-like fringe of white hair bound below their knees, they fitted perfectly into the inhospitable landscape. All were armed with short-handled broad-bladed assagais, with a tuft of hair at the end, and carried oval-shaped shields of white ox-hide threaded with black strips of the same material. Above the head of the leader rose a plume of glorious ostrich feathers, held in place by an encircling band.

'I don't like the look of those gentry,' stated Biggles, as he gazed at them steadily.

'Can't we start up and get away before they reach us?' suggested Algy.

Biggles shook his head. 'Impossible,' he said. 'It would be fatal to try to get off without first clearing a runway, even if we knew that the engine was giving full revs, which we don't, and shan't until we run her up. Somehow I can't think those fellows mean any harm, though; they must have seen plenty of white men, and most African natives have learned by this time that it pays to leave them alone. Ginger, take the rifle into the cabin and keep us covered without letting them see it. Above all, don't look scared, anybody, but be ready for anything.'

'If you don't think they mean any harm, why do you say you don't like the look of them?' asked Ginger from inside the cabin.

'Because I didn't notice at first the direction they are coming from,' replied Biggles shortly. 'It's the direction of Karuli, and the emergency landing-ground where you collared this machine, isn't it?'

'It is,' answered Ginger briefly.

'Well, here they are,' continued Biggles. 'Leave the talking to me, although as none of us knows their lingo there isn't likely to be much.'

The black warriors slowed down to a walk a short distance away, and then advanced in a rough half circle.

Biggles raised his hand. 'Stop there,' he called loudly.

Rather to his surprise the order was obeyed. 'What do you want?' he asked curtly.

The leader raised his assagai to his forehead in a curious sort of

salute. 'What you make with my master's aeroplane?' he asked
harshly, in an even, high-pitched voice.

Biggles expressed no surprise at this unexpected question.
'Who is your master?' he asked.

'My master white man.'

'Yes, I'd guessed that, but what is his name?'

'My master say go Insula and find aeroplane.'

A faint smile flitted across Biggles's face as he realized that the
savage was no fool. 'Where is your master?' he asked.

The native pointed with his assagai to the east.

'How far away?'

'Two day—three day march.'

Biggles suspected that the fellow was lying, but he had no
means of proving it. 'You go and tell your master that we're
taking his aeroplane to Insula, where he can have it just as soon
as he brings *my* aeroplane back,' he answered in a firm voice.

'If you no give aeroplane, then we take it,' declared the other
impudently.

Biggles's eyes glinted and his lips came together in a tight line.
'You insolent rascal; you talk to me like that and I'll thrash the
skin off your back. Be off, and sharp's the word.'

The savage did not move a muscle.

'Did you hear me?' cried Biggles, in a voice that cut through
the air like the crack of a whip.

The savage stood his ground. He did not answer, but some of
the others began to mutter amongst themselves.

'Give me that rifle, Ginger,' ordered Biggles quickly.

Ginger leapt out and put the weapon into Biggles's hands.

'Now!' snapped Biggles. 'Perhaps you've heard it said that
Englishmen always keep their word. Think hard on that,
because in one minute by my watch I'm going to shoot at any one
I see within spear-throw.'

Some of the savages began to back away instantly, while the
leader, clearly torn by indecision, looked at them and the white
men in turn. Finally, finding himself alone, he turned and
followed the others in the slow, insolent, provocative manner
sometimes employed by small children when made to do

something against their will.

Biggles's eyes narrowed. 'You cheeky swine,' he snarled, and throwing up the rifle, sent a shot whistling in the direction of the cause of his ire.

The native's pose of indifference disappeared in a flash. Bending low and zigzagging like a snipe, he ran for his life until he disappeared from view behind a slight rise in the ground a quarter of a mile away.

'Start up, Ginger,' snapped Biggles. 'Algy, come and help me choose the best path to get off. There's no wind, so the direction doesn't matter.' He started off at a run, but pulled up again with a jerk. 'Hark!' he cried.

From afar off came the low, powerful hum of aero engines.

Algy threw up his arm, and with finger outstretched pointed to a tiny speck in the east. 'There he is,' he cried. 'It's the Dragon, and it's coming this way.'

'Come on,' yelled Biggles. 'If he catches us on the ground we're done.'

The next few minutes can only be described as hectic. With perspiration streaming down their faces, Biggles and Algy ran along the least obstructed fairway, flinging aside large stones, trampling down small ant-hills, and examining the ground for holes which might spell disaster if the fast-moving wheels of the Puss struck them during the take-off. Then, satisfied that they had a fairly clear run, they raced back to where the machine was ticking over.

'Run her up,' shouted Biggles to Ginger, and running round to the rear of the fuselage, he threw himself across it to keep the tail down while Ginger opened the throttle. The blast of the slipstream as it struck him was as refreshing as a cold shower-bath, and while it lasted he revelled in it. Then, as the roar subsided suddenly, he dashed up to the cockpit. 'How does she go?' he asked.

'She's O.K.,' answered Ginger crisply.

'Then let me have her. In you get, Algy; make it snappy,' ordered Biggles, as the roar of the twin-engined machine suddenly increased in volume. Glancing up, he saw the blunt nose tilted down towards them. As he jumped in and slammed the cabin door behind him, something struck the engine-cowling with a metallic *zip*. It was a spear; the point had pierced the thin sheet-metal cowling, and remained impaled, the haft sticking out at right-angles. There was no time to remove it, for glancing through the window he saw the savages closing in on the machine in a wild charge.

'Hold tight,' he yelled, and shoved the throttle open.

The actual take-off, for the few seconds while it lasted, was a hair-raising affair. Twice the machine was thrown into the air by tufts of grass before it had reached flying speed, and each time, as the wheels returned to earth with a terrifying rumble, they all thought that the machine must break into halves. How it stood up to the strain Biggles could not imagine, but it did, and he sank back with a pathetic smile, shaking his head sadly as the machine finally lifted.

'A little more of this sort of thing and I shall be ripe for a madhouse,' he yelled, as he held the nose down for a moment to get a reserve of speed, and then zoomed high into the air, looking to right and left for the Dragon.

For a moment he could not see it, but as he turned slowly it swung suddenly into his field of view. To his surprise it was two or three miles away, flying in a northerly direction, steadily, as if the pilot intended maintaining his course.

'What's his idea?' shouted Algy, who had also seen it.

'Goodness knows,' replied Biggles. 'I thought he intended going for us.'

'So did I.'

'Maybe he was, but changed his mind when he saw us take off.'

'Are you going to follow him?'

'What's the use? According to Ginger we haven't more than an hour's petrol. I'll bet he's got a full load. If we followed him for more than half an hour we should find ourselves down in the jungle with empty tanks, so that would be a crazy thing to do. We'd better get to Insula and fill up; then we'll do a spot of quick thinking.'

'I'm getting sick of the sight of Insula,' muttered Ginger.

'So am I,' Biggles told him shortly, 'but it's the only port we've got in this perishing wilderness.'

'What about that landing-ground at the repair depot where I pinched the Moth?'

Biggles started. Then he nodded towards the ground where the savages, clustered together, were staring upwards. 'They came from that direction, and I fancy they'll go back that way, otherwise I'd consider it,' he said. 'In any case, though, to be on the safe side we ought to go to Insula first and fill up our tanks, in casy anything has happened to the fuel you saw at the repair depot. We should look fools to arrive there and find that the stuff had all been taken away. Keep your eye on those fellows and see which way they go when they move off. I'm going to Insula.'

9

BIGGLES SUMS UP

'WHAT happened to those savages at the finish?' asked Biggles as the machine ran to a standstill on Insula aerodrome.

'The last I saw of them they were walking away in single file, just as they arrived,' replied Algy.

'Which way did they go?'

'East—back to where they came from, presumably.'

'We mustn't forget they're about if ever we have to land in that district,' declared Biggles. 'I've no desire to finish this crazy business with one of these skewers in my ribs,' he added, pulling out the assagai that had stuck in the engine-cowling.

'Well, now we're here, what's going to be done about it?' asked Ginger.

'I've been thinking about that on the way,' answered Biggles thoughtfully. 'It's a bit of a problem. There's one thing we *must* do, though.'

'What's that?'

'Collect everything that's likely to be useful to us and hide it— make a *cache* somewhere. What I have particularly in mind is the petrol and oil.'

'Why is it necessary to move it?'

'Because I think it's an absolute certainty that sooner or later some sort of attack will be made on this place. Leroux and his crowd are aware that we have got the Puss, and they must know perfectly well that this is our only depot for supplies. They'll realize, unless they are bigger fools than I take them for, that the quickest and surest way to put us out of action would be to remove or destroy this supply of fuel here. That would put the tin hat on things as far as we're concerned, wouldn't it? Immobile, as we should then be, we should be helpless. In fact, I'm not altogether sure that we should even be able to get back to civilization; Malakal and Juba are our nearest points, and they are both a long way away. It may sound pessimistic, but from what I've heard about Africa I doubt very much if we could carry enough food and water to last us the journey if we had to walk, and it would be fatal to start without enough because, barring a lucky shot which might produce fresh meat for us, there is no food to be had. To set out in the hope of living on our rifle would be folly, but in an emergency we might have to do that. That's why I say I should feel happier if we had a secret dump somewhere. Moreover, by removing the fuel it is more than likely that we should make things awkward for Leroux. In the past he has had to rely on a supply of fuel here, or it wouldn't be here; so if he lands and finds it gone he might be in a mess.'

'Yes, I see that,' put in Algy. 'It will be a bit of a sweat, though, won't it—moving it, I mean?'

'I don't think so; there isn't as much as all that, and we needn't take it far away.'

'I feel inclined to raze the place to the ground,' continued Biggles, as they walked towards the bungalow. 'Leave it like the Bosche left some of the French villages when they retired in 1918—you remember? That would make Leroux and Co. scratch their heads, I'll warrant. It's always a good plan to get your enemies guessing; it's far more disconcerting than knowing the truth, even when the truth is bad news. We played that game for all it was worth during the War, particularly over the submarine question. Bosche submarines used to put out and just disappear into the blue; never came back. Did we shout to the world that we'd caught them in a trap and sent them to the bottom? Not likely. We did the brer rabbit trick; lay low and kept on saying nothing. Do you wonder that the Bosche submarine crews got all jumpy? I don't. No doubt they could have heard without turning a hair that their pals had gone to Davy Jones, but the dreadful uncertainty as to their fate got 'em guessing, and the guessing got 'em groggy. When Leroux and Co. turn up here to find out what has happened to Sarda, as they are bound to do before very long, and find the place deserted, stores gone and all the rest of it, they'll get all hot and bothered, particularly when they work it out that we must still be somewhere in the offing.'

'But if you think they're likely to turn up here why not wait for them, and when they arrive, shoot them up?' suggested Algy belligerently.

'For two very good reasons,' replied Biggles promptly. 'The first is that we don't know how long we should have to wait. It might be days, and while we were waiting our nerves would get on edge, particularly as we should have to mount a very strict guard day and night to prevent ourselves from being taken by surprise. I can't think that they'd be such fools as to just stroll on the aerodrome, or land on it, supposing—as they must—that we are here. We might find ourselves besieged by a mob of savages; we know there are at least a score in their pay, and if they have a score they might well have a whole tribe. And the second reason is that, even if we caught them at a disadvantage, we couldn't just open fire and shoot them down or we might find ourselves in court on a charge of murder.'

'But surely they've given us cause enough——'

'Of course they have. *We* know that, but how could we prove it?'

'What about the snake in the cockpit? And the way they doped us, and stole our machine, and——'

'Told in a court of law that would all sound like a wonderful fairy tale,' declared Biggles, shaking his head. 'No, when we step up to a judge with our story we've got to be able to trot out proof.

Nothing counts for anything at law without that. And what about young Marton? Have you forgotten him? As his father is paying for all this, and it looks like costing him a tidy penny, Harry's rescue must be our first consideration. The bringing of his abductors to justice is a secondary affair, although, naturally, we shall do that if we can. Open a couple of tins of bully and some biscuits, Ginger; we might as well eat while we've got the chance.'

'What beats me is what the whole thing is about,' remarked Algy presently, digging into a tin of bully with his penknife.

Biggles shrugged his shoulders. 'I've thought quite a bit about that,' he said. 'A lot of things have happened since we turned up here, but when you come to examine them you'll find that they haven't provided much information beyond the fact that Harry Marton is alive and someone is using his machine. This is the position in a nutshell, as I see it now. Marton landed here on his way to the Cape. For reasons not yet ascertained he was abducted, held prisoner, and his machine confiscated. My own opinion is that it was because he discovered something— accidentally, no doubt—about this place, or Leroux, or the people who are running Insula. Very well! We arrive on the scene and start nosing round. As soon as it became known in the enemy camp that we were going to stay at Insula steps were taken to cause us to remove ourselves; failing that, to remove us. Sarda tried to put us off in the first place by talking of fever and so on, but when he saw that we intended staying he rang up his head-quarters and told them what was happening; whereupon without any loss of time things began to hum. Within a few hours an attempt was made to murder us, which proves how desperately anxious these people must be to get us out of the way. The question is, why? Ostensibly they are running a tobacco plantation. That that is merely a blind to cloak their real activities is certain, for no one is likely to stop them growing tobacco. Just what they are up to—but let's leave that for the moment. The point is, it is perfectly clear that transport plays a vital part in their operations.'

'Why are you so sure about that?' asked Algy, reaching for the biscuits.

'Dash it all, man, look at the trouble they've been at to establish aerodromes and fit them up. They must have at least three.'

'How three?'

'Insula is one, the place where Ginger found the Puss is another, and the one at their head-quarters. Obviously they must have got one there. Then there's the telephone connecting them up. All these things have meant a pretty heavy expenditure of cash, from which we can reasonably infer that the business, whatever it is, is a highly profitable one. They're using air transport remember, which again is by no means cheap. That suggests to me that either speed is very important, or else——'

'Well?'

'Or else it offers a way of concealing the cargo they are carrying. As we know as well as anyone, an aeroplane can get about with less interference than any form of surface transport. You can take it from me that the whole thing boils down to that cargo, and when we have found out what that is we shall know everything. Harry Marton found out what it was, I'll bet. He found out by accident, no doubt, but it put paid to his Cape record.'

'Which means that it is something of an illicit or contraband nature?'

'Definitely.'

'What could it be?'

'The only thing I can think of at the moment is slaves. There's a big business still done in slaves between this part of Africa, the Sudan, and Arabia. Our people have tried to stop it for years; they've curtailed the slavers' activities but they haven't stopped the traffic, not by a long way.'

'Human freight is heavy stuff. What is a slave worth—have you any idea?'

'About a hundred pounds, I believe.'

'By the time they've paid their running expenses, Stampoulos and Leroux are not going to get very fat out of that, carrying only two at a time in a Puss.'

'True enough. But as I said just now, what these people are doing is of secondary importance to us. We've come to get Harry Marton. We've managed to get his machine, which is as much as old Mr Marton hoped for; but in view of what we know we shall have to count the trip a failure if we don't bring the boy back in it.'

'And we can't very well do that until we know where he is,' observed Ginger tritely.

Biggles glanced up. 'There's an awful lot of truth in that, Ginger, my lad,' he agreed. 'The first thing we must do, then, is to find out where he is.'

'And having done that, what are we going to do?' inquired Algy dubiously. 'Are we in a position to launch an attack on the enemy stronghold for the purpose of rescuing him?'

'Frankly, I don't think we are,' admitted Biggles. 'Quite apart from the white men, who are doubtless armed with rifles, there are those toughs we saw this morning to be considered. I'm not exactly aching to get tangled up with a bunch of assagais, and that's a fact.'

'Sez you,' agreed Algy warmly. 'What's the programme, then?'

'We've got to locate this place Karuli before we do anything else.'

'What are you going to do—fly round and look for it?'

'I'm not going to walk, you can bet your life on that.'

'When are you thinking of making a start?'

'We'd better leave it until to-morrow. It's after two o'clock now, and we've got to shift this petrol yet.'

'Then let's get to it,' suggested Ginger. 'I'm nearly asleep on my feet, and the sooner the job's done the sooner we can all hit the hay. This business is getting a lot too much like hard labour for my liking.'

'I'll bring a gang of navvies next time to do the rough stuff,' Biggles promised, smiling, as he put on his hat and walked to the door. He reached it, and was about to step outside, when a movement in the distance caught his eye, and instead of going out he took a quick pace backward.

Algy snatched up the rifle and peered over his shoulder. 'Antelopes, by jingo,' he muttered.

Ginger joined the others, and looking out, saw a herd of long-horned animals grazing peacefully about a mile away near the eastern boundary of the landing-ground. 'What about knocking one of them over and having steak for supper?'

'I think it's a rattling good idea if it can be done,' agreed Biggles. 'It's worth trying, anyway. But you'd better not go wandering off, Ginger; you're tired as it is. Algy, you take the rifle and try your hand at stalking while Ginger and I shift the petrol. If you get one there's no need to drag the whole beast back; cut off a haunch: that will be enough. The rest would go bad before we could eat it.'

'Good enough,' agreed Algy enthusiastically, and with the rifle in his hand he crept out into the coppice.

'Come on, Ginger, let's go and find a good place to dump this petrol,' ordered Biggles. 'We shall have to do it quietly or we shall alarm the game.'

10
ALGY'S ANTELOPE HUNT

ALGY soon covered half the distance that separated him from his quarry, for he had plenty of cover, but thereafter the going became more difficult. He knew that it was hopeless to attempt to get within range of the wary beasts by going across the open aerodrome, and the country on either side was nearly as bare. After he had left the coppice on the edge of which the aerodrome buildings were situated, he had been able to advance by keeping a large clump of bushes between himself and the herd, but he had now reached the end of the bushes, and from there on the ground, in a direct line with the animals, offered no concealment of any sort. He estimated his distance from them to be about eight hundred yards, although in the clear atmosphere it looked considerably less, and he could see them distinctly.

Thinking that it might be possible to achieve success wih a long shot, he slipped his rear sight up to the eight hundred mark and raised the rifle; but he lowered it again immediately, for the heat-soaked air rippled and quivered like disturbed water, making it quite impossible to take steady aim.

'I shall have to get a lot nearer than this,' he mused, and casting about for another way of approach, he saw something that had previously escaped his notice. It was a shallow gully, presumably a dried-up watercourse judging by the dry reeds that lined its banks; it meandered across the landscape, passing within two hundred yards of the antelopes at its nearest point. He remembered seeing it from the air.

Lying flat in the grass, for in order to reach it he had to pass for some distance in full view of the animals, he wormed his way towards the gully, and managed to reach it without alarming the game. He waited for a minute or two to recover his composure, for in the heat of the sun the method of progress he had been compelled to employ was exhausting, and then set off down the gully, picking his way with great care, knowing well that the slightest noise would be fatal to his object.

He was some time gaining his vantage point, for here and there the gully was very shallow, and in such places he had to crawl; but in the end he reached it and wormed his way into the reeds that lined the bank in order to reach the brink and thus command a view of the antelopes. Slowly and with infinite pains he drew himself level with the top and peeped over. There was not an animal in sight. Dumbfounded, for he was convinced that the antelopes could not have seen him, he could only lie and stare. But his quarry might have dissolved into thin air for all the sign there was of them. Then, in the far distance, he saw a tiny cloud of dust slowly settling, and it told him which way the beasts had gone.

'Well, dash my wig!' he muttered, in a tone of mixed disappointment and astonishment. 'That's good-bye to our supper.' Slowly he slid back down through the reeds, and with all need for concealment gone, was about to rise to his feet when he saw something that made him gasp, and sent him squirming into the thickest part of the rushes, where he lay motionless.

Coming up the gully was a line of armed savages, the same, judging by their attire, as they had seen that morning when they had been at work on the Puss Moth. But now, at their head, in an open shirt, shorts, with a solar topee on his head and a rifle crooked in his left arm, marched a white man. No longer was there any mystery about the antelopes' disappearance, and Algy saw at once that to attempt to move would be folly, for to do so without being seen was out of the question; so he could only lie still and hope for the best, although, lying in the thick reeds as he was, he felt it was unlikely that he would be discovered. Nor would he have been except for an extraordinary unlucky chance that completely upset his calculations, and in a few seconds altered every possible aspect of the situation.

The warriors, with the white man striding along in front, held steadily and silently on their way towards the aerodrome buildings which, Algy had no doubt, was their objective, and they were only a few yards away from him when it happened. Without warning, from out of the dry reeds on the opposite bank came a leopard and two cubs, all yawning and stretching like domestic cats that have been asleep on the hearth. Algy nearly froze with horror when he realized that they must have been there all the time, and that during his stalk down the gully he must have passed within a dozen yards of them. However, there was no time to dwell on his narrow escape, for the leopard, looking up, saw the party just below. Its sleepiness disappeared in a flash. With a vicious snarl it crouched low, the very embodiment of feline fury. Another second and it would have charged, but at that moment the white man fired. That the bullet had gone home Algy knew, for he distinctly heard the soft *phut* of the lead striking flesh, and the creature's behaviour proved it. With a frightful roar it leapt high into the air, tearing at its side with its teeth; then, as it struck the earth again, it twisted, and with a single bound sprang straight into the reeds where Algy lay hidden.

His actions during the next two seconds were prompted far more by sheer instinct of self-preservation than lucid thought.

The leopard landed almost on top of him. It saw him at once and turned like lightning, teeth flashing and claws bared, a picture that was to remain clear in his mind for a long time to come. With a convulsive movement he jerked up the rifle, shoved the muzzle almost into the beast's mouth and pulled the trigger. Then, not waiting to see the result, still clutching the rifle, he flung himself over the bank and ran like a hare towards the bungalow.

As he ran two thoughts flashed into his whirling brain. The first was that Biggles would take no notice of the shot, thinking that he had fired at the antelopes, and the second was that the man he had left standing in the gully might shoot at him, for the fact that he was with the natives more than suggested that he was the 'master' to whom the leader had referred that morning during the altercation near the Puss. With this new fear in his mind he crouched low and swerved; and it was a good thing that he did so, for a moment later a bullet tore up the ground close to his feet and zipped away into the air. He swerved again, expecting another shot to be fired, but it did not come, and in a detached way he wondered why. He noticed that the unknown man's rifle was of a heavier calibre than his own, and the report much deeper. Would Biggles hear it? Yes! Algy saw him run out of the trees with Ginger, stand staring for a moment, and then make a dash towards the hanger where the Puss Moth was housed.

Still no shot came from behind, so he risked a glance over his shoulder, and the sight that met his gaze explained why. Strung out along his path of flight, in a direct line between him and the white man and therefore obstructing his view, were the savages, running; but any relief he experienced from the fact that he was no longer under fire was more than counterbalanced by the proximity of the nearest savage, who, evidently a faster runner than his companions, was well out in front of them and only a short distance behind Algy. What was worse, his speed was terrific and he was rapidly closing the distance.

Algy saw at once that he could not hope to reach the bungalow before he was caught, and his back twitched at the thought of the assagai which might pierce it at any moment. There was only one thing to be done and he did it, for the nearer the fellow with the spear got to him the more desperate was his danger.

Still running, he jerked the empty shell out of the breach of his rifle and reloaded. Then he whipped round, dropped on to his knee and took aim. He saw the brawny arm go up, the spear flashing in the sunlight, and he knew that he could not afford to miss—not that he was likely to at such close range. As he glanced along the sights his war-training came to his aid, and his manner changed. Coolly and deliberately he drew a bead on the shining black chest of his would-be slayer, and squeezed the trigger. At the report the savage sprawled headlong, the spear plunging into the ground, where it remained with the shaft pointing towards its owner.

Algy looked at the others, now perilously close; but a rapidly increasing roar made him swing round. The Puss, with the cabin door flapping open, was taxi-ing tail-up towards him. He needed no invitation to join the others inside. He fired two quick shots at the savages, causing one to fall and the others to stop, and then raced to meet the machine. A bullet smacked through it somewhere as he literally tumbled aboard, and then lay, with his head on Ginger's knees, panting for breath. For a few seconds the wheels bumped over the rough ground; then the floor seemed to press upwards into him and he knew they were off.

'Thank goodness for that,' he muttered fervently.

'Where's that antelope steak?' growled Ginger.

Algy glared. 'I'll knock your block off if you talk to me about antelopes,' he snarled. 'I'll let you go next time. Where are we making for?'

'Goodness knows—I don't,' replied Ginger frankly. 'We hadn't thought as far ahead as that when we saw you making a bee-line for home.'

'Then I hope it's to England,' declared Algy. 'These wide open spaces may be he-man's country, but they're not mine—not by a long shot.'

CRASHED BY A RHINO

As soon as he had recovered his breath Algy tapped Biggles on the shoulder. 'Where are you making for?' he asked.

'Karuli,' answered Biggles without hesitation.

'Are you crazy?'

'Possibly.'

'Haven't we had enough trouble already without shoving our heads into the lion's mouth?'

'We aren't going to shove our heads into anything of the sort.'

'Sounds like it to me.'

'Maybe, but I believe that at the moment the lion—as you call him—is on Insula aerodrome.'

'You mean, you think that tall fellow with the sallow face and black moustache who fired at me is Stampoulos?'

'Either him or his head man. He looks Greek enough, anyway. While he and his cut-throats are at Insula seems to me to be the right moment to go to Karuli.'

'To try to rescue Marton?'

'You don't suppose I'm going there for my health, or for the sake of somewhere to go, do you? What happened to your antelope hunt? It seemed to go wrong somewhere.'

'It certainly did,' agreed Algy emphatically. 'First I bumped into Stampoulos and his crowd of stiffs, and while I was wondering which way to go a leopard bumped into me. Between the lot of us it was quite a merry party while it lasted.'

'What happened?'

'I let drive at the leopard and Stampoulos let drive at me.'

'You scored and Stampoulos missed, eh?'

'That's about it.'

'And then you decided it was about time to go home.'

'I did, and without stopping to pick flowers on the way. That bunch of savages with flattened-out bill-hooks settled all doubt in my mind about that. What happened to them after I got aboard, did you see?'

'The last I saw of them Stampoulos had joined them and they were all marching towards the bungalow, carrying two of their number, as they say in story books.'

'I expect they'll look for Sarda.'

'In which case I hope they'll find him—and plant him. I wasn't looking forward to the job. But the point is, they're a tidy step from home, and as far as I can see they've got to walk, whereas we're getting a ride. With luck we ought to be at Karuli first.'

'You're not so optimistic as to expect to find the place deserted?'

'No, but with the big boy absent, the people in charge—whoever they may be—may not know how to act. If we find the place at all I shall be satisfied.'

'By the way, did you hide the petrol at Insula?'

'We hid pretty nearly everything portable; we'd just finished and loaded the kit-bags in the machine when your gun-shot announced that the hunt was over; although from what you tell us it was only just beginning.'

'We shall have to get a move on if we're going to find this place before dark,' observed Algy, glancing through the window at the sun, which was sinking fast towards the horizon. 'Don't you think it would be a better plan to land at this repair depot place Ginger talks about, to re-fuel, and hide the stuff in the same way as you did at Insula? That would give us two bases where we could get petrol in an emergency, and at the same time put another one of Leroux's landing-grounds out of action. If we go on nobbling his fuel I shouldn't be surprised if he finds himself walking presently, instead of swanking about in our Dragon.'

A furrow creased Biggles's forehead as he considered the proposition. 'I'm inclined to think you're right,' he said at last. 'Quite apart from the points you've raised, we're all tired and it's getting a bit close to sundown for operations. We don't want to get benighted on the open veld.'

'No, by James, that we don't,' agreed Ginger warmly. 'I've already had one go at it and that was one too many. If I've got to look at lions I prefer to see them through nice thick cast-iron bars; or better still, behind a sheet of plate-glass in a museum. I——'

'Don't talk so much,' interrupted Biggles. 'Just keep your eyes open for this repair establishment; remember, I haven't seen it yet.'

'You can't make any mistake,' declared Ginger. 'It's on the south side of a large wood, or forest; I don't know how far it extends because I didn't stop to look when I was there, but it's the first wood you come to.'

'Then that must be it—straight ahead.'

Ginger peered forward through the windscreen. 'That's the one,' he exclaimed. 'It will probably be difficult to see the hut from the air because it's just on the edge of the trees, but the landing-ground is on the south side.'

Biggles throttled back and began a long glide towards the objective, and on reaching it circled twice, both to make sure nobody was about and to pick out the best runway. Then, satisfied that all was well, he landed and taxied slowly towards the hut, which he could now see on the edge of the forest. A trio of ant-hills prevented him from going right up to it, so he switched off, and picking up the rifle, jumped out, watching the door suspiciously. The others followed him.

'I don't think anyone can be at home, or they'd have come out when they heard us coming,' he said confidently. 'Let's go and have a look at the place, not forgetting to keep your ears open. We mustn't forget that Leroux is floating about somewhere with the Dragon, and he might decide to drop in here. I hope he does. I don't like this Puss after the Dragon; feels a bit cramped for elbow room. What the——'

He broke off and spun round as a terrifying noise rose on the still air; it sounded like a cavalry charge and a pig being slaughtered at the same time.

There was no need to look far for the cause of it. Bearing down on them from the fringe of the forest was a rhinoceros. With its great horned snout held low, and its ridiculous little tail switching round in circles, it thundered towards them, squealing in fury, an avalanche of condensed wrath that would have been funny to watch from a safe place.

The three airmen scattered like small boys caught scrounging in an orchard. Algy made for the nearest tree; Biggles streaked for the nearest point of the forest; while Ginger, yelling to the others to follow him, made for the hut. He reached it, only to discover to his unspeakable horror that the door was locked. In an agony of fright he looked back, and to his relief saw that the great beast was not concerned with them. It had continued its charge straight on past the place where they had been and was bearing down on the aeroplane with the relentlessness of a runaway train. He heard Algy, secure in his tree, shout, and then two rifle shots in quick succession; but neither the shots nor the shout had the slightest effect on the berserk monster. With a fearful crash it struck the Puss Moth full amidships, and the machine crumpled up like a match-box that has been trodden on. The noise of the impact seemed to drive the brute to even greater fury, for it snorted, bucked, kicked, and stamped on the wreckage in a rage that was as insensate as it was destructive. Finally, as if satisfied that the life of the strange bird had been crushed out of it, it gave a final snort and trotted off, shaking its head in a vain endeavour to dislodge an elevator that was firmly impaled on its horn.

As it disappeared in the distance Algy dropped down from his tree, Biggles emerged from the forest, and Ginger from the side of the hut from which he had watched the final act of the tragedy. They met near the machine and for some seconds gazed at the tangled wreck in silence.

'Who was it suggested landing here?' inquired Biggles at last, coldly.

'I did,' confessed Algy hesitatingly.

'Then perhaps you wouldn't mind starting to stick the bits of this aeroplane together again,' Biggles told him.

Algy's reply was a roar of laughter, in which presently the others joined. It was, of course, pure reaction, but it relieved the strain.

'It's all very well for you chaps to laugh,' observed Biggles at last, wiping his eyes, 'but it isn't going to be so funny walking home; you take it from me.'

'But did you ever see an aeroplane in such a mess in your life?' protested Algy.

'Never,' admitted Biggles. 'And as long as I live I shall remember the picture of that ugly brute walking off with half our tail on its nose. Well, I hope it carries it about with it for the rest of its life; by that time it should be pretty sick of the sight and smell of aeroplane fabric.'

'I'm not going after it to take it off,' declared Algy.

'And to think I once paid to go to Whipsnade,' murmured Ginger sadly.

Whereupon they all laughed again.

'Well, we haven't got much else left to lose, there is that about it,' observed Biggles ruefully. 'At the rate we're going, we shall be lucky if we finish this affair with a pair of pants apiece.'

He stooped down, dragged the crumpled kit-bags out of the wreckage, and threw them clear. His own came last, and as he moved some mangled three-ply that was holding it, in order to release it, he stiffened suddenly while a puzzled look came into his eyes.

'What is it?' asked Algy who was watching him.

Biggles pulled the kit-bag clear and tossed it out on to the grass. Then he bent down, picked up a piece of the three-ply and put it to his nose, all the while frowning as if he strove to catch an elusive memory.

'I don't know,' he said slowly. 'Queer smell . . . reminds me of something . . . something I've . . . smelt before. Can't think what the dickens it is, though.' Still wearing an extraordinary expression, he allowed the three-ply to fall from his fingers. Then he shook his head as if dismissing the matter and turned to where the others were standing. 'Did you say there was some grub in that hut, Ginger?' he inquired.

'Yes. There's some bully, hard biscuits, and condensed milk,' replied Ginger.

'Then let's go and eat in case an elephant knocks the hut down while our backs are turned,' said Biggles bitterly. 'Combating crooks isn't bad fun, but when all the beasts of the ark join in, the game ceases to be amusing.'

'We can't say we didn't know they were here,' murmured Algy.

'That may be, but I did at least expect them to mind their own business considering that we've never interfered with them. Come on, let's get up to the hut.'

They picked up their kit-bags and walked up to the wooden building.

'It's locked! You can't get in,' cried Ginger, suddenly remembering.

'Can't I! You watch me,' retorted Biggles grimly.

He tried the handle, found that what Ginger had said was correct, backed a yard or two away and then charged. There was a splintering crash as the flimsy lock tore through the woodwork and the door flew open.

'Step in and make yourselves at home,' he said smiling. But the smile faded from his face as, followed by the others, he entered the primitive building. 'I thought you said there was a stock of petrol here, Ginger,' he exclaimed sharply.

'There was,' muttered Ginger weakly.

'Then perhaps you wouldn't mind pointing it out to me,' invited Biggles politely.

'It's—it's gone,' stammered Ginger, staring at the place where the cans had been piled. His eyes switched to the shelf where the food had been. 'So has the food,' he cried.

'So has everything, by the look of it,' said Biggles quietly, looking round the bare walls from which everything of a portable nature had been moved. 'I'm afraid we've arrived on the scene a bit too late,' he went on; 'good thing we weren't relying on that petrol for refuelling, isn't it? It just shows that it doesn't do to count on anything in this business.'

'Somebody must have been here,' declared Ginger.

Biggles eyed him thoughtfully. 'Wonderful!' he said. 'How did you work that out?'

Ginger smiled, for he was accustomed to Biggles's mild sarcasm in moments of anxiety. 'That's how the door came to be locked, too, I expect,' he observed. 'Whoever came here locked the door behind him when he went. It wasn't locked this morning.'

Biggles's eyes were roving round the walls.

'Telephone has gone, too,' remarked Algy, reading his thoughts.

'Yes, but it isn't far away, I fancy,' answered Biggles. 'It cost too much to put up and it's too useful to them to be abandoned altogether. We'll find the wire outside when we look for it.'

'What are we going to do about food?' asked Algy. 'It looks as if someone will have to take the rifle and try to shoot something.'

'No use taking a rifle,' returned Biggles.

'Why not?'

'It's empty, and we've no more ammunition. I fired the last two shots at the rhino. Ginger only took one clip of six rounds when he loaded it in the hangar. You fired one at the leopard, one at the fellow who was chasing you, two at the others, and I've fired two just now. Mental arithmetic isn't my strong point but I am able to work out that that makes six altogether; which means that the rifle is now about as much use as a walking stick—not so much, in fact.'

The others stared at him aghast.

'Then we shall have to fall back on our automatics,' stated Algy.

'Do *you* feel like taking on the denizens of this oversized menagerie with an automatic?'

'No, I can't say I'm keen.'

'Neither am I; and neither, I imagine, is Ginger. It will be dark in about five minutes, anyway.'

'Then we're here for the night?'

'That's about the size of it—unless anyone prefers the open air.'

'And in the morning?' asked Ginger anxiously.

'We'll talk about that when it comes,' replied Biggles, 'but it looks as if we shall have to push on to Karuli.'

'Karuli?' cried Algy and Ginger together.

'It can't be anywhere else, as far as I can see,' declared Biggles. 'We're too far away from Insula, Malakal, or Juba to hope to reach them. To tell the truth, when I saw the Puss Moth go west it struck me that good might come out of evil. Leroux is bound to fly over here shortly, and even if he didn't intend landing in the ordinary way, he would not be able to resist coming down when he saw the wreck on the ground. It looks like a first-class crash, and he would no doubt be overjoyed at the prospect of finding us tangled up in it, having with great consideration removed ourselves from the orbit of operations. Whereupon we could step out and ask him how about it—with our guns. So a half-informed idea was in my mind that we'd wait here for him, keeping an eye open, of course, for Stampoulos and his bodkin-pushers, who might also decide to look in here on the way home. But that was before I knew the food had gone from here. We can't stay now. It might be days before Leroux turns up, in which case we should pass out from hunger while we were waiting. As things are, we've got to move off at the crack of dawn, if only to get somewhere where the supply of vitamins A, B, C, and D are available.'

'And you think the best place is Karuli?'

'Certainly, unless we wander about in the hope that some kind beast will give itself up and invite us to dine off its anatomy.'

Nothing more was said. Darkness fell, and completely worn out by the day's events, they lay down on the floor to get as much rest as the unyielding surface would permit.

12

THE SNAKE IN THE GRASS

I

THE sun was peeping over the horizon when they awoke the following morning, stiff but clear-headed, and refreshed by a sleep that not even the inhospitable conditions of the hut could deny them. Nothing was said about food or water, although they all felt the need of both as they went outside into the clear atmosphere and surveyed the landscape. Except for a herd of small buck far out beyond the landing-ground there was nothing living in sight, so without loss of time they prepared to trek, with their backs to the rising sun.

'How about the kit-bags?' asked Algy eyeing them dubiously. 'Are we going to take them with us?'

Biggles shook his head. 'It will take us all our time to get ourselves where we're going without dragging extra weight about,' he opined. 'There's nothing in them that we really need at the moment, so I think the best plan would be to hide them. We daren't leave them on the ground or the white ants will tear everything to pieces, and we don't want our log-books chewed up. I tell you what: let's sling them in a tree out of sight in the forest; we can use some of the wires from the Puss for the purpose.'

'That's a good idea,' agreed Algy.

Without any more ado they set about putting the plan into action. It occupied but a few minutes, and after they had completed the job to their satisfaction they once more fore-gathered in front of the hut and prepared to move off. Before doing so, however, Biggles made the others wait while he quartered to and fro like a hound on the western side of the hut and some little distance away from it. Presently his persistence was rewarded, and he gave a cry of triumph. 'Here it is!' he shouted, and the others joined him at a run.

'Here's the telephone,' he went on as they came up to him. 'There goes the wire, and the receiver is in this box, I expect.' He pointed to a small wooden box half covered with leaves that rested at the foot of a tree. 'Yes, that's it,' he added, lifting the lid. 'All they've done is to clear it out of the hut in case we found it. They realized that we knew about the hut, of course, because the Puss Moth was taken from here. Incidentally, it must have given them food for thought wondering how on earth we found the place; I imagine Leroux would be hard to convince that he was directly responsible.'

'Are you going to use the 'phone?' asked Algy.

'And tell them that we are somewhere on the line? Not likely!

You see what it is worth to us, though. All we have to do is to
follow the wire and it should take us right up their front door.'

'By James! I never thought of that,' declared Algy.

'That was why I was so anxious to find it,' Biggles told him as
he set off along the track.

For a long way the wire followed the southern boundary of the
forest, about twelve feet from the ground, sometimes fastened to
trees by insulators, and sometimes being carried across gaps by
bamboo poles. Then the timber grew more sparse and in the end
gave out altogether, leaving them facing a dreary expanse of sun-
parched plain with clumps of the inevitable flat-topped trees
dotted about here and there, often forming supports for the
telephone wire. Beyond, at a distance which they were unable to
estimate but which was certainly several miles, great outcrops of
grey stone appeared, increasing in size until they finally merged
in an extensive range of mountains.

Biggles eyed the scene of desolation meditatively. 'We've got
to make those mountains to-day,' he said softly, as if he were
thinking aloud. 'You see what we're up against,' he went on in a
normal voice, turning to the others. 'Lack of water is going to
worry us more than the food shortage, and I think it is extremely
unlikely that we shall find water this side of those mountains; the
colour of the vegetation would probably reveal it if there were
any, and I don't see a spot of green anywhere. There should be
water in the mountains, though, either a spring or a natural
reservoir of rain-water. We're going to need it, too, by the time
we get there; that's why we've got to get across this plain to-day.
Anybody got any suggestion to make?'

There was no reply.

'Come on, then, let's go,' decided Biggles, and taking the lead,
he set off at a steady pace, still keeping his direction by the wire.

For hours they marched while the sun climbed high into the
heavens and tortured them with burning rays of white light that
dried the perspiration on their skins as quickly as it formed. They
did not speak, for there was nothing of importance that called for
comment; in any case, with their mouths parched as they were,
conversation would have been an effort. Game was fairly

common, particularly antelope, giraffe, zebra, buffalo, and the ungainly wildbeeste, which threw up their heads and watched the passage of the three travellers with interest. Once they saw a rhinoceros, standing under a tree attended by the curious birds that live on the ticks infesting its hide, and act, so it is said, as sentinels. Fortunately, the beast was some distance away, and although the birds rose into the air uttering warning cries, it merely contented itself with a series of short rushes in different directions; whereupon, finding nothing on which to vent its bellicose spite, it returned to the tree, and stood gazing blankly with its short-sighted eyes in the opposite direction.

From time to time Biggles looked speculatively at the mountains, now appreciably nearer but still some distance away.

'How far are they, do you think?' asked Algy on one such occasion.

'Five miles, but they're probably farther,' was Biggles's cheerless reply.

Whereupon, without pursuing the subject, they tramped on. They were all getting in a bad way, and although they must have been well aware of it, no one made any comment. Ginger in particular was suffering severely, but not for the world would he have admitted it.

'Any one got the time?' he croaked, after another interminable silence.

Biggles glanced at his wrist. 'My watch has stopped,' he answered. 'How about yours, Algy?'

'Smashed it this morning,' replied Algy briefly. 'It must be about three o'clock at a rough guess,' he added.

'I should say it's about one or half-past,' observed Biggles, glancing at the sun. 'Just a minute.'

He sat down and proceeded to take off his shoes and change the socks over from one foot to the other, inviting the others to do the same. 'It's an old army dodge,' he said, 'and like most army dodges, well worth trying.'

Presently they set off again, making for what looked like a break in the mountains, which they could now see very clearly.

They did not improve on closer acquaintance: the grey granite peaks thrust high into the air, gaunt and stark, without a sign of life.

Suddenly Biggles stopped, staring hard at the ground some distance to the right. Then, turning at right angles, 'This way,' he said.

'What about the telephone wire?' asked Algy in surprise.

'Can't bother about that now,' replied Biggles shortly. 'We've got to find water within the next hour, and anyway, we can always come back to the wire. This is a game path,' he went on, pointing to a definite well-worn track which had been the reason for his sudden change of direction.

The others saw that it was studded with innumerable hoof-marks which had evidently been made when the ground was soft, but had since been baked to brick-like hardness by the sun.

'You think it may lead to water?' asked Ginger, suddenly grasping the reason for Biggles's move.

'I hope so,' returned Biggles. 'I'm no expert tracker, but I seem to remember reading that by years of usage wild animals make definite paths to their drinking places,' he explained. 'We can only trust that this is one. Let's keep going.'

They marched on, nor did they stop or speak again until they were within a stone's throw of the rocks, now dreadful in their appalling desolation. Ginger was clearly very near the end of his endurance. He swayed as he walked; his eyes were glassy and there was a ring of dry dust round his cracked and blackened lips. Algy was in little better case. He could no longer keep his mouth closed and he was drawing his breath in short, painful gasps. Biggles alone seemed anything like normal, but his face was drawn and his lips compressed in a tight, obstinate line.

'Stick it, chaps, we can't be far way from water now,' he said encouragingly. But his heart was sick with anxiety, for he knew that in all their travels they had never been in such a desperate plight. He felt in his pocket and took out his automatic as he continued along the track, looking warily to right and left as he reached the first rocks, shimmering in the noonday sun. His eyes fell on a half-devoured zebra and he redoubled his vigilance.

With every nerve tense, he jumped violently, as, with a snort and scurry, half a dozen long-horned buck leapt up just in front of him and dashed off. For a second or two they bunched as they tried to scramble through a narrow cleft in the rocks. His hand jerked up. *Bang! bang! bang!* spat the automatic.

At the third shot one of the animals fell, but it was up instantly, dashing after the others apparently unhurt. Biggles watched it go dispassionately. Then he turned to the spot from which they had appeared, and a cracked cheer broke from his lips as his eyes fell on a small pool of water. It was stagnant and it looked foul, particularly at the edges where the mud had been stirred up by the buck, which had evidently been wallowing in it.

It was characteristic of him that instead of rushing forward and drinking he first looked back for the others. They were both hurrying towards the spot, Ginger making heavy weather of it some distance behind Algy. Biggles ran into the water beyond the edge of the disturbed area, and filling his topee, went back to meet them. Algy, he could see, would be able to reach the pool, so he passed him and went right on until he came to Ginger, who was beginning to stumble.

'Here you are, laddie, take a sip,' he said. 'Take it gently . . . steady . . . steady . . . that'll do for the present. Feel better?'

Ginger looked up and smiled wanly. 'That's pretty good stuff,' he vowed.

'You wouldn't think so in the ordinary way,' grinned Biggles. Then he took a sip or two himself, allowing the liquid to trickle over his lips with ineffable relish.

'Can I have some more?' asked Ginger.

Biggles passed him the hat. 'Go easy with it,' he warned him. 'You'll knock yourself out if you try taking too much at one go. Come on up to the pool.'

They found Algy sitting by the edge of the water bathing his face; his hat stood beside him, and from it he drank sparingly from time to time.

'I suppose we shouldn't complain,' observed Biggles presently when, their most urgent pangs of thirst assuaged, they were lying by the pool. 'But this is pretty awful stuff. It ought to be boiled to make it fit to drink, but not having a can it can't be done.' He got up suddenly. 'Stand fast everybody,' he ordered. 'Or better still, collect some of this grass and start a fire. You might be able to get some twigs from those bushes over there, but watch out you don't trip over a lion; there's one not far away. I shan't be long.'

He was back in about ten minutes, grinning broadly, and carrying a large slab of red meat in his hand. He nodded approval when he saw that a small fire had been started.

'Where the deuce did you get that?' asked Algy. 'What is it?'

'Sirloin of zebra,' smiled Biggles, laying the meat on a flat rock and commencing to carve it into strips.

'But where——?'

'I'm afraid I've purloined somebody else's supper,' explained Biggles. 'I saw a dead zebra just below as we came up, but until I went back to it I couldn't be sure how long it had been dead. It must have been killed within the last few hours, which suggests to me that a tawny-coated gentleman by the name of *Felix Leo* isn't far away. He'll probably return to his kill at sundown for another snack, so we'd better keep clear of it. We shall have to move off from here, too, before nightfall, or we shall find ourselves holding up the drinking parade. If Mr Leo wants to come and have a drink, I don't feel inclined to stand in his way and argue about it.'

Algy glanced at the sun, already sinking below the peaks of the mountains. 'We'd better see about finding a shakedown, then,' he suggested. 'It won't be long before it's dark. Hadn't we better take some water with us?'

'All we can do is bung up the ventilation holes in our topees and fill them,' replied Biggles, impaling a piece of meat on a stick and holding it to the blaze. 'We needn't go far away. I don't fancy sleeping among these rocks, but we can't be choosers.'

For a little while they busied themselves with their meal, toasting thin strips of the meat and eating it half raw. It was tough and not very palatable, but their hunger was such that these shortcomings did not worry them, and at the end, with their strength rapidly returning, they were quite cheerful. They spent some time cooking what remained of the meat, and then, with Biggles carrying the whole of the unpleasant-looking stock threaded on a piece of wood, and the others each carrying a hatful of water, they set off to find a place where the night could be passed with reasonable safety.

This was more difficult than it first appeared, for although there were plenty of caves and shallow recesses in the rocks, they all looked as if they might already harbour inmates; however, in the end they chose—somewhat hastily, for by this time it was almost dark—a ledge of rock several feet wide which was completely overhung by a low cliff. The last remaining minutes of daylight were spent collecting dry grass and anything that looked as if it would burn. They did not light this, for even if only a small fire was kept going their entire stock of fuel would not last more than half an hour, so they decided to preserve it against emergency, when it might serve as a protection against wild beasts or as a means of illumination in case of any other trouble. The night was then divided into three watches, Ginger taking the first, which is usually reckoned to be the easiest. These dispositions made, they settled themselves down for the night.

II

FOR some time Ginger squatted on a rock and stared into the darkness with restless, anxious eyes. A breathless silence had settled over the land, but it was not the comforting quiet of peace and security; rather was it an uneasy, living silence, a tense hush of expectancy, as if all the wild creatures of the veld were crouching, watching, waiting for something to happen.

Presently a faint hum rose on the air. At first he wondered what it was; but when a tiny, burning pain, as of a stinging-nettle, stung him on the nose, he knew, and he brushed his face irritably with the back of his hand. Then came another, this time on the cheek, and he stirred uneasily although without alarm.

'Confound these wretched mosquitoes,' he muttered angrily, as a dozen stings assailed his neck simultaneously. 'We're going to have a bonny night if this goes on; it must be because we're near that water,' he thought, as he remembered Biggles once saying something about mosquitoes frequenting damp, marshy places, which they made their breeding-grounds.

But in spite of all he could do to prevent it, which was no more than pulling his shirt up round his neck, the vicious attacks of the insects grew steadily more determined and intense, and he glanced behind him, realizing that Biggles and Algy were likely to be severely stung in their sleep; but their quiet, regular breathing reassured him, and he resumed his vigil in silent misery.

The moon, a great lemon-tinted ball of light, crept up slowly over the horizon and bathed the landscape in a pale, eerie glow, insufficient, however, for him to make out more than the broad outlines of his immediate surroundings and the vast expanse of plain that rolled away—to the end of the world, it seemed— from the foot of the hill on which they had made their camp.

Suddenly he stiffened and his mouth grew dry with horror as a dreadful uproar broke out somewhere below him. It began with a ferocious, snarling roar that was instantly drowned in a shrill scream of mortal terror. Then came a frenzied drumming of hoofs on hard earth, punctuated with blood-curdling growls. Another scream, ending in a pathetic, choking sob; then a silence that was quickly followed by a ghastly purring sound.

Ginger shivered, and edged a little nearer to the overhanging rock.

'What the dickens is going on?'

Biggles's voice made him jump, but he was relieved to hear it. 'Phew!' he gasped, moistening his lips and swallowing hard. 'This is awful.'

'What is? What's going on? Something woke me up.' Biggles raised himself into a sitting position.

'Something is being killed, or has just been killed, down below. I thnk it was a lion killing a zebra. I can't see anything, but the noise was shocking. I'm fairly sweating with funk, and I don't mind admitting it. Not only that, but I am being torn to pieces by mosquitoes,' went on Ginger miserably. 'It feels as if they've had most of the skin off my face already.'

Biggles rose to his feet. 'I know,' he muttered. 'I'm nearly bitten to death, too. I was conscious of the things biting me even in my sleep. Whereabouts is this lion do you suppose?'

'I don't know exactly. The sounds came from somewhere out there in the darkness beyond the water-hole. I think we ought to do something about it.'

'What do you suggest we do—tell the lion to go home and not be a naughty boy? A lot of notice he'd take of us whatever we did while he's busy over his supper. We shall have to do something about these mosquitoes, though, or we shall be in a pretty state to-morrow.'

'What the dickens *can* we do about them?'

'Light a fire, that's the only thing. The smoke may drive them away, or at least discourage them; and as the flames may keep the lion at a distance too, we shall be killing two birds with one stone.'

'But we haven't enough sticks to last half an hour.'

'Then we shall have to jolly well get some more. It isn't much use trying to sleep anyway in this fly-bitten, lion-infested bedlam. Hark.'

They remained silent for a few seconds. From the direction of the water-hole came a horrid sound of purring and lapping, both at the same time, like the noise made by a contented domestic cat over a bowl of milk, but magnified a hundred times.

'That doesn't sound very pretty, does it?' observed Biggles quietly.

'What's the brute doing, do you think?'

'Slobbering about in the blood of the wretched creature it has just killed, I fancy. It's some distance away though; moreover, by the time friend Leo has had a good fill of fresh zebra he'll be more likely to think about forty winks than worrying us. At least, we can only hope so.' Biggles brought his hand down sharply on his cheek. 'Dash these pests,' he snarled. 'I'm going down to those bushes for some more brushwood for the fire,' he went on aggressively, taking out his jack-knife and opening it.

'Don't be a lunatic, Biggles,' cried Ginger, seriously alarmed.

'Lunatic or not, I'm going. These little swine are driving me

crazy. The bushes aren't more than a dozen yards away so I
don't think there's any danger—no more than there is here that
I can see. If the lion has ideas about us there's nothing to stop him
putting them into action at either place.'

'That's true, I suppose,' admitted Ginger reluctantly. 'But
somehow it seems safer when we're all together. Wait a minute
while I wake Algy and light the fire. If we're going to light it we
might as well start it off now so that you can have the benefit of it.'

So saying, he nudged Algy, who sprang up with a stifled cry of
alarm.

'What's the matter?' he asked breathlessly. 'Oh, I know; I
guess it's my turn for guard.'

'No, it isn't,' Ginger told him, 'but all the mosquitoes in Africa
are having a stinging competition and they're using us as a
stadium. I fancy the winner is on the small of my back, just out of
reach. Our eyes will be completely closed up in the morning if we
let them go on with it, so we're going to light the fire and try to
smoke them out. Biggles has volunteered to go and get some
more brushwood.'

As he spoke Ginger struck a match and held it to the fire. It
blazed up brightly at once, and cast a lurid glow over the dry
earth, the rocks, and their travel-stained faces. In fact, although
the fire was only a small one, it glowed like a beacon after the
darkness, which naturally had the effect of making everything
outside its flickering radius more difficult to see.

It may have been due, or at least partly due, to this that Biggles
put his foot into it—as the saying is—in the literal sense of the
word. True, he was not looking at the ground. In spite of his
declared assurance, he was by no means certain that he would
not encounter a lion, either the one they had heard or another, so
as he walked towards the bushes his eyes were raised to the
surrounding rocks and not on the ground immediately in front of
him.

He must have put his foot right in the middle of the coiled
python. He did not see it. He felt something soft and yielding
under his foot, and knowing that whatever it was it was alive, he
sprang back; but quick as he was he was too late. In a flash,

almost before he had realized what was happening, the snake, which always seems so slow and somnolent, had coiled itself about him, pinning his left arm and the hand in which he carried his automatic to his side. Fortunately, his right hand, in which he held the knife, was left free, and he at once made a number of wild slashes at the head of the snake as it reared up before him, at the same time letting out a yell that must have been heard a mile away.

Now he knew quite well what everyone knows who has lived in countries where this particular type of snake occurs—that the python is not venomous; it cannot give its victim a poisonous bite, but endeavours to kill it by crushing it in the same manner as a boa constrictor; but this it is unable to do unless its tail is firmly anchored to something substantial, such as a tree or a rock. Even in his present extremity Biggles remembered that there were no trees near. For the rest, he was conscious only of the creature's great weight and the swaying head with its ghastly, flickering tongue a few inches from his face.

His wild yell brought Algy and Ginger to the scene with a rush, and they saw at a glance what had happened. Both carried their automatics, but to use them was clearly out of the question, for it was impossible to put a bullet through the python without a big risk of its also going through Biggles. Admittedly, its head was clear of him, but to hit it as it swayed from side to side would have tried the skill of an expert revolver shot, and neither of them was that.

Biggles, realizing by this time that in his cramped position he could not hope to give the creature a mortal wound, and seeing the others run up, flung the knife clear. 'Go for the tail,' he shouted. 'The tail—the tail—slash its tail.'

Algy heard the steel tinkle against a rock, and darted to the spot where the knife fell, but to his utter and complete consternation he could not find it.

'A light, Ginger,' he screamed hysterically. 'Get a light!'

But Ginger had no light, for after starting the fire he had put the box of matches down on the rock on which he had been sitting. However, he did not wait to explain this, but darted back to the fire, and grabbing a handful of blazing twigs, managed to hold them in spite of the pain until he reached the spot where Algy, now on his hands and knees, was still looking and feeling frantically for the knife.

Fortunately the grass, being bone dry, flared up the instant the twigs fell into it, revealing the knife lying in a hollow of the rock. Algy saw it first, and reached for it, but an instant before his hand closed over it, the python's massive tail, seeking a hold on the same rock, swung round and sent him over backwards.

But Ginger had also seen the knife. Disregarding Algy, he snatched it up with a gasp of relief and flung himself on the creature's tail just as it found the rock. Out of the corner of his eye, in the yellow light of the fire, he saw Biggles fall heavily, still swathed in the python's gigantic coils, so he started hacking at the tail with a fury born of blind panic.

The rest was nightmare. The dry skin, pulsating under his left hand as he grasped it, made him feel sick, but he stuck to his task desperately, vaguely conscious of shouting to Algy to help him. The snake, thus attacked, released its tail-grip on the rock and began threshing about, dragging him with it; but he hung on, still shouting for Algy to help him.

Algy, whose breath had been completely knocked out of him when the snake had thrown him over backwards, rose unsteadily to his feet and threw himself across the black, sinuous body of the creature between Biggles and Ginger. Gripping it with his knees, he pressed the muzzle of the automatic into it and pulled the trigger.

The result was instantaneous. The python, with incredible speed, released its hold on Biggles and turned on him; and taken thus unaware, he sprawled forward as its full weight descended on his back.

At this juncture Ginger, who was still hacking at the tail, behaved with commendable presence of mind. Holding the knife in his teeth, he tore up a double handful of dry grass, held it in the flames for a second, and thrust the whole blazing mass into the snake's open mouth.

Almost before they were aware that the danger had passed,

the python dropped to the ground with a crash and glided swiftly away into the darkness, leaving them all staring at each other, panting for breath and trembling violently from shock and exertion.

'Are you—hurt—Biggles?' gasped Algy.

'Don't think so,' replied Biggles weakly. 'A bit bruised, I think—nothing more. Gosh! What a horror to meet on a dark night—ugh!' He shuddered at the recollection.

'If ever I sleep again in this perishing country it won't be my fault,' declared Ginger emphatically, wiping his hands on a tuft of grass. 'I'd no idea such frightful creatures still walked the earth, or you wouldn't have got me here. No, *sir*. First lions, then mosquitoes, and now snakes—I think it's about time we headed for home and let them have this place as likes it.'

'Let's head back to the fire for a start,' suggested Biggles practically.

He led the way back to where a few twigs still burnt briskly and flopped down limply on the rock on which Ginger had sat during his brief guard. The others saw that he was pale, and knew that he had been more shaken than he had admitted.

'Well?' asked Ginger questioningly, looking at the others in turn.

'Well, what?' inquired Algy.

'What are we going to do?'

'Stay where we are,' put in Biggles shortly.

'What about the mosquitoes?'

'What about them?'

'You said you were going to get some more firewood.'

'Quite right, so I did,' confessed Biggles. 'But I've changed my mind. Of course, there's nothing to prevent *you* from going and getting some——'

'Not me,' interrupted Ginger decisively. 'I've done all the exploring I'm going to do for one night.'

'Look here, it's no use going on like this,' said Biggles seriously. 'We shall have to try to get in a few winks of sleep or we shall all feel like death in the morning. Let's keep double guards; that won't be so nervy as doing it solo. Ginger and I will start. In an hour Ginger will lie down, and you, Algy, will take his place. An hour later I'll lie down and Ginger will have to get up again; and so on. It's heavy going, but it can't be helped; it's better than all of us sitting up all he time, anyway. We shall have to do the best we can with the fire; by keeping it a mere flicker we might be able to make it last for some time, and it can always be made up if any visitors start prowling round.'

'Sounds a good idea to me,' observed Algy.

'And me,' agreed Ginger.

And so it was agreed, and for the second time they settled down to pass the night.

13
WHAT NEXT?

THE stars were still in the sky the following morning when Ginger was awakened by the crackling of twigs to find Biggles and Algy busily warming up the remains of their unappetizing meat supply, and the realization of their position brought him to his feet immediately. It was bitterly cold, and he was glad to stretch his hands to the warmth of the fire.

'Did you see anything during your watch?' he asked Biggles, more for the sake of saying something than for anything else, after congratulations had been exchanged on their survival of a perilous night.

'I didn't see much, but I heard a lot,' grinned Biggles.

'Same here,' nodded Ginger. 'From the grunting, coughing, and splashing, there were enough animals round that water-hole to fill all the zoos in the world six times over.'

'Yes, it was a bit alarming,' agreed Biggles. 'Just sink your teeth into some of this steak, you two, and make the most of it; it may be some time before we get another meal. And don't be too long about it; the sooner we are on the move the farther we shall get before the sun becomes really hot. It's going to be a scorcher again by the look of it, and I'm a bit stiff from the fond embrace of that overgrown worm last night.'

'You're lucky you aren't completely stiff,' grinned Ginger, as he helped himself to the uninviting fare.

It took them only a few minutes to clear up what was left of the meat; they washed it down with a small quantity of the brackish water, and then, tightening their belts, they prepared to march.

'Which way?' asked Algy.

'We'll cut across to the telephone wire again,' replied Biggles. 'It is certain to follow the easiest pass through the mountains. I expect we shall find Karuli the other side of them. If Stampoulos is growing tobacco, and I think he's bound to put up some sort of pretence of doing it, even if the plantation isn't genuine, it won't be on these rocks, that's certain. I don't mind admitting that I'm a bit curious to see this place of his.'

They found the wire without difficulty, and following its course, came to a great gash in the mountains, the floor of which, nevertheless, ascended steeply. They could not see very far ahead, for the ravine pursued a winding course, but that did not worry them; in fact, they were relieved to find such an easy path, for the mountains had by now assumed alarming proportions, and they realized that, but for the telephone wire which showed them the way into the ravine, they would have found themselves faced with an obstacle beyond their power to cross.

In the shade offered by the towering sides of the gorge they made good progress, and a fresh turn showed them that they had nearly reached the highest point. In their anxiety to see over the great watershed they hurried forward, but just before they reached the top they pulled up with one accord as a distant sound was wafted to their ears. They looked at each other expectantly, for it was the hum of an aeroplane.

Biggles turned and raced to the summit, for the walls on either side of them restricted their field of view, and on reaching it turned about and looked back over the plain whence came the sound.

'There he is!' cried Ginger, pointing to a speck in the distance.

'It's the Dragon,' exclaimed Algy as, notwithstanding the distance, his eyes picked out the familiar outline.

'Leroux on his way home,' said Biggles. 'Keep under cover; at the height he's flying he will pass over us very low, and we don't want him to see us.'

In silence they stood and watched the aeroplane approach, roar past a few hundred feet over their heads, and then rapidly diminish in size as it sped on over the unknown country ahead. They were still watching it when the roar of the engine died away suddenly and the machine began to lose height.

'He's going down,' said Biggles. 'That leaves us in little doubt as to the position of Karuli.'

The machine was still in the air when it faded into the haze, but was losing height quickly, and they knew that their objective was not much more than a day's march.

The subject of their attention having disappeared, they dropped their eyes to the country over which they would have to pass, and for some minutes they regarded its wild splendour with admiration. It was, broadly speaking, what is usually described as 'rolling' country: that is, undulating in rather a big way; and whereas the plain behind them had been arid in the real sense of the word, the new panorama on which they gazed was fertile; the herbage was a soft green, and from it rose magnificent trees, singly and in clumps, like the timber in an English park. The reason for such a striking contrast was clearly visible, for coiling across the landscape in mighty sweeps was a broad river. In a general way its course was from north to south, so that it formed as it were a dividing line between the mountains and the fertile country beyond. Indeed, so close to the mountains did it come in one of its serpentine detours that it actually disappeared from view near the foot of the elevation on which the three airmen stood looking down with questioning eyes, to reappear some distance farther on.

'We shan't be short of water again, that's evident,' remarked Biggles, looking down at the river. 'On the contrary, it looks as if there might be more than we want. We've got to cross that river to get to Karuli, and while a bath wouldn't do any of us any harm, in a country famous for its crocodiles, hippos, and other nuisances, I'd prefer to take mine in a nice enamelled tub. By

James! Stampoulos tucked himself away all right while he was about it, didn't he? If he'd searched the whole of Africa—which he may have done for all we know—he couldn't have found a more inaccessible spot, a place less likely to be visited by anyone. On this side he is protected by a waterless plain, a range of mountains, and a river; on the other side by the Congo Basin which, from what I've heard of it, is pretty well impassable. No wonder he used air transport. We should never have got across these mountains if we hadn't struck the pass.' He broke off and glanced back at the towering crags. As he did so his eyes went round with astonishment. 'Great Scott! Look at all this,' he exclaimed.

The others turned quickly and beheld an extraordinary sight. In a wide semicircle amongst the mighty granite crags and boulders was a vast assembly of baboons. Some, most of them females, judging by the youngsters they held in their arms, were sitting still, but others were moving steadily forward with their almost-human eyes fixed on the intruders. Observing that they had been seen, some of these began to voice their indignation by uttering short, sharp barks.

Ginger laughed, for the spectacle was not without humour, and it was plain from their manner as they stood watching that not one of them suspected that they were in danger.

Then one of the baboons, an enormous creature that might have been the leader of the colony, ran forward, chattering with rage and showing its teeth viciously. Instantly, as if it were a signal for a general advance, many of the others began to move forward quickly, leaping from rock to rock with amazing agility.

The expression on Biggles's face changed and he began to back away. 'Let's get out of this,' he snapped. 'I believe these brutes mean trouble. Algy, turn round with me and face them; Ginger, watch the path and tell us if there are any bad places. Look out! Mind your head!'

The last warning came as a result of an unexpected action on the part of the leader of the apes. It had seized a piece of rock and, with unbelievable ferocity, sent it hurtling down towards the now rapidly retreating airmen. It was followed by a dozen others, and presently the side of the mountain was alive with leaping rocks of all sizes.

Biggles abandoned all pretence at finesse. 'Run for it!' he yelled. 'If one of those rocks hits any of us it will mean broken bones at least.'

In something not far removed from panic they set off down the path at a speed which normally they would have regarded as suicidal, for it began to fall away steeply and sheer drops of several feet were common. At one such place, where they could only scramble down one at a time, Biggles whirled round, and seeing that the apes were still following, whipped out his automatic and let drive at the leader. The range was too long for accurate shooting, and the bullets missed their mark, but they made a startling noise as they ricochetted off the rocks, and the apes, who seemed to be fully aware of the danger, slowed down.

'Keep going,' panted Biggles as he raced on after the others.

The ravine had now broken down into comparatively open hill-side although the path was still clearly defined; in fact, there were places where rough steps had been hewn in the granite.

A glance backward showed that the apes were still following, but they had dropped a good way behind and it was clear that the immediate danger was past.

'I don't think they'll follow us much farther now that they see we're going,' muttered Biggles, wiping his forehead with his handkerchief. 'We'd better not stop, though. What a swine of a place this is. What will be next, I wonder?'

He was soon to know.

Breathing heavily, knuckles and shins barked by the swift descent over the rough rock, they reached the level of the river and, turning a corner, saw it almost at their feet, the near side actually washing the rocks on which they stood.

Biggles pulled up with a cry of dismay, looking anxiously from left to right, for although the telephone wire spanned the river, secured on each side by heavy posts, there was no bridge, and the river was a good fifty yards wide.

Without speaking, they walked on until they reached the edge of the water.

'It looks as if we shall have to swim, after all,' observed Algy.

Biggles picked up a piece of loose rock and threw it at what appeared to be a strip of bark floating down the middle of the river. There were several such strips. It submerged instantly, leaving a line of bubbles to mark the place where it had been.

'I'm not swimming in *that* river,' he declared emphatically. 'I'd sooner go back and face the apes. But surely there must be some way across, or the path wouldn't be here. People—those warriors we saw, for instance—must use it. They must have come this way. I've got it! There must be a boat.'

'It's probably over on the other side,' suggested Algy pessimistically.

'No, I won't have that,' replied Biggles warmly. 'Stampoulos and his dart-throwers we know are over this side, so assuming they crossed here, the boat must be over this side, too. We shall have to look for it.'

He was quite right; there was a boat, but it took them half an hour to find it, and even then it could hardly be called a boat. Actually, it was a dug-out canoe of the most primitive sort, being merely a hollowed-out tree-trunk with the ends shaped roughly to points. Moreover, it was rotten, with the freeboard broken down in places almost to the water's edge.

They found it in a peculiar place some distance below the point where the path ended by the river. At the particular spot where they discovered it, lying half in and half out of the water, the river actually flowed through a rift in the foot-hills of the mountains, so that not only was there a steep rocky bank on the side on which they stood, but the wall on the other side was even steeper, making a direct crossing impossible. The distance to the place where the wall broke down again and became the usual reed-fringed bank was not great, but this was in the direction from which they had come, and therefore up-stream. How far it was before the bank occurred again down-stream they had no means of knowing, for a bend hid it from view; nor could they, owing to the interruption of an unscalable cliff, work their way along to a point from which they would be able to see how far they would have to travel that way before they could effect a landing.

For this reason Biggles hesitated after they had tilted the water out of the crazy craft and relaunched it. He eyed the current, which, owing to the narrowing of the river caused by the rocks, was fairly fast, with disfavour. 'Well, which is it to be, up-stream or down?' he asked, unable to make up his mind.

'We shall make slow headway against that current if we try to go up-stream,' declared Algy, 'and this tub leaks like a sieve. I say let's go down.'

'What about carrying the boat higher up and going straight across,' suggested Ginger.

'That's a good idea,' agreed Biggles.

It was, and they attempted to put into execution, only to abandon the project at once when they found that not by their united strength could they lift the water-soaked craft.

'It's no use,' muttered Biggles disgustedly. 'It would need a dozen men to carry it.'

He picked up the crude paddle and, not without difficulty, they took their places—Algy in the bows, Ginger in the middle, and Biggles in the stern. At first they turned the nose up-stream, but the difficulty of making progress combined with the waywardness of the dug-out, which, not being dead straight, went in any direction but the one desired, caused Biggles to change his mind, and as the nose swung he allowed it to come right round until it pointed down-stream, when forward progress become easier.

It was not long before they had an escort. It took the shape of a crocodile which appeared suddenly on the surface of the water a few yards away and watched them malevolently with cold, unwinking eyes. As they passed it turned and followed them.

Algy and Ginger watched it with a sort of fascinated horror.

'Can't you put a bit more beef behind that paddle?' muttered Algy impatiently. 'I don't like the look of that customer.'

'If I push any harder the confounded boat will turn over,' answered Biggles shortly. 'Keep your hands in the boat, both of you.'

Another crocodile appeared, then another and another until

the water was literally swarming with them. The canoe rounded the bend, only to face another one fifty yards farther on, so it was now impossible to land on either side of the gulch.

They all turned pale as one of the saurians deliberately pushed its nose against the side of the canoe, causing it to rock and ship water through one of the gaps in the freeboard; and Ginger did not help to keep the boat steady by reaching for his automatic.

'Put that thing away, you fool,' grated Biggles harshly. 'Wound one, and one swish of its tail would sink us—Ah! you swine!' He raised the paddle out of the water and shifted it over to the other side as one of the crocodiles made a grab at it.

Thereafter, the going, short as it was, became a nightmare of horror that none of them could ever recall without a shudder. They passed through a pool that seemed to be the head-quarters of all the crocodiles in Africa, and they surged about the canoe in a manner that made disaster seem only a matter of seconds. Yet somehow they managed to keep it afloat, and it swerved sideways round the bend to reveal the end of the rock on the far bank only a short distance away. At the same moment the dug-out quivered as if a giant rasp had been drawn across the keel, and instinctively a cry broke from Ginger's lips.

'Keep your head, everybody,' snapped Biggles. 'We're nearly there.'

With agonizing slowness the canoe drifted towards the bank, with Biggles making quick strokes with the paddle as occasion offered, for the crocodiles were now making regular attempts to seize it and pull it into the water.

'Take it gently when we ground,' warned Biggles. 'If anyone tries jumping out we shall capsize.'

Several crocodiles were on the bank, but they all ran down to the water when they saw the canoe approaching. The surge they made as they plunged in caused the water to pour over the side of the canoe, and it began to sink bodily. Realizing the desperateness of the situation, Biggles risked everything on one final effort. He thrust the blade of the paddle deep into the water and hurled his weight behind it. He nearly went overboard as it was torn from his hands, but the stroke had had the desired effect, and the

nose of the frail vessel swished softly into the muddy bank. 'Out
you go, Ginger,' he cried.

Algy leapt ashore just as the canoe sank, but the water was
shallow and the others found themselves standing only a little
more than knee-deep. A splashing rush and they, too, were on
the bank, pale and trembling, while a line of cold eyes watched
them from the river.

Biggles passed his hand wearily over his face. 'I've had just
about as much of this sort of thing as I can stand,' he murmured.

'Are you telling me?' sighed Ginger weakly. 'I shall dream of
this for the rest of my life.'

'Well, let's see where we are,' said Biggles quietly, and ran to
the top of the bank. Reaching it, he fell back a pace, staring, and
there he stood while the others joined him.

Before them, not more than a hundred yards away, was a
native village of low, reed-built, conical-shaped huts. From it
came a shrill cry of alarm. A crowd of warriors armed with spears
and clubs poured out of the huts and charged, yelling, towards
the new-comers.

Ginger's hand flew to his pocket.

'No use, laddie,' said Biggles sadly, shaking his head. 'We
can't fight that mob, so it's no use irritating them. We shall do
better by trying to appear friendly, I think.'

14

ORDEAL BY FIRE

ANY hope they entertained in that direction, however, was
squashed with such speed and violence as to leave them
breathless and flabbergasted. Indeed, with such ferocity was the
onslaught against them carried out that in his heart Biggles felt
certain that the end had come; for the natives, far from stopping
a few yards away as he anticipated, dashed right in, seized them,
and flung them to the ground in a manner that was as violent as it
was unexpected. Their hands were tied behind them, and they

were conducted—dragged would perhaps be a better word—to
a hut and flung inside.

Algy rolled over on to his side and then struggled into a sitting
position. He looked at Biggles reproachfully. 'We ought to have
plugged some of the skunks,' he said bitterly.

'We should all have been dead by now if we had; as full of
spears as a hedgehog is of quills,' Biggles told him coolly.

'I had an idea that the natives of Africa had all been tamed by
now, but I must be wrong,' observed Algy.

'It almost looks like it, doesn't it?' agreed Biggles sarcastically.

'What is their idea, do you suppose?'

'Goodness knows. I can't make it out. There's something
funny about this attack; I'm sure these people wouldn't behave
like this in the ordinary way. Look out, here comes the head lad.'

A shadow had fallen across the low doorway and a moment
later two natives entered the hut. Both were remarkable in
appearance and equally repulsive. The first, who was evidently
the chief of the tribe, was a man of great stature, but he was fat to
the point of bestiality. He was jet black, with short curly hair and
a broad face on which a tiny snub nose with gaping nostrils
looked ridiculously inadequate. His eyes were small, red-
rimmed as if from disease, and set close together, while his neck
would have carried the head of a buffalo. With the two front
claws fastened over one shoulder, a magnificent leopard skin was
draped across his body, caught in round the waist by the beast's
tail. This appeared to be his only garment.

The other was a little wizened old man whose wrinkled face—
or what they could see of it—bespoke a tremendous age. Above
his head, fixed so that it rose above his face, was a mask of
indescribable ugliness, while about his body, in chains, festoons,
and garlands, hung an incredible assortment of articles varying
from old tin lids to human bones and the teeth of animals. A
filthy skirt of coloured grasses hung down from his waist,
completing a picture at which the three airmen gazed in loathing
and disgust. They knew enough of Africa to be aware that he was
a witch-doctor.

'There's getting a *King Solomon's Mines* touch about this

business,' observed Algy, with a courageous attempt at humour.

To this Biggles made no reply, but looking the chief straight in the eyes he asked, 'Do either of you speak English?'

The chief did not answer, but the witch-doctor broke into what sounded like a stream of vituperation, waving his hands to emphasize his remarks. The noise was not unlike the chattering of an angry monkey.

'Apparently they don't,' said Biggles quietly. 'I'm afraid it's going to be a bit difficult if we can't discuss the matter with them.'

That such was the case was soon made clear, for after staring at the prisoners for some minutes the chief withdrew, and the witch-doctor, after removing the one or two odds and ends they carried in their pockets, followed him. Hip-pockets were evidently unknown to him for he overlooked these, so the prisoners were left in possession of their automatics, although as their hands were securely bound they were unable to get at them.

Biggles looked at Algy's wrists and saw that the bonds were strips of green hide, and he knew at once that their chances of being able to free themselves were remote. Still, they could but try, he decided, and was about to roll over in order to attack Algy's with his teeth when a warrior appeared and squatted down in the doorway, watching them closely.

'If that scallywag is going to sit there all the time it's going to be hard to get away,' said Algy, eyeing the new-comer vindictively.

'He is, you can bet your boots on that,' replied Biggles.

Outside a drum began beating fitfully; presently it was answered by another far away. Nothing more was said. Utterly helpless, they could only sit and wait what might befall. Slowly the day wore on. Once or twice there was an excited clamour outside as if something unusual was occurring, but they were left in ignorance as to what it was. They were given neither food nor water, and they all suffered intensely from thirst and from the attentions of myriads of flies from whose attacks they were powerless to defend themselves.

It was nearing sunset when from outside there came a babble

of excited voices, the clamour increasing in volume as if those responsible for it were approaching the hut in which the prisoners lay.

'It sounds as if something might happen shortly,' observed Biggles.

'I hope it does; anything is better than this,' growled Algy. 'If only I could get to my gun I'd give these swine something to yell about.'

A moment later a black form blocked out the light and another visitor entered. They all recognized him at once. It was the leader of the party of warriors who had accosted them while they were repairing the Puss Moth, and he showed his teeth in a flashing grin of satisfaction as he looked down upon them.

'You no talk so big now,' he said boastfully, pricking Biggles's leg viciously with the point of his spear.

'Where's your master?' asked Biggles, ignoring the thrust, thinking that if the white man was about, even if he were an enemy, surely he would not leave them to their fate.

'He no come here,' grinned the native. 'By time he come, two day, three day, you say so-long. My friends outside get much money, much bacca, much beef, much *poshi*, for catching you. You no more shoot at black mans; crocodiles see you finish.' With an ironic smile the man went out.

Presumably he said something to the crowd that had assembled outside, for an absolute bedlam of jeers and shouting broke out. Nor did it cease. Indeed, as darkness fell the pandemonium became indescribable, the clanging of tins and the banging of drums adding to the uproar.

'I should like to make just one small contribution to that din, and that's the good healthy rattle of a machine-gun,' snarled Biggles, as if he could stand it no longer.

'What do you think they mean to do to us?' asked Ginger.

'I shouldn't think about that if I were you,' Biggles told him grimly.

'What about trying to free my hands with your teeth?' suggested Algy. 'There doesn't seem to be anybody on door duty now, and if there was he couldn't see us.'

'At this stage anything is worth trying,' replied Biggles, and turning over on to his side he began gnawing the thongs. He knew it was hopeless from the start, for his teeth could make no impression on the tough hide which, quite apart from anything else, tasted foul, and the smell of it nearly made him sick. 'No use,' he muttered at last, turning away and spitting. 'My stomach will stand a lot, but not the smell of that stuff.'

Outside, the darkness was suddenly dispelled by an orange glare as if a fire had been lighted; it crept through the open doorway and bathed the faces of the prisoners with a lurid glow.

'Looks as if it's getting time for the balloon to go up,' observed Algy philosophically.

'Yes, the fireworks have started,' agreed Biggles. 'Sorry I've got you fellows into this jam.'

'I can't see that you've got us into it,' murmured Ginger. 'I've only one regret, and that is that Stampoulos and Leroux look like getting away with their graft now, and poor old Marton won't see his son again. I'm afraid we haven't much hope.'

'You never know,' declared Biggles, with a conviction that he was far from feeling. 'While there's life there's hope is an old saying, and the more you think about it the more patent becomes the truth of it. When you're dead it's the finish, but until then anything can happen. This isn't the first time I've thought I was sunk, but somehow I've always managed to bob up again.'

'Well, it's nice of you to cheer us up this way,' replied Algy. 'Can you think of anything that *might* save us at this juncture?'

'A herd of mad elephants might charge the village,' suggested Biggles.

'Is there such a thing, do you think?' asked Ginger hopefully.

'Since you force me to say it, I must admit that I've never heard of one,' confessed Biggles. 'There might be an earthquake or a cloudburst, though.'

'Either of which would put paid to our account just as effectively as the stiffs outside,' declared Algy. 'Why pretend? Let us face our end with the cold, calm philosophy of our race, as they say in books,' he added sarcastically. 'Frankly, if they take us to that crocodile pool I shall scream my head off. I——'

'Oh, shut up,' snapped Biggles. 'Here comes the procession, anyway,' he went on quickly as the uproar approached the hut.

Several natives entered. The prisoners were hauled into the open, dragged to their feet, and marched towards an open space in the centre of the village, where the entire population had collected in a circle round three posts that had been let into the ground near a dais on which sat the chief. To these posts the prisoners were led; their hands were untied, and then retied behind the posts.

'Judging from the audience, I should say that this is what in film circles is called a *premiére*,' observed Algy, looking round.

Suddenly the uproar died away; a hush fell upon the scene, and the air was tense with expectation.

'Here comes Father Christmas to do his stuff,' muttered Biggles, looking towards the far side of the circle where a gangway had opened through the spectators.

It was the witch-doctor, clad presumably in his full robes of office. The mask which he had worn earlier in the day had been replaced by another even more monstrous, a ghastly effigy of a crocodile. The head, with gaping jaws, protruded far in front of his face, while the skin hung down his back until the tail dragged along the ground.

This apparition did not walk straight towards the prisoners, but commenced to make short zig-zag rushes to and fro, the end of each rush bringing it a little nearer.

'I suppose we've got to put up with all this tom-foolery,' growled Algy.

'Of course,' answered Biggles. 'The boys must have their fun.'

From somewhere in the folds of his equipment the witch-doctor now produced a short, ivory-handled assagai, and at the same time a dreadful noise that was something between a howl and a scream broke from his lips, the high note being accompanied by a fierce thrust with the assagai at an imaginary enemy.

Slowly but surely he drew nearer. The howls became more spasmodic and the spear thrusts more vicious. A low mutter ran round the spectators, but it died away again to a breathless silence as they saw that the witch-doctor's last rush had carried

him to within a few yards of Ginger. There was a noise like wind
rustling in dry leaves as two hundred throats drew a deep breath.
The witch-doctor's hand went back, assagai poised.

Simultaneously a sudden outcry of voices occurred on the far
side of the assembly, and several natives began running across
the open space shouting as they ran. The witch-doctor swung
round and screamed as if infuriated at this interruption, but the
natives, although they kept clear of him, continued to run.
Others joined them. The chief jumped down from his seat and
shouted something at the witch-doctor, who turned and ran with
a speed that was extraordinary for one so encumbered. In a few
seconds the break-up became a panic which ended in a wild
stampede, and within a minute there was not a single native in
sight.

'Looks as if that herd of mad elephants is coming after all,'
whispered Ginger, through dry lips.

'Something's coming, that's certain,' muttered Biggles, staring at the point where the stampede started.

Presently it came. Out of the darkness into the ruddy glow of
the fire marched a double line of uniformed men. They were
Africans, but they walked smartly, with military precision,
and at their head, in khaki drill tunic, shorts, and a topee, strode
a white man with a walking-stick in his hand.

Biggles took one look at the red fezzes, bandoliers, and rifles
carried at the slope. 'Askaris, by all that's wonderful,' he
breathed.

In military step the party marched across the open space to
where the three airmen stood watching them with thankful eyes.
At a distance of a few yards the officer halted his men and
advanced alone, a jack-knife in his hand.

'Looks as if I've arrived at what is called the crucial moment,'
he observed with a curious smile, as he severed in turn the raw-
hide thongs that held the prisoners to their posts.

'Yes! Believe me we're pleased to see you,' smiled Biggles.

'And I'm pleased to see you.' The officer glanced up. 'My
name is Collison, Seventeenth African Rifles. You're
Bigglesworth, I suppose?'

'Yes, that's my name,' answered Biggles wonderingly.

'Then I arrest you for the wilful murder of Luke Sarda, at Insula, on or about the twelfth of the present month,' said the officer curtly.

Biggles stared at him incredulously for a full ten seconds without speaking. Then a queer, half-hysterical laugh broke from his lips.

'It seems to strike you as funny,' said Collison icily.

'Funny!' Biggles laughed again. 'I think that's just about the best joke I ever heard in my life,' he said simply. 'By the way, if you've got any water handy we could do with a drink.'

15
BIGGLES SPEAKS

'AND now,' continued Collison, when they had all drunk deeply, 'I'm not altogether lacking in a sense of humour, so perhaps you wouldn't mind telling me just where the joke comes in. From my point of view, I found nothing amusing in having to tear myself and my men across that infernal plain in the heat of the day, but we knew it was going to be touch and go whether we got here in time.'

'How did you know that?' asked Biggles.

'The drums told us.'

'And I suppose that's how you knew we were here in the first place?'

'Of course. Every native within a hundred miles knows that three strange white men are in Limshoda.'

'Is that the name of this village?'

'It is. You'd have done well to avoid it: it's got a nasty reputation.'

'We didn't even know it was here, much less know about its reputation,' Biggles told him frankly. 'Are you in a great hurry to push on anywhere tonight?'

'No, we shall have to spend the night here; my men need

a rest.'

'So do we, for that matter,' answered Biggles. 'I'm glad, because I should like to have a few words of conversation with you.'

'I want a few words with you, too, although it is my duty to warn you that anything you may say may be used as evidence against you.'

'That sounds like good old solid English to me,' grinned Biggles. 'Let's find a place to sit down.'

'Are you going to give me your parole?'

'No, I certainly am not.'

'I warn you that if you attempt to escape my men will——'

'That's the last thing I'm thinking about at the moment,' interrupted Biggles. 'For one thing I'm far too tired. All the same, I won't give my parole—not until we've had a chat, anyway. Shall we go to one of the huts?'

'If you knew as much about native huts as I do you wouldn't willingly go within a mile of one,' declared Collison. 'Let's sit by the fire; the smoke will help to keep the mosquitoes away.'

They walked across to where the fire was beginning to settle down into a heap of glowing embers. Beside it, for it was too large for them to sit round it, they sat, or rather squatted, on stools that some of the Askaris fetched from the huts.

'I suppose I may assume that you've been to Insula?' inquired Biggles.

'You may assume what you like, Bigglesworth,' Collison answered curtly. 'But you're here to answer questions, not to ask them.'

'All right, there's no need to be provocative,' replied Biggles quietly. 'We shall both get farther and fare better by maintaining friendly relations than we shall by getting at loggerheads. And let me say this. I realize that your present attitude towards us is in keeping with your instructions, or, in case you are acting on your own initiative, the charge that you have preferred against us. But don't ask me to believe that you've stumbled into this business by accident. Now! The sooner I am able to convince you that you are on the wrong tack, the better will be our chance of winding up successfully the business that brought us to Africa, and the better will be your chance of doing yourself and your regiment a bit of good. So I suggest that either I give you the facts about this affair, or alternatively I'll answer any questions you like; but it will save time if I tell you the story. We've nothing to hide.'

'I've only one question to ask,' put in Collison. 'Did you kill Sarda?'

'I did,' replied Biggles.

'No you didn't, I did,' cried Ginger.

'Very well, let us say that *we* did,' suggested Biggles.

'Then that's all I want to know,' said Collison briefly.

'Maybe its all you *want* to know, but there are a lot of other things you ought to know, and a lot of things you've thundering well *got* to know,' declared Biggles coldly. 'If I'm right in my judgement, the information you hold was furnished by one man. It's his word against ours. Now look, Collison: I've been a soldier. I was a soldier while you were a kid squealing in a cradle, so I'm not ignorant of military procedure. If you're going to take things for granted because a renegade Frenchman shot a cock-and-bull story into your ear, you're heading for a court martial. This is a bigger thing than you imagine. I'm not threatening, but by the Lord Harry, I've been through too much to stand for any nonsense, from you or anyone else.'

At the word 'Frenchman' Collison started. 'What do you know about——?'

'Leroux? More than you do. His real name isn't Leroux, for a start, and he'll be doing a ten years' stretch when this show is finished. I suppose he went and saw you at Juba?'

'Malakal.'

'It doesn't matter where. He told you about Sarda, and sent you off after us. Gave you a lift to Insula to hurry things up, as likely as not.'

'Matter of fact, he did, in his aeroplane.'

'*Our* aeroplane, you mean. Or, to be absolutely accurate, Mr Marton's aeroplane. That machine was bought by Mr Felix Marton, of Birmingham, to enable us to search for his son.'

Collison stared. 'Do you mean that you're here looking for young Marton, the boy who disappeared on a Cape flight a year or so ago?'

'Yes, that's why we're here.'

'Can you prove that?'

'Easily, but it will take a few hours. The documents referring to the matter, with my log-book and small kit, are in my kit-bag at an emergency landing-ground a few miles to the east of this place. We hid them when we pushed on here. If you care to send a couple of runners to collect it and bring it here I'll give you my parole until they come back.'

'Whose was that crashed aeroplane I saw there? We came that way, of course.'

'Harry Marton's, but he didn't crash it. It was stolen by the man who calls himself Leroux.'

Collison's manner changed as he grew interested. 'Stolen? What on earth for?'

'For one of two reasons. Either because Marton had tumbled on the secret activities of a firm, with head-quarters in Cairo, for whom Leroux acts as pilot, or because Leroux wanted the aeroplane the better to pursue those activities.'

'And what are these activities—do you know?'

'Dope running. The biggest dope racket that anyone has ever run in the Middle East is operating between Karuli and Cairo.'

Collison stared. 'What is the dope?'

'*Hashish.*' [1]

It was some seconds before Collison spoke. 'Are you pulling my leg?' he asked suspiciously.

'I certainly am not. This is no time for leg-pulling. Do I look as

---

[1] Hashish *is an insidious drug used widely in Egypt and the Far East, where it is called* bhang, *or Indian hemp. Produced chiefly in Greece, it is smuggled in large quantities into Egypt, where it is in great demand in spite of the vigilance of the special officers whose duty it is to combat the traffic. The history of the tricks that have been employed to smuggle the drug into the country would fill a volume. Most of the big men in the 'trade' are Europeans, chiefly Greeks and Armenians, although the actual distributors are natives. To a vast number of Egyptians* hashish *is what tobacco is to other races, and while the demand for it exists no doubt unscrupulous traffickers will risk imprisonment for the large sums of money successful smuggling produces.*

though I should be likely to waste time talking rubbish?'

'But why didn't you report this to the authorities?'

'Because I've only just discovered what is going on. You see, when I was last at that landing-ground on the other side of the plain, I was standing by the crash when I caught a whiff of an aroma that reminded me of something, something that I had smelt once before. You know how the memory of a smell will persist for ages, and can bring back a scene as nothing else will. At the time I couldn't remember what the smell was, or what it reminded me of. Lacey and I once had a spot of trouble with a Greek in the Red Sea; curiously enough his name was Stampoulos, and he may be the same man for all I know, although it isn't an uncommon Greek name. I saw some *hashish* then, and just now the whole thing came back to me. That Puss Moth which you saw crashed there has been used for a year by Leroux, and the inside of the three-ply luggage compartment smells of *hashish*. Go and smell it for yourself if you don't believe me.'

'But what about young Marton? What happened to him—do you know that?'

'I believe he is within ten miles of us at this moment, a prisoner on Stampoulos's alleged tobacco plantation—which I suspect isn't tobacco at all, but the hemp from which *hashish* is made.'

'Good heavens!'

'You may well look shaken.'

'I think you'd better tell me the whole story,' suggested Collison.

'Certainly,' answered Biggles willingly, and he related the events that had occurred since their arrival at Insula. 'Now look here, Collison,' he went on quickly, when he had finished, 'I know you've only got my word for all this, but I can soon furnish proof if you still feel you need it. Don't lose sight of the fact, though, that we are within an ace of finding Harry Marton, and, frankly, that's all we're concerned with. From your point of view the *hashish* business is, no doubt, a much bigger thing. Well, you can take all the kudos that may be coming on that account. I want Harry Marton, that's all, and I'm going to get him, with or without your consent. To waste time now would be fatal. If once Stampoulos and his crowd get wind of what's happened here tonight, or learn that we are talking together, they'll get into my machine and fly away; and they won't come back. Either that or they'll get rid of everything incriminating that may be about. Either way, Harry Marton will disappear for ever.'

'What do you suggest?'

'I suggest that first of all you send a couple of your men off to fetch our kit-bags; then, that you give us—that is, Lacey, Hebblethwaite, and myself—full rein for twenty-four hours. You can come with us and watch us if you like. At the end of that time, whether we are successful or not, we'll report back to you. You can have my parole on that. That lets you out if we are mistaken—not that I think there is any likelihood of that. Frankly, I should feel happier if you would row in with us, but I see the drawbacks to that from your point of view. If there was any trouble—shooting, for instance—and our plans went wrong, you'd be in the cart when you went back to your headquarters for letting us go. But don't forget this. I'm not going to attempt to apprehend Stampoulos or Leroux. As long as I get young Marton and my Dragon they can go on growing *hashish*, and eating it if they like, until they're blue in the face. That's not my affair. I don't feel inclined to lumber myself up with prisoners, or hang about Africa for weeks waiting for the trial to come on. But I'll do this. You throw in your lot with us and we'll go for a clean sweep—work together for a complete round-up. Then, if we get away with it, I'll take Marton and you can have the *hashish* crowd. I'll give you a written statement describing how Sarda met his death if you like, or I'll come back to Afrca in person and tell the story to a jury. Now make up your mind, for there's no time to be lost.'

'What would be your plan if I agreed to this?'

'Go straight to Karuli just as soon as we've had a bite of food and settle the whole thing one way or the other.'

Inspired by Biggles's enthusiasm, Collison was on his feet in a moment. 'I'm your man,' he said, offering his hand. 'I think I know a true story when I hear one. Between ourselves, I didn't like

the look of that fellow Leroux, but as you must see, I was bound
to follow the thing up.'

'Of course you were,' agreed Biggles emphatically. 'Are you
going to take command, or am I?'

'I suggest that we all go to Karuli together. When we get there
we can scout round and decide on the best course. I shall have to
have proof before I——'

'Harry Marton will supply you with all the evidence you'll
need if we can get hold of him,' declared Biggles grimly. 'Find us
a biscuit or two and a tin of bully, and we'll be ready to trek just
as soon as you are.'

16
THE ROUND-UP

TWENTY minutes later the column was on the march, the four
white men walking in front and the askaris in file behind. In
scouting round the village for signs of the evacuated natives they
had found a path leading in the direction of Karuli, so there was
no danger of losing the way. Smoking had been forbidden, and
the passage of the party was almost as stealthy as that of the wild
beasts that occasionally crossed their path.

For two hours the party marched, and then a small cluster of
lights ahead told them that they were nearing their destination.
Thereafter the party moved with extra caution, the order 'no
talking' being passed from man to man down the column, and
they were not more than a quarter of a mile away from the lights
when Collison gave the order to halt.

'Have you any idea of the lay-out of this place?' Biggles asked
him in a whisper.

'Not the remotest,' was the answer. 'What's your idea of the
best plan of procedure?'

Biggles thought for a moment, eyeing the lights speculatively.
'I'll tell you what I think,' he said quietly. 'If we all go forward,
and anything happens to warn them of our approach, they'll

clean everything up by the time we get there—including
Marton. As likely as not they'll try to do the same thing if you
walk staight up to the place, whether we are with you or not, for
they can hardly refuse you admission. That in itself would look
fishy. At the same time, it's a bit difficult for you as a serving
officer in an official capacity to go snooping about the place like a
spy; I mean, you'd look a bit cheap if they caught you at it. With
us it would be altogether different. I suggest therefore that you
detail all your men except one or two to surround the place. We
will then go forward and reconnoitre. If there is anything to
report, we'll come back and let you know. If you hear any
shooting, or anything in the nature of a rough house, you can
hurry along to the bungalow—or whatever it is—at the same
time blowing your whistle for your men to close in. At present our
great advantage lies in the fact that our presence here must be
absolutely unsuspected.'

'How many people are there likely to be in the bungalow, do
you think?' asked Collison.

'I've no idea,' admitted Biggles. 'It's almost certain that
Leroux is there because we watched him land here this morning.
There is a Greek, who may be Stampoulos, about somewhere,
but the last we saw of him was at Insula. Whether he's got back or
not I don't know, but I should think it's quite likely if he
managed to get across the river.'

'What do you mean? There's no difficulty about that.'

'We had an awful time getting across this morning in that
ramshackle canoe.'

'Why use the canoe? That was abandoned long ago. There's a
flying bridge.'

'What's that?'

'A kind of flat punt affair that goes to and fro on a wire; there's
a rope on it so that whichever side of the river you happen to
arrive at you can pull it over to you.'

'We didn't see it.'

'Possibly you wouldn't unless you knew it was there because it
is some distance above the pass.'

'I see. Well, never mind that now; what do you think of my

idea? Shall I take my party for a look round?'

'I think it's a sound scheme. I'd like to come with you, but I see your point about keeping out of the way for the time being.'

'All right, then; we'll get off. If you hear nothing, wait until we return; if there's a row, come along at the double.'

'That's clear. Off you go, then.'

Biggles touched Algy and Ginger lightly on the arm. 'Come on, chaps. This should be the last act,' he added quietly as he glided away into the darkness in the direction of the lights.

He pulled up in the dark shadow of a tree at a point where the open veld gave way to cultivated country, and beckoned the others to come nearer. 'We've got to watch our step,' he said quietly. 'Remember, we're not alone; we have Collison to consider, which doesn't give us quite the same freedom as we are accustomed to. Still, it's useless to say what we may or may not do until we see how the land lies. The landing-ground must be on the other side of that building, which I take to be the bungalow,' he went on, peering into the darkness. 'The lamps are still alight, so Stampoulos and Co. haven't yet gone to bed although it must be getting late. We mustn't waste time; the lights may go out at any moment, and I'd sooner arrive while they are alight because we shall stand a better chance of learning something. Have your guns handy, but don't for heaven's sake use them unless it becomes absolutely necessary.'

They walked on again, only to stop once more while Biggles examined the crops that now appeared on either side of the path.

'What is it?' breathed Algy, as Biggles fingered the broad leaves of one of the plants that grew in seried ranks as far as they could see.

'It's tobacco all right, there's no doubt about that,' was the mystified answer. 'Stand fast,' added Biggles, and walked several yards into the growth. He was soon back. 'Cunning devils,' he almost hissed. 'There's something else growing in the middle which I take to be hemp; the tobacco round the edges of the field is merely camouflage.'

In silence they crept nearer to the lights that marked the position of the bungalow, and as they drew nearer it became possible to see the dark silhouette of other buildings near at hand. One, a large one, particularly attracted Biggles's attention, and he made his way towards it cautiously.

Another few paces and the crops ended abruptly, leaving them facing a vast, open area, silent and mysterious in the dim starlight, on the edge of which stood the building.

'Here's the aerodrome, and that, I fancy, is the hangar,' breathed Biggles. 'Watch out, there may be a guard.'

They saw no one, however, and it took them only a few minutes to confirm that the building was, in fact, a reed-built hangar like the one at Insula. Moreover, the Dragon was inside with her tanks filled ready for flight, a condition that Biggles ascertained while the others remained on guard. He also found something else, something that gave him a thrill of elation when he discovered it. In the cabin were a number of neat packages, each marked with a number.

'We could get away now if we wanted to,' he murmured, as he rejoined the others. 'In the ordinary way all we should have to do would be to find Marton, but as things are we've got to stay and help Collison to clean up. Let's go and have a look at the bungalow.'

In single file they began to walk quietly towards the building, from which three shafts of yellow light lit up the bare earth outside. From it came the sound of voices, one raised high as if in anger. At the same time a low murmur became audible from another building some distance farther on, a long, low structure, the roof of which was illuminated from time to time by a flickering orange glow, as if a fire were burning somewhere on the other side of it.

'I should say that's the native compound,' breathed Biggles. 'They're bound to employ a lot of labour here, so whatever we do must be done quietly or we shall stir up a hornet's nest.'

Nearer they crept to the bungalow, approaching it from an angle, so that the details of its construction could be seen on two sides. One side, which was, in fact, the end of the building, was in complete darkness, although they could see the black square that marked the position of a window. But the other elevation, which was the front of the house, was ablaze with light which came from three windows. Two were quite small, but the other held their interest, for it ran nearly half the length of the building, and ended at a door, which stood open. So much they could see, although the whole of the front of the house was shaded to some extent by a roof that overhung for several feet, supported at intervals by stout posts, forming the usual shady veranda. As far as they could make out, the room behind it into which the door opened was the main room of the building, for both the door and the long window commanded a broad view of the path, the plantation, and, to one side, the native compound.

Unfortunately, the door was at the far end of the window from where they stood, and Biggles observed that the only way it could be reached without crossing the front of the big window, and thereby risking discovery, was to go round the dark side of the house. He might then crawl under one of the smaller windows, the sill of which was about three feet above the level of the veranda, and survey the interior of the room before going on to the door—not that it was by any means certain that he would find it necessary to enter through that particular door.

At this stage his plans were still rather in the air, because he did not know what the men inside were doing. He realized that if they were engaged in some quite harmless occupation it would be in the nature of an anti-climax to walk into the room and make charges which they would certainly deny. In any case, he decided, that was Collison's job. His primary object was to find out if Harry Marton was in the building, and if so, rescue him before any harm could come to him. Nevertheless, a peep into the lighted room was clearly desirable, and with this object in view he edged his way a little to the right in order to get into the dark shadow on the unlighted side of the building. With the others following him unquestioningly, he crept stealthily towards the wall, approaching it almost at right angles.

It may be that such a small thing as a stone, or a kink in a chain, saved his life, for although he was alert for any emergency, he was certainly not expecting danger from the direction in which it came. The first warning he had of it was a faint *chink* as if a small piece of metal had dropped upon another. At the time his attention was divided between the dark wall which he was attempting to reach, and the door on the lighted side of the bungalow in case anyone came out of it; for which reason his eyes were fixed at his own level and not on the ground. But at the metallic noise, slight as it was, his eyes switched to the point whence it came, which seemed to be on the ground at the base of the wall. At first, all he could make out was a smallish, black shadow, but as he stared at it, trying to see what it was, it moved, and the movement brought it into a new angle of starlight. As if suddenly illuminated from within, two green orbs of light glowed in the darkness.

He did not wait to see what it was, but instinctively sprang backward, colliding violently with Ginger who was close behind him, and who, caught completely unaware, had no time to avoid him. Clutching at each other to save themselves from falling, neither succeeded, but both went sprawling on the hard ground. Simultaneously, there was a deep-throated snarl, a harsh clang of metal and a loud thud.

Biggles was up in a flash, drawing his gun at the same time, eyes feverishly seeking the cause of the débâcle. He saw Algy bending forward, tense as a spring, his right hand out-thrust, and heard his quickly muttered, 'It's all right—don't shoot.'

'What is it?' Biggles gasped, breathing heavily, for the fall had knocked the wind out of him.

'It's a leopard I think, but it's on a chain,' muttered Algy. 'The chain is fixed to something under the window. The brute sprang at you, but you stepped back just in time. That bang you heard was the chain jerking taut; it pulled the beast up short and threw it on to its back. I wonder it didn't break its neck. It's still there, crouching under the window . . . see it? We shall have to go another way.'

Biggles stood for a moment watching the animal while he recovered his breath. 'Are you all right, Ginger?' he asked.

'Yes, I'm all right.'

'Sorry I barged into you like that, but I had to move quickly.'

'So I noticed.'

'Has anyone heard us, do you think, Algy?'

'I don't think so. I can still hear talking going on inside; it sounds as if there's an argument in progress.'

They all went back to the front of the house, keeping in the shadow slightly to one side.

'I'm going to have a look into that room,' declared Biggles. 'Stand still.'

Half a dozen quick steps took him to the edge of the shadow in which they stood, so he dropped on to all fours and crawled quickly to the veranda, taking care to keep below the level of the window. Then, very slowly, he drew himself up until he could see over the sill, and the sight that met his curious stare caused him to catch his breath sharply.

With his hands tied together and fastened to a hook in the wall was a youth whose pale face he recognized instantly. It was Harry Marton. Standing beside him, with the stock of a *jambok* in his right hand and the thongs in the other, was the native who had spoken to them while they had been repairing the Puss Moth, and who, only a few hours ago, had gloated over them as they lay in the hut at Limshoda. From the expression on his face he was enjoying himself.

Seated at a small table in the middle of the room with glasses in their hands were two white men. One was Leroux, and the other was the tall man whom they had last seen at Insula. Both were leaning back in long cane chairs, with cigarettes between their fingers, watching the scene. Leroux was speaking.

'We give you something to remember,' he said. 'Go ahead, Chola.'

Biggles waited for no more. At the spectacle before him all the worry and anxiety he had suffered during the past few days seemed to merge into one searing impulse of cold fury that set his nerves tingling and drew his lips back from his teeth in a mirthless grin.

'Come on,' he snapped over his shoulder to the others, and without waiting for them, dashed to the door.

On the threshold he pulled up short, crouching forward, eyes gleaming, his automatic waving gently like the head of a snake about to strike, as it covered the startled occupants. 'Move!' he snarled. 'Move, one of you! Why don't you move and give me an excuse to blow you in halves, you dirty, crooked rats in white skins. I've had to kill better men than you, and my finger's twitching to fill you full of holes for the pleasure of doing it.' He broke off, nostrils quivering, his blazing eyes never leaving the faces of the two white men, who did not move, but sat staring in a wide-eyed amazement that in different circumstances might have been comical. He heard the others just behind him, and took a pace forward into the room.

'Algy, cut down that boy,' he rapped out in a voice that was as cold and hard as cracking ice. 'Shoot that black devil if he so much as winks an eyelid. Ginger, go and hail Captain Collison. As for you,' he continued, to Leroux and Stampoulos, as the others obeyed his instructions, 'you don't know how lucky you are that Collison is here, or anything I have to say to you, which isn't much, would be said with this.' He flicked the muzzle of the automatic. 'Keep your hands on the table, both of you. One false move is all the excuse I need to hand you what you deserve, and I'm praying for you to make it.' He broke off as Collison, with a file of askaris behind him, hurried into the room, looking from one to the other questioningly.

'Here are your men, Collison,' Biggles told him tersely. 'If you have any doubt as to what their business is, there are acres of hemp growing outside and an aeroplane loaded with *hashish* in the hangar.'

At the word *hashish* Leroux and Stampoulos stirred uneasily. Stampoulos rose to his feet, and opened his mouth to speak.

'You'd better keep anything you have to say for the court,' Collison warned him curtly.

.   .   .   .

An hour later, with the prisoners handcuffed and under armed guard in the room that had been Harry Marton's prison for more than a year, and Collison's askaris rounding up the natives in the compound, the rest of the white men sat round the table recently used by Leroux and Stampoulos. Harry Marton, still looking pale and tired, was telling his story, while Collison, note-book in hand, was making notes.

'There really isn't very much to tell,' Harry was saying. 'As you probably know, I got as far as Malakal without any trouble, and it was just as I was about to leave that I met this villain Leroux. He told me that he was a pilot and had been forced to land near Insula, where he had left his companion who was dying of fever. He asked me to go out and bring him in. What could I do? What would you have done, Bigglesworth?'

'I'm afraid I should have done what you did,' confessed Biggles.

'Yes, of course I had to go,' went on Harry. 'I was ahead of my time, and I worked it out that there was still a chance of getting the record. Leroux said he would come with me to show me the way. Well, we went, and I never had the slightest reason for suspicion. Sure enough, there was a crashed machine lying near the edge of the landing-ground—an old French machine, by the look of it—which Leroux said was his. I landed near it. There was nobody in it, so Leroux said that his friend must have gone down to the rest-house. So to the rest-house we went, where a one-eyed scoundrel named Sarda brought us drinks. How on earth could I have imagined that . . . well, that the drink contained dope?'

'Of course you couldn't,' put in Biggles.

'Well, there I was. I just flopped out and that was all I knew about it. When I woke up I was at this place. Leroux afterwards told me that he and Sarda just carried me back to my own machine and he flew me here the same day. And here I have been a prisoner ever since, compelled to keep my machine in order for their use.'

'I suppose that's why they kept you alive?' suggested Collison.

'Of course. When I arrived here Leroux's mechanic was down with fever, and Leroux himself is no engineer. In any case, neither he nor his mechanic new anything about the rigging of a Puss, nor had they ever seen an engine like mine. So they flogged me and threatened me with death unless I kept the machine in

order for them. Then Barrail, the mechanic, died, and then they
had to keep me. I did what they told me because I always hoped
that sooner or later I'd get a chance to escape. I knew, of course,
that they would never let me go willingly, because I should have
gone straight to the police. Once I escaped, but the natives
caught me and brought me back. I was flogged for it, and after
that a leopard was always kept chained under my window to
prevent me from every trying to escape that way again.'

'We know all about that gentleman; I nearly trod on him
when I was looking for you just now,' smiled Biggles.

'You knew what they were doing, I suppose?' suggested
Collison.

'No, I didn't. I never did find out, but I guessed that it was
something illegal. Sometimes, after I had finished work on the
machine, I was made to do housework, so I knew all about the
telephone. I was working near it the other day when it rang, and
in desperation I answered it, but I only had time to get out one or
two words when Stampoulos came into the room and knocked
me down.'

'All the same, it was a lucky chance, because that's how we first
knew that you were alive,' Biggles told him. 'It was Ginger
ringing up from Insula. It's fairly clear to see what happened,' he
went on, turning to Collison. 'Leroux really did crash his
machine, and what with that and his mechanic being sick, he
was in a mess for transport. He was probably going up to Cairo
by Imperial Airways to report the state of affairs at his
headquarters, or perhaps to fetch another machine, when Harry
happened to land at Malakal and put an idea into his crooked
mind. A crook will always choose a crooked path in preference to
a straight one, so he decided to steal an aeroplane and a
mechanic at one stroke. It was a clever scheme, for there was very
little risk. In nine cases out of ten he would have got away with it,
but Harry happened to have a father who wouldn't take official
reports for granted.'

'And what are you fellows going to do now?' asked Collison.

'If it's all right with you, I propose to hit the breeze for
England, in the Dragon, as soon as it is daylight and your men

come back with our kit-bags. There are four of us now, but we can manage seven, so if you like we'll give you and your two prisoners a lift as far as Malakal.'

'That's fine,' agreed Collison. 'My fellows can march back with the native prisoners, and you can make out your reports at my head-quarters. If you'll do that I don't think any objection will be raised to your pushing straight on home.'

17
IN CONCLUSION

FIVE days later a touching reunion took place at Croydon aerodrome, where Mr Marton senior, who had been notified of their coming, met his son and the three airmen who had been responsible for his rescue. Tears sparkled in the old man's eyes when he put his hands on his son's shoulders and looked into his careworn face. Biggles turned away.

'Yes, I think it's time we were moving off,' observed Algy softly.

But Mr Marton called them back. 'Where are you going?' he asked.

'Well—er, I don't exactly know, but I expect we're going home,' stammered Biggles. 'We've no immediate plans, if that's what you mean.'

'Then what do you say to a little reunion dinner tonight? I've yet to thank you for what you've done, and I'm anxious to hear the whole story; there is also a little—er—business matter to be settled yet.'

'I think that's a fine idea,' smiled Biggles.

'Seven o'clock at the Savoy?'

'We'll be there,' Biggles assured him. 'Good-bye for the present.'

'*Au revoir.*'

'And that's that,' murmured Ginger reflectively, as they walked towards the customs barrier to check in.

'As you rightly remark, that's that,' agreed Biggles.

BIGGLES
FLIES NORTH

I
BIGGLES GETS A LETTER

BIGGLES was whistling softly as he walked into the breakfast-room of his flat in Mount Street, but he broke off as he reached for the letters lying beside his plate. With the exception of one they all bore halfpenny stamps, suggesting that they contained nothing more interesting than circulars, but the exception was a bulky package with Canadian stamps, while across the top was printed in block letters, 'CONFIDENTIAL. IF AWAY, PLEASE FORWARD.'

'What's Wilks doing in Canada, I wonder?' murmured Algy, from the other side of the table.

Biggles glanced up. 'Been doing a bit of Sherlock Holmes stuff with my correspondence, eh?'

'As I happen to know Wilks's fist, and am able to recognize a Canadian stamp when I see one, I put two and two together,' replied Algy casually.

'Smart work,' Biggles congratulated him, with cheerful sarcasm, as he tore open the flap of the envelope.

'Wilks? Who's Wilks?' Ginger asked Algy. He had finished his breakfast and was sitting by the fire.

'Wilks—or rather, Captain Wilkinson—was a flight com-mander in 187 Squadron, in France,' answered Algy. 'He was in South America, an officer in the Bolivian Air Force to be precise, when we last saw him,' he added. 'I wonder what sent him up north?' He said no more but winked at Ginger significantly as a frown settled on Biggles's face, a frown that grew deeper as he turned over the pages of the letter.

There was silence for several minutes. 'Your coffee will be stone cold,' observed Algy at last.

Biggles read the letter to the end of before laying it on the table beside him and reaching for the toast. 'Poor old Wilks is in a jam,' he said quietly.

'I suspected it from your expression,' returned Algy. 'What's the trouble?'

Biggles drank some coffee and picked up his letter again. 'I'll read it to you, then you'll know as much as I do,' he said. 'Listen to this. He writes on paper headed "Arctic Airways, Fort Beaver, Mackenzie, North-West Territories, Canada."

> ' "My dear Biggles,
> ' "I am writing this on the off-chance of it reaching you, but knowing all about your nomadic habits I shall be surprised if it does. As you probably remember, letter-writing is not in my line, so you no doubt guessed before you opened this (if ever you do) that things must be pretty sticky. Believe me, they are all that, and more. To come to the point right away, having heard odd rumours of your adventures from time to time in one part of the world or another, it has just struck me that you might not be averse to starting on a fresh one. I do not know whether it is for fun or for profit that you go roaring round the globe; possibly both; but if you hunt adventure for the sake of it, well, old boy, right here I can supply you with the genuine article in unlimited quantities. But make no mistake. This isn't a kid-glove game for the parlour; it's knuckle-dusters in the wide open spaces; and I don't mind telling you that out here the wide open spaces are so wide that you have to fly for a long, long time to get to the other side of them.
> ' "Before I start on the real story I may as well say that the odds seem to be against my being alive by the time you get this. If I just disappear, or get wiped out in what looks like a genuine crash, find a fellow named McBain—'Bridle' Jake he is called around these parts—and hand him a bunch of slugs from me, as a last service for an old pal." '

'By gosh! Things must be pretty grim for old Wilks to write in that strain,' broke in Algy.

'Grim is the right word for it,' broke in Biggles shortly. 'But don't interrupt—just listen to this.

> ' "You remember I was in Bolivia a few years ago. Well, there was a change of government, and as I didn't like the new one—or maybe the new one didn't like me—I packed by valise and headed north, thinking that the most likely point of the compass where I should find a concern in need of a pilot who had learned to fly by the seat of his pants, and not by these new-fangled instruments. I knocked about the States for a bit without getting fixed up with anything permanent, and ultimately drifted over the border into Canada, which is, I may say, a great country, although I have little to thank it for as yet.
> ' "One day I struck lucky—at least, it looked that way to me at the time, although I am not so sure about it now. I got a charter job flying a mining engineer up to some new gold-fields which were then being surveyed. The concern has since been put over in a big way under the title of Moose Creek Gold-fields Corporation—Moose Creek being the

name of the locality. You may have heard tell of the 'last place on earth'. Well, I can tell you just where it is. Moose Creek. It is well inside the Arctic circle. Why they call it Moose Creek I do not know, for no moose in its right mind—or any other animal, for that matter—would go within a hundred miles of the perishing place. But that's by the way.

' "Having got the low-down about these gold-fields, I had one of my rare inspirations. Moose Creek is eight hundred miles north of the nearest rail-head, and the journey, made by canoe in summer and dog-sled during the freeze-up, takes about six weeks' heavy going. I had saved a bit of money while I was in Bolivia, and it struck me that since there was certain to be a fair amount of traffic to and from the gold-fields, an air line might be worked up into a paying proposition. I counted on flying up staff, stores, mails, machinery, and so on, and bringing back the gold and the people who would rather ride home than walk eight hundred miles. In an aircraft the journey could be done in a day instead of six weeks. To make a long story as short as possible, I put all my savings into the venture, opening up my own landing-field and shed at Fort Beaver, which is the rail-head. I called it Arctic Airways.

' "For a year or so it was touch and go. I was just about broke and preparing to pack up when real gold was struck at the Creek. That sent the balloon up. Traffic jumped. Things began to hum, and it looked at last as if all I had ever hoped for had come to pass. I got into the money, and with my profits I bought a second machine. Then, out of the blue— literally, as it happened—came the smack in the eye; one which, I must admit, I wasn't expecting. Another fellow jumped my claim—the same Brindle Jake that I have already mentioned. It seemed a bit thick after all I had been through, blazing the trail and all that, for someone else to step in and start reaping my harvest. However, it couldn't be helped, and I decided to make the best of a bad show. I figured it out there ought to be enough money in the game for two of us, anyway; as it happened, Brindle had his own ideas about that. He decided that two in the game was one too many—and he wasn't going to be the one to go. From that moment I learned that the gloves were off.

' "I must explain the position in regard to Fort Beaver Aerodrome. (The one at the other end of my run, Moose Creek, belongs to the gold company, so I have nothing to do with that.) There is only one possible landing-ground within fifty miles of Fort Beaver, and that's mine. I bought the land off a fellow named Angus Stirling, who had decided that he preferred prospecting for gold to farming. I paid him cash, whereupon he headed north with his traps and hasn't been seen since. I cleared the ground, put up a shed, and the land became Fort Beaver landing-field. There was never any question about the title of the land until recently; everyone in Fort Beaver regarded it as mine until one day a bunch of toughs rolled up, and, in spite of my protests, without paying a cent, or so much as a by-your-leave, built a larger shed than mine on the edge of my field. A couple of days later two Weinkel Twelve transport planes landed, and out stepped Brindle Jake and his two pilots, Joe Sarton, a tall chap, good-looking in a rugged sort of way, and 'Tex'

Ferroni, a slim, dark little fellow who looks—as, indeed, his name suggests—as if he came from one of the Latin states. McBain himself is a big, broad-shouldered bloke, with odd patches of grey in his hair and beard. That's how he gets his nickname, I am told. A half-breed French-Canadian named Jean Chicot trails about after him like a dog, and I've got my own idea as to *his* real job. I reckon he's McBain's bodyguard. Naturally, I asked Brindle what was the big idea, and you can guess my surprise when he calmly told me to clear off the land. I can't go into details now, but for the first time I learned that there was some doubt as to the title of the land I had bought off Stirling. For some extraordinary reason which I don't understand there seems to be no record of his having paid the Government for it. Anyway, the record has not yet been found, although, being so far away from the Record Office, correspondence is a slow business. He—that is, Stirling—told me that he got the land for a nominal figure under a settler's grant, but it looks to me as if he forgot to register it—or forgot to collect the transfer. The fact remains he didn't give it to me, which was, I suppose, my own fault, for it went clean out of my head. I'm afraid I'm a bit careless in these matters. I took his word for it that it was O.K. There is this about it, though. If I don't own the land, neither does Brindle, although he tries to bluff me that he does.

' "He started operating to Moose Creek right away. I flew up and saw the traffic manager of the gold-fields company, a decent little fellow named Canwell, and lodged a complaint, but it did not get me very far. Canwell's point is—and I suppose he is right—he is only conerned with getting his stuff to the rail-head, and he doesn't care two hoots who takes it as long as it goes, or as long as he gets efficient service. He was born and bred in the north, and he as good as told me that in this country it is up to a fellow to work out his own salvation. If he hasn't the gumption to do that—well, it's his own funeral. That was that.

' "I got my first ideas of Brindle's methods when, a day or two later, one of my machines shed its wing just after it had taken off; yet I'd stake my life that that machine was airworthy the night before because I went over it myself. Brindle or his men tampered with it, I'm certain, but of course I can't prove anything. The pilot, a nice chap named Walter Graves, was killed. I bought another machine and hired another pilot. Two days after taking delivery the machine went up in flames during the night. My new pilot was 'got at' by the other side, and had the wind put up him so much that he packed up. I've no money to buy another machine. The one I have left is a Rockheed freighter which I fly myself. I sleep in it—with a gun in my hand—but I can't stand the strain much longer. One by one my boys have left me, scared by Brindle's threats, so that I have to do my own repairs. That's how things stand at present. Brindle is operating two machines and is gradually wearing me down. I've been nearly killed two or three times by 'accident'. Brindle wants the aerodrome and my shed. I've told him he'll only get 'em over my dead body—and that isn't bluff.

' "The fact is, old lad, it goes against the grain to be run out of the territory by a low-down grafter. I'm fighting a lone hand, for the

'Mounties'[1] have other things to do besides interfering in what, to them, is a business squabble. With one man whom I could rely on absolutely, to take turn and turn about with me, I believe I could still beat Brindle and his toughs. The trouble is, I daren't leave the place; if I did, I'd never get back; Brindle would see to that. Meanwhile, I'm hanging on. I'm in this up to the neck and I'm going to see it through to the last turn of the prop. It isn't just the money that matters now; I won't be jumped out by a crooked skunk. That's all. If you want a spot of real flying, flying with the lid off, step right across and give me a hand to keep the old flag flying. We did a job or two together in the old days. Let's do one more. All the best to Algy (remember that first E.A. he shot down? The laugh was certainly on you that time).

> Yours ever,
> WILKS." '

Biggles's face was set in hard lines as he tossed the letter on the table and picked up the envelope to examine the postmark.

'How long ago was it posted?' asked Algy.

'Nine days.'

'Anything could have happened in that time.'

'I was just thinking the same thing.'

'What are you going to do?' put in Ginger, looking from one to the other.

'That remains to be seen,' replied Biggles curtly. 'For the moment we are just going to Fort Beaver as fast as we can get there. Algy, ring up and find out when the next boat sails. Ginger, pass me that directory. I'll send a few cables. We shall want a machine waiting for us when we land—with the props ticking over. If I can get the machine I want we'll show that blighter McBain how to shift freight. Get your bags packed, everybody, and put in plenty of woollen kit. I've never been to Canada, but I seem to have heard that the winters there are inclined to be chilly.'

'Then let's go and see if we can warm things up,' murmured Algy.

---

[1] *North-West Mounted Police*

2

FORT BEAVER

A LITTLE before two o'clock, sixteen days after Wilks's SOS had been received in London, a Bluewing 'Jupiter' airliner circled low over the cluster of log huts which comprised Fort Beaver, preparatory to landing.

Biggles sat at the controls, Algy beside him, with Ginger braced in the narrow corridor that connected the pilot's control cabin—it could hardly be called a cockpit—with what normally would have been the main passenger saloon. Behind, amongst the luggage in the rear compartment, sat Flight-Sergeant Smyth, Biggles's old fitter and sharer of many adventures.

The 'Jupe'—as Ginger had already nicknamed the machine—was Biggles's first choice, and he accounted himself fortunate in being able to get a commercial transport machine with such a fine reputation. American built, the Jupiter, latest model of the Bluewing Company, was a twin-engined cantilever high-wing monoplane fitted with two 850 h.p. 'Cyclone' engines, one power unit being built into the leading edge of the wing on either side of the fuselage. The undercarriage was retractable. In the standard model there were four mail compartments forward of the main cabin, which normally provided accommodation for eighteen passengers, but Biggles, realizing that eighteen seats would rarely, if ever, be required, had had this number reduced to six, the space thus made available being cleared for freight. As he pointed out to the others, extra passengers, if any, could always travel in the freight compartments. The manufacturer's figures gave the maximum speed of the machine as 230 miles an hour, with normal cruising speed 205 miles an hour.

Negotiations for the aircraft had been carried on by wireless while they were on board ship. Not for a moment did Biggles contemplate taking a machine out with him, although, from choice, he would have preferred a British aeroplane, but that would have meant crating it for an ocean voyage, which is a very expensive business. The result of the negotiations was that when the party had landed at Quebec they had found the machine awaiting them, it having been flown up from the United States by a delivery pilot.

Three long hops had seen the Jupe at Fort McMurray, the base aerodrome of northern fliers, and another long journey northward over the 'bad lands' had brought the airmen to Fort Beaver, which lies mid-way between the north-east arm of Great Slave Lake and the Mackenzie River, some fifty miles south-east of Bear Lake. They all wore heavy flying kit, with the fur outside, for although it was not yet winter it was already cold, and the annual freeze-up could be expected in the near future.

Behind the pilot's cabin, in the main compartment, was piled their luggage—valises and suitcases. Stacked in the freight cabin were bales and bundles of spare parts, chiefly engine components; but perhaps the most striking item was an enormous pair of skis, so long that the ends projected into the doorway of the lavatory, which was situated in the tail. It had been left open for that purpose. These would, of course, be needed when the snow came.[1] Until that time the ordinary retractable-wheel under-carriage would be used.

Biggles regarded the landing-ground dispassionately as he throttled back and prepared to glide in. Since it was the only level piece of ground within view it was unmistakable, although two blocks of wooden buildings on the edge of the field provided confirmation, were it needed.

'What do you think of it?' asked Algy.

'Not much,' returned Biggles briefly.

'I never saw a more desolate-looking spot in all my life.'

'What did you expect to find—concrete runways?' inquired Biggles sarcastically. 'This isn't a European terminus.'

'No, I can see that,' declared Algy warmly. 'Wilks was certainly right about the wide open spaces—although he needn't have used the plural. From what I've seen of this country

---

[1] *Wheel undercarriages give way to skis during winter in all northern countries, where every lake, when frozen, becomes a potential landing-ground.*

from topsides, it's just one big, wide open space, and nothing else.'

'I fancy we shall find something else when we get on the carpet,' observed Biggles, smiling faintly. 'Is that old Wilks I can see, mending his hut?'

Algy peered through the side window. 'That fellow is too tall for Wilks,' he declared. 'And he seems to be tearing the place down, not mending it, anyway.'

Biggles glanced across quickly. 'The dickens he does. That doesn't look too good. However, we shall soon learn what we came to learn.'

Nothing more was said, and a minute later the wheels of the big machine were trundling over the rough surface of the landing-ground, scored in a hundred places with tyre tracks.

Biggles allowed the machine to run to a standstill, and then, using his brakes, turned towards the smaller of the two sets of buildings. Moving slowly and majestically, the Jupiter roared up to where a little group of men stood staring at them from in front of a rough but stoutly built hangar, roofed with corrugated iron.

'Funny, I don't see Wilks,' murmured Algy.

'Which means, obviously, that he isn't here,' returned Biggles.

'Maybe he's in the air.'

'Maybe. We'll soon know. This is his shed, for there is the board with the name of his company on it leaning against the wall. It looks as if it had just been taken down. That being so, what is McBain doing here—for that's who the nasty-looking piece of work in the fur cap is, I'll bet my boots. I don't like the look of things; we'd better leave the engines running in case we want to go up again in a hurry. Tell Smyth to come here and take over, and keep an eye on us. Let's get out.'

As the three airmen stepped down from the saloon door, leaving Smyth in the control cabin with the engines idling, four men walked to meet them. A fifth, obviously an Indian, remained standing near the hangar. One of the four, a little ahead of the others and clearly the leader, was a tall, burly man, whose bristling, square-cut beard was curiously streaked with grey. There was something unnaturally cold about his pale blue eyes, which were set rather far apart, and, as is often the case with pale eyes, looked larger than they really were. Nonetheless, he was a powerful and arresting figure. On his head he wore a fur cap, with flaps hanging loosely over his ears, a check-patterned lumber shirt of blanket-like material, and dark corduroy trousers tucked into half-Wellington boots. A broad belt, with cartridge-pouches thrust through loops, was buckled tightly round his waist.

The man who walked close behind him was an entirely different type, although he was dressed in much the same fashion. Slight in build, undoubtedly good-looking in a rather effeminate way, his delicate features might have passed for those of a woman but for a wisp of black moustache that decorated his upper lip. His eyes, set under finely drawn eyebrows, were dark, but held a quality of restlessness that made it difficult to ascertain what object most occupied his attention—the aerodrome, the aircraft, or the airmen, for he seemed to be watching all three at the same time. The fur jacket he wore was thrown open, revealing a beautifully worked Indian belt, through which he had hooked his thumbs in such a way that the bowie knife which hung on one side could just be seen.

At a distance of two or three paces behind strolled two other men, their hands thrust carelessly into their trousers pockets. One was a fresh-complexioned man of perhaps thirty-five years of age, with a fair moustache; his companion was younger, and as swarthy as the other was fair. Despite the fact that his jaws were working steadily, suggesting the gum-chewing habit acquired by residents in the United States, 'southern Europe' was written clearly on his dark skin.

Before a word was spoken, Biggles, remembering the descriptions in Wilks's letter, could have named them all. The big man was obviously Brindle McBain; the man who walked close behind him, keeping at his heels like a dog, was Jean Chicot. The other two were the pilots, Joe Sarton, the fair man, and Tex Ferroni, the 'slim, dark little fellow'. Wilks's description had been brief, but singularly apt, thought Biggles, as he walked slowly to meet them, at the same time drawing off his gauntlets.

His eyes wandered along the front of the hangar and the adjacent offices, now not more than twenty yards away, hoping to see Wilks, but there was no sign of him or of any member of his staff, despite the fact that the buildings were without question those of Arctic Airways. An atmosphere of desertion, almost of desolation, hung over them.

McBain was the first to speak. Seeing Biggles and his companions walking towards him, he stopped and waited for them to come up. The man with him did the same.

'Ten bucks, stranger,' he demanded curtly.

Biggles raised his eyebrows in genuine surprise. 'Meaning?' he queried.

'Just ten dollars,' returned McBain harshly.

'Yes, I had gathered that much,' nodded Biggles. 'What I meant was, what for?'

'Landing fee.'

'Oh.' Biggles reached the four men, who had formed a little group, and stopped. 'Are you the authorized collector for Arctic Airways?' he asked.

McBain's big eyes rested broodingly on Biggles's slight figure. 'No,' he said shortly, 'I'm collecting for myself.'

'I see. And who might you be?'

'McBain's the name.'

'Mine's Bigglesworth,' returned Biggles evenly.

'Englishman?'

'Guess again and you'll be wrong.'

'Smart guy, eh?'

'No, just as ordinary as they make them,' said Biggles, smiling faintly. 'But aren't you making a mistake, Mr McBain?'

'What gave you that idea?'

'This field belongs to Arctic Airways.'

'Yeah? Well, you're making the mistake. It belongs to me,' grated McBain.

'What gave *you* that idea?' inquired Biggles easily.

McBain hesitated. He took out a pipe and began to fill it. 'What are you doing here, anyway?' he asked in a curious voice.

'Oh, I just dropped in to take a look at my property,' replied

Biggles casually.

The other started. 'Your property?'

'Well, I've just put a lot of money into Arctic Airways, so I seem to have some right to take a look at things at close quarters,' observed Biggles.

There was a moment's silence in which McBain's swarthy companion took out a little bag of tobacco and rolled a cigarette with deft fingers.

'Did you say you'd put money into this concern?' McBain jerked his thumb towards Arctic Airways' hangar.

'That's what I said, Mr McBain.'

'And you've come here to see where your money's gone?'

'No, I've come here to help spend it.'

'You mean—you've come here—to *work*?'

'That's how I figured it out.'

'Then your figgerin' ain't good, Swigglesworth.'

'Bigglesworth, if you don't mind. Awkward name, I know, but it's the best my father could do for me, and as we're likely to see quite a bit of each other, we might as well get things right at the start. It saves misunderstandings later on—if you get my meaning?'

The other nodded thoughtfully. 'Yeah,' he said, 'I get your meaning. Do you know the guy what ran this Arctic Airways outfit?'

Biggles noted the use of the past tense but he did not reveal his anxiety. 'Ran?' he questioned. 'Isn't he still running it?'

'Don't look like it, does it?'

'I haven't had a chance to look round yet, so I can't say. Still, you seem to know. What's happened to him?'

'Say, what do you think I am—a nurse?'

'I hadn't thought about it,' murmured Biggles. 'If Captain Wilkinson has disappeared it looks as if it's time somebody tried to find him, doesn't it?'

'It may look that way to you.'

'Any reason why it shouldn't look that way to you?'

'Plenty.'

'Pity about that; maybe you'll tell me why, sometime.'

'I sure will, and there ain't no need to wait. Get this, stranger. This airfield is bad medicine for visitors, and if you're half as smart as you think you are, wise guy, you'll pull your freight right now.'

Biggles's grey eyes found McBain's and held them. 'That goes for you too, McBain—if you want it that way,' he said in a voice that was as hard and brittle as ice. 'But before you decide how soon you're going, turn this over in your mind. I'm not greedy. There should be plenty of work here for two operators, and if they work together things could go easier for both. I'm willing to go ahead on that arrangement if you are. Naturally, as the field belongs to Arctic Airways you'll have to pay landing fees for the privilege of using it. If, on the other hand, you'd rather have things the way you've been trying to run them——'

'Yeah?' broke in the other, the muscles of his face twitching. 'I guess that's how I'll have 'em, and I'll start by collecting them ten bucks.'

Biggles shook his head. 'Not a cent, McBain,' he said quietly. 'You can't get away with that bluff—not with me. My lawyers in Montreal are straightening out the title deeds of this property, and when we hear to whom it does belong I'll let you know how much you owe Arctic Airways. That's all—except that I'd rather you kept a bit farther away from my sheds.'

Biggles nodded curtly and moved towards what was obviously Arctic Airways' reception office. For a moment it looked as though McBain would intercept him, for he took a pace forward, clenching and unclenching his hands; but then his companion said something to him that the others could not catch, and he stopped, scowling.

Algy and Ginger followed Biggles into the office. There was nobody there, although by this time they did not expect to find anyone. Everything was in confusion. Files had been pulled out and papers were strewn everywhere.

Algy's face was grim as he looked around. 'I don't like the look of this,' he said quietly. 'I'm afraid we've come too late.'

Before Biggles could answer there was a whip-like crack, followed instantly by a splintering thud. Several splinters flew across the room, one striking Biggles on the cheek and drawing blood.

'That was a shot!' snapped Algy, and then darted after Biggles, who had already flung open the door and was striding towards McBain and his companions, who had not moved. The effeminate-looking man, whom Biggles knew from Wilks's description must be Jean Chicot, was sitting on a chock, smiling, a small automatic held in his two hands. McBain and the two pilots were all grinning, but the humour went out of their eyes at the expression on Biggles's face.

Biggles went straight up to Chicot. 'Did you fire that shot?' he snapped.

The half-breed looked up, the affected smile still playing about his thin lips. He shrugged his shoulders and sent a puff of cigarette smoke up into Biggles's face before he replied, at the same time rising slowly to his feet. 'Eet vas an accident,' he smirked. 'I clean my gun—so; he go off. These accidents come sometime—yes?'

Biggles did not answer. His fist flew out in a vicious uppercut. Every scrap of the pent-up anger that was in him went behind the blow. There was a snap like a breaking twig as his fist caught Chicot on the point of the jaw.

The half-breed did not stagger. The blow lifted him clean off his feet. He went straight over backwards and crashed across the concrete apron, his cap going one way and the pistol another. He twisted for a moment and then lay still.

Biggles's face was white, and his lips were set in a straight line as he looked down at him.

'Keep your hands away from your belt, McBain.' It was Algy who spoke. Seeing what was coming, he had whipped out his automatic the instant Biggles struck the blow.

Biggles looked round and saw McBain hesitating; his hands, with the fingers clawed, were a few inches above his belt. 'Plug him if he moves, Algy,' he said grimly. 'If this gang of crooks want it hot, by thunder, they can have it!' Then, to McBain, 'I've killed a lot better men than you in my time, McBain,' he said harshly, 'so I shouldn't lose any sleep on your account.'

'Say, what's going on?'

Biggles spun round and saw that a new-comer had arrived on the scene. There was no need to ask who it was, for his uniform told him that. It was a constable of the North-West Mounted Police.

'What's going on here?' said the constable again, looking suspiciously from one to the other.

'Nothing to speak of,' replied Biggles. 'My friends and I have just arrived by air. For some reason best known to himself—although I've a pretty good idea what it is—McBain objected to our landing and tried to scare us off by getting his half-breed playmate to pull a gun on us, so I had to hit him. That's all.'

The constable regarded Biggles speculatively. 'What are you doing in this out-of-the-way place, anyway?' he inquired.

'Any reason why I shouldn't come here?'

'I don't know—yet.'

'Then you'd better get in touch with your headquarters and find out. If they don't know either, tell them to get into touch with the Department of Aviation—they know. I'm putting money into Arctic Airways, which belongs to a friend of mine, Wilkinson. You probably know him. I want to know where he is.'

'I don't know where he is.'

'Then ask McBain—I reckon he does.'

The constable turned to McBain. 'Where's Wilkinson?'

'Search me, Delaney.'

'When did you last see him?'

'Four days back.'

'Where?'

'Here.'

'What was he doing?'

'Taking off—heading north, I guess.'

'For Moose Creek?'

'Why should he tell me where he was going?'

'And he hasn't come back?'

'I ain't looked for him.'

'You had a good look at the inside of his office, at any rate,' put in Biggles coldly.

'Who said it was me?'

'I do. I saw you come out as we landed.'

'I figger——'

'Wait a minute—I haven't finished figuring myself yet. You knew Wilkinson wasn't coming back, McBain—or you had good reason to suppose he wasn't—or you wouldn't have broken into his office and turned his papers upside-down. Nor would you have started to dismantle his shed.'

'Who said I was dismantling his shed?'

Biggles pointed. 'There's the board—Arctic Airways. I have witnesses who saw you taking it down.'

McBain looked at Biggles evilly. Then he turned to the constable. 'Well, what are you going to do about it?' he inquired. 'I've got something else to do besides stand here gassin'.'

'So have I,' returned the constable. 'You ought to have reported Wilkinson missing, McBain. I shall have to ask fellows going north to look out for him.'

'Don't worry, constable; I'll do that,' said Biggles quickly.

'You mean you're going to look for him?'

'I am.'

'When?'

'Right now. If I don't find him before dark I shall come back here and make another search tomorrow. Meanwhile you might ask McBain to stay in his own sheds; and, while we're away, you might keep an eye on these.'

The constable looked at McBain. 'You stay on your own property,' he said. Then to Biggles, as he moved away, 'Let me know if you find Wilkinson.'

Biggles nodded. 'I will,' he said, and turned towards the Jupiter. 'Come on, you fellows,' he went on quietly to the others, taking no further notice of McBain. 'Wilks must be down somewhere between here and Moose Creek; we've got nearly four hours of daylight left, so the sooner we start looking for him, the better.'

3

A SATISFACTORY TRIP

'So that's Mister McBain,' observed Ginger, as they got back into the machine.

'Yes, and now we know just how we stand,' answered Biggles. 'We shall have to watch our steps with that gentleman. A man with eyes like that was born to be a crook. I must confess that I'm a bit worried about old Wilks.'

'Was McBain telling the truth, do you think, when he said Wilks had flown north?' asked Algy.

'I believe he was. Neither he nor his machine are here, so he must have gone off somewhere, and I imagine Moose Creek would be the most likely place for him to go.'

'He might have gone to Moose Creek and decided to stay there.'

Biggles shook his head. 'I can't agree with that. Knowing the state of things here, if he had to go north my own feeling is that he would get back as quickly as he could. It was quite possible that his machine was got at; anyway, McBain had jolly good reason to suppose that Wilks wasn't coming back, otherwise he wouldn't have dared to take possession of his hangar—for that is what it amounts to, and he would have done it had we not arrived on the scene. If McBain wanted Wilks out of the way— and we know he did—the most certain way to bring it about was to tamper with his machine. Wilks was quite aware of that danger; he told us as much in his letter. It's a hundred to one that he is on the ground somewhere between here and Moose Creek. I only hope the trouble was nothing vital, like structural failure; if it was, then I'm afraid we can say good-bye to Wilks. On the other hand, there is just a possibility that he had to make a perfectly natural forced landing, in which case he would get the machine down somehow. With all his experience the chances are that he would be able to do that without hurting himself, even if he damaged the machine. The only thing we can do now is to try to find out. Fortunately, we've plenty of petrol left in the tanks, so come on; let's get away. All right, Smyth; get back aft, will you.'

As he finished speaking, Biggles took out his map and studied it intently. Both Fort Beaver and Moose Creek were shown, so it did not take him long to work out a compass course, and in five minutes the Jupiter was in the air again, heading northwards, with Algy watching the ground on the starboard side and Ginger on the other.

It soon became evident that the task of picking out an aircraft on the ground, particularly a crashed one, was likely to be a good deal more difficult than they had supposed, for the country was rougher than any they had yet seen in Canada.

For a long time they flew over almost continuous forests of fir, with great outcrops of grey rock thrusting upwards like spurs, while here and there a river wound a tortuous course through gorge and valley. Then the country started to rise, and although the altimeter registered a thousand feet, the Jupiter was soon skimming over the tree-tops. Biggles eased the stick back and climbed slowly to a safer height.

At the end of an hour the forest had become broken into small, isolated groups of wind-twisted trees, and shortly afterwards even these failed to appear, giving way to a dismal panorama of gaunt rock. Ahead, and on either side, mountains towered upwards majestically, their peaks white with the first snow.

'I don't know about a forced landing, but if Wilks had to go down and land on that stuff I should say he hadn't a hope,' observed Biggles moodily, as he stared down at the weather-torn rock. 'From the time we started I haven't seen half a dozen places where there was the slightest chance of getting a machine down without a crack-up. Goodness me! What a country!'

'It looks as if it levels out a bit farther ahead,' remarked Algy, who had turned to look forward through the windscreen.

'Yes, I agree, it does,' returned Biggles. 'But what sort of surface is it? I shouldn't care to have to put a machine down on that stuff. It wouldn't be so bad if you had engine power to fall back on in an emergency—but with a dead stick[1] it would be an

---

[1] Dead stick. A flying expression meaning that the propeller is not revolving.

anxious business. Hello, what's that ahead? That looks like something on the ground there . . . is it? Yes, by heaven, it is! It's a machine. There's somebody beside it—look, he's moving. He's seen us. He's waving.'

The roar of the Jupiter's engines died away abruptly as Biggles cut the throttle and began gliding down to what, by this time, was obviously an aeroplane.

'It's on even keel, anyway,' remarked Algy, who had opened a side window in order to see more clearly.

'It's got its tail cocked up, which looks to me like a broken undercart,' cried Ginger.

'It must be Wilks,' declared Biggles. 'Nobody else would be flying up here. As long as he's all right, I don't care much if he has smashed the machine. Give him a wave.'

With Algy hanging out of the window with an arm outstretched—for to wave literally in the open air when one is travelling more than a hundred miles an hour is practically impossible—the Jupiter dropped lower and lower until at last it was circling in a steep bank at not more than fifty feet above the other machine.

'What's the ground like, Algy?' asked Biggles anxiously. 'Can you see a decent place to get down? It all looks pretty rotten to me.'

'Wilks is pointing. I think he means that there is a place over there where we can get down. He's moving off in that direction— but he's limping. He must be hurt.'

The man on the ground was, in fact, hobbling away from the stationary machine, from time to time stopping to pick up a piece of stone and throw it aside.

'He's clearing a runway for us,' declared Algy.

'So I see,' answered Biggles, with a worried frown. 'I don't relish the thought of getting down on it, all the same.' Nevertheless, he started lowering his undercarriage, which had, of course, been drawn up during the flight. He looked at the ground on which he would have to land, and shook his head.

'We can't leave Wilks down there,' murmured Algy.

'Of course we can't,' agreed Biggles irritably, 'but I don't want to bust a perfectly good aeroplane costing me the best part of forty thousand dollars. Nor do I want to walk home.'

'I don't think it's too bad,' muttered Algy, who was still staring down at the ground. 'Wilks is beckoning, so it can't be as bad as it looks.'

Biggles turned the big machine slowly until it was in line with the runway; then he allowed it to sink slowly towards it. Flattening out a few inches above the ground, he held the stick firmly, holding the machine off as long as he dared.

The Jupiter vibrated from nose to tail-skid as her wheels rumbled over the uneven ground, but they stood up to the strain, and the machine finally came to rest about two hundred yards from the lone figure which at once began hurrying towards them. There was no longer any doubt about who it was.

'Biggles, by all that's wonderful!' cried Wilks enthusiastically.

'Well might you say "by all that's wonderful",' grinned Biggles, as he shook hands with his old war comrade. 'What sort of a country do you call this?'

'It's a grand country when you get to know it,' declared Wilks firmly.

'Maybe you're right,' agreed Biggles doubtfully. 'What happened to you?'

'How the dickens did you know where I was?'

'Just a minute, old boy; let's take one thing at a time,' suggested Biggles. 'I'll tell my story first, if you like. We've been to Fort Beaver—landed there about lunch-time today. We found McBain, and I might tell you that he and I had a few sharp words. He didn't seem overjoyed to see us; in fact, we parted on anything but the best of terms. Constable Delaney blew in while the argument was in progress, and under interrogation McBain admitted that you'd flown off and hadn't come back. In the circumstances we decided that you must have started for Moose Creek but failed to reach it, so we came along to pick up the pieces. What happened to you?'

Wilks's smile faded as he told his story. 'You were right about me starting for Moose Creek,' he said bitterly. 'Somebody was kind enough to put a handful of loose cotton-waste in my second tank and it choked the petrol leads. The engines packed up and I had to come down. As it happened I had enough juice in my gravity tank to enable me to reach this place, which I knew all about, having flown over it several times. Naturally, as it is one of the few places between Fort Beaver and Moose Creek where it is just possible to get a machine down, I had made a note of it. All the same, I was lucky to make it.'

'The cotton-waste was McBain's work, I reckon?'

'Of course.'

While they had been speaking they had been moving slowly towards Wilks's machine.

'Did you knock your leg when you came down?' asked Biggles, noting that Wilks was still limping.

'I hit my knee a crack against the dashboard when we tipped up,' returned Wilks briefly.

'Machine damaged?'

'Busted tyre and a bent prop; luckily, being metal it didn't break. But of course there was no question of getting off again. With a groggy knee I was in no shape to start walking three hundred miles back to Fort Beaver, so I just sat here and waited, hoping that I should be missed and that someone would pass the word to the Canadian Airways fellows. They're a grand lot of chaps, and would have come looking for me when they heard I was down.'

'You would have waited a long time, I'm afraid,' replied Biggles. 'Only McBain and his gang knew that you were missing, and they told no one. Indeed, they were so certain that you were gone for good that they were making free with your office when we landed.'

'The dickens they were!'

'I told Delaney about it and he warned them to keep off, so I don't think they'll touch anything—not for a little while at any rate.'

'I don't wonder they didn't expect me back,' observed Wilks. 'This is no country for a forced landing.'

'So I've noticed,' returned Biggles dryly, as he examined the damaged machine with professional ability. Smyth was already at work on it. 'I see you've got a load on board,' continued Biggles, as he looked into the cabin.

'Yes. I was running some spare machine-parts up to Moose Creek; they were wanted urgently, so I am afraid the people up there will be fed up with this delay. They'll probably refuse to give me any future work as I have let them down once or twice already, through no fault of my own you may be sure.'

Biggles bit his lip thoughtfully. 'It's too late to get the stuff up to them today,' he said slowly, 'but we might be able to manage it tomorrow. I think this is our best plan. We've brought all our tools and spare parts with us; luckily we hadn't time to unload them at Fort Beaver. We'll put all your stuff into my machine and fly it back to Fort Beaver. Tomorrow I'll take it up to Moose Creek. Ginger can come with me. Smyth and Algy had better stay here and get to work on your machine. There's nothing you can't fix up, is there, Smyth?'

'I don't think so, sir.'

'Good. All right, let's get to work. Algy, you'd better stay here with Smyth, and as soon as the machine is ready fly her back to Fort Beaver. We'll leave you some grub and you can sleep in the cabin. I shall take Wilks back with me. He needs a rest. How long will it take you to fix things up, Smyth?'

'I think I can get her finished by this time tomorrow, sir,' was the confident answer.

'Then we'll expect you back tomorrow evening, but don't take off unless you can get back to Fort Beaver before dark; it would be better to stay here another night than risk that. Is that all right with you, Algy?'

'As right as rain.'

'Fine! Then let's see about shifting this cargo into the Jupiter. I'd stay here with you but I don't like leaving Fort Beaver for too long with McBain on the war-path. I'll fly low over you tomorrow on my way up to Moose Creek, but I shan't land unless you signal to me to do so. Come on, let's get to work; we've no time to waste.'

It took them, all working hard, about half an hour to transfer the freight from the damaged machine to the Jupiter, and once this was done Biggles lost no time in getting off, for the sun was already low over the western hills. In a few minutes the Jupiter was roaring back over her tracks.

In spite of the fact that Biggles flew on full throttle nearly all the way, it was practically dark when the scattered lights of Fort Beaver came into sight.

Suddenly Biggles started and stared ahead through the windscreen. 'Don't tell me that McBain has thought better of it,' he jerked out. 'Are those landing flares on the aerodrome, or am I dreaming?'

'They're flares,' declared Wilks, who was as surprised as Biggles. 'I've never known him do that before, and I've had to land after dark more than once.'

Biggles said nothing, but a curious expression came over his face as he stared intently into the gloom. A moment or two later he cut the engines and glided down towards the lights, only to open up again an instant later and roar up into the darkening sky. 'He must take me for a fool,' he snarled savagely.

Wilks stared. 'Who?'

'McBain.'

'Why?'

'To fall into such an elementary trap as the one he has set. Those lights are in the wrong place. Had I landed up the line I should have bashed straight into our hangar. Ginger, drop a signal flare and let's have a look at things. I'd rather trust to my own eyes than McBain's flares—the cunning hound. What sort of fellows can his pilots be to try deliberately to crash another machine?'

The signal light burst below the Jupiter, flooding the earth with its brilliant glare, and the trap was exposed to view. As Biggles had said, a machine trusting to the flares must have crashed to destruction in the Arctic Airways hangar. However, Biggles made no further remarks, but concentrated his attention on bringing the Jupiter down safely, and he succeeded in doing this. Taxi-ing swiftly up to the shed, he opened the cabin door and jumped down, looking sharply to left and right. Not a soul was in sight. And the flares had disappeared.

Without speaking they got the machine safely into the hangar, but they did not leave it.

'Where do you usually sleep, Wilks?' asked Biggles, as he took off his cap.

'I used to sleep in my hut, in a room next to the office; but lately, as I told you in my letter, I have been sleeping in the hangar. It isn't safe to leave the machine.'

'I can well believe that,' answered Biggles, nodding thoughtfully. 'Very well, we'll fix up quarters in the hangar, then the machine will always be in sight. Where's the pantry? I'm hungry.'

'Not so hungry as I am,' replied Wilks. 'I've had precious little to eat for the last three days. By gosh!—that reminds me—I'm almost out of stores. Is there any food left in your machine?'

'Very little except hard tack—emergency stuff—and I don't fancy that. In any case, I don't feel like touching it except in real emergency. You know what happens when you do that. When the emergency arises you go to the locker and find it empty. Where do you usually get your food supplies?'

'At the stores down in the village.'

'Whereabouts?'

'In the main street. There's only one place where you can get grub—the Three Star Saloon.'

'Then I'll go down and lay in a stock. We can't keep running up and down every day. Will you be all right here alone?'

'Why not? I've had to handle things by myself for a long time.'

'Good enough. Then I'll take Ginger with me to help carry the parcels. You get your cooking-things out and fix up sleeping-quarters while we're away. We shan't be long. After we've had a bite we'll have a talk about the position.'

4
AT THE THREE STAR SALOON

IT was a walk of about two miles to the village of Fort Beaver, most of the way being across rough uncultivated country, from which in many places rugged masses of limestone rose up, worn by the storms of ages into fantastic shapes. Still, there was no risk of losing the way, for a vague footpath wound through the boulders towards the occasional yellow lights that glowed feebly from the log or frame huts which for the most part formed the houses.

Nor was there any mistaking the Three Star Saloon, a long building of rough-hewn timber, for three lanterns hung at regular intervals above the broad platform which ran along in front of it, enabling the sign to be read.

Without any misgivings Biggles pushed open the door and went inside. He had not given a thought to the possibility of McBain being there—not that he would have stayed away on that account. Nor did he imagine that the bar would be so well attended as it was. The loud buzz of conversation that greeted the ears of the two airmen as they walked in came, therefore, as a mild surprise.

The room was lighted by several paraffin lamps, mostly of the hanging sort, around which eddied a mist of rank tobacco smoke that set Ginger coughing. Along the entire length of one side ran a counter, or bar, one half of which was devoted to the serving of drinks, and the other half to dry goods—mostly foodstuffs.

Biggles's eyes wandered over the occupants without particular interest. He did not expect to know anyone, nor was he anxious to make new acquaintanceships, for he had no intention of staying. As far as he was concerned the shop happened to be a bar, and his one idea was to get what he came for and depart in the shortest possible time.

With this object in view he started walking down the saloon towards the far end, which, as it so happened, was the section devoted to the sale of food; and he was nearly half-way down before he saw McBain, with the other members of his gang, sitting at a table near one of the two circular stoves which heated the room. He noticed that McBain saw him at the same time, and his conversation ended abruptly. However, Biggles took no notice, but went on until he came to that part of the bar where the counter merged with the food department.

'Give it a name, stranger,' said the barman, who, judging by his clothes, was also the proprietor.

Biggles hesitated for a moment. 'As a matter of fact, boss, I didn't come in for a drink,' he answered in a friendly tone. 'I came in to get a supply of grub, but since you mention it I feel that a drop of something hot would not come amiss while I have a look round to see what you can supply in the food line. Have you got any beef extract or malted milk?'

'Both, though we don't get much call for it,' grinned the proprietor.

'Then we'll help to clear your stock. I'll have a Bovril; you can give me a packet of biscuits to munch with it. What about you, Ginger?'

'I'll have some malted milk,' decided Ginger.

The barman nodded and set about preparing the drinks, while Biggles took an old envelope from his pocket and started jotting down selected items from the things he saw exposed for sale—bread, biscuits, cheese, corned beef, tinned salmon, sardines, dried beans, and the like. By the time the barman returned with the drinks he had made a fairly lengthy list, and this he handed over for the things to be put together while he had his drink.

Ginger picked up his cup of malted milk, and realizing that there would be some minutes to wait, took it across to a vacant seat near the second stove; that is to say, the one other than that at which McBain and his company were sitting. The two stoves were some eight or ten yards apart. Actually, he did not see McBain until he was on the way to the stove, or it is possible that he would not have left Biggles; but having started he saw no reason for turning back, so he went on to the seat.

Several men, trappers or prospectors judging from their

clothes, were sitting near the stove engaged in conversation, but he paid no attention to them, beyond glancing at them curiously, until a name reached his ears. The name was Wilkinson— pronounced Wilkson by the man who had uttered it.

He was an old man, certainly not less than sixty years of age, and he was dressed in the traditional garb of a prospector—thick boots, woollen trousers, and fur jacket. On the back of his head was balanced precariously an ancient and battered hat of the Stetson type. Around his neck was wound a white-spotted red scarf, held together in front—incongruously, Ginger thought— with an opal-headed tie-pin.

'Ay, trust Angus to think o' somethin' for me to do,' continued the old man in a wheezy voice, as Ginger regarded him with sudden interest. 'I'm pullin' out agin termorrer, and I near forgot. "If yer see that feller Wilkson," ses Angus, "tell 'im I forgot to give 'im the transfer, but I've still got it." Maybe 'e'll need it and maybe 'e won't, so I guess I've got to trail across to that pesky airydrome.'

'Leave word 'ere, Mose,' went on one of the others. 'There ain't no call for you to go across to Wilkson yourself. One of us is bound to see 'im sometime, and we'll pass word on about the transfer.'

Ginger butted in. 'Excuse me,' he said, 'but are you referring to Captain Wilkinson of the aerodrome?'

'Sure I am, boy,' answered the old man, stuffing tobacco into a short clay pipe with a grimy thumb.

Ginger realized at once the significance of the old man's message, knowing that the Angus of whom he had spoken could be no other than Angus Stirling from whom Wilks had bought the land; and the transfer to which he referred must be the Government title-deed transferring the property to him—that is, to Angus Stirling. 'That's all right,' went on Ginger, not a little excited by this stroke of good fortune. 'I'm a friend of Captain Wilkinson's. My boss—over there at the bar—is his partner. I'll give him the message. As it happens, we need the transfer. Where is Angus now? We shall probably go and see him.'

The old man uttered a cackling laugh, in which the other men joined. 'Sure, go ahead,' he grinned. 'You'll find him on Muskeg Bend.'

'Where's that?' asked Ginger doubtfully, perceiving that his inquiry had provoked mirth, and suspecting the reason.

'On the south corner o' Eskimo Island,' chuckled the old man. 'Me and Angus are working on a claim there.'

Ginger shook his head ruefully, feeling a bit self-conscious at his ignorance. 'I'm afraid I've never heard of Eskimo Island,' he said, smiling apologetically.

'Don't cher worry about that, son; nor ain't a lot of others,' nodded the old man. 'It's farther north than a lot 'ud care to go; nor me, neither, if I hadn't got Angus with me—for which reason I've to start back termorrer.'

It may have been a movement, or it may have been instinct, that made Ginger glance over his shoulder, and he experienced a sudden pang of apprehension when he saw a man standing so close behind him that he must have overheard every word that had been said. It was the Indian who had been on the aerodrome with McBain's party when they landed.

For a fleeting instant Ginger's eyes met those of the Indian, who then turned suddenly and glided away towards McBain.

Ginger turned quickly to the old man. 'Just a minute,' he said. 'I'd like to bring my boss over here.' So saying, he got up and walked quickly to where Biggles was still standing, checking the parcels as they were piled up on the counter. 'Biggles,' he said quietly but crisply, 'I've had a bit of luck. You remember what Wilks said in his letter about Angus Stirling, the man from whom he bought the land, and not getting the proper transfer?'

Biggles stiffened. 'What about it?'

'Stirling's partner is in here. I've just been talking to him. Apparently they're working a claim together up north, and Stirling asked his partner—that's him, the old man in the slouch hat—to tell Wilks that he still has the transfer. It struck me that we might fly him up and collect it. You'd better come and have a word with him.'

There was no need for Ginger to repeat his suggestion; almost before he had finished Biggles was on his way to the stove. 'Careful,' whispered Ginger, as he followed close behind. 'McBain and Co. are watching us.'

Biggles nodded to show that he had heard, but he did not so much as glance in McBain's direction.

'You're Angus Stirling's partner?' he began without preamble, addressing the old man.

'Sure,' was the brief reply.

'Is it correct that Angus asked you to tell Wilkinson that he still has the transfer of the land he sold him?'

'Ay, that's right enow. That's what he said.'

'I'm glad to hear it,' Biggles went on quickly. 'As it happens we need that paper badly. How far away is this claim of yours?'

' 'Bout fifteen hundred miles.'

Biggles's eyes opened wide. 'Gosh, that's a bit farther than I bargained for,' he admitted frankly. 'Still, that doesn't matter. Is it anywhere in Moose Creek direction?'

'Pretty near due north of it—'bout twice as far, I guess.'

'And you're going back there?'

'Sure.'

'When?'

'Termorrer. I aim to catch the freeze-up. She'll be froze by the time I get to the water.'

In a vague sort of way Biggles realized that the old man meant that ice would have to form over a certain stretch of water so that he could get to the claim where Angus was working. 'How are you going to travel?' he asked.

The old man smiled and turned a bright eye on Biggles. 'There ain't no trains where I'm goin', mister,' he grinned. 'It's canoe to Moose River, where I aim to pick up my dogs.'

'Is Moose Creek somewhere on Moose River?'

'Sure.'

'I asked because I'm flying up to Moose Creek tomorrow,' went on Biggles. 'I reckon to make it in a day. If you care to come along with me that should save you quite a bit of time. Maybe we could go right on to the claim. How does that idea strike you?'

A childish grin spread slowly over the old man's face, and he scratched his ear thoughtfully. 'You mean—you aim to take me up in an airyplane?'

'That's it.'

'Well, I ain't never thought about travellin' that road, but I'll try anything onst. Termorrer, did you say?'

'Yes.'

'All the way to Moose Creek?'

'We'll go right on to the claim if there is any place where I could land. Is there a flat patch anywhere near the claim?'

'Sure.'

'How big is it, roughly?'

'About ten thousand square miles.'

'*What!*'

' 'Tain't nothin' else but flat patch as far as yer can see—when it's froze.'

'You mean this flat patch is ice?'

'That's it.'

'Ah! I understand.'

'Will there be room for the grub?' inquired the old man. 'I've got a fair load to get along—'nough to last me and Angus till the break-up.'

'You can take anything up to a ton,' returned Biggles.

'I ain't got that much.'

'That's all the better. Be on the aerodrome at the crack of dawn and we'll make Moose Creek in one jump. Is that a deal?'

'You betcha.'

'See you in the morning, then.' Biggles turned, and saw McBain's Indian backing stealthily away. 'Was that fellow listening?' he asked Ginger quietly.

'I'm afraid so. I didn't notice him, though, or I'd have warned you.'

'Well, I don't see that McBain can do anything to stop us,' murmured Biggles as they returned to the bar. 'I've got to go to Moose Creek in the morning, anyway, and it won't be much extra trouble to go on to this claim, wherever it is. I'll get the old chap—what did they call him, Mose?—to mark the place on my map when he comes up in the morning. But we'd better finish our drinks and be getting back; Wilks will wonder what has happened to us.'

Biggles paid the score and, subconsciously aware that a curious silence had fallen on the room, reached for the cup that contaned the remainder of his Bovril. Simultaneously there was a deafening roar and the cup flew to smithereens, splashing the liquid in all directions.

For a moment Biggles stared with startled eyes at the spot where the cup had been. Then, recovering himself quickly, he looked round. McBain was standing farther along the bar, a smoking revolver in one hand and a bottle of whisky—which presumably he intended taking away with him—in the other. From the offensive leer on his face, and his heavy-lidded eyes, it was clear that he had been drinking.

No one spoke. The only sound in the room was the soft shuffle of feet as the other men in the bar began to back away out of the line of fire.

'Give me another drink, boss,' requested Biggles quietly.

Silence reigned while the barman prepared another cup and set it on the counter in front of Biggles, whose hand had barely started moving towards it when McBain's gun roared again and the cup flew to pieces as the first one had done.

Unhurriedly, Biggles turned a reflective eye on McBain, who was now holding a glass in one hand while with the other he felt in his pocket, presumably for money to pay the score. The revolver, an almost imperceptible coil of smoke creeping from the muzzle, and the bottle of whisky rested on the bar in front of him.

'Give me another drink, boss, will you?' repeated Biggles, and put his hand in his pocket as if to take out the money to pay for it.

The barman set the cup in front of Biggles and then stepped back quickly.

McBain stood his glass on the bar. His hand moved towards the revolver, but on this occasion things did not go in accordance with his plan. Biggles's hand jerked out of his pocket. There was a double report, the two shots coming so close together that they almost sounded like one. There was a crash of shattering glass and a metallic *ping* as McBain's bottle of whisky splintered into a hundred pieces and his revolver spun along the polished bar before falling behind it.

Dead silence followed the shots. For a full ten seconds McBain stared unbelievingly at the puddle where the bottle had been, his right hand groping for the revolver that was no longer there. The face which he then turned to Biggles was white, mottled with dull crimson blotches. His eyes glared and a stream of profanity burst from his lips.

'What's the matter, McBain?' asked Biggles evenly. 'Any fool can play a game single-handed; you don't mind me joining in, surely?'

The other did not answer. With his big eyes on Biggles's face, very slowly he began creeping along beside the bar, his right hand, with the fingers clawed, sliding along the shiny surface.

'That's far enough, McBain,' Biggles warned him curtly. He knew that it would be fatal to come to grips with the man, who was nearly twice his weight and clearly had the physical strength of a bull. Once in McBain's grip and he would stand no chance whatever. Knowing this, he had no intention of allowing McBain to get his hands on him.

Biggles addressed the bar-keeper. 'What is the usual procedure in a case like this, in this part of the world?' he inquired presently. 'Do I shoot him?'

' 'Ere, wait a minute,' snapped the bar-tender. 'I don't want no shooting 'ere.'

'I didn't start it,' Biggles pointed out.

'I know you didn't.' The bar-tender whirled round and snatched a heavy Colt revolver from a shelf behind him. He turned to McBain, scowling. 'That's enough, Brindle,' he said harshly. 'I ain't taking sides, but you asked for what you got. Now get this. You're always a causin' trouble in my bar. If yer can't carry yer liquor, go some place and learn, but yer ain't bustin' up my bar while I'm here.'

McBain ceased his bear-like advance towards Biggles, and turning slowly to the bar-keeper, called him by an obscene name.

'I'd better plug him and rid the world of a dirty beast,' suggested Biggles, wondering at the back of his mind why McBain's friends did not take a hand. Snatching a glance in their direction, he understood. Ginger's automatic was covering them.

How the matter would have ended it is impossible to say, but at that moment the outside door was flung open, and Delaney, the police constable, stood on the threshold, a carbine in his hands. 'What's the shooting?' he inquired bluntly.

'Only me and McBain seeing who can spill most liquor,' replied Biggles.

'You two at it again?' The constable's eyes went from one to the other. 'See here, stranger,' he went on, observing that Biggles was still holding his automatic in his hand, 'gun-play's finished in these parts—savvy? It went out with Buffalo Bill. This is a law-abiding township.'

Biggles nodded. 'Yes, I've noticed it.' he answered, smiling faintly.

'And I don't want any lip. Who pulled first?'

Biggles shook his head. 'Not me. I can't afford to waste ammunition.'

'McBain shot his drink,' shouted old Mose shrilly. 'I seen 'im.'

'Any more shooting between you two and I'll take away your fire-arms certificates,' declared the constable, eyeing Biggles and McBain in turn. 'And that goes for everyone else in this room.'

'Quite right,' murmured Biggles, putting his automatic back into his pocket and then drinking his Bovril. 'Come on, Ginger; grab some of this stuff. Let's be going.'

As they went out he nodded to Mose. 'See you tomorrow— start at daylight,' he called.

Then the door closed behind them and they hurried back to the aerodrome.

5

GINGER GOES SCOUTING

They said little on the way back beyond congratulating themselves on the discovery of Angus Stirling's whereabouts, and adding a few words about McBain's behaviour.

'One of these days somebody will plug the drunken swine— and the sooner the better,' growled Biggles, as they strode into the hangar and deposited their parcels on a bench.

'I was just beginning to get worried about you,' Wilks told them. 'You were a long time.'

'McBain was there, and he tried to be funny,' replied Biggles, and reported the shooting incident at the saloon. 'But forget about that,' he continued quickly. 'What is far more important, we've got on the track of Angus Stirling. He is working a claim somewhere up north with an old fellow named Mose, who is now in Fort Beaver collecting stores for the winter. Angus actually sent a message to you by Mose—which he gave to us—to the effect that he has got the transfer of the land you bought off him, and you can have it when you want it.'

Wilks sprang to his feet. 'Want it! Why, that document is the key to the whole situation,' he cried. 'With that in our possession we can give Mr Nosey-Parker McBain his marching orders, and call in the police to eject him if he doesn't clear off.'

Biggles nodded. 'That's the way I see it,' he agreed. 'That being so, I've arranged to collect the transfer just as quickly as possible.'

'How?'

'Mose is starting back for the claim tomorrow, so I've offered to fly him up. We'll land at Moose Creek, where I'll dump the freight for the gold people, and Mose can pick up his dog-team. Then I'm going to fly him on to the claim. He says there is plenty of room to get down.'

'That's marvellous,' declared Wilks enthusiastically. 'What a stroke of luck! I reckon I'm about due for a break; your arrival seems to have turned the tide. Is Mose coming up here in the morning?'

'At dawn.'

'Fine!' A shadow of anxiety crossed his face. 'You said McBain was there,' he muttered. 'Did he hear all this? If he did he may try to stop Mose——'

'I think he heard, but I don't see what he can do,' answered Biggles thoughtfully. 'From the way he chipped in over the shooting affair I don't think he has any great love for McBain. We'd better turn in early; we've got a long day in front of us tomorrow. Have you managed to get things fixed up here?'

'Yes, they're a bit rough, but I think we can manage.'

Some of the tinned food was soon opened, and the three airmen, sitting round a candle-lighted table near the big machine, said little more while they enjoyed their overdue meal. At last Biggles set down the tin mug from which he had been drinking quantities of steaming coffee made over Wilks's Primus stove.

'All we want tomorrow is a fine day,' he declared. 'With any luck Algy and Smyth will be back with the other machine. The next day—or the day after—we ought to be back with the transfer. Then, having mustered our forces, we'll see what McBain has to say. He'll find things a bit more difficult now that there are four of us instead of you by yourself. I wonder what the weather's doing?'

'The prophets forecast an early freeze-up,' Wilks pointed out.

'It was clear enough when we came in,' returned Biggles.

'I'll go and have a look at the sky,' offered Ginger, and leaving the table, he walked slowly to the hangar door and looked out.

He shivered a little as he stepped on to the tarmac, for there was a real nip in the air that suggested that frost or snow was not far away. However, the sky was clear, and although there was no moon, the stars glittered hard and bright in the heavens. For a moment or two he stood with his face turned upwards, glad that he would be able to tell Biggles that there was every promise of a fine day on the morrow, and he was about to return to the others when a dull yellow gleam appeared in the darkness not very far away. Instinctively he looked at it, and an instant later realized that it came from McBain's hangar or the workshops or office adjoining it.

'It would be interesting to hear just what's going on there,' he mused. 'Plotting some dirty business, I'll warrant.' The idea flashed into his mind that if his assumption was correct it would indeed be worth taking a little trouble to find out. There appeared to be no risk. 'Shan't be a minute,' he called over his shoulder quickly to the others, and then began walking cautiously towards the light—not in a straight line, but in a curve that would bring him to his objective from the rear.

He slowed down and moved with more caution as he neared the square of yellow light, which he now saw came from the window of one of the smaller buildings attached to the hangar. Step by step he advanced, every nerve keyed up, for he was quite prepared to find a sentry on guard. He decided that if he were challenged he would bolt for it.

But what he had feared did not happen, and a moment later he was crouching against the rough log wall of the hut, from the inside of which came a low, confused murmur of voices. Inch by inch he edged along the wall until he came to the window. He held his breath as he peeped into the room, for there was no blind or other obstruction to interfere with his view.

A glance showed him that four men were in the room, all sitting in various attitudes round a packing-case on which stood various glasses and a black bottle. They were the two pilots, Sarton and Ferroni, Chicot, McBain's bodyguard, and the Indian. McBain himself was not there.

At first Ginger could not hear what was being said, but he found that by pressing his ear close to a chink in the log wall he could follow the conversation fairly well.

Sarton was speaking. 'He's a long time,' he muttered, picking up his glass. 'I reckon you'd better go and look fer 'im, Jean.'

'No. He say "go on",' protested the half-breed. 'I stay here.'

The words had barely left his lips when Ginger heard the sound of heavy footsteps approaching. His heart gave a nervous leap, but his fears were allayed when he heard the footsteps halt on the far side of the hut. There came the sound of a door being opened and closed.

To his satisfaction he found that by placing his eyes level with the chink in the logs he could see into the room, which was far less risky than peeping round the edge of the window, where he might be seen if anyone in the room looked in that direction.

Through his peep-hole he saw that, as he suspected, the newcomer was McBain. Clad in a long and rather dilapidated skunkskin coat—Ginger recognized the fur by the characteristic white blaze—he was standing just inside the door, glaring at the four who were already there. It struck Ginger that he seemed agitated about something, for his face was pale and his movements abrupt. There was definitely an atmosphere of tension in the room, and, if proof of this were needed, McBain's first words confirmed it.

'Waal,' he growled, 'ain't yer never seen me before? What's biting yer?'

'Why—er—nothin', boss,' replied Sarton nervously.

'Waal, go on gassin' and don't stare at me,' growled McBain, dragging off his coat and hanging it on a peg on the inside of a cupboard door which he opened for the purpose.

'We was just figgerin' that you'd been a long time,' continued Sarton, in an explanatory sort of voice.

McBain jerked round with an abruptness that made the other start. 'That's a lie,' he fired out. 'I ain't been five minutes. Get that?'

'O.K. if you say so, boss,' agreed Sarton in a conciliatory way.

'Fact is, I came up here when you did,' went on McBain more quickly. 'I've just bin outside watchin' the weather, that's all. Remember that; if anyone arsts you if I came back 'ere with you, you'll have to say yes or you'll be tellin' a lie. Savvy?'

'Sure,' agreed the others, in a sort of chorus.

'All right,' continued McBain, pouring himself out half a glass of what Ginger took to be neat spirit and throwing it down his throat. 'We're gettin' busy tomorrow,' he added.

'Dey send de gold, ha?' asked the breed quickly.

'In a day or two,' answered McBain. 'About time, too.'

The word 'gold' made Ginger prick up his ears, and a moment

later, for the first time, he saw McBain's activities in a new light.

'I reckon we'd have had it by now if this fool Wilkinson hadn't clung on so long,' went on McBain. 'It was just a fluke he collected and brought down the last two loads that was worth while. These buddies of his may make things harder. I don't like the look of that thin guy—Bigglesworth. He's a wise guy—and smart. But he won't be smart enough for me. I'll tear him in 'arves before I've done with him.'

'Do you think he'd come into the game if we gave him the low-down?' suggested Sarton.

'Not 'im. He ain't that sort,' growled McBain. 'Anyway, four's enough to split, without takin' in four more. I wouldn't 'a' minded one, when Wilkinson was alone, but I didn't trust 'im. No, we'll play as we are. Everything's all set. All we've got to do now is weigh in next time there's a heap o' dust ready to be brought down.'

'I donta like thees new guy, Bigglesworth,' muttered Chicot. 'I think, mebbe, it better if we fineesh heem soon.'

'Wait till Delaney's out on patrol,' said McBain. 'Then we'll see. Are they over there now?' He jerked his head in the direction of Arctic Airways' hangar.

'They all went in; we watched them go,' declared Sarton.

'O.K. Then I'll think about the best way of handling 'em between now and tomorrow. Got the ship ready to start?'

'All set.'

'Everything on board you'll be likely to want?'

'Everything.'

'Then I'll tell yer what to do in the mornin'. I'm goin' to turn in. I'm tired. Don't stay gassin' here half the night.' McBain picked up the bottle, and putting the mouth of it to his lips, emptied it.

The others stood up.

Ginger waited for no more. He had learned more than he had hoped for, so, after backing quietly away until he was what he considered a safe distance from the hut, he hurried back to the hangar, where he found the others just starting out to look for him.

'Where the dickens have you been?' asked Biggles sharply.

Ginger's manner was terse as he waved them back to the table. 'I've been indulging in what is generally reckoned to be a very questionable pastime. Some people might call it eavesdropping, but in time of war, like this, the best people call it scouting. I've been listening to McBain's little party over the way.' He turned and regarded Wilks with a curious smile. 'If you think those guys are here simply to run you off your aerodrome, Wilks, you've been thinking wrong. That isn't what they're after.'

There was a moment's silence.

'What *are* they after?' Biggles almost hissed the words.

Ginger drained his cup of half-cold coffee before he replied. 'Gold,' he said quickly. 'The litle bags of yellow metal which the people at Moose Creek are digging out of the ground.'

Wilks nodded slowly. 'Kick me, somebody,' he said weakly. 'I never even thought of it.'

6

A STAGGERING BLOW

THE stars were still twinkling in the sky, although those in the east were paling, when, the following morning, Biggles, Wilks, and Ginger pulled the Jupiter out of the shed and forced her head to wind ready to take off as soon as Mose arrived. A hearty breakfast, and Biggles and Ginger got into their flying kit, for it had been decided that it would be advisable for someone to remain on guard, and as Wilks was still feeling a bit shaken from his recent crash, he was to be the one to stay behind while the others took the delayed freight to Moose Creek.

While they were waiting they discussed the situation in the new aspect revealed by Ginger's opportune scouting expedition the previous night.

'It would be no use telling Delaney,' remarked Biggles quietly. 'Knowing that there is no love lost between us he'd think that we were just shooting a cock-and-bull story to put McBain and Co.

under suspicion—and you couldn't blame him for that. At this stage it would be better to say nothing. Having got our own clock set right—so to speak—our game is to keep a closer watch on McBain's movements until we've got proof of his intentions.'

'How about warning the people at Moose Creek?' suggested Wilks.

'No use at all,' declared Biggles. 'They'd be less likely to believe us than Delaney. They would think, naturally, that it was simply a scheme to keep McBain out of the air-line business. They might even tell McBain that we had reported them for a gang of crooks, in which case he would guard his movements more closely, making our task of exposing him more difficult. No, at this juncture we say nothing to anybody.' Biggles glanced at his wrist watch as he finished speaking. 'Old Mose is late,' he observed. 'I thought he would be here before this.'

'Who's this coming?' asked Ginger, who was staring in the direction of the village.

'Some one on a horse,' put in Wilks.

'Looks like Delaney—yes, it is him,' declared Biggles.

'He seems to be in a hurry, too.'

It soon became obvious that the Irish-Canadian 'mountie' was making for the Arctic Airways buildings, and a minute later he pulled his horse up and dismounted beside the waiting airmen. His blue eyes flashed to the Jupiter and then came to rest on Biggles's face.

'You pulling out?' he questioned crisply.

'Not exactly,' answered Biggles.

'What do you mean by that?'

'What I say. I'm going away, but not for good. As a matter of detail, I'm going to slip up to Moose Creek with some stuff they're waiting for.'

'Where did you go after you left the Three Star last night?'

Biggles raised his eyebrows at this change of subject. 'I came straight back here,' he said wonderingly.

'Could you prove that?' Delaney fired the question like a pistol-shot.

Biggles smiled faintly, and shrugged his shoulders. 'Well,

naturally I don't clock my movements about, but if you are prepared to take Wilkinson's word, no doubt he's got a rough idea of what time I got back here. You saw how I was loaded up when I left the Three Star; it is hardly likely that I should go for a stroll at that time of night and with that load, is it?'

Delaney switched his eyes to Ginger. 'How about him?' he asked tersely.

'He came with me, of course,' declared Biggles. 'He had as many parcels as I had. What's all this about, anyway?'

'What were you three standing here for when I came along? You looked like you were expecting somebody.'

'We were,' agreed Biggles.

'Who?'

'Mose—I don't know his other name.'

'What did you plan to do with Mose?'

'Fly him up to Moose Creek, and then on to the claim he shares with Angus Stirling. Between ourselves, Delaney, Angus has still got the transfer of this property. If we can get it, it should enable us to give McBain the run-along.'

'I see,' said the constable slowly. 'Well, Mose won't be coming.'

'Why not?'

'He's dead.'

Biggles paled. 'Dead!' he cried incredulously. 'Why, he was as right as rain last night.'

'No doubt he would have been this morning, too, if someone hadn't clubbed his brains out.'

'You mean—he was *murdered*?'

'People don't beat their own brains out.'

'Great heavens!' Biggles's brain raced as he tried to focus the situation in its new aspect. 'You don't think we did it, by any chance, do you?'

'I'm going to find out who *did* do it.'

'Well, we had everything to lose and nothing to gain by his death,' Biggles pointed out. 'We want that transfer badly, and now he's gone we don't even know where the claim is.'

'Yes, I know,' broke in Ginger. 'He told me before you spoke to

him. It was—dash it, what was the name of the place?—Eskimo
Bend—no, Eskimo Island, wherever that may be.'

'By gosh, if we can't find the place, things will look bad for
Angus. Mose was taking up the winter grub,' muttered Biggles.

'If he's on Eskimo Island he will be snowed in for six months
when the freeze-up comes; so, as he won't have much grub left by
this time, he's as good as a dead man,' declared Delaney.

'I'll take the grub up,' stated Biggles. 'I'll find his shack.'

'Then you've no time to waste,' said Delaney harshly. 'The
snow's on the way. Don't all go. One of you had better stay here
in case I want you. I'll go and have a word with McBain.'

'You've no objection to me going to the claim?' asked Biggles.

Delaney thought for a moment. 'No,' he said at last. 'Get back
as soon as you can, though.'

With a curt nod, leading his horse, the constable strode away
in the direction of McBain's shed, where McBain himself and his
assistants were now pulling an aeroplane from the hangar.

As soon as Delaney was out of earshot Ginger swung round to
Biggles. 'McBain killed him,' he whispered tensely. 'That's why
he was so agitated when he came in to the others. I thought his
manner was odd—I mentioned that when I was telling you what
took place in the room.'

Ginger had, of course, described in detail to the others what
had transpired in McBain's hut while he had been watching.

'I wonder,' murmured Biggles. 'Well, if he did, he certainly
had a motive. No doubt he was told by that Indian of the
arrangement I made with Mose, so by killing the old man he
might have reckoned on stopping us making contact with Angus.
So certain was I that Mose was coming with us that I didn't
bother to ask him the name of the place. It's lucky he told you,
Ginger. What's the name of it?'

'Muskeg Bend, on Eskimo Island, he called it.'

'That ought to be sufficient to enable us to find it,' muttered
Biggles. 'The question is, does McBain know that we know where
Angus is? It's no use guessing, anyway. We'll fly up there and let
McBain do what he likes. You look after things here, Wilks. I'll
take Ginger with me. With luck we ought to be back in two or

three days—four at the most. The first thing we've got to do is to
get poor old Mose's grubstake up here, although it wouldn't
surprise me if Angus packs up and pulls out when he learns what
has happened. I imagine that Muskeg Bend isn't the sort of place
where Angus would want to spend the winter alone. Let's see
about fetching this grub.'

The business of fetching the food occupied some time, for it
necessitated a journey to the village; more than one scowl was
thrown at Biggles and Ginger as they walked through Fort
Beaver, suggesting plainly that they were suspected of the crime
that had cost Mose his life, but they took no notice. By the time
they got back to the aerodrome Delaney had gone. So had the
machine—one of McBain's Weinkel Twelve Transports—
which had been outside the other hangar when they had left for
the village.

'Where's that machine?' Biggles asked Wilks as they loaded
the food in the Jupiter.

'It took off about twenty minutes ago, and headed north.'

'McBain go with it?'

'No. Sarton was flying. I think he only had Chicot with him.'

Biggles nodded, but made no comment on this piece of
information as he climbed into the control cabin of the big
machine. He was chiefly concerned with getting to Moose Creek
as quickly as possible. He spent a minute studying his map, then
folded it up and put it away. 'Eskimo Island isn't marked,' he
told Ginger, who had got into the seat beside him. 'We shall have
to ask where it is when we get to Moose Creek. I expect they'll
know up there.'

He started the engines, ran them up, and tested his controls
carefully. Satisfied that all was well, he waved to Wilks, who was
watching them from the hangar, and then with his left hand
moved the throttle slowly forward.

With its engines nearly under full power the Jupiter raced
across the aerodrome, rose steadily into the air and sped away to
the north.

7

THE JUPITER HEADS NORTHWARD

BIGGLES only spoke twice during the next two hours; once, to tell Ginger to keep his eyes open for the Weinkel, and, some time later, to comment on its possible destination.

'I fancy we shall find it at Moose Creek,' he concluded, and in this he was correct.

They roared low over Wilks' Rockheed, which was still standing as they had left it the day before, but receiving the O.K. signal from Algy, they did not land. Biggles tilted the Jupiter's nose upwards as he climbed to his original height.

The country over which they now passed both fascinated and appalled Ginger, who had never seen anything like it before. He realized that he was looking at one of the forbidding sections of the world's surface, a vast area that was absolutely untouched by the hand of man. For the most part it was gaunt grey rock, twisted into a thousand fantastic shapes by vast upheavals when the earth was young, and later cut and scored by glaciers into rifts and gorges both great and small. Occasionally a clump of sparse, wind-twisted bushes mottled the rock; that was all. Once or twice he saw moving objects, which showed that there was a certain amount of wild life even in this wilderness, but the plane was too high for him to identify the animals. Only a small herd of elk did he recognize by their antlers. 'No wonder they call this the "bad lands",' he thought dismally. Instinctively—as most airmen do when flying over such country—he kept a look-out for possible landing places, but he saw none that he would have been willing to try except in the most extreme emergency.

The sun was hanging low over the western mountains like an enormous ball when Biggles picked up the river, which, judging from his map, would lead him to their destination. Soon afterwards the country became a little more open, but they were beyond the world of trees, and the stark barrenness persisted. They passed one or two isolated huts, and then, looking ahead, Biggles saw what he knew must be the gold-field. The river bayed out into a wide lagoon, on the banks of which were clustered a number of huts with corrugated iron roofs. Near them the ground was flat, rather like a marsh, and as they glided down they were able to discern wheel tracks which told them where machines usually landed—for the place could hardly be called an aerodrome.

In ten minutes they had landed and taxied up to the buildings—log huts of the most primitive description—where a man in a fur jacket was waiting for them.

'You Canwell?' called Biggles, guessing that it was the traffic manager.

'You've said it,' was the curt reply. 'You seen anything of Wilkinson?'

'Yes. I'm his new partner. I've brought your stuff along.'

'About time, too. If you fellows can't do better than this, I'll have to find another way of handling my output.'

'We shall do better in future,' Biggles promised him. 'We've had a little trouble, but we're all set now for a regular service.'

Canwell blew a whistle, at which some men appeared and began unloading the equipment. 'I've had one of McBain's machines here,' he told Biggles.

'When was it here?'

'Just now. It's just gone off.'

It struck Biggles as odd that they had not seen the Weinkel on its homeward journey, but he did not comment on it. 'What did the pilot want?' he inquired.

'He has offered to carry all my stuff—*all* of it, you under-stand—at fifteen cents a pound.'

Biggles was a bit taken aback by this 'cut' rate, but he did not show it. A smile broke over his face. 'Why, the fellow's a profiteer,' he said lightly. 'I'll do it—all of it—at twelve cents.'

Canwell registered surprise. 'You *will*?'

'Sure I will. We shan't get very fat out of it, but on the off-chance of you developing into a big concern we'll take a gamble on it—if you'll give us a contract and a monopoly.'

'Sounds fair to me,' agreed Canwell. 'I'll think that over and give you an answer tomorrow. You'll stay here the night,

I reckon?'

Biggles looked at the sun. 'How much daylight have I got left?' he asked.

'What do you mean—how much daylight?'

'Well, what time will it get dark?'

'In about a week or ten days it will get properly dark, not before.'

Enlightenment burst upon Biggles. He realized that they were so far north that the disc of the sun did not drop below the horizon for the whole twenty-four hours, until it went for good for the long winter months. This meant that he could continue on his way without being overtaken by darkness.

'How far is it to Eskimo Island?' he asked.

'Best part of five hundred miles—as *you* travel.'

Biggles was relieved. He had supposed that it was even further.

'What direction?' he asked.

'Due north as near as makes no difference—why, what's the idea? There's only two white men north of us here—Angus Stirling and Mose Jacobs. There aren't two, now I come to think. Mose has gone out for grub.'

Biggles nodded. 'I know. Mose won't be coming back, either.'

'How so?'

'He was murdered last night.'

'The deuce he was!'

'Angus is expecting him back before freeze-up. Well, he won't be coming, which means that if Angus gets snowed in without grub, he's a goner.'

'By thunder! You're right there,' declared Canwell. 'Poor old Angus. He's a bit daft, but I'd be sorry to see him go. Who's paying you to take the grub up?'

'Paying me? Nobody. You don't suppose I'd let a man die unless someone paid me to save him, do you?'

'Nice work, feller. Can I help?'

'You've got petrol here?'

'Sure.'

'Then that's all I want. I'll give Angus his grub, or bring him back if he decides not to stop on.'

'He won't come, I reckon. If I was you I'd drop the stuff overboard near his shack; that'd save you landing.'

'I shall land if I can.'

'Why?'

'He's got a paper I want.'

Canwell's eyes clouded with suspicion. 'What sort of paper?'

'Wilkinson bought his landing-ground off Angus but Angus forgot to hand over the transfer. We've got a fellow trying to jump our claim——'

'Meanin' McBain?'

'Quite right. If we get the transfer we can ask him to find his own field.'

Canwell nodded understandingly. 'I get you,' he said. 'I heard something from Wilkinson about this dirty deal he's trying to put over. Well, you can handle my stuff in future—always provided that you are here on time to take it. Gold doesn't earn nothin' till it's in the bank, you understand, so the sooner it's in, the better. We can't afford to leave it lying about here. I aim to have a big shipment boxed ready to travel tomorrow, so if you're here you can take it down. I guess you'll be tired, though, if you're going up to Angus's shack.'

'Not too tired,' smiled Biggles.

'Fine. I shall expect you back here tomorrow, then. But whatever happens the metal's got to go to the bank, you understand that?'

'You mean—if I'm not here and McBain is, he'll take the stuff?'

'That's what I mean. My job is to make this concern show a profit, so personal tastes don't come into it.'

'Naturally.' For a moment Biggles was tempted to warn Canwell to be careful of McBain, but he thought better of it, realizing that the traffic manager was the sort of man who would take offence at any attempt to undermine a rival's character.

Biggles therefore turned away and attended to the refuelling of the machine. By the time this was completed Canwell had gone back to his work, so Biggles and Ginger climbed into their seats ready to renew their flight northwards.

'The thing that beats me,' muttered Biggles as he started the engines, 'is how Sarton got back past us without us seeing him.'

'He might have gone on to where we are going,' suggested Ginger.

Biggles started. 'Gosh! I never thought of that,' he admitted. 'Still, I don't think that's likely.'

'If he got to Angus first and induced him to part with the paper we should find it difficult to get it back.'

'That's true,' agreed Biggles. 'Well, we shall see.' He turned and looked Ginger straight in the face. 'You know, kid, I really ought to leave you here.'

Ginger opened his eyes wide. 'Why?'

'Because I imagine that the country we shall have to fly over is pretty grim; the sort that if we *do* hit trouble and have to come down, there'll be no getting off again. I doubt if we should be able to get back on our feet. Some of these tough lads, like Angus and Mose, might, but we're not used to it. We——'

'Just give her the gun and let's get off,' broke in Ginger impatiently. 'We're wasting time.'

A ghost of a smile played about Biggles's lips for a moment. Then he lifted a shoulder in an expressive gesture. His left hand felt for the throttle, and in a moment or two the big machine was nosing up into the sky, which had taken on a dull, leaden hue.

'Canwell was right when he said we had no time to lose,' he said.

'Why?'

Biggles nodded towards the sky. 'Take a look at that. It's going to snow before very long—and when it starts it's going to snow for a long, long time.'

8

A GRIM ENCOUNTER

FOR more than two hours Biggles held the Jupiter on its northerly course, flying by compass since there were no landmarks—or rather, no landmarks which could be identified. For the most part the land below appeared to be a sterile wilderness, broken up frequently by mountain groups and ranges, depressing in their utter desolation, their flanks scarred by forbidding glaciers. Several times he made rapid calculations on his writing block, checking compass variation, as was necessary so near the Pole.

At length the ground became concealed under wide stretches of snow, or ice—they could not tell which. These stretches became wider and wider in extent until at last they merged into a continuous landscape of dull white. The sun appeared to be resting, motionless, on a horizon, flooding the scene with a wan light. Stars appeared in the heavens, glittering like chips of blue ice, but it did not get darker.

Ginger shivered suddenly, conscious of a terrifying solitude. He thought of Angus, and marvelled that any man should choose to live in such a place of death, even with the possibility of finding a fortune in gold.

He was about to remark on this to Biggles when a sound reached his ears that caused every muscle in his body to stiffen. He had heard the sound before and knew what it was. It was the unmistakable rattle of a machine-gun. Before he could move, almost before he had thought of moving, the sound came again, this time much more distinctly, and almost simultaneously the Jupiter quivered as if it had been struck by a cat-o'-nine-tails.

Ginger's throat turned dry, and the next instant he was clinging desperately to his seat as the Jupiter soared upwards in a wild climbing turn. Bracing himself against the side of the cabin, he looked out of the window, and was just in time to see a Weinkel Transport go tearing past. The window nearest to him was open, and from it projected what appeared to be a short black stick, from the end of which danced a tiny streak of flame. Behind it was the face of the half-breed Chicot, his lips curled back from his teeth in something between a grin and a snarl.

'Use the signal pistol—it's all we've got.' Biggles's voice was like cracking ice.

Ginger glanced at him and saw that his face was white; his eyes glittered curiously.

'Get a move on,' continued Biggles. 'I'll try to put you into position for a shot. If you can hit 'em it may set 'em alight. You might hit a prop.'

A signal pistol against a machine-gun! Even Ginger was experienced enough to know that the odds were nearly hopeless. 'Need we stop and fight?' he asked tersely.

'They've got the legs of us by ten miles an hour,' was the curt reply. 'Use your pistol. Careful you don't fall out—I may have to throw the machine about.'

Ginger snatched the short large-bored signal pistol from its pocket, and taking one of the thick cartridges from its loop, thrust it into the breech. Forcing the hammer back with his thumb so that the weapon was at full cock, he put his arm through the window and waited. All he could see was sky, but the pressure inside his stomach—a force that seemed to glue him to his seat—told him that the machine was in a tight climbing turn.

Suddenly the Weinkel flashed into view, travelling like a meteor in the opposite direction, streaks of orange flame dancing from the muzzle of Chicot's gun.

Ginger took swift aim and fired, and knew at once that he had missed. A ball of green fire flashed across the nose of the other machine.

Sarton, the pilot, must have seen it coming, for he swerved sharply, which probably spoilt Chicot's aim. As he reloaded Ginger heard the burst of bullets strike the Jupiter somewhere near the tail.

In an instant the Weinkel had disappeared from his field of view, and he could only wait for it to reappear. It needed all his strength to brace himself against the window, for the Jupiter was never still for a moment. Subconsciously he wondered how long the heavy transport machine could stand such handling without falling to pieces.

Again the Weinkel whirled into view, this time coming at him almost head-on. The half-breed was no longer at the window. Apparently he had decided that from the cabin his field of fire was too restricted, so he had climbed up so that the top half of his body projected through the upper part of the fuselage between the wings, a position from which he would be able to fire in any direction.

Ginger realized at once the advantages of this all-round gun-platform, and determined to copy it if his shot missed. He took careful aim at the oncoming machine; unluckily for him, just as his finger was tightening on the trigger, a bullet struck the window frame near his face, and a tiny splinter stung his cheek, causing him to flinch, with the result that his shot went wide. In a flash, following his shot, for which Biggles had waited, the Jupiter whirled upwards and the Weinkel was hidden from view.

Ginger scrambled back into the cabin and grabbed the remaining cartridges—there were only four—and thrust them into his pocket.

'What are you going to do?' snapped Biggles.

'I'm going outside,' returned Ginger crisply.

'Hang on tight.'

'I'll watch it.'

Another moment and Ginger had flung back the emergency trap in the roof and was climbing out. With one hand gripping the edge of the trap, and the pistol ready in the other, he looked round for the attacking machine, and saw it on the opposite side of the narrow circle round which both aircraft were racing. The icy blast of the slipstream smote his face and tore at his body as if he had been naked, and he knew that he would not be able to endure the exposure for long without becoming frozen. Further-more, it was as much as he could do to hang on, for the Jupiter did not maintain a straight course for a moment, for which reason, no doubt, Chicot had failed to score a vital hit.

Twice Biggles took the big machine into position for a shot, but each time the tearing slipstream spoilt his aim. However, it had this effect; the erratic movements of the Weinkel showed that Sarton was nervous of being hit by a missile which would probably send him down in flames, and his jumpiness, combined with Biggles's manœuvring, made Chicot's task no easy one.

Ginger had now only two cartridges left, and determined to make the most of them. He had his automatic, of course, and he knew that Biggles also had one, but he also knew that in air combat such weapons are practically useless. His first chance came when Biggles whirled like lightning and tore straight under the Weinkel, passing under it so close that Ginger instinctively ducked, thinking that he was likely to be knocked out of the Jupiter by the Weinkel's undercarriage. He fired straight up, but the shot, failing to strike a rigid member, went slap through the fabric and out the other side without doing any more damage than making a neat hole which did not affect the Weinkel's performance.

With the tears that the icy blast forced from his eyes freezing on his cheeks, he thrust his last cartridge into the breech. He had to put the pistol in his pocket in order to hang on with both hands while Biggles did an Immelmann turn, but he grabbed the weapon again as the Jupiter came out in the position this manœuvre is designed to effect—on the tail of the opposing machine.

Sarton must have known that Biggles was screaming down on his tail, and in his panic dived to such an extent that, although Chicot continued to fire short bursts at the Jupiter, now not more than twenty yards from his tail, he could not properly control the jumping gun.

Ginger clenched his teeth, and taking deliberate aim, fired down between the whirling circles of the Jupiter's propellers. To his dismay the cartridge misfired. As quickly as his numbed fingers would permit he opened the breech, moved the cartridge slightly so that the firing-pin would strike another place, and fired again. Once more the expected report failed to occur.

By this time the Jupiter was almost immediately above the Weinkel and fast overhauling it; so much so that Chicot was compelled to turn completely round in order to bring his gun—a squat submachine-gun—to bear. Ginger realized with a horrible choking sensation of fear that if Sarton, unaware of their close proximity, pulled his stick back, both machines would collide with such force that they would be reduced to matchwood. He did the only thing that was left for him to do. He flung the now useless pistol.

It was only by a matter of a few inches that he did not succeed in what he hoped to achieve; but a miss, they say, is as good as a mile, and so it was in this case. The pistol struck the port engine cowling just behind the propeller, bounced harmlessly, and then dropped off into space. At the same moment Biggles dragged the Jupiter away from its dangerous position, and Ginger, half dead with cold, slid back into the cabin.

Biggles looked at him inquiringly.

'Missed!' shouted Ginger. 'No more cartridges. Can you put us in that position again?'

Biggles merely nodded. He did not seem in the least perturbed, and something of his calm confidence transmitted itself to Ginger, who smiled as far as his frozen cheeks would permit and then staggered into the main cabin, from where he returned an instant later carrying a foot-square box branded with large black letters:

20 LB. CORNED BEEF

STOW AWAY FROM ENGINES

Not without difficulty Ginger dragged this unwieldy weapon up into his recently held position above the fuselage. Biggles had already begun the Immelmann which starts with a steep climbing turn, so that it seemed to Ginger that the world had suddenly broken adrift from its orbit and was spinning with dizzy speed.

Steadying the box with his left hand, he stared about him through streaming eyes for the Weinkel, and saw it some distance below, circling as if the pilot had temporarily lost them. Then, as if upborne by a current of air, it seemed to float upwards towards him. He knew, of course, that this was simply the effect of Biggles's dive, which had now begun.

Wondering if he would be able to force his fast-numbing

muscles to act when the crucial moment came, Ginger waited for his opportunity. He had a feeling that he was mad, hoping to knock down an armed adversary with a weapon so prosaic as a box of corned beef. Still, by taking a big risk he did not see why it should not be done, and as far as risk was concerned it was a case of neck or nothing now.

With a calmness that surprised him he saw Chicot feverishly reloading his gun; saw him train the weapon on him; saw the tiny spurts of flame start leaping from the black muzzle. Twice he heard the vicious crack of a bullet boring through the machine, and found time to pray that Biggles had not been hit. For a ghastly moment, as the Jupiter suddenly steepened its dive, he feared that he had, and it may have been the horror of this suspicion that caused him to stake everything on one desperate chance. Raising himself on one knee, he waited while the two machines closed up as though drawn by an invisible magnet; then, as the Jupiter swooped low over the Weinkel, he stood upright and with all his force flung the heavy box outwards and downwards. For one terrible second he thought that he was going too, for he almost lost his balance. Dropping on to his knees, he clawed frantically at the smooth fabric; his questing fingers found a rib under the canvas, and although as a handhold this was poor enough, it stayed his progress long enough for him to grasp the edge of the trap and drag himself back to comparative safety.

Now during the brief instant of time in which this had occurred his eyes had never left the box; they had followed its course with a sort of morbid fascination. It was clear from the start that it would not hit the fuselage of the other machine; in fact, he thought that it would not hit it at all. Nor would it have done so but for the fact that at the last moment Sarton must have moved his joystick. The movement was so slight that it could hardly be regarded as such; but it was enough. The Weinkel's wing-tip seemed to move towards the box, which was turning so slowly as it fell that subconsciously Ginger re-read the words on it as they came into view—20 LB. CORNED BEEF . . .

The box struck the Weinkel's wing about four feet from the

tip. The impact occurred just behind the leading edge, and from what immediately happened it was clear that the weight, falling on the main spar where the strain was greatest, caused it to break instantly. The whole wing-tip seemed to crumple up like a piece of tissue paper, twisting back on itself like a worm under a clumsy gardener's heel.

Fortunately, the effect of this was at once exercised on the whole machine. The fractured wing, losing a great percentage of its lift, sagged, causing the machine to fall in that direction. Ginger could imagine the wretched Sarton fighting to right his machine, but in such a case an aircraft is as helpless as a bird with a broken wing. For a second or two the plane zoomed this way and that as the pilot tried to hold his crippled machine on even keel; then the nose followed the dropping wing, and an instant later the Weinkel was spinning earthward.

In fascinated horror Ginger watched it go; he saw the damaged wing 'balloon' as the air rushed into it; saw it rip off at the roots and follow the rest sluggishly, like a piece of torn paper; saw the fuselage spin faster and faster; saw the half-breed flung off and go plunging down beside it, clutching vainly at the air. . . .

He turned away and fell back weakly into the cabin, limp from reaction now that the danger had passed. He felt no sympathy for the two doomed men in the Weinkel, for the fate that was theirs was what they had intended for those in the Jupiter. The poetic justice of it could not be denied. Dragging himself into his seat he turned a white face to Biggles and saw that he was looking down out of the side window, and the roar of the engine died away. From the angle of the floor he knew that the Jupiter was going down. Following Biggles's eyes he was just in time to see the Weinkel hit the snow and crumple to a thousand fragments. A great pillar of fire leapt heavenwards.

Biggles turned an expressionless face to Ginger. 'They got what they asked for,' he said grimly. 'It's no use our risking a landing.'

His hand went to the throttle; his engines burst into their full throated bellow again and the nose of the Jupiter crept up until it was level with the horizon. With the machine levelled out Biggles turned again to Ginger. 'Good work, laddie,' he said. 'You'll find some hot coffee in the thermos; you look as if you need it.'

9

DOWN IN A FROZEN WORLD

FOR some minutes neither of them spoke. Ginger literally gulped the hot coffee, for he was so cold that his lips were stiff and numb. Then he began a vigorous massage of his face and hands to restore the circulation.

He did not expect any great praise from Biggles for what he had done; nor did he get any—which did not mean that Biggles did not appreciate it. Biggles himself did whatever circumstances demanded; Algy did the same, and this example Ginger had learned to follow.

At last Biggles spoke. 'Even now I can hardly believe that McBain would put over a show like that,' he observed bitterly. 'I knew he was pretty bad, but I thought there were limits to how far he would go. Well, it's taught me a lesson. I'll never move without a machine-gun in future. That devil Sarton deliberately waylaid us. But we had better start looking out for Eskimo Island; we can't be far off it, but how on earth we are going to tell where it is or which it is I'm dashed if I know. In some silly way I had imagined that we were going to see an island with water round it, but everything seems to be frozen up. Some snow must have fallen, too, so we can't tell which is land and which is water. Judging by its extent, and the flatness of it, I should say that that's ice under us now. Those humps ahead should be land, but they may be icebergs frozen into the pack-ice. I don't know. This is going to be a lot more difficult than I thought. I'm half sorry I started. Keep a sharp look-out; I'm not going to hang about long and risk running out of juice. This sort of landscape gives me the heeby-jeebies.'

Ginger, somewhat restored, caught his breath as he looked

down at the scene of appalling desolation and loneliness underneath them. He was about to remark on it, to say that they must be off their course since it was inconceivable that a man should leave civilization with all its comforts for such a dreadful place, when one of the engines spluttered, picked up, and then spluttered again.

Biggles was already turning. 'A pretty spot for an engine to pack up.' he muttered viciously. 'I——'

Whatever he had been going to say was left unsaid, for at that moment the port engine cut out dead. But it was not that alone that caused Ginger's lips to part in dismay. The other engine was also spluttering.

A horrid suspicion flashed into his mind. Throwing open the narrow door that led into the freight compartment, he darted in, but was back in an instant, face ashen. 'It's petrol,' he cried, in a high-pitched voice. 'There is petrol everywhere; it's slopping over everything. One of Chicot's bullets must have holed the main tank.'

Even as he spoke the second engine, after a sullen backfire, died out. Both propellers stopped, and a weird silence fell, an unnerving silence broken only by the faint whine of the wind over the wings.

Biggles pumped frantically at the hand-pump that filled the gravity tank; but it drew its supply from the main tank, and the main tank was empty. Nothing happened, so he abandoned the useless task and concentrated his attention on bringing the machine down; it was, of course, already gliding towards the frozen wilderness below.

Ginger looked down to see where they were going. In a subconscious way, without actually thinking about it, he was quite certain that they were as good as dead. He did not lose hope easily, particularly since they had found a way out of so many tight corners, but try as he would, he could think of no possible way out of their present dilemma. Suppose Biggles did manage to put the machine down without breaking anything; what then? The only thing that could get them into the air again was petrol, and that was something they would certainly not find where they were going. To walk all the way back to Moose Creek, a matter of four hundred miles, across such country as they had flown over, was so utterly out of the question that he did not even think of it.

The Jupiter continued to sink with that curious floating feeling customary in such cases, accompanied by the usual soft whine of wind blowing past the wings. As they sank lower it grew perceptibly darker, until, near the ground, the plane was moving through a peculiar twilight, dim, yet light enough to see clearly and for a considerable distance.

The need to choose a landing-place did not arise. The ground was all the same, a never-ending expanse of snow in all directions as far as the eye could see; only to the north a jagged ridge—ice or rock, they knew not which—showed clear and hard against a sky of dark, steely blue.

Ginger braced himself as Biggles flattened out to land. He could see no obstruction, but he had a feeling that the dead-flat surface looked almost too good to be true. Again, there was no way of telling if the snow was hard or soft; if it was very soft, then the wheels of the now lowered undercarriage would certainly sink into it and cause the machine to pull up so suddenly that it would inevitably tip up on its nose.

Nothing of that sort happened. The wheels bumped softly, running through the snow with a gentle hissing sound; then, very slowly in the still air, the tail dragged and the machine came to rest.

For a little while neither of them spok. Biggles yawned and rubbed his eyes. 'Lord!' he muttered, 'I'm tired. I could go to sleep easily.'

'From what I can see of it we shall shortly be going to sleep for a long, long time,' answered Ginger bitterly. 'Strewth! What a place! If I'd just woke up I should have thought I was on the moon.'

Biggles grinned. 'It isn't exactly what you'd call a hive of activity, is it?' he said evenly, feeling for his cigarette case. Then, the reek of petrol warning him of the danger of lighting a match where he was, he opened the door and jumped down.

Ginger followed him, noticing that their feet rested on black

ice under an inch or two of snow. Looking about him, he was
appalled by the stark desolation of the scene. They might have
been the only people on earth. The only familiar object he could
see was a narrow rim of the sun, blood-red, just showing above
the horizon. But it was the silence that affected him most; it
seemed to worry the eardrums, and the noises of Biggles's match,
as he struck it to light a cigarette, sounded like a crash.

Biggles nudged his arm. 'Look!' he said.

Half a mile away two whitish-grey shapes, one large and the
other small, were moving in a tireless lope towards the south.
Ginger started back in alarm as he recognized them for polar
bears, a mother and a cub, but he recovered his composure when
he perceived that they took not the slightest notice of them. They
might have been accustomed to seeing aeroplanes standing on
the ice all their lives. At a perfectly even speed they continued on
their way, leaving a faint wake of smoky breath hanging in the
air to mark their passage. Presently they seemed to fade into the
surrounding gloom, and were seen no more. To Ginger they
seemed like the living spirit of the frozen north, and he shivered
as he turned back to Biggles, for the cold was intense.

'Well,' he said, 'what do we do next?'

'To tell the truth, laddie, I was just wondering,' replied
Biggles. 'There doesn't seem to be an awful lot we can do, does
there? But we needn't give up hope. The position may not be so
bad as it appears at first sight.'

'Well, that's comforting, anyway,' muttered Ginger. 'How
did you work it out?'

Biggles blew a puff of smoke into the still air before he replied.
'First of all, we've got enough grub inside to last us a long time.
I'm afraid it's going to be a bit tough on Angus if we eat it, but
since he is never likely to find us here, and we are unable to find
him, we should be fools to starve ourselves to death on that
account. We have also got the cabin to sleep in. It isn't much
protection against this perishing cold, but it's better than
nothing.'

'And when the grub's all gone?' prompted Ginger.

'Don't be so confoundedly pessimistic,' Biggles chided him. 'I haven't finished yet. As I see it, we've got two fairly sound chances. The first is, obviously, that Algy and Wilks will come to look for us in Wilks's Rockheed. We should hear their machine a great way off in this atmosphere, and if we lit a fire—we could, easily—they could hardly fail to spot it. The place doesn't exactly bristle with illuminations, as you can see. The second chance is that we shall see or hear something of Angus. We must be somewhere near Eskimo Island, and we must be pretty close to the track he would follow if he started off to meet Mose. Not knowing the facts, he might think that he'd had a mishap, and come looking for him.'

'That's true enough,' acknowledged Ginger. 'Gosh! It's cold! I'm going——' He broke off, staring at the sky. He raised a quivering forefinger. 'Why—look! There's a searchlight,' he cried. 'It must be Algy. There's another—three—four—why, there's a dozen. What the dickens is going on?'

Biggles looked round sharply, then laughed. 'I've never seen it before in my life, but having read about it I should say it's the aurora borealis.'

Ginger nodded. 'Of course,' he said. 'I didn't think of that. My goodness! Look how the colours change. I could watch it for a long time.'

Biggles grinned. 'Well, you'll have plenty of opportunity,' he observed cheerfully.

'But *that* isn't the aurora borealis, I'll swear,' cried Ginger emphatically, pointing in the direction of the distant ridge. 'That's a fire, or I never saw one in my life.'

Biggles turned quickly. 'Where do you mean?' he asked tersely.

'Well, that's funny. It's gone now,' said Ginger in a puzzled voice. 'You see those two extra sharp peaks a little to the right? It seemed to be at the foot of those.'

'Are you sure you're not imagining things?' asked Biggles doubtfully.

'I'm absolutely certain I saw a light,' declared Ginger. 'It just flared up, remained steady for a moment, and then went out again. It was as if somebody had opened the door of a lighted room and then shut it again.'

'I hope you are right,' said Biggles. 'If you are, it can only mean one thing—Angus. It is unlikely that there are two men up here. Those peaks must be Eskimo Island! What a stroke of luck.'

'What shall we do?'

'It's no use staying here,' answered Biggles. 'I wonder if Angus is keeping watch for Mose to return. Let's light a fire. We shall soon get an answer if he spots it, in which case we'll load up some food and make for the shack. He'll probably help us to fetch the rest. Come on, let's get a fire going.'

With some pieces of petrol-soaked rag and packing-paper they soon had a bright fire burning at a safe distance from the machine, all the time watching the steely-blue haze that seemed to hang at the foot of the peaks, obscuring the physical features of the island—if, indeed, it was the island.

Nothing happened. There was no answering flame.

'He must have gone inside,' muttered Ginger in a disappointed voice.

'I should feel happier if I had seen the light myself,' said Biggles.

'You can take it from me that there was one,' returned Ginger.

'It wasn't a reflection of the aurora on a piece of ice, or anything like that?'

'Definitely not. What I saw was yellow lamplight.'

'All right. I'll take your word for it. If Angus won't come to us we had better go to him. It's not much use staying here.' Biggles turned towards the machine.

Nothing more was said. They both loaded themselves up with as many of the food boxes as they could conveniently carry, and then set off towards the distant peaks. How far away they were was difficult to judge. Ginger said two miles. Biggles guessed five. As it turned out, he was the nearer of the two, but he was a good deal out in his reckoning.

10

A DESPERATE MEETING

'WELL, I don't know, but those hills seem no nearer to me now than when we started.'

It was Biggles who spoke, and they had been walking for a good hour when he made the observation.

Ginger stopped and set his load down on the thin blanket of snow that covered the ice under their feet. 'I didn't like to mention it, but I also had noticed that,' he said, massaging his lips, on which his breath had caused a film of hoar-frost to form. He turned and looked at the Jupiter, standing alone and forlorn at a distance which he would have judged to be not more than half a mile, although he knew from the length of time they had been walking, and the pace, that it could not be less than three miles.

There was just a hint of anxiety in Biggles's voice when he spoke again. 'Judging by the distance we must be from the machine, those hills ahead must be ten miles away. Still, it's no use sitting down; that won't get us there. Let's keep going.'

Ginger picked up his luggage again.

Biggles was watching him. 'What's the matter—tired?'

'Just a bit,' admitted Ginger.

They said no more, but trudged on towards the still distant hills.

Another hour passed.

'Angus doesn't seem to be about,' observed Ginger. 'I wish he'd show that light again. It would—sort of—cheer one up.'

'By the clock it's somewhere about the middle of the night,' Biggles told him. 'He's probably fast asleep in bed.' He glanced up at the sky.

'What do you keep looking up at the sky for?' asked Ginger. 'That's the twentieth time you've done it.'

'I was just looking at the stars,' answered Biggles. 'It may be my imagination, but it struck me that they weren't quite so bright as they were.'

Ginger glanced up. 'They're not,' he said shortly. 'What's that a sign of?'

'I don't know,' confessed Biggles. 'I know nothing about the meteorological conditions in this part of the world, but if I was nearer home I should say that there's snow on the way.'

'Then we'd better move a bit faster,' rejoined Ginger. 'Things won't look too rosy if we get caught out here in the snow.'

Biggles did not answer, but, picking up his luggage, set off at an increased pace.

At the end of another hour it was apparent that the peaks towards which they were marching were definitely nearer. They could no longer see the Jupiter; it had merged into the vague background.

'Not much farther,' said Biggles brightly, taking a surreptitious glance at Ginger, for he had noticed for some time that he was lagging. This did not surprise him, for he, too, was conscious of an increasing weariness.

They toiled on again, both of them dragging their feet through the snow, whereas at first their trail had been clear cut. Biggles took one of the largest parcels from Ginger's pile and added it to his own. Ginger started to protest, but Biggles silenced him with a word. 'When in a jam, all pull on the same rope,' he added. 'I'm as fresh as when I started.' This was not strictly true, but Ginger was too tired to argue. His hands and feet had begun to pain him.

Another half-hour brought them to their objective, and as Ginger looked at it his heart sank. It was darker than when they had started; the world was bathed in a sort of cold blue twilight, dim, yet sufficient to reveal the silent crags that rose straight up from the frozen sea, and formed the coast-line of the solitary island. The silence was unnerving; so profound was it that it seemed to Ginger that it should be possible to hear the stars twinkling. Nothing else moved. All around was a land of death, as devoid of life as the earth must have once been.

Biggles eyed the cliffs with disfavour. 'I've seen more cheerful spots in my time,' he remarked lightly. 'We can't climb that stuff; we'd better walk along the base until we come to a break.'

They set off again, now following the foot of the cliff, and soon afterwards came to a gigantic gorge, like a vast split in the rock's face. It was not very wide, but the sheer walls were nearly a thousand feet in height, so that the airmen, as they stood at the entrance, looked like two microscopic insects in comparison.

Biggles regarded the chasm doubtfully. Nothing moved. Not a bush or a blade of grass grew; only, here and there, on the rock, a sort of grey lichen or moss. Not a sound broke the eerie silence but their laboured breathing. 'It doesn't seem possible that a human being would willingly exist in such a dreadful place as this,' he said quietly. 'But in the absence of any other way into the island, this must be—what did Mose call it?—Muskeg Bend. If it is, is the shack on the top or at the bottom? Well, I suppose we might as well go in a little way; we can always come back if we find we are wrong.'

They had proceeded a little way into the gloomy ravine when Ginger let out a sudden cry. 'Tracks!' he shouted excitedly. 'This must be the place!'

They hurried towards a long straight mark in the snow, but when they reached it Biggles stopped suddenly. There were two tracks, one wider than the other. 'They weren't made by human beings,' he said firmly. 'I've got it. Those two bears we saw must have come this way.'

Ginger's face fell. 'Confound it,' he muttered, 'I thought we'd struck lucky at last. Hello! What's that?' He looked ahead at a tiny moving object that was floating slowly downward in the still air in front of him. It was not unlike a small grey feather.

'Snow,' said Biggles, grimly. 'That's the first flake. We've got to find Angus pretty soon—or else——'

'How about shouting?' suggested Ginger. 'I should think sound would carry a long way in a place like this.'

'We can try it,' agreed Biggles. 'I think this will be better than shouting, though.' He put his hand in his pocket and took out his automatic. Pointing the muzzle in the air, he pulled the trigger three times at equal intervals.

Ginger flinched as the shots crashed out, reverberating again and again between the towering rock walls. The noise was more like a salvo of artillery fire than mere pistol reports. 'Gosh!' he murmured in an awestruck voice, as the echoes finally rolled away to silence. 'What a din! If Angus is within fifty miles I should think he'll hear that.'

Biggles smiled. 'A little hectic, wasn't it?' he agreed. 'The question is, do we go on or do we wait here?'

'We'd better go on a bit,' suggested Ginger. 'If he comes here he'll see our tracks and follow us. The trouble is, even if he showed a light it is doubtful if we should see it down here in the bottom of this gully.'

They moved on again, pausing from time to time to listen.

They had covered perhaps a hundred yards in this way, with big flakes of snow falling regularly, when Ginger suddenly pulled up short. 'There's something moving ahead,' he said quietly.

'I can see it,' came the swift answer. 'Stand fast. It's a bear. He's coming this way—following the tracks of the others. Don't shoot whatever you do. Gosh, what a monster! He must be the father of that cub we saw. Here, let's get over to one side; he may go past. If he comes for us then we shall have to use our pistols— not that they'll be much use against that brute.'

Dropping their loads, the both ran as fast as they could towards the side of the ravine, giving free passage to the bear, which was following the tracks down the middle, snuffling and grunting to itself as it ambled along without any great haste. When the airmen could get no farther on account of the cliff, they turned to watch.

The bear, an enormous shaggy brute that looked grey in the half-light, snuffled along until it came to the place where the two airmen had stood. For a moment there seemed to be a chance that it would go on, but the human taint seemed to upset it, for it sat up on its haunches and looked around. After a moment or two spent like this, during which time it did not appear to see the airmen crouching against the cliff, it dropped on to all fours again and began following their tracks towards where they waited breathlessly. It moved hesitatingly, grunting and snuffling in the footmarks, occasionally stopping to sit up and look around in a manner which, in a small animal, might have been funny. But a full-grown polar bear is a very large animal, and neither Biggles nor Ginger saw any humour in the situation as the huge beast slowly drew near to them.

Then, suddenly, during one of its sitting-up periods, it saw them. Instantly it raised itself on its hind legs and let out a deep snarling grunt.

'Look out, he's coming!' jerked out Biggles. 'It's no use running. Wait until he gets close and then make every shot tell.'

With his heart hammering against his ribs, Ginger whipped out his automatic and waited. The pistol seemed a futile weapon against such a great beast, but it was all he had.

When the bear was about twenty yards away Biggles let out a yell, which caused it to pull up dead, emitting a rumbling growl deep in its throat. Then, with its head held low and muzzle thrust forward, it came on again.

Biggles took a pace to the right. 'Keep to the other side of it,' he jerked out.

As the words left his lips the beast rose up on its hind legs and ran forward in a stumbling charge. Biggles fired, and a choking grunt told them that the bullet had found its mark. But it did nothing to stop the beast's progress. At a distance of five or six yards Biggles fired again, at which the animal let out a roar and turned to bite at the place where the shot had struck. But its halt was only momentary, for with a roar of fury it darted forward again.

Biggles side-stepped and blazed point-blank at the pointed head, but without stopping its berserk progress. Then, in his haste to step aside, he slipped and measured his length in the snow. In a flash the bear was over him.

To Ginger the moment was one of stark panic. His one conscious thought was that he must save Biggles. Hardly knowing what he was doing, he rushed up to the bear and, thrusting the muzzle of the pistol into the thick fur behind the animal's ear, pulled the trigger. The next instant he was swept off his feet as the bear turned on its new aggressor; a hairy paw caught him a sweeping blow on the shoulder and he went over backwards, the pistol flying out of his hand as he fell. A sickening stench of bear filled his nostrils. A roaring report almost deafened him. Then a great weight seemed to settle on his body, crushing the life out of him. He felt himself being pressed farther and farther into the snow, but he still fought with the panic of despair. Something seized him by the arm and he let out a scream, thinking that it was the bear's jaws. Then the scene seemed to change and he scrambled to his feet, panting and muttering incoherently.

'Ach, now! Take it easy,' said a strange voice in a strong Scots accent.

Ginger stared at a short, broad-shouldered figure, with a rifle in the crook of its arm, that suddenly appeared in front of him. Out of the corner of his eye he saw Biggles picking himself up out of the snow. Then he understood.

'Are you Angus Stirling?' he blurted out.

'Ay, mon, that's me name,' was the casual reply. 'And what might *ye* be doin' in these parts, if I may ask?'

Ginger rubbed his shoulder ruefully. 'We were looking for you,' he said, thinking how silly the answer sounded. 'Did you shoot this brute?' he went on, pointing to the body of the bear.

'I did so,' replied Angus. "'Twas about time, too, I reckon.' Beyond that the bear did not appear to interest him. 'And what might your name be?' he inquired.

'Let's go to your shack and I'll tell you all about it,' put in Biggles.

'Ay, mebbe that'd be best,' agreed Angus, and, turning, led the way up the ravine.

I I

AN UNPLEASANT SHOCK

It was not far to the old Scotsman's cabin, which was situated on the side of a hill which faced south, for which reason it had been seen by the airmen out on the icefield when he had opened the door to bring in some peat for the fire. He told them that he was just going to sleep when he heard the three shots fired by Biggles, and three shots at equal intervals being a universal summons for help, he had at once set off expecting to find Mose, even though it was early for him to return.

After they had shaken the snow from their clothes, Biggles asked the question that was uppermost in his mind. 'What about the weather?' he said. 'Is the snow going to keep on?'

Angus threw some lumps of peat—the only fuel available—into his stove before he replied. 'It might only be an early flurry, and stop again presently, or it may be the real fall,' he said.

'What's your opinion?' asked Biggles.

'I ain't got none; and it would be a wise man as 'ad any in these parts,' was the non-committal reply.

'If it's the real fall—what then?' inquired Biggles.

'We shall all be dead afore the break-up,' returned Angus with disconcerting frankness.

'We've got some food out yonder,' Biggles told him.

'Eh, mon, if this is the big snow it'll be buried afore morning. 'Twouldn't be no use thinkin' o' fetchin' it.'

'And there wouldn't be enough here without it to last us till spring?'

'Not half enough,' said the old man calmly. 'Where's Mose? Did he tell you I was here? What did you come up here for, anyway?'

'I'm coming to that,' replied Biggles, realizing that in his anxiety to try to discover what the weather was likely to do, he had told Angus nothing about his mission. For another moment or two he hesitated, wondering how to begin.

'I've got some bad news for you, Angus,' he said at last.

The Scotsman threw him a sidelong glance. 'Hm?'

'Mose won't be coming back.'

'That means he's dead.'

Biggles nodded. 'Quite right. Mose is dead.'

'How did it happen?'

'He was murdered.'

Angus started. 'Got drunk, I reckon, and talked about—talked too much.'

Biggles noted how the old man checked himself and wondered why. 'No,' he said. 'At least, I only saw him once, and he was sober enough then.' And thereafter he told the whole story; how Ginger overheard him inquiring for Wilks and the events that followed. This involved, naturally, an explanation of the state of affairs at the aerodrome.

'You reckon Brindle done the killin'?' put in the old man shrewdly, when Biggles had finished.

'I'm pretty sure of it,' replied Biggles. 'But that doesn't mean that I could prove it,' he added.

'So you aimed to bring up the grub and get the transfer at the same time?'

'That's it.'

'What happened? How come you to be walking?'

Biggles had to disclose the incident of the air attack by Sarton—not that he had any desire to conceal the fact that he and Ginger had been responsible for the death of Sarton and Chicot.

When he had finished the old man stared at the stove for a long time in silence. 'I reckon you're tellin' the truth,' he said at last. 'I know Brindle. He's bad medicine. Poor old Mose. I never reckoned he'd go out that way. Well, it was mighty kind of yer to come up, stranger, but I guess you was just a day or two too late. You're here, and here you'll stop, I reckon. When the snow stops we'll go and dig out the bear meat; that'll last us for a bit. There's just a chance that we might dig the grub out of the aeroplane; mebbe we could make do with that. And since you're liable to be stoppin', I'll tell yer something else. Mose was a rich man.'

Biggles looked surprised. 'He didn't look like that to me.'

'No? Mebbe he wouldn't. To make my meanin' plain, me and Mose struck it rich.'

Biggles understood then. 'You mean you've found gold here?'

'Ay, mon, dust a-plenty. A power o' good it's like to do us, though, now. Mose had a tidy poke here; he wouldn't take it with him 'cause he was afeared he might get rubbed out for it. Yet he gets rubbed out anyway. Well, it all depends on the weather now; let's see what it's doin'.'

Angus crossed over to the door and flung it open. Outside the world lay still and white under the fresh fall, but it was no longer snowing. Once more the stars were twinkling brightly in the cold blue dome overhead.

Biggles went past him out into the snow, and found that it was only six or eight inches deep. 'This looks like our chance to get the grub up from the machine,' he said. 'We shall have to have an hour or two's sleep first, though. We're about all in.'

'Ay, I can see that,' replied Angus. 'You take a snooze then, while I go out and fetch the bear meat. Then, if you're willin', we'll go to the airyplane.'

Biggles would have preferred to have gone straight back to the machine for fear the snow started again, but there are limits to human endurance, and he was at the end of his.

Angus took some furs from a heap in the corner and threw them on the floor near the stove. 'Make a shake-down out of these,' he said.

Ginger followed Biggles's example in arranging a rough bed on the floor. He threw himself down on it and was asleep in a moment, so soundly that he did not even hear Angus go out and shut the door.

When he awoke he had no idea of how long he had been asleep. It did not seem long, but he knew it must be several hours because a great pile of raw meat was stacked on the far side of the room, the remains of the polar bear. There was more than a man could carry in one load, so he realized that if Angus had made two journeys it must be the next day. Neither Biggles nor Angus were in the room, but it did not occur to him that they were far away, so he got up leisurely and went outside to look for them. Instinctively his eyes went out across the open plain that lay between the shack and the Jupiter, and he was not a little surprised to see two figures moving across it. Presently he made them out to be Biggles and Angus, and what surprised him even more was the fact that they were returning.

'Gosh! What a time I must have been asleep,' he muttered, realizing that the others must have made a trip to the machine. He did not waste any more time in idle conjecture, however, but built up the fire, put the kettle on, and, finding a frying pan, started to fry three large bear steaks, which were just cooked to a turn when the others came in with their loads.

After a hearty meal Angus announced his intention of making another journey to the machine. 'It's a bit of luck, the snow holding off like this,' he explained, 'and we ought to make the most of it. If it starts again it might go on for a week or more.'

The others agreed with this project, for they realized that their lives depended on their getting sufficient food in to last them through the long Arctic winter. Coats and gloves were, therefore, donned, and they set off towards the distant machine.

As they trudged in single file through the snow, with Angus leading, Ginger discovered that he had lost all count of time. With so little difference between day and night he found that he had completely lost track of how many hours or days had passed since they had left Fort Beaver. Not that it mattered. Their actions in future would be ruled by the weather, not by the clock.

Vaguely he wondered what Algy and Wilks were doing, and what they thought of their non-return. As Biggles had said, it was certain that, weather permitting, they would set off in Wilks's machine to look for them, but there were long odds against them succeeding in locating them, with such a vast territory to cover. In any case, once the snow started again it would put an end to any idea of rescue, in which event Wilks and Algy would have to fight McBain as best they could.

The newly fallen snow appeared to have raised the temperature considerably, but it started to freeze again just as they reached the machine, a detail which would, Angus said, make their return trip easier, since it would harden the snow so that they would be able to walk on it, instead of ploughing through it as they had on the outward journey.

To Ginger's surprise the Jupiter was not half buried under the snow as he had expected to find it, but Biggles explained the mystery. On his previous visit, while the snow was still soft, he had brushed it off the exposed surfaces of the machine, so that, on the remote chance of Algy or Wilks finding it, it would be in a condition to fly—provided of course, that it had petrol in the tanks and the bullet hole was mended.

The chances of the machine ever taking the air again seemed so slight that Ginger, although he did not say so, felt that Biggles had wasted his time. He himself thought no more about it, but set to work with the others unloading the remaining stores. This done, he was about to suggest to Biggles that they drained the crank cases of oil, which would be useful in many ways, when he heard the distant hum of an aeroplane. The sound was unmistakable, and his heart leapt when he heard it.

'Good old Algy!' he shouted gleefully.

Even Biggles had flushed with excitement. 'A fire!' he yelled. 'Let's get a fire going!'

They rushed into the cabin and threw out any odd scraps of packing they could find. An old map, a spare pair of gloves, and even the patching fabric went on the pile as Angus put a match to it. A tongue of orange fire leapt upwards, and in a moment the odds and ends were blazing like a beacon.

'It should be possible to see that for fifty miles,' declared Biggles, peering into the sky in the direction from which the sound had come. 'There he is! There he is!' He pointed with a quivering forefinger at a black speck that had materialized out of the dull haze concealing the southern horizon. 'He's seen us!' went on Biggles gleefully. 'I saw him turn. He's coming— coming——' His voice died away in a curious manner.

Ginger, staring at the fast approaching machine, knew why. It was not Wilks's Rockheed. It was McBain's second Weinkel that was roaring low towards them.

12

A ONE-SIDED DUEL

To say that Ginger was flabbergasted would be to express his feelings only mildly. He was thunderstruck. For some reason the possibility of this development had not occurred to him, although he realized now that there was just as much reason for

McBain to come searching for Sarton and Chicot, as for Wilks and Algy to come looking for them.

He turned to Biggles who was still staring at the oncoming machine with an expression of mingled chagrin and disgust. 'He was looking for Sarton, I expect,' he muttered.

Biggles nodded thoughtfully, 'And we were kind enough to light a fire and show him where we were,' he murmured.

'He may still think we're Sarton and Chicot.'

'If he does, he'll realize his mistake when he gets a bit closer,' returned Biggles bitterly. 'Hello—see that turn? He's spotted who we are. It will be interesting to see what he does,' he added. 'He'll hardly risk landing.'

Ginger did not reply. He was watching the movements of the Weinkel with a good deal of trepidation, for he felt that whatever McBain did—assuming that he was on board—it would be unpleasant.

That he was right in this assumption was soon made apparent. The Weinkel banked sharply, and putting its nose down, dived at the stranded Jupiter.

For an instant longer Biggles watched it. Then he let out a warning yell. 'Lie flat.'

Ginger flung himself down just in time. Above the bellow of the Weinkel's engines there came the vicious chatter of a machine-gun, and the line of the bullets could easily be followed by the splinters of ice and flecks of snow that leapt into the air in line with the machine.

As it swept past Ginger clearly saw McBain himself behind the gun, which he had thrust out of the side window of the control cabin.

A stream of belligerent imprecations from Angus made Biggles turn. 'You hit?' he asked anxiously.

'Och, mon, not I,' shouted Angus. 'If I ever get ma' hands on that——'

'You keep down,' shouted Biggles, seeing that the Weinkel was coming back.

Angus's rifle cracked as the Weinkel roared past again, cutting a trail in the snow with its gun. Some of the shots went very near the prone airmen.

'You'll never hit him with that,' Biggles told Angus. 'He'll hit one of us in a minute if we aren't careful. We'd better scatter.'

The third time the Weinkel hurtled past the gun was silent. Instead, a small square object crashed down near the Jupiter; it bounced over and over and came to rest very close to the machine. Biggles started forward with the idea of finding out what it was, but before he could reach it, the Weinkel, which had swung round almost on its wing tip, was coming back. A signal light cut a flaming line through the air; it struck the snow very near the square object, and a sheet of flame leapt upwards.

'It's petrol!' yelled Biggles. 'He threw a can of petrol with the cap off. Now he's fired it with the pistol. He's trying to burn the Jupiter.'

Two gallons of petrol make a considerable flame. The scene was bathed in a lurid glow, but it was soon clear that in this case, at any rate, the Jupiter would not be damaged. Owing to the snow the petrol did not spread far, and the flame was ten yards from the machine.

Seething with impotence, Biggles told the others to get farther away in order to reduce the chances of anyone being hit. It was as well that he did so, for thrice more the Weinkel dived at them, the gun spitting. Another can of petrol was thrown down, and Ferroni, who was actually flying the machine, almost stalled as he turned slowly above the Jupiter in order to allow McBain to take careful aim.

Biggles sprang to his feet and blazed away with his automatic. It is probable that he hit the machine, for it dived away and climbed up out of pistol range. A signal flare came screaming down, but Biggles had not wasted the brief delay; running forward, he had snatched up the can, still nearly full, and carried it clear. The flare burnt itself out harmlessly in the snow.

For the next few seconds the movements of the Weinkel puzzled the watchers on the ground. The plane turned away sharply and began climbing steeply.

'I think he's going,' said Biggles, rising to his feet. 'He's thought better of it. Maybe he was afraid of running out of petrol himself.'

'No, that isn't it,' cried Ginger. 'Look!'

Biggles followed the direction indicated. What he saw made him catch his breath sharply. 'It's Algy!' he muttered hoarsely.

Heading straight towards the scene was a Rockheed Freighter, attracted, no doubt, by the signal flares.

In normal circumstances this would have given Biggles and Ginger cause for jubilation, but now they both went cold with horror, for the Weinkel was racing towards the other machine, and they both knew that whatever Algy might have in the way of weapons, he would certainly have nothing capable of competing with a machine-gun.

'Judging by the way he flies, I don't think Algy has seen the Weinkel,' muttered Ginger, in a hopeless voice.

'He's probably got his eyes fixed on us,' returned Biggles tersely.

Helpless, they could only stand and watch.

The affair—it could hardly be called a combat—was over even more quickly than they had imagined it would be.

The Weinkel, confident, no doubt, of its superior armament, climbed straight up under the tail of the Rockheed, which had now cut its engines and was gliding down slowly, obviously looking for a place to land. An arm appeared out of the window, waving, making it obvious that those inside the machine had not the slightest suspicion of danger.

Ginger groaned aloud in his misery.

Biggles ground his teeth. 'What would I give for a single-seater and just one drum of ammunition—just one,' he forced out through his set teeth.

The two machines were within a quarter of a mile of the stranded Jupiter when the end came; the horrified watchers on the ground saw the whole thing clearly. They saw the Weinkel's side window open and the gun appear; saw McBain take slow and careful aim; saw the jabbing tongues of flame dance from the muzzle of the gun; saw the Rockheed shiver as the burst of fire struck her.

Ginger could hardly bear to watch, but he could not tear his eyes away. A kind of fascinated horror kept them glued to the machine. He was not quite certain what had happened, but it seemed that either whoever was flying it had been hit, or else the controls had been damaged.

The Rockheed fluttered like a wounded bird, careering from side to side with a sickening skidding movement. Its nose swung upward and sagged in turn.

Biggles said nothing. He did not move. With a face nearly as white as the surrounding snow he stared at the swaying machine with brooding eyes. Never in all his experience had he felt so utterly powerless; never before had he found himself in a position where he could do absolutely nothing. Instinctively, aware of the futility of it, he swayed with the machine as if by sheer will power he could correct the faults, leaning back when the nose dropped and pushing an imaginary joystick forward when the machine looked as though it must stall.

It was now so close that they could see the two men in her; could see Wilks fighting at the controls.

'He isn't hit, anyway,' muttered Ginger through dry lips.

Biggles did not answer. He knew the end was not far away.

The Rockheed stalled, came out, and stalled again, this time missing the ground by inches. It was obviously out of control. The port wing sagged as it stalled again at the top of its zoom, perhaps a hundred feet above the snowfield. Instantly it began to fall again, the sagging wing heading towards the ground—the first movement of a spin.

Then, as if by a miracle, the machine righted itself. Neither Biggles nor Ginger could understand why. There seemed no reason for it. The machine turned sluggishly towards them, and the reason for the apparent miracle became revealed. Algy was out on the starboard wing, lying flat, clinging to the leading edge with his hands as, with his body, he counterbalanced the port wing.

The Rockheed swept down like a tired bird, nearly on an even keel, but not quite. The port wing-tip touched the ground first, flinging the snow up like the bow-wave of a ship. After that the result was a foregone conclusion. The whole machine cartwheeled, flinging Algy over and over across the snow. The nose buried itself. The fuselage tipped up, hanging poised for a moment, and then fell back. Movement ceased.

The Weinkel, its engines roaring triumphantly, swept up into the sky. It levelled out, its nose pointing to the south.

Neither Biggles nor Ginger paid any attention to it; they were both racing at full speed towards the crashed machine, which lay about a hundred yards away from the Jupiter.

'Get to Algy; I'll look after Wilks,' yelled Biggles. His great fear was that the machine would go up in flames before he could reach it, for that is what happens all too often in such cases. He tore open the cabin door and disappeared inside.

Ginger went on to Algy, who, he was overjoyed to see, was moving, although ineffectually. Reaching him, he dropped on his knees beside him. 'Algy,' he cried, in a voice high-pitched with anxiety. 'Algy, old man, are you badly hurt?' It's me— Ginger.'

Algy managed to get up on his hands and knees, his head thrust forward. His face was twisted in agony. A long-drawn groan burst from his lips.

Ginger's blood ran cold. The groan convinced him that Algy was mortally hurt. In desperation he looked round for Biggles, but Algy, who apparently divined his intention, shook his head, at the same time groaning again. 'I'm—I'm—I'm—' he stammered, 'on—on—only—winded.'

Ginger gasped his relief and waited for him to recover. There was little he could do. Fortunately, although the symptoms of 'winding' can be terrifying while they last, they do not last long, and once Algy managed to get an intake of breath, he recovered quickly.

'Gosh!' he groaned, smiling wanly. 'Sorry to make such a fuss. How's Wilks? Is he hurt?'

'I don't know,' replied Ginger. 'Take your time. I'll slip across and find out.'

He found that Biggles had managed to get Wilks out of the wreckage. He was sitting in the snow near by, very pale, while Biggles mopped blood from a cut in his forehead. Angus was binding a bandage tightly round his left wrist which, it subsequently transpired, he had sprained slightly.

'How's Algy?' Biggles asked Ginger as he ran up.

'Not bad, apart from being winded. I don't think there is much wrong with him.'

'Snow probably broke his fall,' returned Biggles shortly.

'I expect so,' agreed Ginger.

Algy, his back slightly bent so that one hand rested on a knee, came limping over to them. 'I've had nearly enough of this "farthest north" stuff,' he declared. 'One thing and another, we seem to be in a pretty bad way.'

'Not so bad as it looks,' grinned Biggles cheerfully. Actually, he was so relieved that neither Algy nor Wilks had suffered serious injury that he did not worry about anything else. 'By the way,' he went on, 'this is Angus. Angus, this is my partner, Mr Lacey. You and Wilkinson are already acquainted.' He stood up and looked round.

'Did you see that skunk McBain shoot us down?' grated Algy.

'Saw the whole thing,' replied Biggles. 'He was having a go at us when you arrived on the scene.'

'Did he shoot you down, too?'

'No. Sarton was responsible for that. He's down, too—dead—and Chicot with him.' Briefly Biggles described the incident.

'Well, what are we going to do?' asked Wilks.

'We'd best be makin' tracks for the shack,' chipped in Angus. 'If it starts to snow we may have a job to make it, and the snow's due to arrive at any minute.'

'Do you mean that we're here for the winter?' cried Algy aghast.

'Looks that way to me, mister.'

'I'm not so sure about that,' put in Biggles. 'We may have a chance yet. Had you got plenty of juice in your tanks?'

'Fifty gallons, I reckon.'

'Then if we can find the hole in our tank, and mend it, and swop the petrol over, we can still get back in the Jupiter.'

Algy looked from Biggles to the Jupiter's wheels, more than half buried in the snow. 'You'll never get her off out of this stuff,' he muttered. 'Those wheels must be frozen in by this time.'

'I agree,' answered Biggles, 'but we've got a pair of skis inside, don't forget. If we can jack up the undercart while we get the wheels off, and put the skis on, we might still do it—if the snow will hold off for a little while longer.'

Algy sprang to his feet, his stiffness forgotten. 'Then let's get at it,' he cried. 'It's our only chance.'

'See if you can find that bullet hole, Ginger,' ordered Biggles. 'It's a race against time now.'

13
SOUTHWARD AGAIN

FOR three hours the airmen worked feverishly. Ginger repaired the punctured tank, bemoaning the fact that Smyth, who was an expert sheet-metal-worker, was not there to help him. Algy explained that he had decided to leave him at Fort Beaver— where they had arrived as arranged in the Rockheed which now lay smashed in the snow—for two reasons: first, to leave a guard at the aerodrome, and, secondly, to reduce the load of the aircraft, and consequently the petrol consumption.

The others laboured at the undercarriage, the transformation of the Jupiter into a ski-plane being impeded to no small extent by the cold. However, at last it was done. Ginger had already repaired the tank, so the labourers' task of transferring the petrol from the Rockheed to the Jupiter began.

'Is there anything at the cabin you'll be wanting?' Biggles asked Angus, who was helping as far as he was able.

'Meanin' what?' answered the old Scotsman.

'Well, I take it you'll be coming with us.'

'Na, mon. I'm staying here.'

Biggles stopped work long enough to stare unbelievingly. 'Do you mean that?'

'Ay.'

'You'd rather stay for months in this forsaken place than come back to civilization?'

'Ay, I'll stay.'

Biggles shrugged his shoulders. 'Well, I suppose you know best what you want to do. All right; we'll taxi you back to the shack as soon as we are ready; that will save you dragging the stores through the snow. You can then give us the transfer and we'll get away before it starts to snow.'

Angus cocked an eye heavenward. 'Then ye've no time to waste,' he observed dispassionately. 'Here she comes.'

Following his eyes, Biggles saw one or two big flakes floating downwards languidly. He made no comment. There was no need. The others had seen the dreaded flakes, and were working with desperate speed.

It took them some time to start the Jupiter's engines, for they were stone cold, but a little petrol inserted into each of the cylinders finally did the trick. They all got aboard. A few moments to take the chill off the engines and the Jupiter began gliding across the snow in the direction of the island.

By the time Angus's stores were thrown out for him to collect in his own time, and the old man had returned from the shack with the precious transfer, it was snowing steadily.

The last few seconds on the ground were hectic. Angus heaved into the cabin an object that looked like a small sack.

'What's that?' yelled Biggles, who was itching to be off.

'Old Mose's poke,' shouted Angus.

'Mose's *what?*'

'Poke.'

'He means that it is Mose's gold,' called Wilks.

'What do you want me to do with it?' Biggles asked Angus, not very pleased about the responsibility.

'Mose didn't want the gold for himself. He's got a darter down in Vancouver. I reckon he'd like her to have it. Find her and give it to her.'

'All right,' shouted Biggles, without enthusiasm. He was not in the least concerned about the gold; all he cared about at that moment was getting away.

'Stand clear!' he yelled.

The cabin door slammed.

A parting wave to the old Scotsman, who did not seem in the least concerned about his lonely fate, and the Jupiter swung round. There was no horizon, but Biggles did not hesitate. The engines bellowed, and the big machine raced across the snow. A moment later it rose slowly into the air. The ground disappeared from sight immediately, and Biggles fixed his eyes on the instruments.

'We ought to run out of this in ten minutes,' he told Wilks, who was sitting beside him.

Wilks agreed, knowing precisely what Biggles meant; which was that the snow was coming from the north, and, as it had only just started, and the Jupiter was heading south for Moose Creek, it would quickly pass beyond the snow area. The thought led to another. They had managed to get off safely, but how about getting down—if there was snow at Moose Creek? He asked Biggles this question.

'I hadn't overlooked that,' replied Biggles. 'We'll work that out when we get there. The skids may stand up to a turf landing, but whether they do or not, I'd sooner take the risk—even if we bust the machine—than stay in Angus's shack for six months.'

Wilks nodded. He felt the same about it.

Already the snow through which they were flying was thinning, and a minute later they caught their first glimpse of the ground. Shortly afterwards they ran into clear weather, although the landscape was still snow-covered, the result of the earlier fall. Flying, however, was now a comparatively simple matter, and Biggles, relaxing, began to think of other things. With the major problem answered, that of their escape from being snowed-in, minor worries presented themselves, as usually happens.

'Pity we've lost the Rockheed,' he remarked. 'That leaves us only one machine to operate with.'

'Never mind; we've got the transfer,' Wilks reminded him. 'If we can use that to get McBain off the aerodrome we shall manage all right. By the way, what are we going to do about McBain?'

'What do you mean—do about him?'

'Well, this attack on us. He tried to murder us; are we going to let him get away with it?'

'It's a bit hard to know what to do,' replied Biggles thoughtfully. 'It's our word against his. He thinks we are out of the way, certainly for the winter, possibly for good. He'll get a shock when we turn up. He'll probably accuse us of murdering Sarton, but since the remains of the machine will probably be buried under snow for the next six months, he will have nothing to support his story. We've got a witness in Angus, but he won't be available for six months, either. I think our wisest course would be to submit a report of the whole affair to police head-quarters and let them do what they like about it. Delaney, single-handed, can't do much. There is this; our reputation will at least stand investigation, which is more than can be said for McBain, I imagine.'

They said no more, for it was obvious that the future was so problematical that it was impossible to make plans with any assurance.

The snow on the ground was now very patchy, and while they were still some distance from Moose Creek it died away altogether. Within a few days the snow coming down from the north would bury everything under a deep blanket, but for the present the ground was clear.

'There's just a chance that the Creek will be frozen over,' said Wilks, referring to the almost land-locked stretch of water from which Moose Creek took its name. 'It has been freezing pretty hard.'

'How shall we know?' asked Biggles.

'I always use the lake in winter,' replied Wilks. 'If the ice is safe they shift the windstocking across to it, because the ice has a much better surface than the aerodrome. Being boggy, during the summer it gets churned up by the wheels, and when these ruts get frozen hard in the winter they are awful. However, we shall soon see which it is to be. There's the creek, in the distance. It wouldn't surprise me if we found McBain there.'

'It would surprise him, I'll bet,' grinned Biggles.

'He's been there, anyway,' declared Wilks, who was staring

down through the window. 'There are his wheelmarks on the
ice—at least, those are aeroplane tracks, and it's unlikely that
anyone else has been up here. And there's the windstocking by
the side of the creek; that means it is all right to land on the ice.'

'Well, that's better, anyway. I wasn't feeling too happy at
trying to put this big bus down in a frozen field on a pair of skis.
Can you see McBain's machine anywhere?'

'No.'

'Then he must have gone off again.'

'Looks like it.'

'We'll find him at Fort Beaver, no doubt.'

Nothing more was said while Biggles concentrated on putting
the Jupiter down on the lake on her new type of undercarriage.

To those in the machine the difference was barely perceptible,
apart from the fact that the machine ran a long way before
coming to a standstill.

'What are we going to do?' asked Wilks.

'Refuel, put our wheels back on again, and head south for Fort
Beaver,' replied Biggles shortly. 'There is no telling what lies
McBain will spread about us if we leave him too long alone—
particularly if he thinks we aren't coming back to refute them.'

Leaving the others to attend to the refuelling and the
replacement of the undercarriage wheels, Biggles walked across
to the traffic manager's office.

'Here we are again, Mr Canwell,' he observed cheerfully.

The traffic manager looked up from a book in which he was
just making some entries. 'Sorry,' he said, 'but you are just too
late.'

'Too late—what for?'

'To take the gold down.'

Biggles nodded slowly. 'Ah—of course. I remember. So it's
gone, eh?'

'Yep. Biggest shipment we've ever made in one go. I waited as
long as I could for you. McBain blew in, so I let him take it. I'm
sorry——'

'You will be, I fancy,' put in Biggles dryly.

Canwell started. 'What do you mean by that?'

'Oh, nothing,' murmured Biggles. 'I fancy you would have found us a bit more reliable in the long run—that's all. How long ago did McBain leave?'

'About ten minutes.'

Biggles nodded. 'Right-ho, then. We might as well be getting along, too. See you later, maybe.'

Biggles walked slowly to the door, but once outside he strode swiftly to where the others were waiting for him. 'It looks as if McBain's got away with the boodle,' he said crisply. 'He's got ten minutes start. Not expecting to be followed, he'll cruise; if we run on full throttle we may overhaul him. Get aboard—step on it.'

14
AN UNEXPECTED LANDING

NOT until the Jupiter was in the air, roaring southwards on the trail of the Weinkel, did Biggles settle down to contemplate the situation. The gold was temporarily in McBain's charge: if he intended stealing it, this clearly was his opportunity. In the circumstances it seemed unlikely that he would return to Fort Beaver, where transport from the rail-head would be waiting to take the gold on to the bank at Edmonton. Where, then, would he go? The more Biggles thought about it the more he became convinced that unless he overtook the Weinkel he would never see McBain again. He, with the machine and the gold in it, would disappear. In one way this would be to Wilks's advantage, for the feud for possession of the aerodrome would cease; nevertheless, it was not unlikely that the Moose Creek Company would be so sore at losing the gold dust that they would never again trust gold to an aeroplane, in which case Arctic Airways would die for lack of business. If they could overtake the Weinkel and see where it went they might succeed in bringing the gold thieves to justice, which could hardly fail to cement their friendship with the Moose Creek Company. This opinion Biggles passed on to Algy, who was sitting beside him in the control cabin.

The Jupiter was now once more in the region of day and night, with the 'bad lands' gliding past underneath them. Biggles was staring ahead, striving to pick up their quarry, when Ginger, his eyes alight with excitement, pushed his way into the cabin.

'Starboard!' he yelled. 'The Weinkel's bearing west.'

Biggles did not answer. His eyes switched to the right, far away from the line he had been following. For a moment or two they studied the sky, section by section, before they settled on a tiny moving speck travelling on a south-westerly course at a slightly lower altitude than themselves. It was the Weinkel.

'I was right,' he said crisply to Algy. 'McBain isn't going to Fort Beaver; the course he is on will leave Fort Beaver miles to the east.'

As he spoke he touched the right-hand side of the rudder-bar with his foot, bringing the Jupiter round on a new course to follow the other machine.

For an hour the respective positions of the two machines did not change. Although in the circumstances it was hardly likely that the Jupiter would be seen by the men in the leading machine, Biggles kept at a safe distance, quite satisfied to watch. The only fear he had was that McBain should be carrying more petrol than they were, in which case they might ultimately be compelled to give up the chase for lack of fuel. He was, therefore, more than a little relieved when he saw the Weinkel going down. Grabbing his map, he studied closely the area they were over, then he turned a bewildered face to Algy.

'There's nothing there,' he said.

'Not even a village?'

'Absolutely nothing.'

Algy stood up and surveyed the ground right to the horizon; it was all the same: open prairie broken by wide areas of fir forest, with a small lake here and there. 'No,' he agreed, at the end of his scrutiny, 'there's nothing in the shape of a town or village. What are you going to do?'

That was a question Biggles could not answer at once, for the problem facing him was a difficult one to solve. While the Weinkel was in the air it was extremely unlikely that McBain would see the Jupiter, but once it was on the ground, with its engines stopped, the noise of the Jupiter's engines would certainly give them away. The Weinkel was still in the air, but it was now losing height rapidly, and it seemed only a matter of minutes before it would land.

His brain raced as he sought a solution to the puzzle. Studying the ground intently, he saw that to the right the ground was fairly open, and that it fell away quickly to the left, the locality in which the Weinkel looked as if it would land. It struck him that if he could put the Jupiter down on the high land behind one of the patches of timber, it might be possible for them to watch the Weinkel without being seen. Anyway, it seemed worth trying, so he at once proceeded to put the plan into execution. He cut the engines, and not until the Jupiter's wheels trundled over the turf did the others realize what he had in mind.

The machine had barely come to a standstill before Biggles was out, running for all he was worth towards a line of spruce and fir that hid the whole of the country to the south. They were a mile or more from the Weinkel, so there was little risk of them being seen or heard. Ducking low under the drooping fir branches, they pushed their way to the far edge of the timber from where the country to the south lay open to their view.

'There they are!' Biggles's voice was tense as, keeping under cover, he pointed out the Weinkel, which was now standing on the ground by a small log cabin near the edge of a lake. It so happened, however, that from their coign of vantage the Weinkel was between them and the cabin, so although they could see figures moving, they could not see exactly what was going on.

'I should say they are unloading the gold,' declared Ginger.

'I don't think there is any doubt about that,' returned Biggles.

Several minutes passed during which no more was said; then, not a little to their surprise, the Weinkel's engines suddenly opened up again, and almost before the watchers realized what was happening, the machine had taken off and was racing low over a south-easterly course. The cabin was deserted; or, at least, it appeared to be.

'Gosh! We shall lose them if we are not careful. Come on.' Suiting the action to the words, Biggles led the rush back to the machine.

In three minutes they were in the air again. But the Weinkel had had five minutes' clear start, and an aeroplane can travel a long way in that time. There was no sign of it.

'They were heading south-east. That's the direction of Fort Beaver,' Algy pointed out.

'I know, but I don't get the hang of this at all,' muttered Biggles, with a worried frown. 'If they've hidden the gold, they've got a bit of a nerve to go back to Fort Beaver.'

'Maybe they'll just land to pick up the things that belong to them, and, perhaps, refuel. Then they'll come back, put the gold on board, and go straight on south to the United States,' suggested Algy.

'Possibly,' agreed Biggles. 'Yet, somehow, I don't think that's the answer. It's got me beaten, and that's a fact. One thing is certain; we've got to get back to Fort Beaver ourselves or we shall run out of petrol. Another forced landing would just about put the tin hat on things.'

'Suits me,' agreed Algy. 'A night's rest wouldn't do any of us any harm.'

That closed the conversation for the time being. It was half an hour later before anyone spoke again, by which time Fort Beaver aerodrome was in sight.

'There's the Weinkel,' said Biggles. 'And unless my eyes deceive me, that's McBain and Ferroni standing beside it, talking to—it looks like Delaney.'

'Yes, it's Delaney,' put in Ginger. 'If he is asking them what has happened to the gold we'll be able to enlighten him,' he added.

'It will be interesting to see just what is happening,' observed Biggles smoothly, as he cut the Jupiter's engines and glided down.

Their run in carried them very close to the Weinkel. McBain and Ferroni stared at them as they taxied past.

'Yes, you might well stare,' said Biggles quietly to himself, eyeing McBain and his pilot grimly. 'You didn't expect to see us back so soon—if at all—I'll warrant.' His eyes went past the two crooks and came to rest on something that lay on the ground beyond them. A strange expression crept over his face, but he made no further observation until he had switched off in front of their hangar. 'Well,' he said, in an odd tone of voice, 'what do you make of that?'

'Make of what?' asked the others together.

'Those are the Moose Creek gold boxes that they're unloading,' went on Biggles. 'They haven't stolen the gold after all. They'll never get a better chance.' He passed his hand wearily over his face and then shook his head. 'That seems to knock all our calculations sideways, doesn't it?'

'I—I don't understand it,' blurted Wilks.

'You'd be a clever fellow if you did, I think,' muttered Biggles dryly. 'According to Ginger, those chaps are crooks, waiting for a chance to get their hands on a pile of gold. They've actually had the gold in their possession, with nothing as far as I can see to prevent them from getting clear away with it. Yet they bring it back here and quietly hand it over to the bank messenger—that looks like him coming now—like law-abiding citizens. There's a weak link somewhere in that chain of events. We had better go inside and put our thinking caps on and see if we can find it.'

15

UNDER ARREST

FOR the remainder of the day and far into the night they discussed the problem that seemed to admit of no solution. At daybreak the following morning they resumed the debate. They could talk of nothing else. Biggles broke off long enough to send Smyth to the village, shopping, then he continued the discussion.

'You can't get away from it,' he declared, staring out across the now deserted aerodrome. 'If McBain stays here for ten years he won't get a better chance to lift a load of gold than he had yesterday. If he is a crook, why did he deliver the gold instead of pushing off with it? That's what I want to know. Had he wanted to, he could have been two thousand miles away by now. I give it up.'

'The only answer seems to be that McBain isn't a crook after all,' suggested Wilks.

'I tell you I heard them discussing ways and means of getting the gold,' declared Ginger emphatically. 'You're not suggesting that I dreamed——'

'Of course we're not,' broke in Biggles.

'Maybe the haul wasn't big enough, and they are waiting for another lot,' suggested Algy.

Biggles shook his head. 'That won't do,' he said. 'Why, they might have to wait months. You remember that Canwell himself told us that it was an unusually big cargo of metal; and consider the other circumstances. The freeze-up has set in up north, and it's only a question of days—perhaps hours—before it reaches us here. McBain must know by this time that something has happened to his other machine. He must know that we suspect him of the murder of old Mose. He probably guesses that we have got the transfer from Angus. Any one of those factors should be sufficient to send him scuttling out of this locality as fast as he can go. Why is he waiting? What is he waiting for? If he had hidden yesterday's cargo of gold we might suppose that he is hanging about in order to pick up a second lot before clearing out, but with our own eyes we saw him hand the boxes over. There is something fishy about the whole thing. Talking of gold reminds me that we've still got Mose's "poke" in the machine—the dust Angus handed over to us. We'd better put it somewhere safe pending such time as we can hand it over to the authorities. No doubt they'll find Mose's daughter. I don't feel inclined to tear around at this moment looking for her. We'll tell Delaney about it next time he comes up here.'

'I've got a place where we can hide it,' said Wilks. 'There's a secret cavity under my office floor; I had it specially made for valuables.'

'With McBain and Co. about I think it would be a good thing

if we put it in right away,' declared Biggles.

The small bag of gold was accordingly fetched from the machine and put into Wilks's hiding place. The task done, they returned to the tarmac.

'To get down to brass tacks, what is the next move?' inquired Algy.

'The most important thing is that we now have the transfer.' answered Biggles. 'As far as I can see, there is nothing to stop us from showing it to Delaney, and asking him to order McBain off our property.'

'Yes, I think that is the right procedure,' agreed Wilks.

'Then we'll hang about for a bit to see if Delaney comes along; if he doesn't, then we'll go and find him,' declared Biggles. 'Go and brew a dish of coffee, Ginger. Bring it in the office when it is ready.'

Ginger nodded, got up, and made his way, deep in thought, to the back of the hangar, where the cooking stove had been installed.

The others sat outside the office door, smoking and discussing the situation. They were still waiting for the coffee when, to Biggles's astonishment, Constable Delaney appeared at the entrance to McBain's hangar.

'What do you make of that?' jerked out Algy.

'I wonder how long he has been there,' said Biggles.

'It must have been a long time or we should have seen him go in,' Wilks pointed out.

'I thought everything was very quiet over there,' muttered Biggles suspiciously. 'He's coming over to us now, by the look of it.'

Delaney was, in fact, walking towards the Arctic Airways hangar, followed by McBain and Ferroni.

'What the dickens do *they* want?' growled Algy.

'We shall soon know,' murmured Biggles, rising to his feet to greet the constable. 'Morning, Delaney; looking for something?' he called cheerfully.

Delaney nodded curtly. 'Yes,' he said shortly.

Biggles experienced a twinge of uneasiness. There was

something about the constable's manner he did not like. However, he did not show it. 'Make yourself at home,' he said. 'What can I do for you?'

The constable, carbine across his arm, came to a halt a couple of paces away and regarded the three airmen with an expression of shrewd suspicion. His eyes came to rest on Biggles.

'Were you at Moose Creek yesterday?'

'I was,' replied Biggles frankly. 'Any reason why I shouldn't be?'

'I'll do all the questioning.'

'Go ahead,' invited Biggles cheerfuly.

The constable turned to Wilks. 'Any objection to my searching your outfit?' he inquired. 'I'm searching it, anyway,' he added.

Wilks waved a conscience-free hand. 'Help yourself,' he said. 'Maybe if I was told what you were looking for I could help you.'

'I shan't need any help,' rejoined the constable.

'You've had a look round McBain's outfit for whatever it is you've lost, I presume?' put in Biggles.

Delaney threw him a sidelong glance. 'I have,' he admitted.

'And you didn't find it?'

'No.'

'You won't find it here.'

'You talk like you know what I'm looking for.'

'If I had one guess, and if I hadn't seen the boxes being unloaded on the aerodrome yesterday, I should say it was the Moose Creek parcel of bullion.'

McBain took a quick pace forward. 'What are you suggesting?' he growled.

'Work it out for yourself,' replied Biggles evenly. He turned to Delaney. 'You won't find the Moose Creek gold here,' he said. 'Funny thing,' he went on easily, 'I should have thought that if those boxes had been empty you'd have noticed it.'

'They weren't opened till they got to Edmonton,' returned the constable curtly.

'I see. And what was in them?'

'Lead.'

'Oh!'

'The dust was taken out of those boxes between Moose Creek and Edmonton.'

In a flash Biggles understood the meaning of McBain's detour. The gold had been taken out of the boxes at the cabin, and lead substituted. There was one thing he did not understand, though, and this for the time being remained a mystery.

'I thought the boxes were always *sealed* at Moose Creek?'

'Quite right,' returned the constable. 'When these boxes were taken out of McBain's machine the seals were intact, or I should have noticed it.'

'If the seals were unbroken, then lead, not gold, must have been put into the boxes in the first instance.'

'Any reason why the Moose Creek outfit should send out a parcel of lead?'

'None that I can think of.'

'Nor me.'

'I don't see how or where *we* could have got near it,' protested Biggles.

'You're the only other outfit besides McBain's that was at Moose Creek yesterday—and here. That being so you're under suspicion till the dust's found,' said Delaney firmly.

While he had been speaking he had walked into the office, his keen eyes scrutinizing the walls, floor, and furniture. He came striding towards a cupboard when he stopped dead in his tracks, in the middle of a small rug. He stamped. The boards rang hollow. In a flash he had bent down and whipped the rug aside, disclosing the trap-door of Wilks's secret locker.

'Hello, what's this?' he exclaimed.

Biggles remembered Mose's gold, which had temporarily escaped his memory. He saw their danger instantly, and hastened to try to rectify the oversight, but his very haste was in itself suspicious.

'Oh, yes—I forgot—there is some gold in there,' he said quickly.

Delaney started. His eyes hardened and he reached for his revolver. 'Oh, yeah? Just remembered it, eh?'

'Believe it or not, but that's the truth.'

'A pile o' gold's the sort of thing you easily forget—huh?'

'I was waiting for you to come along to tell you about it,' said Biggles, realizing with dismay how thin the story sounded.

The constable knelt down, lifted the trap aside, put his hand into the aperture and lifted out a heavy doeskin bag. As he stared at it, turning it round and round, his whole manner became tense. Suddenly he tossed the bag on to the table and, whipping out his revolver, covered the three airmen menacingly. 'So that's it, eh?' he snarled. 'You dirty skunks! Stand still.'

'Why, that's the sort of poke old Mose allus used,' cried McBain. 'He allus used doeskin.'

'Yes, and his initials are on it,' grated Delaney. 'Now we know who killed Mose—and why. This isn't the dust I was looking for—but it'll suit me better than the other.'

'Just a minute, Delaney, you've got this all wrong,' protested Biggles desperately. 'Don't jump to conclusions. I know how this must look to you—naturally; but you're making a mistake. I can explain it.'

'you wouldn't have the nerve to suggest that this isn't Mose's poke, I reckon?'

'Of course not. We were going to give it to you to hand over to his next-of-kin—he has a daughter——'

McBain burst into a roar of laughter. 'By thunder, that's a good one! It's your turn to tell one, Delaney.'

The constable's lips were dragged down at the corners. 'So you killed an old man for his poke, did you?' he sneered.

'Angus Stirling gave us that gold yesterday when we told him that Mose was dead,' said Biggles quietly.

'What's this? You trying to tell me that you saw Angus yesterday?'

'I *am* telling you.'

'Oh—shut up. He's on Eskimo Island, and he's froze in.'

'He may be now, but he wasn't yesterday.'

As he spoke Biggles realized with increasing horror just what the fact of Angus being frozen in was likely to mean to them. Not for six months would it be possible to make contact with him. As a witness he might as well not exist. The only scrap of evidence they had in support of their story was the transfer, and even so there was nothing to prove that Angus had given it to them with his own hands.

Delaney jerked his head towards the door. 'Get going,' he said.

'Where to?' asked Biggles.

'You'll see,' was the harsh reply. 'We've got a place for your sort.'

'But——'

'Cut it out. Anything you've got to say you'd better save for the court.'

'Wait a minute. There's another one of 'em,' cried McBain suddenly. 'Where's the kid?'

As if in answer, the Jupiter's engines burst into life.

Delaney cursed and dashed outside, but the big machine was already on the move. 'Stop!' he yelled. Seeing that his words had no effect, he blazed away with his revolver. McBain and Ferroni joining in with theirs.

'You kill that kid and it will be the worst day's work you've ever done!' shouted Biggles furiously. In the swift sequence of events he had forgotten about Ginger and his coffee-making. To his heartfelt relief he saw the Jupiter run across the aerodrome untouched. A faint smile played about the corners of his mouth as he watched it climb into the air. 'You'll have a job to catch him now,' he told Delaney, with savage satisfaction.

The constable whirled round furiously. 'You won't crow so loud presently,' he snapped.

'Nor, I fancy, will you,' replied Biggles, with a good deal more confidence than he felt.

'That's enough. March,' ordered Delaney. 'Any one of you who tries to make a break won't know what hits him.'

16

GINGER ACTS

WHEN Ginger had gone through to the rear of the hangar to make the coffee he had little reason to suspect the desperate events that were soon to follow. As it was, he whistled softly under his breath as he waited for the pot to boil.

There is an old oft-used proverb to the effect that a watched pot never boils and, while this may not be literally true, there is no doubt that whoever first coined the expression had good reason for it. So it was with Ginger. Impatient to return to the others, he was about to pump more pressure into the Primus stove when the sound of voices reached his ears. From the loud and concise tones he realized that visitors had arrived, and unfriendly ones at that. With pardonable curiosity he decided to find out who it was; meanwhile the pot could take its own time to come to the boil.

He did not go round to the front of the office. Had he done so, this story would certainly have ended differently. A few paces from where he stood a small square window allowed light to enter the back of the office, and towards this he made his way.

A description of the scene which met his astonished eyes is unnecessary. He was just in time to hear Delaney accuse Biggles of the murder of the old prospector. And, looking from the tense faces of his friends to the grim countenance of the constable, he realized the desperate nature of the trap into which they had unwittingly fallen. He forgot all about the coffee. The trend of the conversation, which he could hear distinctly, banished everything from his mind except the dire necessity for immediate action. While he had his freedom he might be able to do something. Just what he hoped to achieve he did not know; he had no time to think about it; he only knew that if all four of them were put behind prison bars anything could happen, and for this reason he decided to avoid arrest if this were possible. But how?

On the spur of the moment he could think only of the machine. If he could get it into the air he would be safe—anyway, safer than in any hiding-place on the ground. He lingered only long enough to assure himself that Biggles and the others were, in fact, under arrest; then, dropping everything, he retraced his steps to the rear of the hangar and so reached the machine, which, in accordance with their usual custom, during the hours of daylight, had been left on the tarmac.

Working quietly and methodically, he made his preparations for a swift take-off. He realized that there would be no time to run up the engines; once they were started the noise would bring Delaney out with a rush—as we know was the case.

The whir of the self-starter was the first sound that broke the comparative silence, to be followed almost at once by the choking back-fire of the engines as the propeller jerked into life. With the left wheel braked hard, Ginger slowly opened the throttle. The nose of the big machine swung round until it was facing the open turf. With both wheels free he risked a glance at the office, determined to remain where he was as long as possible in order to reduce the risks of taking off with cold engines; but the sight of Delaney racing towards him settled the matter. Picking a mark on the far side of the aerodrome in order to hold the machine straight, he pushed the throttle wide open. He heard the whang of a bullet somewhere behind him, but he paid no heed to it; indeed, there was nothing he could do now but hold straight on.

His heart missed a beat as the port engine signified its disapproval of this treatment by coughing twice in quick succession; but then it picked up and the Jupiter bored up into the still air.

At a thousand feet he turned, wondering which way to go. Looking down, he could see the little group outside the office staring up at him; watching, he saw Biggles wave, and he derived some comfort from the gesture, for he was by no means sure that he had done the right thing.

Still circling, and climbing steadily for height, he switched his thoughts to the immediate future. Where ought he go? What ought he to do for the best? It occurred to him to go to Edmonton, or some other big town, and there lay the whole story before some important official—if he could find one; but he soon dismissed this plan as too risky. He thought of Angus. If only he could get hold of Angus, and fly him back, the Scotsman's story would confirm their own; then he remembered the snow. He might be able to reach the shack; he might even be able to land without hurting himself or seriously damaging the machine; but once the wheels had sunk into the deep snow no power on earth could get the Jupiter off again. He could see no point in going to Moose Creek, even if the snow had not yet reached there. Canwell would be unable to do anything even if he was willing to come back to Fort Beaver, which did not seem likely. Where else could he go with any hope of finding evidence to bear out the story which he imagined Biggles would tell—the true story?

He remembered the log cabin where the Weinkel had landed on its way down from Moose Creek. Thinking about it, he realized that in some way it was connected with the gang— possibly a hide-away in an emergency should their plans miscarry. It had appeared deserted when last he had seen it. It had this advantage; it was not far away. Provided he could locate it, for he was by no means confident that he could, forty minutes should be ample time for him to reach it. There was just a chance that he might find something there: a clue, perhaps, that would lead to something more important. Anyway, he decided, there was no harm in trying. It was better than submitting quietly to arrest at Fort Beaver.

Satisfied that he was at least doing his best, he swung the Jupiter round until its nose pointed to the north-west, the direction of the cabin.

Looking down, he observed the sterile desolation of the country below and was conscious suddenly of the loneliness. Not without alarm he passed over several patches of fresh snow; however, the sky was fairly clear except to the far north, where a heavy indigo belt of cloud promised more snow in the near future.

He picked up a landmark which he recognized, a diamond-shaped wood, and flew on with more assurance, watching for others. Soon afterwards a silver gleam, almost on the horizon, caught his eye, and presently he made it out to be the lake on a bank of which the log cabin was situated.

Ginger flew on, feeling that it was no use doing anything else; for, if anyone was below, the roar of the Jupiter's engines would make any attempt at concealment futile. He picked out the cabin; it looked pathetically forlorn, he thought, in its lonely surroundings; still, he was relieved to see that there was no sigh of movement near it.

Cutting the engines, he began gliding down, passing, on his way, the higher ground where they had landed while they were trailing the Weinkel. A sleek animal was running low along the edge of the wood. As he got lower he realized it was a wolf. Presently it turned into the timber and was lost to sight. For a moment or two he wondered if it were better to land where they had landed on the previous day, or to go on to where the Weinkel had come on the same occasion. However, there seemed to be no point in giving himself an unnecessary walk, apart from which he did not like the idea of walking about in wolf country. True, he had an automatic in his pocket, but he preferred to avoid using it as long as possible. For these reasons he went on to the cabin, which he was now seeing at close quarters for the first time.

If the cabin was McBain's, and presumably it was, since he had called there, the reason for the selection of the site—apart from its isolation—was at once apparent. On the southern side stretched a wide expanse of open prairie land, large enough for any type of aeroplane to land on in any sort of weather. He noted this subconsciously as he lowered his wheels and glided towards it; actually, he was more than a little concerned with putting the machine down safely, for a broken undercarriage at this stage was the very last thing he wanted.

With his nerves braced with anxiety he flattened out for the landing; but he need not have worried: the wheels rumbled for a moment, the tail dropped, and the machine came to rest about a hundred yards from the cabin, which he now saw was an almost new, well-constructed building.

He did not bother to taxi up to it. There was no real need to do so. Switching off the engines, he glanced round to make sure that everything was in order, then he opened the door and jumped out. For a moment or two he stood watching the building keenly, feeling certain that if anyone had been there he would by this time have shown himself. However, as there was no sign of life, he started walking briskly towards it.

He was still about twenty yards away when a sudden noise pulled him up short. He stood quite still, his eyes running over the building, seeking the cause of the sound, which was very slight, and like the creaking of a tight door or a window being opened. Seeing nothing, he concluded that the sound—if, indeed, he had actually heard anything—was a natural one, such as a piece of loose board giving way, or two branches rubbing together in the belt of fir which began just beyond the hut and skirted the northern edge of the lake.

He was about to move forward again when a shadow flitted across the one window that faced in his direction. This time he knew that there was no mistake; someone was in the cabin. And an instant later all doubt was removed when the light flashed on the window as it was opened. He had no time to think. Regretting his rashness, he looked swiftly around for cover, for the furtive manner in which the window had been opened was at once suggestive of danger; but there was nothing, not even a bush behind which he might hide.

He opened his mouth to call a greeting—but the sound did not reach his lips. Still staring at the window, he saw something emerging; a split second later he realized what it was—a rifle barrel. He braced his muscles to jump aside, but such movement as he made was still little more than an impulse when the rifle cracked. For a brief instant he swayed on his feet. Then he crashed forward on his face and lay still.

The cabin door was thrown open and an Indian, a smoking rifle in his hands and a leer of triumph on his face, strode towards the motionless figure with cat-like tread. A few paces away he halted and looked carefully around, presumably to make sure that there had been no witness of what had transpired; then, as if satisfied that all was well, he leaned his rifle against a tree stump, and drawing a short curved knife from his belt, advanced confidently towards his victim, who was still lying as he had fallen. With his lips parted in a savage smile, the Indian bent over Ginger.

17
A NEW PERIL

WHILE these events were in progress, Biggles and his two companions had been marched by Delaney towards Fort Beaver. It was a grim journey. Algy raged. Wilks strode along, glowering his annoyance. Biggles was irritated, but endeavoured to preserve a calm front. The fact of the matter was, not one of them realized the real seriousness of their position. They were angry at being taken to the jail like common felons, but this, at the worst, would only be temporary. It had not yet occurred to them that they might not be able to prove their innocence of the crime for which they had been arrested. Nor did they imagine it possible that they would be tried by any but an official court of law.

Approaching Fort Beaver, McBain hurried on ahead. Biggles attached no special significance to this at the time, but before very long he realized what the man's purpose had been. Except for this, things might have turned out differently.

The first indication of McBain's errand—although this was not made apparent until some minutes later—occurred while the prisoners were still some distance from the town. Several men appeared, hurrying towards them in a manner that was definitely hostile, if not openly threatening. Muttering and casting malevolent glances at the prisoners, they joined the party. Others appeared, with a sprinkling of slatternly-looking women amongst them. At first vague murmurings were heard; then insults and imprecations were thrown at the three airmen.

Accustomed to civilized administration of justice, Biggles was amazed. He had not supposed that they would be condemned without a fair trial. He noticed that Delaney looked worried, and remarked on it.

'You keep close to me; I don't like the look of things,' said the constable. 'I'd turn back if it wasn't too late. If this crowd decides to take things into their own hands you won't stand a dog's chance. I don't know what's set 'em off like this.'

'McBain, probably,' replied Biggles, suddenly understanding, for he could see the man deliberately egging the crowd on to take the law into their own hands.

Yells, and not a few curses, reached the prisoners' ears. Presently a stone was thrown.

Algy looked at Biggles with startled eyes. 'I don't like the look of this,' he said anxiously. 'Delaney shouldn't have brought us here knowing that the crowd might behave like this.'

'He didn't know. McBain is responsible.'

'The sooner we are under lock and key, the better I shall be pleased,' declared Algy. 'Things look ugly.'

More and more men were hurrying out from the village to meet them and the noise swelled in volume. Above the medley of sound, odd phrases would be heard.

'String 'em up, the dirty murderers!' yelled an old man with a ferocious expression. 'String 'em up like we did in the old days.'

'Murdered Mose for his poke. Hand 'em over, Delaney,' roared another.

'A rope. Fetch a rope, somebody.'

'Hoist 'em up.'

'Old Mose once did me a good turn; now I'll do him one.'

'Hang 'em, hang 'em! Hang 'em!'

These were typical of the threats hurled at the three airmen by the crowd as it surged round them and their escort.

'That's it, hang 'em!' roared McBain.

Delaney halted and held up his hand for silence, but the gesture produced little or no effect. 'Get back to your work, all of you!' he bellowed. 'If this is a hanging job the right people will look after it.'

Those who heard the words only redoubled their demands for the prisoners to be handed over to them.

Delaney was past the stage of being worried. His face was pale and his manner distraught; it became increasingly clear that the situation was beyond his authority or ability to control. 'I can't do nothing with 'em,' he told Biggles hoarsely.

'You've got a rifle, man; why don't you use it? The law's on your side,' Biggles pointed out harshly. Inwardly he was disgusted at the revolting exhibition of hysteria which the cunning McBain had been able to foster.

'They'd tear me to bits if I so much as fired a shot into the air,' yelled Delaney above the uproar.

'I suppose it doesn't matter what they do to us?' sneered Biggles.

A stone was thrown. As it happened it was Delaney that it struck. It caught him on the temple, making an ugly wound. At the sight of the blood the noise died down for a moment, and the constable seized the opportunity provided by the lull to voice another protest. 'What's gone wrong with you?' he shouted furiously. 'What's the idea? Would you hang a man without a fair trial?'

'Yes!' bellowed a red-headed miner. 'Give 'em a trial and the lawyers will help 'em to dodge the noose. We've seen it happen before. Old Mose made his home in Fort Beaver; then it's up to us in Fort Beaver to see justice done.'

'Hear, hear! Hurrah!' shouted the crowd. 'They killed Mose.'

'Who said they killed Mose?' roared Delaney. The stone seemed to have stung him into action.

'Brindle McBain says so,' screeched a woman.

'He seems mighty anxious to get 'em hanged,' answered Delaney. 'It strikes me that he's a sight *too* anxious. Maybe he's got a reason.'

All eyes turned to McBain who, for a moment, looked uncomfortable. 'If they didn't do it, why did you arrest 'em?' he demanded shrewdly.

This was a poser the unfortunate constable found it difficult to answer, a matter which the crowd was not slow in observing.

'Come on, boys. String 'em up!' yelled McBain. 'They'll get off else.'

'You've got one chance; it's a poor one, but I'll try to bring it off,' Delaney told the airmen through set teeth. 'We've got to humour them. Anything so long as we can cause a delay. Maybe later on they'll come to their senses.' He faced the crowd, hands aloft. 'All right,' he shouted. 'If they killed Mose then they'll hang, but I ain't standing for murder. Let's take 'em down to the Three Star and hear what they have to say.'

McBain objected, declaring that this suggestion was only a trick to get the airmen away. A discussion followed and in the end McBain was over-ruled. Possibly the blood on the constable's face had sobered the crowd somewhat. If Delaney had been struck, it was not likely that the whole affair would be allowed to pass without someone being called to account when the chief constable of the area arrived—as he certainly would, sooner or later. Possibly Delaney's aggressive attitude had something to do with it. Be that as it may, the crowd, still grimly demanding the prisoners' lives, quietened down somewhat, and the procession moved off in some sort of order towards the Three Star Saloon.

Another delay occurred at the entrance, where the proprietor, fearful, no doubt, of damage to his property, endeavoured to keep the crowd out. But once a number of people get out of hand they seem to lend each other a sort of false courage to do what in normal circumstances they would not dare do. The door of the saloon was forced open and the crowd surged inside like a wave rushing through a breach in a sea wall. The proprietor took up his position behind the bar, revolver in hand, to prevent looting. He threatened to shoot the first man who attempted to touch a bottle without first paying for it, and from his manner he meant it. Delaney got up on the bar itself, made the prisoners line up under him, facing outwards, and from this commanding position, supported by his carbine, he called the crowd to order. Satisfied, perhaps, that it was now getting its own way, the uproar subsided, and presently a comparative silence fell. McBain and Ferroni, smugly complacent, pushed their way to the front near the prisoners. McBain bit the end off a cigar, spat the end away, and lighted it.

'Make it short and sweet,' he demanded.

'One more word from you, McBain, and I'll put you under arrest, too,' snapped the constable.

'Yeah?' drawled McBain. 'For what?'

'For inciting a crowd to riot.'

McBain laughed as if this was a huge joke, and such was the power of his personality that the crowd laughed with him. He blew a cloud of smoke in the direction of the prisoners. 'How are you going to try 'em—all together or one at a time?' he questioned. 'Not that it makes much difference,' he added casually.

'You can leave that to me,' replied Delaney crisply. 'I'll say my piece first—but I want you all to know that this isn't a legal——'

'Cut out the legal stuff,' shouted a young farmer. 'We want the man—or the men—who killed poor old Mose, and we're going to have him. And when we're satisfied that we've got him we're going to *hang* him. Am I right, folks?'

A roar of approval greeted these words.

Delaney held up his right hand. 'All right,' he said. 'I'll start. First of all, most of you know by now that a packet of gold has been stolen in transit between Moose Creek and Edmonton. Brindle McBain and his pilot flew the gold down, and I saw him hand the boxes over with my own eyes. What was inside those boxes I'm not prepared to swear because my eyes can't see through half-inch timber. But I'll swear this: the seals what was put on each box at Moose Creek hadn't been broken.'

'What's all this got to do with Mose?' drawled McBain in a bored voice.

'Yes, let's stick to the business,' muttered several others.

'I'm coming to that,' announced Delaney. 'I was asked to locate the metal, so I started by inquiring at the aerodrome. First I searched McBain's outfit, where I found nothing. I then went on to Arctic Airways outfit where I found more than I bargained for. I found, hid under the floor, six bags of gold-dust, done up as a single poke, them bags being the same as we all know Mose made for to carry his dust in. His initials was burnt on to the hide to prove that they was his. Mose must have struck it rich. I didn't know he had such a poke; he didn't say nothing about it when he was here a week or so ago; but it seems as if somebody else must have known. We all know Mose was murdered, and how he was murdered—now we know *why* he was murdered.'

'That's where you're wrong, Delaney,' put in Biggles quietly.

'I can't think of no better reason for killing a man than a heavy poke,' snapped the constable.

From the chorus of jeers that broke out it was evident that the crowd thought the same.

'On the strength of that poke I arrested every one in the outfit where it was found,' continued Delaney. 'And unless the prisoners can explain how they came to be hiding a murdered man's poke, particularly as at least one of 'em was with Mose on the night he was killed, then I reckon any court would find 'em guilty. This ain't a properly constituted court and nobody here has any right to take the law into his own hands. These prisoners will have a proper trial, but, as I say, unless they can prove that Mose *gave* 'em his poke—which I doubt—then they'll hang.'

On a point of law Delaney was, of course, incorrect, but none of the airmen thought it worthwhile to argue. They knew as well as anyone how damning the evidence was, and Biggles, for one, could not find it in his heart to blame the crowd for its line of thought.

'It is one of the privileges of British justice,' he said loudly, 'that no man is condemned without being allowed to make a statement in his own defence.'

'I reckons we've heard enough,' sneered McBain.

'You shut your face, McBain,' cried Delaney angrily. Then to Biggles: 'Speak up,' he cried. 'You'd better get up here where everyone can see you.'

Biggles climbed up on the bar and faced the sea of scowling faces in front of him. Perhaps it was his quiet manner, or the steadiness of his eyes, that had some effect on the crowd. A hush fell.

'First of all,' he began, 'let me say that I don't blame any one of you for feeling as you do, or for thinking as you do. Were I amongst you, and another man was standing where I am now, faced with such evidence as has been given by Constable Delaney, I should say "that man killed old Mose for his poke". But I should be wrong.'

The expressions on the faces of some of his hearers changed, suggesting that the words had had the desired effect. Biggles noticed it. Delaney noticed it, and breathed a sigh of relief, realizing that if once the hot indignation of the crowd could be calmed they would be more likely to listen to reason and allow the law to take its course in the usual way.

But another man had noticed it too—McBain. And he perceived, apparently, that if Biggles were allowed to continue, his plans for the swift and easy disposal of his enemies might even yet fail.

'Don't take any notice of him,' he sneered. 'He reckons we're a lot of suckers. Let him talk and he'll put one over. Come on, boys, we're wasting time. We know he killed Mose, and he ain't goin' to get away with it.'

'Cut the gas!' snapped Delaney, but his words were drowned in a fresh uproar started by the more headstrong elements of the crowd. The cry went up, 'Lynch 'em!' and it was echoed on all sides. The mob surged forward towards the prisoners.

'Stand back!' The bar-keeper was on the counter, the muzzle of his heavy revolver threatening the upturned faces below. 'You'd better get 'em down to the jail, Delaney,' he said in a swift aside. 'I'll hold this rabble. Go the back way.'

Biggles and the others did not know it, but the proprietor of the Three Star was a retired sergeant of the 'mounties', which no doubt accounted for his partisanship on the side of the law. The habits of twenty years are not easily cast aside.

Delaney looked at the now clamouring crowd, and what he saw convinced him of the futility of further argument. He turned to Biggles. 'If we don't make the jail they'll hang you, and I shan't be able to stop them. Follow me. If you try to get away I'll plug you.'

Algy and Wilks, now pressed by the crowd, climbed up on to the counter. Instantly there was a yell of 'Stop 'em', and a shot was fired from somewhere in the rear of the mob. The bar-keeper's left arm fell limply to his side. Without a word he blazed back at the man who had shot him. The red-headed miner collapsed in a heap on the floor. Pandemonium followed. A revolver barked again and the bar-keeper pitched head first into the crowd. Delaney, white with fury, shot the man who had fired. He waited for no more. 'Come on,' he yelled, and dashed to the rear of the bar, followed closely by the prisoners.

There was a brief respite as they dashed pell-mell out of the back door of the saloon, for most of the crowd was inside, and those who had run out of the front door had not yet had time to get round to the rear.

'The jail is our only chance,' snapped Delaney. 'If we can get inside we may be able to hold it. This way.'

They dashed down the rear of some frame buildings and cut back into the main street of the village, just as the crowd surged into sight round the end of the saloon. Several shots were fired, but they went wide, flecking up the earth or ripping splinters from the wooden buildings.

The constable and his prisoners did not stop. With Delaney leading, they raced towards a heavily built log cabin which stood in the middle of the track facing the direction from which they had come. A single iron-barred window plainly announced its purpose.

Delaney was feeling in his pocket for the key even before they reached it. He was fumbling with the lock as the crowd, led by McBain, poured into sight. McBain fired, and a bullet thudded into the logs. Biggles fired four quick shots over the heads of the crowd, and while it did not stop their progress, it delayed the leaders long enough for the constable to get the door open.

They all rushed inside, Delaney slamming the massive door behind them and locking it.

'Where did you get that gun?' he asked angrily.

'It was the bar-keeper's,' answered Biggles simply.

The constable did not pursue the subject. He closed two shutters on the window and bolted them, but a dim light still came through the numerous cracks in them.

'Well, we've made it,' he said moodily, 'but I don't know what good it's going to do us. We can't hold it for ever. McBain's got that crowd into a good enough state for anything.'

'Well, at least it gives us breathing space,' replied Biggles, looking round the single large room which comprised the jail. 'I reckon we've got one chance left.'

'What's that?'

'Ginger.'

'You mean that kid who got away in the 'plane?'

'That's right.'

Algy looked up. 'Gosh! I'd forgotten all about him,' he confessed. 'What can he do, do you suppose?'

Biggles shrugged his shoulders. 'Goodness knows. But he'll do something, you can bet your life on that. By the way, I wonder what became of Smyth? He must have seen Delaney marching us towards the village, and guessing what had happened, found some place to hide. He'll take care of himself. I'm more worried about Ginger. I should like to know what he's doing at this moment.'

18

TRAPPED!

'WELL, whatever it is he's doing, he'll have to be quick about it,' remarked Delaney coldly.

'You think the crowd will attack us here—in a Government building?' asked Biggles.

A bullet thudded against the side of the cabin; a splinter of wood jerked out into the room.

'There's your answer,' said Delaney.

From a safe place Biggles looked through the barred window at the sky, now pink-flushed with the approach of sunset. He could not imagine what Ginger was doing or where he had gone, but as Delaney had said, if he was coming back he would have to be quick, if for no other reason than that it would soon be dark.

Biggles looked back at the constable. 'Curious situation, isn't it?' he observed. 'Are we allowed to defend ourselves? I mean, if we kill anyone in defending our lives, are we liable to be charged with murder?'

'Not while I'm here, I reckon,' relied Delaney dubiously, as though he was not quite sure himself. 'It's McBain who is causing the trouble; but for him I think the others would clear off.'

'Why don't you go out and arrest him?' suggested Biggles.

The constable started. 'That's an idea,' he confessed.

'They're not likely to shoot *you*,' urged Biggles.

'Maybe not, but they're likely to shoot you if I open this door,' returned Delaney grimly.

He ducked as a stone whirled through the window. It struck the opposite wall with a crash, and fell to the floor. They all looked at the missile and observed at once that there was something unusual about it. Biggles picked up. 'Hello,' he said, 'this looks like a message.'

A piece of paper had, in fact, been tied to the stone with a piece of string.

Delaney, asserting his authority, took it out of Biggles's hands, unfolded it, and, in the fast waning light, read something that had been written on it.

'What is it?' asked Algy, unable to restrain his curiosity.

'It's from that fellow of yours—Smyth,' said Delaney. 'He says he's found and saddled my mare and is going to Blackfoot Point for help. . . . There's an officer and four troopers there,' he added, by way of explanation. 'Somebody in the crowd must have given him the tip.'

'How far away is this place?' asked Biggles.

'Twenty miles—a bit over.'

'Well, that's a hope, anyway; but twenty miles—it means that if Smyth gets there we couldn't expect help much before dawn.'

'And I reckon that'll be about six hours too late,' returned Delaney. 'What are they up to outside?'

There was little need to ask. While the foregoing conversation had been taking place the crowd had surged round the jail, and the demands for the prisoners had reached an alarming pitch of frenzy. 'We want the men who killed Mose' was the gist of the cries.

'Bring 'em out, Delaney, or we'll tear the jail down,' yelled a strident voice.

'This is Government property and I'll plug the first man who lays hands on it,' roared the constable. 'Go home, the lot of you.'

'Not till we've hung the murderers,' was the reply.

'You won't come in here while I'm on my feet,' declared Delaney wrathfully.

The crash of another bullet against the door was the answer.

'Look here, Delaney, you'd better go,' suggested Biggles. 'There's no sense in your getting killed from a mistaken idea of duty. Leave us to it. We'll hold 'em off as long as we can.'

'The Force has never lost a prisoner yet and I ain't going to be the first,' was the curt rejoinder.

'Get a log, somebody,' came from outside. 'Bring a log, and we'll soon have the door down.'

The words were taken up on all sides. 'A log—a log.' McBain's voice could also be heard demanding torches.

By this time it was quite dark, so the need for some illumination was easily understood.

'Well, I'm afraid it means bloodshed,' said Delaney regretfully. He took up a position beside the window and waited.

'Here they come with a tree,' he answered presently, and levelling his revolver, fired two shots.

There came a yell from outside. The two shots were answered by a dozen, and Delaney staggered back, clutching at his shoulder.

'Have they hit you?' cried Biggles anxiously.

'Got me through the shoulder,' snarled the constable, leaning back against the wall.

Biggles went to the window, shouted out that the constable had been hit, and demanded a truce while bandages were fetched.

A howl of execration was the reply, and he ducked back just in time to escape a fusillade.

'Their blood's up,' groaned Delaney. 'Nothing will stop 'em now. I know. I've seen this sort of thing before.'

'Maybe we'd better surrender,' suggested Biggles. 'I don't like this idea of you losing your life to save us.'

'I've never lost a prisoner yet, and I ain't starting now,' returned Delaney obstinately.

Biggles shrugged his shoulders.

A moment later the building shook as a heavy weight struck the door with a crash.

Delaney cursed, and snatching up his revolver with his left hand, emptied it into the middle of the rough-hewn pine logs from which the door was made.

The shots were followed by a sudden silence.

'They've killed Fred,' said a voice charged with passion. Instantly such a yell arose as made the others weak by comparison. Again the building shook as the attack on the door was resumed.

Biggles's jaw set. Revolver in hand, he crept to the window and peeped out, hoping to see the man who had been responsible for the riot. But if McBain was there he was too wise to show himself. Four men were just lifting the heavy log which was being used as a battering-ram. The eyes of the spectators were on them. Biggles took careful aim at the nearest man's arm and pulled the trigger. The man staggered, and released his hold on the log, which fell on the feet of the next man to him. Again Biggles fired, shooting at the legs of the other three. Another man fell, and there was a general dash for cover. Biggles jumped aside as the answering shots came, and coughed as the acrid smell of cordite drifted back into the room.

Several times as the night wore on the attack was resumed, but on each occasion it was beaten off by the defenders.

'With luck we shall just last one more attack,' announced Delaney during a pause.

'How so?' asked Biggles.

'I've only one cartridge left.'

'And I've none. My gun's empty,' said Biggles quietly, tossing the now useless weapon on the floor.

'What do you reckon the time is?' asked Wilks, who had spent most of the night leaning against the wall smoking, since there was nothing he could do.

'Can't be far short of dawn,' said Delaney. 'I wonder what they're up to out there. They seem to be sort of quiet.'

'We shall soon know, I fancy,' replied Biggles, as the sound of stealthy footsteps, accompanied by furtive muttering and whispering, came from outside.

There came a sudden rush, and then again silence.

An orange light flickered on the window frame, faint at first, but growing rapidly brighter. A crisp crackling told the defenders the worst.

'They've set the place on fire,' gasped Biggles.

'That's the end of it, then,' announced Algy calmly. 'Either we go out or we stay here and fry.'

'Of the two I prefer to go out,' said Biggles.

'And me,' nodded Wilks.

Delaney swore soundly, but it did no good. Smoke oozed under the door and eddied in through the window. Presently they were all coughing.

Delaney went over to the door. 'I'm sorry,' he said, 'but I can't do any more. If you can save yourselves, do it, but if you should get clear give yourselves up at the nearest police post. I shall be after you again, else.'

Biggles nodded. 'We're ready to stand our trial when the time comes,' he said. 'But I'm afraid the crowd thinks otherwise. Come on. Let's get it over.'

Smoke and flames poured into the room as Delaney threw open the door against which faggots had been piled. A yell went up.

'I'll go first,' said the constable, and took a running jump over the blazing faggots.

Biggles followed. Almost before his feet touched the ground on the far side of the fire many hands had seized him and borne him to the ground, where, helpless, his wrists were tied behind his back. He was then dragged to his feet and marched off.

The same fate befell the others, and presently the three of them were assembled in the middle of a jubilant throng. Only the constable had not had his wrists tied together. He remained with his prisoners, protesting in the strongest possible terms at the crowd's behaviour, but he might as well have saved his breath for all the effect the words had. The crowd had nothing against him, so beyond a certain amount of horse-play he was left alone.

A shout went up for ropes, which were soon produced, whereupon a move was made up the main street, the crowd surging along with the prisoners in its centre.

'Where are we going?' Biggles asked Delaney, who was walking beside him.

'There ain't no sense in telling you lies,' answered the constable. 'There's a tree up on the top there, on the way to the aerodrome, with a convenient branch.'

'Thanks,' replied Biggles, not without bitterness.

The eastern sky had already been grey with the approach of dawn when they had evacuated the jail; by the time they reached the tree—which was, in fact, near the edge of the aerodrome—it was comparatively light.

The prisoners were led under a branch, which projected at right-angles from the trunk. Three ropes, with nooses already made, were thrown over it.

'It's hard to believe that this is really happening, isn't it?' said Algy, looking at the tree and then at the eager crowd in a dazed sort of way.

'It is,' agreed Biggles.

'Silly sort of way to die,' complained Algy.

'And all my fault for bringing you out here,' muttered Wilks, in a voice heavy with remorse.

'Rot!' said Biggles. 'You've nothing to blame yourself for. It's just a bit of luck that nobody could have foreseen. My greatest regret is that that hound McBain looks like getting away with it.'

'No use trying to get the crowd to listen to us, I suppose?' suggested Algy without enthusiasm.

'Not the slightest,' returned Biggles. 'I should have tried it had there been any hope of them listening, you may be sure. Look at 'em. They won't even listen to Delaney, who most of 'em must have known for years. No, I don't usually give up easily, but I must confess that there seems to be no way out of this pickle.'

A noose was slipped round his neck. Turning, he watched the others being treated in the same way, regardless of Delaney's frantic expostulations.

'Keep your eyes on McBain, Delaney,' called Biggles loudly. 'He's the man who murdered Mose.' Then, quietly to the others, 'Poor old Ginger. Looks as if he's not coming back after all.'

19
A LIFE OR DEATH STRUGGLE

WHEN Ginger had fallen outside the remote cabin he had not been killed. He had not even been hit by the shot which had been fired at him. He felt the whistle of the bullet as it passed his cheek, and the shock had caused him to stumble. And even as he stumbled he realized with a lightning flash of inspiration that the moment he recovered himself he would be a mark for a second shot. So he dived headlong to the ground.

This was, primarily, an act of pure self-preservation, for in this position he offered a smaller target than in any other, and he was well aware of it. In moments of extreme peril the brain often works faster than at any other time, and hard upon Ginger's first thought came another, the recollection of a trick that is as old as the hills. Men have practised it from the beginning of time. Animals still practise it—some regularly. Indeed, after one of them has the ruse been named—playing 'possum. In short, Ginger feigned death hoping that the man who had fired at him would be deceived and might give the pretended corpse a chance to turn the tables.

Lying absolutely still on the turf, Ginger heard the cabin door open, heard someone emerge and walk towards him. It was a nasty moment, and it required all his fortitude to remain as he was, because, for all he knew, the man was even then sighting his rifle to make sure of his work. It was not to be wondered at that Ginger's scalp tingled—almost as if it was conscious of what was about to happen to it.

The grass rustled as the unseen man approached. There was a momentary pause, then a hand closed over the back of Ginger's head, and he knew it was time to move.

With a grunt he sprang to his feet, looking wildly for his attacker, and saw a man whom he recognized at once—the Indian member of McBain's gang.

With the scalping knife in his hand, the Indian had instinctively started back at Ginger's unexpected return to life; but the withdrawal was only momentary; with his smile of victory replaced by a snarl of disappointment and anger, he leapt forward again to attack.

But the brief respite had given Ginger a chance to get his balance. His right hand flew to his pocket and came up grasping his automatic, but before he could pull the trigger the Indian, with a lightning sweep of his left arm, had knocked the weapon aside so that the bullet crashed into the end of the cabin. What was more, the blow knocked the automatic clean out of Ginger's hand; it described a short flight through the air and came to rest on the turf some ten yards or more away.

Ginger did not attempt to run, for he knew that the fleet-footed Redskin would quickly overtake him. In desperation, he leapt forward to seize the arm that held the knife; he did this before the Indian had time to recover fully from the blow he had struck at the automatic, with the result that they both went down with a crash, Ginger falling across the arm which he had seized so that the knife was not six inches from his face. To prise the weapon from the Indian's hand would be, he knew, beyond his strength, so he resorted to a method which he once saw employed during a fight between two drunken miners. He used his teeth. Taking the bones in the back of the brown hand between his jaws, he bit with all his strength. Under the excruciating agony the Indian let out a scream, and the hand jerked open convulsively. But before Ginger could possess himself of the knife, the Indian, with a tremendous effort, flung himself sideways, with the result that they both rolled over away from the weapon.

Both were now disarmed, but of the two the Indian was the

heavier and Ginger knew that in the end this must tell against him. The automatic was his only chance. Somehow he must reach it, although, having by this time rolled over several times, he was by no means sure of its exact whereabouts. Meanwhile, all his strength was needed to keep the Indian's hands from his throat.

For perhaps a minute the struggle continued without marked advantage on either side. Sometimes the Indian was on top, and sometimes Ginger, who, knowing what his fate would be if he weakened, was now fighting with the fury of despair. He managed to get on top again, but before he could break free and make a dash for the automatic the Indian had flung him off again, this time with such force that he rolled some distance away. He was brought up by a stone against which he struck his head with a force that made him gasp. Yet even in his sorry plight he had the wit to realize that it was a stone, and that a stone can be a useful weapon in emergency.

By the time his wildly groping hand had found and closed over the stone, the Indian was more than half-way towards him, so slightly raising himself, he flung the missile with every ounce of his fast-waning strength, and then twisted sideways.

The stone caught the Redskin full in the mouth, producing an animal snarl of rage and pulling him up short, spitting blood. For a brief moment his sombre eyes blazed into Ginger's; then they went beyond him, and he darted forward.

Ginger was on his feet in an instant, and it took him not more than a split second to see what his adversary was after. It was the rifle which had been left against the tree stump, and which Ginger now saw for the first time. To reach the weapon first was obviously impossible. Frantically his eyes scanned the short turf, seeking the automatic. He saw it, made a rush for it, and reached it at the precise moment that the Indian grabbed the rifle. Both weapons came up together and two reports rang out, one following the other so closely that the sounds blended. But Ginger's shot had been fired first, by an interval of time so short as to be immeasurable. But it was enough.

Where the rifle bullet went Ginger did not know. It had not hit him, and that was all that concerned him. He was staring at the Indian, whose behaviour was unlike anything he had ever seen before. At Ginger's shot he had appeared to throw the weapon up into the air before taking several running steps backward, then he fell and finished up flat on his back.

Ginger, gasping for breath, concluded, not unnaturally, that he had killed the man. Reeling with exhaustion, he took a pace towards him, whereupon to his amazement and dismay the Indian sprang to his feet and dashed away.

Ginger was in no mood to let the man get away; he represented too big a danger. Jerking up his weapon, he let drive at the running form, and missed. At least, the Indian continued runing; furthermore, as he ran he twisted and turned in a manner that made shooting almost a waste of powder. Three times Ginger fired without any of the shots taking the slightest effect, and by that time the Redskin was out of effective pistol range. Still running, he disappeared from sight in the belt of timber that skirted the water's edge.

With a grunt of mortification Ginger dropped the muzzle of the automatic and walked across to where the rifle was lying; on picking it up he perceived the cause of the Indian's strange behaviour. His—that is, Ginger's—first shot had not hit the man; it had hit the rifle. By a strange chance the bullet had struck the trigger-guard, and the force of the impact had, of course, knocked the weapon from the man's hands. Also, it must have spoilt his shot. Considering the matter, Ginger could not make up his mind who was the luckier—he or the Indian.

Looking at the sky he saw that the day was fast drawing to a close, so he made his way towards the open door of the cabin in order to pursue the quest that had brought him to the spot.

He did not intend to stay long. The surprise of his encounter with the Indian had left him not a little shaken; moreover, he was rather worried for fear the Indian would find some means of turning the tables on him; he saw that it was going to be difficult to search the cabin thoroughly and at the same time keep a close watch on the trees in which the Redskin had disappeared. To make matters worse, the light was failing. It would soon be dark, and the possibility of his being benighted in the cabin had not previously entered into his calculations. He still hoped to avoid it, particularly as the Indian was at large. Standing the rifle against the door, ready for action should it be needed, he looked around.

The first thing he saw was a fur coat hanging from a peg on the opposite wall. Its presence gave him something of a turn, for he recognized it at once from its unmistakable white blaze. It was McBain's. He had worn it, he recalled, on the night of the murder of old Mose. What it was doing there he did not know, but it seemed evident that McBain had either left it behind by accident or else he had lent it to the Indian—probably the latter. Anyway, he reflected, its presence proved, if proof were needed, that McBain was closely concerned with the cabin even if he did not actually own it.

A preliminary examination of such objects as were in view revealed nothing more of particular interest. There were a few pieces of furniture, mostly home-made, and of the roughest possible character. A packing case, on which were strewn some odds and ends of food, served for a table. Two chairs, a bench, an iron stove of the covered-in variety, a heap of firewood, a lamp of the hurricane type, a small pyramid of stores—that was all.

In the ordinary way Ginger would have looked no further, for there was nothing suspicious about such articles; indeed, they were more normal camp equipment, and it would have been more surprising had they not been there; but two circumstances combined to make him feel sure that there was more in the cabin than met the eye. In the first place, why had McBain's machine landed there when there was every reason to suppose that it had the gold on board? Secondly, why had the Indian been left there? McBain was not the sort of man who would do anything without a good reason, certainly not when he was in the middle of a carefully prepared scheme. The presence of the Indian indicated that there was something in the cabin that needed guarding, and, in the circumstances, what could be more likely than that it was the gold?

Satisfied that his reasoning was correct, Ginger broke off in his ruminating and looked steadily in the direction of the trees, but there was no sign of the Indian, so without further loss of time he proceeded with the search. If the gold was there, then he would not rest until he had found it, he decided.

There was no question of there being a concealed cavity in the walls, for they were of solid tree-trunks set one above the other in single thickness. The roof was of split pine, through which daylight showed in many places, and clearly offered no hiding-place. There remained only the floor, and this, as far as it was visible, was solid enough.

Ginger regarded the heap of firewood reflectively. 'If the gold is here it is under this pile,' he told himself confidently as he began dragging the branches aside. It took him some time to get down to floor level, for he was still rather worried about the Indian, and he broke off from his task several times to study the landscape. However, at last he pushed the remaining few branches aside and dropped on his hands and knees, feeling for the trap door which he felt certain was there. He could hardly believe it when he discovered that nothing of the sort was there. Again and again he examined the floor inch by inch, but in the end he was compelled to admit to himself that he had been mistaken. The floor at that point was as solid as the rest.

Half sick with disappointment, he stood up and stared down at the spot as though he still found the obvious truth difficult to believe. If the gold was not there, he thought with fast sinking hopes, then it must be buried somewhere outside, in which case he would be very lucky indeed if he found it. It might be anywhere within a hundred yards, which meant that he might dig for a week, or even a month, without striking the spot. The more he thought about it the more depressed he became. It was infuriating to be so near and yet so far, for he was still convinced that the gold was there. He began to hate the sound of the word.

Remembering the Indian, he crossed again to the window and looked out over the darkening landscape. Somewhere out there was the Indian, he mused, unless he had started off on foot for Fort Beaver to warn the others of what had happened, which did not seem likely.

He started as a thought flashed into his mind. The Indian! He would know where the gold was hidden. What a pity he had got away; otherwise he would have made him divulge the hiding-place. Perhaps he was not far away—perhaps—Ginger caught his breath as the idea took root. 'It's my only chance,' he muttered. 'I've got to find that blighter. I've got his rifle, so it shouldn't be very difficult.'

Three swift strides took him to the door, where he had left the rifle. He put his hand out for it, confidently, only to draw back with a little gasp of amazement. He stopped, staring at the place where it had been—where he was certain he had put it. But it was no longer there.

20

LOST

GINGER's first sensation on discovering his loss was one of utter amazement. He was incredulous. It was followed by one of doubt. In his mind he was absolutely certain that he had leaned the rifle against the doorpost. True, he had performed the action subconsciously, for at the time his thoughts were concentrated on the interior of the cabin; but, nevertheless, casting his mind back—as one often can in such circumstances—he had a clear recollection of standing the weapon against the doorpost as he surveyed the interior of the room. Was it possible that he had been mistaken? Had he, without thinking what he was doing, moved it again afterwards? He could not remember doing so, but it was just possible. With a frown of perplexity lining his forehead, he looked at all the likely places in turn—the walls, the table, and even the stove. But there was no sign of the rifle.

As he stared, almost bewildered, vaguely into his mind came stories he had read of the stealth with which an Indian could move; skill in the art of self-effacement, born of a thousand years of inter-tribal warfare, had been the theme of many of the stories he had read in his not-very-distant school-days. Without giving the matter serious thought, he had always regarded this alleged cunning with a certain amount of scepticism. It made good reading, but that did not necessarily mean that it was true. It now began to look as if it were. Somehow the Indian must have crept up to the cabin and recovered the rifle. There was no other explanation.

For nearly a minute Ginger stood still, deep in thought, conscious that the loss of the weapon completely altered the circumstances. It meant that he would have to abandon his recently formed plan, for to go out into country which he did not know, armed only wih a pistol, to look for a man who probably knew every inch of the ground, and was, moreover, in possession of.a rifle, would be sheer lunacy. Still pondering, he became aware that it meant a good deal more than that. If the Indian was still in the vicinity, which seemed most likely, the chances were that he would remain as near to the cabin as possible, covering the door, waiting for him—Ginger—to step outside. With a fresh twinge of alarm, he perceived that he would not be able to get back to the machine without running the gauntlet of the Indian's fire.

Reproaching himself bitterly for his carelessness, he looked up, and saw that he was standing in line with the small window, not much more than a loop-hole, that looked out from the rear of the cabin. Instinctively he stepped aside. He was only just in time. A bullet ripped a splinter of wood from the side of the window and buried itself with a crisp *zut* in the opposite wall.

Although thoroughly startled by the narrow margin of his escape, Ginger realized that the shot settled any remaining doubt as to the whereabouts of the weapon. The Indian had got it, and the direction from which the shot had come gave him a rough idea of his position; and since the ground on that side of the cabin was level as far as the trees, he realized that the Indian had probably taken up a position on the edge of the wood.

Ginger, keeping well away from the window, examined the situation in this new light. He no longer entertained the idea of going out to look for his enemy. He was more concerned with preserving his life, and the machine; and he experienced a fresh pang of apprehension when the thought flashed into his head that the Indian might, under cover of darkness, set fire to the Jupiter, or put it out of action in some other way. At all costs he must prevent that, he thought desperately.

Still racking his brain for a solution to the difficult problem with which he was now faced, he fell back on his old resort. What would Biggles do in such a case? A careful reconnaissance near the door confirmed his belief that it was possible, by making a rush, to reach the machine; but the idea of becoming the fugitive, leaving the Indian in command of the situation, was repugnant to him, quite apart from which it meant, definitely, that his mission had failed. In any case, it was nearly dark, and his common sense told him that it would be an act of the greatest folly to try to find his way back to Fort Beaver in the dark. Even if he found the aerodrome, which was not very likely, the business of landing the big machine without lights of any sort was a responsibility he preferred not to shoulder. If he started and lost his way, the machine would probably be wrecked in the inevitable forced landing when his petrol was exhausted. Having seen the country, he knew that it would be hopeless to try to get down anywhere in the inhospitable region between the place where he was and Fort Beaver. If he crashed it might be months before he was found. He might never be found.

To make matters worse, it had turned bitterly cold, and there was a feeling of snow in the air. Torn by indecision, he tried to make up his mind what to do for the best. Suppose by a miracle he did get back? What then? He would be in the same predicament as the others. Fortunately, he did not know that their plight was as desperate as it actually was, or his anxiety would have turned to something worse.

Now as he stood near the cabin door busy with these worrying thoughts, he perceived something which hitherto he had not noticed, possibly because up to the present moment it had held no significance. Not far from the door there was a depression, a slight fold in the ground. As a feature of the landscape it was negligible, but he knew that by lying flat in extended order a regiment could have taken cover in it. He recalled that once, years before, he had watched a troop of boy scouts practising taking cover in just such a trifling depression. At the time he had not known that the depression was there. From the edge of the field where he stood it could not be seen, when the scouts stood up they appeared as one would expect to see them, a definite and unmistakable party of human beings; yet when they lay down they disappeared from sight as if the ground had opened and swallowed them up. After they had gone, his curiosity was such that he had examined the place, and was amazed to find that the depression was so shallow that he was by no means sure when he had reached it.

Standing on tiptoe, Ginger now tried to see how far the depression extended, but was unable to do so with any degree of certainty; but he saw that it swept round in such a way that if it persisted in its course it would pass near the northern extremity of the wood in which, if his deductions were correct, the Indian had taken cover.

He made another critical survey of the weather, for he knew that he could not afford to leave it out of his calculations. Should it begin to snow in earnest, then that would be the end of the undertaking. It might be the end of everything, for the machine would certainly be snowed in, in which case he would be marooned as effectively as if he were on a desert island. The sky was about three parts covered, with occasional stars beginning to twinkle through the broken masses of cumulus. Still, visibility was fairly good. It had settled down to a deceptive twilight, and he knew from experience that, as far north as he was, it would get no darker; it might even get lighter, for the northern sky was faintly suffused with the mysterious ever-moving glow of the aurora borealis; he knew that should the sky clear the rays would become stronger, and reflect more light over the landscape.

Filled by doubts and misgivings, for he was by no means certain that he was doing the right thing, he darted swiftly to the depression, where he threw himself flat on the ground and endeavoured to make out what course the shallow place of concealment took. But it merged into an indistinct background, and his scrutiny told him nothing. Behind him, the cabin showed up against the sky as a square black silhouette. The machine, looking forlorn and deserted, stood about a hundred yards to his right.

Now that the moment had come to leave these recognizable objects he hesitated, but comforted himself with the thought that if anything went wrong he could return to them. Anyway, he decided, he would keep them in sight as long as possible. Stealthily, sometimes crawling, and where the depression was particularly shallow pulling himself along flat on his stomach, he began to make his way along the fold, pausing from time to time to listen or take a surreptitious peep at the cabin. For he had not overlooked the possibility of the Indian playing the same game as himself. He knew that it was not at all unlikely that his enemy was even than endeavouring to creep unseen to the cabin; but what the Indian would not expect, he told himself, was that he had left it. In fact, if that were so, then of the two positions he preferred his own, for it seemed to hold a certain advantage.

He had made his way for what he judged to be about two hundred yards when a gust of wind brought a flurry of snowflakes with it. He stopped at once, almost overcome with dismay. It was no use going on. Not that there was much point in going back, he reflected bitterly. If there was going to be a heavy fall it would mean the end of everything. 'Still, I suppose I shall be better off inside than out here,' he thought morosely, as he stood up in the whirling flakes, knowing that there was no longer any need for him to remain prone. The snow effectually blotted out everything outside a radius of a few yards. Turning up his collar, he walked swiftly towards the cabin—or, since he could not see, where he imagined it to be.

It surprised him to find how far he had gone. Surely he should have reached the cabin by now? He began counting his paces. When he reached fifty he stopped, knowing that he must have passed his objective. Irritated, but without any alarm, he began to retrace his steps. Presently he broke into a run, only to pull up abruptly as he realized that he was lost. Even then he was not unduly perturbed, for he knew that the cabin could not be more than a hundred yards from where he stood. There was no need for him to lose his head, he told himself. Obviously, the thing to do was to retrace his steps in the thin mantle of snow which now covered the ground. But he soon discovered that this plan, while satisfactory in theory, was, in fact, impracticable, for his trail was obliterated almost as fast as he made it.

He did not attempt to deceive himself any longer. He knew that he had not the remotest idea of where he stood in relation to the cabin. He did the only thing left; he started quartering up and down, this way and that, counting his steps so that he did not go too far in any one direction.

A sharp blow in the face pulled him up with a jerk. Indeed, he staggered back, hand to his face, for the blow had hurt. What had he walked into? It was certainly not the cabin. It was not the machine, for there was no projection on it so sharp as whatever it was that had struck his face. Holding his hands in front of him, he moved slowly forward, feeling his way. They encountered the object, and he knew at once what it was. The blunt end of a twig. His hands groped their way along it until they were met by a tangle of branches, and finally the trunk of a tree. He realized that he had wandered to the wood, but what part of it he had no means of knowing.

And while he stood there, thrown into confusion by his discovery, the snow stopped as suddenly as it had started. The moon broke through the clouds and shone whitely on the snow that lay like a spotless sheet over everything. He saw the cabin and the machine. With a sigh of relief he took a pace forward, for the thought of getting back to the cabin was still uppermost in his mind; but then he backed hurriedly, realizing that the hazard was more dangerous than the one he had first embarked upon. There was no sign of the Indian. Not that he expected it. But that did not mean that his enemy had gone away. On the contrary, in view of the uncertainty of the weather, he would be even more anxious to recover the shelter of the cabin.

Still turning the matter over in his mind, his body stiffened suddenly as a dreadful cry was borne to his ears. It was the howl of a wolf, and at the long-drawn-out cry his blood ran cold. Of course there were wolves there! He had seen them when he had first landed there with Biggles, when they had been following McBain. All the gruesome stories he had heard about wolves pursuing and tearing lonely travellers to pieces rushed through his mind. One wolf, two wolves, or a pack, he hated the whole tribe. He was terrified of them, and he knew it.

Again came the ghastly howl, nearer this time, and before it had come to a quivering end it was taken up by another.

Ginger forgot the Indian. He forgot everything. His one idea now was to get inside the sheltering walls of the cabin and shut the door. The next instant he was flying for his life across the snow in the direction of the haven of refuge. A score of paces, and a chorus of howls broke out behind him. A frantic glance over his shoulder told him the worst; a line of black shapes had broken cover some distance higher up the wood and were streaking after him, running diagonally in such a way that they would, he knew, cut him off before he reached the hut. Hardly knowing what he was doing, acting from an instinct of self-preservation rather than thought, he swerved away from his original objective and raced towards the machine. He ran as he had never run before, for he could hear the soft patter of footsteps and the panting breath of his pursuers.

And as he ran Ginger knew that his life depended upon a circumstance so trivial that he could not have imagined it. The wolves were so close behind that he knew that if the cabin door of the Jupiter was shut he would not have time to open it and get inside before they pulled him down. He could not remember whether he had closed it or left it open. Nor could he see until he was within a dozen paces whether it was open or shut. It was open. With a last convulsive effort he took a flying leap at the aperture and slammed the door behind him just as the leading wolf launched itself through the air. It struck the door with a crash that made the machine rock. Ginger, on his back, still half crazed with panic, snatched out his automatic and blazed at the door from the inside. There was a shrill yelp, followed instantly by a dreadful snarling and scuffling. He knew all about wolves killing and eating one of their number that was wounded or incapacitated, and that is what he imagined was going on outside. He hoped it was true. Nothing would have given him greater pleasure than to see the wolves tearing each other to pieces.

Panting, he made his way through into the cockpit, where he sank down in the control seat to consider the situation in its latest form. He was tired. He was cold. He felt weak and hungry. In fact, he was sick of the whole business. Things seemed to be going from bad to worse, and it is not surprising that he found himself wishing that he had never undertaken a mission which was fast proving to be beyond his ability to fulfil. He could hear the wolves outside. Looking through the side window he could see them, some sitting on their haunches staring up at the cockpit, others sniffing round the undercarriage. One, bolder than the rest, made a leap at the window, only to fall back again as Ginger's pistol cracked. Again came the ghastly business of the wolves devouring their wounded companion.

Ginger felt that he was safe where he was. He would, he decided, stay there until the morning; as soon as it was light enough for safe flying he would abandon his project, and return to Fort Beaver, no matter what the result might be. Searching about, he found a few pieces of broken biscuit in the pocket on the inside of the door, and it was while he was munching these ravenously that he noticed a change in the behaviour of the wolves. One of them, sniffing about some distance from the rest, suddenly threw up his head and let out its hateful howl, after which it loped off towards the log cabin where, as Ginger now noticed for the first time, several wolves were already prowling. One by one the others broke away from the machine and joined the party now circling the hut.

Ginger watched them with a new interest, wondering what it was that had attracted their attention. At first he thought that they had simply found his trail, the scent he had left behind when he had started off on his last ill-fated enterprise; but then, seeing that they were all looking upwards, he, too, raised his eyes. Then he understood. Conspicuous against the snow on the roof was a dark object. Even as Ginger watched he saw it move, and he was no longer in any doubt as to what it was—or rather, who it was.

It was a man, and there was only one man likely to be in such a place at such a time. The Indian!

21
THE PRISONER SPEAKS

HOW long the Indian had been there, or how he had got there, Ginger, of course, did not know. He did not particularly care. One thing was certain, and that was what concerned him most. The man was 'treed' by the wolves as effectively—in fact, more effectively—than he was himself. His plight was a good deal more precarious.

Twice, as he watched, Ginger saw the Indian slip, and climb back to the ridge by what seemed to be an effort. He wondered why the man had not fired at him, or why he did not fire at the wolves. Watching the man's hands as he clung to the ridge, he suspected the reason; and presently he became fairly certain that his assumption was correct. The Indian had not got the rifle with him. Either he had dropped it in his haste to climb on the roof out of reach of the wolves, or he had accidentally let it slip after he was up. Either way, as far as Ginger was concerned, the effect was the same. If the man was unarmed it put a very different complexion on the whole situation, and he began to take a fresh interest in the proceedings; particularly when, a minute or two later, he heard what he took to be a cry for help.

Opening the side window quietly, he looked out. 'Hi!' he yelled. 'Have you got the rifle?' The words seemed strangely loud in the icy silence. The wolves stopped their prowling and stared at the machine.

'No . . . on ground,' came the reply, rather faintly.

'Can you hold on until the morning?' was Ginger's next question.

'No.'

'Why not?'

'Too cold. Die with cold here,' came the tragic

announcement.

It did not occur to Ginger to doubt the word of a man whose position was obviously far too precarious for him to hope to gain anything by lying. 'Hold on!' he shouted.

The last thing he wanted now was that the Indian should die, and carry the secret of the gold with him to the grave—or, as seemed more likely, into the stomachs of the brutes prowling below, who appeared to sense that, of the two men, this was the one more likely to satisfy their appetites.

It did not take Ginger long to make up his mind what to do. There was, in fact, only one thing he could do; for, whether the Indian died or not, he had no intention of taking on the pack single-handed, on the ground, armed only with a pistol. And he lost no time in putting his plan into execution. The self-starter whirred. It did not surprise him when the engines refused to start, for he knew that they must be stone cold. However, it was only a matter of time.

Actually, it took him nearly ten minutes to get the first kick out of one of the propellers. A minute later one engine started with its customary roar. A streak of blue flame shot out of the exhaust. He did not bother about the other engine. One, he hoped, would be sufficient for his purpose. And he was right.

If he had any doubts as to how the wolves would behave in the face of a roaring aero-engine they were soon dismissed. Even before the machine moved, most of them were skulking towards the wood, and by the time it was half-way to the cabin, with Ginger making the night hideous with occasional bursts of throttle, they were in full flight. Slowly, on the alert for any sign of treachery, he taxied the machine right up to the cabin wall and then switched off. 'Stay where you are until I tell you to move,' he called to the Indian; and then, jumping down, he picked up the rifle, which he could now see lying near the cabin wall half buried in snow.

'All right, come down,' he said curtly. 'Be careful what you are doing or you'll get shot.'

He stepped back as the Indian slid off the roof, bringing a small avalanche of snow with him, and fell heavily to the ground.

Ginger did not take his eyes off him for a moment, but he saw that, unless the man was a clever actor, he was at his last gasp. He was so stiff with cold that he had difficulty in getting him to his feet.

Ginger, stooping down, took the Indian's knife from his belt and tossed it, with the rifle, into the machine. He kept him covered with his pistol, and with some difficulty managed to get him into the hut, where he allowed him to sink down again near the stove. Still keeping one eye on him, he lit the lamp, by the light of which he saw that the man was really in a bad way. There was blood on his left arm, from which he assumed that his bullet must, after all, have wounded him. The stove, he discovered, was out, but he did not bother about lighting it. The lamp would give a certain amount of heat.

'Now,' he said, turning to his prisoner, 'I am going to ask you some questions. If you are wise you will answer them truthfully. You can understand English, I think?'

'Sure,' returned the Indian weakly, with a soft American accent.

'Where is the gold?'

The Indian did not reply.

'Where is the gold?' asked Ginger again.

'Gold? No gold.'

'Don't lie to me!' snapped Ginger. 'You know the gold is here. I know it's here. You'd better remember where it is—unless you want to go back outside to the wolves. You needn't be afraid to speak. McBain won't worry you.'

The Indian started, and Ginger knew that his shot had gone home.

'By the time this business is over McBain will be hanging by the neck,' he announced confidently. 'He is probably under arrest by now.'

The Indian looked up. 'What for, huh?' he asked.

'For murdering Mose Jacobs. You were in that too.'

'No! No—no! Not me!' flashed back the Indian quickly.

'We'll talk about that presently,' declared Ginger. 'What I want to know first of all is where McBain has hidden the gold.

Speak up. You'd better tell me what you know. It's your only chance of escaping the rope.'

The Indian looked worried, but he did not answer.

'They'll make you speak when they try you for murdering Mose,' went on Ginger remorselessly. 'You killed him, didn't you?'

'No.'

'Was it McBain?'

'Yes, McBain,' agreed the Indian sullenly.

'How do you know?' fired back Ginger.

'I know.'

'How do you know? Did McBain tell you?'

'No. I guessed. Then I found the——'

'The what? Come on, out with it.'

'He hit Mose with—the butt end of his gun.'

'How do you know?'

'I saw him cleaning blood and hair off his gun afterwards.'

'What did he clean it with?'

'A towel.'

'Where did he put it?'

The Indian hesitated.

'Come on,' prompted Ginger.

'He put towel under some sacks in the corner of office.'

Ginger was more than pleased about this piece of additional evidence—always assuming that the Indian spoke the truth, and he could think of no sound reason why he should lie. 'Of course, there is a way you can save your own neck if you like,' he went on insinuatingly.

'How?'

'By turning Queen's Evidence. You tell the truth to the police and maybe they'll let you off. If you don't tell all you know it makes you as bad as the actual murderer. Remember that when we get back to-morrow.'

The Indian started. His dark eyes sought Ginger's. 'Back – to-morrow?'

'Yes. You're coming back with me. What else did you think you were going to do?'

Again the Indian did not answer.

Ginger was not particularly concerned about the Indian's fate. What he wanted was all the evidence he could muster against McBain, particularly the gold that would prove his guilt, so he spent some time in planting in the Indian's mind the idea that if he confessed all he knew there was a chance that the law would take a lenient view of his association with McBain. He assured him that McBain would certainly be hanged, and in this belief he was sincere. 'If you won't tell me where the gold is, you'll jolly soon tell Constable Delaney when he gets his hands on you,' he concluded. 'For the last time, where is the gold?'

The Indian turned his face slowly towards the stove. 'Under there,' he said simply.

Ginger could have kicked himself for not thinking of it; or rather, for overlooking such an obvious place. Looking at the stove now, he saw that it stood on a small piece of thin iron sheeting, which had probably been supplied with the stove. Seizing the upper part, he dragged it aside. He swept the iron sheeting away with his foot and a cavity was revealed. Reaching down, his hand came into contact with a small bag, or sack, of harsh material. He dragged it up into the room, and knew from its weight that it contained gold.

There were eight sacks, each tied and sealed. On the side of each one was printed in black letters MOOSE CREEK GOLDFIELDS INC. There was only one other thing in the cache, a small iron object, and for a moment he wondered what it could be; but when, on the base, he saw the brand of the Moose Creek company, he understood. 'A spare seal, eh?' he murmured. 'So that's how McBain was able to do the trick. And he came here to do it. Well, when we get back to Fort Beaver with this little lot several people are going to get a shock.'

The Indian said nothing. Ginger, having obtained what he wanted, had nothing more to say. The only thing that remained was for him to wait until daylight and then get back to Fort Beaver as quickly as possible.

The lamp had taken the chill off the room, but it was by no means warm, and although the Indian had recovered somewhat he looked far from happy. Ginger examined the wound in his arm; it was only a flesh wound, but sufficient to cause the Indian to lose a good deal of blood, which, with the exposure he had experienced on the roof, accounted for his weakness.

Ginger remembered McBain's fur coat. He did not need it himself, but it struck him that his prisoner would be more comfortable in it, so he lifted it from its peg intending to hand it to him. As he took it down, something sharp pierced his forearm, bringing an exclamation of pain and surprise to his lips. The object, whatever it was, seemed to be in the sleeve, so thinking that it was possibly a thorn, he examined the sleeve carefully in order to remove it. He was some time finding the object, but at length he located it in the turned-up fold of the sleeve. Taking it out, he regarded it for some moments in silence, an extraordinary expression on his face. He glanced quickly at the Indian, but the man's back was turned towards him and it was clear that he had not noticed the incident. Slipping the object quickly back into the turn-up of the sleeve, he spread the coat over the shoulders of his prisoner.

The night passed as slowly as any he could remember, but at long last the grey dawn for which he had waited shed its feeble light through the window. There had, of course, been no question of going to sleep with a dangerous character like the Indian in the room.

He went over to the window and looked out. Nothing moved. There was no sign of the wolves.

'Well, it's daylight and I don't see any wolves,' he told the Indian.

'The wolves go back into the wood at dawn,' was the cold reply. 'They not come out again now.'

'Well, come on; on your feet. We'll get along,' ordered Ginger.

The Indian pleaded to be left behind, to be given his freedom, swearing that he would never work for McBain again. But this was something Ginger was not prepared to grant. He compelled his prisoner to help him to carry the gold across to the machine.

When the last of it was safely on board, he closed the hut and made the Indian sit beside him in the Jupiter, reckoning that

once in the air the Indian would be powerless to do any harm—
unless he deliberately did something calculated to crash the
machine and kill them both, which hardly seemed likely.

It took Ginger some time to start the engines, for they were
very cold, but in the end he got them going, and just as the first
rays of the rising sun flashed up over the horizon the Jupiter
roared into the air on its return journey to Fort Beaver.

Had Ginger known what was happening there his cheerful
confidence would have received a rude shock. As it was, he was so
pleased with the success of his mission that he hummed softly to
himself as the landmarks he recognized slipped away behind.

'They must have wondered what has happened to me,' he
thought seriously.

22

AT THE ELEVENTH HOUR

As we know, the others had more than once wondered what had
happened to him. But now, as they stood under the fatal tree
with the end so near, he slipped from their minds.

It was Biggles who knew first that the machine was coming; his
keen ears picked up the drone of the motors before he saw it.

'Here comes Ginger,' he said, by which time others in the
crowd had heard it too.

There was a quick babble of excited conversation. The
immediate preparations for the hanging were temporarily
abandoned, and several people pointed to the fast approaching
Jupiter.

'Never mind about that,' shouted McBain. It was almost as if
he sensed that the oncoming aeroplane was a danger to the
success of his plans. Ferroni, who was with him, raised his voice in
a demand that the hanging should be proceeded with, but the
attention of the crowd was distracted by the behaviour of the
machine.

At first it seemed that the pilot was going to glide straight to the aerodrome and land, but at the last moment the machine turned suddenly, as if the pilot had observed the crowd and wished to see it at close quarters. Straight over the tree at a height of not more than fifty feet the Jupiter soared, and then went into a tight circle. The watchers on the ground could see the pale face of the pilot looking down at them.

'Come on; ain't yer never seen an airyplane before? Let's get on with the hangin',' roared McBain. But the noise of the Jupiter's engines so drowned the words that only those in his immediate vicinity heard them.

'What does he think he's up to?' Delaney asked Biggles, who was watching the side window of the control cabin.

'I don't know,' he answered, 'but I rather fancy that he is going to throw something out. Yes, he is,' he went on quickly, raising his voice, as a bulky object blocked the cabin window. 'Watch your heads, everybody.'

The next moment a dark object was hurtling downwards, turning slowly as it fell. There was a yell of alarm from the crowd, each member of which took steps to make sure that it did not hit him; only the prisoners and Delaney remained still, eyes on the falling object, which finally crashed to earth in the middle of the scattered spectators, but, fortunately, without hitting anyone.

The actual moment of impact produced a curious effect: so curious, in fact, that it is doubtful if anyone of the watchers had the slightest idea of what had happened. There seemed to be a sort of brilliant yellow flash, almost like a tongue of flame, which licked along the short turf for a brief moment before it disappeared. The phenomenon had occurred about ten or twelve yards from the tree.

'What the dickens was that?' ejaculated Algy.

'Goodness knows,' replied Biggles, who was still staring at the spot; he could see a small, buff-coloured object, and beside it a yellow streak. Then the crowd converged on it and it was hidden from his view. There was an excited whisper, almost a hiss, and then a shout went up.

Delaney had run forward with the others. 'Stand away there!' he ordered crisply.

Curiously enough, the crowd gave way to him, as though it once more respected his authority. Mass hysteria is a strange thing; it can die down as quickly as it can arise; and thus it was in this case. It was as if the crowd had been shocked by what it saw on the ground.

Delaney perceived his opportunity, and was not slow in taking advantage of it. 'Stand clear!' he snapped. 'Don't touch it, anybody. And that goes for you, too, McBain,' he went on curtly.

One of the first to reach the fallen object had been McBain, and he stared at it as if he could not believe his eyes. Delaney stooped and picked up something from the ground; it looked like a piece of torn sacking. 'Moose Creek Goldfields!' he cried in an amazed voice. Then, a tone higher, he added, 'Boys, it's the Moose Creek gold!'

The words were received with a loud buzz of excitement, and every one pressed forward to see the pile of yellow dust that had burst from the bag when it had hit the ground.

Delaney placed two men on guard over the gold. They obeyed without question. Then he strode to where the prisoners were still standing, the ropes around their necks. The crowd, its anger melting in the face of this new mystery, surged after him.

'What do you know about this?' Delaney asked Biggles sternly.

'Not much more than you do,' replied Biggles. 'I suggest that you let the boy tell his story in his own way. Here he comes, now.'

Ginger, who by this time had landed, was, in fact, marching towards the crowd; and he did not come alone. In front of him, covered by his automatic, walked the Indian, draped in a long skunk-skin coat.

The crowd fell silent as it watched the approach of this curious procession. On all faces was astonishment not far from incredulity.

Straight through the crowd to where Delaney was standing Ginger marched his prisoner, the spectators forming a lane to allow them to pass. His eyes opened wide when he saw the dangling ropes and for whom they were intended.

'What's the idea?' asked Delaney, the words sounding

strangely loud in the hush that had fallen.

'I've brought back evidence to prove that my friends, who have been arrested for the murder of Mose Jacobs, or the theft of the Moose Creek gold, or both, are innocent,' cried Ginger. 'I have brought back the gold,' he went on. 'Some of it you have seen.' He pointed in the direction of that which lay on the ground. 'The rest is in the aeroplane.'

'Where did you find it?' asked Delaney.

'I found it under the floor of a cabin up on the edge of the bad lands—where the thief had hidden it until such time as it suited him to collect it. This Indian was left on guard over it, and he will tell you to whom the cabin belongs. It belongs to Brindle McBain.'

McBain, white with passion, pushed his way to the front. 'What are you saying?' he snarled.

'I'm saying that you stole the gold,' answered Ginger in a hard voice. 'Instead of flying it straight down here you landed at your cabin, broke the seals of the boxes, took out the gold, substituted lead which you had already prepared, and then resealed the boxes. Here is the seal with which you did the job.' Ginger handed Delaney the duplicate seal.

'That's a lie!' roared McBain.

'We shall see,' retorted Ginger imperturbably. He raised his voice. 'Does anyone here recognize the coat the Indian is wearing?' he asked.

A dozen voices answered: 'It's McBain's.'

'Do you deny that the coat is yours, McBain?' asked Ginger.

McBain hesitated. It was quite certain that he could not deny it without proving himself to be a liar, for the peculiar white blaze on the coat would have identified it in ten thousand.

'This coat was in McBain's hidden cabin,' declared Ginger, taking the garment from the Indian and tossing it carelessly to its rightful owner, who caught it and flung it over his shoulder.

'Now,' continued Ginger, 'I want to recall something to the minds of those who were in the Three Star the night Mose was killed. Are the two men here who were sitting by the fire talking to Mose when I joined in the conversation?'

The two men pushed their way to the front.

'You would remember what Mose was wearing that night?' Ginger challenged them.

'I reckon so,' they agreed.

'Very well. You will remember that after the row between my friend, Major Bigglesworth, who stands over there, and McBain, we went home. Mose and McBain were still there.'

'That's right. I was there myself, so I can vouch for that,' declared Delaney.

'After that, who went out first—Mose or McBain?'

'McBain.'

Ginger turned to McBain. 'Did you ever, from the moment you left the Three Star, see Mose again?'

'No.' McBain's denial was emphatic.

Ginger nodded. 'I see,' he said. 'On the night Mose was murdered I believe I am right in saying that you were wearing the coat you now have on your arm.'

Again McBain hesitated. It was as if he suspected a trap, but could think of no way of avoiding it. He could not deny that he had worn the coat, for nearly every man present had been in the saloon that night, and must have seen him in it.

'Well, what if I *was* wearing it?' he snarled belligerently.

'Has anyone else but you ever worn that coat—except the Indian who was wearing it when I arrived here?'

Again a moment's hesitation. The atmosphere was electric.

'Had anyone but you worn the coat it is likely that it would have been noticed, isn't it?' prompted Ginger.

'It's my coat, and nobody else has had it—if that's what you're getting at,' grated McBain.

Ginger pointed to the turn-up at the bottom of the fur sleeve. 'Just feel in there and take out what you find,' he said quietly. 'And then, since you did not see Mose again after you left the saloon, perhaps you will tell us how it got there.'

Like a man in a dream, almost against his will it seemed, McBain's finger went down into the turn-up. The silence was such that every member of the crowd might have been holding his breath. A look of relief passed over McBain's face as he found what was evidently an insignificant object; with a short laugh he took it out and looked at it. As he did so his face blanched. Yet the object was simple enough. It was merely an opal-headed tie-pin.

'Does any one recognize that pin?' called Ginger loudly.

Had he said, 'Does anyone *not* recognize that pin?' there would have been fewer to answer. Nearly everyone present recognized it, and knew to whom it belonged—the murdered prospector.

Delaney raised his hand for silence. Then he took a revolver from the hand of a man standing near him. The man did not protest.

'McBain,' said Delaney, 'I reckon I know why you were so anxious to lynch three innocent men.'

The crowd surged forward, muttering ominously. Nor did it heed Delaney's orders to stand still. Possibly that fact that most of the men felt that they had been duped by McBain had something to do with it. Be that as it may, McBain evidently suspected what his fate might be and it rather seemed as if he lost his nerve. Accompanied by Ferroni, with a wild rush he swept those who stood around him from his path, and drove a lane through the outskirts of the spectators, heading for safety.

'Stop!' roared Delaney above the uproar, but the fugitives took no notice.

'Look out, they're making for the machine,' shouted Biggles. 'And the gold's in it. If you don't stop them they'll get away and take the gold with them.'

McBain and Ferroni were, in fact, running like hares towards the Jupiter, which was still standing out in the middle of the aerodrome where Ginger had left it. And it seemed likely that they would have succeeded in their object but for an unexpected development.

From the far side of the aerodrome, riding at a gallop, came five uniformed figures.

Delaney yelled a warning. He had now reached the outskirts of the crowd, a position from which he dare use his revolver without the risk of hitting the wrong man, and although he emptied it at the fast retreating figures, the range was too long and the shots did not touch their mark. But they served another purpose, just as useful. They gave the oncoming horsemen at least an inkling of what was happening, as was revealed by the manner in which they swerved to cut them off.

McBain and his pilot swerved too, but they could not hope to compete with horses. Seeing that they were trapped they both drew their revolvers and tried to shoot their way to the machine. They did succeed in emptying one saddle, but then a fusillade of shots rang out and McBain pitched face downward on the turf. Ferroni, evidently seeing that his case was hopeless, threw down his weapon and raised his hands above his head.

The crowd started running towards the new scene of action.

'Here, Delaney, haven't we been trussed up like this long enough?' asked Biggles reproachfully.

The constable took out his jack-knife and cut the prisoners free. 'That kid of yours was just about in time,' he said gravely.

'He usually is,' grinned Biggles. 'Who are these newcomers?'

'Captain Lanton and the troopers from Blackfoot Point,' answered Delaney. 'That mechanic of yours must have got through to 'em. Phew! What a report I shall have to make. You'd better not go away; the Captain will want to see you too.'

25
CONCLUSION

'I SUPPOSE you are no longer in any doubt as to who killed old Mose?' Biggles asked Delaney as they walked across the aerodrome towards the Jupiter, near which the crowd had reassembled.

'None whatever,' replied Delaney.

'Then in that case I assume we are no longer under arrest?'

'No, you're free as far as I'm concerned.'

'Then if it's all the same to you we'll get our machine inside its hangar, and tidy things up a bit. I suppose I ought to fly up to Moose Creek and tell them there that the gold is safe.'

'Better not go away until you've had a word with the Captain,' advised Delaney.

They stood still as a little procession passed them, carrying a body. They learned that it was McBain, and that he was dead. A bullet had gone through his heart, killing him instantly. Ferroni, with handcuffs on his wrists, was standing near the troopers, towards whom Delaney now continued his way.

'You'll find us in Arctic Airways shed if you want us,' Biggles told him, as their paths separated, the airmen making for the Jupiter with the object of putting it in the shed. This they did, after which, over a hastily prepared meal, Ginger gave an account of his adventures at the cabin. When he had finished, the others, for his benefit, described what had happened in Fort Beaver.

They were concluding the meal with coffee when Delaney and his superior officer entered. At the officer's request Biggles narrated the entire story of their adventures from the time they had received Wilks's letter in London. The tale took a long time to tell, but both the officer and the constable listened breathlessly, particularly when Biggles related the events that had occurred near Angus Stirling's cabin.

'And what are you fellows going to do now?' the officer asked, when at last the story was told.

'As far as I can see our work is finished,' answered Biggles. 'The transfer which we got from Angus Stirling settles any doubt as to who owns the aerodrome, and now that there is only one line operating between Fort Beaver and Moose Creek, the goldfields people will be glad enough to use it. Anyway, they should be grateful for the recovery of that last consignment of metal, because, but for Arctic Airways, they would have lost it. I reckon that Canwell, when he hears what has happened, ought to give Arctic Airways a contract for handling all their freight.'

'I think so, too,' agreed the officer. 'I know the chairman of the company; I'll have a word with him about it at the first opportunity.'

Which, in fact, he did a day or two later, with the result that the contract was soon forthcoming, as well as an offer of extra finance for spare equipment should it be required.

And that is really the end of the story. Wilks implored the others to remain on at Fort Beaver and share the profits of his enterprise which had been so nearly wrecked, but Biggles was adamant in his refusal to tie himself to any one spot. However, they stayed on until Arctic Airways was reorganized on proper lines, which did not take very long, for Wilks found no difficulty in getting staff once McBain and his gang had been removed.

Wilks flew the party back to Quebec in one of the two Jupiters the firm now possessed, and it was there that goodbyes were said.

'Let me know how things go on,' shouted Biggles from the deck of the ship that was to take them back to England.

'I will,' promised Wilks. 'Thanks for coming over.'

'Don't mention it,' grinned Biggles. 'It's been a pleasure.'

BIGGLES
IN THE
SOUTH SEAS

A WORD TO THE READER

THE reader of the ensuing adventures of Biggles and his comrades in the South Seas may think that the part actually played by Biggles scarcely warrants the title of the book, since others were as much concerned as he. For example, there was Sandy Macaster, the real instigator of the whole business, whose knowledge of local conditions was such that Biggles, recognizing the value of experience, was often guided by him, and so took what may sometimes appear to be second place. Again, there were the two Polynesians, Shell-Breaker and Full Moon, whose peculiar skill and initiative were not only invaluable, but more than once saved the situation. So while Biggles was virtually in command of the expedition, being a wise leader he was prepared to take the advice and accept the service of those better acquainted with dangers of which he had had little experience.

W. E. J.

THE ISLANDS

TAHITI is the largest of the Society Islands, so named by that famous navigator, Captain Cook, after the Royal Society, for which he did much valuable work of exploration and research in the Pacific Ocean—then called the South Sea.

The Marquesas, a group of eleven wild and rugged islands, were so named in 1594 by their Spanish discoverer Mendana, who had been sponsored by Don Garcia Mendoza, Viceroy of Peru. He named them Las Islas Marquesa de Mendoza—or the Islands of the Marquis of Mendoza. Today they are known simply as the Marquesas.

The vast collection of coral atolls known as the Paumotus lie about five hundred miles to the south of the Marquesas. They are true 'South Sea Islands'. The native name Paumotu means literally 'a cloud of islands'. Set in a coral sea, they were for many years the dread of mariners, by whom they were named the Dangerous Isles, or, sometimes, the Low Archipelago, on account of the fact that the islands are sometimes only a few feet above the sea at their highest point. During hurricanes seas have been known to sweep right across them, with appalling loss of life.

I

BIGGLES MEETS AN OLD FRIEND

It was a perfect morning in early spring, when Major James Bigglesworth, better known to his friends as Biggles, with his two comrades, the Honourable Algernon Lacey, M.C., and 'Ginger' Hebblethwaite, turned into Piccadilly on their way to the Royal Aero Club where they had decided to take lunch. They walked slowly on the Park side of the great thoroughfare, enjoying the sunshine, and it was with some reluctance that they finally crossed over to the Club entrance.

A short, slim, clean-shaven man, with bright red hair closely cropped and a somewhat bellicose expression on his sun-tanned face, was standing at the top of the steps smoking a battered briar pipe and gazing reflectively across the greensward opposite. Biggles glanced at him casually, and was about to pass on when he stopped abruptly and swung round, staring hard. 'Great Scott!' he exclaimed. 'If it isn't the greatest of all Scots—Sandy Macaster, the boy himself. And how's Sandy?'

The little man with the red hair snatched his pipe from his mouth. His eyes opened wide. 'Biggles! By the beard of St Andrew! The one and only Biggles. And the fair Algernon— none other. What's this—a reunion party?'

'It begins to look like it, doesn't it?' smiled Biggles, introducing Ginger. 'Meet Captain Macaster,' he said, 'otherwise known as Sandy. Sandy was in our squadron in France—until he hit a telegraph pole on the wrong side of the lines. I never heard how you came to do that, Sandy; I don't think we've met since. I have a faint recollection of somebody telling me that you were leading a life of ease and luxury on a South Sea island.'

'Then whoever it was he was a liar,' asserted Sandy promptly. 'For I've found neither ease nor luxury in the parts I've been travelling.'

'But what are we standing here for?' asked Biggles. 'This seems to be an occasion for celebration. Have you had lunch, Sandy?'

'No. I was just thinking of going into the Air Force Club for a change.'

'How about joining us? If we go in right away we can get a table near the window. You can tell me about the prize coconuts you grow—or is it bananas?'

'I don't grow coconuts and I hate the sight of them; so would you if you'd had to chew as many as I have,' muttered Sandy, as they went in through the swing doors and settled themselves at a window table laid for four.

'What are you doing in England?' inquired Biggles, as he passed Sandy the menu card. 'Are you home on holiday?'

'Holiday! What's a holiday? I've never heard of it,' grunted Sandy, passing back the menu card. 'I think I'll sink my teeth in a steak if it's all the same to you.'

The others gave their orders and Biggles once more turned to Sandy. 'Then what brings you home?' he asked.

'If you want to know the truth, I'm looking for money.'

'Then you've come to a bad place, laddie,' declared Biggles seriously. 'There are about nine million people in this burg and they're all doing the same thing—looking for money.'

'You seem to have found some, anyway,' suggested Sandy pointedly.

'Oh, we've managed to pick up a little here and there,' admitted Biggles lightly. 'If you're short I can let you have a bit.'

'A bit's no use to me, old comrade,' returned Sandy sadly. 'I need a tidy wallop—not just a loan, mind you. I'm trying to get a little company together.'

'What exactly do you mean by a tidy wallop?'

'I should need about five thousand pounds.'

Biggles whistled softly. 'Jumping crocodiles!' he exclaimed. 'What do you want to do—buy a whole island for yourself?'

'I don't need an island,' snorted Sandy. 'I could have a thousand if that was all I needed. The seas down south are stiff with them; you can just go and help yourself. No, my idea is a wee bit more ambitious than that.'

'Well, go ahead—maybe we can help.'

Sandy's face lit up. 'Ye really think you can put me in the way of finding the cash?'

'It depends on what you want to do with it, old son. If my memory serves me, some of your ideas in the old days were not exactly what I should call overloaded with sanity. I'm a bit more cautious myself than I used to be, so I'm having nothing to do with any wild-cat scheme.'

Sandy set down his knife and fork with studied deliberation. He leaned forward and started into Biggle's face. 'Would ye call a hatful o' pearls a wild-cat scheme?' he hissed.

Biggles smiled. 'Come, come, Sandy. Not a *hatful.*'

'A hatful I said, and a hatful I mean,' declared Sandy indignantly. 'And none of your finicky seed-pearls, either. It's *pearls* I mean, pearls the size of peanuts—maybe larger than that.'

'Well, that sounds marvellous,' admitted Biggles. He shook his head sadly. 'But I'm afraid you're going to have an awful job persuading the stiffnecks in the City of London that these pearls really exist. Have you got any with you?'

'If I had I shouldn't be here,' snorted Sandy. 'But I've *seen* them.'

'You don't mean that somebody *else* saw them, and told you about it?'

Sandy set down his tumbler with a bang. His slight Scotch brogue became more pronounced under the strain of his enthusiasm. 'I tell ye, mon, I've seen 'em—wi' me own eyes. Now d'ye understand that?'

Biggles nodded. 'Pardon my scepticism, old sharp-shooter— but when you saw 'em, why didn't you slip a few into your hat?'

'For a thundering good reason. Get me a wee drop o' whusky and I'll tell ye the story; then maybe ye'll understand.'

Biggles passed the order to a steward, laid his cigarette-case open on the table, selected a cigarette, and lighted it. 'Go ahead, Sandy,' he said. 'I haven't heard a good story in years.'

'If ye're no goin' to believe me, than I'm wasting me time a-tellin' ye,' grumbled Sandy.

'You'll stick to facts—no romancing?'

'I'll tell ye just the plain sober honest truth—every word of it,' said Sandy emphatically. 'Now, this was the way of it. The person who told you that I was down in the South Seas was right up to that point. I couldn't stick civilization—or maybe civilization couldn't stick me. Anyway, I couldn't get the sort of job I wanted; the people who gave away the sort of job I had in mind had no time for a feller whose sole qualifications were flying and fighting. Ah weel! I should worry. I just sold everything I had—which wasn't much—and bought myself a third-class passage to Papeete, in Tahiti, which is the sort of head-quarters of those who live on, or around, the Islands. Honest men and the scum of the seven seas, gentlemen and roughnecks, traders and beachcombers; white men and black men, brown men and yellow men, the odds and ends of every seaport in the world get together sooner or later at Tahiti. On the whole they're a good crowd—but tough, mind ye. You wouldn't expect them to be otherwise. But there are some skunks among them, too—bound to be.' Sandy took a reflective sip of his drink before he continued.

'It's a good spot, Tahiti—which, incidentally, in case you don't know it, is one of the Society Islands. They belong to France now and, being French, nobody bothers much about anything—you soon get that way in the South Seas. There are a lot of Chinese there: they're all over the Islands these days; but on the whole they're a decent, harmless crowd. The harbour is a fascinating place; all sorts of shipping, mostly schooners for island trading, old and sun-bleached, but tough—like their skippers. Copra, which is dried coconut, is the chief trade, although there is still a fair amount done in shell and pearls. All the pearls that are found around the islands are brought to Papeete, where they are sold to the agents of the Paris jewel firms. But I must get on with my story.

'Well, I drifted around from one island to another, sometimes doing supercargo on one of the island schooners, sometimes helping a trader to run his store, and sometimes doing nothing at all. The trouble is, you don't have to do anything if you don't want to; you can usually find somebody willing to keep you for the sake of company. If not—well, you can always manage somehow. But I didn't want to stay down there for the rest of my life—don't get that idea. There were times when I'd have given the whole blessed boiling of islands, pearls, and lagoons complete, for a glimpse of old Scotland on a misty day. I wanted to make a fortune, easily if possible, but I wanted one, anyway, so that I could come home for a bit when I felt like it. There were plenty of fortunes about, but they always just seemed to miss me. More than once I had one almost in my grasp, but it always just slipped out of my reach.'

'How?' asked Ginger, who was very interested.

'How? Oh, I could sit here all day if I started telling you hard-luck stories. But I'll give ye an example. One day I spotted an old diving-suit in a trader's store on one of the Paumotus. He agreed to lend it to me on the understanding that if I found pearls I was to give him a third. That suited me. I went off to a chap I knew who had an old lugger and made the same deal with him. So I had a boat and a diving-suit, and could keep a third of all the pearls I found. I did well. I worked like a slave for nearly a year, doing most of the diving myself, by which time I had a nice little bag of pearls—enough to keep me comfortably for the rest of my days even with a third share. So I pulled up my mudhook and made for Papeete. The next day a cyclone hit me. I got ashore at Mareita on a bit of driftwood, with most of the skin burned off my back by the sun. I went to hospital to grow a new hide. The pearls were back where they came from—on the bottom of the sea with the lugger. Another time I was supercargo on a schooner when we found ourselves becalmed near a Marquesan skin-diver, working with a pal in a canoe. They'd got about thirty big shells, unopened, in the bottom of it. Having nothing better to do than whistle for a wind, I offered them two old pipes and a stick of tobacco for the shells. They jumped at it, naturally, for you can open a thousand shells without finding a pearl. In the long run it's shell that makes the money, not pearls; there's always a demand for it. In case you don't know, shell is the source of mother-of-pearl. It's worth from a hundred to four hundred pounds a ton, according to quality. Well, I squatted down on the deck and started to open the oysters, to see what the luck was like. Incidentally, I'd better tell you that the South Sea oyster isn't a little squib like a Whitstable native; it's a big fellow, weighing several pounds. There was nothing in the first one. There was nothing in the second one, either. Presently I had twenty-nine shells opened on the deck and not so much as a seed pearl for my trouble. There was only one shell left, and I hadn't much faith in it. It was the smallest of the lot—you always take the biggest first, whatever you are handling, even if it is only a plate of shrimps. Well, I cut the shell open and ran my fingers through the muck inside. There was something there. I thought it couldn't be a pearl because it was too big. It was about the size of a thrush's egg. I took it out. It was a pearl, such a pearl as you never saw in all your life. There it lay on the deck, gleaming with all the iridescent fire that a pearl has when it first comes out of the sea, and is still wet. In Paris it would be worth maybe five thousand pounds. It was the loveliest thing you ever saw in your life, with just a faint tint of rose in it. I couldn't believe my eyes. I just sat there blinking at it like an owl, sort of dazed and limp. At that precise instant a slant of wind hit the schooner. She heeled over. I went over. So did the pearl—into the sea. I let out a yell as it rolled gleaming across the deck, and flung myself after it. I grabbed—just a tenth of a second too late. My fingers hit the deck not more than an inch behind it. Lying there I could see it going down into the blue depths like a little white electric light. I tell you, I nearly howled. But it was gone. After that I began to think that there was something in the old saying about pearls bringing bad luck, and sooner or later going back where they came from. My trouble was, the pearls always went back before I could sell them. But let me get on with the real story.

'About eighteen months ago I was flat broke, so I took a job as supercargo with a fellow named Louis Castanelli, a dirty little Corsican. He had got a bad name—oh, I knew all about that. You soon get to know about people in the Islands. But I'd no choice. As I say, I was broke. Nothing else was available, and he was just off round the Marquesas and the Paumotus in his schooner, the *Avarata*, a dirty tub with cockroaches and coprabugs squinting at you out of every crack in her warped deck. I'll tell you about these tropical cockroaches one day—they'll eat the soles off your feet if you don't watch out. Well, we set sail in Papeete Harbour, and off we went for a cruise that might last from six to nine months.

'Castanelli was even worse than I expected. He's a crooked, foul-mouthed little swine, and his crew of eight native boys, whom he'd picked up some time in the Solomons, were not much better. Maybe that's why he selected them. As a rule the native boys are good—anyway, the Tahitians, Marquesans, and Paumotuans. But those with Castanelli were a bad lot. I heard later that they'd all done time in Australia for cannibalism—and that didn't surprise me. I knew I was in for a rough trip, but if I'd known how bad it was going to be I'd have stayed on the beach at Tahiti. Not until we were at sea did I discover how much booze Castanelli had below. I knew he couldn't drink it all, so I guessed what it was for. It was his "trade" stock. Now selling spirits to natives is against the law, and quite right, too. Unfortunately, knowing no better, the natives will always buy it, so crooked traders get round the law by all sorts of dodges—putting brandy up in scent-bottles, for instance. The stuff is traded as perfume, or hair oil—but the natives put it inside, not outside. I spoke to Castanelli about it and he admitted it. He didn't bother about camouflage like scent-bottles. He sold the stuff straight. I told him that I didn't agree with that sort of business. We had a row, at the end of which I threatened—foolishly, perhaps—to report him to the first French governor I saw. I say it was foolish, because, knowing Castanelli, I might have reckoned that he'd take steps to see that I never got near the authorities.

'Well, we went on, me keeping to myself and Castanelli drinking most of the day with his gang of Solomon Island cut-throats. You might ask me how we got anywhere in such circumstances. The answer is, drunk or sober, Castanelli's boys were good sailors. All the Island boys are like that. They can weather a big sea in a canoe, and make a landfall two thousand miles away without a compass—and that's no lie. First we worked round the Paumotus, which is a long chain of low-lying coral atolls, sometimes called the Low Archipelago; the old navigators used to call them the Dangerous Isles, which was a good name, because navigation there is as tricky as anywhere in the world. We went on towards the Marquesas, which are an entirely different proposition, being volcanic rock covered with jungle. Scientists reckon that the islands are the tops of the mountains of a sunken continent, and that's just what they look like. They're all jumbled up with mountains thousands of feet high—some of them are pretty big too—but I must get on with the story.

'Now the two groups of islands may look close together on the map—and so they are, comparatively speaking. But they're over five hundred miles apart—not very much when you're in the South Seas, because distances there bear no relation to distances at home. It's all on a much bigger scale. The Pacific is a big place, don't forget, and you can sail before a wind for six thousand miles without seeing so much as a reef. Now it happened that we had got a bit to the east of the Marquesas on account of making the most of a useful breeze, but we were beating up towards them when we made out an island which even Castanelli said he didn't know—and he reckons to know every reef and atoll between the Galapagos and the Ladrones. Not that we paid much attention to that. There are islands everywhere in the Pacific, and if you called at 'em all you wouldn't get anywhere. We shouldn't have called at this one, anyway, because it was pretty certain that there was nobody on it. And this is where the story really begins—and where my life nearly ended.

'Castanelli had been drinking for days, so I'd got into the habit of taking the ship's position. I'm certain that when we passed

that island Castanelli didn't know where we were to within five
hundred miles. That's important—you'll see why presently.
The sea was flat calm, but there was a swell. There nearly always
is a swell in the Pacific, but it may be so big that you don't see it. It
was midday, and blinding hot. The island, an atoll, had drifted
away astern. I had taken our position and put the sextant down
near the wheel, in case Castanelli sobered up and decided to
check my readings. Making a mental note of our longitude and
latitude, and thinking that I'd enter it up in the log later on, I lay
down on the deck and stared down into the sea, waiting for a
wind. And there I lay, staring down into the blue water, thinking
about Castanelli, and myself—anything. And it was while I was
lying there like that I saw something that shook me from my
Adam's apple to my insteps. The bottom of the sea—where there
hadn't been any bottom, you understand—suddenly came up.
It came up to within five or six feet of our keel, hung there for a
moment or two, and then slowly sank down out of sight again.
You won't argue with me when I say that I couldn't believe my
eyes. I thought that the sun had got me at last. But I lay there
staring, waiting to see if it happened again. It did. Everything
was quiet. There was no perceptible movement. Then suddenly
I realized what was happening. The bottom of the sea wasn't
moving, of course. It was the schooner. Although you couldn't
see it, the *Avarata* was rising and falling on a forty or fifty foot
swell. As she came up, the sea bottom disappeared. As she went
down, the coral came up to meet us. No wonder I was shaken, for
we were in shallow water. If the swell got any worse we should
come down on the coral with a crash that would crumple us up
like a busted eggshell. I let out a yell. Of course, I had no means of
knowing how far the shallow water ran. We might have been
simply drifting over the top of a submerged peak. I didn't know.
I still don't know. But it was clear that we couldn't stay there. It
meant manning the longboat and towing the *Avarata* clear—and
quickly.

'My yell brought up Castanelli at a run—and the boys. They
were not so drunk as I thought they were. I shouted "Man the
boat!" Castanelli wanted to know what the blankety-blank

for—and well he might. I told him to come and look. We all stood there staring. The bottom of the sea came up, a marvellous sight, blue, red, green, and purple coral, like—well, you'd have to see it to understand. But there wasn't only coral. There was something else. Shell! Thousands of oysters, the size of dinner-plates, lying in pairs—because the oysters were open. They open to eat, and when they do that you can see the gleam of the mother-of-pearl inside. The whole floor of the sea was covered with gleaming disks of shell, lying flat or sticking out of the coral like big swallows' nests. I felt myself go weak as I realized that in shell alone I was looking at a fortune. It was the sort of thing the old hands dream about. And that very fact warned me to glance at Castanelli. It was a good thing I did. I was only just in time. There was such a look on his face as I hope never to see on any man's face again—and his hand was in his side pocket where I knew he kept his gun. "I reckon there ain't enough here for the two of us," he said, with an ugly grin. I jumped aside just as he fired. The shot missed me.

'Now just imagine my position. We were in the middle of the Pacific, in water crawling with sharks. Castanelli had a gun and was bent on murder. I wasn't even armed. His eight boys were with him, their knives out. I couldn't run. I couldn't hide. There was nowhere on the ship where I could take cover without being shot full of holes. You won't find it hard to believe that I told myself my number was up. But I had one card left to play. If I couldn't get the pearls, then I would see to it that Castanelli shouldn't—that is, if he didn't know where we were. As I told you, I'd noted our position although I hadn't entered it up in the log. The sextant was still standing by the wheel where I had put it down. If I could reach it before he plugged me it should go over the side, for without it he would have no means of ascertaining where we were. I made a dash for it. He fired, but missed again. I fairly yelled with joy as I snatched up the instrument and heaved it over the rail. Castanelli fired again, but at that moment by the grace of God a squall hit the schooner. I fell. So did Castanelli. But the gang, with their knives in their hands, were at me. I decided that I'd rather drown than be carved into slices, so over the side I went, and swam for all I was worth. What with the way now on the schooner, and me swimming, by the time Castanelli had got to the rail I was too far away for accurate shooting. He kept on firing, of course, but although some of the shots splashed the water over me, not one hit me.

'But he wasn't going to let me get away—not if he could prevent it. I saw the boys making sail, and round they came at me. But the wind was now blowing half a gale. You get squalls like that in the Pacific. Twice they brought the schooner past me, but what with me ducking and diving, and the schooner rolling, Castanelli's shooting was all over the place. Pretty soon he had to pack up chasing me and keep his head into the wind, or he'd have capsized his schooner. Now, I thought, as it drew farther away from me, I'll just drown comfortably by myself. You see, it wasn't much use hoping. What could I hope for? Imagine it. Out in the middle of the Pacific, no land in sight, sharks in the water, and a gale blowing up. No so good, eh?'

'Pretty grim,' admitted Biggles.

'You're right, that's just what it was,' declared Sandy, taking another sip at his drink. 'I hadn't even a hen-coop to hang on to, as most people seem to have in a shipwreck,' he went on. 'But there was this about it: the water was warm. It always is down there, and if you can keep afloat, and the sharks leave you alone, you can hang on for hours. I soon stopped swimming. I kicked off my clothes and floated, keeping an eye open for dorsal fins. I saw one or two, but apparently they weren't man-eaters—they're not all killers, you know. The schooner disappeared over the horizon and I was all alone on the rolling deep—a position in which I hope never to find myself again. Night came. The squall passed. The sea began to go down, and I was still floating. Presently I began to wonder why I troubled to float; it was only prolonging things. However, it's funny how you hang on to life, even when everything seems hopeless. I couldn't hope to be picked up. In those waters there is, maybe, one ship for every hundred thousand square miles of sea, so to expect one to come my way at that moment was to expect too much. Years might pass before one came along. But my luck was in, for all that. I might have got into a current running to the North Pole, or to South America, instead of which I struck one running towards the island we had passed. I saw it at dawn, quite close. It lay so low, and I was so low in the water, that I could only see the tops of the palms; they appeared to be growing out of the water, but I knew that where they were there was land, and I struck out towards them. Funnily enough, having resigned myself to my fate I had ceased to worry; but now that I had a chance I got frightened again, terrified that the palms might slide past without my being able to reach them after all.

'I just made it, although the surf nearly finished me. I shan't forget those last ten minutes. Nearly every atoll has a reef round it. The lagoon is inside. But it isn't always possible to get to the lagoon, because once in a while there is no opening through the reef. You'd have to see the combers breaking on a South Sea reef to understand what they're like. If ever there was a case of an irresistible force meeting an immovable mass, that's it. A wave of a hundred thousand tons of water comes roaring along, majestic, invincible. You'd think that nothing could stop it. Then the coral grabs at the bottom of it and tears its foundations away. The mountain of water hangs for a minute in mid-air, and then crashes down with a noise like thunder. It spreads itself out into a boiling sea of foam, like white lace; then it rolls back, and there is the reef waiting for the next wave. And so it goes on year after year. Occasionally the sea seems to go mad and hurls its entire fury on the coral. That's when a hurricane comes along. I hope you never get caught in one. A man or a boat caught in the surf would be smashed to pulp. Well, I kept on swimming until I found a gap in the reef. The sea picked me up and flung me through—just in time, for a shark was very interested in me and had been keeping me company for some minutes. I finished up like a piece of wet rag on the beach.'

'Was anybody there?' asked Ginger, quickly. He had followed Sandy's story with intense interest.

'There was not,' replied Sandy. 'Robinson Crusoe's island was a hive of industry compared with mine. He did at least find a footprint on the beach. I found nothing except sea-shells and coconuts. My great fear was that there would be no fresh water. Fortunately there was; there usually is, although where it comes from in the middle of so much salt is a question I can't answer. So I had a drink, nibbled a coconut, and staggered around the new establishment to see what I'd struck. It was very pretty, there's no doubt of that; the lagoon was something to make you gasp; but I wasn't concerned with beauty. For let me tell you this: Robinson Crusoe stuff may be all very nice to read about, but when you find yourself fixed that way it gives you a funny sort of weak feeling in the tummy. The more I realized that I was likely to spend the rest of my days by myself, the less I liked it. You see, knowing about the pearls, for the first time in years I had a real object in living. I kept a weather eye open for Castanelli's schooner, in case he came back; but I never saw him again, which leads me to think that I was right in assuming that he didn't know where we were when he tried to kill me. Otherwise he would certainly have been back for the pearls.'

'How long were you there?' asked Ginger.

'Only three months. Oh, I was lucky, there's no doubt o' that. I was taken off by a couple of Marquesans from Rutuona in a canoe; a boy and a girl named Breaker of Shells and Full Moon—at least, those are the English equivalents. They are easier to remember than the native names. They had been out fishing for albicore, got caught in a squall and carried out to sea—not that it worried them much. That sort of thing is always happening to them. They are as much at home on the sea as on land. They can swim as soon as they can walk, so always being used to the water they have no fear of it. Anyhow, they spotted my island and came ashore for a few fresh nuts. Instead, they found me. They thought it was no end of a joke. I was certainly glad to see them. They took me back to Rutuona with them.

'It took me two months, hopping from island to island in a canoe, to get to Nuku-hiva, the biggest island of the group, where I had to wait another three months before Pierre Loubert came along in his schooner and took me to Tahiti. I found that Castanelli had been back and gone off again, having reported me as lost overboard in a gale. From the fact that he went off again so soon, I fancy that he went to look for the pearl-bed—as he was bound to. What man wouldn't, with a fortune waiting to be picked up? But without knowing the exact position he might as well look for a particular grain of sand on a beach. I knew where the bed was, of course, and I'd have told him if the fool hadn't tried to kill me. There was just a chance that he might find the island if he looked long enough, but even that would be a tall order.

'The end of the story is that I tried to get one of the island skippers interested in my find, offering to go fifty-fifty. But there was nothing doing. You see, the trouble is that every loafer and beachcomber in the South Seas has a tale to tell about a wonderful pearl-bed. You are always hearing such stories, but nobody believes them. They just laugh at you. And to tell the honest truth, if I hadn't seen the pearls with my own eyes I should have laughed at anyone who tried to pitch me a yarn like that. There were plenty of such beds years ago, but they've all been worked out—at least, that's what people think. I'd picked up a small pearl or two on Rutuona; the natives made me a present of them when I left; they enabled me to get a little money, but not enough to fit out an expedition of my own, with diving-gear, which I should need, because with that weight of water going up and down it would be too dangerous for skin-diving. The boys would be willing to try, no doubt, but it wouldn't be fair to ask them, although a good Paumotuan will go down over a hundred feet and think nothing of it. The only thing left to do was to go to Australia to see if I could raise the money there. I was afraid Castanelli would come back to Tahiti, and if we met face to face one of us was likely to get killed and the other arrested for murder. But it was just the same in Australia. One or two people were mildly interested, but they wanted to know too much. They wouldn't put down the money without my telling them where the pearl-bed was, and that was something I wasn't prepared to do. I had just enough money left to bring me back to England, where I thought people might not be so sceptical—but——'

'You haven't succeeded?' murmured Biggles.

'No.'

'Frankly, I don't think you will. I'm afraid the proposition is too much of a gamble for most people.

'Gamble!' cried Sandy, angrily. 'It's no gamble. I could go straight to the spot.'

Biggles took out his notebook and pencil. 'How far is it from Tahiti to your island—what's the name of it, by the way?'

'It hasn't a name as far as I can make out.'

'All right. For the sake of argument we'll call it Sandy's Island. How far is it from Tahiti?'

'Getting on for eight hundred miles.'

'And the lagoon? Is it a safe anchorage?'

'As safe as anything in the South Seas.'

'Could you land a flying-boat there?'

'You're not thinking of *flying*?'

'Why not?'

Sandy scratched his head. 'No reason, I suppose. I've just never thought of it that way. It would probably be more expensive than using a schooner.'

'It would be quicker.'

'It would certainly be that.'

'Could we dive from a flying-boat?'

'Certainly—in calm weather, of course.'

'You've done some diving?'

'Plenty.'

'You'd know all about the sort of kit to get?'

'Of course.'

'Then if we provided the flying-boat and paid all expenses, would you be willing to split the profits?'

'Would I? You bet I would!' cried Sandy, enthusiastically. 'You provide the equipment; I'll provide the pearls, and we'll split the profits four ways. How's that?'

'Suits us,' agreed Biggles, without hesitation, glancing at Algy and Ginger in turn.

'When would you be ready to start?' asked Sandy.

'Just as soon as we can get the equipment together. I'll give you a cheque. You go off and see about the diving-gear, and anything else you think we might need—but keep the weight down as far as you can. I'll attend to the machine.'

Sandy swallowed the rest of his drink at a gulp. 'I'm on my way,' he declared. 'The pearls are as good as ours.'

'Don't forget to bring your bowler hat to measure them in,' smiled Biggles. 'We shall be satisfied with nothing less than the hatful you spoke about at the beginning.'

2

AN ENCOUNTER WITH CASTANELLI

ALTHOUGH they did not waste a single day, it was nearly two months before the expedition arrived at its first temporary base in the South Pacific; for not until Biggles had examined the situation closely did any of them realize the difficulties involved in getting an aircraft to the Islands. In the first place there were papers to arrange, although this was fairly simple compared with the business of getting the machine where they wanted it. And there was, of course, the matter of selection of the ideal type of aircraft.

Now there are two ways of getting an aeroplane to a given destination; it can be shipped there or it can be flown under its own power. Contrary to general belief, in the case of a distant destination it is less expensive to ship a machine than fly it, for which reason new machines destined for Australia from Great Britain or American usually arrive on board ship. Naturally, this is not the case with specially organized flights, or the regular air lines.

The machine chosen for the arduous duties that would be required of it was a 'Scud' twin-engined flying-boat, a high-wing monoplane with long-range tanks that had been built for a company proposing to operate a coastal service round Great Britain. The company, however, had failed financially, and the machine was put on the market. Biggles snapped it up cheaply, a most satisfactory bargain considering that it suited their purpose admirably.

It was at this juncture, when ways and means of getting the machine to the South Seas were under discussion, that Sandy, having bought such equipment as he considered necessary, suggested that it might be a good thing if he went on ahead and made such arrangements as now appeared not only desirable but imperative. He pointed out that the arrival at Tahiti of an aircraft the size of the flying-boat could hardly fail to create a sensation, a state of affairs that it would be better to avoid if possible. He proposed, therefore, to cable an agent in Australia to forward a supply of petrol and oil to the British island of Raratonga, which is on the main shipping line to Australia. He would go direct to Raratonga, and leaving a supply of petrol and oil for the machine when it arrived, would arrange for the transport of the rest by sea to Vaitie, one of the smaller of the Cooke islands, which had a large, almost landlocked lagoon that would make a perfect anchorage for the machine while it was being refuelled, after it had been flown up from Raratonga. At Vaitie the machine would pick him up, with the fuel, and go on in a single straight flight to Sandy's Island. These arrangements were made to prevent unnecessarily long oversea flights, involving risks which were better avoided.

This plan was adopted, more for the reason that it was the best one so far suggested than because it was ideal. In Biggle's opinion it was far from ideal, but for want of a better one he accepted it. The 'Scud' was therefore put on board an Australian-bound steamer calling at Raratonga, and Biggles, Algy, and Ginger travelled with it.

Sandy had departed for Raratonga immediately on the approval of his plan, taking the stores and equipment with him, so that when the others arrived there nearly a month later they found that, in accordance with the programme, he had already departed for Vaitie, having chartered a native lugger for the purpose. He had, of course, left a supply of fuel and oil at Raratonga, more than enough to enable the machine to fly to Vaitie.

A week of hard work had been required to put the machine in an airworthy condition, so that when it arrived at Vaitie it carried three rather weary airmen, who were not in the least pleased to discover that Sandy had been involved in a mishap which seriously affected their schedule. He was there, as was the petrol and equipment, but his arm was in a sling; and the story he told, apologetically, was this. He had arrived at Vaitie, which was uninhabited, well ahead of time, and learning that the native skipper of the lugger, a Polynesian named Namu, was going on to Tahiti on business, and would call at Vaitie again for fresh water on the way back, he thought it would be a good plan if he went along with him—having nothing more to do—and pick up such news as he might, particularly anything concerning Castanelli. The point was — and in this the others agreed— that there had been a long delay in which there was just a chance that Castanelli had discovered the pearl-bed. If that was so, the news would certainly have got back to Tahiti. So Sandy had gone. One of the very first people he had seen on stepping ashore at Tahiti was Castanelli himself. Before he could get back to the boat trouble had been caused—deliberately, of course—by Castanelli's Solomon Island boys, and although he had tried to avoid it, in the mêlée he had been stabbed in the arm. Naturally, he had been tempted to report the matter to the governor of the island, but, realizing the danger in which he stood, he had gone straight back to the boat and persuaded Namu to return to Vaitie. He had got back to Vaitie all right, but he was still incapacitated by his arm. He had only just got back. Namu and his lugger were still there. That, briefly, was Sandy's story.

Biggles examined the wound as saw at a glance that Sandy was not fit to travel, nor would he be for the next ten days. The gash was an ugly one and looked inflamed, while Sandy himself was feverish. To go on in such circumstances was to court trouble, for wounds heal slowly in the tropics, and should it turn out that medical attention became necessary, the expedition would have to be abandoned at the very outset of operations. Rather than risk this Biggles resolved to delay the final journey to Sandy's Island until it was clear that the wound was healing satisfactorily. It was an unfortunate beginning but it could not be helped.

Instead of doing nothing while they were waiting, Biggles

suggested that, as the lugger was still at Vaitie, two of them
might go to Tahiti to pick up any news that might affect the
expedition—assuming, of course, that the Polynesian was
willing to make the journey for a monetary consideration. He
would not use the aircraft for fear of attracting undesirable
publicity to themselves in Tahiti. The weakness of Sandy's
scheme had been that he was known to Castanelli, but this need
no longer apply. And so it came about that the night following
their arrival at Vaitie saw Biggles and Ginger on the lugger
bound for Papeete Harbour, Tahiti. Algy had been left behind to
look after Sandy, but with instructions to risk the consequences
and fly him to Tahiti should the wound become worse.

Three days on the open sea in a small boat was a new
experience for Ginger; he was rather nervous at first, particularly
when sharks kept them company, as they often did. However,
fair weather and a favourable breeze prevailed, and they sailed
unobtrusively into the famous island harbour of Papeete on the
evening of the third day. Ginger was breathless at the tropical
beauty of the coastal scenery as they sailed along it, and as soon
as they were ashore he would have explored it further. But
Biggles pointed out that they were not visiting the island for
pleasure, and declared his intention of returning to Vaitie as
soon as their inquiries were complete. Ginger took what
consolation he could from the fact that there would be plenty of
time for exploration when they got to Sandy's Island.

With the object of pursuing the inquiries forthwith, Biggles
directed his steps towards the Restaurant du Port, as Sandy had
advised. It was nearly full, and Ginger gazed at the extraordinary assortment of humanity it held with fascinated interest.
There were a few well-dressed tourists, mostly Americans,
brawny island skippers, bearded down-at-heel white men of
many nationalities, islanders of every shade between black and
yellow, Chinese traders, and good-looking Polynesians, some
with hibiscus or other tropical blossoms tucked behind their ears
or into their hair. Odd words of English, French, German, and
unknown languages reached Ginger as he followed Biggles
across the room.

Biggles found two seats in a corner and ordered some food. 'It's rather hard to know where to start making inquiries,' he said, above the babble of conversation. 'Namu said he would come along if he could manage it, after he had finished some business he has to attend to. I hope he does. I think he could help us.'

'You haven't told him anything about Castanelli?'

'No, but he knows that in some way we are concerned with him. Apparently he was with Sandy when he got knifed in the arm, and although Sandy didn't tell him any details, he no doubt drew certain conclusions. In any case, he probably overheard enough scraps of our conversation at Vaitie to give him an idea of how the wind blows.'

Ginger had taken a liking to the big, athletic, open-faced Polynesian skipper, and he said so. 'I think we might have done better had we taken him into our confidence,' he murmured. 'He would be better able to deal with this situation than us. He must hear all sorts of gossip. Ah! here he is, coming in now.'

Ginger noticed that more than one pair of curious eyes followed the Polynesian across the room as he walked straight over to the table where Biggles and he were sitting. He pulled out a chair and sat down. 'You look for Capitan Castanelli, *peut-être?*' he said softly, in an odd mixture of English and French.

Biggles regarded him thoughtfully for a moment without answering. Then he nodded. 'Yes, we are interested in Castanelli,' he said.

'Bad man.'

'So I believe.'

'*Très mauvais.* Be on your guard.'

'Why? Do you know any reason why he should have anything against us? He doesn't even know us.'

'That one make trouble with everybody. He make trouble yesterday. He pull out in the morning.'

'You mean—he's in Papeete now?'

'Yes. His schooner *Avatara* is down in harbour. He back from Rutuona. He sail at dawn. Him plenty stores on board now.'

'What was the trouble?'

'He steal boy from Rutuona. Yesterday boy get ashore here

and run away. Castanelli catch him and beat him pretty hard. Say he signed on for voyage and try to desert. Haul him back.'

'You say he is sailing in the morning?'

'Yes, Governor tell him to clear out.'

'Where is he going?'

'He not say. Nobody knows except Castanelli and his boys. They wink and grin when anybody ask.'

'How did you learn all this?'

'My boys talk on waterfront—plenty gossip.'

'But what happened about the boy Castanelli stole from Rutuona? Has he still got him?'

The Polynesian shook his head. ''Fraid he have to go with Castanelli. Everyone afraid of Castanelli.'

'Even the Governor?'

'Maybe. Castanelli make much trouble.'

'But that's a scandalous thing,' cried Ginger, indignantly.

'I savvy bymeby that boy Shell-Breaker he jump overboard.'

Ginger started at the name. Biggles frowned and stared into Namu's face. 'What name did you say?' he asked, tensely.

'Shell-Breaker.'

'You mean—the boy Castanelli took from Rutuona?'

'Yes.'

In a flash Biggles understood. Castanelli had been to Rutuona. In some way he had learnt that Shell-Breaker had picked up Sandy, and must therefore know the approximate position of the island. Now, with the boy and stores on board, he was going in search of it.

'I think it's a good thing we came here,' Biggles told Ginger grimly. 'That's as much as we want to know. We'd better get back to Vaitie right away.' He glanced over his shoulder to ascertain the cause of a disturbance that had started near the door. A sudden silence fell. All eyes were on a short, thick-set man, with an Italian cast of countenance, who was advancing slowly down the room. His smooth, swarthy face was flushed, his eyes were half closed, and from the way he fingered his sleek black moustache he was evidently enjoying the mild sensation his appearance had created.

Namu had half risen to his feet, but he dropped back again into his seat and touched Biggles on the arm. 'Castanelli,' he whispered nervously.

'What about it?' asked Biggles. 'You've nothing to be afraid of, have you?'

'Maybe you not understand. If Castanelli go for me I do nothing.'

'Why not?'

'Castanelli white man. Me hit Castanelli I get into bad trouble.'

'Ah, I understand,' nodded Biggles, counting out some change to pay the bill. He looked up, however, as out of the corners of his eyes he saw that the Corsican had halted at their table. He was looking down at Namu with an expression of sinister animosity.

'What for you go sneaking round my schooner—eh, you scum?' he grated.

'I no go near your schooner, Capitan Castanelli,' answered Namu quickly.

The corners of Castanelli's mouth came down in an ugly snarl. He drew back his fist. 'You lying——' he broke off and stared belligerently at Biggles who had risen swiftly to his feet.

'Just a minute,' snapped Biggles. 'This is my party. I don't remember inviting you.'

There was dead silence in the room.

Castanelli glared at Biggles. 'You seet down,' he gritted viciously.

'Who do you think you are talking to—one of your boys?' asked Biggles, curtly.

'Get out of my way.'

'What do you think you are going to do?'

'Pulp zis scum.'

Biggles shook his head. 'Oh, no, you're not,' he said evenly. 'If there's any pulping to be done I'll take a hand.'

Castanelli's eyes opened wide. 'Do you know who I am?' he snarled, in a voice that was evidently intended to intimidate.

'Yes, I know who you are and what you are,' returned Biggles evenly. 'Your name's Castanelli, and you're just a cheap bully who thinks he owns the Islands. Now get away from my table.'

Castanelli's arm moved like lightning. His hand flashed to his pocket. It came up with a knife in it.

Biggles snatched up a glass of ice water from the table and flung it in his face. He took a swift pace forward. His left jabbed Castanelli in the solar plexus, and, as the Corsican's head jerked forward under the blow, Biggles's right fist hooked his jaw with a crack that sounded as if someone had broken a cricket stump across the middle.

Castanelli grunted, staggered, and went over backwards, taking with him a table at which a young American tourist had been sitting. The American jumped aside in the nick of time. 'Oh, boy, oh, boy!' he breathed. 'What a beauty!'

Nobody else in the room moved. The proprietor stood nervously wringing his hands, but made no attempt to interfere. Biggles remained where he was, watching Castanelli slowly pick himself up.

The Corsican clambered to his feet and shook his head. His little eyes, glinting with hate, flashed round the room at the witnesses of his discomfiture. They came to rest on Biggles. For a moment he hesitated, breathing heavily. 'I shall see you again some time,' he hissed through his teeth.

'Wait for a dark night when I'm looking the other way, eh?' sneered Biggles. 'You crooked little swine! Go and get on with your work of trading liquor round the islands.'

Castanelli glanced again round the room. Several people were smiling, but their smiles faded quickly when the Corsican's eyes came to rest on them. Castanelli slowly put his knife away, walked quietly to the door, and disappeared into the darkness.

Instantly a babble of voices broke out.

'Time somebody handed him that,' declared a down-at-heel beachcomber in a dirty cotton jacket with no collar or tie.

'Then why didn't you do it?' asked Biggles, coldly. 'You look as if you've had plenty of time.' He turned to the others. 'Come on,' he said. 'Finish your drinks and let's go.'

While he was waiting for them a tall fair-haired man,

obviously a Scandinavian, in a well-worn skipper's uniform, came across and held out his hand. 'I'm Sven Orlaffsen,' he said. 'Good work, boy. I own the *Caramayo*. If I can do anything at any time just let me know.

'Thanks, Orlaffsen,' returned Biggles. 'I'll bear it in mind.' He turned and walked towards the door, watched by everyone in the room. 'Have you finished your business?' he asked Namu as soon as they were outside.

'Yes, boss. I've finished.'

'Ready to sail?'

'When you say.'

'Good. I'm going to find the Governor and ask him to inquire into this business of Shell-Breaker,' declared Biggles. 'We've got to get that boy out of Castanelli's hands.'

Namu was staring across the moonlit harbour. 'It's too late,' he said.

'Why—what do you mean?'

'Castanelli make sail. There go his schooner.' Namu pointed.

Following the direction indicated, Biggles saw a schooner moving slowly towards the harbour mouth. Water still dripped from her anchor. 'He didn't waste much time, did he?' he said bitterly. 'I'm afraid we can't do anything about it now. But I have a feeling we shall meet that gentleman again. We'd better get back to Vaitie.'

They began walking towards where the lugger was moored.

3

GINGER HAS A FRIGHT

ON their arrival at Vaitie they found Sandy's arm much improved, but he was definitely alarmed by their news that Castanelli had got hold of Shell-Breaker.

'I can tell you what happened,' he declared furiously. 'Castanelli was cruising about looking for the shell-bed and put in at Rutuona for fresh water. He would be bound to put in there because it is one of the biggest islands in the group, and at the same time the one nearest to the area where I went overboard. The natives must have told him that I had been there; you can't blame them for that. Very little happens on the Islands, and my staying there would be regarded as a first-class piece of news. Naturally, Castanelli would make inquiries and so find out the names of the boy and girl who picked me up. He was too wise to lay hands on the girl; white men have lost their heads for less— even in recent years; but he got hold of young Shell-Breaker and carried him away. His stores were probably low, so he came back to Tahiti to refit before going on to the pearl-bed. I'll bet you any money that is what happened.'

Namu, who had been listening to the conversation, nodded. 'Yes, he bring plenty stores, and new diving-suit,' he said.

'How do you know he's got a diving-suit?' asked Sandy sharply.

'I sell my copra to Sing Hoo. I know Sing Hoo has diving-gear. When I go this time, no diving-suit. I say, "Where diving-suit?" Sing Hoo say, "Castanelli buy it." '

'Well, that's plain enough,' declared Biggles. 'We needn't argue about it. It looks as if we'd better get along right away; we can still get there before Castanelli.'

'All the same, it's a pity he's got that boy with him,' muttered Sandy with a worried frown.

'It depends on how much the boy has told him,' returned Biggles. 'I suppose he'd tell everything?'

'I'm not so sure of that. Marquesans can be a funny lot. Their fathers were cannibals, don't forget; in fact, there are still whispers of cannibalism. If they like a white man they'll do anything for him; if not, you could cut them to pieces before they'd speak. Shell-Breaker might have told the truth, but on the other hand he might have led Castanelli up the garden path.'

'Will Castanelli call at Rutuona on the way to your island, assuming that the boy has told him where it is?' asked Biggles.

'Bound to. It's a long run to the island. He'll want fresh water. His boys will want fresh nuts.'

'Then how about going on to Rutuona and waiting for him to

turn up? If the natives would help we might make him give up Shell-Breaker,' suggested Ginger. 'We could still get to the island first.'

'There's something in that,' declared Sandy. 'By this time Castanelli will be thinking that he's got clear away. The last thing he'll think of is that we've got an aircraft, and that we might get to Rutuona first.'

'At any rate, it's worth trying,' decided Biggles. 'We'll get to Rutuona for a start, and see how the land lies. We'll leave the final decision until then.'

The 'Scud' floated on the placid lagoon ready for an immediate take-off. What petrol and stores were not immediately required had already been hidden by Algy while the others were away, so as it was still forenoon there was nothing to delay their departure. After thanking him for his assistance, they said good-bye to Namu and his crew of three grinning boys, and took their places in the machine. The engines were started, and in a few minutes her keel was cutting a creamy wake across the limpid surface of the blue water. Biggles was at the joystick, with the chart and a compass-course pinned on the side of the instrument-board.

For hours they flew on at a comfortable cruising speed over an illimitable expanse of sea, sometimes passing an island which looked like an emerald lying on blue velvet. On one occasion they flew high over a tiny black speck which Sandy declared was a native canoe. Late in the afternoon he pointed to a spot on the horizon. 'Schooner!' he shouted. 'That must be Castanelli.'

Not long afterwards a faint blur appeared ahead. Sandy had already announced that they were approaching Rutuona, a fact which he was able to deduce, he said, by the colour of the sky in that direction; instead of the customary deep blue it held a suspicion of reflected green. That he was correct was soon made manifest when the distant blur crystallized into a line of jagged peaks.

'That isn't my idea of a South Sea island,' stated Ginger, as they drew nearer.

'The Marquesas are not South Sea islands in the generally

accepted sense of the word,' Sandy told him. 'Most islands are coral formations, and lie low, like the Paumotus. The Marquesas are a wee bit terrifying at first; some of them stick straight up out of the sea for a thousand feet or more. But most of them have good beaches, although they run up to wild crags in the interior, which, for the most part, is a mass of jungle.

'Any snakes?' asked Ginger. 'They're my pet aversion.'

'No, but there are some nasty ten-inch centipedes that you'll do well to leave alone. In fact, you'd better not touch anything until we've had a stroll round. I'll show you what to leave alone.'

By this time the machine was gliding down, and Sandy went forward to show Biggles where to land. 'There's the village,' he said, pointing to a few palm-thatched shacks on the edge of a bay. 'There's another village on the far side of the island, but it doesn't amount to much; this is the centre of the island's social life. You can come down anywhere in the bay; there are no rocks or anything, but keep an eye open for canoes.'

Biggles circled slowly round the village, losing height, and then dropped the nose of the machine towards the blue bay, which was bounded on one side by a long, curving strip of golden beach.

Ginger regarded the scene through a side window, spellbound with delight. 'What a paradise!' was all he could say.

'Yes, I reckon it's as near Paradise as anywhere on earth,' agreed Sandy. 'But like every paradise, there are serpents.'

'Serpents?' queried Ginger. 'You said——'

'Losh, I'm not thinking of snakes,' declared Sandy. 'It's a bit hard to explain,' he went on. 'Nature is seldom prodigal without throwing in a snag or two. Breadfruit and bananas grow on those hills—but so do poisons. There are orchids in the woods—and there are sandflies, which bite like fury and leave a spot of blood where they bite. There are pearls in the sea, but there are also sharks, and other unpleasant things. Living coral is one of the loveliest things in the world, but don't scratch yourself on it, or you may be poisoned. And on top of all that, there's sickness. A hundred years ago there were more than ten thousand people on this island; now there aren't more than two hundred. The rest have died from the diseases white men have brought, like consumption, or from leprosy brought by the Chinese. A few more years and all the natives will be gone; a tragedy, for they are just big lovable children. The curse of it is they know they're dying, and they don't care. They'll hardly bother to pick the breadfruit and coconuts. But don't let's talk about it.'

By this time the 'Scud' was on the water, taxiing towards the village where a little crowd of natives stood dancing with excitement.

'This is the first time an aeroplane has landed here, I guess,' remarked Sandy, putting his head out of the window. '*Kaoha*,' he roared.

The excitement on the beach was intensified, and it was clear that Sandy had been recognized—not a difficult matter in view of his red hair. Several canoes were launched, and by the time the voyagers were near the beach ready to disembark the 'Scud' was surrounded by natives of both sexes and all ages, some swimming and some in canoes. They greeted Sandy joyfully by name, calling him Andie. He in turn spoke to several of them personally, and the air was full of delighted greetings of '*Kaoha*'. Leaving the 'Scud' riding at anchor on the still water, the airmen climbed into the willing canoes and were soon on the palm-fringed beach.

Sandy took an old, heavily tattooed native by the arm and pulled him towards Biggles. 'Let me introduce you to Chief Roaring Wave,' he said, and shouted with laughter at the alarmed expression on Biggles's face as the Chief smelt him carefully before rubbing noses. 'The Chief doesn't speak much English, but he knows French, although he prefers to use his own Marquesan,' went on Sandy. 'I know a bit of the lingo so we shall get on all right.'

Biggles noticed that several young men kept in the back-ground, and he called Sandy's attention to the fact. 'They look as if they'd rather hit us on the head with a war club than be friendly,' he observed.

Sandy spoke to the Chief, who answered with a pantomine of actions; then he turned again to the others. 'Roaring Wave says they're afraid of being kidnapped,' he said. 'That's the result of Castanelli coming here and running off with Shell-Breaker.'

'Tell him that we are going to try to get Shell-Breaker back,' answered Biggles.

Sandy spoke again to the Chief, and once more translated for the benefit of the others. 'He says everything on the island is ours,' he announced. 'He means it, too—you needn't doubt that. They'll give you anything, these people. He says he's having a house prepared for us right away, and will give a feast to-night.'

'It's all right about the house, but I'm not so sure about the feast,' returned Biggles. 'If that was Castanelli's schooner we saw he ought to arrive here soon after dark. Rather than get involved in a party, we ought to watch for it.'

Sandy had another long conversation with the Chief. 'He understands,' he said, turning to Biggles. 'He is going to send some warriors up into the hills to keep watch, and will warn us when the *Avarata* shows up. Hello! There's little Full Moon, Shell-Breaker's girl friend. She was with him when they picked me up, you remember.'

A pretty girl of about fifteen years of age, in a light blue *pareu*— the single garment common to both sexes—her brown skin glowing with health, ran up, laughing, and seized Sandy's hands without any suggestion of shyness. '*Kaoha! Kaoha*, Andie,' she said, over and over again.

Sandy pulled her hair affectionately. 'We're going to get Shell-Breaker back,' he told her.

At the mention of her lost friend her face clouded. '*Aue!*' she said sadly. 'I weep for him.'

'Come on, let's get some food ashore,' broke in Biggles. 'We'd better bring a few presents for the Chief, too. We can then make ourselves comfortable for the evening.'

Many willing hands helped them with the light task, and they were soon in the 'house' the Chief had placed at their disposal.

'How far are we now from your island?' Biggles asked Sandy.

'Twenty to thirty miles, not more.'

'Wouldn't it be better to use this place as a base?'

'I'm afraid we should use too much petrol going to and fro. We might have a lot of journeys to make, going out and back every day, and it would soon use up what we've got. If we go across to my island it wouldn't even be necessary for us to fly; we could just taxi out to the pearl-bed every morning—at least, in calm weather. Then again, I doubt if it would be wise to let too many people know what we are doing. There is always a chance of a schooner calling, and these people in all innocence might give our game away.'

Biggles nodded. 'I think you're right,' he said. 'We'll go on to your island as soon as we've settled our account with Castanelli.'

The light meal was soon over, and Ginger, unable to contain his curiosity, strolled outside and walked slowly along the deserted beach to a point beyond the village, which consisted merely of a few palm-thatched huts set in a grove of towering coconut palms. The sea was flat calm. The sun was going down, leaving the sky a pale egg-shell blue. The fronds of the palms, quivering in the last breath of breeze, came gradually to rest. The silence was almost uncanny. Before him stretched the beach, devoid of life except for innumerable hermit crabs that snapped their shells at his approach before bolting into their holes among the rocks. Farther on, the way appeared to be barred by a huge landslide of rocks that had fallen from a cliff above. Remembering Sandy's warning he went no farther, but had stopped to gaze at the scene when there came a patter of footsteps behind him. Looking round he saw that it was Full Moon, carrying a primitive fishing rod.

'Plenty *tupa*,' she said, smiling, pointing at the crabs. 'Plenty fish, too. You watch.' She took Ginger's hand and walked on to the rocks, clambering over them until she found a place that suited her, when, baiting her hook with pieces of shrimp, she soon had a number of small fish flopping on the rock, giving each one its native name as she hauled it out, making Ginger repeat the names after her.

Ginger, enthralled, could only gaze down through the crystal-clear water at the strange world below. He could see every cranny and crevice in the rocks, about which darted shoals of brightly coloured fish, appearing to float in air. Once he saw a huge eel, fully fifteen feet long, with a terrifying face, glide smoothly out of a dark cavern and disappear under an overhanging ledge. He was still watching the spot for it to reappear when he became aware that Full Moon was no longer chattering and, looking round to ascertain the cause of her silence, he saw that she was gazing fixedly at a gloomy cave in the rocks near to which they had passed in order to reach the place they now occupied, and which they would have to re-pass to reach the beach. He, too, stared at the cave, and experienced an unpleasant sensation akin to fear when he saw something move.

A wild shriek from Full Moon split the silence. Facing the village and cupping her hands round her mouth she screamed, '*Feke—feke—feke!*'

Instantly four or five men dashed out of their houses and raced towards the spot, each carrying a long fish-spear. They shouted excitedly at Full Moon as they approached, but she only pointed to the cave. '*Feke,*' she said again.

The men formed a rough semicircle round the front of the cave, while Ginger, who was wishing himself farther from the scene, moved back, although he could not get very far on account of the face of cliff that backed the rocks. With a sinking feeling in the pit of his stomach, he could only watch the cave, whence now darted out long arms towards the natives. Full Moon joined him. '*Ta-ta-ta-ta,*' she rattled out. 'We are not afraid of the ugly beast. See, that is my brother.' She pointed to one of the natives. 'He has killed many *feke. Pakeka!* We will kill this one, too.'

'What is it?' asked Ginger, although he had already a pretty good idea.

'Debil fish. Big Debil fish.'

Ginger pressed himself back against the cliff as the huge octopus slowly emerged from the cave to give battle to the prancing warriors who menaced it. Never in his life had he seen such a horror. It was a hugh, dark-purple mass of flesh, covered with warty excrescences, with a head rather like that of an elephant. In it were set two enormous slate-grey eyes, gleaming with demoniac hate. Eight arms coiled and groped out fourteen or fifteen feet in front of it. Ginger was only a few yards from their extremities.

The natives stood their ground, slashing and stabbing furiously, but the octopus advanced. Once a slimy arm touched Ginger's leg, and at its icy touch he cried out. One of the warriors slashed it off, but the piece of tentacle still clung to his leg, until with a shudder of loathing he tore it away.

The natives now launched a furious attack, ripping and slashing with their knives as well as spears. Several of the coiling arms were severed or mutilated, and to Ginger's unspeakable horror the beast began moaning and groaning in a dreadfully human manner. But the fight was nearly over. The warriors rushed in and thrust again and again into the quivering body until it ceased to move.

Full Moon danced with joy. 'We will eat him,' she cried, laughing into Ginger's face.

'You can—but not me,' declared Ginger, who was nearly sick at the thought. 'Phew, what a brute! I think I'll go back and join the others.'

Leaving Full Moon helping to cut up the carcass, he returned to the house through the gathering twilight. But before he could describe his adventure a tattooed warrior came racing down the hill towards them. 'Atanelli, he come!' he cried.

'He means Castanelli,' declared Sandy. 'We'd better go and hear the news.'

4
THE RESCUE PARTY

THERE was no need to go far, for most of the village had assembled on the beach, and the warriors were chattering with excitement. Sandy listened for a moment or two. 'That's awkward,' he said, turning to the others. 'It's Castanelli all right, but he has put into a bay on the far side of the island. I ought to have thought of that. He is probably afraid to come in here, in case somebody sticks a spear into him. Some of the young bloods are talking about doing it. I've told them not to; we don't want murder done—at least, not while we're here.'

'Well, what's the best thing to do?' asked Biggles. 'How far is it round the coast to this bay?'

'You can't get round the coast—except, of course, by canoe. I should say it would be between fifteen and twenty miles.'

Biggles whistled. 'As much as that? How far if we cut across the island?'

'Seven or eight miles, but it isn't easy going. I've never done it, but I've been part of the way. It's the dickens of a pull across that central ridge; it goes up to over three thousand feet, you know. And it's dangerous; not only on account of falling, although if you miss your step you might drop a thousand feet before you hit the jungle underneath, but there are wild animals.'

'What sort of wild animals?' asked Ginger.

'Bulls and dogs. The dogs are the worst. I'm only speaking from hearsay, but I've heard tales about a pack of white dogs that run wild on a plateau somewhere up there. It's a tame breed gone wild; the dogs must have been left behind by a trader or a whaling-ship years ago. Cats go wild in the same way on many of the islands.'

'I can't think that they'd be likely to worry us,' replied Biggles. 'But I leave it to you. Is the trip practicable? We don't want Castanelli to get away with that boy if we can prevent it.'

'I'll ask Roaring Wave,' answered Sandy, walking over to the Chief. He was soon back. 'Yes, he says it can be done,' he announced, 'but it's tough going. He will let us have some boys who know the way to guide us.'

'Then the sooner we start the better,' declared Biggles. 'What about weapons—had we better take rifles?'

'We don't want to clutter ourselves up more than is necessary,' returned Sandy. 'And we don't want to start a gun battle. We've all got revolvers. They ought to be enough.'

'All right. Then tell the Chief we are ready to start.'

In a few minutes they were on their way, escorted by half-a-dozen warriors with torches, and soon found themselves following a trail up a steep mountain-side, hemmed in on both sides by impenetrable jungle, all the more sinister on account of the flickering torches.

Crossing a brook Ginger felt a hand slip into his, and looking down to see who it was he was amazed to find Full Moon. '*Kaoha*,' she said, smiling, showing her white teeth. 'Me come.'

Ginger regarded her bare feet in alarm. 'You'll get your feet cut to pieces,' he said.

'No cut,' declared Full Moon. 'Plenty hard—run on coral.'

Biggles, hearing talking, turned round. 'Here, what are you doing?' he asked, as his eyes fell on Full Moon.

'Oh, leave her alone,' put in Sandy. 'You needn't worry about her. In fact, she may come in useful. Shell-Breaker is her friend, don't forget.'

'All right, if you say so,' returned Biggles briefly, and went on up the trail, which now followed the course of the brook. Wild flowers, including many species of orchids, grew in luxuriant profusion among giant maidenhair ferns, and hung in garlands from tree-ferns. Thousands of guinea-pigs scampered away in front of them.

The path became steeper and steeper, climbing higher and higher above deep gorges, and skirting fearful precipices. The breadfruit-trees and coconut palms were left far below. The trail disappeared under enormous boulders, and it was often necessary to leap from rock to rock.

Looking back while passing across an open space, Ginger saw that they were on the saw-like ridge of what must once have been the crater of a volcano. Far below lay the anchorage, the 'Scud', her white wings reflecting the moonlight, looking like a minute winged insect inside the sweep of the bay. Beyond, the open sea gleamed like quicksilver, stretching, it seemed, to eternity, far beyond the concern of mortal men.

The path went on up. Ginger had climbed many mountains, but never one like this. It seemed as if the earth itself had exploded, pouring out its rocky heart and leaving it in every conceivable fantastic shape. Now in single file, the torch-bearers, unconcerned, skirted a chasm so deep that Ginger dared not look down it. He remembered it afterwards for a long time. It haunted him in his sleep. But he struggled on along the jagged ridge, clutching at handholds whenever they offered. Full Moon leapt lightly from rock to rock, laughing at Ginger's nervousness.

It was the summit, or rather the apex, of the ridge, and thereafter the trail began to fall quickly towards a deep, basin-like depression, clear of trees, which Ginger suspected was the crater of the extinct volcano. Reaching the centre of it, the warriors extinguished their fast-expiring torches and sat down to rest. Ginger was glad of it, and threw himself down beside the others. Hardly had he done so when he was brought to his feet again by the blood-curdling howls of what sounded like a wolf-pack in full cry. The warriors also sprang up in alarm, and took refuge behind the white men. 'The dogs—the dogs!' cried one.

'By gosh! They're right. Here they come!' snapped Biggles, jumping up and taking out his automatic as a pack of white dogs, ghostly in the moonlight, burst into view. They ran straight at the party.

Ginger grabbed Full Moon and thrust her behind him, at the same time levelling his weapon. Shots rang out. A great white beast was nearly on him. He fired point blank, and then side-stepped, dragging Full Moon with him away from the howling animal, which was instantly set upon by others and torn to pieces.

The crater rang with the crash of shots and the snarls of wounded animals. The warriors had lighted their torches again, and flinging handfuls of dry grass on them soon had a fire blazing. The dogs backed away and sat down in a circle, tongues lolling, like a ring of ghosts; some had dragged away their wounded companions, and these they now devoured with much snarling.

'Well, what do we do next?' Biggles asked Sandy, who was in earnest conversation with the warriors.

'The boys say they will have to make fresh torches; the dogs won't face fire,' answered Sandy.

'I'm pleased to hear it,' returned Biggles grimly. 'Otherwise we look like being stuck here till morning.'

The natives were already collecting bunches of dry grass, and these they now tied on the ends of sticks while others kept guard. However, the dogs made no attempt to attack again, and when the fresh torches were lighted, flooding the scene with a ruddy glare, they began to slink away. The retirement became a rout when the natives began hurling firebrands and rocks at them.

Once the crater had been crossed the path dropped quickly, and the party was soon once more hemmed in by jungle. Soft moss flourished under foot. Nothing more was seen of the dogs. Ginger reached for an exquisite feathery flower, intending to give it to Full Moon; but the girl seized his arm and pulled it away. '*Puke*,' she said quickly. '*Puke.*'

Sandy looked round. 'Hi, don't touch that!' he shouted. 'It's *puke.*'

'What's *puke*, anyway?' inquired Ginger.

'You touch it and you'll know—and you'll never forget,' returned Sandy. 'It stings like fury. Stinging-nettles are balm compared with that stuff.'

Ginger went on thoughtfully, a trifle resentful that South Sea islands were not living up to the reputation with which he had credited them.

Another hour of steady walking, the last part accompanied by a heavy shower of rain, brought the party once more to the region of coconut palms. The natives stopped and put out their torches. One of them spoke quickly to Sandy.

'They say the bay is just ahead through this palm-grove,' he translated.

'I'll go forward and reconnoitre,' said Biggles, and disappeared between the towering boles of the palms. He was soon back. 'They're quite right,' he said. 'The schooner's there, about a hundred yards from the beach. There's a light on her, but I can't hear a sound, so I don't know whether the crew is on board or not. I can see a bit of a village a little way along; they might be there.'

'I should say Castanelli will be on the boat, and the boys in the village,' said Sandy. 'The boys would come ashore if Castanelli would let them, to drink brandy.'

'Brandy?'

'I mean native brandy—they make it out of the coconut flowers.'

'I see. Well, it doesn't matter. I'm not standing any nonsense from that swine Castanelli. It's no use mincing matters with fellows of his kidney. If he wants trouble he can have it. There are some canoes on the beach, so I propose taking one and going over to the schooner to demand Shell-Breaker. In fact, we can all go in one canoe. Ginger and I will tackle Castanelli. You, Algy, guard our rear in case his boys are about. And you, Sandy, had better remain in charge of the canoe. Tell our boys to stay where they are until we come back.' When he had finished speaking Biggles began to move forward towards the sea, which was soon seen shimmering through the palms.

There was no sign of life as they finally emerged from a dense shade of breadfruit-trees near the beach. A fire smouldered near the village; only this and the schooner riding at anchor on the bay revealed that human beings were in the vicinity. Silently they made their way along the beach to where three rather dilapidated canoes were lying, and launched the one that appeared to be in the best state of repair. For a moment or two it floated on the moonlit water with hardly a ripple, and then, under the impetus of the paddle Sandy had picked up, it forged towards the schooner, leaving behind it a wake that gleamed like living fire. Nobody spoke as the canoe came quiet under the schooner's counter. The only sound was the soft drip of water from Sandy's paddle.

Biggles reached up and swung himself abroad. Ginger and Algy followed him. Sandy remained in the canoe. 'Stay here, and keep your gun handy; if you have to use it, be careful, or you may hit one of us,' Biggles told Algy, and then walked towards the companion.

'Who's that?' roared a voice, as they reached the bottom of the steps.

Biggles opened the door of the cabin from which the voice came, and was met by the reek of tobacco-smoke and brandy. The yellow light of an oil lamp was half smothered by the fumes.

A cheap deal table occupied the centre of the cabin; on it was a chart which Castanelli had apparently been studying. He rose slowly to his feet, staring incredulously at Biggles and Ginger standing in the doorway. Then, ripping out an oath, he thrust the table aside. 'What in thunder do you want?' he snarled.

'I've come for that Rutuona boy you've got aboard,' answered Biggles curtly.

'Oh, you have, have you?' grated Castanelli, panting with fury.

'That's it,' nodded Biggles. 'Are you going to hand him over or do we take him?'

'I'll see you——,' began Castanelli.

Biggles cut him short. 'All right—that's enough,' he said. 'We'll take him. Go and find him, Ginger.'

Ginger turned and walked along the narrow corridor, shouting the boy's name. He was answered almost at once by a weak voice from the direction of the stern. He found a door and tried it, but it was locked. 'Are you in there, Shell-Breaker?' he called.

'Yes, in here,' came the voice.

Ginger put his heel against the lock and, bracing himself against the far side of the corridor, kicked out with all his strength. The door burst open. A foul stench assailed his nostrils, but he could see nothing, for the place was in darkness. Striking a match, he saw a native boy facing him. He looked weak and emaciated. 'Are you Shell-Breaker?' asked Ginger.

'Yes—me Shell-Breaker.'

'Good!' Ginger told him. 'I've come to take you away. Come on.' He walked back down the corridor with the boy following him.

'It's all right, here he is,' he told Biggles, who was still standing at the door of Castanelli's cabin, now holding an automatic in his hand.

Castanelli was mouthing like an animal, spitting out the most blood-curdling threats.

'If I have any further trouble with you, you blackguard, I'll close your foul mouth for good and all,' said Biggles coldly. 'Stay

where you are. You show your head on deck and I'll knock it off.'
He turned to Ginger. 'Get the boy into the canoe,' he ordered.

They went up on deck and found Sandy staring towards the
beach, where a canoe was just being launched by several
shadowy figures. 'Looks like Castanelli's crew coming back,'
observed Sandy. 'What shall we do about it? They'll make
trouble.'

'No trouble,' said a small voice from the water, near the side of
the canoe.

'Looking down, Ginger saw the smiling face of Full Moon.
'What are you doing here, you little monkey?' he asked.

'I show you,' said the girl, and disappeared under the water
like a fish.

'Into the canoe, everybody,' ordered Biggles. 'We'll get back
to the beach.'

By the time they had pushed off, the other canoe was already
moving rapidly towards the schooner. Castanelli appeared at
the rail of the ship and, seeing the other canoe coming, shouted
something.

'What did he say, Sandy?' asked Biggles, for Castanelli had
used a language unknown to him.

'He told his boys to sink us.'

'Is that all? Well, let them try it.'

The battle which appeared imminent did not take place,
however. The schooner-bound canoe, in accordance with
Castanelli's order, swung round to intercept the other, but when
it was still several yards away a commotion occurred which those
in the other canoe could not at first understand. There was a
sudden splashing in the water, a sharp crack of breaking wood,
and the canoe capsized, throwing its occupants into the water. A
peal of girlish laughter floated across the water above the
guttural cries of the Solomon Island boys.

'*Ta-ta-ta-ta*. Full Moon sink canoe,' chuckled Shell-Breaker,
and slid into the water.

Ginger watched for him to reappear but did not see him. 'My
gosh, Sandy, you were right when you said these people were like
fish,' he remarked.

They left Castanelli's crew swimming towards the schooner and went on to the beach. When they reached it they found Full Moon and Shell-Breaker waiting for them.

'Good!' said Biggles. 'I think that settles our business, so we may as well start back.'

Several natives had appeared from the direction of the village, but they were disposed to be friendly, and after a short conversation with Shell-Breaker they returned to their huts.

Biggles led the way back to where their own boys were waiting for them, Shell-Breaker's appearance causing a minor sensation.

Before starting on the return journey Sandy distributed some biscuits and chocolate which he had brought for the purpose. 'Atanelli, he ask plenty question, eh?' he asked Shell-Breaker.

'Yes, he say I show him island where you stay long time.'

'Did you tell him where it was?'

'No. I say island plenty far, but he say me plenty liar. Say make me show.'

'Well, you won't have to show him now,' answered Sandy, patting the boy's shoulder. 'You are coming back to the village with us.'

Castanelli's voice, still cursing, reached them faintly as they set off up the hill-side.

Dawn had broken by the time they reached the central crater, and this may have accounted for the fact that they saw no signs of the wild dogs. Moreover, being daylight, their task was much easier than it had been in the dark. Nevertheless, it was a weary party that finally marched down through the coconut-grove into the village, where Shell-Breaker was received like one returned from the grave.

Tired out, the others retired to their hut, and having arranged with Roaring Wave for a watch to be kept for Castanelli's schooner, should it come that way, they passed the rest of the day in sleep, having postponed departure for Sandy's island until dawn the following day.

GINGER woke up with a wild shout ringing in his ears. Startled, and still in a daze, he sprang to his feet, conscious of impending trouble. Running to the door, which overlooked the bay, he stared out, and saw that dawn had not long broken, for a faint flush of pink still diffused the pale azure sky; the palms stirred uneasily and a ripple spread across the face of the tranquil water as the dawn-wind caressed it. He looked first at the 'Scud'; it was still at its moorings, rocking gently as the ripple reached it. Then another movement caught his eyes. A brown figure was racing along the beach. It was Full Moon. 'Atanelli, he come!' she cried.

'What's that?' asked Biggles, from inside the hut. He had risen, and was putting on his jacket.

'It's Full Moon. She says Castanelli is coming,' answered Ginger.

Two steps brought Biggles to the door. 'Where is he?' he asked.

'I don't see him,' replied Ginger. 'Yes—look!' He pointed to a rugged mass of rock, a small islet which stood near the mouth of the bay, from behind which now appeared the schooner, all sails set to catch the light breeze before which it moved over the water as silently and gracefully as a bird. It heeled a little as the wind freshened, and came straight towards the beach as if Castanelli intended coming close inshore before dropping anchor.

'What's he doing? Why doesn't he shorten sail?' asked Sandy, who had now joined the others outside the door.

The schooner itself supplied the answer. It suddenly swung round and bore down on the 'Scud'.

'Look out! He's going to ram us!' cried Biggles.

For a moment a sort of panic prevailed, everybody acting as he thought best. Ginger dashed down to the water and struck out for the 'Scud', for the nearest canoe was some distance away. Full Moon joined him, slipping through the water with the effortless ease of a fish, the blue *pareu* she wore clinging to her lithe body like a skin. 'What you do?' she asked Ginger naïvely.

'Cut the cable,' gasped Ginger. 'Atanelli ram her.'

'Me cut,' said Full Moon, smiling, and went on at a speed which left Ginger far behind.

It was only about a hundred yards to the 'Scud', but to Ginger, in his haste, it seemed more like a mile. Long before he reached the machine he saw Full Moon swarm nimbly up the anchor rope and sit astride the nacelle. Her knife flashed in the bright sunlight. But by this time the schooner was only a cable's length away and travelling fast before the swiftly freshening breeze.

Fortunately, the wind came from the sea, so as soon as the cable was severed the 'Scud' began to drift inshore. Instantly the *Avarata* altered its course to follow, leaving no possible room for doubt as to Castanelli's intention. The direction of the 'Scud's' drift being inshore, however, lessened the distance Ginger had to travel. It came towards him broadside-on, threatening to force him under water, but he grabbed a wing-float and hung on. His weight on the float caused the wing to tilt down, and upon it he now climbed, squelching water and gasping for breath, for the fast swim had taken the wind out of him. Full Moon was still sitting on the nose of the machine watching the approaching schooner helplessly. Yelling to her to hold tight, Ginger ran up the wing, across the centre-section, and then to the tip of the far wing, which was, of course, nearer to the schooner. He knew that if the *Avarata* struck the flying-boat her sharp bows would crush it beyond all hope of repair, and for a moment or two it seemed as if nothing could prevent this from happening. There was no means by which Ginger could move the 'Scud' out of the track of the schooner. There was no time to start the engines. Castanelli evidently realized this, for his swarthy face was wreathed in smiles as he stood at the wheel with his boys around him.

But Ginger knew something that Castanelli did not know; that a flying-boat, owing to its shallow draught, rests on water as lightly as a feather, so that a child standing on a firm platform can move it. Ginger had no platform to stand on, for he was standing on the machine itself and therefore unable to move it. But he knew that if he could reach the schooner's bows before they struck the machine he would be able to fend the flying-boat away. It was now clear that the schooner would strike the 'Scud's' seaward wing, so he stood still, hands out, waiting. He nearly went into the sea when the machine tilted suddenly, as somebody else climbed on board, but there was no time to see who it was.

At the last moment the bows of the schooner seemed to bear down on him like a monstrous guillotine. With the curious faculty for noticing details which comes to one in such moments, he saw that the iron anchor was still dripping water and mud. Bracing his feet as far as he was able on the main spar, which he could feel under the fabric, he leaned outwards and clutched at the schooner's bows with both hands. Instantly the wing under his feet seemed to slide away from him as it took the weight of the schooner transmitted through his body. For a second he hung on, his body as rigid as a steel spring; then the 'Scud' began to swing round and he knew that he must fall. Even so he gave a final thrust with his feet. The wing shot away from under him and he fell head-long into the sea. A noise of rushing water filled his ears. A great black shape swept past him, and he struck out away from it into a strange world of profound blue. His lungs felt as if they must burst. He became sure of it. They could not endure such agony. He felt his body rising, but by this time he was too far gone to swim. Flashes of white light began to dance in front of his eyes; they grew brighter and brighter; then, almost with the violence of an explosion, his head broke the surface of the water and he filled his lungs with a mighty gasp.

For a moment or two he could only paddle feebly, just able to keep himself afloat; but then, as his strength returned to him, he looked round, and saw the scene through a sort of hazy blur. Full Moon was a few yards away, streaking towards him. Nearer to the beach was the 'Scud', undamaged, with Biggles standing on the wing looking in his direction. The schooner was some distance away, her canvas fluttering as she came round.

Ginger would never have got to the machine or the beach unaided, for he was completely exhausted; indeed, he was half drowned; but Full Moon came to his assistance and made him put his hand on her shoulder. Biggles, seeing them coming, disappeared into the cockpit of the machine, and a moment later, to Ginger's surprise, the engines started up. As he reached the 'Scud', Sandy dragged him on board; Full Moon followed; and not until then did he see the need for urgency. The *Avarata* had turned about, and was once more bearing down on them.

'Good work, laddie,' said Sandy. 'And that goes for Full Moon, too.'

'Why doesn't somebody shoot that skunk?' gasped Ginger, in a pained voice, staring at Castanelli, who was still at the wheel of the schooner.

'Because we don't want to start a pitched battle,' returned Algy, who was busy stowing gear into place.

Ginger saw that Shell-Breaker was also in the machine, and looked at Sandy inquiringly.

'If we leave him behind Castanelli may get hold of him,' explained Sandy, as the engines roared and the machine began to move forward.

'Gosh! we're taking off,' cried Ginger.

'There's no sense in sitting here and letting Castanelli ram us,' shouted Algy. 'He means business. Biggles says he's going to clear out and save any further trouble.'

Ginger nodded and sat down with a jolt as the machine bumped badly. 'What's going on?' he asked anxiously.

Algy was staring forward over Biggles's shoulder, a startled expression on his face.

'What is it?' asked Ginger, now thoroughly alarmed, and got up to look.

One glance, and there was no need to ask further questions. The 'Scud' was taking off straight into a sea which, except for a miracle or superb pilotage, would capsize them. He could guess what had happened. On account of the direction of the wind, Biggles had been compelled to take off towards the open ocean, unaware that outside the bay a choppy sea was running. And because the machine was heavily loaded it was taking an unusually long run. Now, when the size of the waves could be seen, it was too late to stop. To attempt to turn the machine at the rate it was now travelling would have been the most certain way to wreck it. So Biggles dared not turn, nor dared he throttle back, for the way the machine now had on it was sufficient to carry it into the white-crested breakers that surged across the mouth of the bay. So he could only go on, trusting that the machine would lift before it struck the curling combers.

Ginger held his breath as the machine tore on at ever-increasing speed to what looked like certain destruction. Neither Sandy nor Algy spoke. Not a muscle of Biggles's face moved. Twice he jerked the joystick back in an attempt to 'unstick' the machine, but here again, by a sort of bitter irony, the very calmness of the water in the bay defeated him; for a heavily loaded machine needs the 'kick' of a small wave to break it clear from the surface of the water.

The machine roared on, over water that was now suddenly turbulent. A green-flecked, foam-crested breaker, curling over at the top, reared high in front of it, and then swept down as if determined on the flying-boat's destruction. Biggles jerked the stick back into his stomach in a last effort to avoid the liquid avalanche. The machine lifted, but only sluggishly. The wave broke. There was a mighty cloud of spray. The machine shuddered and rocked. Then a force seemed to rise up beneath it and fling it into the air. For a moment it hung, rocking, like a bird that has been wounded, while the propellers threshed the air; then, just as it seemed that it must stall and fall into the breakers, the engines picked it up and it rose into the air. The danger was past.

Ginger sank down limply on a case of bully beef. The others did the same—except the two Polynesians, who had been blissfully unaware of the danger.

'Hey, mon, that's one way of taking off,' growled Sandy.

'It's one I don't like,' remarked Algy bitterly.

Now that the machine was steady, Ginger stood up and began wringing the salt water out of his clothes. Looking out of the side window he saw the island fast disappearing astern, with the schooner looking like a toy boat on the water. 'I'm glad to be out of that,' he remarked. 'I don't mind an occasional shock, but I don't like too many in quick succession. And without any breakfast, too,' he added plaintively.

'Don't worry, we shall be at the island in a quarter of an hour or twenty minutes,' announced Sandy.

'Does Biggles know where it is?'

'I gave him the bearing yesterday.'

'Then if it was correct he'll find it,' declared Ginger.

In ten minutes the island came into view, and in as many more the 'Scud' was gliding down to an anchorage in a lagoon so perfect that Ginger was enchanted. He looked at Shell-Breaker and Full Moon and smiled, noting that they seemed to be taking their first flight not only calmly but as a matter of course. He remarked on this to Sandy.

'Everything the white man does is marvellous,' Sandy told him. 'There can be nothing more wonderful to them than a box of matches or a gramophone. They've seen so many wonders in their time that they are past being astonished.'

Biggles turned round and laughed quietly as the machine ran to rest on the calm water of the lagoon. 'Well, here we are,' he said cheerfully. 'What did you think of my take-off?'

'Nothing,' declared Sandy. 'I was too scared even to yell.'

'You were no more scared than I was,' returned Biggles. 'If ever I was sure my number was up it was when that big wave reared up and grabbed at us. But let's forget it. I hope that now we are here we shall have a little peace. Where had we better moor the machine? The nearer it is to our camp the better.'

'You can't do better than over there, near that group of palms,' replied Sandy. 'The water is fairly deep right up to the bank, so we can step straight out of the machine on to more or less dry land. That's where I had my hut—over there.' He pointed to a low, palm-thatched shelter near the trees.

'And you lived there for three months?' murmured Ginger, thoughtfully.

'I did,' agreed Sandy, as Biggles taxied the machine slowly to the place he had indicated.

Presently the engines idled, and then stopped, leaving the machine floating on water so clear that it was hard to believe that it was there.

Biggles climbed out on to a bank of coral. 'We'll tie up here,' he said. 'Then we'll get everything ashore we're likely to need and so be ready to start work in the morning.'

The machine was accordingly made fast by the bows to a projecting piece of coral, a safe mooring as there was not a ripple on the water. Stores and spare petrol were put ashore and then carried to Sandy's hut, which on inspection was found to be serviceable enough to provide them with all the shelter they needed. Shell-Breaker and Full Moon helped in the work, their light-hearted chatter lending an atmosphere of gaiety to the scene. The diving-gear was left on board, as it would be needed the next day.

'Which way does the pearl-bed lie?' asked Biggles.

'Over there,' answered Sandy, pointing. 'By this time to-morrow we ought to be raising the shell.'

'By jingo! I've just remembered something, remarked Algy. 'Who is going to open all the oysters?'

Sandy laughed. 'Open them? That's all right if you've only one or two, but you don't bother when you are dealing with the number we shall have to handle. We'd better rot them out, as it's called—that is, dump them on the beach. When the fish die the shells open. Then you feel inside to see if there is anything there. If not, you tip the stuff into a bucket and stir it up. If you happen to have missed a pearl it falls to the bottom. Incidentally, you never open an oyster and throw the refuse into the sea while diving is in progress. It attracts undesirable visitors—such as sharks.'

'Doesn't all this rotting fish stink?' questioned Algy.

'Stinks like nothing on earth, but if we keep it to the leeward side of the island it won't worry us.'

While this conversation had been going on they had been preparing a meal, and now they sat down and enjoyed it. Ginger was in favour of making a raid on the pearl-bed right away, but Biggles vetoed this, as he said he wanted to look over the machine and get everything arranged in camp. In any case, Sandy announced that he would be some time assembling the diving-kit.

Ginger amused himself exploring the lagoon with Full Moon and Shell-Breaker. The only word that he could find to describe it was 'fairyland'. What impressed him most was the transparent blueness of the crystal-clear atmosphere and the delicate blue of the sky in contrast to the emerald green of the palms and deep clear turquoise of the water, through which swam hundreds of fish, some large, of every colour of the rainbow. Here and there, close to the reef, which was half hidden under a sun-filtered cloud of spray, great pieces of snow-white coral rose out of the sea; from where he stood they looked like icebergs. The floor of the lagoon was a kaleidoscopic world of mystery, the home of coral of every hue and shape—pink, blue, green, yellow, every colour of an artist's palette was there, unimaginably lovely; delicate antennae of rose or azure curled upwards like living plants; some were shaped like fans, some like cones, and others like gigantic toadstools. It was a brilliant world, yet soft and harmonious, magical, and almost unbelievable. Once Ginger saw a huge slug, two feet long, crawling on the bottom, and he shuddered, remembering Sandy's words about beauty and horror going hand in hand. Full Moon, noting his disgust, dived into the water and, swimming without effort to the bottom, picked up the slug and brought it to the surface, laughing loudly at Ginger's expression of loathing. She threw it away and climbed out, shaking the water from her skin like a dog.

Ginger judged that the island was three or four miles long, but not more than three hundred yards across at its widest part. On the lagoon side the water was as smooth as a lake, but on the other side the surf thundered in a cloud of glinting spray, and the coral was strewn with countless thousands of shells, of all shapes, sizes, and colours, with the skeletons of fish, and even the teeth of sea-monsters. The waves were constantly throwing up more.

On the island itself there was not much vegetation except for the palms, which often grew to the water's edge, within reach of the spray. Lush grass and flowering shrubs covered the highest part of the atoll, however, although it was not more than twenty-five feet above water-level, recalling to Ginger's mind Sandy's remark about atolls sometimes being swept by hurricane seas.

For the rest, the island was empty of life except for thousands of hermit crabs, that snapped in and out of their shells with a noise like hailstones falling, and a few sea birds. Towards evening, when the tide began to ebb, the silence was eerie, and in the trance-like calm that fell, Ginger, depressed by the utter loneliness of the scene, walked slowly back to the others. Even Full Moon and Shell-Breaker were subdued. He found a brisk fire burning, and the cheerful atmosphere of a picnic about the camp.

Biggles called to him. 'You're taking the first watch,' he said. 'I'm not risking Castanelli creeping in on us in the dark.'

'Good enough, Chief,' acknowledged Ginger, squatting down on the coral sand with the others. 'This place is certainly the end of the world,' he observed, thoughtfully. 'I'm not so sure that I should like to be stranded here, after all.'

6

'TILL THE ROPE BREAKS'

THE following morning, at break of day, after a night made restless by crabs which insisted on invading the hut, the party boarded the flying-boat with the object of visiting the pearl-bed. Sandy, Full Moon, and Shell-Breaker had paid no attention whatever to the crabs, but the others, moving about, had disturbed them, so they were all rather tired. However, it was a perfect morning for their project, for even the open sea was flat calm, as could be seen by the complete absence of spray on the reef surrounding the lagoon.

Under Sandy's guidance Biggles taxied cautiously towards the opening, for although there were no waves the tide poured through the narrow passage with considerable force. It was, Sandy declared, the only opening in the reef, so as the tide ebbed and flowed the water poured in and out with the power of a mill-race. However, Biggles held the flying-boat's bows in the current without difficulty, for he had two engines, and owing to its shallow draught the flying-boat did not feel the tide as a boat would have done.

As soon as they were on the open sea Sandy pointed. 'That's the direction,' he said. 'It's hardly worth taking off. It will be easier to stay on the water, but we must keep a look-out for reefs—you never know where they are going to pop up in these coral seas.'

To Ginger, sitting astride the nacelle, this taxiing over blue water in the manner of a speed-boat was exhilarating, and he sang with joy as he gazed at the water ahead for possible obstructions. For a quarter of an hour they drove steadily towards their unseen objective, and then Sandy told Biggles to slow down, for they were near the spot. Naturally, as it was not marked in any way he could not be certain of it to within a few hundred yards, for at sea even instrument-readings are only approximate; so Biggles throttled back to dead slow to allow Sandy to take soundings. But Sandy did not succeed in finding the bottom. 'It must be somewhere about here,' he said. 'Cruise around for a bit; keep her slow.'

Biggles manœuvred the flying-boat as Sandy had requested while the others, choosing what they thought the best positions, gazed down into the tranquil depths, looking for the sea-bed.

'All right, Biggles, stop her!' called Sandy. 'Let her drift. We needn't waste petrol.' He took a long look at the island and compared it with their position. 'It's just about here somewhere,' he said again. 'The trouble is, the sea is normal; there's no swell—at least, not as much as when I was here last. That ought to make diving easier, but it makes the place harder to find.'

Biggles throttled right back, leaving the engines just ticking over, so that the 'Scud' rested motionless on the limpid surface of the water, her drift being imperceptible. Several minutes passed in silence, while the whole party gazed down into the depths beneath them.

'If any one could see us they'd think we were crazy,' declared Biggles at last, laughing. 'Looking for the bottom of the sea in a flying-boat. That would make a funny picture.'

'You don't doubt that it's here?' demanded Sandy stiffly.

'Good gracious, no,' replied Biggles promptly. 'It just struck me as funny, that's all.'

'Hello, what was that? I think I saw something,' cried Ginger.

Full Moon looked up into his face and smiled. 'Me see,' she said, and with hardly a ripple slipped into the water.

Ginger watched spellbound as the girl lay on her face on the surface, her head below the water, scrutinizing the depths. Then, suddenly, she sank, and started swimming down with an easy breaststroke, and a barely perceptible movement of her legs. Ginger could see her clearly, for the water was of such purity that it seemed to be neither air nor water; but he found it difficult to believe his eyes as he watched Full Moon behaving as though the water was her natural home. She went so low that her body became no more than a shadow, a disembodied wraith; occasionally a shoal of fish would pass about her. For a moment she actually disappeared from sight, and Ginger drew a deep breath of relief when he saw her coming swiftly upward. Her hand broke the surface first; in it she held a huge oyster. Her head appeared, and she drew in her breath with a long whistling sound that Ginger was to come to know well.

Sandy let out a yell of triumph when he saw the shell. 'There you are!' he cried. 'The bottom can't be more than twenty fathoms. I know why we can't see it. The sun is still too low. It was straight overhead when I first spotted the bed.'

'Yes, that might account for it,' agreed Biggles.

Full Moon tossed the shell on board, and scrambled up herself. She spoke excitedly to Sandy in Marquesan, pointing at the same time.

'She says the bottom under us slopes like the side of a hill,' Sandy translated. He pointed towards where the girl had indicated. 'She says it's shallower over there. It must be as I thought. The place I spotted is the top of an under-water mountain. Take the machine over a bit, Biggles.'

As requested, Biggles gave the engines a burst of power which carried the 'Scud' towards the desired locality. 'Stop her—you'll do!' cried Sandy. 'I can see bottom. There it is. I should say it isn't more than six or seven fathoms.'

The other, looking over the side, saw that he was right. The bottom of the sea could be seen plainly, exactly as Sandy had described it, gleaming with half-open oyster-shells.

Sandy turned at once to his diving-suit and began to get into it. His face was serious. 'Diving is a dangerous business,' he said gravely. 'Never forget that. There isn't an insurance company in the world that will insure a diver. We needn't dwell on what *might* happen—there are all sorts of things down there that it's best not to think about. There's only one thing I must mention. One of the worst dangers is the big clams, as big as a bath and weighing over half a ton. The trouble is, they sometimes lie wide open to feed. If a diver steps into one of those—well, he's down for good unless somebody comes down and cuts his leg off. That's why I'm glad we've got Shell-Breaker and Full Moon with us; they'll know what to do if that happens.' He gave each of them a hatchet and spoke a few words in Marquesan. They both nodded. Their faces, too, were now serious.

Algy and Ginger had already been trained in the business of fastening up the diving-suit. 'Remember the signals,' said Sandy, as he picked up the heavy helmet. 'There's one I hope you'll never get, and that is four tugs on the line. That means pull till the rope breaks. It's the forlorn chance. It's a million to one against its ever being needed, but if you do get it you'll know that I'm fast on the bottom, so pull—and pull till the rope breaks. But don't ever pull unless you get a signal. You heard that, Biggles?'

'Yes, I heard you, Sandy,' replied Biggles quietly.

'Good. Right-ho, screw me up,' continued Sandy, and the helmet sank down into its socket.

Ginger and Algy screwed up the nuts, and Sandy dragged his lead-soled feet to the ladder that had been let down beside the hull. He stopped for a moment while his head remained above water, and smiled through the glass. Then he disappeared. Algy was already turning the handle of the air-pump that was part of the equipment. Ginger paid out the life-line.

A minute later a sudden slackening of the line told him that Sandy was on the bottom, and he nodded to Shell-Breaker, who at once lowered a large wire basket for the shell. Full Moon, hatchet in hand, lay staring down into the depths.

Several minutes passed; then Ginger felt a single tug on the line. 'Haul up the basket,' he told Shell-Breaker, and presently it came into view with twenty or thirty huge oysters in it. Under Biggles's direction Shell-Breaker tipped them out on the cabin floor and again lowered the basket.

This was repeated several times, so that by the end of an hour there was a considerable pile of oysters in the cabin, spread about to balance the weight. Sandy had cleared the very shallow place, and had moved a short distance away into rather deeper water, but not deep enough to inconvenience him. Occasionally he could be seen crossing a patch of light-coloured coral, or sand, Ginger was not sure which; but against the darker background it was no longer possible to see him. Comparatively speaking, the water was still shallow, which had this advantage: Sandy could be brought up quickly without risk of the paralysing cramp which is the bane of diving in deep water, and involves long delays while the diver is brought up in stages so that his body may become accustomed to the change in pressure.

Ginger was relieved when he got the signal that Sandy was coming up. A few minutes later his head broke the surface and he climbed laboriously into the flying-boat. His helmet was unscrewed and removed. 'We're not doing so badly, eh?' were his first words, accompanied by a smile. 'I've come up for a wee bit of a rest.'

'What's it like down there?' asked Ginger.

'Pretty fair,' replied Sandy non-committally. 'There are one or two nasty precipices that it wouldn't do to fall over—just like you get on an ordinary mountain. The coral worried me a bit. It's all shapes, some of it bad—sort of craggy. I have to keep my eye on the life-line and air-tube all the time to make sure they don't get fouled. It's surprising how the current drags them about. You'd better keep them fairly taut. It's the easiest thing in the world to get your line tangled round a lump of coral.'

Sandy did not remove his diving-suit as he declared his intention of going down again. 'Another spell like the last should see us with about as much shell as we can carry,' he remarked.

'Keep an eye on the weather, Shell-Breaker. You'll know when it's likely to start blowing. We don't want to get caught in a squall.'

Actually, there was no sign of a change in the weather. The sea remained dead calm, and after a short rest Sandy stood up and prepared to resume his task.

Three-quarters of an hour passed. It seemed much longer to those waiting on the aircraft; but, as Biggles remarked, it probably seemed even longer to Sandy. However, the shells continued to come up, the 'Scud' noticeably settling deeper under their weight.

'We've got enough,' said Biggles, at last, regarding the pile. 'I'm not sure that we haven't got too much.'

'Too much?' queried Ginger.

'If it started to blow we might find ourselves in a mess. I don't think we could get the machine off the water with this load, and that, to my way of thinking, is going a bit too far beyond the margin of safety. However, the weather looks settled enough,' he added, glancing round the sky.

'Sandy will be up any minute now,' said Ginger, feeling the life-line as though he were fishing, hoping to receive the expected signal.

Several minutes passed, but there was no signal.

'It's a long time since we had any shell up,' observed Ginger at last.

Nobody answered. The minutes passed slowly. Biggles glanced at the watch on the instrument-board. 'He's been down over an hour,' he said, presently.

'He seems to be moving about; I can feel the line twitching,' said Ginger. 'He isn't caught by one of those confounded clams, anyway, or he wouldn't be able to move.'

Full Moon was lying on the hull, staring down into the water. She had not spoken for some time. Suddenly she drew the knife which she carried inside her *pareu*, and putting it between her teeth, slipped over the side. Her head dipped downwards, and she began to swim.

Ginger looked at Biggles.

Biggles shrugged his shoulders. 'I suppose she knows what she's doing,' he said.

'By gosh! she's coming back in a hurry,' said Ginger, sharply. Full Moon literally flung herself out of the water on to the flying-boat. '*Feke!*' she cried shrilly. 'Big *feke!*'

'*Feke!*' My God! She means an octopus!' cried Ginger aghast. His face blanched. 'What can we do? Shall we pull him up?'

'He said don't pull unless we got a signal,' said Biggles in a hard voice.

'Andie fight *feke*,' said Full Moon simply. 'Me no fight—get caught in life-line.'

'You keep pumping, Algy,' said Ginger, and started to haul on the line. But there was no slack to be taken up. The line was taut, vibrating slightly.

'This is dreadful. Can't we do something?' Algy panted, for he had been pumping steadily for some time.

'We'd better give him a minute. He may be able to fight it off,' said Biggles, whose face was colourless. 'If he wanted us to pull he'd send a signal.'

'Maybe the thing's got his arms pinned to his sides,' suggested Ginger.

'Wait!' ordered Biggles.

After that nobody spoke for a full minute. Ginger stood like a statue, holding the rope.

'Shell-Breaker, can you go down and see what's happening?' asked Biggles.

Without a word Shell-Breaker dropped the rope that controlled the basket and drew his knife. He was about to dive into the water when a yell from Ginger stopped him. 'He's pulling!' he shouted. 'One—two—three . . . *four*. That means pull till the rope breaks.' He bent his back and pulled, but he might have been trying to lift a mountain for all the effect it had. 'Biggles! Shell-Breaker—help!' he cried.

They all rushed to his assistance, but not even their united efforts could make the line give an inch.

'My God! We shall tear the air-pipe if we pull any harder,' cried Biggles, in a hoarse voice. 'Keep pumping, Algy. Now, altogether—*pull*.'

They threw their weight on the rope until it twisted and oozed water under the strain. But it did not move.

'It's no use. It's holding him down,' muttered Biggles through set teeth. 'We'll try once more. Full Moon—come and pull!'

With four of them now on the rope they pulled until the perspiration dripped from their faces and the machine tilted right over on her side under the one-sided pressure. But the rope might have been tied to the bottom of the sea. It did not give an inch.

Biggles straightened his back and moistened his lips. 'He signalled that we were to pull until the rope breaks,' he said in a curious voice. 'Well, he's coming up or I'm going to break the rope. It's his only chance now.' He seized the life-line and reefed it round the two steel centre-section bracing struts. 'You hold the rope where you are, Ginger,' he said tersely. 'Cover your face in case it breaks and snaps back. Don't go overboard. Hang on everybody.' He jumped into the pilot's seat. His hand closed over the throttle. The gentle ticking of the engines became a roar. The machine surged forward, the life-line tautening like a bow-string. The flying-boat went right over on her side with her wing-tip in the water under the terrific pressure, and then began to move in a slow circle.

'What are you giving her?' yelled Ginger.

'Half-throttle.'

'The rope doesn't move. Go on.'

'We'll capsize the ship.'

'No—*go on*.'

The roar of the engines became a bellow.

'It's coming—it's coming!' screamed Ginger.

Biggles gave the throttle a moment of full power. The engines roared, and the aircraft jibbed like a young horse that feels the spurs for the first time. The sea was a churning whirlpool of foam.

'It's coming!' yelled Ginger again, hanging on to the rope. His eyes were bulging out of his head with the strain as he heaved and pulled.

Biggles suddenly cut the throttle and dashed to his assistance.

Shell-Breaker also seized the rope. 'All together!' cried Biggles. '*Heave!*'

The dripping line began to come in, a foot at a time. 'We've got more than Sandy at the end of this rope,' declared Biggles grimly. 'Thank God it's a brand-new one. Stand by with that chopper, Shell-Breaker.'

Foot by foot the rope came in, the flying-boat lying on her beam ends under the one-sided weight.

Full Moon had been kneeling, staring down into the water. Suddenly she sprang to her feet. 'Andie, he come,' she shrilled. 'He come with *feke!*' Knife in hand, her lips parted, showing her teeth, she looked what she was, a savage, but ready to fight against something she knew and understood only too well.

A long tentacle broke the surface and coiled menacingly. Ginger ducked as it swished over his head.

'Never mind that; keep pulling!' yelled Biggles.

'It's dragging us under,' screamed Ginger.

'Keep pulling!' shouted Biggles again. 'Here he comes. The beast is hanging on him. Hold the line.' Biggles dropped the rope, and snatching up Shell-Breaker's hatchet, began slashing at something just under the water.

'Mind you don't cut the line!' cried Ginger.

Biggles did not answer. A severed tentacle floated up, still coiling and uncoiling like a lasso. Another writhed up and curled itself over the fuselage so that the machine nearly went right over. Biggles severed it with a blow, the blade sinking into the plywood. He snatched it out. Both Shell-Breaker and Full Moon were slashing with their knives; nearly in the water, they were taking the most desperate risks. Ginger hung on the rope. Bending forward to take fresh purchase he had a fleeting glimpse of two great lustreless eyes, as large as saucers. He saw Biggles whip out his automatic and blaze between them, firing shot after shot until the weapon was empty.

Ginger went over backwards at the recoil of the boat as the weight suddenly fell from the line. He saw a mass of grey-coloured flesh floating away amid pieces of severed tentacles. For a frightful moment he thought that Sandy had gone, too. Then he saw the diving-helmet appear above the water as Biggles and Full Moon reached down and dragged Sandy up. He fell motionless across the hull.

'Get his helmet off!' shouted Biggles, and dashed to the cockpit. The engines roared and the 'Scud' surged forward.

'*Mako* finish *feke!*' cried Full Moon delightedly, pointing to the water in which several sharks had suddenly appeared; they were fighting for the remains of the octopus. But Ginger was no longer concerned with it. With trembling fingers he removed the helmet from the motionless figure, to disclose Sandy's face, ashen and streaked with blood. 'He's dead!' he cried.

Algy dashed into the cabin and returned with the emergency brandy-flask. He poured a little of the spirit between Sandy's pallid lips.

By this time the 'Scud' was racing towards the entrance to the lagoon at a speed only just short of flying speed. She did, in fact, leave the water an inch or two more than once. Without slackening speed Biggles tore through the opening of the reef on to the still water of the lagoon, and brought the machine to a standstill at her anchorage. Then he switched off and helped the others to carry Sandy ashore.

As they laid him gently on the sloping beach of powdered coral and shell he opened his eyes and gazed at the blue sky above with an expression on his face which Ginger never forgot. 'Ye saved the shell all right, I hope?' he said, weakly.

'Why, you old skinflint, of course we did,' answered Biggles, with a catch in his voice. 'We've got you, that's all that really matters. All right, boys; let's get this diving-gear off him. Do you feel well enough for us to take it off, Sandy?'

'Aye, I'm a wee bit bruised, nothing more.'

Which was, the others soon discovered, an understatement of fact, for he was bruised from head to foot. Vivid red bands showed where the creature had gripped him with its tentacles. However, he was not seriously injured, and he was soon sitting up, sipping a drop of 'whusky'—just to pull him together.

'Well, I suppose this means the end of the show?' said Biggles.

'Why?' demanded Sandy. 'Nothing of the sort. That's all part of the day's work in a diver's life.'

Ginger stared incredulously. 'Do you mean—you'd go down there again?' he asked unbelievingly.

'Certainly. I'd feel safer now than I did before.'

'How on earth do you make that out?' asked Algy.

'Because there won't be any more big fellows like that one. He would be king of the roost over a big area. If you have killed him, as I expect you must have done, it will be safe down there as it is here. These devil fish are the real kings of the ocean; other fish know that and keep out of the way.'

'The sharks finished off the pieces,' Ginger told him.

'They would,' grinned Sandy, rising stiffly to his feet. 'The truth is, I was a fool. There was a deep sort of dell-hole in the coral. I didn't much like the look of it, particularly as there were no small fish about, or young octopus. You can usually see plenty of the little fellows, but they don't trouble you; they scramble about the rocks like big spiders. I thought it was odd that they had all disappeared. But there were some big shells in the hole, so I took a chance. In a way I was lucky, because the first feeler settled round my helmet. I guessed what it was, so knowing the tricks of the trade I put my arms straight up to prevent them from being pinned to my sides. A good thing I did, for the next tentacle went round my waist. If my arms hadn't been free I should have been finished, but as they were, I could fight. The scrap must have lasted twenty minutes. It seemed like hours. I could see the thing staring at me from a cave. He was only using four arms on me, so I guessed he was anchoring himself with the others. It was no use my signalling to be pulled up while he was holding on to the coral with four arms; it would have needed a battleship to shift him. But I reckoned that if I could slash one or two of his arms he would bring the others into play, and so weaken his hold on the bottom. My greatest fear was that the line or air-tube would get tangled up with the tentacles—that would have been the end. Luckily, you had kept them taut, as I suggested. It was a rare fight between the two of us down there on the sea floor. I cut the ends off two of his arms, and I saw him bring out two more. I was tempted to signal to you to pull me up, but I wanted to make sure. But I was weakening, and he knew it. He was trying to drag me towards him all the time. I could see his eyes. You don't know what a temptation it was to go forward and plunge my knife between them; it became a sort of obsession, but it would have been fatal. Every now and then the brute squirted out a lot of sepia so that I couldn't see his arms—or anything else, for that matter. He beat me in the end. I was whacked. My arms were like lead from holding them up. Then he got my left arm pinned to my side, and I knew that it was only a question of time before he got the other. By then he had managed to drag me to within a couple of yards of him, so I gave the four tugs. And that's all I remember.'

Biggles drew a deep breath. 'It was a grim business,' he said. 'I don't like the idea of your going down there again.'

'A day's rest and I shall be as right as rain,' declared Sandy. 'Why, mon, there's a fortune down there on the bottom, and a fortune is always worth a bit of risk.'

'Well, we'll wash out for to-day, at any rate, and see how you feel to-morrow,' decided Biggles. 'What shall we do with all this shell?'

'Haul it across to the west side of the island and spread it about on the beach above high-water mark. In a day or two we shall be able to see what the luck is like. There isn't a more exciting game in the world than opening shell, knowing that any one might hold a small fortune.'

'Right-ho,' agreed Biggles. 'We'll have a bite of lunch and then, while you take things easy, we'll shift the shell.'

7
AN AMAZING DISCOVERY

SANDY was bruised rather more than he had at first pretended, and it was two days before he felt able to continue diving. The others were so alarmed at his terrible experience that they were half-inclined to abandon the project; but Sandy would not hear of it, insisting that now the big octopus was no longer there, there was nothing more to fear; and as he was the one most concerned the others gave way. So on the third day they again taxied out to the diving-ground, where Sandy made several descents, but by lunch-time he was showing signs of strain, and Biggles decided to suspend operations until the following day, as time was no object. Sandy admitted that he had nearly cleared the shallow area, and in future it would be necessary for him gradually to work deeper as he descended the slopes of the under-water mountain. Not that he ever intended to go really deep. He admitted frankly that deep-sea work was beyond his strength, ability, or inclination; at the same time he pointed out that it would not be necessary, for if the shell they had already gathered yielded the harvest which might reasonably be expected, it would be both easier and safer to spend part of the proceeds in fitting out a schooner with an experienced crew, and hiring expert Japanese divers from Thursday Island, near the north Australian coast, the head-quarters of some of the finest divers in the world. They themselves could superintend operations from the flying-boat, which would at the same time enable them to keep in touch with Tahiti. The work they were engaged on would then no longer be a secret, but as they would have reaped the cream of the bed this would not matter. There would be no need for any of them to take further risks. And this was so obviously sound, common-sense reasoning that the others agreed without demur.

As they taxied back towards the island after abandoning work for the day, Sandy suddenly looked up with a smile. 'Here, I'll tell you what!' he cried. 'Let's spend the afternoon examining our first day's catch. The oysters will be dead by now, so apart from the stink, which will not be pleasant, the job should be easy.'

A cheer from Ginger greeted this proposal. 'That sounds a fine idea,' he declared.

'We'll stack the shell on the beach as we clean it and get a schooner to pick it up later on,' continued Sandy. 'It's worth real money, so we might as well have it. In fact, if the pearls don't turn out too well we may be glad of it.'

And so it was agreed, and after a picnic lunch the whole party went over to the west side of the island, no very great distance, where the shell had been spread out to rot.

Sandy and the two Polynesians laughed at the expressions of disgust on the faces of the others as they approached the now dead oysters. 'It's a good thing the wind is blowing the stink straight out to sea; if it dropped altogether, or blew the other way, you'd know the meaning of the word "fug",' said Sandy, smiling. Then, suddenly, his smile faded, to be replaced by a thoughtful frown.

'What's the matter?' asked Biggles, who was watching him.

'A thought just struck me,' returned Sandy, shaking his head doubtfully. 'I'm not sure that we were altogether wise to rot the shell, after all. This stink will be noticeable twenty miles out to sea, and anyone who has ever smelt it never forgets what it is.'

'You mean—Castanelli might get a whiff of it?'

Sandy nodded. 'Yes,' he said.

'In which case all he would have to do would be to follow it up in order to discover the place where it starts from.'

'You bet he would.'

'Hm, that's rather a pity, but it can't be helped now. We won't do it again. In future we'll open the shell and bury the refuse as soon as we have finished with it.'

'Aye, that's the best way.'

Sandy was carrying a pail and an empty biscuit-tin, and on reaching the shell he filled the bucket with sea-water and, watched with absorbed interest by the others, he commenced operations. He picked up the shells one by one, and holding them over the bucket explored the interior with his fingers before tipping the remains of the dead oyster into the pail. The empty shells he tossed on one side for Shell-Breaker to stack into a neat pile. In this way he had opened nearly forty shells, tossing each one aside with a grunt of disappointment, before he let out a wild whoop and held up a small white object that appeared to glow with inward fire. It was the size of a small pebble. 'Well, there's number one,' he declared, as the pearl passed quickly from hand to hand. 'Now we've broken our duck we shall probably get on better.'

'What's that one worth?' asked Ginger.

'I'll hit the buyer on the nose if he offers me less than five hundred pounds for it,' swore Sandy.

'You're going to be a long time getting a hatful at this rate,' put in Biggles, smiling.

'Don't you be in a hurry,' answered Sandy seriously. 'You never know how things are going to pan out at this game. You can open a thousand oysters without finding a seed pearl, and then find six in succession. We're bound to find one or two real big 'uns in all this shell, or I'm going to be very surprised.'

As if to confirm his statement the very next shell yielded five small pearls—not very valuable, Sandy admitted, but they all added to the harvest. And so the work went on.

A high spot occurred when Sandy suddenly held up a huge, heart-shaped gem. He was even more excited than the others. 'That's something to write home about,' he declared enthusiastically. 'One day that's going to sit on a queen's crown, or a princess's tiara, and when you see pictures of it in the paper you'll get a kick out of remembering that it was you who helped to fish it up from the bottom of the sea. That pearl is worth five thousand pounds of anybody's money.'

'It's lovely,' breathed Ginger.

'It will never again look so lovely as it does at this moment,' muttered Sandy regretfully.

The work continued, the little heap of pearls in the tin growing steadily larger, and the empty shells making a big mound near the scene of operations. When the last shell had been examined and thrown aside, the total catch was found to be five large pearls of considerable value, nineteen of medium size, one 'double button', or two pearls joined together, and a double handful of seed pearls—small pearls of no great value.

'Well, that's a pretty good average, so we can't complain,' said Sandy, with satisfaction. 'If that little lot doesn't fetch twenty thousand pounds I'll eat my hat.'

'What are these cultured pearls one hears so much about?'

asked Ginger. 'I've heard that the Japanese run sort of oyster farms to produce them. They put bits of grit inside the shells, or something, to encourage the oyster to spread the nacre over them.'

'Pah!' Sandy made a grimace of disgust. 'Don't talk to me about cultured pearls. They're not in the same class as real pearls. You'll soon be able to buy 'em at Woolworth's at ten a penny.'

'What's wrong with them?'

'Nothing much, when they first come out of the shell. But they're made too fast, and like most things that are made in a hurry they don't last. They lack the fire of the others, and they're liable to peel. A pearl is made up of a number of skins, like an onion, you know.' While he was speaking Sandy's fingers were groping about in the slush at the bottom of the pail, searching for any pearls that might have been overlooked.

'By jingo! That reminds me,' cried Ginger.

'Of what?' asked Biggles.

'That shell Full Moon fished up when she made her first dive. I kept it by itself. I put it over there by that tree and forgot all about it. I'll go and fetch it.' He ran across to the palm he had indicated and came back with the half-open oyster in his hand. 'I'm not very hopeful,' he said, eyeing the shell disapprovingly, for compared with some of the others it was very small, and diseased in places. The outside was covered with barnacles, and it was obviously of great age. He sat down on the sand and plunged his fingers into the corruption that a few days before had been a live oyster. Suddenly he stiffened and looked up at the others. His eyes opened wide. His face turned pale and his breath came quickly.

'Aha—that's how it gets you when you feel the first one,' declared Sandy.

Ginger slowly withdrew his fingers and held up an enormous round pearl, the size of a marble. It was not white, but pink, and as it lay in his trembling palm it gleamed with an uncanny light, as if it were imbued with life.

Silence fell. It was broken by Sandy. 'Sweet Andrew of

Scotland!' he breathed, white-faced, staring at the pearl as if it exerted an irresistible fascination over him. 'I've seen some pearls in my time, and some beauties among 'em, but I've never seen anything like that. That baby is going to cause more than a flutter when it reaches Paris.'

Ginger had tossed the shell aside, and was about to speak when Full Moon uttered a little cry. She was staring at the shell, which gaped open. The others looked, and saw something pink gleaming between the lips of the shell. In a silence broken only by the harsh rustle of the palms Ginger picked it up and slowly withdrew a second rose-tinted pearl. He laid it on the palm of his left hand with the other. The two made a perfect pair.

Sandy seemed to have difficulty in speaking. 'Look at 'em!' he croaked. Then again, 'Look at 'em! Look hard, boys, because you're looking at something you'll never see again as long as you live—no, not if you live to be a million. I tell you, men have been pearling in these seas for years, some of 'em for half a century, without ever seeing anything like that. Not many men alive have seen one pearl of that class, let alone two. It makes me feel funny inside to look at 'em.'

'Now we can have one each.'

'Each?'

'One for us, and the other for Full Moon.'

'What!' Sandy nearly choked. 'Part a pair like that? You can't do it. It would be criminal. Those two pearls were born together, and must always stay together. Don't you realize what it means to have a pair—no, maybe you don't. Either of those pearls alone would be worth ten thousand pounds, but as a pair you could ask your own price—and get it. Kings have pawned their kingdoms for less.'

'Yes, they'll have to stay together,' agreed Biggles.

'But what about Full Moon?'

The girl pursed her lips. 'Me no want,' she said simply. 'You buy me red beads at Lo Sing's store, maybe?'

'Sure we will,' agreed Sandy.

'You'll give her a sixpenny string of pearls for one of *those*?' cried Ginger indignantly.

'She'd rather have 'em. She said so herself, and she means it.'

'Well, it seems a raw deal to me,' grumbled Ginger.

'Me happy,' cried Full Moon cheerfully. 'Me plenty bead.'

'Well, if you say so,' agreed Ginger reluctantly. 'You help yourself to anything in Lo Sing's store that you like when we get back to Rutuona, and let these skunks pay the bill.'

Full Moon clapped her hands delightedly. 'Plenty brilliantine, plenty face-powder,' she cried.

Ginger looked horrified, but Sandy grinned. 'You wait and see her when she comes out of the store,' he chuckled. 'She'll look like a French doll, and stink like a chemist's shop for a couple of days, and kid herself she's the cat's whisker. Then she'll go swimming and forget all about it.' He got up. 'We might as well be getting back,' he said. 'I can do with a nice cup of tea to wash this stink out of my throat. We'd better find a safe place for these pearls. We won't put them on the 'Scud' till we go for good, in case of accidents.'

They walked back by the side of the lagoon to the camp, where before doing anything else Sandy buried the tin containing the pearls in the soft sand under a conspicuous crag of sun-bleached coral. 'They should be all right there,' he said, as he rejoined the others, who were preparing tea.

When the meal was over, Biggles leaned back and lit a cigarette. Sandy lit his pipe. 'I call that a pretty good day's work,' he said. 'Another load or two and we're all set for an easy life. All I ask is that the weather holds.'

'And the food-supply,' put in Biggles. 'We're getting a bit low. I didn't reckon on six mouths to fill when I made up the list of stores.'

'We ought to help it out with fish,' replied Sandy. 'There are plenty in the water. There's a line and some hooks over there; I brought 'em for that purpose. Full Moon and Shell-Breaker know the sorts worth eating.' He turned to the two Polynesians. 'You kids go and get some fish,' he ordered.

Shell-Breaker and Full Moon sprang to their feet, and picked up the fishing-equipment.

'Hold on, I'm coming with you,' Ginger told them, and

overtook them as they walked away along the beach of white coral sand.

They went on for some distance, and after examining several places Full Moon stopped at a tiny cove, where the coral dropped sheer into a pool such as Ginger had often tried to imagine. Not a ripple disturbed its surface, and shoals of fish could been seen swimming lazily in the crystal-clear water. From the coral edge to the pool was a drop of anything from two to twenty feet, but there were plenty of natural steps leading down to the water. A final touch of artistry was supplied by a little group of palms, one of which hung far out over the pool, the fronds touching its faithfully reflected image.

Full Moon baited a hook with a piece of shellfish, of which there were vast numbers clinging to the coral, and was soon pulling fish ashore as fast as she could throw out the line. Ginger took a turn, and added to the ever-growing pile of fish of all shapes, sizes, and colours that lay flapping on the bank. 'We've got enough,' he said at last. 'It's no use killing the poor brutes for the sake of killing them, and it's more like hard work than sport, anyway. I doubt if we shall be able to eat all we've got, as it is.'

'Me swim.' Full Moon threw the line aside and went into the water like an otter. Ginger watched her for a minute as she turned easily this way and that far under the water, as much like a mermaid as a human being could be. Then he began peeling off his shirt. 'I'm going to have a spot of this,' he told Shell-Breaker, who was collecting some fallen coconuts. Kicking off his canvas shoes he went to the edge of the water and looked for the girl. The ripples made by her entry into the pool were lapping gently against the coral; he could see the bottom clearly, but of Full Moon there was no sign. He waited, a feeling of uneasiness fast becoming anxiety as the girl did not reappear. 'Hi! Shell-Breaker!' he cried, in a high-pitched voice. 'Something's happened to Full Moon.'

The boy dropped the coconuts he was carrying in his arms and ran to the edge of the pool, his eyes scrutinizing every section of it in quick succession. A puzzled look crossed his face. He stared out towards the open lagoon for a minute, and then started working swiftly round the edge of the cove, examining the rough coral walls as he went. The alarm plainly depicted on his face did nothing to allay Ginger's anxiety, which by this time was not far short of panic.

Suddenly Shell-Breaker drew himself up and dived into the water. Ginger ran to the spot. For a moment he could see nothing owing to the wavelets caused by Shell-Breaker's plunge; then, as they rippled away and splashed against the coral, he looked eagerly for the Polynesian. There was no sign of him. Ginger stared and stared again, unable to believe his eyes. A minute passed . . . two minutes, and still Shell-Breaker did not reappear. Ginger knew that not even the Polynesian can stay under water much longer than that, and a terrible fear took possession of him. Never had he felt so utterly helpless. He ran a little way along the coral bank to get a better view of the place where the boy had disappeared, but all he could see was a dark area, as if the water deepened.

It was now more than five minutes since Full Moon had dived into the pool, and he knew that no human being could survive such an immersion. 'An octopus has got her,' he thought, sick with horror, and filled with loathing of the beautiful spot where, nevertheless, death lurked.

He was about to run back to the others in order to tell them what had happened when the water suddenly parted and a head appeared. It was Full Moon. She let out a ripple of laughter.

'Here, what's the game? You nearly frightened me to death,' cried Ginger, angrily, but breathing deeply from relief.

Full Moon's answer was another peal of laughter. 'Me swim,' she called, blowing bubbles on the surface of the water.

'You're not a woman, you're a fish,' sneered Ginger.

Shell-Breaker appeared. They both swam to the edge of the coral where Ginger stood. Full Moon held up a brown hand. 'Come,' she said.

'Where?' asked Ginger suspiciously.

'Me show.'

'Show what?'

'Bottom of sea. Bottom of sea beautiful.'

'I can see all I want of that from here,' declared Ginger.

'Come,' said Full Moon, again. 'Me show.'

Shell-Breaker joined in. 'Yes, we show,' he said. He pulled himself up on the coral and motioned Ginger to dive. 'Take plenty breath, come with me.'

'No fear.'

'White man afraid—ha.'

Ginger flushed. 'I'm not a blinking eel if you are,' he snorted. 'Anyway, I'll show you if I'm afraid.' He took a deep breath and dived. He was about to turn upwards when he became aware that Shell-Breaker and Full Moon were on either side of him, beckoning as naturally as if they were on land instead of under water. He followed them, and saw that they were swimming towards a gloomy cave, about twenty feet under the water. He waited for no more, but turning away shot to the surface and pulled himself up on the coral with his legs dangling in the water.

The two natives appeared. Full Moon looked hurt. 'You afraid,' she said, reproachfully. 'You come—plenty air.'

'Air?'

'Plenty air in cave.'

'What about *feke*?'

'No *feke*.'

'Right! I'm coming.' Again Ginger took a deep breath and dived. He saw that the others were beside him, swimming easily towards the cave, and this time he followed them. To say that he was frightened as he went through the gloomy entrance would be to put it mildly, but he set his teeth and swam on grimly behind the two figures which were gliding through the water in front of him, still beckoning. His endurance was nearly exhausted. He felt that he must breathe or die, but he knew that he had already come to far to get back, so he could only go on, hoping that Full Moon's promise of 'plenty air' was correct. Panic seized him as something clutched his arm, and he tore it away, only to see that it was Full Moon trying to help him along. She shot upwards. He followed, and a moment later his head broke the surface. For a little while he could only gasp; then, looking about him, he saw Full Moon and Shell-Breaker sitting on a ledge of coral in what was clearly a cave, but such a cave as he could never have imagined. He swam up to them and climbed out, and not until then did he realize fully the wonder of the scene about him.

The cave was only a short one, and led to a larger cavity in the coral, the roof of which was above water-level. The beauty of it struck him speechless. It was ethereal, a fairy grotto, blue beyond anything he had ever seen, a deep, unreal, cerulean blue. The water was pure ultramarine, and glowed like blue fire. The drops of water that fell from his legs were blue sparks. At first he could not make out where the light came from; then he perceived that it came through the tunnel, and was refracted by its passage through the water. The result was extraordinary. It was as if the place was illuminated by hidden blue electric lights. He dipped his hand into the water; instantly it glistened silvery-blue, as though he had plunged his hand into cold blue fire rather than water. The whole grotto was charged with such a supernatural light that the appearance of a sea-nymph would not have surprised him. Indeed, the two Polynesians looked more like sirens than human beings.

For some time he sat still, enchanted by the scene, staring at the pellucid sapphire water through which tiny fish moved lazily over a background of white sand, and the iridescent dome overhead. And as he looked a strange feeling came over him that he was no longer on earth, but was a celestial being sitting in a blue cloud.

'This is certainly the most incredible place I have ever seen,' he told the others at last. He knew, of course, that coral is built up by countless millions of minute sea creatures, and that through the ages whole islands have been constructed by this means. Flotsam, such as seaweed, is thrown upon them by the waves; in time it rots and a speck of mould is formed. On this, sooner or later, a seed is washed by the sea, or dropped by a bird; a plant grows, dies, and rots in turn to provide a further quantity of soil capable of supporting a larger plant. This he knew, and he realized that thus had grown Sandy's Island. What he may not have known was that in course of time the coral-makers die; the massive home that they have built loses its strength, and ultimately decays. Coral formations are not necessarily solid; cavities are left; and when the coral is dead these are enlarged by the constant action of the water. Such cavities, or holes, may be small or they may be large. The one in which Ginger found himself was exceptionally large, being between thirty and forty feet long and half that distance in width. From the level of the water to the roof was about twenty feet, and he perceived from the direction of the cave that the grotto was actually under the island; in fact, he judged that the roof could not be more than a few feet below the spot where a few minutes before he had been standing high and dry. In these circumstances it was obvious to him that it would be possible to dig down into the grotto from the outside, and the fact that the air he was breathing was sweet and fresh supported his theory. He could not see them, but he knew that there must be flaws in the coral through which the air could percolate.

At last he rose to his feet. 'I could sit here for hours,' he said, 'but we must be getting back, or the others will wonder what has happened to us.'

Now that he knew the secret he was no longer afraid. He dived into the water, striking out vigorously towards the entrance; the others joined him, and together they shot up to the surface of the pool. 'By gosh! We'll bring the others along here,' declared Ginger, shaking the water off himself. 'But we won't tell them anything about it yet; we'll keep it a secret until they come, and give them a surprise.'

Helping the others to carry the fish, he accompanied them back to the camp.

'You've been a long time,' said Biggles.

'We've been having a swim,' admitted Ginger casually.

8
MONSTERS OF THE DEEP

On each of the next two days they were up at dawn, and quickly away to the pearl-bed, making the most of the ideal weather which Shell-Breaker repeatedly warned them might not last, for the season of storms was approaching. Both Shell-Breaker and Full Moon shared Sandy's confidence that there would be no more *feke* in the locality, and they often swam down to him to keep him company, sometimes bringing a shell up with them. Their behaviour was that of two children on holiday. They teased Ginger so much about his nervousness of the water that on one or two occasions, when Sandy was up for a breather, he dived with them and tried to swim down near them; but he soon discovered that it was much harder than it appeared. Full Moon had told him never to look up when he was deep down in the water, because the distance to the surface was always exaggerated, and somewhat frightening. It was better, she said, to imagine that one was only just under the surface. This, however, only induced Ginger to test the truth of it, and although he was only about thirty feet deep he was appalled by what he saw, and shot upwards in alarm. Under the expert tuition of the two natives, his ability to swim down and remain under water increased rapidly, and by the end of the second day he was disporting himself with them.

He took a last plunge, determined to get down to forty feet and so break his own record. Exerting every ounce of strength he knew that he had succeeded, and was just turning to swim upwards when he saw a shadow pass slowly over a patch of white coral immediately underneath him. He was not particularly alarmed, for he assumed that it was either Shell-Breaker or Full Moon, coming down to tease him, as they often did, and he looked up to see which of them it was. To his unspeakable horror he saw a shark curving round, about twenty feet above him. It was looking straight at him. It was not an ordinary shark, but an enormous brute well over twenty feet long and dirty-white in colour.

He gave himself up for lost. He had no knife to defend himself, not that he thought for a moment that he would be able to use one even if he had. The most dreadful thing of all was that he had to go up towards the creature. He could not stay down for he was at the end of his endurance, and he knew, from previous experience with no danger threatening, that his lungs would be bursting by the time he reached the air. Struggling desperately to keep away from the great fish he began to rise. With ghastly deliberation the shark turned towards him.

It was then that he saw Shell-Breaker and Full Moon coming down, for the scene was as clear as if they were on land. Shell-Breaker was swimming with unbelievable speed straight towards the shark. Ginger was still rising, but his strength was fast ebbing. In a nightmare of horror he watched. He saw the huge brute begin to turn over on its back in order to seize him, as a shark always must to bite its prey; he saw Shell-Breaker flash low across its head, saw him strike, and saw a dark stain spurt from the wound. Again Shell-Breaker struck. The shark turned swiftly, its mighty jaws agape, but by this time Full Moon was underneath and she drove her knife upwards into the shark's stomach.

Ginger struggled upwards through water that was no longer clear, but stained with ugly brown patches that he knew must be blood. He saw no more, for the picture became blurred before his eyes; he was conscious only of a terrible sensation that the shark's jaws could close over his feet at any moment. He was at his last gasp when he reached the surface, to be dragged aboard by Algy and Sandy.

For a few seconds he could only lie on the cabin floor, getting his breath in great gasps, almost overcome by nausea caused by shock. 'Are they up yet?' he managed to get out at last, referring to Shell-Breaker and Full Moon.

'Not yet,' said Sandy.

'But—there's a shark—down there.'

'I know, we saw it. The kids went down after it,' returned Sandy.

'But it will kill them.'

'Not on your life,' declared Sandy, confidently. 'They're brought up on that sort of thing. A Marquesan is more than a match for a shark. Occasionally one gets grabbed, but that's only when the attack catches him unprepared from behind. Once they see it, I'd bet on the Marquesans every time. Shark-hunting is a sport with them.'

'It doesn't sound like sport to me,' muttered Ginger, staggering to his feet in order to see what was happening in the water.

Full Moon's head broke the surface, and she scrambled aboard. '*Aue*! He was bad, that *mako*,' she muttered.

Shell-Breaker followed a moment later, and Ginger saw that his shoulder was bleeding. 'By heavens! he's been bitten,' he cried.

'No, it's only a graze,' answered Sandy quickly. 'A shark's hide is like sandpaper—he must have bumped into it.'

The two Polynesians sat breathing heavily on the flying-boat, talking swiftly in their own language.

'What are they saying?' asked Biggles.

Sandy translated. 'They haven't killed it. A swordfish butted into the fight and attacked the shark, which made off, with the swordfish after it. The kids say it was the blood in the water that brought it. Incidentally, they swear the swordfish was bigger than the shark.'

'But they're not as dangerous, are they?' asked Ginger.

'I wouldn't say that,' returned Sandy. 'They don't attack human beings as often as sharks, but when they do—well, it's good-bye. That sword of theirs isn't just an ornament. There's more than one case of a swordfish sticking its sword right through the bottom of a ship.'

Ginger looked incredulous.

'You don't believe it, eh? Well, you go and look up the Admiralty records. A swordfish once attacked a Plymouth ship called *The Fortune* and put its sword through the copper sheeting, a three-inch hardwood plank, and twelve inches of oak—*and* punctured an oil-barrel on the other side of it. A British man-of-war—I forget its name—was once holed by a swordfish and had to make for port with all its pumps going. Don't you get the wrong idea about swordfish, young feller.'

'Then we'd better be moving,' put in Biggles. 'I hate to think what one of the brutes could do to a ship like this, with only a fraction of an inch of metal between us and the water.' He turned quickly, as there was a loud splash in the water some distance away. 'Hello! What's going on?' he ejaculated.

They all stood staring in the direction of the sound. There was nothing to indicate what had made it, but a patch of foam on the surface of the sea told them that they had not been mistaken.

'Look!' cried Ginger shrilly.

The warning was unnecessary, for everyone on the flying-boat saw what he had seen. A huge grey shark, either the one that had attacked Ginger or another, leapt high out of the water, so high that it seemed to hang in the air before falling back into the sea with a mighty splash. And it was not alone, for an instant later a giant swordfish broke the surface in the same place. It was fully twenty-five feet long.

'*Apau!*' cried Shell-Breaker, alarm in his voice. 'Go! Go fast!'

'Better get moving, Biggles; he thinks it's dangerous,' said Sandy quickly. 'And if he thinks it's dangerous you can bet your life it is.'

Biggles dashed to the cockpit, while the others started feverishly clearing the gear that was lying about. Sandy was still in his diving-kit—without the helmet, for he had been resting—but he soon had it off. Glancing up, he saw the swordfish again break the surface less than a hundred yards away. It was coming directly towards the flying-boat. 'Look out, everybody, he means business,' he shouted. 'I'm afraid he's spotted us.'

The first engine started. The second followed. But the 'Scud' had only just started to move when it received a terrific shock that half lifted it out of the water. Everyone was thrown down. What was worse, Biggles was hurled across the cockpit, and the machine, left to its own devices, yawed wildly before he could regain the joystick.

An instant later the giant fish broke surface about thirty feet away. Biggles jammed the throttle wide open, using one engine only in order to turn the machine away from the fish; but before the aircraft could gather speed there was another violent shock. Something crashed against the hull, and five feet of sword appeared in the cabin, missing Sandy by a few inches. It was withdrawn swiftly, leaving a gaping hole through which water started to pour. Algy flung a towel on it and tried vainly to stem the flow. 'Tell Biggles to take off!' he yelled. 'We shall sink in a couple of minutes.'

Ginger dashed forward to the cockpit. 'Get in the air!' he shouted. 'We're holed.'

'I'm trying to,' snapped Biggles.

Ginger saw the swordfish turning on the surface not fifty feet away. 'He's coming again!' he yelled and, whipping out his automatic, fired shot after shot at the mighty beast. Whether he hit it, he never knew; not that it really mattered, for by this time the 'Scud' was moving over the water faster even than the fish could travel. He hurried back to the others, to find the cabin in a state of chaos. In spite of their efforts to prevent it, the water was still pouring through the hole and the floor was already awash. 'Tell Biggles to keep going,' shouted Algy. 'If he can get off, the water will run out.'

Ginger dashed back to the cockpit and told Biggles what was happening.

'I can't get her off,' said Biggles tersely. 'I've tried. What with all that shell, and the water, she won't take it.'

'What shall we do?'

'Jettison everything. Chuck the diving-gear overboard— that's the heaviest.'

As he shot back to the cabin Ginger glanced through a side window and saw that they were still a good two miles from the island. The 'Scud' was taxi-ing at terrific speed, but not fast enough to lift. 'Everything over the side,' he yelled. 'Get the diving-gear over. It's our only chance.'

Sandy did not hesitate. He dragged the diving-kit, with the forty-pound leaden boots, to the side. It disappeared from view. The helmet followed. The pump, lines, everything portable went over the sides into the deep blue sea. Ginger began bringing the oysters out as fast as he could, but Full Moon stopped him. 'No!'

she cried. 'Me go,' and without giving the slightest warning of her intention she went like an arrow into the sea. Shell-Breaker followed.

'Stop—stop!' screamed Ginger.

'You needn't worry about them,' snapped Sandy. 'It's only a mile to the island, and a mile is nothing to them.'

The 'Scud', relieved of her excess load, rose slowly into the air, becoming more and more buoyant every moment as the water poured back through the leak and fell into the sea. By the time she skimmed low over the reef all the water had gone.

Biggles circled over the lagoon. He beckoned to Ginger. 'Tell the others that we shall sink if I land on deep water,' he said. 'I'm going to put her down near that sandy part, and beach her. Get out as fast as you can as soon as I touch. The lighter she is the higher up the beach she'll run. We'll get the shell out of her and drag her higher as soon as we're down.' Ginger returned to the others and gave them Biggles's message. 'We'll jump clear as soon as she slows down enough for it to be safe,' he said. 'Stand by. He's going down.'

Biggles brought the big machine in as slowly as he dared. But her keel was no sooner touching the water than water began pouring through the hole. Straight towards the beach the 'Scud' raced, sinking lower and lower into the water, and slowing down appreciably as water poured through the leak.

Fifty yards from the beach, while the machine was still travelling at a good twenty miles an hour, Ginger jumped overboard, and coming to the surface struck out along the creamy wake. Algy and Sandy had followed him, for he could see their heads bobbing up and down just in front of him. The 'Scud' held on her way, and slid smoothly up the shelving coral sand.

By the time the others had reached him Biggles was waist-deep in water at the cabin door dragging out the shell, but as soon as the rest of the party joined him he got back into the cockpit and by opening the throttle in short bursts gradually got the machine up on the sand inch by inch as the shell went overboard. When everything portable had been taken out of the aircraft he switched off and examined the damage. 'Well, I suppose you

BIGGLES IN THE SOUTH SEAS

have to take this sort of thing as it comes, in this part of the world,' he observed philosophically. 'I was fully prepared for the machine to be knocked about a bit on the coral, so I brought some sheet metal along, but I must say that I didn't make allowances for fish trying to get on board.'

'The sword came right through into the cabin and missed Sandy by an inch,' Ginger told him.

'You evidently need armour plate in these parts,' smiled Biggles. 'Never mind. It will mean a day's work patching up the hole, but nothing worse, I hope. We can fix it up well enough to get home, and as far as I can see, now that we have finished pearling, there's no particular hurry.'

'Confound it! Of course we shall have to go home now that we've lost the diving-kit,' muttered Ginger in tones of disappointment.

'It looks that way to me,' admitted Sandy. 'I suppose those kids are all right?'

'Yes, here they come,' Ginger told him. 'I've been watching them for some time, otherwise I'd have made Biggles taxi out to pick them up, hole or no hole.'

The two natives were not in the least exhausted by their swim. '*Kaoha*,' they called, smiling, as if the whole thing was a huge joke.

'All in the day's work as far as they're concerned,' murmured Sandy. 'Well, we'd better see about heaving all this shell up high and dry. I'll spend tomorrow opening it, while you're mending the ship. The kids will help me.'

Biggles nodded. 'That's the idea,' he said. 'If the oysters open up as well as the last lot we shall have made a good thing out of the trip. I suppose you'll buy a schooner, Sandy, and come back for more?'

Sandy rubbed his chin. 'I'm not so sure,' he said. 'I'd like to, of course, but in the past my luck with pearls hasn't been too good. Something usually happens to upset the blessed apple-cart. I think we'd better see about getting this lot home before we talk about more.'

'All right, you old pessimist,' agreed Biggles. 'By tomorrow evening we ought to be back in Rutuona. Come on, let's get the shell ashore ready for an early start in the morning.'

9

THE LUCK CHANGES

THE pink of dawn the following morning saw them all at their respective tasks: Biggles, Ginger, and Algy working on the machine, cutting a length of sheet-metal and preparing rivets to seal the hole in the flying-boat; and Sandy, with Full Moon and Shell-Breaker, opening the oysters with their knives. The two natives were a little way along the beach, where the previous day's catch had been dumped. Every now and then a triumphant yell from one of them, or from Sandy, announced the finding of another pearl. And so the day passed pleasantly enough. By the time the blue of the sky was fading the 'Scud' had been repaired to Biggles's satisfaction, and only a few more oysters remained to be opened. The yield of pearls was not quite as good as the first day's catch, owing to the fact that, although there was a two days' haul, there were not so many oysters, for Sandy had been working in deeper water and progress was consequently slower. Moreover, he had to come up to rest more often. However, he declared that the pearls were well up to average, and although he had not realized his promise about filling his hat with pearls, there were certainly enough to half-fill a hat when the seed pearls were included. He was quite prepared to continue operations with a new diving-suit if the scheme met with the approval of the others. Biggles promised to consider it, for, as Ginger pointed out, there was no reason why they should not go on after they had refitted.

'What about you kids going and catching some more fish for supper?' suggested Sandy, putting the pearls in the *cache* with the others.

'A fish nearly made a meal of me,' laughed Ginger, with a wink at Full Moon and Shell-Breaker, whom he had already thanked for their courageous rescue. Picking up the fishing-line he accompanied them to the pool where they had had so much luck on the previous occasion.

The sky was ablaze with all the colours of a Pacific sunset as Biggles walked across to make a final survey of the 'Scud'. Happening to glance at his instrument-board he stared hard at it for a moment, and then hurried back to where Sandy and Algy were sitting.

'What's wrong?' asked Sandy, after a glance at his face.

'I don't like the look of the barometer,' Biggles told him, with a worried frown.

Sandy glanced round the sky. 'It looks settled enough,' he said.

'I don't know anything about that; I'm talking about the aneroid. It's down to thirty.'

Sandy started. '*What?*'

'I said it was down to thirty, and still falling.'

Sandy rose quickly. 'We'd better get packed up,' he said. 'When the barometer falls like that it means there's going to be a blow, so we'd better get the machine afloat ready for a snappy take-off. I'd feel inclined to take off right away.'

'We can't.'

'Why not?'

'I don't think we can move the machine until the tide comes in and lifts her.'

'Well, let's try,' returned Sandy, emphatically. 'At Rutuona I don't think we should take any harm, even if a real snorter came along, but if we were caught out here the machine would be pulp in about five minutes. The seas will come right over the reef if it blows hard. Hark at it now.'

There was as yet only a slight breeze, but already the combers were pounding on the outer wall of the reef with a roar like distant thunder. Columns of spray rose high into the air.

'They're getting it now, somewhere,' muttered Sandy. 'I've heard the combers talk like that before.'

'All right,' agreed Biggles. 'Let's get down to the machine and see if we can move her. Where are the kids? It's time they were back. Algy, you'd better go and see if you can find them. Tell them not to trouble about the fish—we shan't need it if we're going.'

Algy went off at a run in the direction in which Ginger had disappeared, while the others hurried to the machine. Biggles put his weight against the bows and pushed, but the 'Scud' did not move. 'She's still resting on the sand,' he said. 'Another ten minutes ought to see the water high enough to lift her off. By James! Take a look at the gap in the reef.'

Sandy looked in that direction. The entrance to the lagoon was a swirling smother of foam. 'Aye, it's coming right enough,' he said.

'If we're not away in ten minutes it will be dark before we get to Rutuona, anyway,' went on Biggles anxiously. 'I don't like the idea of night flying over the open sea, or of trying to get down without any landing-lights. That bay is too exposed to be of any use to us; we should have to find somewhere under the lee of the island.'

Sandy said nothing. He was staring along the beach.

Biggles turned and saw that it was Algy. He was alone.

'What the dickens are the kids doing?' shouted Sandy. 'We're waiting to push off.'

'I can't find them,' answered Algy.

'What do you mean—you can't find them? They must be on the island somewhere.'

'I've been from one end of it to the other but I couldn't see them,' returned Algy. 'I found Ginger's shoes, and some fish they had evidently caught—but there was no sign of them.'

'Where did you find Ginger's shoes?'

'Just a little way along, on the coral, beside a cove.'

Biggles looked at Sandy. 'What the deuce can they be up to?' he muttered. 'Where are they likely to be?'

Sandy shook his head. 'Don't ask me. Ginger won't have come to any harm, though. Shell-Breaker and Full Moon will see to that—they know what they're doing.'

'I hope they do,' replied Biggles. 'Well, we can't go without them. I think the machine's afloat, so we'll get all ready to take off the moment they arrive.'

A quarter of an hour passed. The sun was now going down in a blood-red glow, misty and threatening; only the rim of it remained above the horizon. Presently it disappeared in the sea. Darkness fell.

'Well, that knocks on the head any idea of going tonight,' said Biggles quietly. 'What's happened to those kids? I'm getting worried about them.'

'Something's going to happen to the machine if we don't do something about it,' cut in Algy. 'Look at the reef.'

For the first time since their arrival seas were sweeping right over the reef into the lagoon. Angry ripples surged across the normally still water, so that the machine, now afloat, moved up and down uneasily.

'We'd better get some more anchors on her,' said Biggles seriously, as he watched the 'Scud' rocking.

'Half a dozen wouldn't hold her if it's a real blow,' returned Sandy. 'She'll tear herself to pieces in no time.'

'There's nothing else we can do,' answered Biggles. 'Get some lumps of coral, the biggest you can lift, and we'll make extra anchors fore and aft. We've plenty of rope.'

'As you say, that's the only thing we can do,' agreed Sandy.

'I think you'd better go and have another look for those kids, Algy,' went on Biggles. 'Sandy and I will fix the machine up.'

Algy nodded and hurried away.

It was half an hour before he returned, by which time the 'Scud' was riding uneasily at six anchors, any one of which would have been sufficient to hold her in an ordinary sea. 'I can't see a sign of them anywhere,' he said. 'Ginger's shoes are still on the coral. He must have taken them off to bathe. I'm sorry to say that I'm afraid something serious has happened.'

Biggles was silent for a moment. 'Yes,' he said, slowly. 'Something has happened or they'd be back before now. Something happened to them in the water. It's hard to believe that they can all be drowned. On the other side of the island, in the open sea, they might have got carried away, but I can't see that happening in the lagoon.'

'I wonder if a shark could have got them?' muttered Sandy.

'Not all of them, surely? At least one of them would get back to the shore—not that I think Ginger would go far away from it after his recent experience. The only thing I can think of is that they went off to the reef, and were either dragged off by a big wave, or tried to swim and were unable to get back. Well, we can't do anything about it. If it were daylight we might fly round and look for them, but in this darkness we shouldn't see anything unless we were on the water, and taxi-ing is out of the question. I couldn't get the machine through those seas pouring into the entrance to the lagoon—not that it would be of any use if I could. She wouldn't live for a minute in the sea that's running outside. Hark at it!'

The deep incessant boom of the mighty combers told its own story. There was something frightening about the way they hurled themselves on the reef with a power that caused the island to tremble. The palms were beginning to lash to and fro in the wind.

'Well, it's no use standing here,' said Biggles at last.

'It's not much use doing anything else that I can see,' murmured Sandy.

'We'll make another search,' decided Biggles. 'It's better than doing nothing. Algy, you take the eastern end of the island. Sandy, you take the middle. I'll do the western end.'

So they parted, each heading for his allotted beat, calling loudly the names of the missing.

Biggles was away for an hour. He got back to find that Sandy and Algy had already returned. He did not trouble to ask them if they had any news, for it was obvious that their search had been as unsuccessful as his. 'Well that's about all we can do,' he said bitterly. 'We'll stand by until the morning. If the machine looks like being damaged we'll try to get her off and head for Rutuona. I can cruise round until it's light enough to see to land. I think we've enough petrol. Otherwise, from what you've told us, Sandy, if the machine is smashed up we're likely to spend the rest of our lives here.'

The night passed slowly, but at long last the eastern sky began to turn pale; and with the coming of dawn the fury of the storm increased. Huge seas were now sweeping right across the reef and flooding into the lagoon. Waves lashed the coral beach which a few hours before had been so silent. The 'Scud' strained at her moorings, throwing herself about like a terrified animal.

'She won't stand much more of that,' said Biggles, grimly. 'Stand fast, and I'll go and have a look at the barometer.' With difficulty he waded waist-deep to the cockpit. He glanced at the instrument board and came back—or, rather, was thrown back by the sea.

'What is it?' asked Sandy.

'Twenty-nine.'

'Sweet spirit of Scotland, then it's coming,' declared Sandy.

'If we don't go now we're here for good,' returned Biggles. 'Look at the lagoon. I couldn't have believed that such a sea could have got up in so short a time. And it's getting worse. I'm by no means sure that I can get the machine off, even now, but it's now or never. Well, what shall we do? You've a say in the matter as well as me.'

'We'd better go. We can always come back later and look for the kids,' voted Sandy. 'There's no sense in just standing here and watching the machine break up in front of our eyes. She'll start dragging those anchors presently, or else tear herself to pieces. The sea is getting worse, and if I know anything about it it's going to be a lot worse before it's better. I've had one long spell on this island and I don't want another, but that's what it will mean if we lose the machine.'

'All right,' said Biggles. 'Get aboard. Be careful, there's the devil of an undertow. It nearly swept me off my feet.'

Fighting their way through the waves they managed to get to the machine and drag themselves on board. Biggles started the engines. 'Cut the ropes fore and aft,' he shouted above the din, for what with the noise of the engines, the crash of the waves, and the lashing palms, it was no use speaking in a normal voice. 'You get to the bows, Algy. Yours will be the last rope. Don't cut till I give the signal. I'll wait for her to swing round with her nose into the sea. Right, Sandy.'

Sandy's knife came down on the last rope that held the machine by the stern. Instantly the 'Scud' swung round, dragging at the single rope that held her by the bows. She bucked so violently that Algy needed all his strength to hold on.

'Right!' yelled Biggles, and opened the throttle.

Algy's knife came down across the rope. It parted with a twang that could be heard above the gale. He clambered aft, and fell headlong into the cabin as the 'Scud' rose to the next wave. He lay where he fell, for it was impossible to stand.

The 'Scud' was racing through a blinding cloud of spray that made it impossible to see anything else, so that Biggles had to fly by feel alone. Twice he was sure they were gone, as the machine plunged into a trough, but each time she rose miraculously to the next wave. Then a sea struck her sideways across the bows, and she yawed into a trough. There was no question of turning. The machine would not answer to her controls in such conditions. But a momentary lull gave Biggles a chance, and he took it. He raced the 'Scud' straight along the bottom of the trough, and as the next wave rolled towards him he jerked the stick back, knowing that if the machine did not rise they were all doomed. Not until all seemed lost did the machine unstick. She staggered off the water, the wave snatching at her keel as it broke under her. The next moment the machine was climbing up through a cloud of spray that hid the reef from sight.

Biggles settled himself back in his seat and tightened the safety belt. To say that he actually headed for Rutuona would not be strictly true. The wind was across, so in order to reach the island he had to turn his bows towards the open ocean and drift sideways. He noticed that the barometer was down to 28.50.

Rutuona came into view, an oasis of whirling trees in a white-flecked ocean, and he looked anxiously for a landing-place. As far as he could see there was only one, a narrow strip of water that ran far inland between two rugged cliffs, like a Norwegian fiord. He nosed the machine towards it, and was thankful to see that the protected water was comparatively calm, although the air was full of flying debris, palm-fronds and the like. There was also a fair amount on the surface of the water. How much of it was soft enough to give under their keel, and how much was solid, it was impossible to determine. But it was no longer a matter of saving the machine. Their lives were in peril, and in such circumstances he was prepared to lose the machine if they could all get ashore safely. Exploring the creek with his eyes he determined to take the machine to the far end of it, where a scree ran right down to the water's edge, forming a natural slipway.

He brought the machine in under full throttle, and even so his ground-speed was negligible. The keel struck the water; the hull veered sideways as a wing-float caught in a tangle of floating bushes, and they came to rest in a still larger tangle that had been caught up by a projecting crag. More debris was floating towards the place, so that in a few seconds the 'Scud' was hemmed in by it. The bottom of the scree was about twenty yards away.

Biggles switched off and turned to the others. 'Well, here we are,' he said evenly. 'And here we look like staying for a bit,' he added. 'I shouldn't have minded had it not been for the kids. Still, I suppose it's no use talking about that now. We couldn't do more than we did. We'll go back and look for them again as soon as this wind drops a bit.'

'It's going to take us some time to get out of here,' declared Sandy. 'It will mean a couple of days' work cutting a channel through these bushes, unless we can get to Roaring Wave and persuade him to lend us some labourers. I don't think there will be any difficulty about that. I reckon we are about six miles from the village.'

Biggles nodded. 'About that,' he said. 'I think we'd better try to get along, and see what Roaring Wave says.'

'If you don't mind we'll stay here until the wind drops,' grunted Sandy. 'We should get our skulls stove in by falling coconuts before we'd gone a hundred yards. A coconut grove is no place in a gale of wind, believe me.'

'Of course,' agreed Biggles. 'I forgot that. As you say, we shall just have to sit here until the wind drops. I hope nothing falls on top of us; half the greenstuff on the island seems to be blowing over our heads. By the way, where did you put the pearls?'

Sandy blinked. 'The pearls?' he stammered. 'Didn't you bring
'em?'

'No, I left it to you.'

Sandy's face was a picture. He shook his head sadly. 'I always
was an unlucky son of a gun when there were pearls about,' he
muttered miserably. 'They must be still under the rock where we
left them.'

Biggles dodged a whirling palm-frond. 'Pretty good,' was all
he said, but there was more than a suspicion of sarcasm in his
voice.

10

WHAT HAPPENED TO GINGER

HAD Ginger told the others of the existence of the fairy grotto
they would have guessed at once where he was, in which case
their attempts to get into touch with him might well have ended
in tragedy. So, although it was hard to believe at the time, it was
really just as well that Ginger had withheld the information.

He had no intention of going to the grotto when, with Full
Moon and Shell-Breaker, he had set off at Sandy's request to get
some fish. Naturally, they made their way to the same cove
where they had done so well on the previous occasion, and they
soon had a good supply of fish flapping about on the coral. So
quickly were they supplied with all the fish they were likely to
need that Full Moon's suggestion of a swim in the pool was
promptly taken up, and they were soon all splashing about in the
pure water. In these circumstances a visit to the grotto was
almost automatic. Full Moon shouted that she was going, and
took a header. The others were on her track before the splash had
subsided, and together they swam through the short cave into
the fairyland beyond. Laughing from sheer light-heartedness
they climbed up on the ledge where they had sat before, and
reaching down kicked spray into the air with startling results, for
it flashed like a myriad blue sparks. However, the best fun must

come to an end, and for a time they sat talking in low tones about their exquisite surroundings.

At last Ginger got up. 'It's time we were getting back,' he said. 'In fact, we've stayed too long already. I have an idea Sandy was waiting to fry those fish for supper. The sun must be going down. The water is turning mauve. Incidentally. I believe it is getting rough outside; look at the ripples coming in.'

For a moment or two longer they stood watching the colour-transformation that was taking place before their eyes; then Ginger balanced himself on the ledge, hands together, ready to plunge. He was looking over his shoulder at Shell-Breaker, who he suspected from previous experience might push him in, and so he did not see what Full Moon saw. Her wild scream filled the cave with sound.

Ginger spun round, not a little alarmed. 'What's the matter?' he cried.

Full Moon pointed at the water. '*Mako!*' she said.

Ginger turned again, and saw an enormous triangular fin projecting above the water just inside the entrance to the cave. It was moving forward, slowly.

For a full minute Ginger could only stare, stunned to speechlessness. It was the first time he had seen a shark inside the lagoon, and his skin curled with horror at the realization that a few minutes earlier he must have been swimming about in close proximity to the monster. 'What are we going to do?' he cried in dismay.

Shell-Breaker made a grimace. 'Me stay,' he said.

'But the *mako* may not go for a week.'

Shell-Breaker shrugged his shoulders. 'Me stay,' he repeated resolutely.

Ginger looked back at the shark. Its back projected out of the water not ten feet from where he stood. The creature was so huge that it seemed almost to fill the pool inside the cave. In the confined space it looked larger than a whale. They were safe where they were, for the ledge was between two and three feet above water-level, but to put hand or foot in the water would obviously be committing suicide in a very unpleasant manner.

'We're trapped,' thought Ginger, aghast. 'We're trapped as effectively as if the cave had closed up.' Which in a way was true. 'Why has the brute come in here?' he asked Shell-Breaker.

'Big storm at sea, maybe hurricane,' replied Shell-Breaker. 'When big fella sea come fish swim in lagoon and stick head in hole.'

'What can we do about it? You know more about this sort of thing than I do.'

Shell-Breaker merely made another despairing gesture. 'Me stay,' he said yet again.

'Can't we kill it, or drive it out somehow?'

'*Aue*! No kill. Outside plenty water, me kill. In cave, no kill. *Mako* plenty *kai-kai* me.'

Ginger stared again at the shark's huge dorsal fin, standing upright like the sail of a boat. 'Heavens above, what will the others think when we don't go back?' he muttered.

Full Moon squatted down on the coral. She picked up a loose piece and hurled it at the shark, screaming what was obviously an insult in her own language.

The creature moved its great body languidly, showing the dirty grey of its stomach.

'Maybe you pray white man's god,' suggested Shell-Breaker thoughtfully.

Ginger said nothing. He was thinking. He saw the mauve tint of the water deepening and knew that the sun had nearly set. He visualized the others coming to look for them, searching the island from end to end, but there was nothing he could do to relieve their anxiety. At first he found himself regretting that he had not told Biggles about the grotto, but on second thoughts he was glad he had not, for in that case Biggles would certainly have sought them there and, not knowing the cause of the delay, would have encountered the shark.

Ginger had been in many difficult and dangerous situations, but he could not imagine anything more fantastic than the one in which he now found himself. He had been locked up more than once, but never before had watch been kept by such a terrible guardian. The thought that appalled him was that the shark might stay there for days, a week, or even longer, in which case they were all likely to starve to death, for there was no question of entering the water while the shark was there. In the fast-fading light he saw that there was now a definite movement in the pool, which previously had been absolutely motionless. The water surged to and fro with a regular movement that could only mean that a big sea was running outside. 'I think you are right about the storm,' he told Shell-Breaker.

'Storm pass, *mako* go,' replied Shell-Breaker briefly.

'How long do you think the storm will last?'

'Two day—three day—maybe.' Shell-Breaker held up all his fingers. He seemed resigned to their predicament.

Ginger leaned back against the wall of the grotto and watched Full Moon relieving her feelings by pelting the shark with lumps of coral; but the great fish did not seem to mind in the least. Swiftly it grew dark. They were, of course, without any means of illumination, so it was now certain that they would have to remain in the cave all night at any rate, for even if the shark departed they would have no means of knowing it until daylight came again. The darkness was intense. The only sound was the eerie gurgling of the rising and falling water. At last Ginger sat down and cupped his chin in the palms of his hands, prepared to pass what he suspected was likely to be the longest night of his life.

In this he was correct. The night seemed like eternity. Indeed, the first reflection of morning light was so long in coming that he began seriously to wonder if the mouth of the cave had fallen in. It was possible, he reflected, for the movement of the water was now much more pronounced, and it was clear that a storm was raging outside. Not once did he close his eyes, although he longed to. More than once he found himself nodding in spite of the discomfort of his position, and when that happened he struck the coral with his hands to keep himself awake, for he was terrified of dozing and falling from his perch into the water. In the end the thing became a nightmare, and he hardly knew whether he was awake or dreaming. But at long last the first suspicion of light came through the tunnel, and he breathed a sigh of relief to know that the passage was still open. But the light was no longer blue; it was grey, dull, and depressing.

He looked along the ledge and saw that both Full Moon and Shell-Breaker were sleeping peacefully, as if there was no such thing as danger, and he envied their happy-go-lucky natures. He awakened them and directed their attention to the water. Side by side they sat and watched the grey light spreading further into the cave, until such time that it was possible to see all the water inside the grotto. At last the matter was no longer in doubt. The shark had gone. Ginger could have shouted with relief and satisfaction, but his optimism received a rude check when Shell-Breaker announced calmly that the *mako* might still be in the cave. That, Ginger realized, was a possibility that would always exist, for it was impossible to see in the cave without entering the water. They waited for a little while, but when the shark did not reappear Shell-Breaker stood up. 'Me go,' he announced casually.

'But suppose you meet *mako* in the cave?' asked Ginger.

'Me fight. Kill *mako* maybe. Maybe *mako* eat me.'

Ginger shook his head in horrible indecision, realizing that he would have no means of knowing what had happened inside the cave unless he himself went in and found out.

'Me go,' said Shell-Breaker again. 'You stay. If *mako* gone, me come back.'

Ginger did not like the idea of Shell-Breaker taking such a desperate risk on his behalf, but such was his fear of the shark that he raised no objection, comforting himself with the thought that even if he went with the native, and they encountered the shark, he would be more likely to get in the way than be of any assistance. Full Moon said nothing, but the instant Shell-Breaker had dived into the water she put her knife in her *pareu* in such a manner that she would be able to get at it easily, and followed him.

With what trepidation Ginger watched the two forms disappear into the cave can be better imagined than described. He became a victim of every sort of pessimism. He fancied that the swirl of the water suddenly increased, as if a struggle was going on inside the cave. He imagined that he could see dark shadows moving just inside the entrance. The minutes passed with nerve-racking slowness. Then one of the shadows materialized and sped towards the ledge, and a moment later Shell-Breaker's head appeared above the water. 'Come—come plenty quick!' he shouted.

'Has the *mako* gone?' cried Ginger, the muscles of his face stiff with fear.

'Come quick, keep close, plenty big wave,' was all Shell-Breaker answered, and kicking off from the coral with his feet, he streaked again towards the cave.

Ginger braced himself. Never in all his experience had he hated anything as much as the task that lay before him. But Shell-Breaker had gone, and clearly expected him to follow, so with a shudder of apprehension he dived in and struck out in the wake of the vague form which he could see some distance in front of him. Every moment he was prepared to see the shark loom up, but even this fear was soon half forgotten in a more pressing peril.

Unseen currents were forcing him against the coral side of the cave. Twice he was carried back nearly to the grotto by a surging flood of water, and then sucked towards the open lagoon by the tremendous backwash, as helpless as if he had been a piece of seaweed. He could only fight to keep himself clear of the rough coral, which would have torn his flesh had he collided with it, but at last an unusually vicious backwash shot him clear into the open and he struggled to the surface. He was almost spent, and clutched at the shoulder of Shell-Breaker who was waiting for him. The native at once struck out for the coral bank, against which waves were dashing in impotent fury.

How he got up the bank Ginger never knew. He had no clear recollection of anything except Shell-Breaker pushing him from behind and Full Moon dragging him up by the hair. Finally, a mighty wave cast them all up together, and they landed clear of the breakers bleeding from a dozen scratches. Shell-Breaker was in even worse case than Ginger, in spite of his ability in the water. Staggering to his feet he pointed to the centre of the cove, where, as the water rose and fell, a dark fin projected. Ginger was nearly sick with horror when he realized that the shark must have been there all the time, and he had been within twenty yards of it.

'*Mako* leave cave—plenty big fella sea,' muttered Shell-Breaker.

Looking about him Ginger perceived for the first time the full force of the storm. The wind, which had now reached gale force, clutched at his body, and beat the palms so far over that their fronds swept the ground. The reef was hidden under monstrous seas that broke with a roar like thunder and flung spray a hundred feet into the air. The surface of the lagoon was being whipped into a smother of foam. Overhead the sky was flat grey.

Ginger's heart sank, and he uttered a cry of despair, for he knew that the 'Scud' could not live in such a gale. The force of the combers crashing on the beach was such that he knew without looking that if the flying-boat was still there it must be a tangle of fabric, wire, and three-ply. What were the others doing? He shouted to Full Moon and Shell-Breaker that he was going, and bending forward into the wind he set off at a laborious run towards the camp. He soon came within sight of it—or of where it had been. There was nothing there. Only a pile of fallen palms, and a few scattered wooden cases, showed where the camp had been. Of Biggles, Algy or Sandy there was no sign. Ginger let out a cry of despair. 'They've gone!' he shouted.

Heedless of the protests of Shell-Breaker and Full Moon, he forced his way along the beach just out of reach of the waves, looking for what he dreaded to find—the remains of the mangled flying-boat; but to his infinite relief he could see no signs of it. 'They must have gone when the storm started,' he told himself hopefully, and in order to confirm that they had not taken refuge elsewhere he dragged himself up the incline towards the centre of the island, ducking and dodging as coconuts and palm-fronds whirled past him.

Not until he reached the ridge did he realize the full fury of the hurricane, for it was coming from that side of the island. The sea was a succession of giant combers, their tops torn into spray, which made it impossible to see more than a few hundred yards. The waves, rearing high into the air, flung themselves towards the place where he stood. Already the whole side of the island was submerged, the waves breaking far above the place where their first load of shell had been stacked. As for the shell, it had all been swept away. More terrifying still, the whole island shook under the impact of the rollers, and in many places water-spouts shot high into the air from coral that was above the water-line. At first Ginger could not understand what caused this; then he realized that the sea was pouring under the island, into caves such as the one he had just left, and under the tremendous pressure was bursting through flaws in the coral. Every now and then a mass of coral would be flung into the air, as if by an explosion. Finding it difficult to remain on his feet, Ginger dropped on to his hands and knees, and clung to some low-growing shrubs to prevent himself from being blown away.

Not until a mighty comber broke and raced up to the spot where he knelt, so that the foam surged right across the ridge, did he realize that he was in peril. Vaguely to his memory came something Sandy had said about big seas sweeping right across the islands. He turned his head to see what the others were doing and saw Shell-Breaker forcing his way towards him.

As soon as he saw that Ginger was looking at him the Marquesan beckoned vigorously, and pointed to the palms. Knowing that there must be a reason for this Ginger made his way towards him, clutching at such handholds as he could find to check his headlong progress. He could no longer see Full Moon. Shell-Breaker's mouth was opening and shutting, and he knew that he was shouting, but he could hear nothing; the wind was snatching the words from his lips as fast as they were formed. The native, realizing the futility of attempting to speak, could only point towards a mass of coral, under which he crouched, and there Ginger joined him.

The Marquesan cupped his hands round his mouth and shouted into Ginger's ear. 'When wind drop, big seas come.'

Ginger reversed the process. 'Bigger than these?'

'Yes, waves come right over island.' As if to confirm Shell-Breaker's words a giant wave did at that moment sweep right across the ridge and reach the lagoon on the far side.

'Come!' shouted Shell-Breaker.

Ginger followed him to the palms. The nuts had ceased to fly, for they were all on the ground. He saw Full Moon clinging to one of the thickest boles. She had evidently been busy, for a series of notches had been cut in the smooth trunk nearly up to the swaying crown. She still gripped her knife in her hand. Round her body was a length of rope which she must have found on the site of the camp. She was now knotting it into a double coil.

When she saw Ginger and Shell-Breaker coming she arranged the coils round her body and the trunk of the palm, and indicated that Ginger was to go with her.

Ginger, still not quite sure what was expected of him, joined the girl at the palm. She did not speak. She pushed him inside the coil of rope, and, starting to climb, motioned him to do the same. So, with the rope round both their bodies, and the trunk of the palm between them, they began to mount.

To Ginger it was a nightmare journey. The violent swaying of the palm, the tearing of the wind, the noise, and the flying debris were beyond human imagination; and as they mounted slowly towards the threshing fronds, the imminent prospect of a fall into the depths below did nothing to allay Ginger's fears.

Full Moon glanced upwards, and evidently decided that they were close enough to the great fronds to make further progress doubly dangerous, for she started tightening the rope, lashing them both to the bole. Ginger could only admire the efficiency with which she went about a task which would have made many experienced sailors pause. Finally, she took her knife and hacked furiously at the trunk immediately above them, so that the chips whirled away in the wind. When she was half-way through it a tremendous gust tore away the crown bodily, and the green mass disappeared into the driving spindrift. The palm, relieved of its dragging weight, at once leapt to a vertical position, and without offering any appreciable resistance to the wind remained more or less stationary.

A minute later Ginger saw the wisdom of her action in cutting off the top of the palm, when another one, not far away, snapped off short just above the roots and disappeared into the seething lagoon. Another followed it soon after. Looking down he saw that the whole island was now buried under a raging sea of water, as the breakers swept it from side to side. Turning his head with difficulty he could just make out Shell-Breaker. He had lashed himself to another palm with his *pareu*, and was hacking at the crown as Full Moon had done. Suddenly it was whipped away, and he was left clinging to the stump, like a bear up a pole. His face twisted into a smile when he saw Ginger looking at him, and Ginger smiled back, although his mood was anything but gay. 'My gosh! these kids have got some courage,' he thought admiringly.

They could do nothing except cling to the tree, and so to some extent prevent the rope from chafing them. An hour passed, two hours, and then, amazingly, there was a sudden lull. The wind died away altogether. Immediately overhead there appeared a round patch of blue sky.

Ginger shouted in relief, but Full Moon shook her head. 'Plenty wind bymeby,' she said. 'Centre of storm. Soon he pass, then plenty wind.'

Ginger understood vaguely what she meant, and soon discovered that she was right, for the lull, which was the centre of the hurricane, did not last long. The blue sky disappeared, and the wind returned with as much violence as before.

Hour after hour it raged, its force slowly weakening as the centre of the hurricane swept on over the ocean, but at a time that Ginger judged to be about four o'clock the gale had dropped to no more than a steady breeze punctuated by occasional gusts. He was more than a little thankful, for he was exhausted with the strain. He was hungry and thirsty as well as tired, for he had had neither food nor sleep for many hours. His thirst was aggravated by the salt spray which still filled the air, but there was as yet no question of leaving his refuge, for as the wind dropped so did the size of the mighty Pacific rollers increase. The whole island rocked under their weight as they streamed across the ridge, carrying all before them. The sand and shell-dust which formed the subsoil, and the herbage that grew on it, were swept away, leaving the foundation of coral exposed. Piles of sand, stone, and seaweed were flung up where before there had been none. Water boiled up through the coral as the seas drove under it. Only a few palms remained standing.

Not until evening did the clouds break and the crimson orb of the sun appear, far down in the west. By that time the waves were subsiding. By nightfall only an occasional breaker managed to reach the ridge, and by then its force was too far spent for it to be dangerous, so Ginger, with Full Moon's approval, made his way stiffly to the ground. He was encrusted with salt; his hair and eyebrows were stiff with it. He ached in every limb.

The others joined him, but they did not share his depression. As far as they were concerned the storm had passed and they had survived, so there was no need to worry any more about it. Even when Ginger pointed out that all the fresh water on the island would certainly be tainted with salt, they only laughed.

Slowly, they made their way through a scene of utter ruin to the site of the camp. It was by no means easy to find, for the whole shape of the island had altered. Masses of coral had disappeared entirely, while sand had been torn from one place and flung up in another. Palms and the fronds that had been stripped from them lay about in wild confusion. Huge masses of seaweed and shells of all shapes and sizes were strewn about over everything. Over them crawled countless crabs, sea-slugs, and other marine creatures, all making their way back to the sea from which they had been thrown.

Dragging the trailing seaweed aside Ginger groped about on the site of the camp and managed to find a few odds and ends. A case of bully beef had been wedged into a lump of coral; a few tins of condensed milk, biscuits, and similar commodities lay half-buried in the sand. Borrowing Full Moon's knife he cut open a tin of beef and another of biscuits, but he soon found that his mouth was too parched to eat, so he made his way to the spring from where they had obtained the fresh water. It was no longer there. The spot was buried under many tons of sand.

Ginger looked at Shell-Breaker with startled eyes. 'If we can't get water we shall soon die of thirst,' he said.

Full Moon only laughed. 'No die,' she said. 'Plenty drink,' she went on, picking up one of the many coconuts that lay on the ground. Taking her knife she cut the top off one with an expert slash, and passed it to Ginger, who was far too thirsty to be embarrassed by his exhibition of ignorance. He emptied the shell and picked up another. Never had anything tasted so delicious as the milky juice. The other two were also drinking, and he derived consolation from the realization that they would not starve or die of thirst while the nuts held out.

For a long time they sat in silence, nibbling a curious meal of bully beef, biscuit, and coconut. When it was finished Ginger gazed out across the moonlit sea for a little while, wondering what had become of Biggles, and deploring the tragic ending of their expedition. Presently, looking round at the others, he saw that they were both lying down, sleeping peacefully. 'I might as well join them,' he thought, and stretched himself out on the damp sand.

11
A RUDE AWAKENING

GINGER was the first to wake in the morning. He opened his eyes and lay still for a minute or two staring at the blue sky, worried by a sense of something wrong. Then, in a flash, he remembered everything. He did not move. There seemed to be no reason why he should. The air was fresh; the breeze was no more than a caress, and the warm sun soothed his tired body. So he lay still on his back, hands under his head, trying to get events into some sort of order. What had happened to the others, he reasoned correctly, was this. When he and the two natives did not return, Biggles would at once make a search. In the ordinary way no great harm would have been done by their enforced absence, but the coming of the hurricane altered everything. In order to save the machine Biggles had been obliged to abandon them, and fly the 'Scud' to a safer anchorage, in which case he would soon reappear. In fact, he might come back at any moment. He did

not believe that Biggles had been taken unawares by the
hurricane, and the 'Scud' destroyed. However, the fact remained that he and the two Marquesans were marooned, and
could do nothing but await the arrival of a rescue party. That
sooner or later it would come he had no doubt.

Full Moon opened her eyes and smiled up at him. Stretching,
she sat up, her eyes wandering out over the lagoon. Suddenly she
stopped, tense, rigid. Into her eyes came the shadow of fear.
'Atanelli, he come,' she hissed.

Ginger sat up as if he had been propelled by a spring, and
followed the direction of her eyes. A schooner, obviously in a bad
way if not actually in distress, was making her way carefully
through the entrance to the lagoon under a few strips of ragged
sail. That it was the *Avarata* was beyond doubt. For a second
Ginger stared at it, hardly able to believe his eyes or make up his
mind what to do. First of all he awakened Shell-Breaker by
striking him on the leg, which happened to be the only part of his
body within reach. 'Shell-Breaker, wake up!' he said tersely.
'Atanelli is here.'

Shell-Breaker sat up, wide awake on the instant. He gazed out
across the lagoon. '*Aue*! Plenty bad,' he said.

'Don't move, they may not have seen us,' said Ginger. 'Let me
think. What is the best thing to do? If he doesn't know we are
here he may soon go.'

Shell-Breaker shook his head. 'No go,' he said. '*Avarata* been in
a hurricane. Plenty damage. He stay long time, maybe.'

'In which case they'll come ashore for water and nuts,'
reflected Ginger. He thought swiftly, looking about for some
place of concealment. 'Let us get over the other side of the ridge,'
he said at last, in desperation, and began squirming through the
debris towards the far beach. Every moment he expected to hear
a shout announcing that they were discovered, but if they were,
no sign of it was given, and they crawled over the ridge where, of
course, they could not be seen from the lagoon. As soon as they
were out of view of the schooner Ginger got up and ran to the
farthest end of the island and, finding a hiding-place among the
coral, turned to watch the schooner. It was just dropping anchor

in the lagoon. The tattered sails lay about the deck. Over them walked the Solomon Island boys, in a listless fashion, as though they were exhausted. Castanelli was leaning against the wheel.

Having nothing else to do Ginger lay still, his eyes on the schooner, anxious to know what Castanelli would do next. There was just a chance, he thought, that the Corsican might depart after a short rest, for the sea outside the lagoon was going down fast. But this hope was soon squashed. Having got the deck of the schooner more or less shipshape Castanelli ordered a dinghy to be lowered—his voice reached the watchers clearly—and he was soon being rowed to the island by two members of his crew.

Ginger bit his lip. 'I'm afraid we're in for a bit of bad luck,' he said. 'Castanelli must know that this is the island near the pearl-bed; even if he doesn't recognize it he must know that it is somewhere in this district. He may have got the taint of rotting oysters either before or after the hurricane blew up; maybe it brought him here.'

Neither Full Moon nor Shell-breaker had anything to say about this, so, continuing watching, they saw Castanelli step ashore and commence a systematic search along the lagoon side of the island. He soon found the wrecked camp, and stood smoking a cigar while his boys dragged the debris aside to disclose the remains of the stores. Suddenly he stooped and picked something up, something that flashed in the sunlight. Ginger knew what it was. The shell that had been stacked on that side of the island had been strewn all over the place; he remembered seeing several among the seaweed. Castanelli had found one, and Ginger realized that it would settle any doubts in his mind about the last occupants of the island. Mortified, but helpless to prevent it, Ginger watched Castanelli show the shell to his boys before tossing it on one side. Fortunately, it did not occur to Ginger that the pearls might still be in the *cache*, or his depression would have been worse, for the Corsican was standing within a yard of the spot where they had been buried.

Castanelli stayed on the island for about an hour, at the end of which time he got back into the dinghy and was rowed to the schooner, which lay about a hundred yards from the shore.

Again Ginger hoped fervently that he would go, for now that the island was devastated there appeared to be no reason why he should stay; but no move was made to suggest that Castanelli had any such intention.

All the day the schooner remained at anchor, its captain sometimes on deck supervising the repair of gear and sails, and sometimes out of sight below. As the day wore on Ginger became more and more worried. But he was still convinced that Biggles and the others had departed as soon as the hurricane had announced its approach, in which case they would be certain to return. He knew that they would be anxious about him. For some reason or other it did not enter his head that he had been given up as lost. What alarmed him most was the thought that Biggles might return at any moment. Apart from the presence of the schooner, the surface of the lagoon was strewn with obstacles, palm-trunks and the like, which Biggles might not see, and if he struck one in landing the aircraft would unquestionably be wrecked.

But when the sun began to sink into the western ocean and there was still no sign of the 'Scud' Ginger knew that there was little likelihood of his returning that day, and for the first time serious doubts entered his mind about the flying-boat's survival of the hurricane. It might easily have been blown out to sea, he thought miserably. On the other hand, it might have reached Rutuona safely, and Biggles was only waiting to make sure that the weather had cleared before he returned, in which case he ought to try to stop him. He turned to Shell-Breaker. 'How long would it take us to get from here to Rutuona in a small boat?' he asked.

Shell-Breaker thought for a moment. 'One day—two day, maybe. Depend on sea and wind.'

Ginger pointed to the dinghy, now moored under the schooner's counter. 'How long in that boat?' he asked.

Shell-Breaker, by words and actions, indicated that if they started at nightfall it might be possible to reach Rutuona by the morning of the following day. In reply to another question by Ginger he declared that he would be able to find his way across the intervening ocean.

'Then if Atanelli no go by night, we steal boat,' announced Ginger.

The others agreed that they were ready to put the plan into execution, so Ginger told Shell-Breaker to gather some nuts together, which they would pick up after they had succeeded in getting the dinghy. It looked simple enough, he thought, as he gazed across the lagoon at the schooner. Castanelli would hardly consider it necessary to set a watch in such a place. The swim was only a short one, and under cover of darkness the removal of the dinghy ought to present neither difficulty nor danger. Ginger's only fear, although he did not mention this to the others, was that the shark might still be in the lagoon. The idea of swimming in water that harboured such horrors as he had already seen became more and more repugnant to him; however, he was prepared to take the risk.

The short twilight faded and darkness fell; only a single light showed where the schooner lay at anchor. Ginger did not move at once; he was anxious to put the plan into execution as quickly as possible because the sooner they started the earlier they would reach Rutuona, but he decided that it would be wise to give the schooner time to settle down for the night. He could tell by the diminishing noise of the breakers on the reef that the sea was still going down, for which he was thankful. He was fond of the water, but not so much as to make him look forward with pleasure to a trip in an open boat across a stretch of ocean during the hurricane season.

At last he rose to his feet. The moon had not yet risen, but the stars were like lamps hanging from the blue dome of heaven, and provided ample light for their purpose. Indeed, more would be dangerous. At the last moment he turned to Full Moon. 'There is no need for us all to go,' he said quietly. 'You gather all the nuts you can carry and take them out to the place where the reef joins the island.' He pointed to the spot. 'As soon as we've got the boat we'll come round and pick you up.'

Shell-Breaker agreed that this was a good idea, so they set off, leaving Full Moon to make her own way to the rendezvous. They reached the edge of the lagoon and waded quietly out into deep water, where they began to swim, using a steady breast-stroke that made the least noise. In a few minutes the dark silhouette of the schooner could be seen, and it was possible to make out that the solitary light came from a porthole—probably Castanelli's cabin, thought Ginger. As they drew nearer their strokes became slower and their approach more cautious. Shell-Breaker found a piece of driftwood, and resting his hands on it pushed it slowly in front of him, paddling with his feet only. Ginger looked for a similar piece, but unable to find it had to go on without any cover. His toes curled with shock when he saw a long black object on the water in front of him, but to his unspeakable relief he discovered it was only the bole of a floating palm.

They were now only a few yards from the schooner's side, and from the dinghy. All remained quiet. Not a soul was in sight. Ginger swam quietly to the boat, rested his hands on the stern for a moment, listening; then, hearing nothing, he pulled himself into it. It lurched under his weight, so in order to balance himself he dropped forward on his hands and knees. He landed on something soft, something that moved violently as his hands touched it, and too late he knew what it was. A man had been lying in the dinghy all the time, probably asleep. He awoke with a wild yell. Ginger tried desperately to get back into the water, but a pair of vice-like hands gripped his throat and he was forced down under a hot, reeking body. What happened after that he did not know, for he was too near to suffocation. Subconsciously he was aware of shouts and a general uproar; then something crashed against his jaw and the world exploded in a flash of blinding light.

He could not have been unconscious for many minutes, for when he came round he was lying on the deck of the schooner, in an area of light cast by a lantern, the centre of several spectators. Blinking, he raised himself on his right hand, and looking up saw Castanelli grinning down at him. The others were his crew of shock-haired native boys.

'Get up,' ordered Castanelli, in his soft, purring voice.

Ginger did as he was told. He was still somewhat dazed and his brain was whirling with shock, but the thought uppermost in his mind was: What had happened to Shell-Breaker? He could not see him, so he assumed that he had escaped, in which case he could only hope that he had not been seen, otherwise his capture was only a matter of time when daylight came.

'So we meet again—yes?' sneered Castanelli.

Ginger did not answer.

'Where are your pals?' asked Castanelli coldly.

'I wish I knew,' returned Ginger bitterly.

'You speak lies wiz me, eh?'

Ginger shook his head. 'No,' he said wearily. 'They disappeared in the hurricane. That's all I know. I was trapped in a cave by a shark at the other end of the island so I don't know what happened. I only just had time to climb into a palm before the seas swept everything.'

Castanelli was silent for a moment. The obvious sincerity of Ginger's words, and the tone of voice in which he said them, evidently made an impression on the Corsican. 'Get plenty pearls?' he asked smoothly.

'We got a few,' admitted Ginger, who saw no reason to lie. 'We might have got more but a swordfish holed our ship and we had to jettison the diving-gear to save it from sinking.'

'Where are ze pearls?'

'On the ship, wherever that is.'

'You know where ze bed is, eh?' leered Castanelli.

'Yes, roughly,' admitted Ginger.

'You show me in ze morning—yes?'

'I'll think about it,' promised Ginger, who was anxious to gain time to think, for his brain was still in a whirl and there were now so many factors to be taken into consideration.

Castanelli drew his knife and fingered the point significantly. 'You tink hard about it,' he suggested softly. 'And when you tink, remember zis. My boys Solomon Island boys. You know what zey eat in ze Solomons? Zey eat men—yes. And my boys are very, very hungry for fresh meat. You tink hard about zat.' He said something to his crew in a language which Ginger did not understand. Rough hands seized him and dragged him to the companion. Down the stairway he was bundled, and along a corridor. A door was opened, and he was pushed into the same evil-smelling compartment from which he had once rescued Shell-Breaker. It was pitch dark. The door closed and a bolt was shot. For a moment he stood listening to the soft pad of retreating bare feet; then he sat down on the damp board floor to think.

12

DISASTER

In spite of his insalubrious quarters Ginger eventually fell asleep. His head ached from thinking and from the blow he had received. It was not unnatural, too, that he was depressed, for the whole expedition, which had started so well, had suddenly gone to pieces. Its members were scattered, he knew not where. The island was a wreck. The shell had been lost. Full Moon was presumably still on the island, where she might escape harm as long as Castanelli did not find her. As for Shell-Breaker, anything could have happened to him. He, too, might have been captured. On the other hand, he might still be in the water near the schooner, although it was more likely that he had swum back to the island and rejoined Full Moon. There was always a chance that he might have been seized by the shark which was probably still in the lagoon. With one thing and another, in a few hours disaster had overtaken the party at the moment when success seemed assured. Ginger was not accustomed to look on the black side of things, but it is not to be wondered at that as he stretched himself out on the damp, evil-smelling boards, he was a prey to melancholy. He felt that he could do nothing. He was not even armed, for his automatic had been taken from his pocket. But so weary was he that not even his dismal thoughts, and the innumerable cockroaches that swarmed over him, could prevent him from sinking into a sleep of exhaustion.

He was awakened by an uproar on the deck above him. He could hear the Solomon Island boys jabbering in their own language, and Castanelli cursing like a maniac; but what it was all about he had no means of knowing. Getting on his feet he was relieved to find that his cubby hole of a prison was at least provided with a light, a small circle of thick glass let into the deck, and the fact that it was now dull grey suggested that the hour was dawn.

Hardly had he made this observation when there was a patter of bare feet in the passage outside; the door was thrown open; without any preamble two of the Solomon Island boys entered, seized him, and hurried him up on deck, where Castanelli was standing, white with rage, spitting like an angry cat. The Corsican eyed his prisoner malevolently through half-closed eyes as he advanced slowly towards him. His fingers were opening and closing like claws. 'Who else was on island wiz you?' he grated.

Ginger did not answer.

Castanelli flew into a fury. Indeed, he lost control of himself. 'Who take my dinghy?' he screamed.

Ginger drew a deep breath. So that was it. The dinghy had gone. Then Shell-Breaker and Full Moon, or one of them, must have returned to the schooner after he had been captured, and succeeded where he had failed. The knowledge gave him new hope and he allowed a smile of satisfaction to cross his face. Which, in the circumstances, was a mistake. Castanelli noted the smile. Already beside himself, he snarled like a wolf as he struck Ginger a blow across the face that sent him reeling into the scuppers.

Ginger picked himself up slowly, wiping blood from his lips.

Castanelli stood watching him, panting with suppressed rage. 'Who was wiz you last night?' he purred, advancing towards Ginger again.

To attempt to conceal the truth was futile, and Ginger realized it. Obviously, someone had been with him or the dinghy could not have been stolen. 'Shell-Breaker,' he said quietly, hoping by this time that he was far away.

The Corsican eyed Ginger with such an expression of hatred that he fully expected to be murdered on the spot. 'Zat sneaking little kanaka,' breathed Castanelli. 'Where he go?' he screamed, with such violence that Ginger took a pace backwards.

'To Rutuona, I hope,' he replied. 'If he started early he should be nearly there by now.'

Castanelli caught his breath and looked round the sky. Ginger could read what was passing in his mind. He was trying to work out if it would be possible to overtake the dinghy before it reached the larger island. And Ginger could have answered the question for him. It was not, for there was not a breath of wind; the open sea, as well as the lagoon, was as flat as a millpond. Not a cat's-paw ruffled the water; there was not a cloud in the sky, nor anything else to suggest that a breeze was on the way.

Castanelli was not slow to realize this, and the knowledge did nothing to improve his temper. On the contrary he flew into a fresh paroxysm of passion. Taking Ginger by the throat he forced him back against the mainmast and drew his knife. 'I show you my way wiz puppies,' he ground out through his teeth.

Ginger knew that he was within an ace of death, but he did not lose his head. He knew that in his present state of mind the Corsican was capable of anything. 'Kill me and you will never find the pearl-bed,' he said.

Castanelli hesitated, and nodded slowly as the truth of this statement penetrated into his frenzied brain. He lowered his arm. 'Ah,' he breathed. 'Ze pearls—yes. I tink I keep you alive for a leetle while.' He released Ginger suddenly and rapped out an order at the boys who were standing round, watching the proceedings with amused interest. The way they jumped to obey their bullying skipper revealed their fear of him.

They ran to the longboat, and in a few minutes it was on the water by the schooner's side. Six of them got into it and picked up the oars. 'You come wiz me,' Castanelli told Ginger, and they got into the boat, which was quickly rowed ashore.

Ginger wondered what the man was going to do, but he was not left in doubt for very long, for as soon as they were ashore the boys started collecting the shell that lay strewn along the beach at high-water mark. Now that the sea had gone down Ginger saw that there was quite a lot of it lying high and dry, and still

more in the shallow water. That which had been on the far side of
the island had apparently been thrown right over the ridge when
the waves swept across. So Ginger thought, idly, for he was not
particularly interested. He watched four of the boys throwing
the shell into a pile; another was carrying it to the longboat, and
a sixth was collecting nuts.

Castanelli, taking Ginger with him, began rummaging about
on the site of the camp, putting together anything worth saving,
the remains of stores and a few odd pieces of tackle. Occasionally
he asked a question, but there was little Ginger could, or would,
tell him. From the speed at which the Corsican was working he
judged that he was anxious to get the work finished, in which
case it was not unreasonable to suppose that he had no intention
of remaining in the lagoon. Perhaps he had Shell-Breaker in
mind, and was anxious to get away in case he returned with
assistance. Thus ran Ginger's thoughts as he watched Castanelli
delving about among the seaweed and other rubbish.

The sun climbed up into an azure sky, and as the day
advanced the island shimmered in the heat. Ginger continued
watching Castanelli's activities in a disinterested fashion, turning over in his mind the possibility of escape. There seemed little
chance of it. He had not overlooked the grotto as a hiding-place if
he could get away, but the chances of this were remote. For one
thing Castanelli was watching him closely, and the butt of a
heavy revolver protruding from his hip pocket discouraged the
idea of making a dash for it. In any case, the boys were working
on the beach between him and the cove, so to reach it without
being intercepted was manifestly impossible.

His interest quickened as Castanelli approached the spot
where the pearls had been hidden; it was now half covered by a
pile of seaweed which had wrapped itself round the coral.
Castanelli dragged some of it aside with his hands, and cleared
the remainder with his foot, and was about to turn away when
something caught his eye. He went back and reached down.

Ginger's heart stopped beating for an instant, and then raced
in a burst of palpitation. In spite of the heat he felt a chill creep
over him. Sticking up out of the sand was the top half of a tin. It

was a biscuit-tin, and he recognized it instantly. It was in such a tin that Sandy had put the pearls, and there could hardly be two such tins in the same place. The waves had washed most of the sand away, and so partly uncovered it. For a brief moment he hoped that Castanelli would not see it, but when it became obvious that he had he prayed fervently that he would not trouble to investigate it. But the Corsican was leaving nothing that was worth taking away. Without the least suspicion of its contents he kicked the sand aside with his foot and dragged the tin from its bed. Without even glancing at Ginger—whose face might have betrayed the secret, for it was as white as death—he tossed the tin amongst the others. Ginger almost gasped his relief as it spun through the air, for while Castanelli did not know what it contained there was always a chance that he might recover it. But his hope was short-lived. The lid either fitted loosely or struck one of the other tins, for as it rolled into the pile the top flew off, and its contents streamed in a gleaming cascade across the sand.

Castanelli had already half turned away, but his eyes remained on the tin just long enough to see it fly open. For a second he stood like a man petrified, his little eyes bulging in their sockets; then he let out a hoarse yell, shouted something in a language Ginger did not understand, and in a moment was on his knees, picking up the pearls with trembling fingers and putting them back into the tin. Once he paused to turn to Ginger a face flushed with exultation. He was panting with excitement. His crew ran up, and gave vent to their feelings in a series of staccato ejaculations.

Ginger, sick to the very soul, could only watch helplessly. The appearance of the tin had been as great a shock to him as the sight of the pearls had been to the schooner captain. Why or how they had come to be left behind he could not remotely imagine. It was unbelievable, incredible, and he could have wept with mortification. Everything had looked black enough before, but now he was swept by a wave of depression that left him weak with misery. But behind the depression there grew a fierce hatred of the man who was now chuckling with glee, and he began to understand why so many crimes had been committed for these gems of the sea.

At the time of Castanelli's startling discovery the longboat had just left for the schooner with the first load of shell. The two boys who had gone with it, seeing the commotion ashore, now shouted to know what it was about, and their companions joyfully informed them. The work of unloading was hastened, and the boat was soon flashing back towards the silver beach.

There was still a big pile of shell lying there, and when the boys started loading afresh Ginger marvelled at the mentality of a man who, with a fortune already in his pocket, could bother about a few hundreds of pounds extra. However, Castanelli evidently saw no reason why he should not have the shell as well as the pearls, for he remained on the island supervising the work until the last shell had been collected. Occasionally he glanced at Ginger, whose downcast face seemed to amuse him; he was no longer vindictive, but smiling with supreme content. 'Why you not tell me ze pearls still here?' he questioned once.

'I did not know myself,' returned Ginger, with such bitterness that the Corsican laughed aloud.

'Your friends save me all ze trouble,' he murmured. 'Alway ze way wiz pearls,' he added cryptically, tossing Ginger a coconut. He had already punctured one, and after drinking the milk was crunching the soft spongy flesh.

Ginger was in no mood for eating, but he drank the milk with relish, for his throat was parched.

The sun was touching the horizon by the time the last few shells, and the remainder of the stores, had been thrown into the longboat. The rowers took their places. For some time Ginger had been hoping that Castanelli would go, leaving him marooned on the island, because he felt sure that sooner or later Biggles would return to look for him. But this hope did not materialize. Castanelli looked at him thoughtfully for a moment or two with a curious expression on his face, and then motioned him to get into the boat. Ginger obeyed, and the Corsican got in behind him. From the way he looked round to make sure that nothing had been left behind it was fairly clear that he had no intention of returning. The boat was pushed off, and cut an ever-spreading ripple across the still water as it sped towards the schooner. Ginger watched it with the calm of utter despair. All day he had been listening, hoping to hear the familiar roar of the 'Scud', but in vain. Now that night was closing in it certainly would not come until the morrow—if then—and by that time anything could have happened.

As they climbed up on the schooner's deck a slant of wind sent a succession of curving ripples sweeping across the lagoon, and the schooner rocked gently. Castanelli let out a yell of triumph, and Ginger's mouth turned dry with bitterness as he realized that even nature was playing into the Corsican's hands. First the hurricane, which had driven the 'Scud' away and disclosed the pearls and now a breeze just when Castanelli most needed it. With a fair wind the schooner would be a hundred miles away by the next day, so even if Biggles did return it would avail him nothing.

Castanelli, the pearl-tin under his arm, went below, but was soon on deck again without it. In a vague sort of way Ginger noted that the wind appeared to have had an immediate effect on his plans where he himself was concerned, for after speaking in a low voice to the crew he turned to his prisoner with such an expression on his face that Ginger felt a qualm of alarm.

'You no like my ship? I tink you best stay here,' purred Castanelli.

Ginger drew a deep breath of relief. Nothing would have suited him better, but he did not say so.

'But perhaps you talk too much,' went on Castanelli smoothly. 'I am very sorry, but I tink you talk no more.' Then, with a nod to the crew, he turned and walked towards the wheel. Four of the boys ran to the capstan, and a chain clanked as the anchor came up. A sail bellied out against the fast-darkening sky.

Two of the repulsive-looking Solomon Islanders had re-mained beside Ginger, who, interested in watching the schooner get under way and approach the entrance to the lagoon, barely noticed them. But when he felt them lay hands on him he turned sharply to see what they were doing. Not until then did a terrible suspicion come into his mind. One of them had tied a length of rope round his waist, and the other was now attaching the loose end to a piece of rusty iron piping. For a moment Ginger could only stare in mute horror, still refusing to believe what his eyes were telling him, but when the natives started dragging him towards the side of the ship there was no longer any doubt as to their intention. He knew that they were going to throw him overboard. The piece of iron was to take him to the bottom.

As soon as he realized this he began to struggle violently, trying to free himself from the rope, but the natives seized him, and in their powerful hands he was helpless. One dragged his arms behind him, and the other whipped up his feet, so that he could not even kick. As helpless as a rabbit in the hands of a poacher he was carried to the rail. One of the natives grunted, and he was swung into the air. He made a last frantic clutch at the rail, but his hand missed it by a foot, and the next instant the water had closed over his head. Even before he could get to the surface and fill his lungs he felt the weight of the iron take effect and drag him down. Struggling with a desperation near to madness he seized the rope, but the iron was far below him and he could do nothing to check his descent. He felt the weight of the water pressing on him. Then, suddenly, the downward movement ended, and he knew that the iron had reached the bottom. Frantically he dragged at the rope. All around him was darkness.

13
WHAT HAPPENED AT RUTUONA

BIGGLES was still at Rutuona with Algy and Sandy. His difficulties were not so alarming as those of Ginger, although he suffered considerable anxiety on his account, but they were bad enough. To start with, his fears had been only too well founded when, during the hurricane, he had expressed a hope that no debris would fall on them. A palm-stem had crashed down on the port wing-tip, and while the wing had not been torn off the leading edge had been crushed, so that flying was out of the question until it had been repaired. Lighter matter, such as brushwood, had been piled up around the *Scud*, so that by the time the hurricane had passed the machine was almost buried.

For those on board to get ashore had been no easy matter, for the flimsy rubbish would not support their weight and at the same time it made swimming impossible. In the end they had piled rubbish upon rubbish and then trampled it down until it formed a bridge of sufficient strength to carry them. By this time it was dark, and they passed the night in even more discomfort than Ginger, who was, of course, in the grotto, where he was at least free from the disturbing attentions of the myriads of mosquitoes that attacked Biggles, Algy, and Sandy as they rested in a swamp by the edge of the creek in which the machine had come down.

As soon as it was light they had set off for the village, hoping that it would not take them more than an hour or two to reach it, since by their reckoning it was not more than six miles away. But unexpected difficulties presented themselves. Biggles had seen many jungles, but never growth so impenetrable as that which fringed the creek. It was impossible to move in any direction without hacking every inch of the way with their knives—an exhausting business in the heat; apart from which their faces were soon covered with spots of blood from the vicious bites of sand-flies. Then, just as they thought they were through, and not more than a quarter of a mile from the beach, which they knew ran all the way to the village they came to an obstacle which not even Biggles's agile brain could devise a means of crossing. It was the mouth of the river, which was not so much a river as a swamp; a stagnant lake which had formed in the low ground at the foot of the hills. Had it been only water it would have been a simple matter to swim across, for the distance was not more than a hundred yards; but there was more than that to consider; the water was choked by a riotous growth of water-lilies, great pink blooms which in different circumstances would have been objects for admiration. The fact that the huge, flat, fleshy leaves were the homes of revolting-looking centipedes, nearly a foot long, did not make the prospect of trying to swim across any more agreeable. However, it was obviously impossible to swim, for the thick white roots of the lilies formed an almost solid mass under the water, and as they were too pliable to bear any weight the only alternative was to go round.

So, blood-stained and weary, they had to start hacking a new path inland along the edge of the swamp. The depressing part of the task was that they did not know how far the swamp extended, although Sandy held the view that it could not be far on account of the hills which rose steeply no great distance away. And in this assumption he was correct. A few hundred yards and the swamp began to narrow, until at length they came to a place where a fallen breadfruit-tree offered a passage across. By this time it was nearly dark. Far from reaching the village in a few hours they had been all day in a jungle, and had covered less than a mile.

They crossed the swamp by means of the tree just as the sun was setting, only to discover when they were on the other side that the jungle was again so thick that it was useless even to think of going on until daylight came. Even so, Biggles was in favour of pushing on, but Sandy declared that it was madness. Even if they did not wander into a swamp as deadly as quicksand, which was probable, they would certainly lose their way in the darkness, and make so little progress that the labour was not worth while. After considering the matter the others were reluctantly compelled to agree. So, again beset by countless mosquitoes and surrounded by alarming phosphorescent fungus, they remained in the fallen tree prepared to pass another night of misery.

'I'm beginning to understand why pearls are expensive,' remarked Biggles grimly, as he slapped at the insects that were settling on his face.

As the night wore on these became so bad that he lit a fire and sat in the smoke, although the pungent reek of the wood was nearly as hard to endure as the bites of the mosquitoes.

'I wouldn't mind so much if I knew that those kids were all right,' he muttered once. 'I can't imagine what could have happened to them.'

Neither Sandy nor Algy replied. Perhaps they both hesitated

to express their views.

Slowly the night wore on, the swamp-water glowing with phosphorescent light as unseen creatures moved about in it. Strange noises came from the tree-ferns; not even Sandy knew what made them. Great moths flitted silently across the fiery area, and once an enormous bat gave them all a fright by dashing itself against the tree. The darkness was incredible; it hung over them like a weight. In the silence invisible creatures crept and rustled. Once Algy dozed, to awake from a fitful dream with the feeling that something was crawling on his leg. By the light of the dimly burning fire he saw a reddish-brown centipede, ten inches long, clinging to his bare ankle. With a convulsive shudder he tore it off with a quick jerk and flung the thing from him. A double line of scarlet spots rose on the place where the centipede had been; his ankle began to swell; and it remained painful for many days. Sandy puffed at his pipe incessantly, and Biggles smoked all his cigarettes.

'Thank heaven, I believe it's getting light at last,' muttered Algy, after a long silence. 'One more night of this and I shall be ready for the madhouse. These South Sea islands aren't all that they're made out to be.'

Biggles stood up stiffly. 'Well, let's be moving,' he said, and although it was still only grey twilight he commenced cutting a path down the far side of the swamp towards the beach.

The others joined him. The strain of the last two days and nights was beginning to tell on them, and they were all nearly exhausted by the time they staggered from the undergrowth on to the open sand, where they spent some minutes looking for water; but there was none except that of the swamp, which they would not touch.

'Never mind; let's get along. We ought to be in the village inside a couple of hours,' murmured Biggles, and with dragging feet they set off along the sand. They stopped at the first coconut palm they reached, and, hunting about, found several nuts that had been dislodged by the hurricane. They drank the milk greedily and, strengthened by its cool sweetness, made better time for the rest of the journey.

They had nearly reached the village when Algy stopped suddenly, staring at something ahead. The others, following the direction of his eyes, were just in time to see a native disappear like a shadow into the dense shade of the trees. It was not an ordinary native, such as those they had previously met in the village; he was smeared from head to foot with white chalk or mud, put on in the most fantastic designs.

'Something's happening here,' muttered Sandy, looking worried.

'What do you mean? What could happen?' inquired Biggles.

'You saw that chap? He was in war-paint—and he was carrying a war club. I haven't seen such a thing in years. He means business, or he wouldn't be got up like that. They take these things very seriously. It's against the law, anyway. They are not allowed to do any of this war stuff nowadays, because once they start they're not responsible for their actions. There you are! Hark at the drums.' A hollow booming sound echoed weirdly through the jungle. 'If you listen you'll hear others answering it,' declared Sandy. 'They're calling the warriors together. Something must have happened since we were here last; I only hope some fool hasn't been causing trouble or we may find ourselves in the cooking-pot presently. When they get the war fever on them they're not particular who they kill.'

'But they're not cannibals, surely?' put in Biggles unbelievingly.

Sandy threw him a sidelong glance. 'Not one of them would admit it, and I doubt if any of the youngsters would have anything to do with "long pig",' he muttered. 'But I wouldn't trust the old 'uns. I'll warrant plenty of the old men here pine for the days when the enemy was served up for supper. The authorities have done everything they can to suppress cannibalism, and generally speaking they've succeeded, but once in a while there are rumours of it back in the hills. Mind you, these people were never cannibals for the sake of it; they've all the other food they need; it was just a custom to eat a part of some particularly hated enemy.'

'Well, it's no use messing about,' declared Biggles. 'We'd

better go and see what's going on.'

Two more natives appeared just in front of them. Both were in war-paint, and both carried war clubs. They bolted like rabbits at the sight of the white men, who soon reached the village and marched straight into it. Only two or three women were in sight. The drums had stopped booming.

Sandy walked up to an old woman and spoke to her in her own language, but she only sniggered. He turned to Biggles. 'They're all hiding in the bush,' he said. 'I'll bet the whole lot of them are within earshot, but they won't show up for fear we report them.' Cupping his hands round his mouth he yelled for Roaring Wave.

A few moments later the bushes parted and a slim figure stepped out. A white band encircled his forehead and his chest was painted with a hideous magical device. Algy clutched Biggles's arm. 'Great heavens!' he cried incredulously. 'It's Shell-Breaker!'

'Shell-Breaker, come here,' ordered Sandy sternly.

The boy approached, nervously.

'What for you make war?' asked Sandy curtly.

'Make war on Atanelli,' muttered Shell-Breaker sullenly.

'Ask him where the others are,' Biggles told Sandy.

Sandy spoke to the boy in his own tongue, whereupon Shell-Breaker broke into a torrent of explanation, waving his hands to add expression to his story. At last he broke off from sheer exhaustion.

Sandy drew a deep breath and turned to the others. His face was a picture of wonderment and dismay. 'Ginger's a prisoner on Castanelli's schooner,' he said.

'*What?*' cried Biggles and Algy together.

'Shell-Breaker's story rings true enough,' went on Sandy. 'And there doesn't seem to be any reason why he should lie to us. He says this is what happened. After they had finished fishing they went for a swim in a cove and discovered a grotto; the entrance was under water; however, they swam in and sat on a ledge. While they were there a shark appeared in the entrance and trapped them. They had to stay there all night. In the morning the shark had gone so they swam out, only to find that we were no longer there. Then the hurricane hit the island and pretty well wrecked it. No sooner had the hurricane moved on than Castanelli sailed into the lagoon. They waited until dark and then tried to pinch the schooner's dinghy. Ginger was caught in the act and taken aboard. Shell-Breaker got to the reef, but came back later on and got the dinghy and rowed it single-handed to Rutuona. Full Moon stayed behind to watch what happened. Shell-Breaker only got here about an hour ago, and his story has sent everybody war-mad. Roaring Wave has sworn to have Castanelli's blood. They've got their big war canoe all ready; apparently they were just going to start when we turned up.'

Biggles listened to this story in silence, his first expression of relief on hearing that Ginger was still alive changing slowly to one of amazement. 'If Ginger is on Castanelli's schooner we've got to get him off,' he said slowly. 'I'm relieved to learn that nothing more serious has happened.'

Algy looked dubious. 'It might be harder to get Ginger back than it sounds,' he muttered. 'Castanelli's got a tough crew, and there are only three of us. The machine is out of action, anyway. In any case, with Ginger on board, we couldn't shoot the schooner up.'

'I wouldn't say that the "Scud" is out of action,' returned Biggles quickly.

'But you can't fly it with a busted wing.'

'I didn't say anything about flying it; there's no reason why we shouldn't taxi it across to the island, if we can get it clear.'

'I don't want to raise difficulties, but Castanelli will hear our engines,' Algy pointed out. 'All those toughs of his are armed, and they're likely to sink the "Scud" before we could get it near enough to board them. We must look at the thing sanely. To suppose that we could taxi right up to the schooner without one or more of us being hit would be expecting too much. We've got to get Ginger off, of course, but getting the "Scud" sunk won't help us.'

Biggles nodded. 'I agree,' he murmured. 'It would need a dozen men to take that schooner by force, unless surprise tactics were employed. We've no proof that the schooner is sill there, if it comes to that. There ought to be some way in which we can use these Marquesans.' Biggles thought for a moment. 'I don't like the idea of their going without us,' he continued. 'If there is a general attack Ginger is as likely to get hurt as anybody.'

'That's true,' remarked Sandy. 'Once they start on a job they're apt to go crazy. Why not taxi the machine across and take a bunch of them with us? We could get ten or a dozen in the cabin at a pinch.'

'Why not take the whole blessed war canoe in tow?' suggested Algy.

'By gosh! that's an idea!' cried Sandy.

'We might as well do both,' Biggles pointed out. 'We could put some of them in the machine and tow the canoe as well. How many will the canoe hold, Sandy?'

'I don't know; I haven't seen it; but judging from others I've seen it will probably carry thirty or forty. But we shall have to watch what we're doing. If we once set these boys on to Castanelli there will be no holding them, and if they kill him we shall be answerable for it.'

'That doesn't worry me,' declared Biggles. 'We've a witness to prove that Ginger is on board, a prisoner, so we should be justified in trying to get him off. What worries me most is the time limit. How long is Castanelli going to stay in the lagoon, even supposing he is still there? It's going to take us some time to get the machine clear, don't forget. It's after midday already. Whatever we do it is going to be dark before we get to the island.'

'Aye, that's true enough,' admitted Sandy. 'I agree with you, I think it would be dangerous to let these Marquesans go without us. I reckon our best plan would be to explain the position to Roaring Wave; if he falls in with us he could lend us some men to get the "Scud" out of the creek. After that it wouldn't take us long to get to the island. We could tow the canoe most of the way. Then, when we got near the island, we could let the canoe tow the machine. In that way we should make no noise, and we might be able to get right up to the schooner without being seen.'

Biggles nodded. 'That's it,' he said. 'If we towed the

Marquesans nearly to the island they would still be fresh when
we got there. If we find that the schooner has gone, the only thing
we can do is to repair the wing as quickly as possible and fly
round as long as we have any petrol left.'

'That sounds like common sense to me,' agreed Sandy. 'I'll go
and have a word with Roaring Wave, or tell Shell-Breaker to go
and fetch him.' He turned to Shell-Breaker, who still stood by
him, and spoke to him at some length.

Shell-Breaker dashed off into the trees, where his voice could
be heard raised in a long harangue. His speech was concluded in
a pandemonium of yells, and a few moments later about
threescore painted warriors, some carrying clubs and some
spears, burst out of the bushes.

'They're a pretty tough-looking crowd to try to keep in order,'
observed Biggles, regarding the striped warriors with misgivings.

'You leave 'em to me,' said Sandy confidently, going to meet
them. Somehow he managed to pick out Roaring Wave, and
held a brief conversation with him. At the finish the Chief gave a
shout and disappeared again into the bushes, followed by his
pack. 'It's all right,' said Sandy, returning to the others. 'In fact,
I believe the old man is tickled to death that we are going into the
business with him. One thing is certain; they hate the sight of
Castanelli, and once they get started there will be no stopping
them.'

'Where have they gone now?' asked Algy.

'To get the canoe,' replied Sandy. 'Here they come.'

Both Biggles and Algy stared in astonishment as from
underneath the trees appeared the grotesque painted prow of an
enormous canoe. It was a beautiful piece of work, carved from
end to end in a regular pattern, gleaming with oil. It was not less
than forty feet long and needed nearly forty men to carry it. In
dead silence the warriors carried it down to the water and
launched it on the bay.

'Come on,' said Sandy.

'Where to?' asked Biggles.

'Back to the "Scud", of course. There is no sense in walking.
The canoe will have us there in half the time.'

'That suits me,' agreed Biggles.

In a few minutes the three white men were seated in the stern of the canoe, staring at the broad painted backs of thirty natives, in a double row, fifteen on each side, each holding a beautifully carved paddle. Their weapons lay at their feet. Roaring Wave stood in the bows, looking ahead. He raised his spear and pointed. Instantly thirty paddles dug deeply into the water, and the canoe streaked forward like an arrow. Roaring Wave's spear fell, and the flashing paddles dipped again. And so it continued, the paddles keeping perfect time with the strokes of the spear.

'By jove! This is something like travelling,' murmured Algy admiringly.

'You bet it is,' answered Sandy. 'Think what this bay must have looked like years ago, with perhaps fifty canoes like this one all sweeping out to sea in formation to make a raid on a neighbouring island. It must have been a sight worth watching.'

In less than an hour they were at the creek, where Sandy, pointing to the 'Scud', explained to the Chief what was required. After that there was nothing more to do than sit in the canoe and watch the natives hacking at the brushwood and other debris with their heavy, keen-edged knives. At first they worked from the canoe, but as the 'Scud' was neared many of them got into the water and tore the stuff away with their hands. As soon as a fairway had been made Biggles climbed on board, and the others followed him. He went forward into the cockpit and made ready to start the engines, knowing that this would not alarm the natives, who had already seen the machine on the water near the village.

It was a long, tedious business getting the machine entirely clear, and darkness was closing in by the time the work was nearly complete. At length a line was thrown to the canoe; the natives took their places and towed the aircraft into the clear water in the middle of the creek. The canoe cast off, and was eased alongside, whereupon Sandy climbed up on to the centre section and explained the plan in detail, to make sure that it was understood. The engines were then started. Ten of the natives were transferred to the 'Scud' to reduce the drag of the canoe, which was then taken in tow. Slowly, with her engines roaring, the aircraft taxied towards the open sea. The ancient war-chant of the Marquesans rose into the still air.

Biggles glanced at Sandy and smiled; but he would not have done so if he had known that at that very moment Ginger was just being dragged down to the bottom of the lagoon.

14
OUT OF THE DEPTHS

WHEN Ginger had been dragged down to the bed of the lagoon he knew that nothing short of a miracle could save him, and although he still struggled to free himself he felt that it was hopeless. From the moment he had realized Castanelli's intention he had given himself up for lost, and he can hardly be blamed for that. But there is an old saying to the effect that while there is life there is hope, and never was the truth of it better demonstrated.

His senses were fast leaving him when his outflung arms collided with something soft. It might be thought that with death imminent his fear could not be greater than it already was, but at the touch of that unseen body his fear became blind terror, which in the circumstances is hardly to be wondered at, for he knew only too well what horrors dwelt in the warm waters of that sapphire sea. Again came the touch; he struggled violently, but, nevertheless, something long and soft wrapped itself about his legs, gripping them firmly. That it was an octopus he had no doubt whatever. It was the culminating horror, and as far as he was concerned, it was the end. There is a limit to what human consciousness can stand without collapsing.

His next sensation would be difficult to describe. It was, perhaps, more curiosity than anything else. He was quite sure that he was now dead; he did not see how it could be otherwise; but death appeared to be taking a form so strange that he was amazed. In the first place, he was still conscious of his body, for his stomach hurt him excruciatingly. And he was still able to think, although his thoughts were vague and disjointed. Where was he? What was happening? He wondered. It was all very confused. But presently he found himself able to think more clearly, and he discovered that his eyes were open. Or he thought they were—he was by no means sure. As far as he could make out he was lying head downwards on a shelving slope of coral. That seemed natural enough. It was only to be expected. But what was his face doing out of the water? He was sure it was out of the water, but not more than an inch or two. Phosphorescent wavelets were lapping against the coral just below his eyes. He could hear them as well as see them. Water was also running down the coral and dripping into the wavelets. He noticed with surprise that it was coming out of his mouth and nostrils, but on thinking it over he realized that there was nothing strange about that, after all, for he must have swallowed vast quantities of water.

He could see the wavelets more clearly now, and discovered that the scene around him was becoming more solid, and at the same time the pain in his stomach became more intense. He realized that it was due to a heavy weight on his back, a weight that rose and fell regularly. He was lying face downwards, and every time the weight fell the pain in his stomach became almost unbearable. At last it became so bad that he groaned. He knew that he had groaned because he distinctly heard the sound, and it added to his amazement. Instantly the weight on his back occurred again with increased violence, and at the same time something seized his arms and dragged them upwards. It had the result of sending more water gushing from his mouth. His arms were lowered and then raised again, as if someone was using them as pump-handles; and all the time the dreadful weight was on his back, forcing his stomach against the hard coral. He groaned again with the agony of it.

At last he could stand it no longer. Not even in death could he endure such agony. With a sudden wrench he tore his arms free from the grip that held them by the wrists, and with a tremendous effort flung the weight off his back. Clutching at the coral he dragged himself back from the water and at the same time twisted into a more horizontal position. He looked up. At first he could see nothing except a star-spangled sky, and the black silhouette of rocks against it. Then, close at hand, a dark form moved like a shadow. 'You plenty better bymeby,' said a small voice.

Again it would be difficult to describe Ginger's sensations at the sound of that well-remembered voice. For a moment he could do nothing but vomit water in a fearful fit of retching, but when the spasm passed he felt more normal, and he looked again at the dark figure. 'Full Moon!' was all he could say, in a voice heavy with wonderment.

Full Moon knelt down beside him. 'You feelum better bymeby,' she whispered. 'One time I reckon you plenty dead——'

'But where have you come from?' asked Ginger, sitting up, and feeling his stomach tenderly. He saw that a jagged piece of coral pressing into it had caused the pain.

'Me on schooner all long time,' answered Full Moon.

Ginger sat silent for a moment, trying to force his aching brain to assimilate this piece of information. 'On the schooner?' he got out at last. 'You mean you were on the schooner when they threw me over?'

'Yes. I stay on schooner all day, hide under sail.'

Ginger shook his head. The business was becoming more and more unbelievable. 'Where is Shell-Breaker?' he asked suddenly.

'He take dinghy and go Rutuona plenty quick,' returned Full Moon.

'But how did you get on the schooner?'

Full Moon explained. 'When you get hit on head by Atanelli, Shell-Breaker swim fast under water. He tell me. We go back. Shell-Breaker take dinghy. I stay see what Atanelli do. Me hide in sail, see everything. See Solomon boys throw you overboard. Me swim down, but you kick like debil-debil. I cut rope, but reckon you die plenty quick, so I pull you on reef.'

Ginger was still inclined to believe that the whole thing had been a ghastly nightmare, but he saw that the rope was still round his waist, with a short end hanging to it, and he knew that it must have happened. For a little while he was so overcome by the simple devotion of the two Marquesans that he could not trust himself to speak. 'Full Moon, one day I thank you for this,' he said at last, huskily. 'I think you're wonderful.'

Full Moon laughed. 'What for wonderful?' she asked, naïvely. 'Me no run away when plenty trouble. Me glad when you go overboard; no longer wonder how save you from schooner.'

'Well, I reckon you're a brick,' declared Ginger.

'What is brick?' inquired Full Moon curiously.

Ginger could not find an adequate answer. 'Never mind,' he said, and stood up, shakily.

'We stay here,' said Full Moon. 'Shell-Breaker he come back bymeby with long canoe.'

Ginger looked round. 'Did you say we were on the reef?'

'Yes, on reef.'

'Atanelli gone?'

'Yes, he make sail.'

'One day I'm going to give myself the pleasure of shooting that scoundrel,' declared Ginger.

'Yes, me kill, too,' answered Full Moon, cheerfully.

Ginger had to kneel down again as he was shaken by another spasm of retching. He still felt deadly sick as a result of all the salt water he had swallowed, but after a time he got up and announced that he was able to get to the island. The moon had just come up, and he looked along the reef, which hitherto he had not examined very closely. He had a horror of entering the water again, but examining the reef he saw that it was possible to get to the island without swimming. He suggested this to Full Moon, who agreed that it was the best way.

'Any *feke* on these rocks?' asked Ginger, cautiously.

Full Moon saw nothing unusual in the question. 'Maybe,' she said, eyeing the reef with professional eyes. Then she shook her head. 'No *feke*,' she decided. 'Plenty crab. No crab if *feke* here.'

'Well, that's something to be thankful for, at any rate,' muttered Ginger, to whom an octopus was one degree worse than a shark.

'We walk now,' suggested Full Moon. 'You drink plenty coconut water you feel better bymeby.'

'Yes, I could do with a drink,' agreed Ginger, whose mouth was parched from swallowing salt water.

Full Moon cut the remains of the rope from his waist. Then, hand in hand, they walked slowly up the moonlit coral to the top of the reef, where they pulled up dead, staring unbelievably. Instead of finding only the sea stretching to the horizon they saw a schooner standing straight towards the entrance to the lagoon. It was not more than a hundred yards away.

Full Moon recovered her presence of mind first. 'Atanelli, he come back,' she hissed, and dropped behind a large piece of coral.

Ginger was too stunned to speak. It was the very last thing he expected. Taking his cue from Full Moon, he dropped behind another large piece of coral, but quick as he had been he was too late. A yell on the schooner told him that they had been seen.

Full Moon sprang to her feet. 'We run plenty quick,' she said tersely and set off along the reef towards the island, jumping from rock to rock with the sure-footedness of a mountain goat.

Ginger followed as fast as he could, but he had by no means recovered from his recent terrible experience, and his legs tottered under him. Seeing his condition, Full Moon waited and helped him over the most difficult places, but they were still some distance from the place where the reef joined the island when a rifle barked, and a shot tore away a piece of coral unpleasantly close to them. Looking back, Ginger saw that the schooner was already passing through the entrance to the lagoon, and although it was moving slowly the longboat was swinging over the side. Another shot zipped viciously into the coral and he ran on. He knew all about the difficulty of shooting accurately by moonlight, but he took no chances. Actually, he was more concerned for Full Moon than for himself.

Jumping from rock to rock they sped on, taking advantage of such cover as was available, and Ginger's weakness was almost forgotten in the face of the new peril. Castanelli—for Ginger had no doubt as to who was doing the shooting—continued to fire from time to time, but although some of the shots came close they did no damage. But by the time the two fugitives had reached the island the longboat was racing across the lagoon, the rowers bending to their oars under Castanelli's furious encouragement.

Ginger and Full Moon did not stop. The reef joined the island at its narrowest end, and it was clear that if Castanelli and his crew reached the island in time to cut them off from the wider end their capture was only a matter of minutes. The far end of the island was not only wider, but more rugged, and offered better hiding-places.

Ginger now led the way, making for the far side of the ridge where they could not be seen from the lagoon, and were therefore out of the danger of Castanelli's rifle. The going was not easy, for debris flung up by the hurricane lay everywhere—palm-fronds, piles of seaweed, and masses of coral—and detours had often to be made. However, they reached the wide end of the island, where Ginger, risking a peep over the ridge, saw the longboat being hauled up on the beach. Castanelli was already standing on the white sand, his rifle under his arm.

'Confound the fellow, what the dickens does he want to come back here for?' muttered Ginger angrily. 'I wish to goodness I had a rifle.'

Full Moon made no comment. Perhaps she knew the futility of wishing.

Ginger thought rapidly. To remain hidden indefinitely on the island was clearly impossible. They might climb up into one of the few remaining palms, or find a place among the coral that would offer them cover for a little while; but once daylight came discovery would only be a matter of time. Had their presence on the island not been known to Castanelli the matter would not have been so difficult. In that case there would be no deliberate search. But now it was known that they were there, it was obvious that the schooner captain would search every nook and cranny; and he would not desist until he had found them. The Corsican had already revealed himself to be a cold-blooded murderer, so in the event of capture Ginger knew what to expect. Castanelli would make certain next time. On the whole island there was only one place where they would be safe, and that was in the grotto. Even the Solomon Island boys might search for weeks without finding it. It was their only chance, and he told Full Moon so in a low voice. She had already realized it, and now set off towards the cove, picking up coconuts on the way. Ginger, perceiving the wisdom of this precaution, did the same. He knew that they might have to stay in the grotto for several days.

He expected no trouble in reaching the cove; his only fear was that the shark might still be there, a contingency he preferred not to contemplate. But again he was to be disappointed, for just as they reached the cove a mop-head rounded a corner of the coral, the swimmer actually landing at the spot where Ginger had climbed up many times. It was one of Castanelli's crew. Why he had chosen to swim ashore and choose that particular place he did not know; he could only suppose that the fellow had suspected what they would do, and saw a way of putting himself in his master's good graces by out-flanking them.

Ginger and Full Moon were just inside the tiny, semicircular cove when the native pulled himself ashore, and they could only crouch back into a depression in the coral trusting that they would not be seen. For a minute the native stood where he had come ashore, water dripping from his black body; then he let out a yell which made Ginger flinch. At first he thought that the native must have seen them, but when he made no move in their direction, and the shout was answered by another not far away, he realized that this was not so. The man was merely letting the others know where he was.

Ginger prayed that he would go. If he would disappear only for a minute or two, it would give them all the time they needed to reach their grotto refuge. The man did, in fact, move a few paces forward to the edge of the cove, but it was only to climb up on the highest point of coral from where he could command a view over the whole of it, and some distance beyond. And there he evidently intended to remain, while the others, spread out across the island, drove the quarry towards him. Or so he imagined. Ginger could hear their shouts as they drew nearer. He felt Full Moon reach for her knife, but he pressed her back, knowing that it was absolutely out of the question to get anywhere near the man without being seen. And if once they were seen the end was a foregone conclusion. So they remained where they were, Ginger hoping that the search would presently be abandoned, at least for the time being.

A minute passed—five minutes—and then footsteps could be heard approaching. A second native appeared, followed shortly afterwards by Castanelli, conspicuous in a dirty suit of white ducks with a rifle under his arm. 'You no see?' he said to the waiting boy.

'No see, boss.'

Castanelli sat down on the coral. 'They not far away,' he said confidently. 'We wait daylight.'

Ginger's heart sank. Their luck seemed to be absolutely dead out, but there was nothing they could do about it. He had lost all count of time, one reason being that he had no idea how long he had been unconscious. The moon passed its zenith and began to sink, and still they crouched in their narrow hiding-place. A deadly weariness began to creep over him. That some of the natives were still carrying on the search he knew, for he often heard them shouting to each other. The situation became one of those evil dreams that go on and on, repeating the same thing over and over again indefinitely. All the time Castanelli sat on the rock, smoking innumerable cigars. Ginger had never hated anyone quite as much as he hated the smooth-tongued Corsican. He hated him so much that had he possessed a weapon he would have shot him and risked the consequences.

At long last the moonlight began to fade. A lavender streak, swiftly turning to pink, flushed the eastern sky, and Ginger knew that discovery was now only a matter of minutes. He looked again at Castanelli still sitting on his selected seat; it was obvious that he had no intention of moving. He was, however, looking the other way, presumably watching the boys who were still carrying on with the search. One only remained with him, and he, too, was looking in the same direction.

Ginger put his lips close to Full Moon's ear. 'We no stay,' he said. 'If Atanelli turns he see us plenty quick. We make for grotto.'

Full Moon nodded to show that she understood.

Slowly, for he was as stiff as a rod, Ginger moved from his cramped position, ready to bolt. Full Moon joined him, and in another moment they were both creeping silently towards the water. Half way, neither of the two men on the rock had turned. They were now only a few yards from their objective, and Ginger was just beginning to hope that luck was favouring them at last, and that they would reach the water undetected, when the Solomon Islander turned. There appeared to be no reason why he should. It was almost as if his instinct had warned him that something was moving. He spoke swiftly, touching Castanelli's arm, and then pointed to the fugitives.

Out of the corner of his eye Ginger saw the Corsican reach for his rifle, and he waited for no more. Even as he made a dash for the water Full Moon passed him like a brown streak, but they were practically side by side as they went head first into the water. As he turned to follow Full Moon to the cave Ginger distinctly felt the sharp concussion of a bullet striking the surface. The next moment they were in deep water, swimming through a dim twilight, as the sun was not yet up. Ginger swam by feel as much as anything. Had he not been to the cave before he would never have found it, but he knew where it was, so he dragged himself in and struck out through the inky blackness. Gasping for breath he came to the surface inside the grotto, to find Full Moon waiting for him. They climbed out and sat on their customary ledge, where Full Moon produced a single coconut from under her arm, and again Ginger marvelled at her foresight and ability.

There was just enough light in the grotto for them to see each other. Full Moon smiled, and Ginger smiled back, but in his heart he felt far from smiling. He knew that their escape could only be a brief respite. It was merely a matter of time before Castanelli's boys found the cave, and—well, he did not know what would happen then. He only knew that the Corsican would not go away and leave them there.

'I reckon we stay here long time,' remarked Full Moon

philosophically, cracking one end of the nut against the coral.

Ginger nodded. He said nothing, for the simple reason that he could think of nothing to say. Wondering what devilment Castanelli was devising, he sat and watched the water turn from grey to mauve, and from mauve to blue. Full Moon handed him a piece of coconut and he munched it mechanically, for he was too weary to be hungry.

The girl drew her knife and laid it on the coral beside her. 'I cut Atanelli's throat bymeby,' she announced casually. 'Maybe I eat him,' she added pensively as an afterthought.

In his overwrought state, the picture of Full Moon eating the fat Corsican made Ginger laugh immoderately. The grotto echoed with his laughter.

'You no laugh that way,' scolded Full Moon sharply. 'You laugh that way you get debil-debil in head.'

'I shouldn't wonder at that,' returned Ginger, and for a while they remained silent.

15
TRAPPED!

FOR nearly an hour—or what Ginger judged to be an hour—he and Full Moon sat on the ledge in the grotto, waiting for they knew not what. There was nothing they could do except wait. There was no sign or sound to indicate that their enemies were outside, but Ginger did not attempt to deceive himself. He knew that Castanelli would not leave the island while he and Full Moon were alive, so he waited with what patience he could muster for the Corsican's next move. That something would happen presently he was certain, but what it was he could not remotely imagine. He looked at Full Moon. She was sitting with her feet dangling within an inch or two of the water, apparently quite content, her simple mind oblivious to danger.

Ginger was about to warn her to get higher on the ledge in case a shark or an octopus should seize her feet, for after his recent experiences these dangers were ever in his mind, when with hardly a ripple the water parted and a brown hand appeared. It closed round the girl's ankle. An instant later the mop head of one of Castanelli's islanders broke the surface.

Full Moon, caught off her guard, was nearly pulled into the water at the islander's first tug, but by a convulsive twist of her body she managed to seize a piece of projecting coral and hang on to the ledge. The scream she gave reverberated through the cave.

After the first shock of surprise had passed Ginger moved swiftly. He snatched up Full Moon's knife, and without the slightest hesitation drove it down with all the strength of his arm into the brown shoulder. The hand released its grip on Full Moon's ankle immediately, and the native pushed himself clear of the ledge in a swirl of discoloured water. For a moment his right arm disappeared from sight; then it reappeared, gripping a knife. At the same time he made a rush for the ledge. Ginger saw that if the man once gained his objective their plight would be desperate indeed, and he ran forward with his own knife upraised to meet the attack.

But the attack did not materialize. A lithe brown body slipped past him. It was Full Moon, with her arms raised above her head. In her hands she held a piece of coral rather larger than a coconut. The native saw his danger and, twisting away, prepared to dive, but before he could carry out his intention the coral came down on his head with a thud that made Ginger wince. The islander's body went limp, and then sank slowly in the blue water.

'Me finish him pretty quick,' announced Full Moon, in tones of the greatest possible satisfaction.

Ginger stared at her, for the casual way in which she treated life and death never failed to amaze him. In his heart he knew that he himself would have hesitated to do what she had done— deliberately kill the man. Even when he had struck with the knife he had chosen the man's shoulder as a target when he might have struck him in the head or throat. But Full Moon evidently had no such scruples. With a smile on her face she stood looking down at the body, now lying on the white sand at the bottom of the pool. In a way it pained Ginger to think that she was capable of such an act, although he realized that he had little cause for complaint. It was, he supposed, all a matter of environment. All the years of her life had been spent in danger, real and ever-pressing, so it was unlikely that she would be disturbed by the sight of death. Sandy had once told him that death was held to be a thing of no account in the Islands, where people took a pride in preparing their own coffins and graves, prizing them highly until such time as they fulfilled the purpose for which they were made.

Ginger continued to stand on the ledge with his back to the wall, gazing down at the black figure asprawl on the bottom. He felt that he ought to dive in and pull the body up, but he dismissed the inclination. After all, he reasoned, the man had swum in to kill them, so what had happened had really been just retribution. The thing that concerned him most was the fact that the islander had discovered their retreat. Did those outside share that knowledge, he wondered, or had the man only just discovered the cave, and swum in to explore it?

Full Moon took the knife from his hand. Looking to see why she wanted it he saw her prising off another large piece of coral, presumably for ammunition in case there should be another attack. She sang to herself in a queer minor key as she did so, from time to time glancing over her shoulder at the water. During such a glance her song came to an abrupt end, and she uttered a little cry.

Ginger, following the direction of her eyes, thought for a moment that the islander had come to life; but the dead man still lay in the same place, and he realized that it was a second figure under the water, swimming strongly. It reached the dead man lying spread-eagled on the sand, and paused as if to examine the body. Full Moon stepped forward, with the piece of coral, which she had torn off, raised above her head. Ginger, too, stood ready. But the islander did not come up. Apparently he had learnt what he wanted to know, for after a glance towards the ledge he twisted like an eel and shot back into the cave. Ginger would have prevented this had it been possible, for he knew that the islander would be able to explain to Castanelli just where they had taken refuge; but he could do nothing.

'They know where we are now,' he told Full Moon.

'Maybe Atanelli come,' suggested the girl hopefully, balancing the lump of coral in her hand with eager anticipation.

'Not he,' declared Ginger. 'He no come. He plenty afraid—send boys.'

Full Moon nodded. '*Aue*,' she muttered. 'We kill boys all same, eh?'

Ginger smiled in spite of himself. 'You blood-thirsty little wretch,' he admonished her.

'No blood-thirsty—just kill, that's all,' protested Full Moon.

The minutes passed, but the islander did not reappear. Ginger would have given a lot to know what was going on outside. Whatever it was he would have preferred to know the worst. But time went on and nothing happened. The pool was now a blaze of blue light, and he knew that it was broad daylight outside. As is usual in such cases, the inactivity frayed his nerves, but there was nothing he could do. He fell to wondering what Biggles was doing all this time, but conjecture did not help him. Full Moon, seeing him look often towards the cave, offered to swim through to find out what was happening in the cove, but he would not hear of it.

'What Atanelli he do, you reckon?' she inquired cheerfully.

'I don't know, but you may be sure he is up to some devilment,' replied Ginger, wondering if, now that their whereabouts was known, Castanelli would try to dig down to them from the outside. 'I wish something would happen,' he added. 'This standing here doing nothing is awful.'

His wish was speedily fulfilled. Hardly had the words left his lips when he was flung backwards by a violent explosion that rocked the entire grotto. Acrid fumes and coral-dust filled the air, while the water surged over the ledge with such force that he was nearly swept away. Pieces of coral began dropping from the roof into the water, and it was obvious that the whole place might collapse at any moment.

After her first scream of fear Full Moon clutched Ginger's arm.

'What Atanelli do?' she gasped.

'I'm afraid he is going to blow the place to pieces with dynamite,' replied Ginger, coughing as the fumes of the explosive reached his lungs. 'I suppose he has had to go to the schooner to get it; that's why there has been a delay,' he explained.

'What we do? You say?' questioned Full Moon plaintively.

Ginger did not know what to do. To swim out through the cave would probably mean that they would be shot by Castanelli, who was doubtless waiting for their heads to appear above the water. To remain where they were would invite the Corsican to fire another charge of dynamite and bury them for all eternity in the ruins of the grotto. The walls were already cracking. One more charge would certainly cause the whole place to fall in. Either way they were doomed, but of the two deaths Ginger preferred to remain where he was, if only to deny Castanelli the satisfaction of shooting him. 'We stay here,' he told Full Moon, instinctively crouching back against the wall. 'If we go out Atanelli shoot plenty quick.'

'Me stay,' announced Full Moon philosophically.

There was another nerve-racking period of waiting, but Ginger could now visualize fairly clearly what was going on outside. Castanelli would wait for a few minutes to see if they came out; when they did not appear, he would fire another stick of dynamite and throw it in the hole made by the first, which was somewhere over their heads. That would be the finish.

Ginger put his arm through Full Moon's and leaned back against the wall to wait for the end. He had not long to wait. There was another violent explosion. The flash of it struck downwards through the grotto into the water, to be followed immediately by the splash of falling rock. Parts of the wall caved in. Then, with a loud crack, a large portion of the roof broke away and crashed down into the grotto. The daylight poured in, and it was blue no longer.

So far no rocks had fallen on the narrow ledge on which Ginger and Full Moon crouched. Coughing, Ginger looked up through a cloud of smoke and coral dust at a hole nearly as large

as a dining-room table that had appeared in the roof. Above it
was the blue sky. For a moment or two there was no sign of life;
then Castanelli's head appeared over the edge. A broad smile
spread over his face when he saw the two shrinking figures on the
ledge. 'You come out,' he ordered.

'We'll stay here,' replied Ginger, wondering if he could throw
Full Moon's knife accurately enough to hit the man whom he
hated most on earth.

The Corsican shrugged his shoulders. Quite calmly, as if it
were a cigar, he took from his pocket another stick of dynamite
with a short fuse attached, and a box of matches. He lit the fuse
and raised the dynamite above his head. 'You come out,' he
ordered again.

'No!' shouted Ginger.

There came a sound of distant shouting. Castanelli evidently
heard it, for he looked round over his shoulder. When he turned
his face back to the grotto the smile was no longer on it. Showing
his teeth in a snarl of animal rage he hurled the stick of dynamite
straight at Ginger. It sped through the air, leaving a trail of pale
grey smoke behind it.

Ginger watched it fascinated. He could see that even if it did
not actually hit him it would fall on the ledge. His first
inclination was to jump into the water, for there was no room to
run. Then he saw that the dynamite would hit Full Moon, and
his reaction was instinctive. Like a cricketer taking a catch he
jumped forward and allowed the stick to fall into his hands.
Instantly he hurled it back at the hole whence it came. There was
no time to think, for as the dynamite showed for a moment
against the blue sky there was a terrific explosion, and the next
moment he was on his knees shielding his head from the falling
debris. He dragged Full Moon towards him and did his best to
protect her with his body. The air was full of smoke, and the noise
of falling coral. Brushing the dust from his streaming eyes he tried
to see what was happening. It was not easy, for the shape of the
whole grotto had altered. Pieces of the wall, and the roof, were
still falling, and as they fell into the water, blocking the cave, it
rose accordingly, so that their ledge was awash. Ginger only saw

these things vaguely, for in the horror of the moment it seemed as if the whole world was crumbling to pieces about them. He could still hear shouts outside, but he could see nobody, so he had no idea what was happening; but presently the smoke began to clear, and he could see more plainly what had happened to the grotto. Most of the roof had disappeared, so that he and Full Moon were, so to speak, at the bottom of a rough basin, the sides being composed of coral, some of which was cracked, and only needed a touch to bring it down. In fact, the whole place appeared likely to cave in at any moment. Of Castanelli there was no sign.

Ginger caught Full Moon by the hand. 'Let us try to get out,' he said tensely. 'If any more coral falls we shall be buried.'

But Full Moon only stood like one transfixed, listening, with parted lips and shining eyes. Then, suddenly, she let out a blood-curdling yell, and thrusting her knife into the fold of her *pareu*, started climbing up the wall towards the open air.

'Be careful. You'll bring the whole place down on us,' yelled Ginger, who, in the back of his mind, was wondering what had become of Castanelli.

But for once Full Moon ignored Ginger's frantic appeal. She went on climbing, heedless of falling rocks, from time to time uttering a piercing cry, not unlike those which could at times be heard in the distance. Altogether she gave Ginger the impression of having suddenly gone out of her mind, and he was by no means sure that she had not. That the shock of the explosion had affected her brain was quite possible, he reflected. Prompted by the fear of what Castanelli might do when she reached the top, he again yelled to her to stop, but although she acknowledged his appeal by shouting something in her own language she went on climbing. In the circumstances all he could do was to follow her.

THE TABLES TURNED

THAT something had happened outside was certain, but apart from the possibility of Castanelli's having been killed or disabled by the stick of dynamite which he had thrown back, Ginger could not imagine what it was. Full Moon was already more than half-way up the coral wall, so he exerted every ounce of strength he possessed in order to overtake her, or at least get to the top at the same time. And in this he was successful, for he found a comparatively easy way up, whereas Full Moon had rushed at the wall without troubling to ascertain the least difficult course. Nevertheless, the coral often broke under his weight, and more than once he thought he was bound to fall; but somehow he managed to hang on and, heedless of torn fingernails, dragged himself over the rim. Full Moon was still six feet below, looking vainly for a way up, for she had come to an *impasse*. By lying down he could just reach her hand; this was all the support she needed, and in a few seconds she was lying beside him, gasping for breath and wiping the coral-dust from her eyes with the hem of her *pareu*.

The strain of the last minute had been so intense that Ginger had temporarily forgotten Castanelli and his islanders, but now, remembering them, he looked round to see what was happening. This is what he saw. Near at hand lay two of the Solomon Island boys, terribly mutilated, apparently by the explosion. But it was not this that made him stare unbelievingly. The whole island seemed to be swarming with hideously painted warriors who yelled like madmen as they chased the scattered members of Castanelli's crew. And this was not all. The 'Scud', with her port wing-tip fractured and hanging loose, so that the tip of it trailed in the water, was floating at an alarming angle on the lagoon. More painted warriors were even then jumping out of the cabin doorway into the water. Others were swimming at an incredible speed towards a long, sleek canoe, which was being paddled towards three swimmers who were making for the schooner.

Ginger knew from their mops of hair that two of them were members of Castanelli's crew; the other, swimming much more slowly, was Castanelli himself.

Ginger must be forgiven if he ran up and down in hopeless indecision. He was completely bewildered. He could not make out what was happening. All he could think was that the 'Scud' had returned, only to be attacked by a swarm of native warriors who had arrived simultaneously in the war canoe. And this, it must be admitted, was a reasonable assumption. He perceived also that if his reading of the situation was correct he and Full Moon were likely to be the next victims, yet even in these alarming circumstances he was distracted by a tremendous hubbub that arose from the lagoon. The position was very much the same as when he had first emerged from the grotto, except that the two islanders had succeeded in reaching the schooner before being overtaken by the canoe, which had swung round to intercept Castanelli. But it was not this that had caused the outcry. The canoe was no longer being paddled; it still had a certain amount of way on it, but all the warriors were standing up, the better to see something that was happening in the water. It was they who had caused the uproar by their shouting.

Ginger watched, although as yet he could see nothing to justify the commotion. In fact, he wondered why the paddlers had desisted in their efforts to prevent Castanelli from reaching the schooner. But when the water near the swimming man was suddenly broken by the dreadful triangular fin which he knew so well, he understood. There was no need for them to trouble further. The shark would do what they had intended doing, and at the same time relieve them of the responsibility of the Corsican's death.

With his heart stone cold inside him, and his eyes still on that formidable dorsal fin, Ginger began running towards the beach. The fin disappeared, and the swimmer, with a terrible cry, thrashed the water with his legs. If by this means he hoped to frighten the shark he appeared to be successful, for again the huge fish broke the surface, its fin cutting a curving white wake in the water. Again Castanelli struck out for the schooner. The canoe was only a short distance away, and it was obvious that those in it could save the wretched swimmer if they would; but it was equally obvious that they had no intention of doing so, for they only leaned on their paddles shouting jeers and taunts at the luckless man in the water.

Ginger reached the edge of the lagoon and pulled up dead. He felt that he was going mad, yet he could not tear his eyes from the awful drama that was being enacted before him.

'*Mako*, he plenty *kai-kai* Atanelli,' said a voice at his elbow.

He glanced round and saw that it was Full Moon. Her eyes were shining with delight and satisfaction.

'These *kanakas* plenty *kai-kai* us presently,' he replied curtly, but Full Moon's only answer was a ripple of laughter.

Ginger turned back to the lagoon in time to see the finish of the tragedy. Castanelli was now very close to the schooner, swimming fast and making a tremendous splash with his feet. It looked as if he would escape, after all. The warriors in the canoe evidently thought so, too, for they suddenly dropped into their seats and began paddling furiously towards the ship. But the shark also appeared to realize that its prey was about to escape. The fin disappeared, and the water swirled as it closed over it. Castanelli clutched at a trailing rope and began to pull himself clear; but he was exhausted, and could only hang helplessly, trying to lift his legs above the surface of the water. There came a dark streak near the schooner's side; a terrible scream that was cut off short, and Castanelli disappeared.

Ginger moistened his lips. He was trembling violently and felt sick. Through it all he had an increasing feeling that this was not really happening, that it was all a dream; either that, or he had been killed by the explosion in the grotto. He was prepared to believe anything, however fantastic. He saw the canoe surge up to the schooner and the warriors begin to scramble up her side; a shot rang out, and one of the warriors fell back with a splash. The others went on. Wild yells rent the air.

Ginger turned to Full Moon, who was watching the scene quite unmoved. 'Where these boys come from?' he asked, as a suspicion slowly took shape in his mind.

'Shell-Breaker, he come,' murmured Full Moon briefly.

The sound of running footsteps behind him made Ginger turn quickly. A warrior was racing towards them, brandishing a club. Had Full Moon not warned him who it was he would have thought that the end had really come at last, but as the warrior drew nearer he saw that the girl was right; behind a grinning mask of white clay he recognized the features of Shell-Breaker. He was laughing. 'Plenty finish all time,' he shouted joyfully as he ran up.

'Where Andy?' cried Ginger.

Shell-Breaker pointed. Ginger spun round and looked in the direction indicated, which was towards the 'Scud'. So taken up had he been in watching Castanelli's dreadful end that he had forgotten all about the flying-boat. When he had last seen it it was—or he had thought it was—in the hands of the warriors. Somehow it had not occurred to him that Biggles and the others might be there too, but now, to his unspeakable astonishment, he saw Biggles, Algy, and Sandy standing on the centre section. They waved to him when they saw that he was looking in their direction. Had Ginger but known it they had been yelling at him for the last five minutes, but what with the pandemonium made by the warriors, and the drama in the water, he had not heard them.

As soon as he realized that they were really there Ginger dashed along the beach until he was as near as he could get to the flying-boat. Nothing would have induced him to swim out to it, for it was nearly two hundred yards away, so he could only stand on the edge of the lagoon beckoning furiously. He had just remembered the pearls, and was afraid of what the warriors might do. For he had grasped the truth at last; that Biggles and the war canoe had arrived together, and that the warriors were Marquesans from Rutuona.

Biggles was shouting, pointing first towards the schooner and then to the beach, as if he could not make up his mind which way to go. Ginger could not hear what he said, so he beckoned again, frantically, and wiped the perspiration from his blood-streaked face with relief as the 'Scud's' engines started, and the machine started taxi-ing slowly towards him. Not until it was twenty yards from the beach did Biggles cut the engines, so that at last Ginger could make himself heard. And by that time he knew it was too late, for smoke was pouring from the schooner's portholes and hatches, and the natives jumping clear into the water; the canoe picked them up, and the paddlers backed away from the burning ship.

Biggles was saying something, but Ginger did not listen. 'The pearls! The pearls!' he screamed. 'The pearls are on the schooner. Castanelli found them.'

Too late those on board the flying-boat understood. Ginger dashed into the water and scrambled aboard. 'Castanelli found the pearls!' he gasped. 'He took them aboard with him. They must be in his cabin.'

Biggles said nothing. He jumped into his seat and again the engines roared. The *Scud* whirled round, churning the sea into milky foam, and raced towards the doomed vessel. But long before they got to it all those on the flying-boat knew that the effort was wasted. The schooner was a sheet of flame from stem to stern. It would have been suicide for anyone who attempted to board her.

Biggles cut the throttle and the engines died suddenly, so that the 'Scud' floated motionless on the water. Not far away a wild chant rose from the warriors who were packed in the war canoe; they, too, were watching the end of the *Avarata* with the same glee as they had watched the end of her owner.

'Well, that's that,' muttered Sandy, in a resigned voice. 'I never did have any luck with pearls,' he added, with poignant bitterness.

'Pity you couldn't have got here a bit sooner,' muttered Ginger.

'We should have been here hours ago if we hadn't struck a head wind,' put in Biggles quietly.

Ginger smiled grimly. 'I know all about that wind,' he said, realizing that it must have been the same breeze that had caused Castanelli to change his plan and throw him overboard before taking advantage of it to get away. 'It was nearly the death of me,' he added.

'It was nearly the death of us, with an overloaded machine and a blooming canoe in tow,' remarked Algy.

'Well, I did all I could,' declared Ginger.

'You look like it,' observed Biggles, regarding him curiously. 'You look as if you've been dragged round the reef at the end of a rope.'

'It was worse than that,' Ginger told him. 'I was dragged down to the bottom of the lagoon at the end of a rope. I'll tell you about that later on.'

'You're not seriously hurt, are you?'

Ginger shook his head. 'Only scratches—and shock,' he replied. 'I don't know what happened to you, but when I tell you what *we've* been through you'll think I'm a prize romancer.'

'You mean—you and Full Moon?'

'Yes.'

'Where is she?'

'On the island somewhere. I left her there with Shell-Breaker.'

'Hello, there goes the *Avarata*,' said Algy, in a hushed voice, as with a hiss the still-burning remains of the doomed schooner slid slowly out of sight under the water. A cloud of steam rose into the air and a few pieces of debris floated to the surface; apart from that there was nothing to show that the schooner had ever existed.

'Yes, and there go our pearls,' remarked Sandy, bitterly.

'Wouldn't they be any good if we fished them up?' asked Algy.

Sandy laughed harshly. 'After being in that fire? They'll just be a handful of white lime, that's all.'

For a minute or two nothing more was said. They all stood staring sombrely at the spot where the *Avarata* had disappeared, thinking of the risks and labour that had been in vain.

'Well, I suppose it's no use sitting here moping about it,' said Biggles at last. 'We might as well have a spot of something to eat while we're here and then we'll start back for Rutuona.'

'We shall have to find out what has happened to Castanelli's boys, too,' muttered Sandy. 'The whole business will have to be reported to the authorities, of course. As far as Castanelli is concerned—well, he got what he has deserved for a long time, and I don't suppose there'll be many tears shed on his account. I don't know about his crew; they were a bad lot, but the Governor at Tahiti will want to know what happened to them, so we had better find out—not that I think there is much doubt about it.'

Nobody answered. Once more the engines were started, and the 'Scud' moved slowly—almost reluctantly, it seemed— towards the beach.

17
FULL MOON SPRINGS A SURPRISE

SITTING in the sparse shade of the ruins of their first camp, with the painted natives squatting a short distance away, Biggles told Ginger why they had found it necessary to take the flying-boat to Rutuona, and their subsequent adventures, concluding with a description of the towing of the war canoe in the face of a stiff breeze. When he had finished Ginger told his own tale from the time he, Full Moon, and Shell-Breaker were trapped in the grotto by the shark, thus being effectively prevented from returning to the flying-boat. As far as the others were concerned this was the answer to a problem for which they had been unable to supply a reasonable solution. Shell-Breaker had told them a little, but his account had been so fantastic that they could hardly believe it. Ginger also told of the arrival of Castanelli, and his discovery of the pearls by means of the exposure of the biscuit tin by the waves flung across the island by the hurricane. But when he came to the episode of his being thrown overboard from the schooner, with an iron pipe tied to his waist, Sandy interrupted.

'Here, wait a minute, young feller. Are you sure you didn't dream all this?' he demanded suspiciously.

'Ask Full Moon; she cut me loose and fished me up,' returned Ginger simply.

'Losh! I reckon you'll never go nearer to death and get back again,' declared Sandy.

'You're right,' agreed Ginger. 'I thought I was a goner. When we saw Castanelli coming back I thought it was about the last straw. Naturally we made for the grotto. Castanelli was blasting us out with dynamite when you arrived. Another five minutes and all you would have found of us was bits and pieces.'

'We heard the explosions and it hurried us up,' declared Biggles.

'Well, that's all,' concluded Ginger. 'You saw the finish of the business.'

'Yes, that's all,' said Biggles quietly. 'After what you've been through I should think you've pretty well had enough of the South Seas. We may as well get along home. It won't take us long to put the machine in order. I think we'd better taxi her back to Rutuona and do the repairs there. Of course, if anyone feels like starting the whole thing afresh, and making another raid on the pearl-bed, I'm willing to fall in line. But that's really up to Sandy; he has the dangerous work to do.'

'Nay, laddie, it's up to you,' returned Sandy. 'You provide the cash, so it's your privilege to call the tune.'

'If only we had been able to save the pearls we should have been well out of the whole business, after all,' murmured Algy regretfully.

'That's true—but it isn't much use thinking about that,' answered Biggles. 'As far as pearls are concerned, we are where we started, but none of us has been hurt, and after the narrow escapes we've had we really have no cause for complaint. I only hope there will be no trouble with the authorities. Which reminds me, we'd better have a word with Roaring Wave about the casualties, so that when we tell our story his version of it will agree with ours. I don't think a single one of those Solomon Island boys got away. If there is a survivor, then he is hiding somewhere, and as far as I'm concerned he can stay there. But I should say that Roaring Wave's crowd killed the lot. Incidentally, we shall have to buy some handsome presents for Shell-Breaker and Full Moon. But for their pluck we shouldn't have got off as lightly as we have. We'll turn them loose in Lo Sing's store and let them help themselves.'

'If it hadn't been for Full Moon I shouldn't be here at all,' declared Ginger, looking over to where Full Moon and Shell-Breaker were recounting their adventures to an ejaculating circle of warriors.

Biggles waited until they had finished, and then called them over, when he made a short speech extolling their courage, and concluded by telling them that they could have whatever they liked from the store on Rutuona. 'We lost the pearls,' he said finally, 'but that wasn't our fault.'

Full Moon frowned as if she did not understand.

'No lost pearls,' she said.

Sandy looked up quickly. 'What you say?' he demanded. 'Atanelli, he take pearls on schooner.' He turned to Ginger. 'You're quite sure about that, I suppose?' he went on quickly, with a new hope in his voice.

'Absolutely certain,' answered Ginger. 'I sat next to him in the longboat when we went back to the schooner and he had the tin under his arm. I know the pearls were in it because I could hear them rattling. As soon as we got aboard he took the tin to his cabin—at least, when he came on deck again he hadn't got it, so obviously he must have left them below.'

'And it was immediately afterwards that you were thrown overboard and he sailed away—I think you said?' questioned Biggles quickly.

'That's right.'

'And then Castanelli came back?'

'Yes.'

'Why did he come back?'

Ginger looked puzzled. He had wondered about that at the time, but in the rush of subsequent events the matter had passed from his mind. 'I don't know,' he said.

'Atanelli, he come back for pearls, I reckon,' put in Full Moon.

Sandy rose swiftly to his feet. 'What do you know about pearls?' he asked almost harshly.

Full Moon looked up into his face wonderingly.

'Me take pearl,' she explained.

'You take pearl—how come?'

'Me on schooner,' explained Full Moon. 'I lie in sail. Soon hear plenty shouting on island; boys say Castanelli find pearl. Soon Atanelli he come aboard, bring pearl in tin. I watch along window in deck; see Atanelli put pearl in cabin. When he come up on deck I go through window, take pearl.'

'Where you put tin?' almost shouted Sandy, who was nearly beside himself with excitement.

'Me throw in lagoon.'

Sandy let out a yell. 'Did you hear that?' he cried. 'She threw them overboard. *That's* why Castanelli turned about and came back. He went down to the cabin and found the pearls had gone. No wonder he came back. They're in the lagoon all the time.'

The others were all on their feet. Full Moon looked from one to the other in astonishment; it was clear that she found it difficult to understand why there should be so much fuss over a few pearls. But she grasped the situation. 'Atanelli, he come back for pearl, I reckon,' she said again.

'But why didn't you tell me?' asked Ginger.

'No time,' explained Full Moon. 'You plenty dead, I think.'

'She means that when Castanelli threw you overboard she forgot all about the pearls,' said Biggles.

'Aye. I reckon that's it,' agreed Sandy. 'We'll soon find out for certain.' He turned to Full Moon.

'What place you throw tin?' he demanded.

'I show,' replied Full Moon without hesitation.

All was now bustle and excitement. Sandy yelled to Roaring Wave to man the canoe, and they were soon in it, steering according to Full Moon's directions. At the spot where the schooner had lain at anchor when Ginger had been a prisoner she raised her hand, and the canoe came to a stop. She then got over the side into the water, with her face below the surface, looking first one way and then the other at the bed of the lagoon. Once she turned over again to breathe, paddled a little farther away, and went on with her search.

'What about the shark?' cried Ginger, aghast.

'Look around you,' replied Sandy. 'You needn't worry. If that *mako* shows up here he'll be a dead fish before he knows what's hit him.'

Ginger looked along the side of the canoe and saw a dozen men, muscles tense, hands on the hilts of their knives, ready to dive into the water the instant danger threatened.

At last Full Moon swam back to the canoe and shook the water from her hair. 'Me see,' she said quietly. For a minute or two she clung to the side of the canoe, breathing deeply, each breath longer than the preceding one. As she exhaled she bent her body like a jack-knife to force all the air from her lungs. Finally she took an extra deep breath, and turning head downwards, went down into the depths like an arrow.

Ginger often thought about that moment afterwards, for it was the most dramatic he had ever known. The silent lagoon, the long black canoe with its grotesquely carved prow, and the line of grim, painted faces, with eyes boring into the depths, watching for the dangers they understood only too well. Every man was tense, the muscles rippling under his oiled brown skin.

Suddenly there was a slackening of the tension. Full Moon came into sight, shooting towards the surface, her blue *pareu* clinging to her lithe body. One arm was upraised. In it she held the tin. There was a roar from every man in the canoe as she broke the surface. For a little while she clung to the side of the boat drawing in her breath with that curious whistling sound which Ginger had come to know so well. Then she tossed the tin into the canoe and climbed in herself.

Sandy was on the tin in a flash, and dragged the lid off. 'They're here!' he shouted hoarsely.

Biggles smiled. 'After this trip I shall be ready to believe anything,' he declared.

In a few minutes they were back on the beach, in an atmosphere very different from that of an hour previously. Full Moon was the heroine of the occasion—as indeed she deserved to be. Sandy held the pearl-tin under his arm, declaring that he would not lose sight of it again until the pearls were sold.

'Then let's get back to Rutuona for a start,' suggested Biggles. 'If we get along right away we can be back before dark. The machine is in no case to face another hurricane.'

So they took their places in the 'Scud', allowing Full Moon and Shell-Breaker to travel with them. In fact, much to her delight, Full Moon was permitted to sit next to Biggles in the control cabin and work the throttle. The war canoe was taken in tow, and under an azure sky the 'Scud', with her engines roaring, surged through the entrance to the lagoon for the last time.

A quarter of an hour later Ginger stood up and looked back. All he could see was a few tattered palm-fronds swinging in the breeze. Even as he watched they sank below the horizon, and in spite of its grim associations it gave him a feeling of sadness to think that he would never see the island again. 'I'm coming back here again one day,' he told Sandy confidently.

Sandy chuckled. 'That's what we all say,' he grinned. 'The Islands get you that way.'

The End of the Trail

The return of the warriors to Rutuona with Full Moon, and the story of how Castanelli had died, created a sensation which, Roaring Wave declared, demanded a feast to celebrate it, and preparations were begun forthwith. The white men were the guests of honour, and in the glare of many torches the banquet began. Ginger, seated on a mat between Full Moon and Shell-Breaker, was ready for it, for it was a long time since he had eaten anything substantial. Leaf plates were provided, and Ginger's was heaped in turn with pork and *popoe*,[1] sweet potatoes, shark's sweetbreads, and other local delicacies, to say nothing of unlimited quantities of fruits of many sorts. Every time he paused in eating Full Moon or Shell-Breaker would shout, '*Kai! Kai!*', and push more food towards him. Apart from that there was very little talking, for in Polynesia a meal is something to be taken seriously.

---

[1] Popoe *is the staple article of food in the Marquesas. It is a sticky yellow paste manufactured from the fruit of the breadfruit-tree.*

When all had eaten to repletion the guests reclined on their mats, while the children rushed out to eat what was left over, as was their privilege. Then, in the orange light of the flickering torches, the warriors began to recount their version of the end of the *Avarata*. Ginger did not hear the finish. Worn out, he retired from the scene, and, flopping down on the floor of their hut, was instantly asleep.

It was broad daylight when he awoke, to find that the others had been at work on the machine for several hours, and the job of mending the broken wing was nearly complete. By noon they were ready to depart. When they walked down to the beach with their belongings they found all the people of the island gathered there—men, women, and children sitting on the sand. As the white men approached they began singing their moving song of farewell:

> 'Farewell to you,
> You go to a far-distant land.
> There you will stay, and you will weep for me.
> Ever I shall be here, and my tears will fall like rain.
> The time has come. Farewell.'

Many of the singers were sobbing. Full Moon and Shell-Breaker, dressed in the flimsy finery they had selected at Biggles's invitation from Lo Sing's store, sat apart from the others, weeping unrestrainedly, their *pareus* lifted to their eyes. Their distress was so affecting that it was all Ginger could do to keep his own tears back. He ran over to them and held their hands.

'*Kaoha*, my friends,' he whispered huskily. 'I shall not forget you. One day I shall come back.'

They clung to him, imploring him to stay, but the others were calling, and in the end he had to tear himself away. With his eyes misty with tears he ran down the beach and splashed out to the machine. The engines were started. The cabin door slammed. The engines roared and the 'Scud' carved a trail of foam across the bay for the last time. As it rose into the air Ginger sat silent at a side window, his heart heavy with grief, taking his last view of Rutuona.

Sandy clapped him on the shoulder. 'Don't worry,' he said.

'You'll come back. Once you have been to the Islands you can't ever forget them, and one day they will call you back.'

There is a little more to tell. The 'Scud's' first landfall was Tahiti, where Sandy, who knew the Governor well, made a full report on the loss of the *Avarata*, and the death of her captain. The others confirmed his statements, which were accepted without question. Indeed, the Governor hinted that in his opinion Castanelli was well out of the way, for his illegal practices, including the selling of liquor to the natives, had been known for some time, but it had been difficult to obtain evidence to convict him. Several leading Parisian pearl-buyers were in Papeete, and to them Sandy sold most of the pearls, retaining only the very largest, for which he thought Biggles would get a better price in Paris. Nevertheless, those sold on the island not only paid for the entire expedition but left an ample margin for division among the partners.

Sandy remained in Tahiti, announcing that he was going to buy a schooner and set up as a trader; but the others suspected that the lure of pearls would be too great for him, and it was far more likely that he would fit out his schooner for another raid on the pearl-bed.

By the time they reached Australia the machine was too badly in need of a complete overhaul for them to consider flying home in it, so Biggles sold it for what it was worth to an operating company and out of the proceeds bought three tickets for air travel to England.

'It will be a change to sit still and let somebody else do the work,' he remarked with a smile, as they all went aboard.

BIGGLES
AND THE
BLACK MASK

BIGGLES REMEMBERS

BIGGLES sat at his desk in the Air Police office at Scotland Yard studying the periodical report on International Civil Aviation.

He had looked at one page for so long that Ginger, working at a filing cabinet, remarked: 'Isn't it about time you turned over the page? What's on your mind?'

'I'm thinking,' answered Biggles, pensively.

'About what?'

'I'm wondering if it's possible for a man with a crooked streak ever to straighten out.'

'And what conclusion have you reached?' inquired Air Police Sergeant Bertie Lissie.

'I'd say it may be possible while all goes well; but there will always be a weakness. The piece that has been straightened, under pressure, is liable to bend.'

'What induced this profound train of thought, if I may ask?'

'An item of news I've just read here.' Biggles sat back and lit a cigarette. 'I don't know if you've noticed it but since I've been on this job I've sorted out some problems which could have got a non-flying cop bogged down. I'm not flattering myself by implying I'm smarter than the next man. No. It happens that I've been in aviation a long while, and in that time I've seen all sorts of pilots, and aircraft, come and go. It's also my luck to have a memory. That can be reduced to one word. Experience. That, more than once, has enabled me to see the ground when the overcast looked solid.'

'You still haven't answered my question, old boy,' returned Bertie. 'Why this sudden burst of philosophy?'

'Last month a man named Roderick Canson was granted a licence to operate an air charter company.'

'Any reason why he shouldn't?'

'That is precisely what's exercising my mind. I knew Canson years ago as a flying officer R.A.F. At that time he had one of

those crooked streaks I mentioned a moment ago. Naturally, I'm
bound to wonder if he still has it. We all have our weaknesses,
and I'm aware that I have mine. But I've never sunk to robbing
my brother officers.'

'Did he?'

'He did. And, moreover, he got away with it. Don't ask me
how. I could only conclude it was a glib tongue or the charm he
could turn on. Anyhow, he got away, twice, with a reprimand. I
must admit he was popular in the mess although he wasn't my
cup of tea. He talked too big. Really big men don't talk big. He
was also that rare thing, a good pilot who is also a clever
mechanic. He could do anything with his hands. It was an
education to watch him at a bench. He was also the most
plausible liar I've ever known. They say that to be a good liar you
must believe your own lies. Canson told a tale so convincingly
that I fancy he could do that. He was always hail-fellow-well-
met. He spent money freely—as things turned out, not always
his own. He was a queer mixture.'

'He must have been.'

'I believe his real trouble was vanity. I suppose you'd call him
good-looking. He certainly fancied himself. But a man who has
his hair artificially waved like a corrugated iron roof isn't my
idea of a man. When I knew him he sported one of those fair,
fluffed up moustaches. Nothing wrong with that. But he never
stopped fiddling with it—like a girl who can't leave her hair
alone. It may be significant that the lower ranks called him Foxy.
Foxy Canson. And as you may have noticed, when troops coin a
nickname for an officer it's generally on the beam.'

'What mischief did he get up to?'

'The first time he slipped up—as far as I know—was over a
bag of coal.'

'*Coal!*'

'The stuff you put on the fire. Why coal, you may ask? Canson
was married. A nice-looking girl. I sometimes wondered how she
put up with him. They had permission to live off the station so
they rented a cottage not far away. One day his batman, going
out on his motor-bike with a sack on the carrier, was stopped at

the gate. The sergeant of the guard asked him what was in the bag. It turned out to be coal. From the Service dump, of course. The man said he was taking it to Canson's house. He, and Canson, were put under open arrest. At the court martial it was revealed that this pinching Service coal for Canson's private use had been going on for some time. The airman pleaded he had been ordered to do it and couldn't disobey an order. This, a reasonably valid defence, was accepted; and possibly because it would have been difficult to punish one without the other. Canson got off with a caution as to his future conduct. His popularity and charm may also have had something to do with it.'

'I wouldn't call that a very serious charge,' said Ginger.

'Maybe not, but it provides a line to his character. I may be a harsh critic, but I hold the view that if a man will steal a small thing, given the opportunity he will help himself to something bigger. To get an airman involved was to me unpardonable.'

'Absolutely,' murmured Bertie. 'Only a stinker would do that.'

Biggles went on. 'Canson's next effort had an even nastier smell. He was Mess Secretary. After a while some officers, including myself, began to look hard at their mess bills, particularly their wine accounts. I for one was sure I hadn't had the drinks for which I was charged. Naturally, there were complaints, and these eventually reached the ears of the Group Captain commanding the station. He called for the books and got the Accountant Officer to audit them. Then the truth came out. Canson, if you please, had been having some of the wine, ordered for the mess, delivered at his house. The deficiency he had squared up by overcharging officers on their mess bills—a pound or two here, a pound or two there. He was, of course, put under close arrest. This time I was sure he'd be handed his bowler hat.'

'Don't say he got away with that,' said Bertie.

'Nearly. All he got was a severe reprimand, and as he could hardly remain on the station he was posted to Iraq. That was the last I heard of him.'

'Marvellous what some fellows can get away with,' murmured
Ginger, cynically. 'How did he manage it?'

'Don't ask me. He put up some cock and bull story about
intending to pay for the wine out of his winnings at cards in the
mess. He was in fact a first-class bridge player. He had no money
of his own. For all I know he may have gone straight after that;
but now you'll understand why, when I saw he'd managed to get
a licence to run an air operating company—well, it gave me
something to think about.'

'Where is this?'

'He's taken over the abandoned American training aerodrome at Millham, in Suffolk.'

'Any other particulars?'

'Yes. He's started with two machines, an Auster Autocrat and
a de Havilland Dove. What sort of business does he hope to do
with a *Dove*, a twin-engined eight seater, with a pay load—if my
memory serves me—of 1,500 lb. and a range of 700 miles?
There's another angle to that. From where has he got the money
to start a venture like this? You can't buy aeroplanes with
chicken feed. When I knew him, although he talked as if he was a
millionaire, Canson never had any money; he spent his pay as
fast as he drew it. That, maybe, is what caused the trouble.'

'He may have got some rich uncle to put up the money,'
suggested Bertie.

'It's possible. He was glib enough to talk Eskimos into buying
refrigerators. Even so, how and from where does he hope to get
enough passengers to fill a *Dove* to capacity? You can't pay your
way, let alone make money, flying with empty seats.'

Ginger came in. 'What this boils down to is, you're suspicious.'

'I wouldn't go as far as that. It would be going too far. Let's say
I'm a bit puzzled. I'm not questioning Canson's ability to run an
air charter concern. He's a good pilot and he must know the
regulations. He may have turned over a new leaf. Knowing what
I do I may be prejudiced; but on his past record I'm bound to
wonder if he's the right sort of man to be doing what he's taken
on.'

'What you really mean is, there may be more to this than

appears on the surface,' guessed Ginger.

'Put it that way if you like.'

'One thing in his favour is, he must have left the Service with a clean sheet or he wouldn't have got a licence. Surely someone would check up.'

'I wouldn't be too sure of that. I've already told you he had a way with him. In ten minutes he could make black look white; and on top of that he had a knack of making friends in high places.'

'Well, what are you going to do about it—if anything?'

'I feel like dropping in at Millham to have a close look at the sort of business Canson is doing. I mean, if he's getting any customers. He can't last long without any.'

'Why bother?' questioned Bertie. 'Why not wait for him to make a boob. If he's up to any funny business we shall know about it eventually.'

'Perhaps. Perhaps not. He's a clever fellow. And he has, or used to have, ambitious ideas. Anyhow, you know how it is. If he does get away with something there'll be the usual outcry. What were the Air Police doing? Why didn't they spot it? That would mean a rap on the knuckles for me. I'd rather satisfy my curiosity *now*, before anything happens. If everything is above board we can forget it. I know it isn't very nice to go through life being suspicious of people but that's why we're here; and in this case Canson, with blots on his copybook to my certain knowledge, has only himself to blame. That's what I tell some of these youngsters. One black mark can stick all your life.'

'When are you thinking of going?'

Biggles glanced at the window. 'It seems a fair sort of day; it might as well be now. I'll take you with me. Two pairs of eyes are better than one. Ginger, you'd better finish that filing job. You might ring up the hangar and get the Auster pulled out ready.'

'I'll do that,' said Ginger.

. . . .

It was a little after eleven o'clock when the Air Police Auster arrived over Millham aerodrome, a pre-war rural airfield that had been abandoned because it was not large enough to take modern military jet aircraft. For a time, before being given up, it had been used as a practice emergency landing ground for pilots under training in piston-engined machines. There was still one permanent hangar, with the original tarmac apron in front of it, and a cluster of administration buildings. A wind-stocking on its pole and the usual white chalk circle indicated that the flat, treeless area, was still a landing ground for aircraft. Two machines were standing on the tarmac. Three men, near them, were looking up at the new arrival.

'Not exactly falling over themselves with activity,' observed Bertie, casually, as they lost height.

There were no formalities, Biggles landed, ran on to the buildings, switched off, got out and with Bertie walked on to meet a man now coming towards them. 'It's Canson,' he said in a low voice. 'Leave the talking to me until we see how he shapes.'

For a moment Canson did not appear to recognize Biggles. A puzzled expression dawned on his face as he said: 'Haven't we met before, somewhere?'

'We have. Bigglesworth's the name. Remember?'

'Of course. How could I forget. What are you doing nowadays? I seem to remember someone telling me you'd got a flying job for the government—an inspector of some sort.'

'Quite right. Meet one of my assistants—Bertie Lissie. He was with me when I had 666 Squadron.'

'Had you any reason for inspecting my little show here?' inquired Canson, with raised eyebrows and a faint smile.

'No. Noticing your registration I dropped in to see if everything was all right.'

'No trouble here, my good fellow. Everything goes according to plan—as they say.'

Biggles took a casual look round, his eyes resting for an instant on a Rolls parked in the shade of the hangar. 'It must have cost you a pretty penny to set yourself up in this sort of business.'

Canson smiled broadly. 'Me?' Don't be silly. Where do you

suppose I'd get the cash to buy aeroplanes?'

Biggles looked mildly surprised. It was not affected. 'Oh, so it isn't your company?'

'Good Lord, no. I'm merely manager of air operations and chief pilot.'

'Does that mean you have assistant pilots?'

'Not yet. At present I'm on my own; but I'm looking for the right fellow to help me. But why are we standing here? Come into the office and have a drink.'

'Thanks.'

They went in. Canson produced bottles and glasses from a cupboard.

'You don't appear to be very busy at the moment,' prompted Biggles.

'You've come on the wrong day, my dear chap. Had you come on a Monday you'd have seen a different picture.'

'Why Monday?'

'That's the day we do business.'

'Do you mean you can fill the Dove with passengers?'

'Fill it! We've got a waiting list.'

'How do you manage that?'

'I can see you don't understand the sort of business we're running here. I'd better explain. Do sit down. This company is a subsidiary of a new travel agency called Sunnitours Ltd., head office in London. It was formed to cash in on the current tourist boom. More and more people are looking for cheap holidays on the Continent. We provide them.'

'Where?'

'We hope to expand, but at present we have only two regular runs, to Switzerland and the French Riviera. I have nothing to do with the bookings. All that's done in London. One reason why we're able to do really cheap holidays is because the company has its own hostels—you know the modern holiday camp sort of thing. We give an all-in price for a week, although this can be extended. It's all very simple. Bookings are made from Monday to Monday. At eight o'clock on Monday morning the tourist party assembles at the London office. After passports and so on have been checked a fast coach brings the party here. I fly them to their destination, where they are met by another coach which takes them to their quarters. I then fly home the previous week's party. It runs like clockwork.' Canson spoke enthusiastically and was obviously well satisfied with the success of the scheme.

'Where does the Auster come in?'

'For a possible emergency. That's another part of our service. Should any member of a party fall sick, or have an urgent reason for coming home, I fly out and collect him, or her, as the case may be. We specialize in family parties—mum, dad and the kids. By foolproof organization, and without the heavy overhead expenses of the big regular services we can do a really cheap job. Of course, we don't pretend to be one of these luxury affairs.'

'I see that,' said Biggles. 'There's one thing I'm not clear about. When you bring your customers home where do you land for Customs examination?'

'Here. We've got that laid on.'

Again Biggles looked surprised. 'Do you mean you have a Customs and Excise officer *here*?'

'When required. Not a full-time officer. He'd have nothing to do most of the time. The day a party is due in we notify Customs and they send an officer along to meet the plane. Then he goes home. We have to pay for that, naturally, but it works out cheaper than using an airport, where we should have to pay landing fees and lay on another coach to take people home. A lot of headwork has gone into this. The only way a show like this can be made to pay is by cutting expenses to the bone, and that's what we've done.'

'I can see that,' agreed Biggles.

'We're giving people the cheapest overseas holidays they've ever had. I handle the actual flying. The bookwork, inquiries, publicity and so on, is done in London. That's not my line.'

'What about ground staff?'

'All I want here, apart from myself, is one competent fitter and a rigger who knows his job. I've been lucky enough to find just the chaps I needed.'

'Very good,' congratulated Biggles. 'Whose bright idea was

this?'

'Mine. It struck me one day and I got down to working out the details. There were a few snags, mostly concerned with Air Traffic Regulations, but I got over them. When I was ready I took the scheme to Sunnitours and told them I could handle it. They jumped at it. Up to that time they were doing their tours by train, boat and motor coach.'

'So the show looks like being a financial success?'

'Can't be otherwise.'

'What happens if you have a crack-up? It can happen.'

'That's all covered by insurance, of course. Matter of fact that's our heaviest expense.'

'All very interesting,' said Biggles, getting up and rubbing out his cigarette. 'It shows what can be done by people with brains, imagination, and a flair for organization.'

'That's what I told Sunnitours. Now they can see it for themselves.'

'Well, we'll be getting along. Thanks for the drink and for showing us how things can be done. I hope the show keeps going well for you.'

'No reason why it shouldn't. I've got it all buttoned up.'

Still chatting they walked back to Biggles's Auster. A last word or two and the machine was in the air, heading for home.

2

SUSPICIONS

BIGGLES flew on. He did not speak. His expression was pensive, serious.

For some time Bertie did not break his train of thought; then he said: 'Well, old boy, what do you make of all that?'

'What can we make of it? Canson's story sounded reasonable—anyhow for the most part.'

'He seemed frank enough. He struck me as being a very decent fellow.'

'Of course he did. I warned you to be prepared for that. Good looks and charm always were part of his stock-in-trade.'

'He could look us straight in the face.'

'That, contrary to what you may have read, is nothing to go by. If all crooks looked crooked they'd be easier to catch.'

'I noticed you didn't tell him you were a cop.'

'I saw no reason to volunteer the information.'

'You didn't spot anything wrong?'

'Not exactly wrong, but one or two things struck me as odd. I was surprised by the Customs arrangement; but I think it must be true. Knowing it might be checked he'd hardly dare to invent such a lie, however good a liar he might be. I can't help feeling it's all *too* good, too easy, to be true. Put it like that. I suppose the company, as it's being run, could be made to show a profit; but Canson, on his own admission, is only an employee, and as such he wouldn't earn the sort of money he likes to talk about. That Rolls parked against the hangar must be his. Could he run a Rolls on the salary he's likely to get for the job he's doing—or says he's doing?'

'You think that's sufficient evidence for suspicion?'

'Hardly. There's another item that is. Now I'll tell you something you don't know. You saw those two men on the tarmac—Canson's ground staff?'

'Yes.'

'One of them is the airman who was involved in Canson's little coal racket. The other was acting clerk in the office of the Mess Secretary when he faked the wine accounts.'

'Oh here, I say. That's a bit of a coincidence.'

'If it is a coincidence.'

'You don't think——'

'Listen. Both those men knew, and had good reason to know, about the trouble Canson got in when he was in the Service. They gave evidence. One would have thought that Canson, knowing they knew the sort of man he was, would never want to see them again. Now then. Both men—whose names I forget— must have been in Canson's confidence when he was, in plain English, a thief. That makes all three of them crooks. Each man

knows what the other is. Now we find them together. Don't ask
me to believe that's pure coincidence. If it isn't coincidence then
Canson must have organized it. Why?'

'To have men by him he knew he could trust.'

'I'd say it goes farther than that. If Canson had something
underhand in view it would be easier to use men whom he knew
could be persuaded to go off the rails, than honest men who
might jib.'

'I see what you mean.'

'I hope Canson's memory isn't as good as mine. Of course,
when he recognized me he'd remember I was on the station when
he got into trouble. The court martial and so on. But I don't
think he made allowances for me spotting his two assistants as the
men who were mixed up in the dirty work. It was a long time ago.
I'd like to think Canson is now on the level; I wouldn't make
trouble for him if he is. But I can't help feeling a bit uneasy.
There's something about this business, several things in fact, that
don't quite add up. If I knew nothing about Canson's record I
wouldn't give the matter another thought; but knowing what I
know I'm bound to wonder if there's a wasp in this innocent-
looking pot of jam.'

'Then you don't intend to drop it?'

'I shall think about it and, if only to satisfy myself, make a few
inquiries. I may have worked out what they will be by the time
we get home.'

Nothing more was said, and an hour later they were back at
Scotland Yard. Ginger was there. 'Well, how did you get on?' he
questioned.

'Let's go to lunch. I'll tell you about it while we eat because I
shall have a job for you presently and you'll need to have your
clock set right.'

This was done, and back in the office Biggles explained his
plan.

'First you, Ginger. Now you understand the position this is
what I want you to do. Look up the address of this Sunnitours
concern and go to see them. Find out the earliest date you can
book for one of their air holidays; never mind where it is.'

'What if they haven't a seat in the near future?'

'Ask them to put your name on the waiting list. There may be a cancellation. Give them our home phone number so they can let you know.'

'And if there's a seat vacant now, or next week?'

'Take it.'

'You mean, I'm to go with the party?'

'Of course. All you have to do is keep your eyes open for anything unusual—that is, not strictly within regulations. See how the thing works. The reason I'm sending you is because Canson doesn't know you. If what he told us is true he'll be flying the Dove. Keep an eye on him. It would be no use me going because from the moment he saw me he'd be suspicious—if he has any reason to be suspicious.'

'This means I shall be away for a week.'

'Oh no. You're not having a week's holiday. Assuming I shall know your address before you depart, the day after your arrival I shall send you a telegram, or get the Sunnitours office to send one, saying your brother Jack has met with a serious accident and you are to come home at once. You will tell the manager of the hostel. He will inform Canson who, if he lives up to his guarantee, will fly out in the Auster and fetch you. In this way we shall have covered the full service, so if there is anything, any irregularity, anywhere, you should be able to spot it.'

'I get the idea. What are you going to do?'

'Wait here for you, to see if you have anything of interest to report. In the meantime I shall do a bit of checking up on Canson's story. I want to know the names of the directors of this Sunnitours Company. At a pinch I could get that from the Board of Trade. I shall check at the Air Ministry when Canson left the Service, and why. Bertie can do similar checks, at the R.A.F. Record Office, on the two ex-airmen Canson has working for him. It will also be necessary to find out from the head office if Canson really has this Customs arrangement, that he can get an officer laid on when he wants one. We've plenty to do here. If it all comes to nothing we shall have done nothing worse than waste a little time. My mind will be at rest as far as Canson is concerned.'

'Shall I start now?'

'You might as well. You're not likely to get a seat in a plane right away. That is if Canson told the truth when he said he was booked to capacity and had a waiting list. Of course, there's always a chance that he might run an extra tour to thin out the number of people waiting.'

Ginger made a suggestion. 'Instead of wasting time why shouldn't I follow the Dove on its next trip in one of our own machines? I could check its course and movements.'

'I want more than that. You could keep a closer watch on the Dove from the inside of the cabin, than from the outside.'

Ginger nodded. 'True enough. I'll see what I can make of it.' He went to the telephone directory for the address of Sunnitours Ltd. and departed on his mission.

Biggles looked at Bertie. 'Right! Let's get on with what we have to do.'

Said Bertie: 'I understand you to say you weren't suspicious. All this sounds to me as if you were mighty suspicious.'

'All I'm trying to do at this juncture is satisfy myself that there's no reason to be suspicious.'

'Surely it would be easy enough to search the Dove next time it comes in from abroad.'

'It would, but if we found nothing we should have told Canson that we suspected him of running a crooked show. Let's clear up some of the details.' Biggles reached for the telephone.

By the time Ginger returned, two hours later, Biggles was in possession of most of the information he needed. Far from doing anything to justify his suspicions it tended to ease them although there were one or two things that provided food for thought.

It was learned that Canson, a Flight Lieutenant at the end of his last overseas tour of duty, had retired from the R.A.F. at his own request, which as an officer he was of course entitled to do. It was also learned that the two airmen now in his employ had left the service at about the same time. The R.A.F. Record Office had provided the information that their names were Tomlin and Rawlings. Both had secured their discharge on medical grounds.

There was an odd feature about this, Biggles thought, discussing the matter with Bertie. Tomlin had only recently been re-engaged to complete his time for pension. Why had he suddenly changed his mind? Was it another coincidence that both these men, now working for Canson, had left the Service at the same time?'

In the matter of the Customs officer visiting Millham aerodrome Biggles was mildly surprised, because it was unusual, to learn that such an arrangement had been made.

Then Ginger came in with his story. Everything had gone well. The Sunnitours offices appeared all they were said to be. It was evidently a going concern, several people being there making inquiries. He had been attended to by an efficient young woman who had explained how the service operated. There was no vacant seat for the time being, but should a single booking be cancelled he would have it. She would let him know. He had given her his telephone number. He had brought back with him some brochures giving particulars of the firm's activities. One of these gave the names of the directors of the company. They were Smith, Buchonnet and Kronfelt. Smith managed the London office. Buchonnet looked after the French terminus at Nice and Kronfelt the Swiss end at Geneva. From these airports private cars and coaches took the passengers to the hostels and, for an extra charge, to places of interest.

'It all looked fair, square and above board,' concluded Ginger.

'It could well be,' said Biggles. 'The company may be sound, but that doesn't rule out the possibility of Canson running a racket on his own account. Let's not forget that this air transport angle was his scheme. He put it up to Sunnitours and they, to use his own words, jumped at it. Anyhow, that seems to be all we can do for the moment. I'll have a word with Gaskin to see if these three men running Sunnitours have been in trouble at any time.'

'So after all this you're still suspicious,' challenged Bertie.

Biggles frowned. 'Yes,' he admitted. 'I can't shake out of my bones a feeling that there's something wrong somewhere.'

'A hunch?'

'Not entirely. I suppose it stems from my knowing what Canson used to be, and I'm still a believer in the old saying, a leopard can't change his spots.'

'In other words, give a dog a bad name and hang him.'

'What else can you do with a bad dog? Let him run wild to bite somebody else? Since you appear to be critical tell me this. Why should Canson give up a career in the R.A.F., which carries security and a pension at the end of it, for the job he's doing now? He's the type who must have money, and plenty of it. He now owns a Rolls. How did he get it? Sunnitours has to work to a tight margin to show a profit, so I doubt if his salary can be as much as he was getting as a Flight Lieutenant in the Service. Does that make sense?'

Nobody answered.

Biggles went on. 'There's one other thing that puzzles me. Now I've had time to think, I wonder why Canson hasn't yet fixed up a second pilot. The cockpit of the Dove, as I remember it, has dual controls, with seats for pilot and co-pilot who can also act as radio operator. If he has a second pilot working with him, as he should, why did he duck the question when we were talking about staff? One would have expected his co-pilot to be at Millham when we were there. If he was he kept out of the way. I can understand Canson trying to cut running costs, but—well, as I've said before, there's something about this set-up that doesn't ring as true as it should. However, there's nothing more we can do for the time being. I can't go back to Millham asking more questions without Canson realizing I'm suspicious about what he's doing there. Whatever else he may be he isn't a fool. There's nothing more to do here so we might as well knock off and go home. I've a few things to do there.'

Events moved faster than could have been anticipated, for they had not been long in the flat when the telephone rang. Biggles answered. He handed the receiver to Ginger with a brief 'For you.'

Ginger took the call. 'Yes, Mr Hebblethwaite here . . . That's splendid . . . Thank you . . . I'll be there. Pay in English money when I arrive . . . Passport. Yes, I understand that. Money . . .

You can. Good. Where? . . . I see. Right. Good-bye.' Ginger,
smiling, hung up.

'That's a drop of gravy,' he said, turning to the others. 'As you
may have gathered, that was Sunnitours. Same girl I spoke to.
She says they've got enough bookings to make up a load for
tomorrow. Destination France. Land Nice airport. I have to be
at the office at eight o'clock sharp, with my passport. I hope
you've got some francs. I have some, but perhaps not enough to
see me through.'

'I can fix that,' said Biggles. 'What did she say about money?'

'She said if I ran short of francs the car driver who meets the
plane will let me have some in exchange for English notes.'

'That's illegal for a start, although it's a common wangle,'
declared Biggles. 'Did she give you an address that will find you?
I'm thinking of the telegram.'

'She told me the hostel was just behind Cap d'Antibes.
Address, Bureau Sunnitours, *près* Cap d'Antibes, Alpes
Maritimes.'

'Good enough,' said Biggles. 'You'd better get your things
together. You won't be away long so you won't need much in the
way of kit. By the time you get back you should be able to answer
some of our questions.'

3
GINGER SETS OFF

THE following morning Ginger arrived at the offices of Sunnitours Ltd with a few minutes to spare. His only baggage was
contained in a featherweight air-travel handbag and consisted of
pyjamas, a clean shirt and his toilet things.

Against the kerb outside the office was an old Rolls-Royce that
had been converted into a station wagon. He assumed, correctly
as it turned out, that this was the transport that would take them
to the aerodrome. The driver, in a flamboyant uniform, with the
name of the company on the front of a peaked cap, stood waiting

beside the vehicle.

Some of the passengers had already assembled. They were a couple with two children, a young woman, alone, and a lad in his late teens who, Ginger learned later, was a bank clerk going abroad for the first time. It also transpired they were all making their first trip by air: for which reason Ginger envied them their new experience. The first flight is always an occasion.

He announced himself at the counter, was given his ticket and paid for it. The ticket was actually a small folder of the 'all-in' type; that is, covering travel, food and accommodation for the period named. He had to show his passport, sign a form to the effect that he had nothing to declare in contravention of Customs, and that was that. Perfectly straightforward.

The last two passengers, a young married couple, arrived a few minutes late. Their formalities completed everyone was given a neat packet of sandwiches to serve as lunch on the plane. The whole party then went out to the car. Luggage was stowed by the driver. Everyone got in, Ginger at his request being allowed to sit next to the driver, and they were on their way.

Once out of the traffic Ginger was soon in conversation with the driver, a cheerful cockney who talked about everything under the sun, from politics to football. Ginger learned nothing from him, his work consisting simply of taking passengers to and from the aerodrome.

On an open road the car arrived at Millham just after eleven o'clock, pulling up close to the tarmac on which stood a Dove aircraft with its twin engines idling. Two men, one in mechanic's overalls, stood by it. When everyone was out of the car another man, evidently Canson, came out of the office, walked to the machine and climbed into the cockpit. One of the other men now showed the travellers into their seats, four on each side of a central gangway. All were in good spirits, chatting and comparing notes as if they had known each other all their lives. During this period Ginger watched everything closely. He also took an interest in the aircraft, because he had never flown the type. With toilet and other conveniences it seemed to be ideal for the job it had to do. He had learned at the office that there would be no intermediate stop.

He was now to learn the answer to one of Biggles' queries. Canson did not fly alone. The man who had shown the passengers into their seats now got in beside him so he was obviously going with them, either as co-pilot or radio operator, perhaps both. Who was he? Ginger wondered. As there was no one else about he thought he must be one of the two men Biggles had named as ground staff, Tomlin or Rawlings. Could it be that one of them now held a pilot's licence? It was possible, he decided.

The man remaining on the ground, the one in overalls, closed the door. He stood back, made a signal: the engines raised their voices and the aircraft moved forward. Conversation in the sound-proofed cabin died away as the passengers realized they were about to be airborne. They smiled at each other to hide any nervousness they may have felt. However, once in the air, they were soon talking again. The two children, unconcerned, began to unwrap their lunch sandwiches. They may have made an early start and it was now getting on for noon.

Of the flight to the South of France nothing need be said. It was a perfect summer day; under a flat blue sky visibility was excellent; the air was still, and once the machine had taken some altitude it was as steady as a barge on a river.

Ginger took a paperback novel from his pocket and settled down to read, looking out occasionally at the panorama spread out below, which he knew intimately, to satisfy himself that the aircraft was on course. He did not expect anything of interest to happen during this part of the programme, and nothing did. He had to suppress a smile at some of the remarks made by his companions when, over Southern France, the landscape changed and began to look 'foreign'—grey mountains, arid hills often with a castle or village perched on top.

Knowing the cruising speed of the aircraft he had already worked out the approximate time of arrival, and he was not far wrong. At four o'clock the Dove, presumably having received permission to land, touched down on the impressive new airport at Nice, its perimeter almost washed by the blue waters of the

Mediterranean. He put his book away, for from now on he would have to use his eyes and probably his wits. His intention was to watch Canson, where he went and what he did, at all events as far as this was possible. He realized it would not be easy. He had given the matter a lot of thought. He had no idea of what Canson did on these occasions. If he went to the hostel, so well and good; but if he did not he could see no useful purpose in going there himself except perhaps to sleep. Would Canson and his co-pilot remain together or would they separate? If they parted he would obviously not be able to watch both.

Another question that worried him was this. Would there be members of a previous tour waiting to be taken home? As this was an extra trip he thought not, but he couldn't be sure, therefore it was difficult to make a plan. He didn't care about the people. He was not interested in them, feeling sure they would be genuine holidaymakers. The problem really boiled down to this. If there were passengers waiting Canson would turn round and go straight home. He might do that in any case. If no one was waiting Canson would probably stay the night and return home the following day. If he stayed it would be difficult to keep in touch with him. Aside from this, as a civilian he would not be allowed the free run of the airport buildings, as would Canson, a professional pilot with an aircraft on the airfield. He would have to wait for him to leave and then follow him.

By the time the party had been passed through Customs, and had been met by a man in the Sunnitours uniform who guided them to a waiting coach, he had made up his mind what he would do. There appeared to be no one waiting to be taken home so the chances were in favour of Canson staying for a while, if not for the night. The two pilots had not emerged with the party. He didn't know where they were. He could only assume they had gone to check in. Anyway, he couldn't see them. He decided to stay and watch.

With this in mind he went to the coach driver, a Frenchman who spoke some English, and asked if it would be all right if he didn't go on the bus as he would like to have a look round Nice, and perhaps do some shopping, while he was there. He would provide his own transport to the hostel later. He knew it was no great distance to Antibes; a matter of twelve miles or so. In fact, he could see the Cape, at the western end of the bay, from where he stood.

To his relief the man, a jovial type, raised no difficulty about this. Indeed, he was most helpful, giving precise directions for finding the hostel. That was all Ginger needed to know. Not wishing to be cluttered up with his case he gave it to the man who put it in the coach with the rest of the luggage.

He waited for the coach to depart and then, free to do as he liked, took up a position behind a line of taxis from where he would be able to watch the main exit and at the same time keep an eye on the Dove in case it should take off. He could make no provision for that. The reason why he kept behind the taxis was because he did not want Canson to see him in case he recognized him as one of the tourist party; he might wonder why he had not gone in the coach to the hostel. Actually, Ginger did not think he would be recognized, because at Millham Canson had got into his seat with hardly a glance at the passengers. However, he was taking no risks that could be avoided.

He had a long wait. Planes came in and departed but Canson did not appear. What could he be doing? Having a meal in the restaurant? Drinking in the pilots' room? The Dove had not been moved. It was no longer possible for it to get back to England in daylight so it began to look as if it was there for the night. He had almost given up hope of seeing either of the two pilots in whom he was interested when they appeared together, carrying their travelling bags, which suggested they intended spending the night in Nice.

Somewhat to Ginger's alarm they walked straight towards him; but it turned out this was only to hire a taxi. They came so close that he heard the order they gave to the driver. Ruhl Hotel. The door slammed and away they went. From force of habit he noted the registration. He took the next cab in the line and gave the same order. Now he knew where the two pilots were going there was no need for him to follow their car. He knew the famous Ruhl Hotel at the far end of the Promenade des Anglais. It was one of the largest in the town; also one of the most expensive. Obviously Canson intended to do himself well.

In spite of all this Ginger was by no means happy. He could see difficulties ahead. If the men he was following went into the hotel and remained indoors what could he do? It would be practically impossible to keep an eye on them. If they left the hotel later, and went different ways, it would only be possible to shadow one of them. That, he decided, would have to be Canson. He was a trifle disappointed that so far their behaviour had been perfectly normal.

His taxi reached the hotel just as the two men were going in. That meant there was no longer any urgency. He foresaw another wait, possibly a longer one. He paid his driver and found a seat on the broad terrace overlooking the promenade and the sea beyond, choosing one that commanded a view of the hotel exit. As usual the terrace was well patronized, some people, English from their conversation, having a late tea. He attracted the attention of a waiter and followed their example, prepared for anything, or nothing, to happen.

Darkness had fallen, although of course the promenade was a blaze of artificial light, when Canson and his companion came out. They wore hats so they were evidently going somewhere; but they were without their travelling bags, from which Ginger assumed they intended to stay the night at the hotel. At the step down from the terrace to the pavement they paused, and he heard Canson say: 'Don't change too much money at the Casino. See you later.' This struck Ginger as an odd remark to make. Had Canson said, don't *lose* too much money at the Casino, it would have been more easily understood.

'I'll watch it,' answered the other, and turning to the right walked away.

Apparently Canson had an afterthought, for he called: 'Oh Rawlings. I should be back in about an hour so don't be late.'

Rawlings raised a hand to show he had heard.

Canson turned to the left and went on.

Ginger got up and followed, having noted that Canson's co-pilot was one of the men Biggles had named as being employed at

Millham airfield. He was not surprised. He had learned something. Apart from the name it was obvious the two men were on more intimate terms than their relative positions at the aerodrome would suggest.

At the point where the pavement turned left, on the opposite side of the road, at a corner of the gardens named Jardin du Roi Albert, there is a permanent taxi rank, and for a moment Ginger thought Canson intended to hire one; but he walked straight past and into the gardens. With rows of palms and shrubs it was easy to keep in touch from a safe distance.

At the far end of the gardens, however, at the busy Place Messina with its streaming traffic and pedestrian crossings, it was not so easy, and he had to close up a little. His interest was mounting, for the general direction was away from the modern buildings, fashionable cafés and tourist attractions. Clearly, Canson was not out for pleasure. Was he making for the big new bus terminus?

It was soon revealed that he was not, and Ginger became even more interested, although a little worried, when his quarry turned into a narrow, badly lighted street, into the quarter that is known as the Old Town. And it is old, very old. It is visited often enough by curious tourists in daylight; but seldom by night. There was just enough light for Ginger to read the name of the street, or rather, alley. Ruelle François Leroux. In France it is a custom to name streets after persons; but as these are sometimes changed it can be confusing.

The origins of Nice, this part of Nice, are lost in the dim past. In its earliest days it was probably no more than a tiny fishing village. It became a Greek settlement. Long before the birth of Christ the Romans took it over. A castle was built on a near-by hill for its protection, but all through the early Middle Ages it was taken, ravaged and sacked by invaders, raiders and pirates. It was besieged by the infamous Mediterranean corsair Barbarossa. Later it changed hands many times, being held by Turks, the kings of Sardinia, by French and Italian dukes and counts. In 1860 it became officially French. We are speaking of course of the Old Town, not the new modern city, one of the largest in France.

The result of more than two thousand years of strife and bloodshed is a labyrinth of ancient buildings, many of them dilapidated, huddled together for defence below what is left of the castle. The houses are tall and the streets narrow to provide shade in the heat of summer. There are holes and corners never reached by the sun. The place has the queer, cold, sour smell of age. To a visitor entering from the new town the atmosphere can be sinister. It has reason to be so, for even in the last war on dark nights knives flashed, and more than one Nazi sentry who ventured in was never seen again. Here a Resistance worker, or an escaped prisoner, could find a safe hideout. This atmosphere appears to affect the many cats that slink furtively round corners or glare down balefully from walls and windows.

Today, of course, the tourist has nothing to fear. The people who live in this strange little world may be poor, but that is all.

This is a digression, but it is important that the reader should have a rough picture of the sort of place into which Canson's steps had taken him.

Ginger hurried on, determined not to lose sight of the man he was following, now only a vague shadow in front of him. He realized that if he lost him he would be lucky to find him again. There were very few people about; an occasional pedestrian. There was no traffic. The street was too narrow for wheeled vehicles. What, he wondered, could Canson be doing in such a place at such an hour? Canson obviously knew, for he strode on purposefully, taking one turning after another in the maze, with the result that Ginger had soon lost all sense of direction. Was this intentional? Had Canson perceived that he was being shadowed? If these tangled little streets had names they could not be read. All Ginger could do was try to memorize conspicuous features when they occurred, but even so he was doubtful if he would again be able to find any particular place.

Canson was about twenty paces in front when he stopped suddenly, causing Ginger to shrink back flat against a door. There was a knock, a sort of double knock, so unusual that Ginger suspected it to be a recognition signal. It was followed by an eerie silence. When he risked a peep Canson was no longer there. In fact, there was not a soul in sight. Where had he gone? It could only be into the house on the door of which he had knocked. Which one was it? He could, he thought, judge it roughly, if not accurately, from the distance between them when Canson had stopped. The question was, how many doors were there? He had passed many doors, sometimes they were close together, sometimes a distance apart. They were always closed. Windows were shuttered.

A street lamp hung from a lopsided bracket a little farther on but the radius of light it gave was limited, and broken by uncouth shadows cast by intervening stonework. One decision Ginger reached without effort. Whatever Canson might be doing there it was not for any good and proper purpose.

He walked on, slowly, alert, step by step, until he reached the house which he thought Canson had entered. It turned out to be a tiny shop. A door was there, and beside it a sheet of plate glass. The interior was unlighted, but by putting his face close against the glass and peering in he could make out what appeared to be photographs, some on stands, some lying flat on a sheet of paper, others pinned to or stuck on a cardboard background. He came to the natural conclusion that it was a photographic establishment.

On the door post he discovered a small notice board, but he was unable to read the words on it; the paint had faded, the board was dirty and the light too dim. It was important that he should have the name of the establishment, perhaps the occupier, and any other information the board might offer. Dare he risk using his petrol lighter? It would provide enough light for his purpose.

He looked up and down the street. He had it to himself. The only sound was the deep growl of a tom cat against the confused murmur of the traffic on a main road not far away. He was feeling for his lighter when his eyes fell on something he had not previously noticed. A yard or so farther on what he had taken to be a shadow was a narrow, tunnel-like cavity; in fact, an arched entrance leading to—what? He couldn't see. The inside was as black as a coal hole. As he stared at it he thought he heard a slight movement. A cat? He peered forward, and held his breath when he made out, just inside, sitting hunched up on the ground, the vague form of a human being. A woman. Dressed in black. Had it not been for the pale outline of the face, which he could just distinguish, he would not have known there was anyone there.

Instinctively he drew back.

A voice spoke, a thin whining voice. Speaking of course in French it said: 'Spare a *sou* for a poor old woman, *monsieur*.'

4
WHAT HAPPENED IN NICE

GINGER breathed again. It was only a beggar. Feeling in his pocket he took out a few coins, and without looking at them, for they could be of no great value, dropped them into the skinny hand that had been held out. '*Voilà, madame*.'

'*Merci bien, merci, monsieur*.'

Ginger would now have walked on, to return later, but the old woman said: 'Can I help you, *monsieur*? You look for someone perhaps.'

Feeling that he should give an excuse for stopping Ginger answered, choosing a name at random: 'I was looking for the house of Doctor Cauvet.'

'He does not live here, *monsieur*. I do not know this name.'

'Thank you, *madame*. I must be in the wrong street.'

Ginger walked on until he came to a side turning and then stopped to think. The old woman was a nuisance. Why had she chosen such a place to squat? There was no likelihood of rain so the question of shelter did not arise. Could there be another purpose? Was she playing the part of a watch dog? It was, he thought, just possible, but hardly likely. He had an idea she would not have spoken had he not become aware of her presence.

This thought led to another. He remembered he had had in his trousers pocket, apart from some French francs which had been given to him as change at the hotel, some English silver; a ten pence piece and a five among others. Taking from his pocket the coins that remained he examined them. The ten pence was not there. He could only have given it to the old woman. What would she think of that? Perhaps it didn't matter. It was a mistake—a careless one—easily made. It could only tell her he was an Englishman.

How long would she remain there? He was still anxious to read the plate on the door so that he would have no difficulty in finding the house Canson had entered, should Biggles decide to look at it; but this would necessitate a light, and he hesitated to use one while the old crone was there. After being told his imaginary doctor did not live there what excuse could he find for that? She would wonder what he was doing. She might tell the occupier, whom she probably knew, of his suspicious behaviour. She might fetch the police.

Happening to look up he could just read, in the light of the next lamp, the name of the street. Rue Baldini. That was something worth knowing, anyway, he told himself.

He waited for a quarter of an hour and then strolled back towards the archway hoping that now the old woman had some money she had gone off to spend it. He was relieved to find she had. At all events she was no longer where he had left her. Good! Now he could get what he wanted. He was feeling for his lighter when a sudden noise, the rattle of a chain and the turning of a key, caused him to turn about and walk smartly away. Ten steps and he turned again, flattening himself against a wall, to watch.

He saw Canson come out and walk quickly up the street. He recognized him by his figure. He now carried an object that looked like a bulky portfolio. He had arrived without luggage of any sort so this obviously had been collected at the house. What was it? What did it contain? were questions that automatically flashed through Ginger's brain. The odd thing was, in his concern about the old woman he had forgotten all about Canson.

The door had been closed, so again he approached, impatient at having so much trouble over such a simple task. For the third time he felt for his lighter.

Then it happened.

A woman's voice said shrilly: 'This is the man!'

Instantly, without further warning, there was a rush and two men were on him. Behind them the old woman in black hovered like a witch.

Ginger struggled desperately, but taken completely by surprise he was at a disadvantage from the start. It had happened in a flash. One of the men had got behind him and was pinning his arms to his sides so that he could not actually fight. The other man came from the front with an arm raised. The hand held a dagger. As he came in and struck Ginger raised a leg and drove his foot into the man's stomach. With a gasp the man staggered back. The dagger clattered on the pavement. The woman swooped on it.

For some reason—Ginger discovered it later—the man behind him spat out a curse and released one arm. This gave Ginger a chance. He could half turn. Using his free arm as the man struck at his face he caught the blow, carried the hand to his face and sank his teeth into the thumb. This is not a very nice trick, but in a close struggle it can be effective because the pain caused is considerable and the victim thinks more of getting free than pressing home his attack.

It worked. The man let out a cry and released him. Ginger sprang clear and raced away up the street. He took the first turning, the next and the next. He had no idea of where he was going but that didn't worry him. All he wanted was to get well away from his assailants. A glance behind showed he was not being pursued so he steadied his pace to a fast walk, heading for a noise of traffic not far distant. Three minutes later he was in the bright lights of a broad street with the sea on the far side. He now knew where he was. This was the Quai des Etats Unis, which might be called an extension of the Promenade des Anglais, so he was not far from the hotel where he had started.

Turning to the right he hurried on and did not stop until he came to the gardens through which he had walked earlier. Finding a vacant bench in the shadow of a palm he sank down on it, mopping his face with his handkerchief, to recover his composure. He was streaming with sweat, for the night was hot and humid. He was still breathing heavily and his hands were trembling from shock. Utterly unprepared for such a murderous attack it had been severe. Such a possibility had not for a moment entered his mind.

It was some minutes before he could think clearly.

He examined himself. He appeared to have suffered no injury, but he discovered a four-inch gash in the upper part of his left sleeve and for the first time realized how narrowly the dagger had missed him. The spot was wet. He pinched it and looked at his fingers. Blood. He was not conscious of any wound, and confirmed it. Then he understood; understood why the man behind him had released his hold. The dagger, deflected when he had kicked the man in front, had run across the fingers of the man holding the arm. No wonder he had cursed and let go!

What amazed Ginger as much as anything was the violence of the attack. It had been a deliberate attempt at murder. There was no doubt about that. He recalled the stories he had heard of how during the war the corpses of victims of the French Resistance had been disposed of by being thrown down old wells known only to them. But why had they been so determined to kill him? They must have been sure he was a spy. How did they know? What had he done? It was the old woman who had given him away. Was it because of the English money he had given her when Canson had been inside? That was careless of him.

Summing up he came to the conclusion that the woman was a sentry, posted in the archway to keep watch for strangers who lurked in the vicinity. She may have seen him stop when Canson had stopped to knock and from this guessed the truth; that he was shadowing Canson. Be that as it may, he thought; that such precautions were being taken could only mean that something ugly was going on in the shop in the Rue Baldini. Canson had been there. He had arrived without luggage and departed with a case. What was in the case? Where was Canson taking it? This would be something for Biggles to work out when he was told the news. At least he had some information to take home.

He still had problems. He didn't know what was written on

the plate on the door of the shop, but decided it would be folly to go back again so soon. That would have to wait. He would have to go to the Sunnitours hostel for the night; for two reasons. If he failed to show up he might be reported missing and that could bring in the police. He didn't want that to happen, anyhow, at this stage of affairs. If they found him it would mean awkward questions. If they failed to find him it would soon be generally known that an English member of the Sunnitours party had disappeared.

He would be known by name. That could lead to more complications. The people in the Rue Baldini might put two and two together. So might Canson. The second thing was, he felt he ought to be at the hostel when Biggles' telegram arrived. He wanted to go home anyhow, and the best way would be to follow Biggles' instructions and allow Sunnitours to take him back to England.

There was a snag about that. Canson was still in Nice. Unless the Sunnitours office in London had some means of getting a message through to Canson in Nice how could Canson fly him home?

Ginger gave it up. Things were getting too difficult. They would have to take care of themselves. Sitting on a bench in the gardens, guessing, would not solve his problems. He got up, walked to the corner where the taxis were parked, and took the first in the line. When he told the driver he wanted to go to Antibes there was some hesitation, but the promise of an extra pound on the official fare did the trick. He was still a little perturbed about what might happen at the hostel.

Thanks to the instructions the Sunnitours driver had given him he had no difficulty in finding the place. Having paid off his cab he went into the main building, set between a row of small but neat bungalows, to be greeted by the driver, now wearing a white apron, and his wife, who between them ran the place, as he learned later. The woman, a buxom, cheerful-looking woman, delighted to learn he spoke French, said they were just getting worried about him. The evening meal was finished and cleared away, but no matter, she would make him an omelet, if that, with cheese and fruit would be enough. Ginger said that would be ample, he hadn't much appetite—which was true. He had had a nasty shake-up, and had not yet fully recovered.

He was told the other members of the party had gone for a walk as far as the sea. He said he would not be going out again and handed in his passport, as is customary, for the police check.

Having had his meal he was shown his room, which turned out to be number five. It was little more than a cubicle but it was fitted with hot and cold water. The walls were thin, being in fact merely plain grey asbestos sheeting, but the furniture, consisting of a bed, a table and a chair, if simple was sufficient. The hostel had obviously been carefully planned at a considerable outlay, and he found it difficult to associate this with what had happened in Nice.

Where did Canson fit in? Up to his arrival in Nice Ginger had assumed, admittedly without justification, that the whole set-up was crooked. He now began to think on different lines. Was the Sunnitours organization a genuine concern in which Canson was running a racket on his own account? Some illegal business which his employers knew nothing about? The caretaker and his wife seemed to be nice, ordinary, honest people.

The affair in the Rue Baldini left no doubt in his mind that Canson was up to something. Why, otherwise, would he associate with potential murderers? It had been too dark for him to see his attackers so he did not think he would recognize them again should he see them. By the same token they would not recognize him. He was not so sure about the old woman. Canson had already left the shop so he couldn't have seen him. Of the man who had seized him from behind he had seen nothing at all. Of the man with the knife, who had been in front, he had only a blurred impression of a thin black moustache on a youngish face under a beret.

Ginger found his bag on the floor. He threw his pyjamas on the bed, got out his toilet kit and had a good wash, after which he felt better. He then sponged the blood out of the sleeve of his jacket and hung it up to dry. There was nothing he could do about the slit in the cloth, anyhow for the time being. In the morning he might find a tailor in the town willing to repair it. The thought occurred to him to put a call through to Biggles to tell him what had happened. But it would be dangerous to use the hostel phone, even if there was one, and as he did not feel like going into the town to look for a public call box he decided against it. He would be seeing Biggles shortly and there was no immediate urgency. It was getting late, anyway.

He was content to get into bed, for he had had a tiring day. He heard his travelling companions arrive home, making a good deal of noise, but he pulled the sheet over his ears and was soon asleep.

5
FOOD FOR THOUGHT

CONSIDERING how his nerves had been rattled by shock Ginger had a good night, but he was awakened rather early by brilliant sunshine pouring through his window. Finding the bathroom at the end of the corridor he had a shower, and feeling refreshed was ready for anything. In the broad light of day he found what had happened in Nice overnight hard to believe. It seemed more like a bad dream.

He went along to the dining-room to find he was the first up of the tourist party. However, he did not have to wait. The coach driver, who with his wife were evidently the caretakers, served him with the usual continental breakfast of coffee, hot rolls, butter and jam. He took the opportunity of asking the man if the pilots of the plane ever came to the hostel. He was told they never came. They stayed near the airport. He would have liked to ask more questions but thought it prudent not to appear too inquisitive. He was anxious to know if the Dove was still on the aerodrome, but he himself would soon be able to check that.

The man, bringing in some toast, noticed the tear in his sleeve. Ginger told him casually that he must have caught it on something, which was near enough to the truth; whereupon the man said he would get his wife to mend it for him right away. The wet patch had dried during the night, so Ginger thanked him, took the things out of the pockets and handed the jacket to him.

By the time he had finished his breakfast it was returned to him with madame's apologies that she had not made a better job of it. He sent renewed thanks. As a matter of detail he could hardly see where the cut had been. Most French housewives are clever with their needles.

By this time the rest of the party had trickled in and were being served with their breakfasts. Ginger stayed speaking with them for a few minutes in order not to appear unfriendly; but as soon as he could conveniently do so he made his way to the town and in the main thoroughfare soon found what he was looking for—a garage. There was no difficulty about hiring a car to go to Nice airport and straight back. He was soon on his way, travelling at a speed faster than he would have wished, although he was in a hurry to return in case the expected telegram from Biggles arrived. It was eleven o'clock when the car came in sight of the aerodrome. A glance told him all he needed to know. The Dove was still there, in the same place.

So Canson hadn't gone home. This rather surprised him. What reason, he wondered, had the pilots for remaining in Nice?

He returned forthwith to Antibes and got the driver to drop him off as near as possible to the hostel. Another car was already standing on the rough gravel drive. A frown creased his forehead as he observed the registration that it was the car Canson had taken when he had left the airport to go into Nice; but before he could consider what this might imply he saw Canson, alone, come out of the hostel. This startled him. So the car was not a coincidence. What was Canson doing there? The caretaker had said he never visited the hostel.

As Ginger walked past the car he glanced in it. The driver was in his seat smoking a cigarette, and Ginger had a twinge of alarm when he saw a young man, with a wisp of black moustache, wearing a black beret. Was this the man . . .? but Ginger comforted himself with the thought that the description would fit a million Frenchmen. He went on to where, looking anything but amiable, Canson stood waiting for him; in fact, staring at him harder than was polite. Why stare? What was he looking at?

Canson greeted him curtly with the words: 'Where have you been?'

Ginger's eyes opened wide. 'To Nice. Why? Is something wrong?'

'You've kept me hanging about——'

'*I've* kept you?'

'Yes. I've had a message from London, a phone call. Your brother is seriously ill and you're to go home at once.'

'That's too bad. What stinking luck.' Ginger was thinking, so instead of sending a telegram Biggles had got in touch through the Sunnitours office.

'Naturally, I came to see if you would decide to go home, in which case I'd fly you.'

'Thanks. I'm sorry. But how was I to know——'

'Why did you rush off to Nice so early?'

'To have a look round.'

'The caretaker here tells me you were in Nice last night.'

'That's right.'

'Did you get involved in some sort of accident?'

'No. Why?'

'Madame here tells me you ripped your sleeve. She mended it for you.'

Ginger's uneasiness was rapidly becoming alarm. Why this interrogation? 'Yes,' he said. 'It was most kind of her.'

'You should be more careful. Remember, we're responsible for you while you're here.'

'I'm perfectly capable of taking care of myself,' retorted Ginger.

'What were you doing in Nice, anyway?'

'Having a look round. Exploring if you like. It's a civilized city, isn't it?'

'I suppose so. But let's not waste any more of my time. I'm due back. Do you want to go home?'

'I suppose I shall have to.'

'All right. You can come with me. Get your baggage. To save

time I've got your passport. The police were here checking when I arrived. Here it is. Take it, and keep it handy. We don't want a hold-up at the airport.'

'Thanks. I'll just get my things. Shan't keep you more than a couple of minutes.'

Ginger walked quickly to his room with his brain racing. Had he made a slip somewhere? What was the purpose of this questioning? Clearly, Canson was suspicious. How suspicious? Of what? Why? He remembered the driver of Canson's car. Was it the man who had tried to knife him in Nice? It was an uncomfortable thought. Canson obviously intended to use the car to take them both to the airport. At least, that was the declared intention. But once he was in the car where would it take him? So ran Ginger's thoughts, wildly, as he flung his things in his bag. If anything happened to him, should he fail to return home, Biggles would soon be looking for him. One of the places he would check was here, the hostel. Could he leave a message— in case?

There was no question of writing a letter. He daren't leave it here. He wouldn't have a chance to post it. There was no time for that, anyway. Canson, already impatient, was waiting. He would wonder what he was doing.

Ginger, thinking desperately, could see only one way he might get a message to Biggles should he come to the hostel and look over his room. It was a slim chance but it was better than no chance at all. He could write on the wall. Somewhere inconspicuous, where the woman cleaning would not notice it. To write it in clear English might do more harm than good should the caretaker or his wife notice it. He could write it in code, using one of the simple rough and ready methods Biggles had sometimes used in an emergency. Put the first letter of a word last and add any two letters. To decode, delete the last two letters and then put the last letter first.

Ginger whipped out his pencil, and choosing a spot on the wall where the shadow of the window curtain fell, wrote swiftly:

HOTOSPAN HOPSEL UERIX ALDINIBEL ICENOR
                                                        GINGER

He was thinking, of course, that should Canson not go to the airport he would be taken to the scene of his overnight adventure.

This done he snatched up his bag and went out. 'Okay,' he said briskly. 'I'm ready.'

'Is that all the luggage you've got?' asked Canson, looking with surprise at Ginger's bag.

'It's enough for a warm climate,' returned Ginger.

They got in the car. It turned and set off, heading for Nice, Ginger wondering if he had been wise to accept Canson's invitation. But he felt in duty bound to follow Biggles' orders and return home as arranged.

As they sped along the coast road with the blue sea on their right, thoughts continued to race through his head. If Canson was not actually suspicious he was behaving in a very odd manner. The man in the driving seat: was he really the man with the knife? If he was had he been brought along to identify him as the spy in the Rue Baldini? What had put Canson on the track? Where had he slipped up? Had he in giving the old woman money made a bigger blunder than he had supposed? It would suggest he had not been long in France or he would have put the English coins away to prevent confusion.

Canson broke into his thoughts. 'I see from your passport you're a student.'

'Yes.' This was the occupation shown in Ginger's civil passport. Why, Ginger wondered, had Canson troubled to read his passport? He must have seen his address, Biggles' flat in Mayfair.

This was quickly confirmed.

'I see you live in Mount Street,' remarked Canson, his eyes on the road ahead.

'Yes.'

'Expensive area.'

'What about it?' inquired Ginger coldly, feeling that Canson was getting too personal.

'Oh, nothing. I just thought that if you can afford to live in exclusive quarters you could afford a holiday on the same lines, instead of the cheapest on the market.'

'Have you any objection?'

'Of course not. Don't be so touchy. I was only making conversation.'

Nothing more was said, which suited Ginger, who wanted to think.

He was a little surprised, and it must be admitted more than somewhat relieved, when the car turned into the airport. That could only mean they were really going home. The car was dismissed and they walked on, Ginger wondering why Canson carried no baggage. Had he brought his bag in earlier? He was thinking particularly of the bag he had carried away from the photographic shop in the Rue Baldini.

He noted that Canson seemed to be well known to the airport officials most of whom gave him a nod or word of greeting. For that reason perhaps Ginger was only given a cursory glance in the Customs office. He was not asked to open his bag. He showed his passport and they proceeded to the aircraft. It was all easy and casual.

Just as they reached the Dove, Rawlings got down from the cabin. It struck Ginger that he did this hurriedly, as if unprepared for their arrival. He had a screwdriver in his hand, and it seemed to Ginger, who in his nervous state was keyed up to be suspicious of anything, that he tried to prevent the tool from being seen, holding it straight down by the side of his leg. No comment was made about this. Canson merely said: 'Everything ready?'

'All set,' answered Rawlings.

Canson turned to Ginger, saying: 'Get in. You'll have the cabin to yourself.' He smiled bleakly. 'You're getting VIP treatment.'

'Sorry to cause you so much trouble,' returned Ginger.

'No trouble at all. I was going home anyway.'

Ginger got in, taking his bag with him, and dropped into a seat.

During the next few minutes, while final preparations were made for departure, his eyes were busy. He could see no other luggage so he assumed Canson and Rawlings had put their stuff in the luggage compartment, which, after all, was natural enough. He was still puzzled about Rawlings' screwdriver. What could he have been doing in the cabin with such a tool? Screws may have needed tightening; but where were they? He couldn't see any.

The engines had been started. Both Canson and Rawlings were in the cockpit. The machine taxied slowly to a runway. There was a brief delay, apparently while they waited for permission to take off, then they were away, with the sparkling Mediterranean on their left and the gaunt grey peaks of the Alpes Maritimes to their right. Airborne, the Dove turned slowly north.

Now that he had plenty of time Ginger settled down to do some serious thinking, to sort out, he hoped, his doubts and suspicions, and to try to make sense of the events that had occurred during his brief stay on the French Riviera.

He was concerned, and perhaps a little worried, by Canson's questioning, but he was not alarmed for his personal safety. He would have been had he been taken to the Rue Baldini, or anywhere else in the Old Quarter of Nice. But he was now in a British aircraft bound for England, and even though Canson might be engaged in an illegal practice he could not imagine him resorting to physical violence even were he given the opportunity, which in the circumstances seemed unlikely. He assumed they would land at Millham.

Perhaps because he was anxious to see Biggles and make his report the flight seemed a long one, and it was with satisfaction that from an altitude of about six thousand feet he saw the grey waters of the English Channel creep up over the horizon. The white cliffs of Dover, one of the best known landmarks in the world, enabled him to make a rough guess at the course the aircraft was taking, and although Canson was keeping well to the east he saw no reason to change his opinion about their objective.

They were opposite the Thames estuary and beginning slowly to lose height when the door opened and Canson came into the

cabin, evidently leaving Rawlings in control. Taking the seat
next to Ginger on the opposite side of the gangway he looked at
him with a peculiar expression.

'Everything all right?' he inquired.

'No complaints,' answered Ginger, wondering what was
coming next.

'To save any argument when we're on the ground I want you
to tell me something while we can talk here in private,' went on
Canson.

'What do you want to know?'

'Last night, in Nice, you went into the Old Town.'

'Correct.'

'What took you there?'

'Call it curiosity.'

'Why did you go to the Rue Baldini?'

'Did I?'

'You did.'

'In that slum, to me one street was like another,' parried
Ginger.

'If I say you went to the Rue Baldini you wouldn't deny it?'

'No. So what?'

'You gave an old woman some money?'

'Okay. So I gave an old woman some money. What about it?
It was my own money.'

'I want to know why you went there.'

'Why do you want to know?'

'Don't quibble. I'm asking the questions. What were you
looking for?'

'Just a minute,' protested Ginger. 'I can go where I like. What
are you getting at?'

Canson's voice took on a harder note. 'Answer my question.'

'Why should I?'

'Because I say so.'

'And who do you think you are to question where I go and
what I do? What makes you so certain that I was in the Rue
Baldini, anyhow?'

'This,' replied Canson softly. Reaching out he took the lower part of Ginger's right hand sleeve and turned it over to show the cuff buttons. There should have been three. There were only two. Opening his left hand Canson very deliberately put a button on the spot where the missing one had been torn off. It matched—exactly.

Ginger realized of course what had happened. The button had been pulled off in the struggle, when his arms had been held. One of his assailants had found it.

'Is that your button?' asked Canson coldly.

'It looks like it.'

'You know damn well it is.'

'Very well. So it's my button. What about it?'

'That,' replied Canson succinctly, 'is what I'm asking you. And you'd be well advised to give me the answer. Now, what were you doing in the Rue Baldini?'

'I'll give you two guesses.'

Canson got up. 'Okay, if that's how you feel. We shall be landing in about ten minutes. That'll give you time to think things over. Some friends of mine will be meeting us. You may find them less patient than me.'

He went back to the cockpit.

6

MR X

THE arrival of the Dove over its base at Millham found Ginger looking at the ground with considerable interest. The plane had come straight in without landing at a Customs airport for inspection. This could only mean, or should mean, that an officer would be here to carry out the check—that is, if Canson's story of how his machines operated was true. Seeing no preparations Ginger began to wonder. It seemed preposterous to call in an officer for one passenger. Yet he found it hard to believe that Canson would dare risk losing his licence by flagrantly breaking regulations. If he did that it meant he was seriously concerned about something.

The fact of the matter was, after Canson's threatening behaviour he had been relying on Customs officials to get him out of trouble. Now it looked as if there would be no inspection. Canson had said friends would be there to meet them. As they glided in he could see only one man, presumably Tomlin, the other mechanic, as he wore overalls.

Ginger was uneasy, but not seriously worried. He was now convinced that Canson was engaged in a big-money racket, but he could not believe that he would go so far as to murder him. Yet what else could he do to silence him? It would, he thought, be interesting to see what happened next. Come what may he was determined to see the business through, although he would of course have preferred to make his report to Biggles and leave the next move to him.

The afternoon was well advanced when the Dove touched down and without stopping taxied straight on into the hangar, a procedure for which Ginger was unprepared, so unusual was it. Before he had time to realize what this might imply the door had been opened and Canson stood there, a pocket-sized automatic in his hand. Using it to wave him down Canson said in a brittle voice: 'All right. Come on out.'

Ginger could only comply. There was no point in remaining in the aircraft, anyway. But he felt obliged to register a protest, as the natural thing to do. 'What's the big idea?' he demanded, in a voice high with indignation.

'You'll see,' answered Canson curtly.

'You'll be sorry for this,' promised Ginger. 'I'll report you——'

'Don't argue.'

Ginger jumped down.

Instantly he was seized by two men who, although he hadn't seen them, must have been waiting in the hangar. He did not resist, knowing it to be futile. With the mechanic there were four of them, including Canson, who kept him covered at short range with his automatic. The mechanic, approaching from behind, put a scarf, or a bag, over his head, blindfolding him.

'Walk,' ordered Canson.

Ginger, guided by a man on either side holding an arm, walked, his chief reaction to this treatment being astonishment that Canson should go to such lengths. He did not have to walk far. He was bundled into a car, still with a man on each side. The doors slammed. It moved off.

He made only one remark during the drive that followed. Speaking calmly he said: 'Would you mind telling me what this is about? Who do you think I am?'

The answer he got was: 'You'll find out.' He did not know the voice, so he did not know if Canson was in the car.

As near as he could judge he was travelling for about twenty minutes. This told him little, because the car might have gone straight to its objective, or, on the other hand, it might have gone round in circles to confuse him. He tried to memorize the turns, but this is harder to do in practice than in theory. Again, little reliance could be put on this. The car might be crossing its own tracks. During the journey he saw nothing.

It came to an end. He was pulled out. He was marched up steps. He counted four. Then floor covering under his feet told him he was in a house. Then came stairs. Fourteen. The scarf was removed and he found himself in a bedroom with his two guides. For the first time he was able to have a good look at them. As they backed to the door one said: 'Don't try to leave by the window. The dogs are savage.'

They went out. Ginger heard the door locked. He went straight to the window hoping to get an idea of his whereabouts. He learned little. He saw he was in a country house of some size standing in its own grounds. It was, as far as he could see, surrounded by trees. They cut off his view. A gravel drive disappeared from sight into them. He tried to open the window in order that, by leaning out, he would get a wider picture: but it was fixed by an anti-burglar device which needed a key to open it.

He understood the warning about the dogs when there walked into his range of vision, close to the house, three Alsatians. He was not likely to invite their attentions because, as he had

realized from the stairs, he was on the first floor, with a long drop
to ground level. He could not see what was immediately below
the window.

He sat on the bed to think about the whole situation.

One thing was clear. This was no minor racket run by Canson,
who might, or might not, be in the house. He didn't know. Not
that it mattered particularly. Up to the moment it had been
supposed that Canson was the head man of the show. Ginger
now had doubts. It began to look as if he had broken into a
criminal organization on a much larger scale than there had
been reason to suspect. There was big money behind it. The
house he was in, for instance. Aircraft are expensive both to buy
and maintain. There was the house in the Rue Baldini, in Nice.
There might be another establishment in Switzerland, since the
company's planes went there. It was not surprising that Ginger
began to wonder how far the ramifications of the organization
extended.

What was going on? What were these people doing? He still
had no idea. There were several of them in it. Smuggling? It
would have to be on a big scale to be worth while. Drug running?
On a small scale it wouldn't pay all these people; yet on a big
scale the Anti-Narcotics Bureau would soon get wind of it. He
would have heard about it at the Yard. A spy ring? That was
possible because it could have the backing of a hostile government. But would Canson, who after all was British, sink as low as
that? Crime was one thing. Treason, a very different matter.

Ginger was alone for about an hour. Then his two guards
reappeared to say they had come to take him downstairs.
Someone wanted to see him. This was said quietly, without
threats or a hint of violence.

Ginger went with them, downstairs, presently to be shown
into a large, comfortable room, expensively furnished as a
library. There was one person there, a man seated in an arm-
chair with both hands resting on an ebony, gold-mounted
walking-stick. He was dressed in a single garment; a loose-fitting
dressing-gown of black velvet. But the most unusual, not to say
disconcerting, thing about him was the fact that he wore a black

silk mask. For this reason only the lower part of his face could be seen; but the impression Ginger got was of a frail, elderly man, possibly an invalid.

He made a signal to the guards to retire. When they had gone he indicated another arm-chair and said in a pleasant, cultured voice: 'Sit down young man. I want to talk to you. Would you care for a drink?'

'Thanks. I would very much like a cup of tea,' answered Ginger, who realized this was where he would have to keep his wits about him. He had a vague idea of the purpose of this interview. It would, he suspected, be more of an interrogation. And it soon turned out he was right.

The man touched a bell at his elbow. It was answered. Ginger couldn't see by whom as the door was behind him.

'Mr Hebblethwaite would like some tea,' said the man in the mask.

'Yes, sir.'

The velvet glove method, thought Ginger. While they were waiting he said: 'I have also some questions to ask you, if you're the man responsible for having me brought here. If the purpose of the mask you're wearing is to intimidate me, it fails.'

'Its purpose is to prevent you from seeing my face.'

'After what has happened you have good reason.'

A tray with a pot of tea, cakes and biscuits, was put on a small table within easy reach of Ginger's chair.

'Do please help yourself,' said the man. 'And now let us get on. I am going to ask you some questions, and it will save trouble all round if you will answer them briefly and truthfully. According to your passport you are a student. What are you studying?'

'My passport is my private property, and the particulars it gives are no concern of yours,' answered Ginger stiffly.

'That is where you are mistaken. Let us put it this way. For whom are you working? Could it by any chance be a newspaper?'

'Instead of asking personal questions don't you think it's time you gave me an explanation of——'

'All in good time. I shall get the answers to these questions, you may be sure. I hoped you would save my time, and your own, by providing them here and now. Be reasonable, and try to see things from my point of view. I run a big business, a secret business if you like, for which I take every possible step to prevent my methods becoming known to my competitors. You have chosen to interfere. Let us start at the beginning. You went to France with the deliberate intention of prying into my affairs— no, don't waste your breath denying it. Naturally, I am anxious to know what interests you represent. It is also of importance to me to know what gave you the idea that the Sunnitours Travel Agency might not be all that it purported to be.'

'Isn't it? I gathered the impression it was a genuine concern; and I still have no reason to think otherwise.'

'That's very interesting. Then why didn't you go to the Antibes hostel with the rest of the party?'

'I thought I was free to go anywhere. There was nothing in the rules about staying under supervision. I decided to have a look at Nice.'

'And instead of staying in the sophisticated quarter, as would have been natural for a tourist, you went directly to that most insalubrious area, the Old Town. Why?' The speaker's eyes never for a moment left Ginger's face.

By this time Ginger was convinced of one thing. His questioner was worried, or he wouldn't go to this trouble to ascertain who he was and why he went to Nice.

Said Ginger: 'I wouldn't say I went directly to the Old Town. When I left the plane I took a taxi. It dropped me on the front. After that I really had no idea of where I was going.'

'Why did you choose the Rue Baldini?'

'Where's that?'

'In the Old Town. The street where you had some trouble.'

'I see what you mean. I didn't choose to go there.'

'What made you decide to go there?'

'If anything it was the pilot of the plane.'

'That's very interesting. How did it happen?'

'I thought I recognized him. I saw him turn into a dark street and wondered what there was in it worth seeing. A night club, or something of that sort, perhaps.'

'I'd like to believe that. But wouldn't it be more correct to say you followed Mr Canson?'

'Who's he?' inquired Ginger, feigning ignorance.

'The pilot.'

'Well yes, I suppose that's right. I've already said so.'

'What made you stop where he stopped?'

'To see what there was there. To look where he'd gone. I can't see anything strange about that. There was an old woman sitting in an alley. I didn't see her until she spoke. She begged for money. I gave her some and went on.'

'Then you came back. Why?'

'I didn't want to lose my way. I decided to go back to the main road. The next thing I knew I was set upon by a couple of ruffians. The old woman was in with them. She must have fetched them from somewhere. I managed to get away.'

'And ran for your life.'

'Wouldn't you?'

The man smiled.

Ginger perceived that Canson had lost no time in telling his questioner all that had happened in Nice.

The man went on. 'I see you're a smart lad; but not smart enough, I'm afraid, to undertake that sort of job that took you to Nice. Who sent you?'

'Why should anyone send me?'

'That's what I'm asking you.'

Ginger decided to take a new line, and in a way carry war into enemy country. He might be able to give the man opposite more food for thought. It was dangerous, but his position could hardly be worse than it was.

'All right,' he said. 'I'll be frank with you. The man responsible for me going into the Old Town was Canson.'

'Ah! So you knew his name all the time.'

'I did. But when he was first mentioned I decided it wasn't for me to say what I knew about him.'

'What do you mean by that?'

'Do you insist on knowing?'

'I do.'

'Very well. I recognized Canson at the aerodrome. We were in the Air Force at the same time, so, naturally, I knew about his record. But perhaps you knew about that.'

'About what?' The masked man was frowning.

'His court martial.'

'What did he do?'

'He had been in trouble before for helping himself to government property, but his worst effort was when, as Mess Secretary, he faked the accounts of other officers to pay his own mess bill.'

'Indeed. I find that most interesting. Go on.'

'At Millham I was surprised to see he was still flying. Later, seeing him in Nice, I wondered what he was up to.'

'I see. And you decided to do a little private detective work, eh?'

'Say I was curious. I'm still on the Reserve of Officers.'

'What did you discover?'

'Nothing.'

'Is that true?'

'Absolutely. You know what happened. I lost sight of him in the Old Town and I didn't see him again until he came to the hostel this morning to fetch me.'

'That reminds me. Who sent the message asking you to come home?'

'Ask Canson. He told me he took the message over the phone, but he didn't say who sent it. Of course, he may not have known. Someone must have gone to the Sunnitours office in London asking if it was possible to get a message through to me. That could have been one of several people.'

'Are you saying you didn't expect to see Canson at the hostel?'

'I am. Why should I? It was a surprise to me. And now I've told you all I know will you please tell me what all this is about? And as you brought me here by force perhaps you'll be kind enough to find me transport to the nearest railway station. I'm anxious to get on home.'

'There's no hurry. I'm glad to be able to tell you your brother is out of danger.'

'I'm relieved to hear it,' returned Ginger, knowing this was a lie, as he had no brother. 'And after all this isn't it time you told me your name, for future reference?'

'Call me Mr X.'

'You're making this sound very melodramatic. Is it necessary?'

'Very much so,' was the dry retort. 'But forget about that. In the circumstances there appears to be no reason why you shouldn't return to Nice and finish your holiday. That's up to you. We can't expect Sunnitours to lay on a special plane, but no doubt Mr Canson will be going back to Nice in a day or two.'

'It seems hardly worth while.'

'You could stay here, handy for the aerodrome, until a plane is ready.'

'I'd rather go home.'

Mr X shook his head. 'I'm sorry, but I can't allow you to do that.'

'But this is monstrous. You can't hold me here against my will!'

'I'm afraid I shall have to.'

'Why?'

'Purely as a safety precaution to protect my business. I shall have to make further inquiries about you.'

'You've no right to keep me here.'

'It isn't a matter of right, young man. It's a matter of necessity.'

'Haven't I told you enough?'

'No. What you have told me sounds plausible but I'm not altogether satisfied.'

'Aren't you afraid I shall kick up a fuss about this?'

'Not in the least. If my inquiries about you confirm your story I shall recompense you for any inconvenience I may have caused you. If, on the other hand, you turn out to be a spy, I shall have no alternative than to see you are never able to report what you know to anyone. I trust I have made myself clear. That's all for now.'

Mr X touched a bell.

The guards came in. Ginger was returned to his room.

7
BIGGLES IS WORRIED

A LITTLE after nine o'clock the morning after Ginger's departure, as soon as he thought the Sunnitours office would be open,
Biggles sent the message as arranged. He had discussed this with
Bertie and reached the decision that the most satisfactory way to
do this might be through the Sunnitours organization which
would be in touch with both Millham aerodrome and the hostel
in the South of France. At all events he would speak to them and
accept their advice.

He called them on the telephone, and having explained the
fictitious accident asked that Mr Hebblethwaite be brought
home forthwith. Somewhat to his surprise, and certainly to his
gratification, the office manager, to whom he spoke, could not
have been more helpful. He said he would attend to it at once. It
could be left to him. He would speak to Mr Canson, the pilot.
They could expect Mr Hebblethwaite home some time later in
the day.

This was easier than Biggles had expected. He thought some
excuse would be made for a delay. Well satisfied he thanked the
manager for his co-operation and congratulated the travel
agency on its efficiency.

What he did not realize, of course, was that Canson was still in
Nice. When the manager had said he would call him on the
phone he supposed it would be at Millham aerodrome. The
whole idea of the scheme was that Canson would fly out in the
Auster, which he said was maintained for such emergencies, and
bring Ginger home. In that way Ginger would have seen the full
service in operation. Not for a moment did it occur to Biggles that
Canson might still be in Nice, and that Ginger would be flown
home in the machine used for the outward journey. The Dove.

So easily can misunderstandings occur to thwart the best laid plans.

Later, when he realized what had happened, he blamed himself for departing from the original project, which was to make contact directly with Ginger by telegram and leave him to make the arrangement about coming home. However, Sunnitours had the facilities, and seemed so anxious to oblige that he did not hesitate to accept their offer.

It was not long before he had cause to suspect that something had gone wrong.

As they had nothing urgently needing attention he suggested they might fly over Millham and check the time of departure of Canson's Auster—as they supposed. This would give them a rough idea of the time Ginger might be expected back.

They did this, Biggles' only fear being that Canson would have left for France before their arrival over the airfield. This apparently had not happened, because when, flying high, they cruised past, the Auster could be seen standing on the tarmac. The engine was dead. There was no one in sight, but Canson's Rolls could be seen standing beside the hangar.

Biggles saw nothing strange in this. His only remark was 'He's late getting away. If he leaves it much longer it'll take him all his time to get back before dark.'

'I can't see the Dove,' said Bertie.

'It's probably in the hangar,' returned Biggles. 'If it isn't wanted there would be no reason to bring it out.'

From which it may be judged that Biggles still had no suspicion of the truth.

He flew on for a little while and then made a wide sweep back. Nothing had changed. The Auster still stood in the same place, engines silent. There was no sign of activity.

'Considering I told the man at Sunnitours that the matter was urgent Canson seems to be treating the job pretty casually,' said Biggles irritably. 'I'm beginning to wish I'd sent the wire direct to Ginger.'

'Maybe they're busy in the London office and the message to Canson got held up,' offered Bertie by way of explanation.

'It could hardly have been held up all this time. But this is like Canson. He never hurried over anything unless it suited him.'

Again Biggles flew on, anxious not to give the impression that he was hanging about in the vicinity of the aerodrome in case Canson should wonder what the machine was doing. This time he was away for about twenty minutes. When he returned it was to see a man get into the Auster, start the engines and taxi slowly into the hangar.

'There's something wrong about this,' declared Biggles.

'Absolutely.'

'If that aircraft was going anywhere today there'd be no point in putting it back in the hangar.'

'It looks to me as if the fellow who's just put it away is going off duty,' observed Bertie. 'There he goes, on a motor bike. Why not land to see what goes on?'

'No. What reason could we give Canson for turning up again so soon? We couldn't ask him what we want to know. To land would do more harm than good.'

'Canson may not be there.'

'His car's there.'

'True enough.'

I think our best bet is to go to the Sunnitours office and make inquiries there. They're bound to know what has happened. There may be a simple explanation.'

'You don't think anything could have happened to Ginger?'

'Of course not. How could anything have happened to him? No. It's just that the arrangements Sunnitours said they'd make haven't worked out. One can't rely on anybody any more.'

Biggles headed for home. By this time it was after two o'clock, so they had lunch before going on by taxi to the Sunnitours office.

'We shall have to be a bit cagey about the questions we ask,' said Biggles, as they went in. 'I hope we don't bump into Canson. That would throw a spanner in the gears. There's just a chance he might be here.'

'We saw his car at Millham.'

'He could have got here by now.'

In the event this awkward situation did not arise.

To the smiling girl who came forward to attend to them Biggles said: 'I'm the man who rang you up this morning about bringing home Mr Hebblethwaite, who was on yesterday's tour to the Riviera. His brother——'

'Oh, yes. I know all about it,' broke in the girl, brightly.

'Good. I've just looked in to make sure you were able to fix things up.'

'Don't worry. Everything's been taken care of.'

'Can you give me an idea of what time I can expect Mr Hebblethwaite home?'

'I can't say exactly. Some time this afternoon, or this evening at latest. It would depend on what time the plane started. The pilot, Mr Canson, was anxious to make an early start.'

Biggles looked puzzled. 'Are you sure of that?'

'I wouldn't say so if I wasn't sure. I spoke to Mr Canson myself, soon after you rang up. He said he'd slip along to the hostel, pick up your friend and fly him home.'

'I don't quite understand. If he was at Millham how could he slip along to the hostel——'

'But he wasn't at Millham. I caught him at his hotel in Nice.'

'You mean . . . he didn't come home last night.'

'That's right. He stayed in Nice. He often does that.'

'I see,' said Biggles slowly, understanding now why the Auster was still at Millham. 'I suppose that means he'll fly home in the plane he took out.'

'Exactly. It was lucky he stayed, otherwise it would have meant a special journey.'

'That's what I imagined would happen. Not knowing the facts, perhaps I was anxious, I jumped to the wrong conclusion.'

'You'll find it'll be quite all right,' asserted the girl cheerfully. 'We'll have your friend home as soon as possible. Mr Canson may be back a little later than usual because of his having to go to the hostel at Antibes to collect him. It's some little way from Nice. Then again, there's always a chance that Mr Hebblethwaite may have gone out, in which case he'd either have to wait or go to look for him, perhaps at the beach.'

'Of course,' agreed Biggles. 'I realize that. Well, thanks very much for being patient with me.'

'It's been a pleasure. That's what I'm here for you know. Don't worry. The plane might be back any time now, if it isn't back already.'

'How will Mr Hebblethwaite get to London? Can you provide transport?'

'Naturally. It's part of our service. No doubt Mr Canson will fix that.'

'Good. That's a load off my mind. Thanks again.'

'Don't mention it.'

Biggles and Bertie went out into the street.

'What do you make of that?' asked Bertie, as they waited to pick up a cruising taxi.

'I don't quite know what to make of it, and that's a fact,' answered Biggles thoughtfully. 'I'm pretty sure of one thing. That girl was telling the truth as far as she knew it. If there was anything funny going on she wouldn't have been so frank.'

'But you're not altogether happy about it?'

'I am not. Things haven't worked out as I planned; but how was I to know Canson would stay the night in Nice? Even so, if he did what he said he would do I should have thought Ginger would be back by now. There's something about this that doesn't quite add up. I'll tell you what. You fly down to Millham and cast an eye over the tarmac to see if the Dove is back. Don't go too low. There's just a remote chance that it had engine trouble and dropped in somewhere to get it put right. I'll go to the Yard and wait in the office in case Ginger turns up, or phones to say he's at home.'

'Good enough, old boy.'

They took the first taxi that came along and went to Scotland Yard. There Bertie took his own car to get to the operations airfield. Biggles went to his office, and before doing anything else rang the Operations Room to order an aircraft to be ready for Bertie when he arrived. There was nothing more he could do.

Thinking the matter over it was easy to understand how his plan had miscarried; but he still could not see how the ultimate result had been affected. It simply meant that Ginger would return in the Dove, which was on the spot, instead of being fetched in the Auster kept for emergencies. It seemed not unreasonable that Canson would spend the night in Nice.

Time passed. There was no word from Ginger. He was getting really worried when Bertie walked in.

'Well?' queried Biggles quickly.

'The Dove's back.'

'It is!'

'Yes. I think it must have been back some time. It wasn't on the tarmac. It had been pulled into the hangar, but the doors were wide open so I could just see its tail.'

'Was anyone about?'

'Not a soul.'

'Was Canson's car still there?'

'No. It had gone.'

Biggles sat back, shaking his head. 'There's still something about this I don't understand. If Ginger came home in the Dove he should be here by now. Put it like this. I rang Sunnitours this morning just after nine. The girl has told us she spoke to Canson, in Nice, right away. He said he'd go straight along to pick up Ginger. Allow half an hour for him to get to Antibes and the same time to get back to Nice airport. The Dove should have got away by ten-thirty. Call it eleven o'clock. The Dove cruises at a hundred and eighty. Giving it four hours to get home it should have touched down at Millham by three. It's now after seven. Surely it wouldn't take Ginger four hours to get here from Millham?'

'There may not have been transport available.'

'The girl in the office said transport would be provided. What about Canson's car? If he didn't bring Ginger to London he could have run him to the nearest railway station. Anyhow, had there been a delay Ginger could have phoned us to say he was back and might be late.'

'I think you're worrying yourself unnecessarily. What's on your mind?'

'I'm beginning to wonder if Ginger came home in the Dove.'

'Oh, but here, come off it, old boy. With the Dove already at Nice, why on earth shouldn't he come home in it? Canson was bound to come home. There'd be no sense in sending out the Auster.'

'Forget the Auster. It wasn't sent out. We know that. We saw it.'

'Okay, laddie. Have it your way. I still say Ginger will turn up presently with a perfectly natural explanation to account for the hold-up.'

Biggles shrugged and lit a cigarette. 'Well, there's nothing more we can do for the moment. We'll hang on. I agree, there's still a chance he may walk in.'

A long pause. Then Bertie said: 'If anything fishy happened on the flight Ginger may be doing a spot of scouting at Millham.'

'Yes, I suppose that could happen,' conceded Biggles. 'But I find it hard to believe.'

'Why?'

'Because if Ginger saw anything irregular he'd come back here hot foot to let me know.'

They waited until eight-thirty. Ginger did not come. They went home to the flat hoping they might find him there. He was not there.

'It's no use kidding ourselves any longer,' said Biggles grimly. 'He's not coming home tonight or he'd have been here before this.'

'When Canson went to Antibes to fetch him he may have found he'd gone out for the day.'

'He wouldn't go out for the day.'

'Why not?'

'Because he was expecting a telegram from me.'

'Yes, of course. I'd forgotten that. It was just an idea. What are we going to do about it?'

'We'll go out and have a meal. If he isn't here when we get back we'll start thinking seriously.'

'I say it's too soon to get upset. After all, you know how messages can get scrambled. I'd make a bet he's still at the hostel wondering why you didn't send the telegram.'

'I hope you're right. It's too late to do anything tonight, but if he isn't back by the morning I'm flying to France to cast an eye over this hostel set-up. The first thing is to satisfy ourselves he isn't there.'

'And if he isn't?'

'We shall have to find out what time he left, and with whom.'

'If the show is crooked we can't expect the people in charge of the hostel to tell us anything.'

'There were other people on the flight. They can't all be crooked. We could rely on them to tell us all they know about Ginger's movements.'

'Before we dash off why not have a word with the Sunnitours office here in London. They'd know if Ginger flew back in the Dove.'

'I don't see why they should. All they'll know is what Canson cares to tell them. They might believe him, but I wouldn't.'

'Then let's tackle Canson and get the truth out of him.'

'I've already said, the last thing you're likely to get out of Canson is the truth,' declared Biggles. 'The more he knows the less likely will he be to talk. He's a dead loss. Once he is suspicious of us the harder will it be to get to the bottom of this business. Let's go out and have something to eat.'

8

THE MYSTERY DEEPENS

BIGGLES went to bed late, having waited in vain for Ginger. He was up early, still to no purpose. Bertie, hearing him moving about, rose to find him brooding over a cup of tea and a cigarette.

'So he hasn't come,' said Bertie.

'Not a sign.'

'What can have happened to him?'

'I've been turning over in my mind the possibilities, but it's all guesswork. He may have tried watching Canson and went too far. That would lead to trouble. The devil of it is, if that did

happen, it could have been in France or in England. We don't
know, and the only way we shall find out is by trying both ends of
the Sunnitours airline for a clue. I feel like trying the hostel at
Antibes first. We do at least know he went to France, but we
don't know if he came back. I'll ask the switchboard at the Yard
to let the Air Commodore know what we're doing; then we'll get
cracking.'

By seven o'clock they were on their way. They landed at Nice
at eleven. After the usual formalities, simplified by their Interpol
carnets, they took a taxi and went straight to the hostel. Doors and
windows were open but there was no one about. As they paused
to survey the place a woman came out to shake a duster. She was
a buxom, cheerful-looking housewife type who smiled when she
saw them.

Biggles addressed her, speaking of course in French. '*Bon jour,
madame*. Do you work here, if I may ask?'

'*Oui, monsieur.*'

'I think a friend of ours is staying here. As we were in Nice we
thought we would call on him.'

'Everyone has gone to the beach for the day, to bathe.'

'Ah, yes. I should have expected that.'

'What is the name of your friend?'

'Monsieur Hebblethwaite. You know him? He arrived with
the last party from England.'

'Certainly. But he is not here now.'

'Where is he?'

'He has gone home.'

'So soon?'

'His brother is ill.'

'Did he tell you that?'

'No. Monsieur Canson, who is the pilot of the plane. He came
here to fetch him.'

'When was this?'

'Yesterday morning.'

'What time?'

The woman shrugged expressive shoulders. 'I couldn't
say exactly. It was soon after breakfast, when I had mended

his coat.'

'Monsieur Hebblethwaite's coat?'

'Yes. Then he went out for a little while. When he came back Monsieur Canson was here, waiting, very annoyed because he was ready to fly back to England.'

'Why did you have to mend the coat?'

'The sleeve was torn. A long cut.'

'Did he say how that happened?'

'He told me he did it in Nice, before he came here.'

'Then he didn't come straight here from the airport with the rest of the party?'

'No. He asked my husband, who drives the car that meets the plane at the airport, if he could take a walk in Nice and find his own way here when he was ready.'

'That's right, *monsieur*,' said a man who had come out of the building to join the party. He wore a white apron.

'Are you the driver?'

'*Oui, monsieur*.' The man grinned. 'One of my jobs. I told the young man he could do anything he liked. I gave him exact directions for finding us before I left him outside the airport. He must have stayed in Nice for a long time. It was late when he got here.' The man winked. 'I think perhaps he had a little fun.'

'Why do you think that?'

'He has a bruise on his face.'

The woman came back. 'Dinner was finished when he came, but he had some food and then went to bed.'

Said the man: 'I noticed the tear in his jacket and said *madame* would be happy to mend it for him.'

'And then what happened?' prompted Biggles, finding the people friendly and frank.

The woman continued. 'He was up early for his coffee. Then he went out. He came back in a taxi.'

'Do you know where he went?'

'No, *monsieur*. He did not say. In the meantime Monsieur Canson had arrived. He told me that Monsieur Hebblethwaite might wish to go home and he had come to fetch him. He was angry at being kept waiting.'

'Did he have to wait long?'

'No. But he was in a hurry. He asked me for the passport of Monsieur Hebblethwaite to save time when he came.'

'Did you give it to him?'

'Yes. I had taken the particulars.'

'Then what happened?'

'They spoke for a little while. Then Monsieur Hebblethwaite packed his bag and they went away together in Monsieur Canson's car.'

'And you haven't seen him since?'

'No. He must have decided to go to England in the plane.'

'Ah well. It is a pity we missed him. He may have guessed we would come to see him. Did he by any chance leave a message?'

'Not with me,' said the woman.

Her husband shook his head. 'He said nothing to me.'

'I wonder if he left a message in his room, in case we came? He has sometimes done that.'

'I don't think so.'

'Would you mind if I looked, to make sure?'

'Look, *monsieur*, if you wish, but I don't think you will find anything. I've cleaned the room ready for the next visitor. Number five. Come, I will show you.'

They followed the woman to the room Ginger had occupied. There she left them, saying she would have to get on with her work. If they wanted her they would find her in the kitchen.

Biggles' eyes went round the room with its simple furniture. It was spotless. The bed had been made, the floor polished. The window was wide open.

'Nothing here,' said Bertie. 'Did you really expect to find anything?'

'I thought there was just a chance. Ginger must have got into some sort of trouble in Nice or how did he tear his jacket and get a bruise on his face? It struck me that if he was in danger, knowing we'd follow him up he'd leave us a clue.' Biggles' eyes were going over the walls. He was near the window when a breeze moved the curtain. 'What's this?' he said sharply, taking a pace forward.

They read Ginger's message together, in silence, decoding it.

'So that's it,' breathed Biggles. 'He ran into trouble in Nice, presumably at the address he's given us. He must have followed Canson to it. Why else should he have gone there? The fact that he wrote this, obviously for our benefit, can only mean that he didn't feel safe, even here. I'd like to know when he wrote this—if it was when he first came home or after he had spoken to Canson. That could be important, particularly if it was the result of something Canson said when he came to fetch him.'

'Canson himself may have learned something here, from Ginger's passport. That was a queer thing to do—collect his passport. Was it really to save time?'

'No. He wanted to see the particulars in it.'

'He could have done that on the way out, or when they were checked at Nice Airport.'

'The obvious answer to that is, the need had not arisen. If that's right, it follows that he wanted to see it as a result of something that happened in Nice.'

'Something to arouse his suspicions.'

'That, I'd say, is the answer. The big question is, where did Canson take Ginger when he left here? Was it to the airport—or to this address Ginger has given us in Nice.'

'Let's go and have a look at it.'

'That's our next move, as we're here. There's one thing I am sure of. Whatever is going on the caretakers here know nothing about it. If they were aware of anything crooked they wouldn't have talked as freely as they have, or I'm no judge of human nature.'

At this juncture the woman came back. 'Have you finished, *messieurs*? I must close the window now.'

'Yes, thank you, *madame*. No doubt we shall see our friend when we get back to England. May I offer you a little *pour boire* for being so helpful.' Biggles slipped her a tip.

'*Merci, monsieur.*'

'*Au revoir, madame.*'

'*Au revoir, messieurs.*'

They went out. Their taxi was waiting. 'You can take us to Nice, now,' ordered Biggles.

'*Oui, monsieur.* The address?'

'The Rue Baldini.'

The driver hesitated. 'I can't take you all the way.'

'Why not?'

'The Rue Baldini is too narrow for traffic. It is in the Old Town.'

'Then take us as close as you can get.'

'Certainly, *monsieur.*'

They set off on a pleasant drive along the coast road. Little was said on the way, and conversation was kept to general subjects as it would be overheard by the driver, who for all they knew might be able to speak English. He stopped at the entrance to a narrow street on the fringe of the Old Town. '*Voila, messieurs. Rue Baldini.*'

Biggles paid the fare and he departed.

'Now,' said Biggles. 'We'll take it slowly, goofing about like a couple of tourists who have never seen such a place before. We're looking for a photographic shop, but when we come to it don't look too hard. It may be nothing very much, but it may be red hot.'

'I get it,' said Bertie.

They strolled down the street, sometimes stopping to gaze at a unique feature. There were quite a few people about, mostly women with empty shopping baskets going to, or coming from the near-by market with baskets piled high, long sticks of bread projecting.

'This must be it,' said Biggles softly, as they reached their objective. 'There are not likely to be two photographic shops in a dive like this.'

On the occasion of Ginger's visit night had hidden the blemishes, but in the broad light of day the establishment presented a depressing picture of the drab, squalid dilapidation that results from age and neglect. Most of the buildings in the street were in much the same state so there was nothing remarkable in this. An old woman dressed in faded black sat in the entrance to an alley close by eating a piece of bread and olives which lay at her side on a scrap of newspaper.

Biggles paused only long enough to glance through a dirty

glass window at a display of fly-speckled photographs. He succeeded, where Ginger had failed, in reading the words, almost obscured by dirt, on the plate by the door. They were: *Armand Mattio. Photographe Gravure.* He merely glanced at this in passing and joined Bertie, who had strolled on.

After dawdling a little way they came to a turning to the right. Biggles took it and stopped, lighting a cigarette.

'Well?' queried Bertie.

'I didn't learn much. The shop is run by a man named Mattio who calls himself a photographer and engraver, or a photographic engraver, which I take to mean he can make etchings from his portraits. By the look of the place he doesn't do much business.'

'I'll tell you one thing. When I turned to wait for you that old dame had poked out her head to see where we were going.'

'What else has she to look at apart from the odd stranger? Old women will do that in any village at home.'

'Well, what do we do?'

'You mean, to find out if Ginger was brought here?'

'Yes.'

'There's nothing we can do about it. We've no right to barge into the house and to ask questions could only do more harm than good. Yet somehow Ginger must have been involved in the place or he wouldn't have left that message. What did he expect us to do about it?'

'Maybe he didn't expect us to do anything; it could have been his way of passing on a piece of useful information.'

'That may be the answer, but I have a feeling that when he wrote on the wall he was expecting trouble. Why write on the wall? Why not a note? I'd say he was pressed for time. Canson was waiting for him. We know that. They had a conversation, but what it was about we don't know. I'm pretty sure it was after that, and possibly as a result of that, Ginger wrote the message. He knew that if he didn't come home we'd come here; and that can only mean he thought there was a chance he might not come home.'

'Yet you say there's nothing more we can do here?'

'Nothing. If we knew for certain Ginger was in that shop it would be a different matter. We could call in the police. But for all we know he may have gone back to England in the Dove. Come to think of it we should be able to settle that at the airport. Someone must have checked him out. The National Security officer would want to see his passport and the Customs people look at his baggage. Let's try it. We'll forget this place for the time being.'

They found a way out of the Old Town and on a boulevard picked up a taxi. In twenty minutes they were at the airport.

Using his Interpol papers Biggles started his inquiries, and without any difficulty learned all he wanted to know: the time of departure of the Dove with its one passenger whose passport was in the name of Hebblethwaite. There were two pilots, both well known at the airport. Their names were Canson and Rawlings.

'So Ginger *did* go back with Canson after all,' said Biggles, when he was alone with Bertie in the reception hall. 'We must assume the machine went to Millham. The question is now, did Canson go straight there and ask for a Customs check or did he make a landing at a proper Customs airport? We should be able to work that out when we get home.'

'You're not going back to the Rue Baldini?'

'There's no point in it. I'm going flat out for home. It seems that Canson's old pal Rawlings has managed to get a pilot's ticket.'

'What I don't understand,' said Bertie, 'is this. If Ginger flew to England with Canson why didn't he come home, or at any rate get in touch with us somehow.'

'I don't understand it either,' returned Biggles. 'That's the next problem to be solved. Let's get on with it.'

The flight home was uneventful, but it was late evening before they were in the Air Police office at Scotland Yard, having confirmed that Ginger had not returned to the flat.

Using two telephones they got busy checking all Customs airports at which the Dove (giving its registration) might have landed on the way to its base. This produced no result. Biggles then asked the head office of Customs and Excise to ascertain if

Millham had requested the services of a special officer. The answer was no.

All this took a good deal of time, and they were both showing signs of weariness when Biggles finally sat back and lit a cigarette.

'So that's that,' he said. 'So Canson had the brass face to land at home without going through Customs. How long does he think he can get away with that sort of thing?'

'We could nail him on that. We know the Dove is there. I saw it.'

Biggles shook his head sadly. 'He'll have an excuse ready you may be sure. He'd get away with a fine and we still wouldn't know what he'd been up to. We'd have shown our hand for nothing.'

'It beats me that he dare risk dodging Customs. Why?'

'If you're asking me I'd say because he had Ginger on board and wasn't giving him a chance to speak to anyone. It's pretty clear now that Ginger must have slipped up somehow. Canson's got him and he's not letting him go. I only hope it's nothing worse.'

'But look here, old boy, we shall have to do something about this.'

'We'll deal with it tomorrow. We've had a long day. We couldn't do anything tonight, anyhow. Let's go home and sleep on it.'

9

WHAT NEXT?

THE next morning Bertie's first question was: 'Any word from him?' There was no need to mention Ginger by name.

Biggles shook his head. 'Nothing. I don't like it.'

Over an early breakfast Bertie asked: 'Have you any bright ideas?'

'I have some ideas, but how bright they are remains to be

seen,' answered Biggles. 'Lately my bright ideas seem to drift off the beam. I thought it was a bright idea to send Ginger on a trip with Canson but it doesn't look very bright at this moment. Let's face it. I didn't foresee a situation like this and I couldn't have imagined it.'

'You knew Canson was as crooked as a corkscrew.'

'I knew he used to be, which isn't quite the same thing. I was working entirely on suspicion. I'd no proof of anything underhand. Canson is one of those men who are never content with what they've got, and knowing that I thought he might be working some minor racket on his own account. In view of what's happened it begins to look as if I was wrong. This is a bigger thing than I suspected. It must be, or Canson would never have gone so far as to interfere with Ginger. At least, as Ginger hasn't reported back we can only conclude that's what has happened. Had it been possible for him to get in touch with us he would have done so. He wouldn't leave us in the air like this.'

'You really think Canson has got him?'

'What else are we to think?'

'Let's suppose you're right. What does Canson hope to gain by it?'

'I wouldn't know.'

'Where could Canson keep him? He must live somewhere but I can't see him taking him home.'

'Neither can I. He could hardly lock him up at the aerodrome; there's no building suitable for that. If he isn't there he could be anywhere. I have a feeling there's more to this business than we know; that Canson isn't alone in whatever it is he's doing.'

'Well, what are *we* going to do about it? It's time we were doing something.'

'For a start I'm going to Paris.'

'Why Paris?'

'To have a word with Marcel Brissac of *la Sûreté*.'

'Couldn't you phone him?'

'No. There's too much to say. I want him to understand exactly what has happened. He can lay on a man to keep an eye on that shop in the Rue Baldini, in Nice. That fits somewhere into the jigsaw. I'll give him a description of Canson in case he goes there again. I'll also give him the registration of the Dove. If he knows it's under suspicion he'll watch it every time it enters France.'

'Are you going alone?'

'I am. I have a job for you. It may lead to nothing but it's the only thing I can think of. I'm reckoning that if Canson has got Ginger put away somewhere he'll go to see him from time to time. He'd hardly leave him to starve to death. The chances are that when he goes—in fact, wherever he goes—he'll use his car. You can't mistake it. Big crooks love big expensive cars. It's one of their weaknesses. Vanity, of course. This is what I want you to do. Take the Proctor and fly over Millham. If the Rolls is there, watch it. See where it goes. As long as it keeps out of heavy traffic, and there isn't much traffic on that secondary road that serves the airfield, that shouldn't be too difficult. Failing the car you can watch the airfield for any sort of activity. Keep high, and don't circle too close. Play cagey. A sudden burst of aviation could set Canson wondering what it's about.'

'Leave it to me.'

'Right. There's no hurry for you. I don't suppose Canson will be on the job before nine o'clock. It might be a good idea if you took the pistol-grip camera with you to get oblique shots of any place Canson visits. Apart from having a record for future identification we could study the pictures at leisure.'

'I'll do that.'

'I'll ring Marcel's office to let him know I'm coming. We can't fix any time for getting together again because neither of us knows when we shall be finished. Whoever's back first can go to the Yard and wait.'

'How long do you want me to watch Millham?'

'I'll leave that to you. Say, until you see something worth reporting. If nothing happens, carry on as long as possible even if it means refuelling. Let's go. If this doesn't get us anywhere I shall have to see the Air Commodore and report Ginger missing.'

Presently they went their respective ways, Biggles to the Yard to phone French police headquarters on the private line, and

Bertie, in his own car, to the Air Police hangar to prepare for his reconnaissance.

When, some time later, he arrived over Millham, the place looked dead; or at any rate deserted. The hangar doors were closed, which suggested there was to be no flying in the near future. He cruised on and, circling high, watched the airfield from a distance. This was a simple matter, as the weather had remained fine, with the only cloud a few flecks of cirrus far above. Visibility was good. On the country roads there was little traffic.

Shortly after ten o'clock he saw a man, presumably one of the ground staff, arrive at the airfield on a motor cycle. The rider parked his machine, entered a building and soon afterwards came out dressed in overalls. He opened the hangar door and disappeared inside, evidently to do some work, for he remained there.

A little while after this another man arrived in a small car. He did precisely the same thing, joining the man in the hangar.

It was nearly an hour before anything else happened, and Bertie, who had kept at a distance, was getting a little bored when he saw a big car travelling slowly up the accommodation road that led to the administrative buildings. Having plenty of altitude he cut his engine for silence and glided close enough to be able to recognize a dark green Rolls. Canson's car. It went on to the hangar. Someone, too far off to be identified, got out and went into the hangar. Bertie sheered off, making S turns to keep the aerodrome in sight.

He was thinking he might have done better on the ground, and even considered landing in a near-by field to continue his investigation on foot, when he would be able to get nearer. It was as well he did not do so, because after a few minutes he saw the Rolls moving off in the direction from which it had come. He kept his eyes on it, feeling more comfortable, knowing that with the car in motion the driver would be less likely to hear him and would probably pay no attention if he did. Determined not to lose his quarry he risked losing a little height, confident that Canson would never suspect he was being shadowed from the air.

He didn't attempt to guess where the Rolls might be going. It could be anywhere. As long as it went somewhere, that was all that mattered. His only fear was that its destination might be in a big town, where he would almost certainly lose it in the traffic. Great was his satisfaction, therefore, when after covering about five miles, during which distance it passed through the little village of Millham, it turned into a short drive which ended at what can best be described as a mansion house; a large building of mellow red brick with outbuildings, extensive gardens, a broad lawn and some fine ornamental trees and shrubs.

Bertie was now alert, for this could only be the objective of the vehicle he was following. He was also mildly surprised, for to run such an establishment would obviously be an expensive undertaking; not the sort of place a man in Canson's financial position could afford. It began to look as if Biggles' theory, that Canson was engaged in a bigger enterprise than had at first been supposed, was right. And he was not alone in it. There was big money involved.

Keeping well to one side, flying at a speed only just above stalling point, he watched the Rolls stop at the front door. The driver was admitted. Bertie would still have been unable to swear that the man was Canson; but it was certainly Canson's car, and that was all that mattered. Canson would not be far away from it. This, for the moment, was as much as Bertie needed to know.

Half turning away he opened a side window and picked up his camera, the 'pistol' type used for shooting oblique photographs, lying handy on the seat beside him. Holding it at the ready he flew across the front of the house, quickly taking shots from different angles. He flew on for some distance before he turned and came back, this time taking snaps of the back of the house. After this he did not turn, but carried right on, feeling he had done enough. To remain near the house might well cause anyone inside to wonder what the aircraft was doing. In any case he could not expect to learn much more if he hung about. Canson might stay in the house for hours.

What he decided to do, and what in fact he did, was fly back to base and hand in his photographs to be developed. He had a cup of tea while his tanks were being topped up, and then, really to occupy himself knowing that Biggles would not yet be back from France, he made another sortie to Suffolk.

Flying high he first passed near the house in the park. The Rolls was no longer at the door; but he spotted something he had not previously noticed, concentrating as he had on getting the photographs. Animals were wandering about on the lawn. Using binoculars he made them out to be dogs. He counted five. Why so many? he wondered. Was the place a kennels, for training police dogs, guide dogs for the blind, or something of that sort? He decided that Canson, or his friends if they were anything like him, would not be interested in work of that nature.

He went to the aerodrome, and flying straight across observed an Auster on the tarmac with two men working on it. He couldn't see the Dove, but Canson's Rolls was parked in its usual place in the shade of the hangar. As it seemed likely that it would remain there for some time, perhaps for the rest of the day, he decided not to linger but return to base, which he did. In the Operations Room he spent some time studying the prints of his photographs, which were now ready. He learned nothing more, but he was well satisfied with them. The light had been good so they were clear and sharp. He tried to think of a way of learning the name of the house without going to the district; he considered ringing up the post office at Millham village, or the police-constable should there be one; but in the end he decided against it as an unnecessary risk. If word leaked out locally that inquiries were being made about the house only harm could come of it. It could wait.

The time was now getting on for two o'clock, so leaving the prints to dry—they were still damp—he went to the canteen and had a leisurely lunch. Afterwards he collected the prints and drove back to the Yard to await Biggles' return.

It was nearly four o'clock when Biggles walked in.

'How did you get on?' asked Bertie.

'All right. I had a long talk with Marcel. He understands the position. He's promised to lay on an experienced man to keep an eye on the Rue Baldini. He'll check up on anyone who uses the shop. He may recognize someone of whom he has a record. We can leave that end to him. How about you? Did you have any luck?'

'I think so. Canson came to the aerodrome in his Rolls. He didn't stay long. Afterwards I was able to track him to a big house only about four or five miles away. I got some pretty good shots of the place, front and back. Here they are. Have a look at 'em.'

'I suppose you don't know the name of the house?'

'No. I know nothing about it. I thought it better not to start making inquiries until I'd seen you. I could only have got particulars on the spot.'

'No matter. We'll soon deal with it when we're ready.' Biggles was sitting at his desk studying the photographs through a magnifying glass. 'Are these dogs I see on the lawn?' he questioned.

'Yes.'

'Alsatians?'

'That's what I took them to be.'

'H'm. Very interesting. One dog can be a pet but no one keeps a pack without good reason—particularly of Alsatians. Could you find this place again from ground level?'

'Easily. No trouble at all.'

'Our next move, then, will be to have a closer look at it. Ginger may be there. It's quite certain now that he can't get back or he'd have been in touch before this.' Biggles was still looking at the photographs. 'These dogs present a problem. If they're allowed to run loose all day and night, getting near the house is going to be quite a business.'

'Are you going to apply for a search warrant?'

'No. Not yet, anyway. We haven't enough evidence to justify it. Remember, we're now faced not with one problem but two. We have to find Ginger, and we've also got to see what it is these people are up to. Canson is up to something and he's not alone in it. It looks more and more like big business.'

'Are you going to tell the Air Commodore how things stand?'

'I may have to, later, but at present I'd rather not. I put myself on this spot and I shall get off it under my own steam, if it's possible.'

At this point of the conversation there was a knock on the door and a uniformed constable came in.

Biggles looked up. 'What is it?'

'There's a gentleman below asking to see you.'

'Tell him I'm busy.'

'He says it's urgent.'

'Did he give his name?'

'Yes. It's Mr Canson. Mr Roderick Canson. He says you know him.'

The face that Biggles turned to Bertie wore an expression of utter incredulity. 'Well, so help me,' he breathed. 'I'm used to surprises, but this is one out of the top flight.'

'By gosh! He's got a nerve, coming here,' growled Bertie.

'That's where you're wrong. It isn't nerve. It's vanity. Plain swank. He thinks he's smarter than we are but he's not satisfied to let it go at that. He's got to prove it.'

'To us or to himself?'

'Both, I'd say.'

'He must be sure of his ground.'

'His type always are. Well, we'll see.' Biggles turned to the constable. 'All right. Bring him up.'

Quickly gathering the photographs that lay spread on the desk he put them out of sight in a drawer.

10

CANSON MAKES A PROPOSITION

CANSON came in beaming. 'Hello—hello there, so this is where you do your sleuthing.' He selected a chair, dragged it up to Biggles' desk and sat down.

'Make yourself at home,' said Biggles, with frosty sarcasm.

It appeared to be lost on the visitor. 'I've got a bone to pick with you, Bigglesworth,' he stated belligerently.

'Then get on and pick it. I'm busy.'

'When you dropped in at Millham why didn't you tell me you were the big noise in the Air Police?'

'I don't go around shouting my business. You said you'd heard I was employed by the government. What more did you want? Who told you I was in the police, anyway?'

'Nobody told me. I worked that out for myself.'

'Is that what you've come here to tell me?'

'Not by a long chalk. I've come here to do a deal with you.'

'I don't do deals with people I don't know.'

'Don't know?'

'Well, say, people I don't like, if you'd rather have it that way.'

'You haven't forgotten that once we lived on the same station?'

'No, and I haven't forgotten what happened there.'

Canson made a deprecatory gesture. 'Oh, come now, don't say you're like the elephant that never forgets.'

'Suppose you come to the point.'

'Very well. You live with a young man named Hebblethwaite. Right?'

'Say he lives with me. What about it?'

'He's one of your assistants.'

'If you say so.'

'You sent him on a Sunnitours trip to check what I was doing.'

'Did he tell you that?'

'There was no need for him to tell me. It was too obvious. I'm not a fool, you know. I'll admit that at first I didn't know who he was or what his object might be; but when on his passport I saw the address Mount Street I made it my business to find out why a chap living in an expensive flat should choose the cheapest possible trip abroad. Who else lived at the address? Why, none other than Inspector Bigglesworth. And what was my old messmate Bigglesworth doing now? Top pilot of the Air Police. Then I knew why I had been honoured by his presence at my poor little airfield at Millham. It was as easy as that.'

'Very clever.'

Canson's expression hardened. 'You didn't just drop in, as you said. Just as a matter of detail, to satisfy my curiosity, what were you hoping to find?'

'You know, so why ask me? What were you doing with Hebblethwaite's passport?'

'As a visitor from overseas he had to hand it in when he got to France. When I went to the Antibes to bring him home he wasn't there, so to be ready I collected it for him; and as I had nothing to do I happened to glance at it. What gave you the idea I might be misbehaving myself?'

'You seem damned anxious to know that. I haven't said I was interested in what you were doing.'

'You must have been or you wouldn't have had me followed in France. But let it pass. I'll come to the point. Hebblethwaite hasn't reported back.'

'How do you know?'

'Because he's staying with a friend of mine, one who will see he doesn't get into any more mischief.'

'What you mean is, you've got him locked up somewhere.'

'Well, something like that.'

'And you've got the brass face to come here and admit it?'

'Why not?'

'I've a good mind to arrest you here and now.'

Canson sneered. 'You know better than that. I know what you can do and what you can't do. You can't keep me here without making a charge. What will it be?'

'Abduction.'

'And just how are you going to prove it? You can't, and you know it. But let's not waste time arguing about that. You arrest me and it's likely to be too bad for Hebblethwaite. I take it you want to see him again?'

'It'll be too bad for you if I don't.'

'All right. Let's understand each other. I have a proposition to make. This is it. You give me your solemn oath that you won't poke your nose any farther into my business, either now or in the future, and I'll undertake to see that your young friend is returned to you, A1 and fit for full flying duties, before midnight. That's fair enough. It'll save us both trouble. Call it a gentleman's agreement. Is it a deal?'

Biggles stared at Canson stonily. 'So you've still got the damned impudence to call yourself a gentleman.'

Canson flushed slightly. 'Why not?'

'A man who fakes the mess bills of his brother officers to pay his own isn't my idea of a gentleman.'

'So you've still got that stuck in your gizzard. Well, I'm not concerned with your opinions. I repeat, is it a deal?'

'I don't make deals with people like you.'

'You realize what that means?'

'What does it mean?'

'It means you're forcing me to take drastic action. You won't see Hebblethwaite again. It's as simple as that. I've got a good job and I intend to keep it. Neither I, nor the people for whom I work, are prepared to have our organization upset by you, or anyone else, because you've got a bee in your bonnet over something that happened years ago. Purely on that account you assume I'm doing something illegal.'

'Aren't you?' inquired Biggles blandly.

'You try to prove it.'

Biggles went on evenly: 'In the presence of a witness you've threatened to murder a police officer.'

'What are you talking about? I didn't say anything about murder.'

'Then what were you saying?'

'There might be an accident.'

'Such as?'

'Hebblethwaite might fall out of an aircraft crossing the Channel. That, as you know, has happened before today. It can be proved that he booked an air trip to France and later asked to be flown home to see a sick relation. The Sunnitours office will swear to that. We do our utmost to take care of our passengers but accidents will happen. If people do silly things, such as opening a door when the aircraft is in flight, that's their funeral.'

Biggles remained unruffled. 'You're a worse scoundrel than I

took you for, and that's saying something.' He reached for a
cigarette from the box on the desk.

'Thanks, I'll have one of those,' said Canson.

'You will not.' Biggles closed the box. He went on: 'I find
myself wondering how far these friends of yours, as you call them,
would trust you, if they knew as much about you as I do.'

'Never mind what they think. I'm doing the talking now,'
retorted Canson, showing signs of anger.

'I think you've said enough.'

'Then you're not going to play!'

'Not with you. And if that's all, if you don't mind I'll get on
with my work.' Biggles touched a bell push.

'That's your last word?' growled Canson.

'It is.'

'All right, if that's how you want it. But you'd better think it
over. And you needn't bother to have me followed. I'm going
home. I have a flat not far away from here. This is the address.'
Canson tossed a card on the desk. 'My phone number is on it. If
you have second thoughts about my proposition you have only to
give me a ring.'

'I wouldn't count on that so don't wait in,' returned Biggles
coldly.

The constable entered. 'Show this gentleman out,' said
Biggles, with slight emphasis on the word 'gentleman'.

Canson went without another word.

As the door closed behind him Bertie burst out: 'Well of all the
infernal audacity!'

'Take it easy.'

'That rascal must have a hide like a rhino, coming here with
such a proposition.'

'He must be worried, for all his high and mighty attitude, or he
wouldn't have come here at all. He was on safe ground and he
knew it. We shall need more concrete evidence than we have at
present before we can charge him with anything. But we'll get it,
don't worry. He, and the gang he's working with, are rattled.
They know we're suspicious, and someone has had the bright
idea of using Ginger as a hostage to stall us off. I'm pretty sure

that so far, at any rate, not knowing how much we know they'll think twice before they resort to deliberate murder.'

'What about this talk of fixing an accident?'

'Bluff.'

'Then you don't think Ginger is in danger?'

'I didn't say that. Of course he's in danger. But I'm talking of the present situation.' Biggles shrugged. 'How far these people will go if they get really desperate remains to be seen. Then, of course, they might do anything. Meantime, they've got Ginger. They know we know that. Not being fools they must realize that if he disappears we shan't rest till we've brought them to book.'

'But what are we going to do, old boy?' Bertie was deadly serious.

'Tackle them from the angle where we have the edge on them.'

'Meaning what, exactly?'

'Through the house you tracked Canson to at Millham. They don't know we know about that. I say *they* because it's obvious that Canson isn't working on his own. I'm prepared to gamble on Ginger being in that house. Where else could he be? Dash it all, they can't have many establishments. I'm going to see inside this place at Millham.'

'How are you going to get in?'

'Break in.'

Bertie looked startled. 'But here, I say, old boy, you can't——'

'Never mind what I can't do. If Ginger is in that house I'm going to get him out before I do anything else.'

'When?'

'Tonight. There's nothing to be gained by delay.'

'You're serious about this?'

'I was never more serious.'

'Are you going to tell the Air Commodore what you have in mind?'

'No.'

'Why not?'

'Because he'll forbid me to do it. That would knock out my middle stump. As I don't break orders I should have to abide by his decision. This is a case where I keep my mouth shut.'

'You're taking one hell of a risk.'

'Of what?'

'Well—er—of getting fired. When the Air Commodore hears what you've done he'll blow his top.'

'I can't help that. I hope he'll never know.'

'What a headline for the newspapers if the house turns out to belong to an innocent party. Police turn housebreakers, and all that sort of thing. They'd be out for your blood.'

'I'd resign, anyway, if Ginger lost his life. I sent him on the job. Now stop quibbling. I've made up my mind. You stay out of this if you don't like it.'

Bertie looked hurt. 'Here, I say old boy, that's a bit thick. You know me better than that. Where you go I go. So we're going to do a spot of house-bashing; that's if you don't change your mind and apply for a search warrant.'

'It's no use. We'll never get one on the grounds we have to offer. It would take too long, anyway. Suppose we did get one. It would mean going to the front door to serve it. We might as well ring up Canson and warn him. No. Complete surprise is our best bet. If we knew for certain that Ginger was in the house it would be a different matter; but we're not.'

'Okay. You know best. You're not forgetting the dogs?'

'I am not.'

'If they're allowed to wander about loose in daylight they'll certainly be on the job after dark.'

'I hope they are. Then they can be dealt with.'

'By whom?'

'You.'

Bertie looked shocked. 'You're not going to ask me to knock them off?'

'Don't be silly. What do you take me for? But let's get on with it. We haven't too much time. For a start I want you to slip out, find a shop where they sell meat and buy a couple of pounds of liver.'

'Did you say *liver?*'

'I did.'

'What sort of liver?'

'Any sort—pigs, sheep, cows, chickens—I don't care.'

'What the devil do you want liver for?'

'The dogs. Dogs love liver.'

'But wait a minute. You can't poison——'

'I haven't said anything about poison. If you can think of any way of getting through a barrage of Alsatians without a sound I'd be happy to consider it. I know of only one way. Putting it nicely, call it a tranquillizer. I call it dope. While you're out I shall go down to the lab. and ask them to let me have something guaranteed to put a pack of hounds to sleep for a couple of hours or so. I'll take their advice on it. They should know.'

'How are you going to feed this stuff to the bow-wows?'

'That's the job I have for you.'

'Here, now, wait a minute. I'm not——'

Biggles raised a hand. 'It's all right. Don't get in a flap. They won't have a chance to bite you. All you have to do is glide over low, low enough to make sure you don't miss the target but not too low, and scatter the bait on the big lawn in front of the house. You'll do this after dark, of course. If the dogs are about they'll soon wind it. You needn't come back. Fly on and land on the aerodrome. Canson has no night-flying facilities so everyone should have gone home long before you get there. Canson will be in his flat here in London. I shall go down by car to the airfield and pick you up. Put a gun in your pocket. You may need it before the night's out.'

'Sounds like you're going the whole hog.'

'I'm prepared to, if necessary. We don't know what we may have to face in that house. It may be a den of thieves. With bare hands we'd get the worst of the argument.'

'This sounds like going flat out for trouble.'

'In for a penny in for a pound, as they say. Ginger will be relying on us to get him out and I'm not going to let him down. I've always been prepared for one of us to go west by accident; that's on the cards; but Canson's hint of murder has got me savage, and I'm taking no risks of that while I'm on my feet.'

'Absolutely. I'm with you.'

'Fine. Then we understand each other.'

'Have you made a definite plan?'

'Not definite, but I know what I aim to do, which is get inside that house. Just how that's to be done will depend upon circumstances, what we find when we get there. It won't be easy. People who take the precaution of laying on a pack of guard dogs aren't likely to leave the doors and windows open. I'll talk to you more about it when I meet you on the airfield. You press on and get the liver. I'll go to the lab. and get the dope.'

Bertie departed on his errand. It took him a little while to find what he wanted, and when he returned with his parcel it was to see Biggles' desk spread with old newspapers. On them lay a knife, some phials, and an open case containing a hypodermic syringe.

'Here's your meat,' said Bertie, putting his package on the papers. 'The stuff's pretty bloody. I call this a disgusting business. I like my liver cooked.'

Biggles unwrapped a gory-looking mess. Without a word he sliced the liver into fairly small pieces. This done he injected each piece with a dose from the phials. He then wrapped the lot up in a clean sheet of paper and handed it to Bertie.

'Here's the gubbins,' he said. 'You know what you have to do with it. Don't hang about near the house, but don't miss the mark or the dogs may end up by smacking their lips over *our* livers. Don't make more noise than you have to. That's all. See you later. I can't say exactly when I shall get to the airfield. You'll have to wait for me.'

'Right you are, old boy. I'll be pressing on.'

Bertie went out.

II

DARK WORK

As soon as Bertie had gone Biggles washed the stains of the liver from his hand and on the intercom telephone put a call through to the office of Detective Chief-Inspector Gaskin, CID, with whom he so often co-operated. Having made contact with him he asked if he could spare the time to come to his office for a few minutes.

Presently the detective's burly figure filled the doorway. When he saw the bloodstained newspaper still lying on Biggles' desk he took his pipe from his mouth long enough to ask: 'Where's the body?'

'There isn't any body—yet,' answered Biggles. 'This gore isn't human. It came from a beast of some sort. It doesn't matter. Sit down.'

Gaskin sat, knocked out his pipe in Biggles's ash-tray and refilled it with tobacco from a well-worn pouch. 'What's on your mind?'

'Plenty,' Biggles told him. 'I've lost Ginger.'

'Oh, and how did that happen?'

'I sent him out to tail a suspect. Something must have gone wrong. He's now in the hands of a gang who have threatened to murder him if I don't lay off.'

'What are you going to do about it?'

'Get him back.'

'How?'

'That's why I asked you to come here. I need your help. Could you find me an efficient housebreaker for a few hours, one who can be relied on to keep his mouth shut?'

Gaskin, always imperturbable, showed no surprise. 'Since when did you decide to start cracking cribs?'

'Tonight.'

'Bit unorthodox, isn't it?'

'I've no alternative.'

'Looks to me as if you're dead set for trouble in a big way. You get copped house-breaking and they'll tear your hide off.'

'Can't help it. They're welcome to my hide if they want it.'

'What's the idea?'

'I've muscled into what may turn out to be a big thing. So far I haven't been able to get the details; but the point is, the gang have got hold of Ginger and are holding him as a hostage. Either I pack up or they've threatened to throw him out of an aircraft into the Channel.'

'Could they do that?'

'Quite easily. They have aircraft. It would look like an accident and I couldn't prove it wasn't. As I don't want that to happen, before I deal with these swine I've got to get Ginger out of their hands.'

'Do you know where he is?'

'I think so. I have reason to think he's in a big house in Suffolk, not far from the private aerodrome these crooks are using.'

'Then all you have to do is trot along with a search warrant.'

Biggles shook his head. 'No use, for several reasons, one of which is I haven't a shred of evidence against the man who owns the house. I don't even know his name. I only *think* Ginger is inside. I don't know it for certain.'

'So you're going in to see?'

'What else can I do? If I take another step against this gang I may be sending Ginger to his death. They may be bluffing, but I daren't risk it. There are guard dogs, Alsatians, round the house, but Bertie has gone on ahead to drop from the air a lot of doped meat which I hope will put them to sleep for a while. Then I break into the house. Not having had much experience at this sort of thing, and not having the right tools for the job, I've decided to take a professional with me—if I can find one. I thought you might know one. How about it?'

Gaskin exhaled a cloud of blue smoke. 'I suppose you know what you're doing? You get caught at this and there'll be hell to pay.'

'I'm perfectly well aware of it. Hell can burn the roof off the Yard for all I care as long as I get Ginger back.'

'Okay, if that's how you feel about it.'

'Well, do you know anyone, not behind bars at the moment, who for a consideration would undertake to get me inside this house? He needn't come in with me. As soon as I'm inside he can hoof it.'

'Are you reckoning on making an arrest?'

'No. Anyhow, that isn't in my programme. I haven't a clue as to what I may find, and I don't particularly care. I'm simply concerned with getting Ginger. The rest can wait.'

Gaskin thought for a minute. 'I think I know the man for you if I can get hold of him at such short notice. He's going straight now—or so he tells me, although I wouldn't care to bet on it. He's a quick-witted little cockney known in the business as Badger.'

'His name doesn't matter.'

'All right. I'll see what I can do. How long can you give me?'

'At a stretch, a couple of hours.'

Gaskin looked at his watch. 'Eight o'clock. He should be in the Red Lion. It's his usual time for a snifter. I'll send someone along to fetch him. He'll come if he knows it's for me.' The detective hesitated. 'How are you getting to this place?'

'By car.'

'Would you like me to come along with you?'

Biggles' eyes opened wide. 'That's mighty kind of you but I can't drag you in.'

'Nobody drags me anywhere. You may need help.'

'That's more than likely, but I'm not letting you risk your pension on my account. No, thank you.'

'I was only reckoning on standing by, as a witness, say, in case anything went wrong. Someone ought to know where you are in case you don't come back. What's the name of this house?'

'I don't know.'

'Stiffen the crows! You're taking on something without knowing much about it.'

'I know where the house is and that's enough for me.'

Gaskin got up. 'Well, think about it. I'll see what I can do. I'll be back.' He left the room.

Biggles waited, killing time by again studying the photographs until he had memorized the premises from all angles.

It was an hour before Gaskin came back. With him he brought a pale, undersized, seedy-looking individual with nervous, restless eyes.

'This is Badger, the man I told you about,' announced Gaskin. 'Have you told him what's afoot?'

'I've given him a rough idea but you'd better tell him

yourself.'

Biggles looked at his proposed accomplice. 'A couple of hours out of town there's a big country house. I have photos of it here. You can see them. Inside the house is one of my assistants, a police officer. If I don't soon get him out he's liable to be murdered. I've been warned that may happen. Who occupies the house, and how many people there are in it, I haven't the remotest idea; so I'm not denying there may be risks. My plan is, I shall take you to the house. All you have to do is get me inside. Having done that you'll be free to do what you like. You can go home or you can wait for me to bring you back to town. The job's worth fifty pounds. I don't know how long it will take; maybe minutes, maybe an hour. Whatever happens I'll see that no blame attaches to you. I'm prepared to swear you were acting under my orders. Is that all clear?'

'Clear as daylight, guv'nor.'

'Any questions you'd like to ask?'

'No.'

'Very well. How about it?'

Badger turned his head to look at Gaskin. 'You tell 'im what I told you, Chief.'

To Biggles, Gaskin said apologetically: 'He's being awkward. He's not happy about it.'

'Why not? Isn't the money enough?'

'It isn't the nicker. He says he doesn't know you, and he's a bit cagey about working for people he doesn't know.' Gaskin smiled whimsically. 'He trusts me; trusts me like a father. He says he'll do it if I come along to see he's kept in the clear if the thing boils over. Naturally, he's a bit sensitive about his past record.'

Biggles looked uneasy. 'You put me on a spot. It's up to you. It'd suit me to have you with us in case I needed a witness to confirm the reason——'

'Then say no more about it. You've helped me more than once so I owe you——'

'You don't owe me anything.'

'All right, all right; keep your hair on. When do we start?'

'The sooner the better. Does that suit you, Badger?'

Badger nodded. 'Just one thing, guv. How about dawgs?'

'You don't like dogs?'

'It ain't that. Dawgs don't like me.'

'There are some dogs,' admitted Biggles. 'But by the time we get there I hope they'll be in no state to express what they think about strangers. A friend of mine has gone on ahead to distribute some doped liver.'

'That's what I like to hear.' A slow smile softened the ex-burglar's face. 'Excuse me, but it comes to something when the bogies themselves take me out to do a job. I shall remember tonight, and not 'arf.'

'I hope you'll forget it,' replied Biggles. 'It shouldn't be necessary for me to tell you that I'm acting without authority. The only reason I'm doing it is in the hope of preventing a murder faked to look like an accident. Now, is there anything else before we start?'

'I'd like to 'ave a squint at them photos.'

'Here you are.' Biggles spread them over the desk.

Badger scrutinized them with a critical eye. 'You say you ain't never bin inside this joint, guv?'

'I have yet to see it from the outside.'

'That don't make it no easier but I reckon I shall manage. Okay, guv. That's enough.' Badger swept the prints into a heap.

Biggles put them back in the drawer. 'Right. Then we might as well move off. Where are your tools?'

Badger unbuttoned and opened his jacket to reveal a waistcoat with numerous pockets, some of queer shape, some bulging. From the tops of one or two projected the handles of tools. 'This is my working outfit,' he stated with a hint of pride. 'The Chief 'ere knows all abart 'em.'

'Your equipment doesn't include a gun?' queried Biggles.

Badger looked horrified. 'Gun! Me! Not on your nelly. When I'm copped I come quiet. The Chief'll tell you that.'

'That's right,' confirmed Gaskin.

'Let's get along,' said Biggles. 'We've some way to go. My car's outside.'

Two minutes later they were on their way.

The journey was uneventful, and with little traffic on the roads at such a late hour the car made good time, arriving at the airfield a little before midnight. Bertie was there. He must have heard the car coming, because when it ran to a stop at the end of the road he appeared out of the darkness; or, rather, into the moonlight, since the sky was clear and the moon well up.

'You've been a long time. I thought you were never coming,' he complained.

'I had things to do.'

'I see you've brought the Chief-Inspector along. What-cheer, Inspector.'

'He offered to give us a hand—and will probably regret it. He also found a craftsman to help us. Meet Badger, who once made a speciality of getting in and out of other people's houses. Where's the machine?'

'I parked it by the hedge about a hundred yards on. I thought I'd better not leave it too close to the buildings in case anyone came along. There's no one here. Everything's locked up.'

'Good. How did you get on?'

'All right, I think. I glided over as low as I dare. The last I saw of my disgusting cargo it looked like making a direct hit on the lawn.'

'What time was this?'

'Ten o'clock. That should give the bow-wows time to find the stuff, get it inside them and give it a chance to work.'

'Did you see them?'

'No. The moon was still low and much of the lawn was in shadow.'

'Did you see anything at all of interest.'

'No. There were lights on in the house, most on the ground floor but I noticed one upstairs. I got an impression that some lights on the ground floor, close together, came from one big room.'

'We'll have a look at them from ground level. You'd better drive, Bertie. You know where we're going.'

They all got into the car, Bertie at the wheel. He drove slowly through the village which, as was to be expected at midnight, was mostly in darkness, and, cruising on quietly, soon afterwards allowed the car to come to rest tight into a broad grass verge, with a hedge on the far side and a belt of fir trees beyond.

'We're alongside the property,' he said. 'The entrance to the drive is where the trees end about twenty yards on.'

Still sitting in the car Biggles said: 'I think the best thing for you, Inspector, would be to stay here in the car in case someone should come and wonder what it's doing. The village constable would, if this turned out to be on his beat. We'll run it on the grass. Then we can switch off the lights. With everything quiet you should hear if we run into trouble.'

'As you say. It's your show.'

The others got out. 'Let's have a look at the house,' said Biggles. 'Badger, you keep close to me. Bertie, you act rear-guard—not too close but keep in touch.'

'Right.'

'We'll take the easy way in. No need to poke our eyes out trying to push through these trees in the dark.'

They walked on to the drive entrance. There was a gate. It was shut, but not locked. They went in, closing it behind them, and moved on, turning half right to get into black shadow of the conifers. The house stood the best part of a hundred yards away but already the lights were in full view. A series close together at the end of the left wing supported Bertie's belief that it was one big room. Light came from a window on the first floor and a glim over the front door suggested a lighted entrance hall.

It was a fine summer night, warm, moon and starlight, without a movement of air. In a way these conditions were ideal for the work on hand in that any sound of movement near the house would be heard; but they also operated in reverse; any sound made by the approaching party would be heard by anyone, or anything, outside the house; for Biggles was not forgetting the dogs, and was not prepared to take chances with them until it was confirmed that they were out of action.

Making no more noise than shadows the intruders advanced towards the house, always taking advantage of the cover offered by the trees, some isolated specimens, others clustered in small groups. Badger kept at Biggles' heels; Bertie tracked them at a distance of ten or twelve yards. In this order they drew near the objective.

Under the low, spreading arms of a fine old cedar on the very edge of the lawn, Biggles stopped, his eyes making a thorough reconnaissance of the scene. The lawn, rectangular in shape, perhaps half an acre of it covering the full frontage of the house, lay bathed in moonlight. A single object was conspicuous. It was a small hump. It lay near the border of a flower-bed on the side by which they were approaching. It did not move. It was impossible to say what it was. It might have been a pile of dead leaves swept together by a gardener. It could have been a heap of earth.

Biggles brought Badger forward and pointed. 'What do you make of that?'

Badger stared. 'Looks to me like it might be a flamin' dawg.'

That was what Biggles was thinking.

His eyes were still focused on the object when Badger's fingers closed on his arm like a vice, and he breathed hoarsely: 'My gawd! Look what's coming.'

From round the end of the house had appeared what was undoubtedly a dog. An Alsatian. It walked slowly, often stopping to sniff the ground.

Badger would have bolted had not Biggles held him. 'Stand still, you fool,' he hissed.

12

THE RAID

BIGGLES spoke without taking his eyes off the animal. It was evident that it had not seen them, or suspected they were there, for it was still walking on, more and more slowly, hardly more than a step at a time. Once it appeared to stumble. In this way it wandered on until it reached the original object that had attracted Biggles' attention. It smelt it. Then it sat on its haunches beside it. It raised its chin and yawned.

A minute passed. Two minutes. Biggles stood frozen rigid. Beside him Badger was breathing fast.

Then the dog lay down.

Biggles pulled Badger closer to him and whispered: 'I think it's had its medicine. Keep still.' But he remained motionless for a full five minutes before he took a cautious pace forward. Nothing happened. He took another.

Slowly they edged nearer. This could not be avoided because the dog, or two dogs as it presently transpired, lay directly between them and the house. They made as wide a detour as was possible, but it was curtailed by a brick wall, which Biggles knew from the photographs was the boundary of a walled vegetable garden. As they reached the nearest point, still with his eyes on the danger, Biggles took out his automatic pistol. The two dogs, lying stretched out on the grass, could now be plainly seen. They did not move.

'They're asleep,' he breathed, putting the gun back in his pocket.

'I 'ope to gawd they stay asleep,' growled Badger. 'You didn't tell me you'd brought that thing.'

'What thing?'

'That gun. I'd never 'ave come if I'd a known. I bar shooting, always 'ave.'

'Don't worry. It was only in case of emergency. You may not mind taking on Alsatians with your fists, but I do. This is no time to argue about it.'

'How many of these flamin' dawgs are there?'

'I don't know for sure. About six, I think.'

'Cor, blimey! Where are the rest?'

Biggles had to admit he didn't know. To comfort his nervous assistant all he could say was: 'Wherever they are they should be out for the count. Dogs keep together, so if these two found the dope the others should have had a share.'

'I don't like dawgs,' muttered Badger. 'Anything else I don't mind: but not dawgs when they're this size.'

'Forget it.'

'I wish I could, guv'nor.'

'Let's press on.'

Taking infinite care, eyes and ears alert, they crossed a flower-bed and did not stop again until they were hard against the wall of the house.

'I'm out o' practice, that's my trouble,' murmured Badger, mopping a sweating forehead with his sleeve.

'This is where you get some,' returned Biggles cheerfully, beckoning Bertie to come forward.

'This is it,' he said, when they were all together. 'Now, Badger, this is where you find what you think is the best place to get us inside. Once you've done that you can go back to the car. What would you do if you were on your own?'

'If I was on me own the first thing I'd do would be to see who's in that end room with the lights on. It's always a good thing to know who's abart.'

'That's a sound idea,' agreed Biggles. 'You two wait here while I slip along to see what goes on. From the strength of light I don't think blinds or curtains can have been drawn. Badger, instead of standing still, wasting time, you might explore the possibilities of getting in somewhere at this end. I shall come back here. Bertie, I'll leave you to take care of Badger. Keep your eyes open for a dog that may still be on its feet. Shan't be long.'

Keeping as close as possible to the wall of the house Biggles made his way as quickly as circumstances allowed to the far end of the mansion, passing the steps leading up to the front door on the way. As he drew near the first lighted window a faint murmur of voices told him there were at least two people in the room. The windows were closed so the sound was muffled, and although he paused to listen he could not catch the words. A final step revealed there were curtains; but they were of a light material and had been carelessly drawn, leaving gaps between them. Leaning forward he looked between the nearest into the room.

He had no idea whatever of what he might see and he hadn't wasted time on futile speculation. He was prepared for almost anything—except for what he saw. It was this. Between two men, who had their backs towards him, stood Ginger.

When Biggles had recovered from the shock, which did not take long, his eyes explored the room. A glance showed that it was large and expensively furnished; but in this he was not interested. His eyes came to rest on one side of the fireplace. Seated in an arm-chair facing the others in the room, a glass in his hand and a bottle on a small table beside him, was a man dressed in a black dressing-gown. He wore a black mask. He was talking as if in argument, using a hand in the continental manner to emphasize what he was saying. The other hand rested on the handle of a black cane.

Biggles would have liked to hear what the conversation was about, but this was denied him. He could judge the situation pretty well. Ginger was being questioned and the two men beside him were guards. Who these two men were was unimportant. The great thing was, Ginger was there, and he appeared to be in good shape. This was as much as Biggles really wanted to know.

Withdrawing, he hurried back to where he had left the others. He found Bertie alone. 'Seen any dogs?' he asked tersely.

'No.'

'Where's Badger?'

'Working on a window. The kitchen, he thinks. There are bars, but he says they're soft iron and he has a tool that'll cut through 'em like butter. He'll have a couple of 'em out in five minutes.'

'I hope he's right because we've no time to lose. I've seen Ginger.'

'Where?'

'He's in the end room; being questioned I imagine. There are three men with him. This is our chance to get him, while we know where he is. He may not be there long. If he's moved we'd have to search the whole house for him. Take me to Badger.'

'This way.'

Half a dozen steps and they came to Badger working on a ground floor window at waist level. Actually, the room inside turned out to be what is known as semi-basement.

'How's it going?' asked Biggles.

'Shan't be a tick. Do you know if they 'ave any burglar

alarms?'

'I have no idea.'

'Then it looks as if you'll have to chance 'em.'

There was a brittle *snick* as metal bit through metal. 'That's it,' said Badger, removing the second bar and thrusting it into some near-by shrubs. 'Is that 'ole big enough for you? I can easy cut out another.'

'Plenty big enough.'

'You know how to slide through? Feet first, never head first.'

'Okay. Now you've done your job you can go back to the car. We can manage now.'

'I'd better make sure o' that.'

'How?'

Badger produced a torch and directed the beam inside the room. 'Like I thought,' he said. 'The kitchen. You'd look silly if you got in, after I'd gone, and found someone had locked the kitchen door.'

'I didn't think of that.'

'In this business you 'ave to think of everything. I'd better make sure.' Badger slid through the aperture he had made and disappeared. In seconds he was back. 'All clear,' he reported. 'I've opened the door. The key's on the inside. There's a long corridor the other side. I'll give you a tip. Put the key in your pocket. Then, if you run into trouble and come back this way you can lock the door behind you.'

'I'll do that. Now you get back to the car. Tell the Inspector Ginger is inside. I've seen him. We're going in after him. I'll be back as soon as I can. That's all.'

'I get it,' said Badger, and faded away into the dark shadows.

'Let's go.' Biggles, torch in hand, went through the window. Bertie followed. They went straight to the door. Biggles opened it, took out the key and put it in his pocket. He looked into the corridor. 'All clear.' Leaving the door open behind them, together they walked on in the direction that would bring them to the far end of the house.

A short flight of stairs took them to the level of the ground floor rooms. A door covered with green baize filled the passage; but it was only a swing door to cut off the staff rooms and they went on, presently to arrive in the hall, a large entrance hall with the front door on the left. It was lighted by a hanging chandelier.

Torches, no longer needed, were put away. Biggles pointed to a door on the far side of the hall. 'That must be the room where I saw Ginger. Listen.'

They stood still. From the far side of the door came a murmur of voices. 'Good,' breathed Biggles. 'It sounds as if he's still there. This is it.' He took out his gun.

'What are you going to do?'

'The only thing we can do. Open the door, walk in and demand Ginger. You back me up. Quick work and bluff, before they realize what's happening, should do the trick. Ready?'

'All set.' Bertie took out his gun.

'Keep close.'

Biggles crossed the hall to the door. He took the handle. Slowly and quietly he turned it. The door yielded to his pressure. He pushed it open and strode forward a few steps. The position was exactly as when he had last seen it.

'Don't move, anybody,' he rapped out. 'Anyone who moves will be asking for trouble. Come on, Ginger. I want you.'

The man wearing a mask was the first to recover from what must have been no ordinary shock. At all events, he was the first to speak. His expression did not change.

'Just a moment,' he said calmly. 'Indiscriminate haste is quite unnecessary. Would I be right in thinking you are Inspector Bigglesworth?'

Whatever surprise Biggles felt at his name being known he did not show it. 'You might and you might not,' he answered stiffly.

'I'd like a few words with you.'

'Some other time. At the moment I'm in a hurry.'

'It could be to your advantage.'

'We'll discuss things later.'

'You're giving yourself unnecessary trouble, I do assure you,' said the man in black, showing no emotion. 'Please put that pistol away. As a police officer you would hardly dare to use it, and it does not impress me. You have my word for it there will be no violence on my part.'

Biggles did not answer.

Without hindrance Ginger had already moved to a position behind Bertie, who had followed Biggles into the room. No one else had moved. It seemed that with the pistol covering them no one was anxious to be the first to take a chance.

Biggles went on, quietly, but with iron in his voice: 'If you are wise you will all stay here. If anyone gets hurt it will be his own fault.'

No one spoke. No one moved.

Biggles backed to the door. He waited while the others went through, followed them and closed the door behind him.

'Keep going, Bertie,' he said tersely. 'You know the way. I'll watch the rear.'

The retreat was continued swiftly and without a word until the kitchen was reached, when Biggles said: 'Make it snappy. They may try to cut us off from outside.' Taking Badger's tip he locked the kitchen door behind them. Another minute and they were together outside the house.

'Make for the car,' ordered Biggles. 'Keep close to the trees. Watch for dogs. Take it steady.'

As they crossed the end of the lawn a dog appeared, but it wandered about aimlessly and to everyone's relief took no notice of them. There was no sight or sound of pursuit.

'I think they've taken your advice, old boy,' said Bertie.

Apparently Biggles was not so sure of it, for he merely answered: 'Keep going.'

When they were half-way to the road there was an unexpected development. A car with blazing headlights turned into the drive and raced on to the house. They paused to watch it.

'That's a Rolls,' observed Bertie. 'It's either Canson's car or one like it.'

'He's arrived at a good moment,' returned Biggles cynically. 'They can now all put their heads together to work out how we knew about the house, and how we got in.'

They watched the car stop at the front door. A man got out, but he was too far away for recognition. The front door was opened to let him in.

They went on and without trouble reached the car, on the verge where they had left it. Gaskin was standing by the bonnet. Badger was inside.

'Well, how did it go?' questioned Gaskin.

'Easy. No bother at all. In fact, I have a feeling it was *too* easy. It will surprise you to know we got quite a civil reception, so civil that looking back I can't help thinking there was something phony about it. I expected something very different.'

'No shooting?'

'It wasn't necessary.'

'Thank God for that. We're on thin ice as it is. This is no sort of a lark for respectable police officers. Are you sure they didn't come after you?'

'If they did we saw nothing of them. We've got what we came for so let's forget it.'

'I was a bit worried when a car went past at a hell of a lick a few minutes ago. I thought it turned into the drive.'

'It did. It must have been Canson. They let him in. Did he see you here?'

'I dunno. If he did he didn't stop.'

'If he did notice the car, when the people in the house tell him what has happened he'll guess what it was doing here. We'd better get on. He may come back.'

'I can tell you this,' put in Ginger. 'Canson carries a gun.'

'All right. Let's go. Bertie, you drive. Take us back to the airfield. You know the way.'

When the car was moving Gaskin said: 'I still don't know what all this is about.'

'If it comes to that, neither do I,' confessed Biggles. 'I'm hoping Ginger will be able to help us.'

'I'm afraid I can't help you, either,' put in Ginger. 'Something big is going on, that's fairly obvious, but I still haven't a clue as to what is being transported between this country and the Continent, or vice versa.'

'How about picking up one of the gang and making him talk?' suggested Gaskin.

'I've got to get more evidence before I can do any picking up. You seem to be all right, Ginger. How did they treat you?'

'Very well. Surprisingly well. I've no complaints about that. I can only imagine it was because they wanted to know something and thought I could tell 'em. They were putting on the pressure when you walked in. The head man, whom I judge to be the chap in the mask since he did all the questioning, had just had a phone call; from Canson, I suspect. I don't know what he said, but I think he must have passed on a piece of important information. Maybe that's how the boss knew your name. I didn't tell him. Anyhow, it seemed to upset him.'

'Canson had found out you were in the Force.'

'How do you know?'

'He told us so.'

'*Told* you?'

'Yes. He had the impudence to come to the Yard with a proposition. We didn't bite. That may have been what he reported. It was about you. That was what decided me to get you out of that house right away. But never mind about that now. I'll tell you about it later.'

The car had arrived at the airfield and was slowing down as if to stop; but Biggles said: 'Carry on, Bertie. Right up to the machine . . . that's it. Now switch off all lights.'

Bertie seemed surprised. 'Are we staying here?'

'For a while.'

'What's the idea?' inquired Gaskin. 'We've got what we came for.'

'Not everything,' replied Biggles. 'I'm looking at it like this. At the house we've just tossed a hammer in the gears. What will they do about it? Anything could happen.'

'We're not likely to learn much sitting here.'

'We might learn a lot.'

'How?'

'The gang must be wondering how much we know. They know we know about the house. That must have been a bone-shaker for them. Their problem at this moment must be whether to hang on and bluff it out or get clear while the going's good. If they decided to pull out they may go by air. They have two machines in the hangar. It would be a great help towards our next move if we knew they were left there. That's why, as we're in no great hurry, I suggest we sit here for a bit to see what happens. We've plenty to talk about. I want Ginger to tell me what happened to him.'

Gaskin spoke. 'I'd say what they're doing right now is hiding or getting rid of anything that might be incriminating. They must be reckoning it won't be long before the police arrive.'

'Let's watch what happens. We can't be seen from the hangar. We'll get away before daylight in any case. Go ahead, Ginger and tell us how you got in such a mess. You can take your time.'

13
NOW WHAT?

GINGER told his story, step by step, from the time he had left the Sunnitours office in London. No one interrupted.

When he had finished Biggles asked: 'Do you know how Canson got wise to what you were doing?'

'No. Not specifically. I've thought a lot about this. It may have been a number of small things that aroused his suspicions. Naturally he'd be on the alert. Whatever happened it must have been after we landed in France. He may have noticed at Nice airport that I didn't go to Antibes with the rest of the party. Later he may have seen me on the terrace of the hotel. I had to wait there for him to come out. Maybe it was the English money I gave to the old woman outside the shop in the Rue Baldini. She saw me try to see through the window. She knew I'd arrived just after Canson. He was still inside. From the way she behaved when I was attacked I'm sure she's one of the gang—a sort of watchdog. She may have gone in and told Canson an Englishman had followed him. In the morning someone found the button off my sleeve. It must have been sent along to Canson at his hotel. When he came to fetch me at the hostel I wasn't there.

The driver of the bus may have told him I'd stayed in Nice and
didn't get back until late. He had a look at my passport. I had to
leave it for the police to check.'

'What else could the people at the hostel have told him?'

'Well, in the struggle in the Rue Baldini a knife ripped up my
sleeve. They knew about that although I didn't tell 'em how it
happened. They mended it for me. I slipped into Nice early to see
if the Dove was still there. When I got back Canson was already
suspicious. I knew that from the questions he asked me. He must
have noticed the button missing from my cuff but he didn't
mention that until later. He'd got my passport. He said it was to
make sure I didn't forget it. That was nonsense. He hung on to it
because he knew I couldn't move without it. By that time I'd
realized that things were going to be difficult; but I wasn't
particularly worried; I thought I was safe in going back with him
to England, assuming I'd be able to leave him if I felt like it when
we landed at a Customs airport. But he saw that didn't happen.
He came straight here.'

'You mean—he flew here non-stop from Nice?'

'He did. At first I thought the reason for that was because he
wasn't giving me a chance to speak to anyone; but, of course, it
may have been because he was carrying contraband.'

'Are you sure of that?'

'No.'

'Then why do you think he was carrying contraband?'

'It's really no more than a hunch. But there was one small
incident that made me think. When we got to the plane at Nice
airport, Rawlings—I told you he was co-pilot and how I knew
his name—came out of the cabin with a screwdriver in his hand.
I might not have noticed it if he hadn't looked a bit embarrassed
and tried to hide it. All the way home I was trying to work out
what he could have been doing in the cabin with a screwdriver.'

'Weren't there any screws?'

'Yes, but it took me some time to find 'em.'

'Where were they?'

'The backs of the two front passenger seats had been screwed
on; but the heads of the screws were hidden by an overlap of

material, some sort of fabric, so that unless you were looking for them you wouldn't see them. None of the other seats were like that. Do you happen to know if those screwed-on backs are standard fittings?'

'No. But we can soon find out. Of course, the seats might have been damaged at some time and repaired in Canson's workshop. Did the screws look new?'

'Yes.'

'You couldn't do anything about them?'

'I'd nothing to unscrew them with, if that's what you mean. Even with a tool it would have taken some time, and Canson may have come aft at any moment to see what I was doing. Actually, he did, later on, leaving Rawlings at the stick.'

'And that's all you can tell us about the trip?'

'I think that's the lot.'

'Tell me this,' requested Biggles. 'The fellow in the mask. Did you ever see his face?'

'No. I saw him three times and he was always in the same chair, dressed the same way.'

'Did you hear his name mentioned?'

'No names were mentioned in front of me.'

'Then you know nothing about him?'

'No more than you do. But there's no doubt he's the boss.'

'Why do you think they kept you?'

'I'd say there were two reasons. First, they didn't want me to talk. Even before they knew who I was they weren't giving me a chance to speak to anyone. I was grabbed the instant we landed. Those two men you saw in the room were waiting in the hangar. We taxied straight in. Canson must have sent a signal to the boss warning him to be ready. The second reason, and this may have been more important, was that they wanted me to talk, to tell them who I represented. They thought I might be working for a newspaper. They were really worried. They realized there had been a leak somewhere and were mighty anxious to know where it was. They knew I could tell them if I could be induced to open my mouth. They tried the velvet glove, first, including bribes. But when Canson found out who I really was, and told the boss, as I suppose, he got tough. Tonight, when you walked in, it looked like being the showdown. I was told to talk—or else. By the way, how did you——'

'I'll tell you our side of the story later. Did you tell them anything?'

'As a matter of fact I did drop a hint to the boss about Canson's character.'

'Why did you do that?'

'Partly for something to say but chiefly to cause mischief. From the way he reacted I fancy he knew nothing of Canson's Service record.'

'How did you explain you knew about that?'

'I admitted I'd served in the R.A.F.'

Gaskin broke in. 'Where's all this nattering getting us?'

'Not very far, I'm afraid,' conceded Biggles. 'What in your opinion should be our next move? You have heard how things stand. Would you raid the house?'

Gaskin shook his head. 'They'll be expecting that to happen, so anything there or which may have been there will have disappeared by now—hidden or destroyed. I think you'd better tackle the plane angle. Find out what it's carrying.'

'The same thing applies. Anything it may have had on board when it flew home will have been disposed of. I could grab the plane now, for illegal entry. Ginger would be a witness to that. But it's a minor offence. Canson would get off with a fine and I'd find myself with a dead duck. Another thing. Suppose we were lucky enough to catch Canson with the goods on board. We'd have him in the bag. But, unless he squealed, the rest of the gang, including the big boss, would get away. We'd have nothing on them. When I close the bag I want them all in it.'

'I'd grab the plane when it returns from its next flight abroad.'

'If we drew blank we'd have exposed our hand for nothing. That could happen. They've had a fright, so it's reasonable to suppose they'll lay off for a while, whatever it is they're doing. I feel more inclined to give them a bit more rope, hoping they'll take enough to hang themselves. In other words, leave them to make the next move.'

'Well, that's up to you.' Gaskin relit his pipe.

'Another thing I'm up against is this. How far are the Sunnitours people, the employees of the travel agency, involved? Are they in the racket or do they know nothing about what has been going on?'

Ginger spoke. 'I'd say they know nothing. I mean the people in the London office and the couple in charge of the hostel in Antibes. They've struck me all along as being ordinary decent people. I'd say only the flying people at this end, and the toughs in the Rue Baldini, are in the know.'

Biggles nodded. 'I agree with you. The lower employees couldn't tell us anything.' He raised his head in a listening position. 'Wait! Can I hear something?'

'Like what?'

'A car.'

Silence fell. Ginger opened a door quietly and listened. 'I can hear a car, and it seems to be somewhere close, but I couldn't say exactly where it is. I can't see any lights anywhere.' A long pause and he went on: 'I can't hear it now. It must either have stopped or gone on.' He got back into his seat leaving the door open.

A minute later, from no great distance away, came a curious, low, rumbling sound.

'Can I hear distant thunder?' queried Gaskin.

'What you heard was the hangar doors being opened,' corrected Biggles tersely, scrambling out of the car. He stood motionless, staring in the direction of the hangars. The moon had set and consequently visibility was restricted. 'I could have sworn that noise was made by the hangar doors but I can't see a light anywhere,' he muttered. 'There it is again! It must have been the doors being closed. I'd better have a look to see what goes on. Stand fast. I can do this——'

His voice was drowned as the quiet of the summer night was torn wide open by the roar of aero engines being started. He went off at a run, keeping close to the hedge.

Bertie and Ginger had by now got out of the car. They stood staring into the darkness in which Biggles had disappeared.

'I doubt if he got there in time to see anything,' said Ginger presently, as sounds made it evident that an aircraft was taxiing across the field.

'Sounds like the Dove,' murmured Bertie. 'It's away. There it goes.'

All that could be seen of the machine as it took off was the vague glow of the cockpit.

Within five minutes Biggles was back. 'That was the Dove,' he announced shortly. 'I thought something like this might happen. That's why I waited.'

'Did you see anything?'

'Enough. There were only two people in the machine. One of them we may suppose was Canson, since his Rolls is parked in its usual place beside the hangar. It was his car we heard.'

'Which means he must be coming back,' said Ginger.

'Probably, but not necessarily. He may have arranged for someone to collect the car.'

Gaskin stepped in. 'It's my guess that anything incriminating that might have been in the house is now on its way in that plane to some place else. Where do you reckon Canson's making for?'

'I may be wrong but I shall bank on Nice. We know the gang has a place there. This is where we have to move fast.'

'Doing what?'

'I'm going to follow him in our machine,' declared Biggles. 'Ginger, listen carefully. This is what I want you to do. Take the Inspector and Badger back to London. At the Yard, get on the private line to Paris Interpol office. Contact Marcel. He's not likely to be there at this hour but if he's at home the switchboard operator should be able to put you through to him. If you can't get him first go keep trying. Tell him that the suspect Dove may be on its way to Nice. Ask him to have someone at the airport to check if it arrives. If it does, tail the people in it. He can do that by phone long before the Dove gets there. He's already got a man watching the shop in the Rue Baldini so we should know if Canson goes there. Say I'm on my way to Nice. I'd be obliged if he would fly down and meet me at the airport; then we can decide what to do. Is that clear?'

'Perfectly.'

'I shall take Bertie with me to Nice. If the Dove is on its way there it will of course beat me to it: but if Marcel gives his orders over the phone there should be ample time for someone to get there before it lands. Bertie, how much petrol is there in the Proctor?'

'She's a bit more than half full.'

'That won't see us to Nice. We'll drop in at Paris, Le Bourget, to top up.'

Ginger spoke. 'If you're going to stop at Paris why not take me with you and drop me off there? I could make personal contact with Marcel and tell him what goes on.'

Biggles considered the suggestion. 'No,' he decided. 'It wouldn't save any time and something might go wrong. It would be better if you spoke to Marcel from London.'

'What do you aim to do in France?' asked Gaskin.

'Consult Marcel about the best way to tackle this place in the Rue Baldini. I, personally, have no authority to do anything in France, but when I've put the case to the French police they may do something. As you know, Marcel Brissac is my Interpol contact. Over the other side I shall have to work through him. If he isn't available I might as well come home. I wouldn't think of taking any action in France without the French police. Only they can raid the shop or make an arrest.'

'Can I do anything at this end?' offered Gaskin. 'I'm thinking of the house here.'

'What could you do?'

'I could send down a plain clothes man in a private car to keep an eye on the place. This masked bandit and his pals may pull out.'

'That's quite likely after what's happened tonight. I'd be glad if you'd do that. I can't be in two places at once and my main concern at the moment is Canson and his machine. We should find the answer to the whole business in that Dove.'

'Where can I get you should anything urgent turn up? This is your case and I don't want to butt in without you.'

'As I haven't a clue as to where I might end up I can't answer that. In an emergency you might make a signal to Marcel Brissac at Nice police headquarters. I hope we shall be together and if we have a chance to call there we will. I shall get back here as soon as possible. But that's enough talking. Time's getting on. It'll soon start to get light. We'll press on. See you tomorrow, or the next day, or some time. Come on, Bertie.'

The car waited until the Proctor had taken off and then headed for London.

14
BACK TO NICE

At ten o'clock Biggles was asking Nice airport control for permission to land. He had to wait a few minutes because the airport was already busy, one of the aircraft in front of him being the British Airways early morning flight from London. Bertie remarked that he could see the Dove below them.

'Good. So our guess was right,' said Biggles, as he went in. 'At least we know Canson is here somewhere.'

To their great satisfaction they found Marcel there, having flown down from Paris in his own machine. Smart and dapper in his police uniform he had with him a new assistant, who was introduced to them as Sergeant Jules Picot.

'So Ginger got through to you all right,' were Biggles's first words as they shook hands.

'As you see.'

'I suppose you were at home, asleep in bed?'

'But of course.'

'Sorry to drag you out.'

Marcel shrugged. 'It matters nothing.'

'Were you here before the Dove?'

'Yes. Ten minutes.'

'Was anyone here to meet it?'

'No. They took a taxi. Jules folowed the two men who came in the plane. They went to the shop in the Rue Baldini. He came back to tell me. The shop is still under observation.'

'Had these men any baggage?'

'Nothing.'

'Then it looks as if they don't intend to stay long.'

'Tell me, what is this business?' requested Marcel.

'It's time you knew the whole story,' said Biggles. 'You will know if the men leave the house in the Rue Baldini?'

'At once.'

'Good. Then let's go and have some coffee and a *croissant* and I'll put you in the picture. Now we are in your country it will be for you to decide what to do. The situation is a little difficult.'

Over a light breakfast in the airport restaurant Biggles told the story in detail. 'That is how things stand at the moment,' he concluded.

'So you still do not know what it is these *escrocs* are doing?'

'No. It might be anything. But today, with your help, I hope to get the answer. All I know is there is some illegal traffic going on between France and England, carried on under cover of what I believe to be an innocent travel agency which has a holiday hostel on the coast at Antibes. I have been there, and formed the opinion that the caretakers know nothing about what is happening. I believe the real French headquarters of the gang is the shop in the Rue Baldini; which means you are as much involved in this as we are—if not more so.'

'What shall we do? You're the old dog. I take your advice.'

'The ideal thing would be to catch Canson with contraband on him or in the plane. The trouble is we don't know what we're looking for.'

'I could take him in for questioning.'

'That's risky. If we found nothing on him we should have made it more difficult to catch him. You couldn't detain him. He might demand to see the British Consul and that could lead to all sorts of complications.'

'What else could we do?'

'You could search the plane—on suspicion. It's in your country. But again, if you found nothing, you would have done more harm than good. I believe that the most likely place to find what we're looking for is the shop in the Rue Baldini.'

'Would you like me to make a raid?'

'Frankly, yes. It should settle the matter, one way or the other, at your end of the racket. But I must leave that to you.'

'Very well. There's nothing else?'

'There is just one other thing we might try. As I told you, Ginger travelled in the plane. He had reason to think that Rawlings, Canson's co-pilot, had done something in the cabin with a screwdriver. The only screws he could find were in the backs of the two front seats. I'd like to see inside the backs of those seats.'

'Let us do that. This is a good time. I am within my rights in searching any plane. Jules, fetch a screwdriver from the car and bring it to the plane.'

'*Tout de suite, mon Capitaine.*' Jules went off.

The others walked over to the Dove. There was no one with it. Presently Jules brought the necessary tools. They went into the cabin. Five minutes work and the back, well padded, was lifted from its seating. It disclosed a cavity. There was nothing in it. The back was replaced and the second one tried, with the like result.

Biggles said: 'This is where the stuff is carried. These seats weren't turned out like this by the makers. All we want to know now is what Canson puts in them.'

'If we wait here we may find out,' suggested Bertie.

'No doubt, but after what's happened at Millham we might have to wait a week or more. I can't see Canson carrying anything illegal to England for a while.'

'We will try the Rue Baldini,' decided Marcel.

They were walking back to the reception hall when Bertie said suddenly: 'Here comes Rawlings.'

'Don't let him see us,' said Biggles sharply, turning away.

'He carries no baggage,' observed Marcel.

'Then as he's known to them it's unlikely he'd be checked through Customs.'

Marcel agreed. 'Only if the Customs officers suspected anything would they search his pockets.'

'He may be carrying something. If he is he may put it in the back of one of the seats. I'd wager that is what he'd been doing when Ginger saw him with the screwdriver. We'll give him a minute or two if he goes in the cabin, then jump in.'

From a distance they watched Rawlings walk straight to the aircraft and enter the cabin. They gave him a minute. He did not come out.

'Now,' said Biggles. 'Let's see what he's up to, Bertie you keep an eye open for Canson. He may be about.'

They closed in swiftly on the aircraft. The cabin door had been left open. Biggles, followed closely by Marcel, jumped in. Rawlings was on his knees by one of the two front seats, the back of which had been removed. He sprang to his feet at the disturbance, but was unable to hide what he was handling, packing into the cavity. He could only stand there, staring, his face ashen.

'All right, Rawlings, the game's up,' said Biggles sternly. He walked forward and, stooping, picked up one of the objects Rawlings had been stowing away. It was a wad of bank-notes. English five pound notes. Brand new. There were a number of identical packets. He handed one to Marcel.

'Well, do you want to say anything?' he asked Rawlings.

It was obvious that the ex-airman was no tough. White and trembling he appeared to be on the point of collapse. His tongue flicked over dry lips. He seemed unable to speak.

Biggles went on: 'You'd better come clean or you've had it for a long time. Now then: where did all this money come from?'

Rawlings recovered enough nerve to answer. 'Will I get off if I tell you all I know?'

'That's unlikely, but if you turn Queen's Evidence you may get a lighter sentence. Don't forget you're in France, so the French police will want to know about it. Who does this money belong to?'

'It isn't real money.'

'What do you mean?'

'It's phoney. It was printed here.'

Biggles looked incredulous. 'Are you telling the truth?'

'I should know.'

Biggles compared one of the notes with one from his notecase. He handed them to Marcel. 'This stuff is perfect. Don't get them mixed or we shan't know which is which. Do you want to ask questions?'

'No. You continue. Your English is better than mine.'

Biggles turned back to Rawlings. 'How long have you been importing this stuff into England?'

'Two weeks ago for the first time. Up to then it went to other European capitals.'

'Why?'

'Canson thought it would be easier to get rid of and less likely to be spotted.'

'Where was this lot going?'

'To Switzerland. Geneva.'

'Were you going alone or was Canson going with you?'

'I was going alone and then coming back for him.'

'Where is he now?'

'In Nice.'

'Where in Nice?'

'In the Old Town.'

'The Rue Baldini?'

'So you know about that. Yes.'

'Then you were going back to England?'

'No. We're not going back to England any more.'

'Oh. Why not?'

'Canson's got the wind up. He thinks the game's played out. His idea was to put this lot in a safe deposit in Geneva, take another load with us to the Middle East, sell the plane and disappear.' Rawlings now seemed anxious to ingratiate himself by talking.

'So you were going to double-cross the Boss at Millham, eh?'

'He means nothing to us.'

'What's his name?'

'I don't know for sure. I've never been told.'

'Does Canson know?'

'He may. Ask him yourself. He always refers to him as the Doctor.'

'How many men live in the house with him?'

'Only two, I think.'

'What about your pal Tomlin?'

'He's still at Millham.'

'Were you leaving him in the lurch, too?'

'He had a chance to come with us but he recently got married and wouldn't leave his wife.'

'Did the Boss know you were pulling out on him?'

'No. Something happened at the house last night and Canson reckoned it would only be a matter of hours before the police raided the place.'

'So he decided to save himself and let everyone else take the rap.'

'Yes.'

'Is this stuff actually being printed in the photographic shop in the Rue Baldini?'

'Yes.'

'And that's where Canson is now?'

'Yes. He's scared. He's not likely to go out.'

'How much of this stuff have you here?'

'Canson said twenty thousand pounds worth.'

Biggles nodded. 'Okay. I think that's all we want from you for the time being. You'd better fix that seat back on. Leave the money out.' He turned to Marcel. 'Do you want to say anything?'

'No. We'll take him, and the money, to the police bureau, and then I think we go to the Rue Baldini.'

So Rawlings was taken to the *Commissaire de Police* where he was formally charged and detained, in the first instance on a currency conspiracy. The spurious money was also lodged there pending a decision as to its disposal.

This was followed by a conference in which the whole affair was explained to the Chief of Police. He did not hesitate. He ordered a full scale raid immediately on the shop in the Rue Baldini. He himself would lead it. A plan was made over a large map of the district. This revealed that the shop backed on to an ancient church. Thinking there might be a bolt hole through it two men were sent to cover the exit—a wise precaution as it turned out. It was arranged that two *gendarmes* (armed policemen) would enter the street from each end and so complete a net round the establishment.

Being on French soil Biggles no longer had any say in the matter, but as Canson, one of the suspects, a British subject, was thought to be there, he and Bertie were given permission to watch events with Marcel. This settled the party proceeded to the scene in a police van.

The appearance of the uniformed police in the Rue Baldini, obviously engaged in a serious operation, caused something of a stir, for it was a busy time of the day. One of the first persons to become aware of it was the old woman who was at her usual post in the passage beside the door of the shop. She tried to get in, but Biggles had warned the police this might happen so she was too late. Fighting and screaming she was taken to the police van, parked at the end of the street, which was as near as it could get.

The door of the shop was locked, but the police soon had it down and charged in.

Biggles and Bertie waited outside so they did not see exactly what happened. There was some fighting, but no shooting. Presently two Frenchmen, and Canson, all handcuffed, were brought out and taken to the van. Two men who had tried to escape through the church were also brought in. That was all. With a *gendarme* left in charge of the premises the raiding party with its prisoners returned to police headquarters.

On the way Marcel told Biggles that the culprits had been caught in the act of printing bank-notes in a cellar under the shop. It was equipped with the latest thing in printing machinery. It may as well be said here that the old man who owned the place was a craftsman in the art of photo-engraving. In the subsequent search plates of bank-notes of several nationalities were found, proving how widespread had been his activities. But this was of no great interest to Biggles. He was more concerned with the British end of what now looked like an international network.

No message had come through from Gaskin, so as there was nothing more for him to do in France he told Marcel he was anxious to get back home as quickly as possible. Before he went, however, he would like to speak to Canson, who might now be persuaded to tell the truth about what went on in the house at Millham.

This was arranged, and a few minutes later he was confronting Canson in his cell.

'We've got Rawlings,' he said. 'He's told us all he knows. Is there anything you'd like to say before I return to England?'

Canson glared. 'You always were a cunning devil,' he sneered, spitefully.

'Never mind the compliments. Do you feel like talking?'

'Why should I tell you anything?'

'It might be in your own interest.'

'How?'

'You're in France—remember? You'll be brought before a French court.'

'Aren't you taking me back to England?'

'I can't do that. If you come clean it might be possible to extradite you to England for trial, although of course I can't promise that. An extradition warrant would be a matter between France and England. You stick your toes in and you're likely to see the inside of a French prison.'

'What do you want to know?'

'Whose bright idea was this currency smuggling racket?'

'Not mine. I was out of a job and answered an advertisement.'

'Inserted by the man who lives at Millham House.'

'Yes.'

'Do the travel agency people, Sunnitours, know what has been going on under cover of their organization?'

'No.'

'But you fixed that up, I imagine.'

'I did. The man who engaged me provided the money to buy the aircraft.'

'You were at Millham last night. You know what happened. What are the people there doing?'

'Nothing.'

'You mean—they're staying there?'

'The old man is, anyway. You'll waste your time going there.

You won't find anything.'

'This man who wears a mask. What's his name?'

'He calls himself Doctor Fortescue. It's probably an alias.'

'Does he know you bolted?'

'No.'

'So he thinks you'll be coming back.'

'I suppose so.'

'Is that all you can tell me?'

'That's all I know. I was simply employed as a pilot.'

'And you brought in Rawlings and Tomlin?'

'Naturally. I had to have ground staff and I knew them.'

'These hollow seats in the Dove. Was that your work?'

'Yes. It was left to me how I got the stuff home.'

'One last question. Does your wife know what you've been doing?'

'She couldn't know. She left me long ago.'

'I'm not surprised. All right, Canson. I'll report to the Air Commodore at Scotland Yard what has happened. The rest will be up to him. I'll get along now.'

'May I ask a question?'

'You may, but I won't promise to answer it.'

'I thought this scheme was foolproof. How did you get on to it?'

Biggles smiled wanly. 'You won't like my answer to that but you'd do well to ponder it. Knowing what you got up to in the Service I made it my business to find out if you were now going straight. I took no pleasure in discovering that you weren't. That's all.'

Biggles went out. To Marcel he said: 'That's all I can do here. I'll be seeing you again shortly. Thanks for your help. Now I'll get home and tidy things up at my end. What about the Dove?'

'We shall need it here. You will be able to take it home later.'

'Fair enough. I'd like one or two of those bank-notes to show to the experts at Scotland Yard.'

'You shall have them.'

That was all. An hour later, after a quick meal, Biggles and Bertie were on their way home. They landed very tired.

'I'll just have a word with the Air Commodore to let him know we're home, then I'm for bed,' declared Biggles. 'I've had enough for one day.'

15

SHOCKS

AFTER a night's rest Biggles was on the move early, for, as he remarked, this looked like seeing the end of a criminal affair into which he had stumbled more or less by accident; merely to prove his point that once a certain type of man has resorted to unlawful practices he is unlikely to change his ways.

By the time the early morning cup of tea had been made Ginger was up to date with the situation. He in turn was able to report that as far as Gaskin was aware nothing had happened at Millham House. 'What's the drill now?' he inquired.

'When I saw the Air Commodore last night he said he'd apply for a warrant to search the house and aerodrome buildings; so before we can do anything I shall have to wait for him to come in. While I'm waiting I'll have a word with Gaskin. As he was good enough to hold the fort yesterday he might as well be in at the finish. In fact, if it comes to making arrests I'd rather he did it. I'll suggest he brings one of his experts along to help with the search. We may find anything—or nothing.'

'What are you hoping to find?'

'A parcel of spurious money. That would be all the evidence needed. We know from Canson and Rawlings some was brought over.'

'You know, old boy, I've been thinking,' put in Bertie.

'Good. What have you worked out?'

'There's something I can't work out. According to Rawlings he had twenty thousand quid on him when we grabbed him yesterday.'

'I didn't count it but I could believe that.'

'Very well. If that's the kind of money Canson has been

importing one would have expected the country to be flooded with dud fivers—if you see what I mean. Why haven't we heard anything about it?'

'As far as I know there has only been the usual trickle of forgeries, mostly one pound notes.'

'Doesn't that strike you as odd?'

'I don't know,' answered Biggles reflectively. 'These new dud fivers may not yet have been spotted. They're the most perfect specimens I've ever seen. I'll ask Gaskin if he's heard anything about an unusual number of forged fivers in circulation. Ginger, you say nothing's happened at Millham?'

'Not a thing. According to the man Gaskin put on to watch no one has entered the house and no one has left. There's been no sign of life. He says the place might be dead.'

Biggles frowned. 'I can't understand this. There must be something wrong. After what has happened one could have expected a complete evacuation.'

'Maybe the Boss is waiting for Canson to return.'

'That may be the answer.'

'If they've got rid of everything incriminating they may intend to try to bluff it out,' offered Bertie. 'They won't yet have heard of Canson and Rawlings being arrested in France.'

'It'll be interesting to hear what they say when I tell them that Canson and Rawlings have squealed. Well, we should soon know the answers. The Air Commodore knows I'm waiting for that search warrant so he shouldn't be late in. Let's get on with it.'

They went first to the office at Scotland Yard. The Air Commodore had not yet arrived; but Inspector Gaskin was in and at Biggles' invitation he came up.

'Any news of Millham?' was Biggles' first question.

'Nothing.'

'You've still got the house under observation?'

'Day and night. My man's in a radio car. If anything should happen I'll know within five minutes. It looks to me as if the birds have flown.'

'Could be,' admitted Biggles. 'Tell me this. Have you had

word from the Bank of England of an exceptionally large number of dud five pound notes in circulation?'

Gaskin's eyes opened wide. 'Is that right?'

'I have reason to think so.'

'Then I've heard nothing of it.'

'I take it that if these fakes had been spotted by the banks you'd be told about it?'

'Straight away. We should see the public were warned. If there was any distinguishing mark on the counterfeit notes they'd be told where to look for it.'

'Even if these notes were exceptionally good would they be spotted?'

'Absolutely certain. Are you sure you aren't making a mistake?'

'I can't see how that's possible. For some time now counterfeit English five pound notes have been turned out in large quantities in France and flown here. You can take that as gospel. I've seen the stuff—twenty thousand pounds worth in one consignment. Here's a sample. Take a look at it. I can only think it must be so perfect that it hasn't yet been spotted.'

'So *that* was the contraband that was being carried!'

'That's it.' Biggles went on to narrate what had happened in France. 'I'm sorry I couldn't tell you about it last night but I was all in by the time I got home.'

'And what now?'

'All we have to do is tidy up this end. The Air Commodore is getting me a warrant to search Millham House. I'm waiting for it now. I thought you might care to come along and give us a hand.'

'Sure.'

'When we take the mask off the face of the big Boss there's a fair chance you might recognize him.'

'I shall if he's been in this sort of business before.'

'There may be trouble.'

'Suits me, if that's how they want it. But I'd bet there's no one there by now.'

'We'll see.'

The intercom. buzzed. Biggles answered it. 'I'll be right down, sir,' he said. 'That was the Air Commodore,' he informed, as he replaced the receiver. 'He's got the warrant. I'll go and collect it.'

In a few minutes he was back with the document in his pocket. 'That's all we need,' he remarked. 'Let's press on to Millham. The rest looks a straightforward job. I must confess to some curiosity because there are still one or two aspects of the case that puzzle me.'

'Are you going to fly down?' asked Gaskin.

'I don't think so. There's no desperate hurry and a car might be handier for what we have to do. I'll take Bertie and Ginger with me in our car. I suggest you follow us in one of your light vans in case there are prisoners to bring back.'

'Okay.'

In a few minutes both vehicles were on their way.

When they arrived on the road that went past the house they stopped long enough to have a few words with the man who had been watching.

'Anything doing?' questioned Gaskin.

'Not a thing, sir. Not a sight nor sound of anyone. No one's been in. No one's come out. No postman. No tradesmen. I reckon you'll find the place empty. It looks dead to me.'

'And me, in view of what you tell us. I'm not surprised.'

'Let's go and find out how dead it really is,' put in Biggles. Gaskin got back into his van.

Biggles's car led the way up the drive to the house. It came to a stop before the front door. Everyone got out, and forthwith began a series of surprises which, as Biggles was later to admit, 'fairly rocked him on his heels'.

Approaching the door in a body they did not have to knock, or ring, much less force an entrance. The door was opened wide by an unsmiling man dressed in the sombre style of a footman.

'I take it you are the police,' he said quietly and without emotion.

Biggles confirmed it.

'Then please come in, gentlemen. Doctor Fortescue has been

expecting you. Follow me. I will take you to him.'

The expression on Gaskin's face as he looked at Biggles was comical. 'What the hell!' he ejaculated. 'Is this some kind of a trap?'

Biggles did not answer, but he, too, was looking astonished. A courteous invitation to enter was not what he had expected. Indeed, it seemed more likely they would have to force an entrance.

They followed the manservant across the hall to the door of the big room where Biggles had collected Ginger. He threw it open. 'The police are here, sir,' he announced, and then stood back to allow the visitors to enter.

From inside the room a voice was calling cheerfully: 'Come in, gentlemen. You've been a long time getting here.'

With one exception the room was exactly the same as when Biggles had last seen it. The same man was there, seated in the same chair, his hand resting on the same stick. The only thing missing was his mask. Without it there was revealed the faintly smiling face of a man of perhaps sixty years of age.

Biggles spoke. 'Is your name Doctor Fortescue?'

'My name is Cedric Adrian Fortescue and I was once a doctor by profession.' The voice was that of a man of education.

'That is your real name?'

'My real name. I have never used another.'

'Very well, Doctor Fortescue. I am going to ask you some questions. You are not compelled to answer, and I must warn you that anything you say may be used as evidence.'

'I shall do everything possible to assist you. I assume you have a search warrant?'

'I have.' Biggles produced it.

'Before you start on what would prove to be a tedious and probably futile task may I suggest that you sit down while we have a chat. It would save both time and trouble.'

'I prefer to stand.'

'As you wish. But what I have to say may take a little while. May I offer you some refreshment? I have a sherry which I can recommend.'

'No thanks.'

'You are sure you won't sit down? It is embarrassing to see guests standing while I remain seated. You needn't be afraid that I shall do anything desperate; and I promise I won't attempt to run away. After all, had that been my intention, even if it were possible I could have gone long before you came.'

'What do you mean—if it were possible?'

'I can't walk anywhere, let alone run. You see, I am paralysed from the waist down.'

Biggles could only stare.

'Once my two faithful servants have dressed me and put me in this chair I have to stay in it until they carry me back to my bed,' went on the doctor. 'They are still here. I told them to go, to escape while they could, but to their credit they refused to leave me. I hope you will keep that in mind when they are taken to court.'

For once Biggles was at a loss for words. He had come to the house prepared to battle with a gang of desperate criminals. Instead he found a helpless old man with two passive male nurses. He looked at Gaskin with eyes that asked a question.

Gaskin shrugged and shook his head.

The doctor was speaking again. 'Tell me what you know, or what you suspect, and I will then fill in the details of what you do not know.'

'You have for some time been importing from France, where they are printed, forged English five pound notes. Is that correct?'

'Perfectly correct,' confessed the doctor without hesitation.

'I seized a consignment yesterday in Nice.'

'I warned that silly fellow Canson it would happen if he persisted. But there was no satisfying him. By the way, I didn't know he had a record of dishonesty until the young man standing behind you told me.'

'Why try to throw the blame on Canson? You financed him. Why, if you had as much money as that, did you try to get more by a criminal enterprise?'

'Ah! There you are wrong. I did not do it for money.'

'Do you expect me to believe that?'

'Frankly, no.'

'If it wasn't for money what was it for?'

'For fun.'

'Fun.'

'That's what I said. Call it amusement if you like.' The doctor was smiling at the expression on Biggles' face.

'Do you call it fun to flood the country with spurious notes?'

'Again you jump to conclusions. I am not as wicked as you think. Not one of the notes brought to this country has ever reached the public.'

'What did you do with them? Don't expect me to believe you bought an expensive aeroplane to bring them here merely to burn them.' Biggles' voice was heavy with sarcasm.

The doctor picked up a key from the table beside him. 'In the corner of the room you will see a safe. This is the key that unlocks it. Oblige me by opening it. Then tell me what you see.'

With all his preconceived ideas turned upside down Biggles took the key, went to the safe and pulled the heavy door open. The interior was stacked with bundles of new bank-notes. For some seconds he stood gazing at them. Then he thought he knew the answer to this fantastic state of affairs. The doctor was mad.

'These are all spurious?' he queried.

'Every one. All those that have been imported.'

'What about those you used to pay Canson?'

'I paid him with my own money. I happen to be a very rich man, but, ironically, money is no use to me.'

Biggles walked back. 'But why did you do this?'

'I have told you. For fun. Or, if you like, for something to do. A man must do something, but there is little a man in my state can do. Nothing with a dash of excitement in it. There was a time when to relieve my boredom I did a lot of reading. Mostly detective stories—you know, what are called thrillers. The villain was always caught at the end. This struck me as being a little unrealistic and one day it occurred to me to put the matter to test. As detectives, the story, my own story, should interest you. Are you sure you won't sit down?' The doctor spoke calmly.

There was nothing in his voice or manner to suggest he was not in his right mind.

This time the invitation to sit was accepted. Everyone found a chair.

The doctor took a sip from a glass that stood on a small table beside him.

16
THE STRANGEST TALE OF ALL

'When I was a child,' resumed the doctor, 'my nurse made a remark which I have never forgotten. She said: "You're a lucky little boy. You were born the richest baby in the country." As each of my parents had a private fortune, and I was an only child, it looked as if she might be right; and, in fact, she was, for quite some time. I could indulge in anything I cared to take up. This was mostly outdoor sports and games, and if it is not immodest for me to say so I was good at most of them. I had my own horses, sailing yachts and racing cars. I ran a private plane. Being physically fit and fairly presentable I was able to enjoy life to the full. Not that I was just a playboy. For a profession I studied medicine, and qualified; but I never practised.' The doctor smiled whimsically and went on:

'As my nurse had said, I was a lucky boy. The luck was too good. I should have known it couldn't last. No matter who you are you can't expect Lady Luck to hold your hand all the time. She's liable to get jealous. Then she fetches you a swipe that knocks you off your pedestal.

'My luck ran out in the war. I joined the R.A.F. The powers that be decided I was a little too old for fighter aircraft so it had to be bombers. On my last trip over Germany the base of my spine was shattered by a piece of shrapnel. My second pilot brought the machine home. From that day I have been helpless and never free from pain. I was three years in hospital before being discharged as a hopeless case. Since then life has only been made bearable by pain-killing drugs. Of course, other men were stricken in the same way, but for me, after the life I had led it meant the end of everything. I had nothing to live for. I had all the money in the world but it was no use to me. More than once I contemplated suicide and had everything organized for it.'

'I can understand that,' interposed Biggles quietly.

'Then one day I had a brainwave. It came as I was reading a detective novel. Here was a game I could play without leaving my chair. You may call it stupidity but to me it offered relief from the everlasting boredom to which I had been condemned. In my reading it seemed the criminal was always caught by making a silly blunder. I would pit my wits against the police. It would be an exciting competition to keep my brain active. I hadn't a relation in the world so it wouldn't hurt anyone if I lost the game. It had to be something simple and relatively harmless. Smuggling seemed to be the answer. Naturally, as a pilot I thought of aircraft. There was an unused airfield near at hand. All I needed was a reliable pilot who would obey my orders.'

'What you got was an unreliable one,' put in Biggles dryly.

'I realize that now. I advertised for a pilot. Canson applied for the job. I told him what I intended to do and he fell in with the idea instantly. Unable to get about myself I left him to organize everything. He bought the planes we needed and engaged the necessary ground staff.'

'He chose two men who had been involved with him in shady work in the R.A.F.'

'I know that now, thanks to Mr Hebblethwaite.'

'Whose idea was it to work under cover of the Sunnitours organization?'

'Canson's. I approved. It seemed a smart move in that it provided a reason for our machines to go overseas. He put the scheme up to them and they accepted. Well, for a time all went as planned. Canson made one or two trial runs, bringing in for my personal use only French foods and wines that are unobtainable in this country. Fortunately I am still able to enjoy my meals. There was no trouble so we decided to move on to something more ambitious. The weakness of my scheme was, not needing money I had no incentive to smuggle anything.'

'Then why did you choose spurious money?'

'That was Canson's idea. I didn't much care for it but I let it go. I was under no compulsion to use the forgeries. It was never my intention to foist the notes on the public.'

'Then what was the point of doing it?'

'No point at all, except that I was breaking the law. I had to do that or the game wouldn't have been worth playing.'

'Where and how did Canson meet these forgers?'

'That's another story. This is his version of it. Before he knew me, while staying in the South of France he had occasion to change some French francs into English money. He had won money gambling in the Casino at Nice, and as you know one is only allowed to take a small amount of French currency out of France. He asked the hall porter of his hotel what he could do about it. As a result he made contact with a man who asked him if he would care to buy some forged notes. That's the story he told me. How true it was I don't know. I don't know these people or anything about them. They did not concern me. Nor did it matter to me whether the notes were good or bad. I was smuggling, and I confess I got a kick out of doing something wrong. It gave me new interest in life. Do you believe me?'

'Yes,' answered Biggles. 'I can't see anyone inventing such a fantastic story. But I think it was an extraordinary thing for a man in your position to do.'

'That is how it must strike you, but remember, as you are not in my shoes you are in no position to judge. Then you had to step in and spoil my little game. Where did I make the mistake that put you on the trail?'

'It was nothing you did, if we rule out your choice of pilot.'

'How could I possibly have known he had a bad record in the R.A.F.?'

'You knew he was crooked.'

'How?'

'Had he been straight he would never have joined you in what plainly was a crooked enterprise.'

'Ah yes. I suppose you are right.'

'It so happened that I knew what sort of man Canson was. When I learned he had been granted a licence to operate from Millham aerodrome I wondered what he was really doing. You see, I have the old-fashioned notion that once a man starts swindling, to get money the easy way as he imagines, in most cases he goes on doing it. That was what brought me to Millham in the first place. To attack Hebblethwaite in Nice was a mistake. To bring him here was an even bigger blunder. When he disappeared I was bound to look for him.'

'That is what I told Canson when he reported what had happened in Nice. I had nothing to do with that. I knew nothing of it until Canson told me. I was angry with him. My scheme did not include the kidnapping of police officers.'

'Then why did you hold him a prisoner?'

'What else could I do? I was annoyed and disappointed. I had flattered myself that the scheme was foolproof, so it came as a shock to learn that it was so soon under suspicion. I was anxious to know how it had come about, what had gone wrong. I hoped Hebblethwaite would tell me, but he refused.'

'When Canson discovered he was one of my men you threatened to murder him if I troubled you again. Your criminal ambitions were going rather far, weren't they?'

'Indeed, I did nothing of the sort. This is news to me.'

'That was the message that was brought to me.'

'Not on my orders.'

'But you sent Canson to see me.'

'That is true. But it was only to say you had no cause to worry. No harm would come to Hebblethwaite. His detention was only temporary. Once I knew how you had found me out I would have let him go. The whole point of what I was doing, in my competition with the law, rested on that.'

'Canson told me a very different story. Had he given me your message correctly it's unlikely I would have risked breaking into your house.'

'I was a fool to trust him. He was furious, probably because he had more to lose than I had.'

'In what way?'

'He needed money. I didn't.'

'Why did you wear a mask?' inquired Biggles curiously.

The doctor smiled. 'Vanity, perhaps. I was playing the crook so I dressed up for the part. There is something sinister about a black mask—don't you think? Makes one really feel a rogue.'

'I wouldn't know about that,' returned Biggles dubiously. 'I'll admit I felt a bit of a rogue myself when I doped your dogs. I hope they're all right now.'

'Oh yes, they soon recovered.'

'By the way, Canson and Rawlings are now in prison in France. Where is the other mechanic—Tomlin?'

'I don't know. I think it more than likely that he has bolted.'

'Why should he?'

'He provides an example of how little crooks trust each other. The last time Canson came here he learned Hebblethwaite had been rescued. At first he was inclined to panic. Then he said he would make one more trip to France and return here.'

'He had no intention of coming back. He was out to save himself. Had he not been stopped he would have flown a big consignment of bad notes to Switzerland and deposited them in a bank. He would then have flown to the Middle East, sold the aircraft and disappeared.'

'Tomlin rang me up from the aerodrome and said he was sure Canson had something of that sort in mind. He wouldn't come back, anyway. I didn't care. I could see the game was played out.'

'Why didn't Tomlin go with Canson?'

'He wasn't given a chance. He was at home when Canson departed.'

Biggles glanced at Bertie. 'Now we're getting the facts.'

The doctor sighed. 'So all my beautiful scheme has fallen to pieces. It seems the books are right. No matter how carefully a criminal may plan, sooner or later something goes wrong and the law catches up with him. It wasn't long catching up with me, and I had ample time and money at my disposal. Ah well, it has been an interesting experiment. Well, gentlemen, whatever may happen to me there is one thing I must bring to your notice.'

'Yes?' queried Biggles.

'The two men who live with me in this house, and for many years have devoted their lives to me, have not been guilty of any crime worse than keeping Hebblethwaite here, and that was on my orders. They are good men and have proved loyal servants. I don't know what I would have done without them. I engaged them originally as cook and valet. Yesterday, when I realized what would inevitably happen, I advised them to leave. I offered them large sums of money—real money. They refused to go. They know nothing about my smuggling activities and have had no financial interest in anything I may have done. They may have suspected something irregular was going on but they did not question it. Please keep that in mind if you find it necessary to arrest them. And now, I really can't stand this pain any longer. This is the only cure.'

The doctor picked up a small jar from his table, tipped two tablets into the palm of his hand and swallowed them.

Said Biggles: 'The question at the moment is, what are we going to do with you?'

The doctor smiled. 'I have just answered it for you.' With both hands on the gold knob of his cane, one on the other, he rested his chin on them.

A strange attentive silence fell as they waited for him to speak again, to explain his last remark. Instead, very slowly and deliberately, he withdrew his chin and lowered his forehead to rest on his hands so that his face could not be seen.

Biggles waited another minute. 'Are you all right, sir?' he asked.

Then he caught his breath and hurried forward. He put a hand on the Doctor's shoulder. The body fell back limply into the chair. The cane struck the carpet with a soft thud. Biggles peered into the face that was still smiling, then looked over his shoulder at Gaskin.

'He's answered the question not only for us but for himself,' he said grimly. 'Those tablets must have been a fast-acting poison. He's dead.'

For some seconds nobody moved or spoke. Then Bertie

murmured: 'Wretched fellow. What a pity. What a pity.'

Biggles pressed the bell.

The manservant who had let them in entered.

Said Biggles: 'Your master is dead. He has just committed suicide by poison.'

The man looked stunned.

'The doctor said he had no relations. Is that true?'

'As far as I know, sir.'

Biggles turned to Gaskin. 'Is there anything you want to say?'

The Inspector shrugged. 'No. What is there to say? That was the way he wanted it.'

Biggles spoke again to the servant. 'You have someone to help you to carry him to his room. There is a lot of money in the safe. I am taking the key with me. There will be an inquest. After that arrangements will be made for the funeral. You will stay here pending further orders from me. Is that clear?'

'Yes, sir.'

Biggles beckoned to the others and they filed slowly from the room to the bright sunshine outside.

As they paused on the steps of the house of tragedy Gaskin said in a melancholy voice: 'I don't know what things are coming to and that's a fact. If millionaires are going to start playing crooks just for the hell of it I might as well give up. I can't win.'

Bertie had this to say. 'You know, old boy, had it not been for you happening to know Canson's character this need never have happened. The doctor's little game of beating the police could have gone on indefinitely.'

Biggles shook his head. 'I doubt it. I know the type. Once he found it was easy and the novelty had worn off he'd have packed up. Let's get away. The place depresses me.' He was thinking that what had happened to the doctor could have happened to him.

The cars set off back for London. They called at the airfield on the way but there was no one there. Tomlin, apparently, had bolted.

.   .   .   .

So ended the case of the man who was born with everything a man could want but was denied the one thing that really mattered.

It only remains to be said that the inquest was a mere formality. Biggles and Gaskin gave evidence having agreed to say nothing about the dead man's irregular activities. Biggles's explanation for being in the house was that he was checking up on the ownership of the aircraft. The verdict was a foregone conclusion, for, after all, the dead man had said before witnesses that he had often contemplated suicide: he couldn't stand the pain any longer. Clearly, it had to be 'suicide while of unsound mind'.

Biggles and Ginger attended the funeral in the village churchyard and laid a wreath on the grave of a man who was really a war casualty. There was only one other—from the two men who had given him loyal service.

No charge was made against them and after the funeral they faded away. No great effort was made to find Tomlin. He had played only a minor part, and if the truth must be told Biggles was suddenly sick of the whole affair. In spite of protests from the others he could not shake off a feeling that he was responsible for the tragic death of an unknown war hero.

With Canson and Rawlings it was different. They were the really bad men of the piece. No application was made for their extradition so they were tried in France and Biggles derived some satisfaction from the long prison sentences they, with the forgers, received.

He, accompanied by Gaskin, made one last visit to Millham House. This was to destroy, by burning them in the garden, the spurious bank-notes. With their destruction disappeared the evidence of a rich man's folly.

BIGGLES
AND THE
DARK INTRUDER

I
NO ORDINARY PROBLEM

AIR Detective-Inspector Bigglesworth, chief operational pilot of the Air Police based on Scotland Yard for the investigation of criminal activities in Aviation, entered the office of his chief, Assistant Commissioner Air Commodore Raymond, closed the door behind him, took his customary chair in front of the desk and waited.

The Air Commodore regarded him with pensive, harassed eyes. 'Good morning, Bigglesworth,' he said, without enthusiasm.

'Good morning, sir.'

'That unidentified aircraft was over again last night.'

'I know. I was in the air for hours looking for it. So were my pilots.'

'How did you know it came in?'

'I got a signal direct from the radar boys.'

'See anything?'

'Not a sign.'

The Air Commodore sat back in his chair. 'What do you make of it?'

Biggles raised a shoulder. 'What can we make of it? All I can say, from what little we know, is this. Someone is working on a well-thought-out scheme; which means that an experienced pilot, who is also a first-class navigator, comes into the picture. That much is obvious. More than that would be guesswork.'

The Air Commodore pushed forward the cigarette box. 'Well, something will soon have to be done about it,' he said wearily.

Biggles took a cigarette. 'You tell me what to do, sir, and I'll do it.'

'What can I tell you to do?'

'With respect, sir, that's your problem.'

The Air Commodore went on. 'I've just left the Air Minister. He's getting really worried.'

'What has he to worry about?'

'It's only a question of time before some member of the House of Commons gets wind of what's going on and asks a question that the Minister won't be able to answer. That could happen any day. No Minister likes to admit he doesn't know. It's a reflection on his ability. It's his business to know. In this case it would amount to an admission that our national security precautions are not what they should be.'

'Apparently they're not. Let's face it.'

'Someone will have to take the blame.'

Biggles smiled wryly. 'Yes, and I can guess who that will be.'

The Air Commodore shook his head. 'This is a serious matter, Bigglesworth. Here we have an aircraft that comes and goes as it pleases and we're faced with the disagreeable prospect of having to admit there's nothing we can do to stop it.'

'After all, that's the plain, simple, unvarnished truth. You know it and I know it. If planes could come and go in wartime, with every anti-aircraft device in action, why shouldn't they be able to do it now? We've been over all this before. If I had a reason, I could fly over any country in Europe any night that suited me and probably get away with it. Nothing short of a major operation involving searchlights, guns and fighter aircraft could stop me. Even with all that laid on I'd probably get through. In fact, as you know, I've done it.'

'Is that what you're suggesting I tell the Air Minister?'

'That's up to you, sir. I'm stating a fact and you know it.' Biggles knocked the ash off his cigarette.

'You realize that it isn't only the Minister of Aviation who is losing sleep over this business. The Ministry of Defence, the Home Office, the War Office—they're all asking what's going on. Whatever it is, they want it stopped.'

'I can understand that; but have they put forward any suggestions for stopping it? They're the people with the power to do things.'

'It isn't practicable in peace-time, as in a war, to call in the entire anti-aircraft defences of the country—if that's what you mean. The public would wonder what was going on. Some nervous people might panic, imagining a nuclear war was on the

way. Think what fools we should look if the intruder turned out
to be some hen-brained youth having what he thinks is fun,
taking his girl friend for a sky-ride. We should be the laughing
stock of Europe.'

Biggles shook his head. 'That isn't the answer.'

'It might be.'

'I doubt it. A young irresponsible fellow might play such a
lunatic game once, but I can't see him repeating it. An aircraft
isn't a motor bike. Night flying calls for something more than
nerve. This plane has been over to our certain knowledge at least
six times. Anyway, I'm sure this is no ordinary game. I've
checked every flying club, and the entire list of private owners,
for night flying, with no result. Even if someone was taking a
chance, the machine would, or should, be showing navigation
lights. Moreover, should such a pilot find himself off course he'd
be bawling for someone to give him his position. Not only does
this pilot fly without lights but he ignores signals to identify
himself.'

'His electrical equipment might have developed a fault.'

'That's always possible; but don't let's fool ourselves. Everything points to this being something more sinister than that. This
plane has a definite purpose, and at present, from what little we
know, to try to guess what that is would be a waste of time. I
could think of several possibilities. To me, one thing sticks out
like a sore finger. We're dealing with a pilot who knows the ropes
and all the tricks for dodging anti-aircraft devices. Witness the
fact that he has never crossed the coast twice in the same place.
Which means we can't concentrate on any one particular area.
He never comes at the same time or in any particular sort of
weather. There isn't much we can do with a man like that. I have
four machines. They can't watch thousands of miles of coast. Not
that it would make much difference if I had a hundred planes.'

'He's been tracked, but never for very far. Then he disappears.
How does he manage that?'

'I'd say he glides in high with his engine cut. As soon as he
realizes he's in a radar beam he comes down like a brick and gets
under it. That's when we lose him. And I'll tell you something

else. He has always kept clear of any of the regular air routes—
B.E.A., B.O.A.C., Air France and the rest. Don't ask me to
believe that's a matter of luck. He must have studied the air line
timetables. He's a wily bird, whoever he may be.'

'What the devil can he be doing?'

'Without knowing where he starts his flight, or where it ends, it
could be anything.'

'Could it be a smuggling racket?'

'Possibly. We know it's a small, single-engined job; but even a
light plane can carry a lot of contraband. It would have to be
high-value stuff to make it worth while—gold, precious stones,
paper money, something of that sort. Drugs, perhaps. They're
light and don't take up much room. I gather there's now quite a
market here for dope—heroin, hashish and reefers. There's no
longer any point in smuggling cigars, cigarettes or brandy,
which used to be the coastguards' headache.'

The Air Commodore threw out his hands in a gesture of
despair. 'What are we going to do about it? We shall have to do
something. Of course, what the Security people are most afraid
of is that this might be a way of getting spies into the country, or
the information they gather, out to the people they work for.'

Biggles shrugged. 'Could be. That, I fancy, has always gone
on. It went on right through the war. But this is guessing. It won't
get us anywhere. We shan't know the answer until we get this
crafty bird on the ground. Perhaps not then.'

'What do you mean—perhaps not then?'

'Well, if he was forced down he might set fire to his machine
and disappear before anyone could get to him. If he was shot
down he might go up in flames; in which case we wouldn't learn
much from a few charred bits and pieces. Even then, if this
business has a political angle it might not stop. We would expect
the people behind it to replace the pilot and aircraft.'

'That's cold comfort, I must say,' muttered the Air
Commodore.

'I agree, but it's no use blinking at a possibility because we
don't happen to like it.'

'Well, what *are* we going to do? We shall soon have to

do something.'

'Frankly, sir, I don't know what more we can do. I've carried out the usual routine and a lot more besides. I'll have a conference with all hands right away. We may be able to think of a new approach to the problem.'

'For heaven's sake do something. I'm scared the Press will get hold of the story. When they growl, ministers tremble.'

'And start looking round for a scapegoat,' added Biggles cynically.

'Naturally.'

'And we can guess who it will be. Just one point about that while we're on the subject. If someone starts kicking up a fuss it's likely to do more harm than good.'

'Why? In what way?'

'It will tell the intruder his activities have been spotted and he will tighten up his precautions not to get caught. Left alone, thinking all is well, he may become careless and drop us a clue; something, anything for us to work on.'

The Air Commodore nodded. 'I take your point. Very well. I'll do my best to keep the soft pedal on the business but I can't promise to hold it down for very long. Do the best you can and don't waste any time. Call on me for anything you need. What have you actually done so far?'

'It didn't seem much use waffling about the sky night after night, haphazard, on the off-chance of meeting this fellow who's making a nuisance of himself. I haven't enough pilots or machines for that sort of lark. It seemed to me that our only hope was to know when he was over and the area he was in; so I established direct contact with the radar chaps, and the main airports, and asked them to send me a signal if they saw or heard anything. I would always have somebody standing by. Apart from that, whenever possible I've had a machine on patrol ready to move fast to the district concerned should such a signal be received. It's hard to see what more we can do.'

'And that has had no result?'

'It has worked up to a point. When Algy was out last Wednesday night he picked up a signal that the plane was over.

He rushed to the place where it was said to be, but he couldn't find it. Radar lost it, too. That's what happens every time. This pilot, whoever he is and wherever he's coming from, is no novice at evading tactics. He's bound to realize that we shall be after him and knows what to do about it.'

The Air Commodore nodded. 'That's pretty obvious. Naturally, a good man would be chosen for such a job. That's what makes me think this is no ordinary affair. Well, carry on. Do what you can and let me know at once if you get a line on what's happening. I'll tell the Air Minister that we're doing everything possible to put an end to this intrusion.'

'Okay, sir.' Biggles got up, left the room and returned to his own office.

2

THE CONFERENCE

BACK in is own room Biggles found his three assistant pilots waiting for his news.

'Well, what was all that about?' questioned Algy Lacey.

'I'll give you one guess,' returned Biggles lugubriously, dropping into his chair.

'This intruder?'

'Of course. I was expecting the balloon to go up.'

'I suppose some official sitting with his feet up in front of the fire wants to know what we're doing about it?'

'The Air Minister wants to know why we *haven't* done something about it.'

Bertie Lissie chipped in. 'But look here, dash it all, old boy, what does he think we are—a party of wizards?'

'He, too, has a job to do, don't forget. He's responsible to the Government. Don't worry. The Chief knows our limitations and no doubt he's explained them to the Minister.'

'And a lot of good that'll do if I know anything,' put in Ginger, coldly. 'Let 'em call in the Air Force and see what they can do about it.'

Biggles ignored the remark. 'We can rely on this,' he went on. 'If the Air Commodore gets the sack for failing to do his job properly he won't bleat about it. I mean, he won't try to push the blame on to us. He was a wartime pilot himself years ago so he knows what we're up against. But instead of sitting here moaning, let's put our heads together to see if we can hit on a scheme for nobbling this smart guy, who must think he's got us baffled.'

'It seems he has,' said Ginger gloomily.

'Not yet,' disputed Biggles. 'Take it from me, he'll play his trick once too often, get careless and make a boob.'

'Fair enough. Where do we start?' inquired Algy.

'We'll start with you, answered Biggles. 'You were the last man to get a line on his track. Get out the file, Ginger.'

Ginger produced it and laid it open on Biggles' desk.

Biggles went on, speaking to Algy. 'Three days ago, when you came in you told me what had happened, but let's go over it again rather more carefully to see if we can get a line, if only a rough indication, of what goes on. This plane has been over six times to our certain knowledge—maybe more—and always manages to do the disappearing act.'

Biggles took from the file a sheet of paper on which had been roughly sketched the outline of the south-west corner of England. He picked up a pencil and a ruler. 'Go ahead, Algy,' he requested.

Algy began. 'It was last Wednesday. You sent me to do a night patrol between Weymouth and Land's End. You said, if you remember, that the plane had been reported on both sides of the Cornish-Devon peninsula and it might try that area again; but as I couldn't cover both the north side and the south at the same time I'd better keep to one side or the other.'

'That's right.'

'At 2.0 a.m. I was off the Lizard heading east. It was a fair sort of night, clear, still, starlight, but no moon. There was a thin layer of alto-cirrus but on the whole I'd call it a perfect night for flying. I had climbed to eight thousand, keeping an eye on the

Eddystone Light for a line, when I had a flash from London Airport to say an unidentified aircraft showing no lights was approaching the coast from the south at approximately six thousand. If it held its course it would cross the coast somewhere between St Mawes and Fowey. London had got the tip from the coastguard station at Falmouth. They were still tracking it. Well, that wasn't far away from me, so having asked them to keep in touch and report any change of course I went flat out downhill for the area named. Having height of this mystery bird I thought I might catch up with it and spot it, although if it wasn't showing lights that could only be more by luck than judgement. I'd have to be pretty close.'

'You had your lights on?'

'Of course.'

'Which means he'd spot you before you saw him.'

'Naturally. There I was at a disadvantage, because if he was up to any dirty work, if he spotted me it wouldn't be difficult for him to give me the slip. That's what must have happened.'

'You didn't see him?'

'Not a sign. Inside five minutes, down to six thousand, I struck the coast at a litle port which I took to be Mevagissey, although I couldn't be sure of that because at that hour there weren't many lights showing on the ground, and what there were were scattered. There wasn't much traffic on the road, either.'

'What made you think you were over Mevagissey?'

'I knew it was a fishing port. A number of small craft were putting out to sea and I took them to be fishing boats. Presumably the tide was right.'

'Then what?'

'I went inland for a little way, cruising up and down, searching the sky, but I couldn't find an aircraft. Then I had a signal to say Falmouth had lost the plane in the region of St Austell. It was then losing height fast.'

Biggles nodded. 'That's how he does it every time. Went down to get below the beam, I suppose. Anything else?'

'No. I hung about for as long as my petrol would allow; then I came home.'

'You didn't by any chance see any lights on the ground that might have marked a landing area?'

'Nothing like that.'

'May I butt in?' asked Bertie.

'What is it?'

'I know Cornwall pretty well, and I was only going to say that if this perisher dived below the beam near St Austell he'd have to keep his eyes skinned or he'd bump into the Cornish Alps. He wouldn't be likely to land there.'

Biggles looked puzzled. 'What are you talking about? There aren't any alps in Cornwall.'

'Aren't there, by Jove! That's what they call 'em.'

'Do you mean *mountains*?'

'Pretty nearly. And they keep their snow all the year round. They're whiter than white. I'm talking about the china clay workings. They pile the stuff they don't want in tips running to hundreds of feet high, some of 'em. They look like the peaks of the Swiss Alps. Mention of St Austell reminded me. That's the centre of the china clay industry. That's where this intruder disappeared. No one but a lunatic would try to land there. But there is this about it. If a pilot needed a landmark he wouldn't find a better one than these artificial mountains. They're white and they shine. Moreover, they're the only ones in the country.'

'Thank you, Bertie,' acknowledged Biggles. 'You see the advantage of several heads working together. We'll keep that in mind.' With the pencil he drew a line on his map. 'At all events, if this machine held on its track its objective must have been somewhere in the centre of Cornwall. That ties up with previous reports. All tracks so far known converge on that area. The R.A.F. base at Milford Haven picked up an unknown plane in the Bristol Channel area. It was heading in the same direction.'

Algy spoke. 'If it was over the Bristol Channel where did it start from? Somewhere out in the Atlantic?'

'Could be, if it was based on an aircraft carrier. I must admit that doesn't seem very likely, because if there was a foreign aircraft carrier hanging about our coast the Admiralty would know about it, and want to know what it was doing. But for the moment never mind about where the plane starts from. What we want to know, as it crosses the coast, is where it is going and for what purpose. As far as we can make out, every time it has been picked up an extension of its track would have taken it to about the middle of Cornwall. It doesn't follow that the machine landed there. It could have dropped something and then made for home. But mark this. Whether it landed or simply flew over the objective, there must have been a confederate waiting on the ground either to show the position of the dropping area or to collect what the plane came over to deliver.'

'It seems to me,' said Ginger, 'it's time we had a close look at the middle of Cornwall.'

'It's a big lump of land to watch. Come on, Bertie. You're the expert on the county. Can you narrow down the most likely areas to search, or to keep an eye on?'

Bertie answered. 'I can tell you this. It's all pretty hilly, and there aren't all that number of places for a machine to get on the carpet, anyway at night. It's true that on the north side of the county there's plenty of open ground, by which I mean there are not so many trees there, so I'm told, being discouraged by the Atlantic gales. The south side is different. It's well wooded and at the same time pretty hilly. Of course, there's Bodmin Moor. That's more central and it covers a lot of ground. A pilot who knows his job should have no great difficulty in getting his wheels on the ground, provided he chooses the right place. In the off season for holiday traffic he might even land on the main road, the A30, which runs right across it, mostly dead straight, for what must be the best part of ten miles or more.'

Biggles frowned. 'Bodmin Moor,' he said softly, slowly. 'That name rings a bell with me. Where have I heard it lately?'

Ginger answered. 'You're probably thinking of the police constable who was found there, murdered—let's see, it would be about a fortnight ago. The constable found dead on the road. He was a man named Harley, one of the regulars who did night duty.'

'Ah! That's it. I remember now. I've heard no more about it.'

'No doubt because no arrest has been made. There has been

nothing more about it in the papers.'

'Queer that this should crop up just when we were interested in the place. Can you recall the details, as far as they're known?'

'I think so. Some tourist on his way to the coast via Bodmin saw a bicycle lying beside the road. He stopped and had a look round, but seeing nobody he went on. A couple of hundred yards farther on his headlights picked up a body lying on the road. It was a policeman. He was dead. All he could do was move the body to the side of the road and press on to Bodmin, where he reported what he had seen to the police. They brought the body in. There were several injuries, one on the head. Naturally, at first it was assumed that the constable had been knocked down by a hit-and-run motorist——'

'In that case, surely, the bicycle would have been near the body?' interposed Biggles.

'The answer was found at the post-mortem, when it was discovered that the officer had been shot in the back by a forty-five revolver bullet. That, of course, made it a case of murder. That's the last I've heard of it.'

'Now why should anyone murder a policeman at a spot like that?' murmured Biggles pensively.

'He may have stopped a suspicious-looking character to question him,' contributed Algy.

'I suppose that could be the answer, but it doesn't impress me,' returned Biggles. 'In the first place, why should a suspicious-looking character be walking the road in the middle of the night? Why walk? One would think he'd try to thumb a lift. Again, why was the body so far from the bicycle? Why didn't this supposed suspicious character get on it and ride away?'

'You tell me,' Algy answered. 'What are you thinking?'

'I'm wondering if by any chance this murder could have any connection with our problem. Why was the body so far away from the bicycle? That strikes me as very odd. If you asked me to explain it I'd say the officer wasn't with his bike when he was murdered.'

'All right. What do you think happened?'

'If you're asking for a theory, without any evidence to support it, I'll give you one. The constable was cycling down the road when he saw something unusual. He stopped, and leaving his bike beside the road went forward on foot to investigate. In doing that he took on more than he bargained for. That's the risk policemen take these days. He was trying to get back to his bike when he was shot in the back.'

'But his body was found *on* the road, nowhere near the bike,' argued Algy.

'That's because it was put there. The murderer didn't know the policeman had a bike. He had to get rid of the body so he dumped it on the road, anywhere, hoping it would be assumed that the officer had been knocked down by a car. As in fact it was, at first.'

'But why did the murderer have to go to all that trouble?'

'Because he knew policemen don't vanish into thin air. When this one failed to return from his beat a search would have been made for him. The man who did the shooting didn't want that to happen.'

'He could have put the body where it wasn't likely to be found,' suggested Bertie.

'That doesn't change my argument. It was better to have the body found, or, as I say, there would have been a full-scale search, which was something the murderer didn't want.'

'I can see some weak spots in your theory, old boy,' came back Bertie.

'Such as what?'

'The wounds. If the constable was shot dead there would have been no need to knock him about.'

'That's where you're wrong. You'd expect a man knocked down by a car to have injuries—serious injuries if they were enough to kill him. And it's no use arguing that the wounds were caused before the shooting because if the constable was on the ground it wouldn't be easy to shoot him in the back. Why shoot him in the back, anyway? If the shot was fired to make sure he was dead it might as well have been into his chest, in the heart, or head. No. When that wretched police officer was shot he was trying to get away. His back was towards the gunman. And he

had not then been injured or he wouldn't have been able to run
away. In a word, he was shot first and injured afterwards. Does
that make sense?'

There was silence for a moment. Then Bertie said. 'I know that
road pretty well. The moor is open, but there'd be no difficulty in
disposing of a body where it would never be found.'

'Such as where, for instance?'

'Down one of the old mine shafts scattered about all over the
place. Hundreds of 'em. A local lad once told me there were over
two thousand of 'em.'

'Are you talking about coal mines?'

'No. Metals. Cornwall used to be a great place for metals—
copper, lead, zinc, but mostly tin. The place is fairly dotted with
ruins at what used to be the pitheads. Sometimes the old shafts
have been fenced, but not always, so if you're thinking of doing a
hike be careful where you're putting your feet. Every so often
someone falls into one of these holes. It's a dangerous place for
kids to play, I can tell you.'

'I find that interesting,' said Biggles slowly. 'I imagine these
holes would make it dangerous for a plane to get down.'

'Not if you knew your ground. Of course, the herbage is pretty
rough—heather, gorse, and that sort of thing.'

'Hm. I have a feeling it wouldn't be a bad idea to cast an eye
over Bodmin Moor.'

Said Ginger: 'Does that mean you're going to take up the case
of the murdered constable?'

'It does not. The local police would take a dim view of
Scotland Yard poking its nose in without being invited.'

'Then why bother?'

'There's a chance that the man we're after, this fly-by-night
intruder, may be using the moor for whatever it is he's doing. If
we follow his tracks, those we know have always run in that
direction, and as the moor must be a lonely place it seems the sort
of spot he'd be likely to choose. We've got to start somewhere and
this strikes me as good an area as any. What I'd really like to
know is the exact spots where this unfortunate constable and his
bike were found. If there *is* any connection between this and the

man we're looking for, it should narrow the area to be watched.'

'You'll only get that information by going to Cornwall.'

'I realize that. Just a minute. Let me think.' Biggles paused, toying with his pencil. He took a cigarette and lit it. 'What I'd like,' he went on, 'is a mosaic of this moor on both sides of the road. We could extend the picture later if necessary. I'll tell you what. We can all take a hand in this. Algy, you and Ginger can get the photographs. Take an Auster with a vertical camera and be on the job first thing tomorrow morning—that is, of course, if the weather is right. Visibility will dictate your altitude but around two thousand would be best. Have the pictures ready for me when I get back here.'

'What are you going to do?'

'I shall take Bertie and go to Bodmin by road. I'll have a word with the police there and, if they'll co-operate find out exactly where the policeman and his bike were found. At the same time I'll have a good look at the moor from ground level. I don't think we need bother to find the man who reported the body to the police. They'll have got a statement from him.'

Biggles got up. 'Okay. Let's get on with it. If we don't soon have something to report the balloon will go up and we shall go up with it. Come on, Bertie. We'll get off right away. We can spend the night in Bodmin to be ready for an early start in the morning. With any luck we should be back here by tomorrow evening.'

3

BODMIN MOOR

AT ten o'clock the following morning, with a cigarette smouldering between his fingers Biggles sat on a low, heather-covered mound, beside the road that crossed the expanse of desolate ground he had come to see with his own eyes—as the saying is. Bodmin Moor. It was a fair morning, clear, with an occasional bank of high cumulus cloud drifting on the face of a moderate south-west wind across a blue sky.

As a general view the landscape was not inspiring, but it was much as he had expected to find it. One moor is very much like another. On both sides of the pale ribbon of road, without much traffic on it at this hour, an expanse of rough, flat, mostly treeless, uncultivated ground rolled away to a horizon formed by gently rising slopes.

As with similar areas in Britain, there was a wearisome sameness about the scene, with nothing to catch the eye or hold attention. The heather, tough old 'stick' heather, as it is called in Scotland, was not yet in flower. Only here and there a growth of gorse made a splash of gold. For the rest, one or two ruins such as Bertie had described, roofless walls with perhaps the stump of a crumbling chimney stack, were the only objects, dismal enough in themselves, to break the melancholy picture. High in the air larks were trilling, but apart from these there was no sign of life; no animal, not even a humble rabbit that had survived the killing disease, myxomatosis.

Things had gone as Biggles had planned. After an easy run down from London in the car he and Bertie had spent the night in Bodmin. Nine o'clock the following morning found them at the police station. Biggles had introduced himself, making the excuse for being there that the affair of the murdered constable might have a bearing on another case on which he was engaged; which was true. He did not say what it was.

The Inspector in charge could not have been more helpful. He said there had been no new development in the case of the policeman. They were still at a loss for a motive, and without one it was hard to think of a theory to account for the murder. When Biggles had asked for the scene of the crime to be marked on his map, he was offered the services of a policeman to show him the actual spot where the body was found; which was even better, particularly as the officer detailed to go with them was one of the party that had gone out to bring in the body. He knew exactly where it had lain.

'I don't think you'll find much there,' were the Inspector's last words. 'We've been over the ground thoroughly.'

Biggles answered that he was more concerned with the spot where the murder had been committed than with finding the weapon that had been used.

'The whole thing's a mystery,' concluded the Inspector, shaking his head. 'Why anyone should want to kill poor Harley beats me. He was a quiet, inoffensive sort of chap; rarely had any trouble with anybody except on one or two occasions with a poacher.'

'And poachers don't usually carry revolvers,' returned Biggles, as he left the office.

With the policeman beside him, Police Constable Redruth, Biggles drove towards the scene of the murder. His guide appeared to be a taciturn sort of man. Not until they arrived did he speak, and then it was with a rich Cornish brogue.

'We're coming to the place now,' he said. Then, 'This is it.' He got out and pointed to a spot on the verge. 'Just here. This is where Mr Brunner put the body. He found it lying in the road. He moved it so it wasn't run over by another car. They travel fast on this stretch.'

'I suppose Mr Brunner made a statement?'

'Yes. He's a Mr Peter Brunner; comes from Coventry. He was on hs way to St Mawes for his holidays. He says he looked around but couldn't see anybody. It was a dark night.'

'What time was this?'

'Just after two o'clock in the morning.'

'And where was the bicycle?'

Again the policeman pointed. 'Along there. Same side of the road, lying in the heather. About two hundred yards from here as near as makes no difference.'

'Was it damaged at all?'

'Not a mark on it as far as I could see. Just as if poor Harley had put it down to look at something.'

'By the way, was Mr Brunner alone in his car?'

'Yes. Good thing too. It wouldn't have been a nice experience for a woman if he'd had one with him.'

Biggles looked across the Moor. 'I believe these ruins I can see are all that are left of old mine workings. Are they ever worked now?'

'Never in my time. They're just the same as when I first set eyes on 'em as a boy.'

'What's that long dark-coloured mark I can see over there?'

'Been a fire at some time, I reckon. Picnickers and hikers are always setting the heather alight. We don't bother much. Can't do much harm here unless the smoke's blowing across the road to interfere with the traffic.'

'Quite so. Well, I think that's all. Thanks for coming along. Mr Lissie can run you back to the station now. I'll wait for him here and we'll get back to London.' Turning to Bertie Biggles went on: 'Take the officer back to the station. Collect our things at the hotel and settle the bill. I'll stay here. There's no need for me to come with you. Pick me up and we'll push along home. We'll have lunch somewhere on the road.'

'Right you are.' Bertie got into the driving seat and the car departed the way it had come.

Biggles, alone, found a little heather-covered hump and sat down to smoke a cigarette and survey the landscape pending Bertie's return. The delay, he thought, would at the same time provide an opportunity to do some hard thinking while on the actual scene of the tragedy. Not that he knew much more than when he had set out for Cornwall. He decided not to bother to search the ground in the immediate vicinity because this, according to the Inspector, had already been done by the police. They had found nothing, and he was confident they would have done the job thoroughly.

As he sat there, with an occasional car passing in one direction or the other, a familiar sound overhead made him glance up. He saw what he expected. An Auster. So Algy and Ginger had arrived. Forthwith they began their task of flying up and down. Always at the same altitude, taking in a different stretch of the ground on every run.

With the sound of the engine constantly in his ears, knowing what the plane was doing, Biggles took little interest in it. His eyes wandered over the landscape, not seeking anything in particular but on the off-chance of noticing something, such as a detail out of place, on which to concentrate his attention. He saw nothing to excite him, but because the dark patch of ground was one of the few conspicuous marks in an otherwise monotonous panorama, his eyes more than once wandered back to it. The police constable had said he thought it must be where there had once been a heath fire, caused by careless trippers lighting a fire for a picnic tea. As this is a common occurrence all over the country it seemed a reasonable assumption.

But why there? pondered Biggles. When the driver of a car on a long-distance run stopped to boil a kettle it was usually by the roadside, close to the car. Why did someone walk what Biggles estimated to be at least a quarter of a mile to light a fire? It seemed unlikely that anyone in a car would do that. Of course, he reasoned, it might have been caused by a party of hikers out for a tramp across the moor. No doubt that was a common occurrence. But this fire could not have been caused by a cigarette end tossed carelessly from a car window—a common cause for such fires.

Thus meditated Biggles, moodily contemplating the lonely moor, with the Auster drowning the song of the skylarks as it worked at its photographic routine. He was still sitting in the same place when the car returned.

Bertie stopped and got out. 'I see the boys are on the job,' he said cheerfully.

'Yes. They came some time ago and must be nearly finished.'

'Anything doing, old boy?' Bertie joined Biggles on his hump.

'Not a thing, as far as I can see.'

'What do you make of it?'

'Not much. If we're right in thinking it's somewhere in this locality that our unknown night bird is laying its eggs, the pilot's taking a chance every time he comes over; that's if he actually lands and supposing the ground coverage of the moor is the same everywhere as it is here. Look at it. This old tough heather is long enough to trip up a light plane and put it on its nose. I wouldn't care to try putting an Auster down on it.'

'It may not all be like this.'

'True enough. How do we find out? We'd have to walk a good

many miles to check the entire moor and that would take time. Algy's photos should show any obstructions, rocks and that sort of thing, but I doubt if they'll have a clear enough definition to reveal the height of the herbage.'

'Pity there aren't any grouse here.'

'What have grouse got to do with it?'

'Well, if this was a grouse moor it would be worth while burning the heather off in strips, as they do in Scotland, to produce new young shoots for the birdies to eat. This old stuff is all right for them to nest in, but no grouse-bird, unless it was dying of hunger, would try to make a meal of it.'

'Talking of burning, it looks as if there has been a fire over there.' Biggles pointed. 'That's what the constable thought. He put it down to careless hikers.'

'Probably right. Maybe not. In dry weather a moor can set itself on fire by spontaneous combustion. The sun shining through a piece of glass, a broken bottle for instance, can do it.'

'So I believe.'

'If a fire did start here I doubt if anyone would bother to put it out. It couldn't do much harm.'

'In that case what does put it out?'

'Rain, sooner or later. Have you been across to look at that burnt patch?'

'No.'

'Why not?'

'What could it tell us? There's been a fire. We know that already. It would mean a fair walk and we haven't time to mess about for no serious reason.'

At this point of the conversation, Algy, or whoever was flying the Auster, apparently having spotted the stationary car on the road and two men sitting near it, came over low. Biggles waved. The plane rocked its wings as a signal of recognition and went on its way, heading east.

'So they've finished and are going home,' observed Biggles. 'I think we might do the same. We've a fair run in front of us. It might be as well to have a look at their pictures before we start tramping the moor. They should be ready by the time we get back.' Biggles got to his feet. 'The trouble with this sort of thing is there's always a feeling that you could be wasting your time—looking for something that isn't there. However, we've got to look somewhere and it might as well be here. At least we can tell the Air Commodore that we're trying. I'd like something a bit more substantial to work on before I spend too much time here. At present were working on not much more than a hunch. If necessary we can always come back.'

'But you still think this may be the objective of the bloke we're looking for?'

'I wouldn't go as far as that. I think it *might* be, because from all the sightings that have been made the plane was heading in this direction. We may be barking up the wrong tree. How are we going to find the right one?'

'I can only see one way to check if we're on the wrong track.'

'How would you do that?'

'We could sit here and wait for the plane to come over.'

'That would mean squatting here all night and every night, in all weathers.'

'I'm afraid so,' agreed Bertie.

'If the plane came over at regular intervals, and at one particular hour, the idea might be worth considering. But it doesn't. It has sometimes been more than a month between the reports, so one might sit here for a month to no purpose. Do you feel like sitting here for maybe a month on the mere off-chance of the plane coming over?'

'Frankly, old boy, I can't say the prospect would set me whooping with rapture,' admitted Bertie.

'That goes for me, too. Let's press on home and have a close look at the photos before we talk about doing night shifts in this dreary place. We shall have to be on call at the Yard, anyway, in case there's another report.'

'Then there's nothing else we can do.'

'There might be one thing while we're in Cornwall. The thought has just struck me.

'What is it?'

'When we came here we'd decided there might just be a

remote possibility that there was a connection between the intruder and the murdered constable. The murder isn't our business, but there's one angle, from our point of view, that may have been overlooked by the local police because to them it could have no possible bearing on the case.'

'And what's that?'

'This man who found the body, a traveller from Coventry named Brunner, on his way for a holiday at St Mawes.'

'What about him?'

'He said he had a good look round but didn't see anybody or anything. It was a dark night. But did he *hear* anything? An aircraft, for instance. He might have done. If he did he wouldn't pay any attention to it. Why should he? He'd be concerned only with the body he'd found. A plane at that moment would mean so little to him that I doubt if he'd even mention it in his statement to the police. He was travelling alone, remember. We might even wonder what he was doing on the road at two o'clock in the morning.'

Bertie stared. 'You don't think he could have had anything to do with the murder.'

'I'm suspicious of everyone until he can prove he's in the clear. What I'm really thinking of is this. Did he notice a light anywhere? If a plane intended landing on the moor there should have been a signal light showing somewhere on the ground. That again would have meant nothing to Brunner in the state he must have been in at the time. That's if his statement is true. Come to think of it, we know nothing whatever about this man Brunner. He was alone on the moor on the night of the murder so the police have only his word for what happened. The police don't appear to have questioned it. It might be worth while having a word with him. St Mawes is only a small place, so he wouldn't be hard to find, if he's still there.'

'Does that mean you're thinking of calling on him?'

'Possibly. But we've no time for that now. Let's press on home.'

They got into the car and set off up the long white road.

4
A MATTER OF DEDUCTION

The following morning Biggles was in the office early with the photographic air survey covering the top of his desk. It consisted of a number of photographs taken by a vertical camera from the same altitude. Fitted together like a jig-saw puzzle they made a single picture of an area of ground too large to be contained on a single photographic plate. In this case it was Bodmin Moor, or that part of it with which they were concerned. The road on which the constable had lost his life ran like a ribbon across the middle of it.

With a large magnifying glass in his hand he had been studying the result of Algy's work for the best part of half an hour without comment. He went over it slowly, inch by inch and section by section.

At last he spoke. 'I can't see much that's likely to be of any help to us,' he said. He continued. 'There is just one thing though that puzzles me. Algy, or perhaps you, Ginger, must have noticed this long darkish patch, no great distance from what I take to be the ruins of an abandoned mine. What did you make of it?'

Ginger answered. 'Yes, I saw it. One could hardly miss it. It was the only really conspicuous mark on the heather, which for the most part was pretty well all alike.'

'What do you think it was? What had caused it?'

'I took it to be a place where there had been a runaway heath fire at some time. I can't see what else it could have been.'

Algy agreed.

Biggles nodded. 'That's what the policeman thought, the one who showed us the spot where the murdered constable's body had been found. I didn't question it. But there's something else. On the photograph there's a detail which I couldn't see from where I stood on the road: or maybe the angle from which I was looking had something to do with it. It's plain to see on the photo. I mean this strip of heather that runs parallel with the burnt piece. It seems to be lighter in colour than most of the heather.

Did either of you notice that?' Biggles looked up.

Ginger answered. 'Yes, I had a good look at it.'

'What do you make it out to be?'

'Frankly, I didn't pay any serious attention to it. There was nothing on it. It shows up because the green is lighter, brighter. It was the only place like it as far as I could see; but as I say I didn't give it any serious thought because working the camera I had to watch what I was doing.'

'I noticed it, but I was more concerned with keeping a straight line,' put in Algy. 'I fancy the ground there dipped a bit so it might have been a brighter green as a result of water draining in from the higher ground.'

'Yes, I suppose that could account for it,' murmured Biggles.

Bertie stepped forward. 'Mind if I have a dekko, old boy?' He took over the magnifying glass. 'I've never been on this particular moor, but I've walked on a good many grouse moors in Scotland so I know a bit about this sort of country, if you see what I mean. I imagine all moors that grow heather are very much alike.'

'Carry on. See what you can make of it. There must be a reason for the heather being a different colour and we can't afford to gloss over anything, however trivial it may seem.'

For perhaps a minute Bertie studied the photograph intently. Then he said: 'Shall I tell you what I think this is, what happened here?'

'That's what I'm waiting to hear.'

'Before fire burnt off that patch of heather where it's plain enough to see, there was another fire close to it. Must have been some time ago. In case you don't know, when a fire runs through heather it burns off all the stuff that's above ground but it doesn't kill the roots unless the peat underneath it is very dry, when it may go deep and smoulder for months unless there comes a lot of rain. I fancy what we can see here, this light patch, is young heather shooting up from roots where old woody stuff was at some time or other burnt off.'

'That's interesting,' Biggles said. 'If you're right, it can only mean there must have been two fires in practically the same place.'

'That's what it looks like to me, old lad.'

'Hm. That strikes me as a bit odd. Say, a coincidence.'

'I suppose one could say that, considering how far the fires were from the road. Of course, there may be something in that particular area likely to cause a fire. If a railway crossed the moor, for instance, sparks from the engine would cause fires when the heather was dry.'

'There isn't a railway, so let's not waste time talking about something that isn't there. What else could have done it?'

Bertie, polishing his monocle with a handkerchief, shook his head. 'I haven't a clue, old boy, not a bally notion—unless some silly blighter chucked cigarette ends about.'

'In that case one would expect fires all over the place. Two in the same place looks more to me as if it was done deliberately.'

Nobody spoke.

After a pause Biggles continued. 'It would be reasonable to suppose that what caused the first fire also caused the second. If it wasn't an accident, and we can't see anything to suggest it might have been, then the thing *must* have been deliberate. It follows that if someone set the heather on fire he must have had a reason. You'll notice that both fires were roughly the same size, long and narrow. That can only mean that both fires started when the wind was in the same direction.'

'They run south-west to north-east or vice versa,' put in Algy.

'Say south-west to north-east. South-west is the direction of the prevailing wind. Both strips are long and narrow. Does that suggest anything to anybody?'

Ginger answered. 'A long strip would be handy for an aircraft wanting to land.'

'Good. That's what I was thinking. If I wanted to make a landing strip on the moor that's the shape I'd make it, and the direction, to suit the wind one's most likely to find in this particular part of the country. It might be worth while checking the direction of the wind when the intruder came over. The Met. people would know. I don't say that would prove anything, but it would support the view that a plane could land there—the pilot, of course, having the advantage of knowing he was landing into the wind as he touched down on the strip. In fact, he wouldn't be able to land in any other direction without running into long heather which might tangle with his undercarriage and trip him up. Just a minute. Let me think.' Biggles paused, chin in hands, elbows on the desk. Presently he went on. 'Here, if Bertie is right, we have two strips. They run parallel. One has been there for some time. The other is apparently new. Bertie, you seem to be an expert on these matters; tell me this. When old heather is burnt off how long does it take for the roots to sprout again?'

'It would probably show green the following year.'

'You mean, short stuff.'

'Yes. Very short. Naturally, after that it would get longer every year. Being young, and fresh, and green, it wouldn't be as easy to burn as the old stuff.'

'So in order always to have a clear strip it would be necessary to burn off the old, rank, heather from time to time to keep a safe strip going.'

'Yes. As I say, it would be easier to burn the old stuff than the new growth. But hold hard, old boy. Aren't you forgetting something?'

'What?'

'This intruder chappie, as far as we know, is a night bird. In the dark he wouldn't be able to see the strips.'

'He would if a light was put out at each end of the runway to mark it. That raises a point. Could these lights have been what the murdered constable saw that caused him to get off his bike to investigate?'

Algy answered. 'That's possible. But surely if there had been a plane up to some crooked business the lights would be fixed to point directly upwards so that only the pilot could see them?'

'One would think so,' conceded Biggles. 'But don't forget the constable was on the road, which is on somewhat higher ground. He might have seen the glow, particularly in the absence of any other lights on the moor. He might have heard the plane, even if it was only gliding in.'

'Hold on a tick,' broke in Ginger, who had been scrutinizing the photograph through the magnifying glass. 'I'll tell you something else that gives weight to the theory that these burnt areas might be landing strips. You'll notice there are quite a few obstructions on the moor; the remains of old mine workings and what might be outcrops of rock. Admittedly they're widely scattered, but you'll notice that there aren't any on the runways. Why? Is that a coincidence—or is it?'

Biggles grabbed the magnifying glass. 'By Jingo, laddie, you're right!' he exclaimed. 'Good work. I hadn't noticed that. Either those strips, if that's what they are, must have been sited to avoid any obstructions, or any obstructions that may have been there were moved.' Biggles put down the glass. 'Unless we've run into more than one coincidence, which is always possible, we may have got a line on something here. Well, we've covered the ground pretty thoroughly and I don't think there's any more we can do with these photographs. I have a feeling it's time we had another look at Bodmin Moor.'

'How?' inquired Algy. 'How are we going to find out if we're on the track or merely building up a theory to suit us? Would you like me to slip along in the Auster and try an actual landing on one of these strips?'

'Not on your sweet life,' replied Biggles vehemently. 'That's the last way I'd go about putting the theory to the test.'

'Why?'

'Use your head, chum. If it so happened that we're thinking on the right lines, an aircraft landing on that particular spot could hardly fail to warn the people there that someone is wise to what's been going on.'

'You think there *is* somebody there?'

'Surely there must be if these are landing strips. At least one man would have to be on the spot to take care of things. I can imagine several things that might upset an aircraft. Sheep wandering about, for instance. Apart from mobile obstructions, bearing in mind we're dealing with a night-flyer, someone would have to put out at least two landing lights to mark the limit of the runway. The pilot couldn't do anything about that himself. I can't imagine him using parachute flares. They might set the heather on fire. Apart from that, there's always a certain amount of traffic on the road and it wouldn't be long before someone would want to know what was going on. If this mystery plane we're after is using the moor, he arrives after dark and leaves before dawn, when no one is about; that is, when there are no car headlights on the road.'

'So what are we going to do?' asked Ginger.

'Go down again by road to Cornwall and have a closer look at these strips by taking a stroll across the moor. That shouldn't arouse suspicion if we were watched. It must happen sometimes. There's no need for us all to go. Two should be enough, one to keep his eyes on the ground and the other to take note of anyone else about in the vicinity. Someone will have to be on duty here, anyway, in case the radar boys come through to say the intruder is over.'

'When are you going to start on this jaunt?'

Biggles looked at the clock. 'I might as well start today to be ready for work in the morning. It's a long run and one needs a rest before starting on anything else. I shall take Bertie with me, as he seems to be the expert on moors and what happens on them. We'll put on some old togs and carry haversacks to look like a couple of stray hikers.'

Algy put a question. 'How long are you likely to be away?'

'I can't say. That will depend on what we find—if we find anything. Having got the information we want about these strips, there'd be no reason why we shouldn't come straight back home.'

'You wouldn't stay there?'

'I wouldn't think so; not at this stage of the proceedings. I could always ring up if we were likely to be delayed. I'll let you know where we're staying in Bodmin. Should the intruder come over you can call us and let us know.'

Algy went on. 'There's one thing about this that doesn't line up with you being a couple of hikers. I imagine you won't walk all the way from Bodmin to the moor. It's a long way.'

'Of course not.'

'You'll take the car?'

'Yes.'

'If you stop it beside the road anywhere near these strips, and then get out and start hoofing it across the heather it would knock on the head your pose of being ramblers.'

Biggles nodded. 'You make a point there.'

'Moreover, a stationary car on the road and nobody with it might start the local police making inquiries. You might even return to the car to find it had been towed away.'

Biggles considered the problem. 'Perhaps it would be as well if someone else came with us,' he decided. 'Having dropped us off he could carry on and return to pick us up later. After all, one should be enough here to take care of things for the short time I reckon to be away. Ginger, you'd better come. I'm afraid, Algy, that means you'll have to stand by the phone here.'

'Okay. It'll suit me to rest my feet instead of blistering 'em route-marching through miles of dusty heather.'

Biggles rose, picking up the photograph. 'All right. Let's leave it like that. Ginger, you might bring the car round. We'll slip home to get our kit and have a bite of lunch on the way to Cornwall.'

An hour later the police car was on the road.

Six hours later it was being parked in the garage of the hotel where Biggles and Bertie had already stayed the night.

They had travelled slowly over Bodmin Moor, which, of course, using the main road, the A30, they had had to cross on the way to their destination. Once, for a few minutes, without getting out of the car, they stopped to survey the landscape and reconsider the general picture. With one minor difference it was exactly the same as when they had last seen it; and there was nothing unnatural about the difference. Beyond the burnt strip a man with a dog, apparently a shepherd, was minding a small flock of sheep.

'I can guess what he's doing,' Bertie said.

'Tell us.'

'He's giving his sheep a feed of that new heather. Sheep, like the grouse-bird, are fond of heather when it's short and sweet and tender and juicy.'

'That's a pity,' returned Biggles. 'If sheep have been trampling the stuff down we're not likely to find much. I suppose the old stuff may have been burnt off for no other reason than to feed sheep.'

'Quite likely.'

'In that case it looks as if we're wasting our time.' Biggles drove on.

At the hotel, as they got out of the car Ginger said, 'Shall we need the car again tonight?'

Biggles answered. 'No. Not unless Algy rings up to say he's had a signal that the intruder is over, in which case we'd go back to the moor and keep our eyes and ears open. You might call Algy to let him know we've arrived. Confirm he has our phone number here.'

'Right away.' Ginger went off.

5
FIRST INSPECTION

THE next morning, after an undisturbed night, Biggles and his party were early at work. With sandwiches for the day in their haversacks, and Biggles with binoculars slung over his shoulder, they set off for the objective.

A little distance short of it, before reaching the higher ground, Ginger, who was at the wheel, at a word from Biggles brought the car to a stop. Biggles and Bertie got out quickly. The car went on, to get, and remain, out of sight. This meant going something like two miles, because the road was straight and open to the winds of heaven, that is to say, without any concealing trees or hedges, except an occasional clump of broom or gorse on one side or the other. This manoeuvre, of course, had been arranged before the start.

Ginger's orders were to wait an hour before returning. Then he was to cruise back without stopping unless signalled to do so.

This procedure was to be repeated until the others returned from their on-the-spot reconnaissance, which was not expected to take more than two hours at most.

This was merely a simple precaution against attracting the attention of anyone who might be watching the area with which they were concerned. There were other cars on the road, most of them travelling at high speed and without stopping, there being no reason to do so except in the case of a breakdown. Later in the day a car might stop for a picnic lunch by the roadside, but that was not likely to happen at this early hour.

When Biggles and Bertie were ready to leave, seeing the car coming they would 'thumb' a lift, which would account for the car stopping. All this was on the off-chance of a watcher keeping an eye on the road for anything unusual. It might be that they were being over-cautious, as Biggles stated when the arrangement was being made; but he held the view that the visits of the intruder, should this be its objective, must have been organized by a man who would take every possible precaution against his plan going wrong. He was convinced that if the moor was being used as a secret landing ground there would have to be at least one man on the ground to carry out part of the operation.

With the car disappearing in the distance Biggles and Bertie walked a little way along the road to higher ground, actually close to the spot where the constable had been murdered, as this gave a wider view of the moor. Here they sat, backs to the road, to make a preliminary survey of the ground in front of them before walking across it. There was no apparent change in the landscape except that the shepherd and his sheep were no longer there; or, at all events, they were not in view.

'Apparently sheep don't graze here all the time,' remarked Biggles. 'I suppose they're only driven on from time to time for a free feed.'

'You know, old boy, I found myself thinking about that last night after I'd gone to bed,' Bertie said pensively.

'You mean the sheep? What was there to think about?'

'It struck me there was something a bit odd about it. Only a detail, I must admit.'

'What's odd about sheep on a moor? On most moors you will usually find sheep.'

'I'm not thinking about the bally sheep. It was the dog that somehow seemed wrong.'

'Where you see a shepherd you will always see a dog. And there are a devil of a lot of dogs in the country, of one sort or another.'

'True enough. But a lot of them are specially bred and trained for one particular job. The sheep dog is one of them. He comes from a specialized strain. He inherits from his mum the knowledge of what he's expected to do. That makes him easy to train. I mean to say, a foxhound is bred to hunt foxes and nothing else. If he went after a rabbit he'd be ticked off. Pointers and setters are trained to point game, although some do it by instinct. The job of a bloodhound is man hunting—that sort of thing—if you see what I mean.'

Biggles looked at Bertie curiously. 'Well? What about it?'

'The sheep dog we saw on the moor yesterday wasn't like any sheep dog I've ever seen. Nowadays they're mostly a sort of collie.'

'What breed was the one we saw here yesterday?'

'I don't know. It was too far away. But I can tell you this. It was no ordinary sheep dog.'

'I imagine any dog can be taught to look after sheep.'

'Probably. But why should a farmer in this part of the world use anything but the right sort? It's his business. The wrong sort of animal might do more harm than good, chasing the wretched sheep from hell to breakfast.'

'What did this particular dog look like to you? Make a guess.'

'Well, if you're asking me to guess, the dog we saw yesterday reminded me of a German breed of guard dog. I forget its name.'

'You don't mean an Alsatian?'

'No. Nothing like it. The dog we saw was brown—a kind of chestnut colour. The type I'm thinking of is more like a small, lightly built mastiff. I once knew a feller who had one, but it bit so many people he had to get rid of it. Most sheep dogs are friendly.'

'Hm,' murmured Biggles. 'This is interesting. We'll keep it in mind,' he smiled. 'This is where you can teach me a thing or two.'

'It's my line of country, old boy.'

'That's what I thought. That's why I brought you along. Try to spot something else. Now we'd better start walking.'

Bertie gave the moor a final comprehensive scrutiny through the glasses. 'Not a soul about,' he announced. 'We have the place to ourselves.'

'Provided the ground is level.'

'What is that supposed to mean? You can see the ground is level.'

'I agree that's how it looks from here, but in open country one can never be sure. A fold in the ground, even a slight depression, can hide a crowd as long as they all keep their heads down. I've seen it happen. Even so, that needn't concern us. We've as much right on the moor as anyone. Let's press on.'

They moved off at a steady pace towards the final objective, which was, of course, the burnt heather suspected of being a strip on which a light plane could land. This was no more than a suspicion. The present excursion was to ascertain, if possible, if the ground was being used for that purpose.

It was a fair day, sunny, with only a light breeze, although some threatening-looking clouds rolling up from the south-west suggested these conditions might not last.

'I have a feeling we should have brought our macs,' remarked Bertie. 'This is no place to be caught in a storm.'

Still without seeing any signs of life, except a soaring buzzard high overhead, they reached the blackened area without encountering such a depression as Biggles had thought might occur. They stopped to examine the ground at their feet.

'What do you make of it?' Biggles asked the question.

'Not much, old boy. But I can tell you this. The heather here was burnt when it was bone dry. Notice that the fire has burnt to ground level; sticks and everything. On a grouse moor they'd say this was good burning.'

'Then heather doesn't always burn like this?'

'No fear. On a stiff breeze, if the ground is wet, a fire can sweep through taking off only the tops. They flare up like tissue paper. I get the impression that this fire was started deliberately when the heather was in perfect condition for the job.'

'Anything else?'

'No. That's all.'

'Then let's walk the length of it. The bare ground, having been exposed to wind and sun, has dried out pretty hard, but it might still show wheel marks.'

Moving a few yards apart to cover more ground they walked the length of the strip, stopping where the long heather started, no great distance from what apparently were the ruins of an abandoned mine. They found no wheel tracks, or anything else of interest.

'No luck,' Bertie said.

'If there were tracks they could have been brushed out by someone who didn't want them seen,' mused Biggles. 'Or sheep could have trampled them out. Sheep have been on here. Let's try the young stuff. We may have better luck there.'

They moved on the adjacent strip. It was about the same width and ran parallel. The ground had a covering of bright green fresh young heather from six to nine inches high.

'This wouldn't be too bad for landing on,' observed Biggles.

'Not at the moment,' agreed Bertie. 'But given the right sort of weather from now on it will grow pretty fast, and soon be long enough to make landing risky.'

'This patch was once burnt off?'

'Definitely.'

'And this new growth. How long would it take to reach this stage?'

Bertie looked doubtful. 'It's hard to say. That would depend on the weather and the nature of the ground. Only a man who knew the moor could answer that. I can only say this. Whether this strip was burnt to graze sheep, or make a landing strip, it'll soon be too long for either. Perhaps the chap who burnt the first strip wants to have another patch ready.'

'I take your point. That's what it looks like. I'm no expert on heather but I can see you could be right. Tell me this. If a plane landed here surely it would crush the heather and show marks?'

'It might crush the heather but it wouldn't stay crushed. Heather is tough and springy. It doesn't break off. It bends, and it doesn't take long to get on its feet again. Any marks would soon disappear. Look behind you and you'll see what I mean. Sheep have been on here, as you can see where the stuff has been nibbled, but they haven't left any tracks. We're walking in it, but we're not leaving any marks either. You can see the stuff straightening itself again behind us.'

Biggles stood with both feet together and put his weight on them. Then he stepped aside. The heather sprang erect, showing practically no mark. 'I see what you mean,' he said. 'I'm glad I had someone with me who knows something about heather or I'd have missed that point. Good work.'

Bertie grinned. 'Don't mention it, old boy. Glad I can be useful sometimes—if you see what I mean. One man can't be expected to know everything about everything, so to speak. It so happens that I used to do quite a bit of grouse shooting in Scotland, and where you have grouse you have heather. The birds live on it. Pretty poor sort of diet, you might think, but they seem to do all right on it. That's where I learned to shoot. I mean to say, if you can pull down an old cock grouse whistling over at seventy miles an hour, jinking as he goes, you should be able to hit a thing the size of an aircraft.' Looking past Biggles' shoulder Bertie went on quickly with a change of tone: 'Don't look now, but here comes the shepherd, complete with dog, taking his baa-lambs for a stroll.'

Biggles' expression changed. He frowned. 'Where the devil could he have come from?'

'Search me, chaps. He must have popped up behind us, maybe from one of those depressions you were talking about. Same dog, I think. If that's a sheep dog I'm a bally Eskimo. I don't care much for the look of it. I don't think it likes us.'

On the pretext of turning his back to the breeze to light a cigarette Biggles looked round. Coming slowly in their direction a powerfully built man was bringing up the rear of a small flock of about a dozen sheep. Little could be seen of is face for it was almost covered by an old cloth cap above, pulled down over his ears. He wore a macintosh, with the collar turned up, gumboots, and carried a shepherd's crook. The sheep grazed as they walked. The dog took no notice of them. From its manner it was more interested in the men. With its head held low, and the hair on its neck bristling, it was advancing towards them with a slow but purposeful step.

'See what I mean?' Bertie said softly. 'When a trained sheep dog is doing a job it takes no notice of anything else.'

As the dog came nearer it showed its teeth.

Biggles shouted to the man: 'Call your dog off. It looks dangerous.'

At a word of command from its master the dog, with backward glances, sullenly retreated.

'What do we do?' Bertie asked.

'I don't see that we need do anything.' Biggles glanced at the sky, from which a few spots of rain were falling. 'We look like getting wet. No matter. I'd like to know where this fellow suddenly appeared from. I can only think it must have been from behind those ruins. We'll have a look when he's moved on a bit. If we're going to have a shower, and I fancy we are, we might find shelter there.' Again Biggles looked round the sky as if they were discussing the weather.

The shepherd was still moving on slowly, apparently taking no notice of them.

'Let's make for the ruins,' Biggles said.

They started walking towards them casually, but as the rain quickened they increased their pace to a quicker step and finally a trot. As Biggles remarked, this, in the circumstances, was natural; not that they really needed an excuse for what they were doing.

They reached the old mine, for clearly that was what it was, to find the sprawling brickwork covered more ground than they had expected. As the lower part of the crumbling walls were still standing they had to walk round them to find a way in, to get to the only shelter the place offered. This was a long low shed in the last stages of dilapidation, but at one end of it, for a matter of a few yards, some slates remained on what had been the roof. The only other conspicuous objects were the stump of a chimney stack, built of stone slabs, and a skeleton wooden structure which may have carried the winding gear over the pit.

Hurrying on, they came to what appeared to be the only gap in the walls. It had been half closed by two hurdles.

'This must be where the old man came from,' said Biggles as they went in. 'Yes, this is it. He must spend some time here, judging from the quantity of sheep droppings.'

They walked across a trampled area of heather and tufts of coarse grass between heaps of fallen weed-covered brickwork to the end of the shed, the only place that promised shelter from the rain, which by now had increased to a sharp downpour. Under the remaining piece of roof some of the old bricks had been roughly arranged to form a seat; or that's what it looked like, since there was no other apparent reason for it.

'This must be where the shepherd sits to watch his sheep before he lets them out,' surmised Biggles, seating himself. 'I imagine he closes the exit with those hurdles.' He looked around. 'What's that wire arrangement over there?' He pointed to a length of galvanized wire netting, about five feet high, stretched on posts. It was under what apparently, from some rusting ironwork, had been the winding gear when the mine was working.

'Look's like a fence round the old shaft to prevent anyone from falling in,' conjectured Bertie. 'Or the sheep, if it comes to that. I'll have a look.'

He walked over, and after a quick glance returned. 'Yes, that's it,' he announced. 'I believe all these old pits are by law supposed to be fenced, but not all of them are. I wonder they didn't clear all this junk away. They've even left some of the old wire rope hanging down the shaft, to encourage any kids coming this way to play games and break their necks. Confound this rain. Why didn't we have the sense to bring macs? We look like getting our shirts wet.'

'We didn't bring macs because when we started it didn't look as if we should need them,' Biggles pointed out. 'The shepherd must have seen what was coming and put his on. Can you see what he's doing? We don't want any trouble with that vicious-looking hound of his.'

Bertie stood on a mound of bricks and looked over the wall. 'He's coming this way. Bringing the sheep here, I suppose.'

'How far away is he?'

'About a hundred yards.'

'I have a hunch he's coming to see what we're doing. Keep an eye on him.'

Biggles got up and strode quickly to the old shaft. He considered it for a minute then walked closer to the remains of the pithead gear. He reached out and touched something, then walked back to Bertie.

Hardly had he resumed his seat, and before he could say anything, sheep were pouring in through the gateway, followed by the shepherd and his dog. The man pulled the hurdles together. The dog stopped, bristling, when it saw the two men already there.

Biggles got up. 'I'm afraid I've taken your seat,' he called cheerfully. 'We came in to shelter from the rain.'

'You can sit,' the man replied gruffly, and then stood leaning on his crook.

Bertie, standing in the open, held out his hands palms upward. 'The rain's about finished. No more than a drizzle now. The sun's blinking through already.'

'In that case we might as well get back to the road before another storm blows up,' Biggles said, vacating his seat.

They walked out of the place, the dog snarling at them as they passed.

'Which way?' asked Bertie, replacing the hurdle he had moved to enable them to get out.

'Like I said, back to the road,' answered Biggles. As they strode on through the wet heather Biggles added, 'I think we've learned enough here, as much as we shall learn today, anyway.'

'Well, what do you make of it?' inquired Bertie, as they made for the nearest point of the road. 'I still think there's something fishy about that nasty-tempered dog.'

'The dog isn't the only fishy thing there,' returned Biggles dryly.

Bertie looked at him sharply. 'Ah! You spotted something.'
'Too true. Fasten your safety belt because this is going to shake you.' Biggles held out his right hand. It was black.
Bertie stared. 'What the deuce is that?'
'Oil, laddie, oil. O - I - L. Don't stop. Keep walking. And don't look back.'

6

SINISTER DEVELOPMENTS

FOR a moment Bertie said nothing. He whistled softly. Then he muttered, 'I say, old boy, that's a bit of a bone-shaker. Where was it?'
'On the gears of that winding tackle. That mine is still being used. You don't grease gear wheels that are never likely to be used again.'
'Our shepherd pal must know all about it.'
'Of course he knows. He knows plenty. I'd make a bet he knows who shot Constable Harley. I'd also bet he's watching us at this moment. That's why he's there. There's no other practical reason.'
'The sheep are a blind, eh?'
'That's how it looks to me. And I'll tell you something else. He isn't alone.'
'Why do you think that?'
'Because one man alone couldn't lower himself into the mine. It would need at least two men, one to work the winding gear while the other goes down.'
'Stiffen the crows!' breathed Bertie. 'This certainly is a corker.'
'We haven't wasted our time.'
'Have you any idea of what the mine is being used for?'
'Not the remotest. How could I have? But it's obviously being used for something crooked; something worth while, too, judging from the trouble that has been taken to get the place organized. Don't talk for a minute. I want to think about this

while it's fresh in my mind.'

Nothing more was said until they reached the road. Cars and other vehicles were passing in both directions but their own was not among them. 'We may have to wait a bit so we might as well sit down,' Biggles said, sinking into the heathery verge. He lit a cigarette before he went on. 'We've done a good morning's work, and for the moment I'm content with that.'

'What's our next move?'

'Frankly, I don't know. It'll need some serious thought. The thing bristles with difficulties. Naturally, I'd like to have a closer look at those ruins, but I don't see how we can go back there in daylight. That fellow watching the place can't suspect what we're doing—not yet. But if he sees us there again, unless he's slow on the uptake—and I wouldn't care to gamble on that—it would be a different matter. What excuse have we got for going there? If you can think of a plausible reason I'd be glad to hear it.'

Bertie polished his eyeglass. 'Sorry, but that's got me beat.'

Biggles resumed. 'It seems to me we're in some danger of getting two cases tangled up. The intruder and the murdered constable. It may well be that there's a connection between them; but until we get evidence to support that, we'd better stick to what brought us here in the first place. This damned intruder aircraft. The first question we have to ask ourselves, before we do any more scouting on the spot, is this. Assuming that shepherd is a guard, a sort of watch dog, does he live on the job, in the ruins or possibly down the mine, or does he knock off and go home somewhere? That's important.'

'There doesn't seem much point in him being there all the time,' offered Bertie. 'He'll be there when he's wanted.'

'Another question. Does this old mine belong to somebody who is actually still working it? No doubt the police could tell us that, or find out; but if we go to them we may start something. I'd rather work on my own unless it becomes impossible. I could go on asking questions for some time, but I see Ginger coming so they can wait till we get back to the hotel.' Biggles stood up.

For the benefit of the shepherd, who may have been watching, they made a business of thumbing a lift. The car slowed.

Stopped. They got in. Ginger drove on. 'Any luck?' he inquired.

'Not too bad. We might have done worse,' answered Biggles, who was sitting next to him. 'Pull into the side of the road and stop at the next dip. I've a little job for you.'

Ginger obeyed.

Biggles went on. 'You know we came here to have a look at what we thought might be a landing strip. We've done that. I haven't time now to tell you what happened, but not far beyond the end of the burnt heather there's a pile of ruins. A disused mine—or that's what it looks like. Something's going on there. We don't know what. I hope to find out. When we left the place a few minutes ago there was a man there with a dog and some sheep. What I want you to do is stay here and watch if the man leaves. If he does, note where he goes. Lie in the heather so you can't be seen. Careful of the dog if he comes near you. Here, you'll need the binoculars. Don't let the sun flash on the lenses. I'll leave you my haversack. You may do with the sandwiches. There's no need for us all to stay here. It would mean leaving a stationary car on the road. I'll dash into Bodmin with Bertie for some lunch and come back to relieve you in, say, a couple of hours. Okay?'

'I get it.' Ginger got out, taking the binoculars and the haversack.

Biggles slipped into the driving seat and Bertie got in beside him. 'See you shortly,' he said, and drove on.

'In case you're wondering why I'm doing this,' he went on presently to Bertie, 'I have a feeling that phoney shepherd is a key man in whatever is going on here, so the first thing to find out is where he goes when he leaves here. He knows us by sight, so we don't want to be seen hanging about here. He'd wonder what we were doing. Ginger doesn't matter.'

'Absolutely,' agreed Bertie. 'I'm with you.'

'The devil of it is we can't go back to those old workings—anyway, not in daylight—without the shepherd getting suspicious. We might do some scouting after dark but that would be a tricky business. What we really want to know is, does that fellow live on his job or does he go somewhere to eat and sleep? If he stays where we saw him then obviously he must have some means of subsistence. That's why I've left Ginger there to watch.' Biggles, who was driving only at cruising speed, waved on a car trying to overtake.

'If he's living there it could only be down the mine or we'd have seen more than we did.'

'That might be the answer.'

'If he's anything to do with our intruder he'd certainly have to be on the spot when the plane is expected.'

'Not necessarily. His job might be merely to check on anyone prowling about the place—as he did on us this morning. He wasn't long giving us the once-over; at least, I can think of no other reason for his behaviour. It's reasonable to suppose he'd be about when the plane was expected. But that introduces another factor. He would have to know when the plane was due. How does he know? I don't see how there could be a regular timetable because operations would be subject to weather conditions. Someone, somewhere, must have contact with the pilot of that plane. It would be no use him coming over if the moor was under fog, and that's a common occurrence here.'

'I see no reason why the shepherd, or someone else at the mine, shouldn't be in touch with the plane by radio,' Bertie said.

'I was thinking on those lines. But where's the equipment? I didn't notice an aerial. But I wouldn't expect to. If one was seen by a person wandering on the moor it would look a bit out of place and perhaps start inquiries.'

'An aerial needn't be left out all day,' Bertie pointed out. 'Nobody would see it at night, the time it would be needed. It could be inside what's left of that old chimney stack.'

'Yes,' agreed Biggles. 'You may have something there.' He grinned. 'Jolly good. This seems to be one of your really bright days. Full marks. I feel we ought to have a closer look at that chimney stack. But how? When? It would have to be at night. Carry on. You're doing fine. Tell me something else.'

Bertie smiled. 'Thanks, old boy. There must be something in the atmosphere here that gets the old grey matter ticking. Sorry, but I'm afraid that's the lot for the moment. I'll let you know if another brainwave hits me.'

Arriving at the hotel they parked the car, went in, and still discussing the case had lunch. They then went back to the car and returned to where they had left Ginger. They couldn't see him, but a whistle brought him up from some deep heather in which he had been lying.

'Well, have you seen anything?' questioned Biggles.

'Not a thing. If a man was in those ruins when you left them he must still be there,' declared Ginger. 'No one has come out since I've been here.'

Biggles looked surprised. 'Great grief! He must get bored with sitting there hour after hour with only a bunch of sheep for company.' With a change of voice he went on sharply: 'Wait a minute. Have you been asleep?'

Ginger blinked. 'What do you mean—have I been to sleep?'

'What I say. Lying in the sun you didn't by any chance find yourself dozing?'

'I most certainly did not,' declared Ginger indignantly. 'Why ask such a question?'

'Because if I can't see the man out on the moor, going somewhere, there must be something wrong with my eyes.'

'Where?'

'Close on half a mile from the ruins, making for the road.'

'All I can say is, he didn't come out of those ruins,' asserted Ginger trenchantly.

'Give me those glasses.'

Ginger handed them over.

Biggles focused them on the distant figure. 'Yes, that's our man all right,' he stated, looking at Ginger suspiciously.

'Don't look at me like that,' protested Ginger. 'I'm telling you the truth. I don't know where he's suddenly popped up from but I'd take my oath he didn't come out of those ruins.'

'Where else could he have come from?'

'Easy on the oars, chaps,' put in Bertie. 'I may have the answer to that one. I remember reading in a book, a long time ago, that these early miners made a point of having an emergency exit, a spare hole to get out of, so to speak, in case the bally roof caved in, as in those days it sometimes did. The spare hole also created a draught to let in some fresh air to the poor blighters sweating away with their picks and shovels down below. That sort of thing, if you see what I'm getting at. There may be more than one way of getting in and out of this mine we've got our eyes on.'

'I suppose that could be the answer,' conceded Biggles, thoughtfully. 'The possibility didn't occur to me.'

'If that's the man you saw it's the *only* answer, because he didn't come out of the ruins you told me to watch,' insisted Ginger vehemently.

'Okay—okay. I'll take your word for it. But if there is a spare hole, as Bertie calls it, where is it? Work that one out.'

'You work it out yourself,' challenged Ginger. 'You can see everything I can see.'

By this time the man they had been watching had passed out of sight behind some rising ground not far short of the road.

'Are you sure it's the same man?' said Ginger.

'Almost certain; but I must admit he was some distance off. We can soon settle that. He must be nearly to the road by now. Bertie, nip along in the car and have a look at him. Try not to let him see your face. We'll wait here.'

Bertie drove off at high speed. He was away only a few minutes. He returned in a skidding stop and jumped out. 'No use,' he announced. 'He isn't there.'

'Isn't there?'

'Not a sign of him. All I could see was a car in the distance going the other way.'

'So that's it,' muttered Biggles. 'Someone must have been waiting and picked him up. That's a pity. We missed a chance.'

'Always supposing he *was* the man were watching,' Ginger said. 'What about the dog? He hadn't got one with him.'

'No. Now you mention it, he hadn't.' Even Biggles began to look doubtful. 'There's only one way to settle this,' he decided. 'If that wasn't our man then he must still be at the ruins. Bertie, run Ginger into Bodmin for some lunch. I'll keep watch here. If nobody has come out of the ruins by the time you get back Ginger can walk across and have a look inside. Our smart shepherd has never seen him so it won't matter if they bump into each other.'

This being agreed, Bertie departed, taking Ginger with him.

Biggles made himself comfortable in the heather and with his back to the road settled down to watch the landscape in front of him, paying particular attention, of course, to the ruin. He lit a cigarette and reflected on the unusual problem he had set out to solve. The facts, such as they were, were meagre, but there was plenty of room for conjecture. There were, he saw, two problems involved, the murdered constable and the intruding aircraft. Did they overlap? It was a possibility that could not be ruled out, although the one did nothing to help the other. Indeed, they were likely to cause confusion unless they were considered separately.

Time passed. Nothing happened. To the frequent passers-by nothing could have looked more quiet and peaceful, or innocent, than the open moor.

The sun was well down when the car returned.

'Anything doing?' inquired Bertie as he jumped out.

'Not a thing.' Biggles went on, somewhat gloomily: 'I'm beginning to wonder if we aren't trying to build up a little flimsy evidence to fit what we came here to find. If that shepherd has really gone we may be wasting our time. If he's still in the ruins what can he be doing all this time? It's time we settled the thing one way or the other. Ginger, do you feel like a walk?'

'Suits me.'

'Fine. Then stroll across and see if there's anyone in those ruins. Don't go direct. Make a detour as if you're not making for anywhere in particular. Carry on past the burnt heather and have a look inside the old mine workings as you pass them. Watch out for the dog. As far as we know it's still there. It's a bad-tempered brute, although I shouldn't say that, if it's only doing what it's been trained to do.'

'Is this really necessary?' Bertie asked.

'Well, I see it like this,' returned Biggles. 'If we're thinking on the right lines, if the shepherd isn't there it's unlikely our intruder friend will be over tonight. If he is there, then the plane may come.'

'I see what you mean,' said Bertie.

'Shan't be long,' put in Ginger. 'If I don't get a move on it'll be dark before I get back.' He departed on his errand.

Biggles and Bertie could see him until he reached the burnt strip and turned in the direction of the old mine. After that, what with the failing light, and a tenuous mist that was beginning to form now the sun had gone, they lost sight of him. They could only wait.

When nearly an hour had passed and Ginger had not returned Biggles said, perhaps a little irritably: 'What can he be doing? He should be back by now. I'm getting worried. I shouldn't have let him go alone. Anything could happen out there in the dark.'

'Maybe he's found something,' suggested Bertie, optimistically.

'If he has, I only hope it isn't more than we bargained for,' returned Biggles grimly.

Bertie got up. 'I'd better put on the sidelights or move the car off the road. We don't want anyone bumping into us. This mist, now it's nearly dark, could make driving a bit tricky.' Turning towards the car he stopped, rigid. 'What's that?'

The question was not really necessary.

From somewhere out on the moor, distant but clear in the silence, came the sound of a dog barking furiously. Biggles sprang to his feet. 'We can guess what that means,' he said crisply. 'We'd better get out there if he isn't back here in the next few minutes. Let's get the car off the road for a start.' Moving quickly he joined Bertie, who was already at the car.

Before they could get in they were dazzled by the headlights of an oncoming car travelling in the direction of Bodmin. There was a scraping of brakes. It stopped. A man got out and came over.

'Having trouble? Can I help?' he offered, in a quiet, cultured voice.

Looking at the speaker Biggles saw a tall, well-dressed, clean-shaven man regarding them with a sympathetic smile.

'No, we're all right now, thanks all the same,' he answered. 'We were just moving off.'

'I'm going on to Bodmin and thought if you were in serious trouble you might like me to call at a garage and ask them to send someone out to you.'

'That's most kind of you, but we're all right now so that won't be necessary.'

'As you wish.' The man got back into his car and drove on. Biggles stepped into the road and watched it go.

'Nice feller,' remarked Bertie. 'Not everyone would have bothered to stop.'

Biggles did not answer. Frowning, he returned to the car.

Bertie looked at him curiously. 'I said he was a nice feller. Wouldn't you say so?'

'I wouldn't say anything.'

Bertie looked surprised. 'Why not? Dash it all, he couldn't have done more than he did.'

'I agree with you there. All I know is, he had a damn good look at us.'

'What about it? Why shouldn't he? He was talking to us. People don't usually stand with their backs to you.'

'Yes. You might have thought he was smiling at us, too; but in case you didn't notice it I can tell you the smile didn't get farther than his lips. There was a look in his eyes that told a different story—to me, at any rate.'

'Oh, I say old boy, come off it,' protested Bertie. 'You must have reached the stage of imagining things. You couldn't say there was anything suspicious about him.'

'You could be right; but at the moment I'm suspicious of anyone on this road, day or night. I have an increasing feeling that there's more going on here than meets the eye.'

'Just what are you thinking?'

'First, why did he stop? Drivers don't usually stop at a stationary car beside the road unless signalled to do so. If they pulled up at every car they wouldn't get anywhere. As things are today everyone is in a hurry to get to where he's going. It struck me that that car might be the one that collected our wandering shepherd. I say collected because I feel sure it was no casual pick-up. The shepherd must have known the car would be there.

Remember, it didn't come from the direction of Bodmin or we'd
have seen it go past us here. It came from the opposite direction,
picked up the man, turned and went back.'

'So what?'

'It's my guess the shepherd reported seeing us on the moor—
at the old mine, in fact—whereupon someone came along to
have a look at us. Don't forget we've been on and off this road
most of the day. I suspect someone is wondering why.'

'Any reason for thinking that?'

'Yes. I noticed the gent who offered to help us had a long hard
look at our number plate. Why should he be interested in our
registration? I returned the compliment by making a note of his.
That's why I stepped into the road when he went on towards
Bodmin. Another thing. I'm pretty sure I've seen that man's face
before; but it was a long time ago and his name eludes me. I may
remember it presently, and in what connection.'

'Do you mean he was a crook?' asked Bertie.

'I don't know; but if he was, well, you see what I'm getting at.
But never mind about that now. Ginger isn't back, so it's time we
were doing something about it. He may be in trouble. I only
hope that dog hasn't savaged him. We needn't move the car.
We'll leave the sidelights on. That should be okay. When it gets
really dark we may need them ourselves to mark the position of
the car.'

They set off at a brisk pace across the moor, heading for the
spot where they judged the old mine to be. In the failing light it
could no longer be seen.

They had covered some distance when Bertie laid a hand on
Biggles' arm and brought him to a halt. 'Did you see that?' he
ejaculated.

'See what?'

'I thought I saw a light flash ahead of us. In fact I'm sure I did.
It seemed to reflect on something.'

Biggles stared into the gloom. 'Ginger hadn't got a torch.'

'That's what I was thinking.'

'There's no light there now.'

'No. But unless it was a will-o'-the-wisp there was one.'

'Listen.'

From somewhere in front the sound of voices came eerily through the clammy mist.

'Come on,' snapped Biggles.

They went on as fast as the rough ground and thick heather would allow.

7
TREED

GINGER set off on his solo assignment with the greatest confidence. Nothing could have appeared more simple, and whatever happened he could not see himself in any physical danger. He did not forget the dog, should it still be there; but he regarded this more as a possible nuisance than a threat.

He should have learned that over-confidence can be as disastrous as under-confidence, and it is likely that he took his mission too casually. His only anxiety was, should he be delayed until after dark, with the mist thickening he might have difficulty in finding his way back to the car, even though the lights were on.

He came to the burnt area, and without loitering, knowing that Biggles had already examined it, turned towards his real objective—the old mine workings. There did not seem any particular need for caution, for, after all, this was England and, as far as he knew, common ground, so the question of trespass did not arise.

Reaching the broken-down walls he did pause for a moment or two to listen; but he heard nothing. A strong unmistakable smell of sheep told him the animals were still there; or had been until very recently. Satisfied that all was well, moving quietly he made his way along to the hurdles that barred the entrance, or the exit, as the case might be. They were closed. He stopped. He looked. The only sign of life was a huddle of sheep staring at him. The light was now dim, so what with this and the weed-covered heaps of rubble he found it difficult to see the far side of the enclosure as clearly as he would have wished. He waited for a minute, peering and listening, but there was neither sight nor sound of a human being. Evidently the shepherd was not there. That was really all he wanted to know. Thinking it important that there should be no mistake about this, with a hand resting on the hurdles he whistled softly. When this did not produce any result he said, in a voice loud enough to be heard by anybody present: 'Anyone there?'

There was no reply.

This really answered his question. Nothing more was necessary. The shepherd had gone. This did not surprise him. If, as Biggles had thought, the man had left the place, his absence was to be expected. Still, he was not entirely satisfied. It would be as well to make sure. There was just a possibility that the man, should he still be there, had gone to sleep in the only building, or part of a building, left standing. This of course was the shed where Biggles and Bertie had sheltered from the rain. He could see the silhouette against the sky but he could not see inside it.

Deciding that it would only take a minute to confirm definitely that there was no one there, he pulled the hurdles apart and with every confidence stepped inside.

He had not taken more than three paces when, with a vicious snarl, a dog rushed at him. Where it so suddenly came from he did not know. He did not stop to look. Feeling sure the animal would follow him, and catch him, should he retire the way he had come—for the hurdles would obviously be no obstacle to the dog—he sped to the only place of safety in sight. This was the skeleton wooden structure that had once supported the winding gear over the pit. He scrambled up to the first crossbar, one that braced the whole thing, beyond the reach of the dog, and sitting astride it looked down at the creature below. It had squatted on its haunches and was glaring up at him with an expression of calculated hatred.

Ginger could have kicked himself, as the saying is, for putting himself in such a ridiculous position. He had not forgotten Biggles' warning about the dog, but not seeing it had naturally assumed it was not there. Safe for the moment, from his perch he considered the situation. At first he could not see how he could do anything about it. He had no weapon of any sort, not even a stick, and he was not so stupid as to suppose he could take on a big dog with his bare hands without injury. To be bitten, in such a remote place, could be a serious matter. It was hard to see how he could escape this if he tried to get away. The dog was no mere terrier. It was more the size and weight of a hound.

He tried talking to it in a coaxing voice, hoping to soothe it; but he soon gave that up, perceiving it was futile. The animal bristled in a frenzy of rage.

Looking hard at it Ginger saw, for the first time, that it wore a collar. To this was attached a rope, a tethering line. Following this with his eyes he made it out to be tied to a short post driven into the ground not far away. This explained what up to now had been something of a mystery. Why the dog had not caught him. It had been given enough rope only to cover the entrance; that is, the hurdles. This, he supposed, would be all that was necessary to prevent the sheep from leaving their pen should anyone open the hurdles and leave them open. Just as effectively it would, of course, prevent him from leaving the place by the way he had entered.

He would soon have to do something, he told himself desperately, for deep twilight had closed in and Biggles would be wondering what he was doing. He had already been away longer than had been anticipated.

Thinking the matter over he decided that if he could get down out of reach of the dog it should be possible to find a place where he could get over the surrounding wall and so make his escape. This he resolved to attempt. To be on the safe side it meant moving along the crossbar and descending to the ground by means of the leg at the far corner to which it was joined.

Straddling the crossbar he worked his way across it foot by foot to the far side of the structure, or rig, or derrick, or whatever it might have been called. He took it slowly and carefully, for a fall could have serious consequences. However, all went according to plan and he reached his first objective, the far leg, without any great difficulty. Well satisfied, for the way of escape now seemed open, he took a short rest. Then, clutching the heavy square timber post like a monkey on a stick he started down. This, too, had to be taken carefully, for there was a risk of getting splinters in his hands.

He had nearly reached the ground when something he had not foreseen occurred. The dog, apparently having more than ordinary intelligence, must have realized what was happening. Straining on the rope at its fullest extent, barking furiously, it gave a tremendous lunge. The rope broke and it was free.

Ginger went up his post faster than he had come down; and he did not stop until he reached the crossbar. There, still breathing heavily from shock and consternation, he rested, the dog below, and the sheep in a tightly packed mob watching the performance with their customary foolish expressions—or lack of expression.

It was now a case of as-you-were.

Ginger resigned himself to wait for rescue. Sooner or later, when he did not return, Biggles or Bertie, or probably both, would come to look for him. He might have to wait a long time. He was worried about what would happen when, with the dog loose, they arrived on the scene. There seemed a good chance of one of them being bitten before they realized the danger. To make matters more difficult it was now almost dark; and it looked like being a dark night.

It would not do to print the names he was calling himself for having, with the best intentions, brought about such an infuriating situation. In some circumstances it might have had a humorous aspect; but, it need hardly be said, he saw nothing funny in it. There was no excuse. He had made a blunder.

The cause of the trouble had stopped its frenzied barking and now sat staring up at him. He stared back. There was nothing else he could do. The dog was not likely to move; and he couldn't move.

He nearly fell off his perch when a voice spoke; and it was not the voice of either Biggles or Bertie. It was deep and harsh. It said: 'Where are you? Come out.'

Ginger could just discern a shadowy figure advancing in the dim light. It appeared to limp and moved with the aid of a stick.

As Ginger had been looking at the dog he had no idea of the actual spot from which the man had so suddenly appeared.

'I'm up here!' he said.

'What are you doing?' came back in a peremptory voice.

Ginger bridled at the question. 'What the devil do you think I'm doing, looking for birds' nests?' he answered curtly. 'I'd have thought you could see what I'm doing.'

'Come down!'

'Not on your life,' returned Ginger grimly. 'If that dog belongs to you, get it under control. It flew at me. It's a dangerous brute.'

'You had no right to be here.'

'No right!' Ginger nearly choked. 'This is a National Park' (actually he was not sure of this) 'and I have as much right to be here as you have. You've no right to bring that beast to a public place.'

The man had come closer. He must have had a torch, for suddenly Ginger was half blinded by a bright light turned on him. He shielded his eyes with his hands, but with the light on his face he could not see the man behind it.

'Come down,' the voice ordered again.

'Not me. Tie up that dog. It broke its rope to get at me. If I'd been bitten you'd have heard about it.'

The light was switched off and in the gloom Ginger could see the man joining the broken ends of the rope. It was evident the animal knew him, for it made no protest. Indeed, at a word of command it slunk away and sat down.

Ginger returned to earth.

The man came right up to him. 'Now, young man, what are you doing here?'

Ginger liked the tone of voice still less. 'What the hell's it got to do with you?' he rapped out. 'You talk as if you owned the place. If it comes to that, what are *you* doing here, anyway?'

'Answer me!'

'You can go to the devil,' snapped Ginger. 'Instead of giving me orders you owe me an apology for bringing a mad dog here and causing me a lot of inconvenience. Get out of my way.'

'Where do you think you're going?'

'If you must know, back to the road.'

The man did not move.

'Whats the big idea?' demanded Ginger indignantly, although, as a matter of fact, he was aware of a mounting feeling of alarm. 'My friends are waiting for me,' he added, to let the man know he was not alone.

'Unless you answer my questions I'll let my dog loose.'

Ginger stared. 'You'll do what?'

'You heard me.'

Ginger could feel a loose brick under his feet. He snatched it up. 'You take one step towards that hound and I'll knock your block off,' he threatened viciously.

What the outcome of the affair would have been had there not been an interruption, is a matter for speculation; but at this juncture a voice spoke. To Ginger's great relief it was Biggles. He said: 'What's going on here?' To Ginger he added: 'What are you playing at? We can't wait all night.' Bertie was with him. They moved in through the hurdle entance. The dog growled but did not move.

Ginger answered. 'I was cornered by a hound that must have had a wolf for its mother. Apparently this fellow owns it. Instead of apologizing he's talking as if it was my own fault for coming here.'

'Well, come on,' Biggles said shortly. 'If you must fiddle about looking for a sprig of white heather you'd better choose some other time. White heather wouldn't have been much use had a dog got its teeth into your leg. Let's go.' He turned away.

Leaving the man standing there they left the enclosure and strode on in the direction of the road. Not until they had gone some way did Biggles speak. 'What happened?' he asked quietly.

Ginger told him. 'Phew! Was I glad to hear your voice! That fellow was getting nasty. Was he the shepherd?'

'No. This chap had a beard.'

'I noticed that. I could swear there was nobody there when I arrived. I looked for the dog but couldn't see it. Goodness knows where it came from. It hadn't made a sound. It was tied up, but when it flew at me the rope broke and all I could do was shin up that derrick affair like a blinking squirrel. Then the man appeared.'

'I told you to be careful of that dog.'

'I *was* careful. But how was I to know the brute would come at me like a lunatic tiger?'

'That's no sheep dog,' put in Bertie.

Nothing more was said till they reached the road and were in the car. Ginger asked where they were going.

'Back to Bodmin,' answered Biggles.

'Are we coming back here?'

'I don't know. I haven't made up my mind yet. It needs thinking about. We're up against something. We're looking for an intruding aircraft that comes only at night. I doubt if we shall ever find it in the air. If we did, what could we do about it? Shoot it down? No, that wouldn't do. Our only chance is to catch it on the ground. That means finding its landing strip. It may be here, within a mile of us. On the other hand we may be on the wrong track altogether, although there's certainly something fishy going on here. One thing we can't do is keep dashing to and fro between London and Bodmin. It takes too long and we should wear ourselves to a frazzle. I shan't go back to London tonight. When we get to the hotel we'll ring Algy and tell him we're spending the night here. He'll have to stand by the phone. If he gets a report of an unidentified machine coming over he can call us. That means we shall have to stand by the phone, too. Or one of us. We'll arrange that. I don't expect anything to happen tonight, but there seems to be a certain amount of activity at the mine, so it could happen. But I rather think that if a landing had been arranged it would be cancelled.'

'Why do you think that?' asked Bertie.

'Well, look what's happened today. First, two strangers are seen on the suspected air strip. They also go to the old mine. Later, when it's practically dark, someone else goes to the mine. For what reason would anyone go there at that hour? On the spur of the moment, to provide an excuse, I hinted that Ginger was looking for some lucky white heather; but I doubt if the man there would be taken in by that. Whatever these people may be, they can't be fools. Don't forget our car has spent some time on the road today, and someone may have wondered what it was doing. This, I suspect, is why that considerate gentleman stopped to ask if we needed help.' Biggles told Ginger about the incident as he was not present when it happened. He went on: 'We'll find out who that car belongs to. I've got its number. It was an old Bentley. Registration letters CV, which I believe is Cornwall. The police should know the owner. There can't be many old Bentleys about here.'

'What do we do tonight?' inquired Ginger.

'I had intended walking out to the mine again to have a closer look at it, but after what's happened today it would be risky. We can't go in daylight. If we are seen the people there would wonder what we were up to. That wouldn't make things easier for us. I'll think about it. Let's get back to the hotel. If we got a call that the intruder had been spotted we could always dash out here. That means having the car ready. Bertie, you might see that we're okay for petrol and oil.'

'If you go to the mine don't forget that brute of a dog,' reminded Ginger.

'I'm not likely to forget it. I shall also remember the man who owns it.'

'He's a nasty piece of work, too,' stated Ginger. 'He gave me the impression of being a foreigner.'

'I thought that, too, from what little I heard. But let's press on to the hotel. We can talk there.'

They had gone about two miles when they found themselves at the tail end of a queue of cars. Fortunately it was not a long one. 'Must have been an accident,' Bertie said, getting out to see what was happening. He was soon back. 'I guessed wrong. It's a police road block. They're checking all cars.'

Their turn soon came. A police sergeant held up a hand. Two constables, holding torches, closed in. One of them smiled recognition. It was the officer, Redruth, who had shown them where the body of Constable Hartley had been found. 'So you're still here,' he remarked.

'Looks like it,' Biggles answered. 'Carry on. It's all yours.' He handed over the key of the boot.

After a perfunctory search the sergeant waved them on. 'All right, sir. That's all.'

'What's the trouble? inquired Biggles. 'Not another murder?'

'No, thank God. A prisoner got away from Dartmoor this morning in the fog. He may have helped himself to a car. We're making sure he doesn't come this way.'

'Who was it?'

'Lewis.'

'Cracker Lewis?'

'That's him. You know him?'

'Only very slightly.' Biggles drove on.

Bertie spoke. 'Cracker Lewis! Isn't he one of the two safe-busters the Yard picked up after that bank raid in Hampstead? Shot at and wounded a constable. Got ten years if I remember.'

'That's right,' confirmed Biggles. 'I can understand the anxiety not to let him get away. He had a nice haul of about thirty thousand nicker and managed to tuck it away before he was caught. The money's never been found.'

'No wonder Lewis made a break, with that little lot waiting to be collected,' put in Ginger.

Biggles did not answer.

8
BERTIE BRINGS NEWS

BIGGLES sat alone in the residents' lounge of their hotel in Bodmin trying to put together, and make them fit like the pieces of a jig-saw puzzle, the items they had gathered since their arrival in Cornwall. These he examined one by one in the hope of making a complete picture. He had not succeeded when Ginger came in. He glanced around.

'Bertie not back yet?' he queried.

'Not yet.'

'It's taking him a long time to top up with petrol.'

'He'll be back. Did you speak to Algy?'

'Yes.' Ginger dropped into the seat next to Biggles. 'We had a long natter. I told him we were staying on here and put him wise as to what's happened so far.'

'Had he anything to say about it?'

'Not much. He'll mark time on the phone. I gather the Air Commodore is breaking out in a rash over this intruder business, wondering what we're doing and how long it's going to be before we let him have some definite news. The Minister wants to know what country this plane is coming from and who's operating it.'

'Is that all?' said Biggles with biting sarcasm. 'I'm afraid he'll have to sweat it out. I can't make head nor tail of it. I'm beginning to wonder if we're chasing a wild goose. I'm pretty certain something's going on at that old mine, but what it is I haven't a clue. It may have no connection with what we're looking for. In fact, it may be something perfectly legitimate. It's hard to know what to do next. Even if we're on the right track, to go on wandering about the moor near the mine is likely to do more harm than good. If once we're suspected of being what we are, our birds—if they really are the people we're looking for— will take fright and we shan't see them for dust.'

'What beats me is where that fellow came from who started to cut up rough because I wouldn't answer his questions. I don't see how he could have been there when I arrived or he'd have shown himself when I whistled. It must have been the dog barking that brought him along. But from where? He didn't come through the hurdles or I'd have seen him. He suddenly appeared from nowhere. Could he have come up from the mine? The oil you found on the windlass suggests its being used.'

Biggles shrugged. 'It's possible. How are we going to confirm that there's something going on underground without knowing the depth of the shaft or what's at the bottom? Would you like to go down?'

'I wouldn't mind if you were up top.'

'Stout fella! I'll bear it in mind,' chaffed Biggles. 'I may take you up on that.'

'What's wrong with calling in the police and making a

thorough search of the place?'

'And a nice pack of fools we'd look if there was nothing there. We'd be the laughing stock of the county. For some reason, I don't know why, people love to take the mickey out of Scotland Yard. All I can say is this, we've soon got to get some definite information or we shall have to pack up and go home. I can't see the Air Commodore letting us fiddle about here indefinitely running up an expense account. He'll suspect we're scrounging a holiday at the Government's expense.'

'Rot,' rejoined Ginger tartly. 'Not after what you've done in the past.'

'It's time you realized the past has nothing to do with it. It's the present that counts. While things go well, you're the blue-eyed boy. When they go wrong, there's mud in your eye. What have we found out since we came here? Some burnt heather that might be used as an air strip. A shepherd who minds his sheep with a dog that isn't an ordinary sheep dog. That doesn't amount to much. You go along after dark and a man asks you questions. So what? He may be the owner of the property or he may hold the grazing rights.'

'What about the man on the road who stopped his car to ask if you needed help?'

'That may be unusual but it isn't particularly remarkable. There are such men, although with everyone in a hurry to get somewhere they're getting few and far between. The only thing about that is, as I said earlier, I have a feeling that I've seen that face before. Perhaps not in the flesh. It may have been a photograph. I may be wrong. It was a long time ago, anyway. Well, that about sums up the position as it is at the moment. What else can we do? We shall have to do something or pack it in. Of course, we could sit on that miserable moor and wait for a plane to land on the strip. We might wait for weeks. If we're wrong it would never come. That's no use. Frankly, I don't know what to do. We can't go near the mine again without a plausible excuse; and it would be daft to cruise up and down the road in the car and expect no one to notice it.'

Bertie came in and joined them.

'You've been a devil of a long time,' accused Biggles. 'Is something wrong with the car?'

'No. The car's all right. Don't get steamed up, old boy. It happens I've been busy, all on my own. I struck lucky and picked up some news, although you may not think too much of it.'

'Why?'

'Because it knocks on the head your idea that the chappie who stopped his car to ask if we needed help might have something to do with what's going on on the moor.'

'Come on. Let's have it,' requested Biggles.

'When I went to the garage to fill up, there in front of me was that old Bentley.'

'Are you sure?'

'Positive, old boy. CV registration, and all that. And as if that wasn't enough, there was the man himself paying the pump attendant. He didn't see me. I hung back till he'd gone and watched which way he went.'

'Which way did he go?'

'He took the road that crosses the moor. But hold your horses. I haven't finished yet. When I went back to the pump to top up I asked the chap in charge if he knew the gent in the Bentley. He did. He knew all about him. Known him for years. Regular customer. His people used to be some of the biggest landowners in Cornwall—tin mines and what have you. His name's Sir Humphrey Trethallan. He lives at Hallstone Towers, the old baronial mansion near Hallstone, which I gather is a district rather than a village, a little beyond the northern extremity of the moor.' Bertie broke off, looking hard at the expression on Biggles' face. 'What is it? Have I done something wrong?' he asked anxiously.

Biggles recovered himself. 'No. Oh no,' he said quickly. 'Far from it. You've given my memory the jolt it needed to make the penny drop. It was the name that did it. I thought I vaguely knew the face. It must have been a picture in a newspaper. There was a time, some years ago, when Sir Humphrey's face looked at you from the front pages of the national papers.'

'Matter of fact, the name rang a bell with me,' said Bertie.

'What did he get up to, to get his name in the papers?' inquired Ginger.

'It comes back to me now,' resumed Biggles. 'As I remember it, the case, which raised a first-class stink, was this. Sir Humphrey Trethallan was a well-known playboy in high society. He could afford to be. His father left him a fortune, and he set about going through it faster than his old man had made it. He gambled in a big way, owning a string of racehorses among other things. The parties he threw in London, Paris and Monte Carlo were the talk of the town. All this blew up with a loud bang when he was accused of cheating at cards in one of the swish London clubs. He brought an action against his accuser—Lord somebody or other. He had to, or admit guilt. He hadn't a hope. Other people had seen what was going on. He lost the case and was ruined. There was no criminal charge, but as far as society was concerned he was finished. He had to resign from his clubs and the public appointments he held. All he could do after that was fade away. There was a report that he'd gone to Australia. I was doing charter work at the time, that was before I went to the Yard, so my memory is a bit hazy. Well—well. So he's still alive, rusticating in the ancestral home. In what sort of conditions, I wonder?'

'The pump attendant seemed to think he was the tops,' Bertie said. 'A good tipper, and so on.'

'He would be. That sort of man usually is. Of course, it's easy if you're using somebody else's money,' Biggles ended cynically.

'So that's another clue that's fizzled out,' sighed Ginger.

For some seconds Biggles did not answer. Then he said: 'It would be interesting to know why he came to Bodmin tonight. Was it simply to fill up with petrol?'

'Why not?'

'It meant he had to come across the moor. According to Bertie he went straight back the same way. I can't believe Bodmin is the nearest place where he could get petrol.'

Bertie frowned. 'Have a heart, old boy. I mean to say, dash it all, he's a gent. You can't suspect him of anything crooked.'

'His social position makes what he did in the past worse than rotten. He cheated his own friends at cards. If that isn't crooked I don't know what is. A man who will do a thing like that must have a streak in him that's as crooked as a ruddy corkscrew. Some men have an excuse for going off the rails, but he hadn't. Anyway, I've already said I'm prepared to have a second look at anyone, tourists apart, who crosses that moor at night without a reason. Merely to fill up with petrol doesn't strike me as a very convincing reason. If only to satisfy my curiosity I shall make it my business to check that Bodmin is the nearest place where Sir Humphrey can get petrol.'

'You're wasting your time,' declared Bertie. 'Once a gent always a gent.'

'And once a crook always a crook,' returned Biggles evenly. 'I had an idea of having another look at that moor later tonight, after we've had something to eat. We can still do that. At the same time we can go a bit farther and cast an eye over—what's the name of Sir Humphrey's place?'

'Hallstone Towers.'

Ginger stepped in. 'With what object? What's the house likely to tell us?'

'Well, it occurs to me that if the Trethallans made money out of mining, Sir Humphrey may still own land here. He may even be the owner of these abandoned mines, including the one in which we have an interest. It may be a remote chance, but it's possible he still holds the title deeds. He may have let the land to someone, in which case he should be able to help us.'

'But if these mines have been worked out they can be of no value to anyone,' Ginger pointed out.

'Not as mines, admittedly.'

'What, then?'

'It's no use asking me. That's what I want to find out. I know of one mine that's being used for *something*, otherwise only a lunatic would have oiled the wheels of the winding gear.'

'Are we all going on this jaunt tonight?' Ginger asked. 'I was thinking, shouldn't one of us stay here to keep an ear to the phone in case Algy comes through to say an unidentified aircraft is in the offing?'

Biggles hesitated for a moment. 'We can take a chance on
that,' he decided. 'It shouldn't take us long to do what we have to
do. If a plane should come this way we should hear it. I'll speak to
the night porter and ask him to take a message should one come
through for us while we're out. My plan was for all of us to go,
drop you off at the usual place on the moor to watch the mine and
go on with Bertie to Hallstone Towers. When we've had a look at
it we'll pick you up on the way back. Remind me to have a look at
the map to see exactly where this place Hallstone is. But that's
enough for now. I'm getting hoarse with so much talking. I'm
going to oil my tonsils with some steak and kidney pudding. I see
it's on the menu.'

'That,' said Bertie, 'is music to my ears. The best suggestion
you've made tonight, old boy. Absolutely. I'm flat out for a plate
of pud, anywhere, any time.'

They got up and walked through to the dining room.

9

A SHOCK FOR BIGGLES

IT was ten o'clock when the party left the hotel, Biggles having
made no changes in his plan.

Where the weather was concerned the night could be
described as fair; moonless but clear; the sky half covered with
high cirrus cloud which, as there was no wind to move it, seemed
likely to persist. As Biggles observed, it was a good night for
flying, although while visibility might have been better, it could
have been a lot worse.

'There's plenty of cover behind that cloud layer for an
intruder to slink in,' he said, as he took the road to the moor. 'The
alternative would be to come in low to get under the radar. That
means five hundred feet, or lower. If the pilot tried that we
should certainly hear the machine. Not that we have any reason
to suppose it will come over tonight. That, with us on the moor,
would be too much to hope for. The trouble is, we haven't a clue

as to what this raider is doing. If we had we'd be in a better position to judge when he's likely to come.'

'That, surely, would be governed by weather conditions,' put in Bertie.

'No doubt. But even so, his goings and comings would almost certainly depend on something that has happened on the ground, not necessarily here, but somewhere in the country. Obviously these raids are being made with a definite purpose, otherwise they wouldn't happen. It's no use trying to guess what that purpose is. We've got to find out—don't ask me how—or we could spend the rest of our lives here without getting anywhere. We're still groping in the dark, literally, but if we stick around, with any luck we should spot something that will make sense of the whole business.'

The car, running on sidelights only, made its first stop, as arranged, at its usual place on the moor. The police road block had been lifted, so the road was clear. Ginger got out.

'I reckon we should be back in about half-an-hour,' Biggles told him. 'Stay here. Watch for lights. If any appear at the mine, or anywhere else on the moor, you're bound to see them. Don't try any more exploring on your own.'

'I shan't, don't worry,' returned Ginger warmly. 'I'm not likely to forget that brute of a dog.'

'Okay. This is where we'll pick you up.' Biggles drove on.

Although the map had been studied it took longer to find the house they were looking for than had been anticipated. They found the district without much trouble, but it consisted only of a few widely scattered cottages dotted about a tangle of lanes with banks and hedges on either side. Moreover, there were trees to restrict the view. There was no actual village, practically no traffic on this lonely fringe of the moor, not even a pedestrian to ask the way. Apparently the men who worked in this truly rural countryside went to bed early.

After several false trails, and stops to consult the map, Biggles brought the car to a halt in a lane which ran up a steep hill. From it branched off a tree-lined track; but the existence at the entrance of broken stone pillars suggested that the track was, or had been, a drive leading to a house of some size. Biggles got out and looked for a notice board, a name, or some other means of identification; but he failed to find one.

'I think this must be it,' he told Bertie, returning to the car. 'There can hardly be two big estates here. If this drive leads to a house it shouldn't be far away. I'll walk along and have a look.'

'Want me to stay here with the car?'

'You can't very well stay here. There isn't room for another vehicle to pass should one come along. I think you'd better move on a bit to one of those places were the lane has been widened to allow for two-way traffic. You shouldn't have to go far. Or if you'd rather you can back down to that field gate we passed on the way up.'

'I'll go on a bit,' decided Bertie. 'I don't feel like backing two hundred yards or more down this hill with a sharp bend in it.'

'Please yourself,' replied Biggles. 'I shan't be long. When I come back I'll walk up the hill till I find you.'

'Right-ho.' Bertie slid into the driving seat and went on up the hill.

Biggles walked between the crumbling pillars, and carried on along what may once have been a gravelled drive but was now a mossy track, through tall bracken, with trees and shrubs rising from it. There was not a sound; not a sign of life of any sort, and more than once in the darkness under the trees he had to stop to peer ahead to see what was in front of him. He regretted he had not brought the torch that was kept in the car. He had not expected anything quite like this. However, he carried on, making the best time possible in the circumstances.

It was some minutes before he saw with some relief that he was nearing his destination. A light could be seen through the low-hanging branches of the trees. Going on he saw more clearly what he had been looking for; what he had expeced to find. A large mansion house. It was not possible to make out details, because all he could actually see was the silhouette against the sky. There was no proof that this was Hallstone Towers, but a tall castellated structure at each end suggested it might be. The drive ended, widening, at an ornate canopy over the front door. One light only was showing. The one he had seen. It came from a room on the ground floor and was no more than a slit, a few inches wide, as if curtains had been carelessly drawn. It reflected faintly on the metal parts of a car drawn up near the door.

Biggles considered the place. He could see as much as was necessary. Advancing with caution, keeping near to the overgrown evergreen shrubs that bordered the drive, he went close enough to recognize the car. It was the Bentley. So he had come to the right house. This was Hallstone Towers, and it was at once clear that Sir Humphrey Trethallan's fortunes had not improved with the years. The general impression created was one of melancholy neglect. The drive in front of the house was rutted and overgrown with weeds. What had been a garden was a jungle of briars and nettles. The whole building, what could be seen of it, was well on the way to dilapidation. Part of the guttering had broken loose and was sagging. A broken window had not been repaired.

Biggles was about to turn away, for he had no intention of calling on the owner and he had seen all he needed to see, when someone must have moved across the room with the lighted window. The shadow crossed the slit where the curtains did not meet. Thinking it would be interesting to see who was in the room, and as it seemed this could be done without much risk of discovery, he moved closer to the window. Passing the car he put a hand on the bonnet. It was warm. But he already knew that it had been out: to Bodmin. Reaching the window he inched his head forward until he could peep round the frame; or, more correctly, the curtain.

He saw at a glance that the room, a large one in proportion to the house, was not furnished in a style that might have been expected of a place of such size. In fact, there was very little furniture; no carpet, no ornaments, not even a picture on the walls, which were panelled. In a word, it was in keeping with the outside; all of which suggested that the prosperity of Hallstone Towers had reached its lowest point ever.

There were two men in the room, standing one each side of a small table on which stood a bottle, a siphon, two glasses and a sheet of paper. They were in earnest conversation, but it was not possible to hear what was being said. It loked as though something on the paper was the subject under discussion. One of the men was the owner of the establishment; Sir Humphrey Trethallan. That was to be expected, and Biggles recognized him instantly. Only a few hours earlier he had spoken to him on the main road when the Bentley had stopped to offer help.

The other man he did not know. Or for a moment or two he *thought* he did not know. He was well dressed, even smartly, in grey flannel trousers, a sports jacket and a bow tie. There was, however, something vaguely familiar about his face, and while Biggles stared at it, searching his memory for identification, the man moved his head a little so that the single light in the room fell on it from a different angle. With the change came recognition; and shock; a shock that froze Biggles to the stiffness of a statue.

The man was Lewis. 'Cracker' Lewis; the time-serving criminal who had just escaped from Dartmoor.

Biggles was not unaccustomed to surprises, but this one took his breath away. He could hardly believe his eyes, as the saying is. What could such a man be doing there?

He did not try to find the answer. That could wait. Moistening his lips, which had dried under the shock, he backed away. Once at a safe distance he retreated hurriedly down the drive.

He had not reached the junction with the lane when he heard a car start up behind him. It could only be the Bentley. Within a minute he saw the flicker of its headlights in the trees as it came down the drive. He flung himself into the bracken beside the track and covered his face except for his eyes. He remained motionless as the car went past. There were two men in it. Those he had seen in the room. Sir Humphrey was driving.

As soon as the car was out of sight he was racing after it, not of course with any hope of catching up with it, but, if possible, to see which way it turned on reaching the lane. In this he failed; when he reached the junction it was out of sight. He ran on up the hill, and had to cover nearly a quarter of a mile before he came to Bertie waiting in their own car. 'Has a car come past here?' he panted, breathless after his dash up the hill.

Bertie, looking startled, sat up abruptly. 'No. Nothing has come past here.'

'Then it must have turned the other way. Get the car turned round. I don't suppose we can overtake it now but we can try.'

'What car is it?'

'The Bentley. Don't talk now. Get cracking. Make for the Bodmin road.'

It took a minute or two to turn the car in the narrow lane, to face the direction from which it had come.

'Steady down the hill,' warned Biggles. 'This is no time or place to have a pile-up.'

Nothing more was said until, after one or two halts to check the signposts, the car was on the main highway. The A30. Then, with the open road in front of them and very little traffic Bertie was able to put his foot down. Biggles peered ahead through the windscreen. Two or three cars were overtaken but none was the Bentley.

'I'm afrad we've lost it,' muttered Biggles. 'It must have gone the other way.'

'Had you any reason to think it was coming this way?'

'None whatever; but without giving the matter any serious thought I assumed it was making for the moor. I hadn't much time to think.'

'What happened?'

'When I got to the house the Bentley was standing at the front door. I was on my way back down the drive when I heard it start up. Another minute and it went past me. When I got to the junction with the public road it was out of sight, so I'd no means of knowing which way it had turned. I thought it might have gone up the hill, but apparently it didn't. I then thought it might be making for Bodmin Moor, but it seems I was wrong again.'

'It might still be in front of us.'

'Could be. But I thought it might stop when it got to the moor. Ginger should be able to tell us if it went past him. All right, Bertie, you can take it easy now. Stop when you come to the place where we left him.'

'Who was driving the Bentley—Sir Humphrey?' asked Bertie,

taking his foot off the accelerator.

'Yes,' answered Biggles grimly. 'But he wasn't alone. He had a passenger, and I was more interested in him than in the driver. They were both in the house when I got to it. I saw them through the window. Here we are. This is it. Pull in close.'

Bertie stopped the car with two wheels on the verge. Biggles sprang out. 'Ginger,' he called.

Ginger rose up out of the heather.

'Have you seen that old Bentley go past here?' rapped out Biggles.

'No.'

'You're sure?'

'Of course. I haven't left the side of the road. Several cars have gone past, but no Bentley.'

Biggles drew a deep breath. 'That settles that then. It must have gone another way. Pity.'

'What's all the fuss about, anyhow?' asked Bertie. 'Is it something to do with the passenger in the car?'

'Yes.'

'Who was it? Did you know him?'

'Too true I knew him. Fasten your safety belt. You're not going to believe this. It was "Cracker" Lewis.'

Silence.

Then Bertie said. 'Oh no. It isn't true. Are you sure about this?'

'Of course I'm sure.'

'But it doesn't make sense!'

'It's *got* to make sense, and it will when I've had time to think about it. I have a glimmering already.'

'But dash it all, old boy, I mean to say, how could there possibly be anything in common between Sir Humphrey and that nasty little gaolbird?'

'I can think of something.'

'Like what?'

'Money. A little matter of the thirty thousand quid in notes that Lewis still has salted away somewhere.'

Ginger whistled softly. 'How right you are,' he said softly.

'That sort of money can make friends of the most unlikely people.'

'By the look of his place our charming baronet could certainly do with some of it,' went on Biggles. 'I imagine that's what he's after. What else could it be? But he's not likely to get a share of it for nothing. Does that suggest anything to you?'

Bertie answered. 'Not on the spur of the moment, I must admit.'

'It does to me. But we've been here long enough. Let's move on a bit, as far as that next dip where the car couldn't be seen by anyone on the moor.'

They all got into the car and Bertie drove on some little distance before again pulling into the side of the road. 'What was your idea?' he asked, as Biggles lit a cigarette.

'Simply this. I'd make a wager that Cracker Lewis would be more than willing to hand over ten thousand nicker to anyone who would guarantee to get him out of the country with the rest of his swag. Money's no use to him while he's behind bars.'

'You've hit it,' declared Bertie. 'Hit it right on the boko. Jolly good. But tell me this. I may be a bit slow on the uptake, but how could our noble baronet guarantee to get his crooked pal out of the country?'

'If my guess is right he'd arrange for someone to fly him out.'

'So *that's* what the intruder is doing,' breathed Ginger.

'That's how it looks to me.'

'And you think that's going to happen tonight?'

'I did at first, but now I've had time to think I've changed my mind. There's a snag. I doubt if it will be tonight.'

'Why not?'

'Because there's one little job that will have to be done before Lewis can repay Sir Humphrey for his hospitality. Lewis has only just got out of gaol. He wouldn't have the money on him when he escaped. It'll have to be fetched from where he hid it after the robbery. Maybe that's what the Bentley is doing now. Cracker wouldn't be likely to tell Sir Humphrey where it is and leave him to go alone to fetch it. He might grab the lot, and Cracker, in his position, wouldn't be able to do anything about it. That, I fancy, is why they've gone together.'

'Then all we have to do is call in the police and trap the pair of them when they return to Hallstone Towers with the lolly on them.'

'No. It isn't as easy as that. They may not go back to the house. Think what fools we should look if we raided the house and found nothing or nobody there. We shall have to think of something else. I'd rather be sure of my ground before we jump in. This may turn out to be a bigger business than the capture of one man— Cracker Lewis. Another thought has just struck me. It's this. For a rough guess, without the records, I can think of at least five gaol-breaks over the past six months. None of the men has been recaptured. Where are they? Where have they gone? All of them had one thing in common. They all managed to hide their loot before they were picked up and convicted. In view of what's happened tonight I'd say their chances of being recaptured now are pretty remote. They're out of the country; and the stolen money has gone with them—or some of it.'

'They were *flown* out!'

'That's how it looks to me.'

'And that's what this night-bird has been doing—fetching them?'

'Subject to confirmation, I'd say yes. There must be an organization behind this. These gaol-breakers all knew where to make for once they were free. Hallstone Towers. Remember the police road block? The constable said it was thought Lewis was heading in this direction. They were right; but Lewis didn't have to come as far as this. No. He knew where he was going.'

'You talk about confirmation,' put in Ginger. 'How are we going to get it?'

'That's a problem we now have to work out,' Biggles said. 'It's no use looking for that Bentley tonight. As we know, it was topped up with petrol. It might be anywhere between Land's End and John o' Groats.'

'We know its number. Why not put out a general call for it to be stopped?' suggested Bertie.

'We only *think* we know its number. The number plates may

have been changed. It's easy enough to put on false ones. Sir
Humphrey's no fool. He'd take no chances. From the way this
thing is being run, and I suspect it has been going on for some
time, there are brains behind it. We shall have to decide quickly
what we're going to do; before the car comes back. It might not
be too difficult to pick up Sir Humphrey; but how do we know
he's the head man of the racket? When we strike we want the
whole gang. The man I really want is the man we were ordered
to find; this night-flying intruder. There are some things we shall
have to do right away. The first is to let the Air Commodore
know we've struck a hot trail. Another thing we'd better do, if
we're going to take on a big gang, is provide ourselves with some
guns. I don't feel like taking on men like Cracker Lewis with my
bare hands. We've done a good night's work up to now and I
don't want to bungle it. Let me think.'

10

A PLAN AND A PROBLEM

Nobody spoke for some minutes. They all sat in the car, Biggles
with his eyes brooding over the silent and apparently deserted
moor. At last Biggles moved. He looked at his watch. 'It's getting
on for midnight,' he said, as if reminding himself of the time.

'We've run into a knotty problem,' he went on in a normal
voice. 'It would be easy at this stage to make a mess of things. The
trouble is, practically all we know, or think we know, is based on
surmise. That's no use. We need evidence. Proof. How are we
going to get it?'

'You've seen Lewis with Trethallan,' reminded Ginger. 'Isn't
that proof?'

'No. My unsubstantiated word wouldn't hold up in court. As
things stand we haven't a shred of evidence of Sir Humphrey's
association with Lewis. Whatever we know, or think we know,
we've no case against him. There are two big questions still to be
answered, otherwise we shall be groping in the dark. We know

Trethallan has taken Lewis under his wing. They've gone out together. We don't know where they've gone. I can only think it's to fetch the money that Lewis has got hidden somewhere; the fruits of his last bank raid. A man like Trethallan could have no other interest in that crook. For what other possible reason would he lay himself open to a charge of giving house-room to an escaped criminal? The question is, assuming I'm right, having got the money, where will they go? If we're thinking on the right lines, that Trethallan can arrange for Lewis to be flown out of the country, they should come back here. I doubt if Trethallan can fly himself. We've no record of his having been a pilot, or even a member of a flying club. I can't imagine an aircraft being hidden anywhere on the moor. Where is there to hide it? No. The aircraft will be flown here when it's required. I may be wrong, but it is reasonable to suppose that the machine is the intruder we've been looking for. It comes from abroad and returns to its base. I'm pretty sure this isn't the first time this sort of thing has happened. It has been going on for months, and would account for the utter disappearance of other escaped criminals who had money tucked away.'

Ginger spoke. 'Trethallan must have contact with the plane to let the pilot know when a passenger is ready to be picked up. How's that being done? By radio?'

'That seems the most likely method, unless an arrangement has already been made. Where is the radio equipment? It could be at Hallstone Towers or it could be here, at the old mine, where the operator would be in direct touch with weather conditions on the landing ground. When this pick-up will take place we don't know, and are not likely to know. It may be tonight, although that doesn't seem likely in view of the time. It'll start to get light in a few hours, and there's never been any record of the intruder coming over in the day time. If it isn't tonight, where will Trethallan and Lewis go to wait for zero hour? They'll have to go to some safe place to divide the money. The most probable place would be Hallstone Towers, although it could be here, at the mine. We can't be in two places at once in sufficient force to make an arrest. We might bite off more than we could digest. There must be a sizeable organization behind this racket. Lewis knew where to make for when he was free.' Biggles broke off to light a cigarette.

He continued. 'We know we may have at least four men to contend with, not counting the pilot or crew of the plane. First, there's that phoney shepherd. He knows what's going on. Then there's the tough who tackled Ginger when he was treed by the dog. He's one of them. That's proved by the fact that the dog knew him. Now there's Trethallan and Lewis. We can't expect them to submit without a struggle. The chances are they're armed. We haven't a weapon between us, so we're in no case to take on several armed men. I'd feel more comfortable even now with a gun in my pocket.'

'What about calling in the police?' suggested Bertie.

Biggles shook his head. 'I feel it's too early to call on the police for help. It would be hard to convince them about what's going on. With no concrete evidence to show, that would be understandable. They wouldn't want to make fools of themselves any more than we do.'

'Well, what *are* we going to do?' asked Ginger. 'We shall soon have to make up our minds.'

'You're dead right.' Biggles went on as if he'd reached a decision. 'I don't like leaving this place. Anything could happen, any time. If it should happen that while we were away the plane slipped in and collected Lewis we'd be left standing on one foot. We wouldn't know anything about it; we wouldn't even know that Lewis had gone; and as I've said, we'd have no case against anyone here.'

'So what?'

'I can see only one way to handle this,' Biggles said. 'Ginger, you'll go to Headquarters and tell the Air Commodore how things stand. Come straight back bringing three guns with you. That means if you take the car we shall need another. We'd be helpless here without transport. Anyway, this one has been here on the road for so long that it must be getting conspicuous. Bertie, you'll have to watch Hallstone Towers in case Trethallan and Lewis go back there. I'll keep watch here to check if they come here to rendezvous with the plane, should that have been arranged. Now, this is the order of it. Bertie, you'll slip into Bodmin right away, taking Ginger with you. There you'll hire a car. If you can't find a garage open you'll have to ask the police to find you one; but don't do that unless it's necessary. Maybe they'll let you have one of theirs. You've got your Yard identity card on you?'

'Of course.'

'All right. You'll come back here with two cars. You, Ginger, will then press on for London in our own car. Get back as quickly as you can but don't risk breaking your neck. As long as you're back here tomorrow before dark it will be okay. Nothing is likely to happen in daylight. Got that?'

'Will do.'

'Using the spare car I shall take Bertie to Hallstone Towers where he'll have to plant himself out of sight to watch the place. I shall come back here to watch the moor. Right?'

'Okay. But how do I get back?' Bertie asked.

'I'll fetch you as soon as it's daylight. I don't think you need stay after that. It might be risky, anyhow. I'm sorry to have to split up the party but I see no alternative. It's vital that we should know if anything happens tonight and this seems the only way of doing it. If nothing happens, well, we get a breathing space to plan something for tomorrow night. Is that all clear? Any questions?'

There were no questions.

'Right,' said Biggles. 'Let's get on with it.' He got out of the car. Bertie, with Ginger beside him, drove off down the Bodmin road. Biggles sat down to wait, always watching the lonely stretch of country in front of him.

An hour later two cars arrived together and stopped. One was their own, with Ginger at the wheel, the other a Morris, Bertie driving.

'Good work,' said Biggles. 'Okay, Ginger. Off you go.'

Ginger departed, heading for London.

Biggles got into the second car. 'You know where we're going,' he told Bertie. 'I want to be back here as soon as possible.'

Bertie drove on, and with little or no traffic on the road was soon outside the drive that led to Hallstone Towers. He did not stop there, but on Biggles's instructions went on a little way before pulling up. He got out. Biggles slipped into the driving seat. 'I'll be back to pick you up soon after daylight,' he said. 'Careful how you go.'

'Leave it to me, old boy.'

'Be seeing you.' Biggles returned to the moor, pulling in at the place where they had recently stopped, just off the road. He switched off all lights, made himself comfortable in the heather and prepared for a long wait. In front of him lay the moor. To left and right the road ran on to fade and finally disappear into the gloom.

Would the airborne invader come tonight? was the thought uppermost in his mind. From what he knew he did not think so. He hoped it would not, or he would find himself opposed, single-handed and unarmed, to what would certainly be a dangerous gang. More than anything he wanted to intercept the plane and keep it grounded; to learn its nationality and establish the identity of the pilot. That was what the Air Commodore wanted to know; to learn if the purpose of the intruder's mission was criminal or political—that is, espionage.

Biggles thought he now knew the answer to that. The arrival of Cracker Lewis on the scene had revealed it. Either way it could not be allowed to go on, flaunting both the law and Air Traffic Regulations. So pondered Biggles, as he gazed across the desolate expanse of moorland in the direction of the supposed landing strip. Not a light showed. Always keeping an ear to the sky for the sound of an aero engine, he waited.

Time passed. Nothing happened. There was a little traffic on the road; an occasional long-distance lorry, a milk-collecting truck and a few private cars. He looked hard at all the vehicles that passed, but none was the car with which he was concerned. The Bentley.

By three o'clock time had begun to drag. Not until six would dawn creep up over the horizon. There was nothing to relieve the boredom. Fortunately the weather was mild or the vigil would have been even more tedious.

However, the longest night has to come to an end, and it was with heart-felt relief that Biggles at long last saw a grey streak appear in the eastern sky to tell of the coming of another day. Nothing had happened, and it now seemed unlikely that anything would happen during the next fourteen or fifteen hours. He waited another five minutes, by which time through a misty twilight he could see some distance across the moor; then, rising and stretching his stiff limbs, he got into the car and set off to fetch Bertie, as had been arranged. It would, he thought, be interesting to know if he had anything to report. The most important thing was, had the Bentley returned to the house?

He drove slowly, still keeping an eye on the moor, while it was in view, for any sign of activity. He saw nothing except the rolling landscape. Once clear he increased his speed and in twenty minutes was passing the broken pillars at the entrance to Hallstone Towers. Bertie was not there. He did not expect him to be, so he carried on up the hill to where the lane widened. This was the rendezvous. Bertie was not there, either. This did not worry him. No actual time had been set for the appointment. Bertie would, he was sure, be along at any moment, so he settled down in the car and lit a cigarette, prepared to wait.

After a little while and Bertie had not shown up he felt his first twinge of concern. It was now daylight, and he could think of no reason why Bertie, after a night out, should linger longer than was absolutely necessary. Another ten minutes and concern had become anxiety. What on earth could Bertie be doing? What could be keeping him?

Leaving the car he walked down to the drive. There was nobody there. He whistled softly. This produced no result. Now seriously alarmed he walked a little way up the drive looking for signs of Bertie's occupation. He thought he may have found it when he observed a spot where the bracken had been crushed flat as if someone had rested there. He noticed something else; something that puzzled him. The place was strewn with small chips as if someone had whittled a stick. Would Bertie have done that? He might. Lying near was a fallen branch from which the stick had apparently been cut with a small knife.

Not knowing quite what to make of it, he went on up the drive, as far as he dare without taking a risk of being seen from the house. Peering through the shrubs he saw the house. He also saw something else. Standing by the door was the Bentley. So the owner had returned. It was useful to know that. But where was Bertie? What could have happened to him? Obviously something had gone wrong. But if Bertie had done his job properly what *could* have gone wrong? With the return of the Bentley there was all the more reason to be at the rendezvous to report it.

With his alarm becoming acute Biggles hurried back down the drive and up the hill to the car, hoping to find Bertie there. He was not. It was now evident that something had happened. Moreover, it must have been something serious.

Still hoping Bertie would eventually turn up he got into the car, prepared to wait. He could think of nothing else to do. It would, he thought, be folly to go near the house. In any case, what could he hope to gain by that? So he waited. He waited for half-an-hour. Still Bertie did not appear. He decided it was no use waiting any longer. Had it been possible Bertie would be here by now, he told himself. The fact had to be faced. The plan, for some unknown reason, had come unstuck. It was hard to know what to do for the best. To go near the house in broad daylight would be to risk wrecking everything. Trethallan, should he see him, would recognize him as the man he had spoken to on the road. Lewis, should he, too, have returned to the Towers, would also recognize him as a Scotland Yard detective who had given evidence against him in court.

At the finish of his deliberations Biggles resolved to return to the hotel at Bodmin, thinking there was just a chance there might be a message there from Bertie. Or possibly Ginger, although it was no use expecting him back from London for some hours yet. Apart from that, he needed some breakfast. The keen morning air had given him an appetite, and in view of what had happened it might be a long time before he would get a chance for another meal. Anyway, should Bertie belatedly arrive at the rendezvous and find the car gone he would guess what had happened and in all probability start walking towards Bodmin expecting to meet the car coming back to look for him; or find it waiting on the main road where it crossed the moor.

Reluctantly Biggles started on the return journey. He went dead slow past the broken pillars, hoping against hope that he would see Bertie coming down the drive. In this he was disappointed. He even gave a gentle hoot on the horn. Nothing happened, so he had no alternative than to go on. In due course he reached the road that crossed the moor. The first thing that caught his eye as he gazed across the heather was the shepherd, his dog and his little flock, on the supposed landing strip close to the mine. What did that signify—if in fact it meant anything?

He didn't stop, but carried on to Bodmin and the hotel. There was no message, either from Bertie, Ginger or anyone else.

II
MORE SURPRISES

Biggles had a quick bath to refresh himself after having been up all night, and afterwards some breakfast, all the time wondering what he should do about Bertie. On the face of it there was not much he could do. He felt, naturally, that he should start looking for him. But where? He might be at Hallstone Towers; on the other hand he might not. To go near the house was likely to do more harm than good. To try to gain an entry like a thief would be to exceed his authority, even as a policeman, and land him in trouble. Yet to go to the door to make inquiries would be futile, for if he was there Trethallan would not be likely to admit it. If Bertie was not at the Towers he might be anywhere.

Now in a state of apprehension Biggles felt he could not just sit still and do nothing. He went out, took the car to the garage to have the tank topped up and then made again for Hallstone Towers, thinking, but without much hope, that he might see Bertie, or find a clue to account for his disappearance; possibly even meet him walking back.

He did not meet him. He did not find a clue. He went as far as the rendezvous. He was not there. He waited for an hour. Then, no longer able to deceive himself that there was any hope of Bertie turning up, he cruised back to the moor and stopped in the usual place, the dip in the road where the car could not be seen from the mine. There, not knowing what else to do, he decided to await Ginger's return, although this would not be for some time.

The moor lay as deserted as usual. The shepherd and his flock were no longer there. Why? Where had they gone? He did not waste time in what obviously would be futile speculation.

It had turned three when he saw the car for which he had been waiting coming up the road. It stopped. Ginger got out. He was followed by Algy.

Biggles' eyebrows went up. 'What are you doing here?'

'The Air Commodore insisted on it.'

'Why?'

'He knows the position and thought you might need help.'

'What about the telephone?'

'He's taking over. When he goes home all calls for our section will be switched through to him. That will cover any radar signal that might come through about the intruder being on the job.'

'I see.'

Ginger, who had been looking round, asked the natural question. 'Where's Bertie?'

'I've lost him,' returned Biggles morosely.

'Lost him! How?'

'When I went to the Towers to pick him up he wasn't there. I haven't seen a sign of him since I left him there.'

Ginger grimaced. 'I don't like the sound of that.'

'Nor I.'

'What have you done about it?'

'Not much, I must admit. I've been back over the road to the place where I was to pick him up. I've been a little way up the drive that leads to the house but I daren't go too close.'

'What do you suppose could have happened to him?'

'Your guess is as good as mine.'

'He must have run into trouble.'

'That's fairly obvious or he'd have met me as arranged.'

'What are we going to do about it?'

'Frankly, I don't know.'

'We shall have to do something.'

'I think we'd better wait for a bit to see if he turns up before we do anything desperate. I can tell you this. The Bentley is back at the Towers. I saw it standing by the front door. How long it had been there, of course, I've no idea. Nor do I know if Cracker Lewis came back with it. Did you bring the pistols?'

Ginger fetched a .38 automatic from the car and handed it over. 'I'd better leave Bertie's in the car,' he said.

Biggles put the gun in his pocket. 'That feels better. I have a hunch I shall need this before we've finished here. Now, before we go any farther, what had the Air Commodore to say about all this?'

'He was delighted to learn we'd struck a trail, but was a bit worried when he heard about Lewis being here, thinking we might get hurt. He's a desperate character and it's known he carries a gun. That's why he insisted on Algy coming back with me. He thought we might need help. He did talk about coming down himself, but I said I didn't think there was any necessity for that—not yet, anyway.'

'Never mind about that,' broke in Algy. 'What are we going to do about Bertie? That's what I want to know.'

'That's what I want to know, too,' answered Biggles, grimly. 'Ginger, how long is it since you had anything to eat?'

'Nothing since last night. Knowing you were waiting for me I came straight back without bothering about food.'

'In that case we'd better all go to Bodmin and get a meal while we have the opportunity. Anything could happen, and it may be some time before we have another chance. We'll talk things over; maybe run out again to the Towers to see if there's anything doing there.'

'I know Bertie,' declared Algy. 'Only trouble in a big way would have prevented him keeping the appointment with you.'

'You needn't tell me,' retorted Biggles. 'Let's go. I'm sick of staring at this perishing moor. We shall have to come back to it, of course. Sooner or later that Bentley should come along to bring Lewis to the landing ground. At least, that's how I see it. That hired car can go back to the garage. I don't think we shall need it now. If we do we can always fetch it.'

They got into the two cars and drove off in the direction of Bodmin.

After a wash and brush up, which Ginger needed after his long run, they had a meal, still, of course, discussing the situation. From time to time Biggles went to the hall porter to ask if there was a message for him, but the answer was always the same. No message. Time went on. Bertie did not appear.

The first shades of evening were falling when Algy spoke impatiently. 'This is no use,' he declared. 'Talking is getting us nowhere. We shall have to do something about Bertie.'

'Do what?' inquired Biggles dolorously. 'You tell me. I can't see that we can do anything. To wander about the moor, or hang around the Towers on the off-chance of finding him seems a pretty hopeless business.'

'It'd be better to do that than sit here doing nothing,' Ginger said.

'There's nothing to stop you from trying it, if that's how you feel,' Biggles told him.

'I'd bet any money Bertie is in Hallstone Towers,' averred Algy. 'He isn't on the moor. What is there to do there? If he was free to come home he'd have been here long ago. No. He was spotted prowling about the Towers and taken inside.'

'I'm inclined to agree with you,' conceded Biggles. 'All right. Let's assume he's in the house, presumably a prisoner. What do you suggest we do about it?'

'Go there and get him out.'

'Are you proposing that we break in?'

'Why not?'

'For the very good reason that we've no right to do anything of the sort. If it turned out that Bertie wasn't there, and Sir Humphrey made a complaint, as he probably would, there'd be one hell of a row about it and the Press would shoot us down in flames.'

'To the devil with what we have a right to do! That's no argument.'

Biggles shook his head. 'I doubt if it would work. Hallstone Towers is a big place. It would need a lot of men to search it properly. We don't know how many people there are inside; Lewis for one; there may be others like him. You can bet they wouldn't take kindly to us going through the place without a warrant.'

'Very well. Then let's call in the local police. Tell them we have reason to believe that the escaped prisoner they're looking for is inside. That should be sufficient reason for them to get a search warrant.'

'Even if they agreed that would take time. It'll soon be dark. By the time the police got to the Towers Lewis could be on his way out of the country. We should still be able to prevent that if his departure is timed for tonight.'

'How?'

'By going to the moor and taking up positions near the airstrip. If that plane lands I'll take damn good care it doesn't get off again.'

'We've no reason to suppose tonight is the night,' argued Algy. 'There's been no signal from radar, or the Air Commodore would have been on the phone.'

'It's early yet. There's plenty of time for the plane to slip in between now and five o'clock tomorrow morning. Our job is to see it doesn't get away with it tonight. That's why we're here. If it doesn't come tonight we shall have all day tomorrow to think about it. I'll ring the Air Commodore first thing in the morning and ask for instructions. Let him take the responsibility. Meanwhile let's get to the moor. We're not likely to do any good sitting here.'

'You could run me out to the Towers and drop me off there to see if anything's going on,' suggested Algy. 'No one there knows me.'

'All right, if that's how you feel.'

'And you could put me off at the moor on the way,' offered Ginger. 'I could go across and see if anything is happening at the old mine. We haven't said anything about that.'

'What about the dog?'

'What about it? If he comes for me now I have something in my pocket that'll stop its yapping.'

'I'm all against shooting a dog for doing what it's been trained to do.'

'If it's been trained to bite people, that's its bad luck. I'm not standing for being savaged by any brute, no matter what it's been trained to do. It may not see me. You can put me off at the far end of the moor so that I can work up to the mine from behind.'

'Okay, if that's how you want it. But be careful what you get up to. I've one man missing already; I don't want another. Now let's get on with it. After dropping Algy at the Towers I shall dash back here to see if there's a message from Headquarters. If there's nothing I'll return to the moor and park in the usual place. That's where you'll find me, Ginger, when you get tired of sneaking about in the heather.'

'Fair enough.'

In a few minutes they were on their way. It was still not quite dark, but twilight had taken possession of the scene by the time they reached the moor. The car was stopped at the far end to enable Ginger to get out and approach his objective from a new angle.

'You know the scheme,' Biggles told him. 'I'm taking Algy on to the Towers. That means I shall have to fetch him later, but I don't know exactly when that will be. Come to the road when you've had enough of the moor. You know where I'll be. I'm sorry to split up the party like this but I don't see what else we can do. Be careful.'

Ginger raised a hand. 'Okay.'

Biggles drove on, slowly, still with one eye on the moor, so to speak, and had not gone far when a car, actually a light van, coming towards him pulled up level with a squeal of brakes. He felt for his gun, thinking this was an attack; but he left it in his pocket when he saw the car was not the Bentley. He was not a little surprised when he observed that it appeared to be filled

with policemen. An inspector got out and came to the window
Biggles had opened. 'I thought I recognized your car,' he said in
a voice that did not sound very friendly.

'Did you want to see me?'

'Yes.'

'Is something wrong?'

'Plenty.'

Biggles got out of the car. 'What's the trouble?' he asked,
puzzled by the Inspector's brusque manner.

'You sent us out on a wild-goose chase.'

'*I* sent you out? What are you talking about?'

'Where are you off to now?'

'Matter of fact we're on our way to Hallstone Towers.'

'What for?'

'Oh, just to have a look at it.'

'Hoping to find Lewis?'

'Partly.'

'Well, I can save you the trouble,' was the curt rejoinder.

'How do you mean?'

'There's nobody there except a bad-tempered old bitch of a
woman.'

Biggles blinked. 'How do you know?' Such was his surprise he
had to grope for the words.

'We've been there.'

'You've—been—there!'

'Yes. We've searched the place from top to bottom. It was a
waste of time.'

'Who were you looking for?'

'Cracker Lewis, of course.'

'What gave you the idea he was there?' inquired Biggles,
trying to keep pace with the situation.

'You said he was there.'

'Me! I never told you anything of the sort.'

'You told your chief in London, didn't you?'

'Yes—but . . .' Biggles began to see daylight. 'I think you'd
better tell me how this came about.'

'You made a report to your chief at the Yard.'

'What of it?'

'He was given to understand you'd seen Lewis at Hallstone.'

'That's right. One of my assistants went in person to explain what was going on here and ask for instructions. He brought Sergeant Lacey, here beside me, back with him.'

'Well, I had a phone call from Assistant Commissioner Raymond, who I understand is your boss, to ask me to give you all the help I could if you asked for it. He said he thought you might be taking on more than you could cope with.'

Now Biggles understood. 'And Air Commodore Raymond told you Lewis had been seen at Hallstone.'

'Yes.'

'So you decided to grab him.'

'Naturally.'

'Did Raymond ask you to do that?'

'No. Er, not exactly.'

Biggles shook his head sadly. 'I'm afraid you've jumped the gun, Inspector. Lewis is only a small fish in this swim. Did Raymond tell you what we were *really* doing here?'

'No.'

'Then I'd better tell you in the hope of getting this mess straightened out. We've reason to think Bodmin Moor is being used as a landing ground for an aircraft coming in to fly criminals and their swag out of the country. Lewis is one of them. The man behind the organization, at this end, anyway, appears to be Sir Humphrey Trethallan. It may have been one of this gang who shot your Constable Harley.'

The Inspector looked incredulous. 'Good God!'

'We were holding our hand hoping to grab the lot, including the plane and its pilot, in one cast of the net. If Trethallan learns that his house has been raided by the police—well, it won't have improved our chances of doing that.'

'No. I see that. I'm sorry, but I acted for the best.'

'I'm sure you did. Forget it. Let's deal with things as they stand. You say Trethallan and Lewis weren't in the house.'

'If they were we couldn't find 'em.'

'They *were* there. I saw them. They went off together in a car. I had a notion it was to fetch the money Lewis had hidden away. It has never been found. I posted a man to check if they came back. Incidentally, he's disappeared, and I haven't a clue as to what has happened to him. One of my lads is on the moor now, looking for him, but I wouldn't give much for his chances.'

'When you talk of Trethallan going off in his car do you mean that old Bentley?'

'Yes.'

'Well, they must have come back because it's there now, or it was when we left, standing at the front door.'

'The devil it is!'

'It was there when we arrived.'

'I wish you'd told me you were going there.'

'I would have done had I been able to find you. I went to your hotel but you were out. Thinking we had no time to lose we pushed on to the Towers. What would you like me to do now?'

'Give me a minute to think. What I can't understand is, if the Bentley is at the Towers where the devil have Trethallan and Lewis gone? I had assumed that when the time was ripe for Lewis to be flown out Trethallan would bring him round here in the car and drop him off at the nearest place to the landing strip, which is an area of burnt heather near an old mine. It seems I may have been wrong.'

'Had you any reason to think the plane would be coming tonight?'

'No. But I imagined Trethallan wouldn't want to keep that crook in his house longer than was absolutely necessary. The plane may come tonight; it may not. As a pilot myself I can say that weather conditions for a night landing are okay. I've got to catch that plane on the job. We know it has been coming over regularly. It's giving the Government sleepless nights, thinking the motive might be espionage. If we can nobble that plane it will tell us the answer, and keep Lewis in the country.'

'Can I do anything about it? What are you going to do?'

'Well, after what's happened there's no point in our going to the Towers, so I shall stay handy until my assistant on the moor comes back. He may be able to tell us something. If you're not

too busy you might stand by to give us a hand should the plane
come tonight. If it does it will be before daybreak. We may need
help. There are several in the gang here, not counting Lewis and
the pilot. Crooks like Lewis won't be likely to pack up without a
fight; we can be sure of that.'

'All right. I'll do that,' agreed the Inspector. 'I'd give
anything to get my hands on the rat who murdered poor Harley.
Where would you like us to wait?'

'Follow me. I'll take you to the place where my assistant is to
meet me when he's finished on the moor. We made arrangements
for that.'

'Right. Lead the way.'

Biggles got back in his car and in a few minutes was at the usual
parking place.

The Inspector pulled in behind him.

Biggles got out and walked to his open window. 'Coming
along I was thinking,' he said. 'Did you mean it when you said
you'd do anything you could to help?'

'Of course.'

'Then here's a little job you might do for me. Ask your driver
to run into Bodmin and ask at my hotel if there's a message for
me. Only one man need go. The rest can stay here.'

'Are you expecting a message?'

'No. But there might be one. My chief is in touch with the
radar stations, and if they pick up this unidentified plane they'll
let him know. He'd pass the message on to me. If such a message
came through we should have an early warning of what was
likely to happen.'

'I get it. I'll do that.'

The Inspector gave the necessary order and the car went on its
way, leaving the Inspector and two constables with Biggles, who
said: 'While we're waiting we might as well sit down.' They
found seats in the heather beside the road.

Nothing happened during the half-hour the car was away.
When it returned it pulled up with a dry skid and the constable
driver jumped out, holding a slip of paper. 'Here you are, sir,' he
said. 'Priority signal from Scotland Yard to Inspector

Bigglesworth.'

'That's me.'

'The hall porter was taking the message down when I got there.'

Biggles read it aloud for the benefit of the others who were watching. 'Intruder sighted twenty miles south-west Falmouth on course north-east. Altitude approx. ten thousand. Losing height.' Biggles looked up. 'Good,' he said tersely. 'Now we know where we are. We shouldn't have long to wait. Our best plan, I think, would be to move nearer to what I take to be the landing ground and lie down in the heather. Then, when I give the signal, we'll all rush it together. I expect Trethallan will be along any minute now with Lewis. I'm a bit surprised he isn't here already. He's cutting it fine.' He got up and looked across the moor. 'Hello, what the devil's that?' he exclaimed, pointing to a spark of light that had suddenly appeared.

The Inspector's eyes followed the pointing finger. 'Could it be a landing light?'

'No. It's nowhere near the landing strip.'

'Then it looks as if some damn fool has set the heather on fire,' growled the Inspector. 'Does that lad you've got on the moor smoke?'

'Not often. He wouldn't be likely to smoke on the moor, anyway. He should be back by now. We'd better give him a minute or two or he won't know where to look for me. If he isn't soon here, Algy, you'll have to wait for him. There's no great hurry. On a still night like this we should hear the plane some time before it gets here.'

A couple of minutes passed. 'What can Ginger be doing?' muttered Algy irritably. 'He said he wouldn't be long.'

Biggles shook his head. 'I can't imagine.'

'That fire's spreading,' observed the Inspector. 'If it comes this way we shan't be able to see anything for smoke.'

WHAT HAPPENED TO BERTIE

Algy was right when he said that only trouble in a big way would have prevented Bertie from keeping his appointment with Biggles. That he brought it on himself is not to be disputed, but faced suddenly with an unexpected situation he acted for the best; as Biggles, he was sure, would have approved.

The task he had been set seemed simple enough, and so it would have been had things worked out as Biggles had anticipated. He had assumed, if he hadn't actually taken it for granted, that when Lewis was taken to the landing ground to be flown abroad, Trethallan would bring him in the Bentley to the nearest point on the road. This was a natural supposition, because from the moor to the Towers by road was a distance of some miles; with transport available there was no reason why they should walk, particularly as, after Lewis had been seen off, Trethallan would be anxious to get back to the Towers as quickly as possible. In the event, things did not work out like this. Far from it. What did actually happen, starting at the beginning, was this.

After Biggles had left him Bertie walked down the lane to the drive that led to the Towers. There he paused to look around and listen. All was quiet; dead quiet. Not a sound. So he continued on up the drive looking for a good place in which to conceal himself and observe the Bentley when it returned. That is, *if* it returned. There had been nothing to indicate that it would, but it was a reasonable supposition if Biggles had been right in thinking that the car had gone off to collect the money Lewis had hidden. Obviously, how long the Bentley would be away would depend on how far it had to go.

Bertie, sure that he had plenty of time—as in fact it turned out—walked on until he could see the black bulk of the mansion looming against the sky. Not a light showed anywhere, which made him wonder how Sir Humphrey managed for servants. Were there any? Was the house empty? The fact that no lights were showing proved nothing, he told himself. The staff quarters, if Sir Humphrey did not live in the house alone, which seemed most improbable, might be round at the back. Anyway, it wasn't worth going to any trouble to find out. That wasn't his business.

Going back a little way down the drive he settled on a place from where he would be able to see the front of the house, and as far down the drive as was possible in the dark. It was a moonless night, and the light of the few stars that were showing did not penetrate the leaf-laden branches of the overhanging trees on either side. Tall bracken flourished on the banks. This offered perfect cover, so taking care not to disturb it more than was unavoidable, he made his way into it for a few yards and settled down to wait.

Taking out his penknife he trimmed the bracken that impeded his view. This he did more for something to do than for any practical purpose. For the same reason, finding himself sitting on something hard he investigated and found it to be a fallen branch. The thought struck him that a stout stick would be useful should an unfriendly dog come along, so he occupied himself for some time by cutting a straight length out of the branch that would serve as a weapon in an emergency. He had no other.

He was prepared for a long wait, which was just as well, for so it transpired.

It was after three o'clock in the morning when he heard a car change gear in the lane; coming up the hill. This brought him to the alert. Following the sound with his ears he heard the car slow down as it turned into the drive. A moment later he saw the reflection of the headlights in the trees. It came on. He crouched, peering through the fringe of bracken. It went past quickly in a blaze of light, dazzling after the darkness. He could not see who was in it.

This introduced a factor on which he had not reckoned, although perhaps he should have done. He was able to recognize the Bentley by the shape of its body; but nothing more. This was not enough. What Biggles would want to know was, who was in it? Had Trethallan returned alone or had he brought Lewis back with him? That was the fundamental purpose of the exercise; of his being there.

Blaming himself for his stupidity in not making allowances for this, although in fact it was hard to see what more he could have done without risking discovery, he listened. He heard the car stop. The doors slam. Then the front door opened and closed. After that, silence. For a minute or two he sat still, thinking the matter over, reluctant to leave his job half done. He knew the Bentley had returned. That was something. But it was not enough.

Thinking it might still be possible to complete the most important part of his mission, he got up and made his way cautiously towards the house. When he reached the point where the drive widened as it approached the front door, he saw with satisfaction that his luck was in. A light appeared at a window on the ground floor; as if an electric light had been switched on. A shadow moved across it. Someone was in the room. Who was it? It seemed a fairly simple matter to find out.

He advanced, slowly, keeping close against the shrubs, laurels and the like, which here lined the drive. He had not made much progress when he feared he had congratulated himself too soon. The silhouette of a man appeared against the light and in an instant the light was cut out as if curtains had been drawn. But either they had been drawn carelessly or they did not quite meet in the middle, for when they stopped moving, a gap, a narrow slit of light, was left between them.

This is how they had been, Bertie recalled, when Biggles had described how he had seen Lewis in the house. This was probably the same room. Who was in it now? Was Sir Humphrey alone or had he brought the escaped criminal with him? Bertie resolved to find out.

Holding his cudgel, still with the possibility of the guard dog in mind, step by step he made his way to the window, and after a pause to listen for danger, going down on one knee he applied an eye to the gap between the curtains. One glance was enough to reveal everything, and what he saw took his breath away, although he should perhaps have been prepared for something of the sort.

Trethallan and Lewis were both there. But it was not this bare fact that shook him. On a table between them was an open suitcase, the contents of which had apparently just been emptied on the table. It was money; a heap of bank-notes done up in bundles as they are stored in a bank. Trethallan was counting the bundles, making two piles, one on each side of the table in the manner of one for me, one for you.

So Biggles had been right, was the thought that flashed into Bertie's head as he continued to watch this transaction. They had been to fetch the swag and were now busy 'carving it up' between them.

This did not take long. When the operation was finished Lewis packed his share back into the suitcase. Trethallan went to the panelled wall near the fireplace and slid a section of it to one side exposing a cavity. In this he stacked his share of the loot, and closing the panel returned to his companion.

Bertie, deciding he had seen enough, retired to the shrubs to think about it. There was no need for haste. For the moment there was nothing he could do. It would be some time before Biggles came along to pick him up. He considered walking to meet him; but that would mean a change of plan, which he knew from experience was ill-advised as all too often it ended in a muddle.

What did this mean—what he had just seen? Having achieved their purpose would the two men now part company? Would the next move be for them to return to the Bentley so that Trethallan could complete his part of the transaction by taking Lewis to the moor for his final getaway? If this was so did it mean that the intruder aircraft was on its way to pick up the convict and his money? Bertie hesitated, although thinking on these lines the matter suddenly became urgent.

There seemed to be only one way of learning what the two partners in crime intended to do next. This was to wait, and watch. He thought, and hoped, they would not leave the house. Time was getting on. They would not be likely to do anything in broad daylight. That would give him time to report to Biggles what he had seen. Give them all time to do something about it.

This seemed reasonable, and he decided it was the best thing to do. Had the operation continued to work out as Biggles had imagined it would, and the signs all pointed to that, all might have been well. Instead, they took an entirely different course, one that did not fit into Biggles's scheme at all.

Bertie backed a little way down the drive and took up a position in the bracken from which he would be able to keep an eye on the house, the lighted window and the front door. Should the two men leave the house it would be, he was sure, by this door; and in this respect, at least, he was right.

He looked at the sky. There was still no sign of dawn, so there was no point in going yet to the rendezvous. Biggles would not be there. He would stick to the letter of the arrangement. Had Bertie thought there was the slightest chance of Biggles arriving early he would have hurried to the meeting place to unload his vital information, and leave the next move to him. But Biggles would still be watching the moor, and would not be likely to leave it until daylight put an end to any chance of the plane coming that night.

So Bertie could only wait, which was a pity, although to say this was a mistake would be going too far, and unfair to Bertie, whose state of mind can be imagined.

After some ten minutes or so the light in the room was switched off. A little later the front door was opened. Trethallan and Lewis came out. It was dark, but there was just enough starlight for the figures to be recognized. Lewis carried a suitcase; no doubt the case containing the stolen money. So they were leaving after all. Naturally, Bertie thought they were about to drive off in the car. Indeed, no other thought occurred to him. This dismayed him, for having no transport himself it meant he would lose them. But this did not happen. What did happen struck him at the time as even worse. The two men started walking briskly down the drive. All Bertie could do was crouch back in the bracken, hiding his face, trusting they would not see him. In the event he need not have feared. The men did not reach him. The footsteps stopped abruptly. Holding his breath he waited for them to continue. They did not. Nothing happened. What were the men doing? Where had they gone? After a few palpitating seconds he risked a peep. They were not in sight.

Taken by surprise, and not a little astonished, Bertie realized that only one thing could have happened. The men had left the drive. How? Where? Creeping along a little way he discovered the answers when he came to a much overgrown footpath, leading off through the bushes. Where were they going, and for what purpose? wondered Bertie desperately, thrown into confusion by a development so unexpected. What should he do? It had happened so suddenly there had been no time to think. Should he follow? It would obviously be dangerous; the men might stop or he might run into them coming back; but that was a secondary consideration. It was the difficulty of pursuit in the darkness, not having the least idea of what lay ahead, that made him hesitate. He was afraid of doing the wrong thing. On the other hand, he was in a position, should things go well, to obtain information that could be of vital importance.

It was a murmur of voices some distance ahead that decided him. While he could hear the men talking he would be able to judge where they were, how far they were in front of him. With his hands held in front of his face to protect his eyes from projecting twigs which in the darkness he would be unable to see, he set off along the path.

Soon, to his great relief, the footpath ran across more open ground. This enabled him to see a light that jerked about as if one of the men, probably Trethallan, was carrying a torch. Trethallan, no doubt knowing the ground, would be showing the way. It seemed more than likely that he was on his own property, reasoned Bertie. The light made things easier for him, but that is not to say he was happy. Far from it. On the contrary he was worried. Was he doing the right thing or should he have gone to the rendezvous? But he decided he had gone too far to go back. Having started he might as well see the business through to the end, wherever and whatever that might be.

The path meandered on interminably. He had no reason to

think the journey would be a short one, but he did not expect it to be as long as this. Where on earth could the men be going? He reckoned they must have covered well over a mile, sometimes uphill, sometimes down. Where was it going to end? What could be the object of such an expedition at such an hour?

He still had not suspected the truth when the terrain began to change. The deciduous trees, with an undergrowth of shrubs and bracken, gave way to a stand of Scots pines with a thick carpet of needles under foot. There was less risk here of making a sound that might betray him; but the trees being widely spaced there was more chance of him being seen should the light be turned in his direction. He tried to avoid this by moving swiftly from tree to tree, pausing briefly behind each one before going on. This had the disadvantage of allowing the two men to get farther in front; but this did not worry him while he could still see the light of the torch.

The path, now only faintly discernible, ran up some gently rising ground; evidently a hill, or a knoll. The light disappeared over the top. When he reached the spot, which he had approached with extra caution, it was not to be seen. Apparently it had been switched off as no longer necessary. The reason for this was plain to see. Below the hill the ground rolled away in flat open country for as far as it was possible for the eyes to follow it in a misty gloom. The men he had been following were not in sight. At all events, he couldn't see them. They had completely disappeared. Where had they gone? What was this place?

For a few moments Bertie stared, frowning uncomprehendingly. Then the truth dawned on him. This was the moor. Bodmin Moor. Of course. Trethallan, knowing the ground, had taken a short cut. Biggles had been wrong in his conviction that when Lewis was brought to the landing ground it would be by road, in the car. That the trip might be made on foot had not occurred to any of them, the reason being, understandably, that the distance by road between the moor and the Towers was something like ten miles. It now appeared that cross-country, as the crow flies, for a rough guess it was not much more than two miles.

So there Bertie stood, bemused, staring at the wilderness of heather stretching away in front of him, colourless in the feeble moonlight. He had no idea of which part of the moor he was looking at. To make matters worse he had lost the men. It was reasonable to suppose they were making for the landing strip. But where was it? In which direction? Looking at the moor from a new angle he couldn't even guess. To hope to come on it in the dark by accident was hardly worth considering.

The fact that Lewis was carrying a suitcase now became significant. His share of the money was in it. That could only mean one thing. He would not be going back to the house. He was on his way out. Now. Tonight—or early morning as it was now. Trethallan was with him to act as guide; to show him the way to the old mine which marked the landing ground. Yes, that was the answer. Bertie was sure of it. He could think of no other explanation to account for what had happened.

What should he do? Or rather, what *could* he do? Biggles, he did not doubt, was still on the road, watching. He would not leave until daybreak. That was fast approaching, but as yet there was no indication of it in the sky. Biggles should know what was going on. At once. It was imperative. But how could he get to him?

Bertie fretted. To retrace his steps to the Towers, even if he could find his way—and of this he was by no means sure—would be useless. He would arrive at the meeting place too late. The bird would have flown—literally. The alternative was to walk across the moor to the road. If he could find it. In which direction did it lie? To go the wrong way would only make matters worse. He looked for lights of cars moving on the road; but either there was no traffic at this hour before dawn, or there was just sufficient mist, rising as usual, to reduce visibility very considerably. It was impossible in such conditions to judge distance. The road might be no more than half a mile away, but for all he knew it might equally be two or three miles. He wasn't sure, but the mist seemed to be thickening instead of dispersing.

This question of poor visibility introduced another factor. Would the plane attempt to land in such conditions? He thought not. Thinking as a pilot, first there would be the difficulty of locating the moor, let alone the strip. To put the aircraft down without mishap would be even more difficult. Even if lights were put out to mark the spot, they would hardly be the powerful sort used on commercial airfields. In view of what he was doing the pilot wouldn't risk a crash. Wherefore it seemed that if landing arrangements had been made for that night, it might be found necessary to postpone them; that was assuming Trethallan was in radio contact with the plane. The mist would clear quickly when the sun came up; but then it would be light. Would the plane risk landing in daylight? It seemed highly improbable.

So reasoned Bertie, these thoughts going through his head faster than they take to tell. If the flight had to be postponed, all might yet be well. But he was still undecided about which course to take; to try to find the road, or to go back the way he had come, hoping to find Biggles waiting for him. But that would serve no useful purpose if the plane had come and gone.

Somewhere in the distance a car horn hooted. A welcome and familiar sound. He looked hard in the direction from which he thought it had come; but he could see no light; nothing. However, this decided him. The car that had sounded its horn could only be on the road. He started off at a trot, trusting to be able to keep his sense of direction. Apart from long heather impeding his progress somewhat, there was no difficulty until he came to a peculiar configuration of the ground, and he did not seriously regard this as an obstacle. It consisted of a number of mounds in the manner of enormous molehills, some twenty or thirty feet high. They were covered, like everything else, with heather. What had caused these humps he did not know, nor did he give the matter any consideration. He had only one thing in mind. To get to the road. So he hurried on between them, worried because he had never previously seen this part of the moor, and so could only conclude he was some distance from his objective.

It was not until he came upon some ancient brickwork that the truth hit him. This was the site of another old mine, and the mounds were the tips, the heaps of discarded debris thrown up

when the mine was being worked. Judging from the growth of
heather and weeds that had taken possession of them, this must
have been a long time ago. Anyway, there was no chimney stack
so it was not the mine he knew, the one not far from the landing
strip; so there was no fear of encountering the shepherd's dog.
Having realized the sort of ground he was on he should, of course,
have proceeded with extra care; he knew the danger of such
places, and had in fact pointed them out to Biggles when
speaking of these old mines.

But it is easy to criticize. Bertie's mind was entirely taken up
with getting to the road in the shortest possible time, so he
hurried on regardless. He was looking ahead to mark the next
hillock, in order to avoid it, when without warning his feet went
through the heather into a void. Feeling himself falling he made
a desperate effort to save himself, clutching wildly at the heather.
For a few seconds he clung to it, trying to drag himself back; but
it tore out by the roots and he fell into space, still snatching for
something, anything, that might break his fall. He struck hard
ground with a bump and rolled on, his fingers clawing into loose
shale which, sliding with him, offered no hold.

The end came when his head struck something hard, and the
world exploded in a shower of stars that faded quickly to utter
darkness.

13
THE PIT

WHEN Bertie opened his eyes he was at first conscious of only one
thing. A throbbing head. A little later he saw above him a
circular patch of sky. Still dazed, he struggled into a sitting
position and tried to remember what had happened. Slowly it all
came back. The Towers: the two men he had followed; the moor;
the fall. With broad daylight above, he realized he must have
been unconscious for a long time. He looked at his watch. The
glass had gone, the face was smashed, so it told him nothing.

The next thing he did was to examine himself for injuries and was relieved to find no broken bones. That, he told himself, was something to be thankful for. The only real damage appeared to be to his head, which ached unmercifully. He felt it tenderly and found dry blood on his face. Beside him was the rock that had done the mischief. Close by it lay his cudgel.

At the bottom of the hole into which he had fallen, just below him, was a puddle of surface water that must have drained in. He made his way to it unsteadily, soaked his handkerchief and bathed his head, afterwards leaving the wet rag on as a bandage. This needed effort and he had to rest for a while. His thoughts became more coherent. Had the plane come? Had Lewis escaped after all? It had been near dawn when the accident happened. The moor had been misty. He comforted himself with the possibility of the flight having been postponed.

Calling himself hard names for not looking where he was going, he examined his surroundings and observed that his position might have been worse. Much worse. While he was actually falling, for a dreadful moment he felt sure he had stepped into an old mine shaft, perhaps of great depth. That would have been the end, without any shadow of doubt. He saw that things were not as bad as that, although they were serious enough. The hole into which he had fallen was shaped like an inverted cone, about thirty feet deep, as if there had once been a mine there and a half-hearted attempt had been made to fill it in after it was abandoned. Either that, or the place had been used only for opencast mining. The sides were not sheer, but steep; too steep for herbage, heather or anything else, to get a hold on it. The actual soil was a mixture of gravel and shale.

He sat on the rock which his head had struck. The movement produced dizziness and a feeling of nausea. This suggested concussion, and he thought it prudent to rest for a while before he did anything or he might fall again with more serious results. There was no urgency now that it was daylight, although the others would be in a state wondering what had become of him. Naturally, he was anxious to get out of the trap into which he had fallen, to see where he was, and if anything was happening on the moor. This, he saw, was not going to be easy; but just how difficult it was to prove he still had not realized.

His eyes wandered round. They came to rest on something he had not previously noticed; a hole that appeared to be the entrance to a cave, or more likely, the mine. Originally it had been shored up with timber, but some of this had collapsed, leaving an irregularly shaped opening. He worked it out that this must have been a passage through which waste material had been carried to produce the mounds above.

Still unsteady on his feet he walked over to it and tried to peer inside; but it was pitch dark and he could see nothing. A curious smell reached his nostrils to make him sniff; an unnatural smell considering where he was. It reminded him of an unventilated room with people in it. He even thought he could detect the unmistakable aroma of coffee. This was ridiculous, he told himself, wondering if he was really fully conscious. How could anyone be inside? Thinking it over it occurred to him that the source of the smell might be some distance away. Somewhere there might be another shaft creating a draught. Was this part of an old ventilation system? It could be. He was not a miner, but he seemed to recollect reading that in the early days of mining this sort of thing was constructed to prevent the air in the mine from becoming foul.

At this juncture it did not occur to him to investigate. He was in no state to start exploring. He was in enough trouble without making matters worse. He had no means of illumination except his petrol lighter, and as that might give out he decided it would be folly to take unnecessary risks.

Feeling his strength returning he turned his attention to a more practical project; that of getting out of the place and back on to the moor. What would happen when he got there he did not know; and he didn't particularly care. The thing was to get out and find the road—and Biggles, who would, he was sure, be somewhere on it. He looked up at the sky. Was it merely overcast or was it getting dark? He found that hard to believe. Was it possible that he had been lying there unconscious all day? It did not seem possible; but presently he had to face the fact that it was evening, and the light was fading.

It was not until he made his first attempt to climb out of the hole that he realized, not without a pang of anxiety, that this was going to be more difficult than he had supposed. And he had chosen what he thought looked the easiest place. He got nowhere near the top. Still feeling sick and giddy he looked for somewhere else. But it was all the same. Loose, friable shale and gravel that crumbled under his hands, offering no hold. It poured down on his head in a little avalanche when he reached up at it, blinding him and filling his mouth with dust.

He made several attempts in different places. Always with the same result. Failure. He had a final go, using his cudgel as a prop. He managed to reach the fringe of heather that hung over the rim, but it came away in his hands and he fell heavily, narrowly missing the rock at the bottom. As it was he was severely shaken, with the breath knocked out of him. It was no use, he told himself lugubriously. If he went on like this he would end up by doing himself another mischief. He would have to think of something else; and soon, if he was to get out before dark; it was already twilight.

Again he sat on the rock to recover from his shaking and give further thought to his problem. There must be some way out, he told himself in a sort of desperation. He looked again at the cave, or old mine, whatever it might be. It could be the answer, but the thought of going in, not having the remotest idea of where it would end, and without a proper light, appalled him. The whole thing might collapse and bury him for ever. He had risked death many times, but that would not be a nice way to die.

Looking up at the rim of the hole, so near and yet so far away, a thought struck him. If he could set fire to the heather on top it would be seen over a wide area. If Biggles was on the road it was almost certain that he would see it, in which case he could be expected to investigate. It seemed a crazy thing to do, to set fire to the moor, but he didn't care about that as long as it achieved its purpose. Even if Biggles did not come, someone was bound to see the fire and report it. That might bring the police along, or the fire brigade. He didn't care who came, so long as it was someone; otherwise it looked as if he might be stuck in the hole until some wandering hiker found his bones.

The question was, how to set fire to the heather? He knew from walking through it that it was dry and would only need a spark to set it going. This did not seem difficult. In fact, it should be easy, he decided. There was plenty of heather lying about, stuff that he had pulled out in his original fall and later in his attempts to get out. This could be tied in a bunch. All he had to do then was to light it with his lighter and throw it over the top. That should do the trick, he thought confidently.

Another thought struck him, one that gave zest to his project. If the plane had not been and gone this might be the night for it to come. With the moor on fire it would not be able to land. Even if the actual fire did not reach the landing ground the smoke would deter any sane pilot from attempting a landing.

Enthusiastic now that at last he had something to do, he collected a good bunch of heather and tied it in a tight ball with his necktie, leaving a long loose end for handling it, and for the swing that would be necessary to get it over the rim of the hole. This was the work of only a few minutes. He tried a short practice swing to confirm that his firebrand would not come to pieces in flight. It held together. He collected it, and took out his lighter in readiness for the experiment.

A slight sound behind him made him turn, to see a most extraordinary spectacle. It was the end of a ladder. It was emerging from the cave, obviously being carried by someone. He stared incredulously, not without good cause. A man appeared. He was carrying the ladder on his shoulder. The light was not very good but he was able to recognize the shepherd he had seen when he and Biggles had inspected the supposed landing strip.

A ladder! At that moment it was a more welcome sight than a bag of gold. It seemed too good to be true. The appearance of the man from the cave explained the smell he had noticed. He didn't bother to wonder what the man was doing in the cave. There was only one reason why he should want a ladder; obviously, for the same reason as he himself needed one. To get out of the pit. But would he be allowed to use the ladder? Perhaps not. Not if the man saw him. So he kept perfectly still, hoping the man would not notice him before he had erected the ladder and gone over the top. It was not unreasonable to suppose he would leave it in position against his return.

For a minute it looked as if this might happen. The ladder, one of the aluminium extending sort, took a little while to adjust. It was put up resting against the side of the pit, reaching nearly to the top. This done, the man looked around. For what purpose was not clear. But he looked, and inevitably saw Bertie sitting on his rock. It was his turn to look astonished. He then asked the question that might have been expected. 'What are you doing here?'

'What does it look like?' Bertie answered with a trace of sarcasm. 'I fell into this damned hole, cracked my skull and haven't been able to get out. Am I glad to see you with a ladder!'

The man advanced slowly, for the moment saying nothing. He appeared to be at a loss for words, as was understandable. But it was soon evident that he was not to be taken in by Bertie's casual manner.

'What were you doing when you fell in?' he asked suspiciously.

'Taking a walk on the moor. What else would I be doing?'

'What were you looking for?'

'The road. It was misty and I lost my way. I'd like to get along if you don't mind. My friends will be looking for me.'

'Where are they?'

'Waiting on the road, I imagine. Which is the nearest way to it?'

'They're not on the moor?'

'Not as far as I know.' The instant the words had passed his lips Bertie realized he had made a mistake.

The man confirmed it. 'In that case I'm afraid they'll have to go on waiting for you.'

'What do you mean?'

'You're not using this ladder.'

'Why not?'

The man did not answer. He walked back towards the ladder.

'But look here, I say . . .' Bertie started to follow, but when the man took a revolver from his pocket and pointed it at him he stopped.

'Stay where you are,' growled the man, and walked on.

Bertie said: 'All right, if that's how you want it, you disagreeable fellow.' He flicked on the lighter and held it under his fireball. As soon as it was well alight he hurled it over the rim of the pit. A brisk crackle told him it was doing what he had intended.

The man must have heard it, or seen the flicker of the flames, for he spun round. 'What are you doing?' he demanded angrily.

'I've done it, old cock,' answered Bertie, calmly. 'You won't lend me your ladder so I'm letting my friends know where I am.'

For a moment he thought the man was going to shoot him; from the way he pointed the revolver he must have contemplated it. But he thought better of it, perhaps because the sound of the shot would be heard. 'Do you want to set the whole place on fire, you fool?' he shouted furiously.

'Yes,' replied Bertie. 'That's the idea. You've got it.'

The man drew a deep breath, and after a pause, with many a backward glance strode quickly to the ladder. He withdrew the extension, put it on his shoulder and hurried to the cave. At the entrance he stopped only long enough to shout, holding up the revolver: 'You try to follow me and you'll get this.' He went on into the cave.

Bertie was no coward but he had more sense than to follow a man with a gun into a place where he would be at a hopeless disadvantage. The man would see him against the light and no doubt carry out his threat. Inside the cave the report of a shot would be muffled.

So he sat on his rock trying to work out what this strange occurrence might mean. What had been the man's purpose? What did he intend to do now?

He coughed as a wave of smoke rolled down into the pit and the pungent reek of burning heather bit into his lungs. More was coming down. There was nothing he could do to stop it.

He hadn't thought of this.

14

TOUGH GOING FOR GINGER

WHEN Ginger left Biggles for his walk across the moor, had anyone asked him exactly what he was going to do he would not have been able to answer. He had a vague idea of getting as close as possible to the old mine, and by using his eyes and ears learn if there was any activity. He felt that the near-by landing ground was the centre of things, and therefore most likely to yield results. Not that he expected to find Bertie there. In his heart he agreed with Biggles. That was too much to hope for. But he thought there was just a chance, however remote, that he might overhear a conversation that would give him a clue as to what had become of him, or better still, where he was. So he carried on across the moor with hope, but without much confidence, that he was not wasting his time.

Twilight had given way to darkness, but it was not a bad sort of night. There was no wind, merely an occasional slight breeze, this being of the sort known as variable. There was no threat of rain. The sky, judging from a sprinkling of early stars, was clear. He would have called conditions for night flying fairly good. What he would do should the intruding plane come in while he was out on the moor, he didn't know. He hadn't thought as far ahead as that. If it came it would probably be later, after he had returned to the road to meet Biggles. If he found nothing of interest, that would be fairly soon. That was his intention. He had no wish to spend more time alone on the moor than was necessary for his purpose.

He stopped several times to look around, bending low to get the configuration of the horizon against the sky, for the ground was strange to him. He had never seen this part of the moor. He was, he reckoned, roughly a mile east of the abandoned mine that was really his objective. As he had said, he thought it more prudent to take this roundabout course rather than walk to it directly across the open heather, when he might be seen by anyone on the watch for strangers.

For some time he could see the road, or rather, the lights of traffic on it; but when the ground began to fall away he was denied this advantage, his view being blocked by the higher ground that intervened. This did not worry him much because he knew, or thought he knew, the general direction. He was also aware that nothing is easier than to lose one's sense of direction on a wide expanse of open ground without a landmark. If he was afraid of anything it was a sudden fog, a not uncommon occurrence on any moor. It was not until later that he became a little uneasy.

Thinking he had gone far enough out to bring him in behind the mine he began to swing towards the left. It was soon after this, peering through the gloom, that he made out an undulating skyline, as if there was a range of low hills in front of him. He had never noticed them from the road; but he thought nothing of it because he was now looking at the moor from an entirely new angle.

Coming to the first hill, it occurred to him that instead of going round it, as he could have done, if he went over it he would get a wide view from the top; so he continued straight on up the slope. It was not much of a climb, anyhow. On the summit he paused to survey his surroundings. There was little to be seen; no life, no movement. All he learned was that there were other similar hills close by. Whether this was a natural or artificial formation he didn't bother to speculate. He was only concerned with what he was doing, and with keeping his sense of direction.

For as far as he could see the moor lay grim and silent, open to the winds of heaven. Not a light showed anywhere. He appeared to have the world to himself. It looked anything but inviting. However, that was how all moors looked after dark, he ruminated, as he started down the far side of the slope to continue on his way. A few seconds later he was brought to an abrupt halt by the last sound he expected to hear at that particular spot. Human voices. He was astonished. He was also a little alarmed, realizing he was in no position to take on a gang single-handed should they come in collision. As men do not normally talk to themselves there were at least two men not far away. There might be more, and he could not imagine they were anything but enemies.

Again came the murmur of voices. The trouble was, he could not decide the spot, or even the direction, from which they were coming. There was nothing remarkable about this. Any sound coming out of the darkness in conditions such as those in which Ginger found himself are always difficult to locate. They seem to have a ventriloquial effect, as anyone who has ever tried to mark down a corncrake at night will have discovered. The bird is never at the spot where its call is heard.

Ginger stood motionless, listening intently. At this moment, far from trying to see the men who were speaking, he was more anxious to keep clear of them. Again came the voices, muffled, but one raised as if in anger or argument. He stared but could see nothing. Where were these men? What could they be doing, out on the moor without a light? They sounded close; or, at all events, not far away; but just too far for him to catch the words. He should, he thought, be able to see them. To go on would be to risk walking into them.

His nerves tingled when there came a shout.

This was followed by an even more startling event. Out of the ground—or so it appeared—not far in front of him a blazing brand shot into the air. It fell in the heather. Flames leapt up. There came another shout. Then silence; a silence broken only by the crisp crackle of burning heather as the flames began to spread.

Ginger stood as if spellbound. What did all this mean? Not surprisingly he could make nothing of it. There was no more talking but certain curious sounds suggested a struggle. Loose rock or shale clattered as it fell. What should he do? Get away from the place while the going was good? That seemed the most sensible course. But curiosity held him rigid. He had set out to look for signs of activity but he was not prepared for anything like this. Creeping flames were now throwing a lurid light on the scene but there was still no sign of the men. What had become of them? He stared at the point where the fire had started. He could see it clearly. Beyond was a dark area . . . apparently something that had prevented the fire from spreading in that direction. What was it? Water? No, that would have reflected the light of the fire. What had become of the men he had heard talking? Had they been there he must have seen them. It was all very strange: incomprehensible.

Sheer curiosity determined Ginger to take a chance and investigate. He had been hoping for something to happen, he brooded. Well, he had found something. Why run away? He had a pistol in his pocket. He took it out. His mind made up, he went on down the hillock, and making a detour to by-pass the slowly advancing line of fire he crept on until he was in a position to see what was beyond it. What he saw was a hole in the ground; a gaping pit. He could not see into it but he could hear someone coughing. Creeping forward to the edge he looked down and saw a face looking up. A man with a bandage round his head was leaning on a stick.

Ginger did not recognize him. He watched the man, using his stick, make a run at the side of the pit as if trying to get out. He slid back. He fell. He rose and looked up. He must have seen Ginger's face looking down at him for he called: 'Hello, there! I say, can you get me out of this?'

That, of course, did it. Ginger recognized Bertie's voice. The shock made his brain reel. 'It's me, Ginger,' he managed to get out.

'Jolly good. Never more pleased to see you, dear boy,' came back Bertie. 'You don't happen to have a rope on you?'

'No. Can't you get out?'

'Have a heart! Would I be here choking to death if I could? Do something about it. Buck up. That nasty shepherd fellow isn't far away and he's got a gun.'

Ginger tried to think. It wasn't easy. It was all very well to say get me out, but how was it to be done? 'What can I do?' he asked desperately.

'Make a rope with your shirt, trousers, anything.'

Ginger threw off his jacket and took off his shirt. With his penknife he cut it and tore it up. The sleeves made two strips, the body two more. These he knotted together, all the time wondering if the material would take Bertie's weight. This done, lying on the brink of the crater he lowered the linen line. It was too short. Bertie couldn't reach it.

'You'll have to chuck me *your* shirt to make it long enough,' panted Ginger, coughing in a waft of smoke.

'Here it comes,' Bertie took off his jacket, ripped off his shirt, rolled it round a stone and tossed it up. While he waited he put on his jacket.

Ginger repeated the operation he had performed on his own shirt and tied the two together. After testing it for strength he lowered one end.

By using his stick as a support Bertie was just able to reach it. He hung on, and thrusting his feet against the wall began to climb. Ginger hauled. At the last moment, just as Bertie was within reach of the top, the shirts began to tear. Ginger seized him by the collar of his jacket and dragged him bodily over the brink. Panting, they collapsed in a heap.

'Thanks, laddie,' gasped Bertie, as they untangled themselves. 'I'd been in that beastly hole long enough.'

Ginger looked at him. 'What have you done to your head?'

'I tried breaking a rock with it but it didn't work. The rock was harder than my skull.'

'Are you all right otherwise?'

'I think so.'

'Can you walk? We've some way to go.'

'I'll have a shot at it. Where are we going?'

'To the road. Biggles will be there.'

'How far is it?'

'A mile, at least.'

'Give me a minute to get my breath and I'll be okay,' Bertie said.

While they rested Ginger said: 'How long have you been in that hole?'

'Since early yesterday morning.'

'Good lord! How did it happen?'

'I fell in, like a silly ass, not looking where I was putting my feet.'

'Whom did I hear you talking to?'

'That phoney shepherd. He found me there; popped out of a hole like a ruddy rabbit. He had a ladder but he wouldn't lend it to me to get out. He had a gun, so I couldn't argue.'

'Where is he now?'

'He went back down his burrow, which I fancy is a bolt-hole, to ask, I imagine, what should be done with me.'

'What were you doing when you fell in?'

'Tracking Trethallan and Lewis. They left the house together on foot and took a short cut to the moor, where I lost them. Lewis has a suitcase full of money with him. I saw them sharing it out. Trethallan left his in the house. I saw where he put it. On the left-hand side of the fireplace there's a head carved on the panelling. It pulls out. There's a drawer behind it.'

'Where are Trethallan and Lewis now?'

'I don't know for sure but I think they were making for the old mine. I believe it has a link with this one.'

'If that's where they've gone it looks as if the plane may come over tonight,' Ginger said.

'That's what I was thinking. But I say, look at the jolly old fire I started.'

'I've been watching it. If you feel up to it, it's time we were moving. If the fire spreads much more it'll cut us off from the road. We shall have to go round it as it is.'

The fire was in fact creeping towards the road on a widening front, throwing up clouds of smoke.

Ginger set off at a brisk pace.

Bertie was soon lagging behind. 'Take it easy,' he complained. 'The old head spins a bit and I'm still a bit groggy on my pins. I can't go at that ding-bat you're setting.'

Ginger waited impatiently, and it was soon evident that Bertie had understated his condition. He struggled on, but he was obviously making heavy weather of it. To make matters worse the fire prevented a straight walk to the road and they had to make a wide 'dogs-leg' to get round the end of it. They then began to feel the effects of the smoke.

The end came when at last Bertie sank down. 'It's no use,

laddie, I can't make it,' he panted. 'Sorry, but I'm done. You'd better go on alone.'

Ginger realized that Bertie had made light of his injury. He was all in, and the violent exertion was doing him no good. On the cinema or television screen it is common to see a man who has been clubbed unconscious with the butt end of a revolver, or some other heavy weapon, rise to his feet within seconds, and resume fighting as if nothing had happened. In real life that does not happen. A man so wounded is usually a bed case in a hospital for at least twenty-four hours, often longer.

Ginger was in a quandary. Bertie was now being sick, and that, he knew, was an almost certain symptom of concussion of the brain. What could he do? He couldn't leave him there, for should he lose consciousness and the fire turn that way he would be burned to death. He would have to get him to a safe place even if he couldn't get him to the road—still a quarter of a mile away as near as he could judge. What he did was give him an arm to help him along.

This worked all right for some distance, with Bertie leaning more and more heavily on his shoulder; but then he fell and made no attempt to get up. Ginger knelt beside him but could get no response. He saw he had an unconscious man on his hands. He himself was leg-weary from dragging his feet through long heather.

He looked up in desperation. A car with its headlights on was going down the road at high speed. It didn't look very far away. He knew it couldn't be Biggles, whose car would be stationary, probably off the road showing no lights. No matter, if he couldn't find Biggles someone else might come along to give him a hand. He was afraid Biggles might have left the rendezvous to look at the fire.

Leaving Bertie as he lay he ran towards the road shouting: 'Help. Biggles. Help' at the top of his voice. He didn't care who heard him. He had only one thought and that was to get Bertie off the moor. The heather tripped him and he often stumbled. Once he fell, but he scrambled on, still shouting, regardless of an increasing pall of smoke as the breeze veered.

He had nearly reached the point of exhaustion when he heard an answering hail. Vague figures took shape in the smoke. He could no longer shout. His mouth was so dry that the sound that left his lips was more like a croak.

A man ran up and caught him by the arm.

It was Biggles. 'What the hell do you think you're doing?' he demanded angrily.

'Thank God you've come,' gasped Ginger.

'What's the trouble?'

'Bertie. He's unconscious—back there—in the heather.'

'How far?'

'Two hundred, three hundred yards.'

By this time more figures had closed in, some in police uniform. Ginger pointed. 'He's over there. You can't miss him.'

Biggles sent Algy with two police officers to bring him in. 'How did all this happen?' he said shortly. 'You were supposed to keep quiet. Where did you find Bertie?'

Breathlessly Ginger explained. 'In a pit, an old mine shaft or something of the sort. He was following Trethallan and Lewis to the moor, and in the dark he fell in. He saw them in the house together counting money. Lewis took his share with him in a case. Trethallan put his in a drawer which is opened by pulling on a dog's head carved in the panelling on the left of the fireplace. That's what Bertie told me.'

'Is he badly hurt?'

'I don't know. Not too badly I think. He was conscious when I found him. He struck his head on a rock when he fell.'

'How the devil did you find him?'

'I heard voices. The shepherd was with him in the pit. He had a ladder to get out. And a gun. After an argument he went off into the hole he came out of. Bertie thinks it's a bolt-hole from the mine we know.' Ginger paused for breath.

'Could you find this pit again?'

'Yes. That's where the fire started.'

'How did it start?'

Ginger explained how Bertie had lit the fire as a signal for help. 'That's how I was able to find him.'

Algy and the policemen came back carrying Bertie.

'Let's get to the cars,' Biggles said tersely. 'The sooner he's in hospital the better.'

As they hurried to where the cars had been left, speaking to the Inspector, Biggles went on: 'Does your driver know the way to the hospital?'

'Of course.'

'Then he can take him in. It only needs one man. He can come back here afterwards. If we have a gang to deal with, and I think we have, we shall need all the hands we can muster.'

Bertie, still unconscious, was lifted into the back of the police car and it departed on its ten-mile journey.

As the sound of its engine faded another became audible. It was the drone of an aircraft, still distant.

Biggles looked up at the sky for possible navigation lights, but failed to find any. 'That must be the plane coming now,' he rapped out. 'We've no time to lose.'

15

ENTER THE INTRUDER

STILL talking to the Inspector, Biggles went on: 'The first thing we have to do is settle who is going to take charge of this operation. If we both give orders we may get in a muddle. This is your territory. How do you feel about it? It's up to you.'

'You started, so you'd better carry on,' replied the Inspector, generously.

'If that's all right with you. All I want is that plane. You're welcome to Lewis and anyone else you can catch. Be careful. We know one of 'em has a gun. We'll go to what I believe is the landing ground but someone will have to cover that bolt-hole Bertie spoke about. Ginger, you're the only one who knows where it is. A constable had better go with you. Lie low and wait. Should the Inspector blow his whistle join us. You know where we'll be. You're sure you can find the place?'

'Can't miss it. That's where Bertie started the fire so it can only be at the far point of the burnt heather.'

'Right. Off you go. Hurry. Don't use your pistol unless you have to for self-defence.'

Ginger, and an officer detailed by the Inspector, moved off, walking quickly.

'Where do you think the gang will be?' asked the Inspector.

'Probably at the old mine, waiting for the plane to land. When they see things have gone wrong, they may go down the mine and try to get clear by using another exit. My man who was hurt believes there is one. But let's get into position,' Biggles concluded, starting off in a direct line for the landing strip. He was followed by the Inspector, Algy, and the one remaining constable.

'You'd better tell us exactly what you want us to do,' the Inspector said as they marched across the heather.

Biggles answered: 'We'll get as close as we can to the landing ground in long heather, then lie down and wait.'

'And as soon as the plane lands we rush it—is that the idea?'

'No. Not quite. We shall have to wait for Lewis to show himself when he joins the plane. I don't want anyone to move till I give the word. You make sure of Lewis. He's got a load of money on him and may fight to keep it. I'll take care of the plane and the pilot. You stay with me, Algy. There may be more than one man aboard, a navigator or crew.'

'What if it takes off again?' queried the Inspector.

'Once its wheels are on the ground I'll see it doesn't do that,' returned Biggles, cogently.

'How do you know where it will stop?'

'If I've got this worked out correctly it'll come in from the far end of the strip in order to finish its run as near as possible to the old mine workings. That's where the others should be waiting. When we move it'll have to be fast, because if I know anything about this sort of exercise the pilot won't stay on the ground longer than is absolutely necessary. He'll know that's where he's most vulnerable.'

The Inspector cocked an eye to the sky. 'I can't hear him.'

'He's probably cut his engine. We shall hear him when he gets lower. An aircraft can't glide without making a certain amount of noise. Look! The landing lights have been switched on. That's all the proof we need that the plane is coming here.'

The actual lights, two at each end of the strip, could not be seen. They had apparently been set to show directly upwards, with some sort of shield to prevent them from being seen by anyone on the road. It was on the far side that their reflections could be seen on the heather.

'Won't the pilot sheer off when he sees the moor on fire?' questioned the Inspector.

'That remains to be seen. No doubt he'll wonder what has happened, but unless he gets a warning signal I imagine he'll carry on. There may not have been enough time to cancel the trip, which must have been organized some time ago, before the pilot left his base. The decision about landing will be up to him. I imagine he'll take the landing lights being on as an okay signal to come in. The fire is some way off, and there's no smoke on this part of the moor to interfere with visibility. Talk quietly, now. We're getting close.'

Biggles, leading, stopped in an area of long heather as near the landing ground as he thought it advisable to go. 'This'll do,' he said. 'Everyone lie down and keep quiet.'

'I can't hear the plane,' whispered the Inspector.

'You will,' answered Biggles confidently. 'It's no use looking for lights. He won't be showing any.'

They waited for what seemed a long while, so long that Biggles began to get anxious.

'I'd say the pilot doesn't know what to make of the fire,' whispered Algy.

Biggles agreed. 'I suppose we must remember, too, that he had a lot of height to slip off.'

A little later Algy said softly: 'I can hear him. Here he comes.'

Faintly through the still night air came the whistling hum of a gliding aircraft. At the same time a small moving light, as of a hand torch held low, appeared near the old mine workings, less than a hundred yards away.

Biggles did not move.

Thereafter events happened quickly, one following on the other. The hum of the gliding plane became louder as it drew near. Then, suddenly, it was there; a small, single-engined high-wing monoplane, low over the far end of the runway. All that could be seen of it was, of course, its silhouette against the sky; but there was something about it that made Biggles stare.

'Great grief!' exclaimed Algy. 'It's fitted with floats. What the devil——'

'Must be an amphibian,' muttered Biggles.

'Looks like a modern improved version of the old German *Storch*.'

'Don't talk. Watch.'

The plane came on, losing speed and height. Its floats—or rather, the wheels that were in them—touched, and it ran on to a good three-point landing which the watching pilots could appreciate. It came slowly to a stop. A touch of throttle brought it round in its own length, facing the direction from which it had come, ready for take-off. There was no wind. A side door was opened and a man stepped down, leaving the engine ticking over with the smooth precision of a well-oiled sewing machine. This made it evident that the pilot did not intend to stay long. He stood still, looking towards the old mine. Was he alone, or was there someone else in the plane? was the question uppermost in Biggles' mind.

Meanwhile, other things were happening. The landing lights went out, their purpose having been served. Two men, one carrying a suitcase, walked quickly towards the plane.

'Let them get together,' Biggles told the Inspector. 'When we go, you take the two coming now. You can leave the pilot to us.'

The Inspector nodded.

The pair who had come from the mine reached the plane. There was a word or two of crisp conversation. Something changed hands.

'Now,' said Biggles, and jumping up ran towards the aircraft.

He did not suppose that a party of four men would not be seen, but half the intervening distance had been covered before a startled exclamation made it clear that that was what actually had happened.

Biggles broke into a sprint as the little group scattered. By the time he had reached the plane the pilot was half inside. He seized him by the legs and dragged him out, struggling. Algy went to Biggles' assistance and between them they got him on the ground, still kicking to get free. Algy knelt on him and showed him his gun saying: 'Keep still or you'll get hurt. The game's up.'

'Hold him,' ordered Biggles, and taking out his automatic rose to his feet. He fired two shots through the float into the nearside tyre. There was a hiss of escaping air and the machine settled down with a slight list. Satisfied that the aircraft wouldn't be able to get off with a flat tyre, he returned to Algy to find the pilot now on his feet. Apparently realizing what had happened he no longer struggled. He shrugged as if resigned, but said nothing.

Biggles got into the cockpit and switched off. Coming back he looked towards the mine to see how the others had fared. In dealing with the pilot he had not been able to see what had happened. The constable was coming towards them with a handcuffed prisoner, and carrying a suitcase.

'Where's the Inspector?' asked Biggles sharply.

'He's gone after the other man. We got Lewis but the other one got away.'

'Which way did he go?'

'Over there.' The constable pointed to the mine. 'He's gone after him.'

'Are those the Inspector's handcuffs or yours?'

'The Inspector's.'

'Have you got yours on you?'

'Yes.'

'Good. Handcuff these two prisoners together.'

This was done, Lewis cursing viciously. 'I told him there was something wrong,' he snarled.

'Told who? Trethallan?'

'Go to hell.'

Another constable ran up; the one who had taken Bertie to hospital. 'I heard shooting,' he said. 'Anyone hurt?'

'No,' Biggles told him. 'We're all right. I'll leave the two of you to take care of these prisoners while I go to see if the Inspector needs help.'

'We should be able to do that,' answered one of the policemen.

'Right. Come with me, Algy.' Biggles set off at a run towards the mine buildings, from where now came the frenzied barking of a dog. He had to dodge a small flock of panic-stricken sheep and made for the broken wall.

'Where are you, chief?' he called, reaching it.

'Here.' The Inspector appeared. 'I can't find him but he must be here somewhere,' he growled.

'He may have gone down the mine.'

'Do you feel like going down to see?'

'Not me, thank you.'

'Nor me.'

'Who was it—Trethallan?'

'I think so, by his figure. It was the damn smoke or I'd have caught him. Some came this way and got between us. That was the last I saw of him. From the row that blasted dog made I was sure he came in here. Lucky it's tied up.'

'Was no one else here?'

'Not a soul.'

From some little distance off came the crack of a pistol shot.

'I think I know what that means,' Biggles said. 'Someone's made a break through the bolt-hole; the old shaft that connects with this one.'

'Then let's get there.'

'Not to worry. If it's Trethallan, and he's got clear, I fancy I know where we shall find him.'

'Where?'

'At home.'

'Why should he go home after this?'

'Where else can he go? He's got a good reason for making for the Towers. His share of Lewis's money is there. He'll need it. But before we do anything about that you'd better get the prisoners to the station. We can't take them with us. Afterwards we can go on to the Towers.'

'Yes, we'll do that. How many prisoners are there?'

'Two. Lewis and the pilot of the plane. There's a suitcase there, too. I think we shall find Lewis's swag in it.'

'Good. Let's get along.'

They were leaving the ruins when Ginger came hurrying up with the officer who had gone with him. With them, handcuffed, was a prisoner. It was the shepherd—so-called.

'We got one of 'em,' announced Ginger. 'They got out of the pit with a ladder.'

'How many?'

'Two. We grabbed the first one over the top and while we were struggling with him the other climbed out and got away. He pulled a gun and had a crack at us.'

'Did you recognize him?'

'No. What with it being dark, and the smoke, it wasn't easy to see anything.'

'Did he look like Trethallan?'

'Could have been, but I wouldn't swear to it. It was impossible to see anything in the bottom of the pit.'

'Which way did he go?'

'That way.' Ginger pointed.

'That'd be the direction of the Towers,' said the Inspector. 'We'd better get along there as soon as we've cleared up here.'

The party made its way back to the plane, where the other two constables were waiting with their prisoners.

Biggles went to the pilot. 'Where did you start from?' he asked casually.

'I have nothing to say,' was the curt answer, in a pronounced foreign accent.

'Maybe you'll change your mind when you've had time to think about it,' returned Biggles. 'I'm a pilot myself, and my advice to you is, tell us all you know. It'll pay you in the long run.'

'I lost my way and had to make a forced landing.'

Biggles shook his head. 'You'll have to think of a better story than that.' He turned to Lewis. 'Do you know where you were going?'

Lewis spat. 'No. And I wouldn't tell you if I did, copper.'

'Well, you know where you're going now, anyway,' Biggles told him evenly. 'Come on, Inspector, let's get along.'

The entire party walked to the road where the cars were standing. On the way the Inspector asked Biggles what he was going to do about the plane.

'It can stay where it is for the moment,' decided Biggles. 'I'll have a closer look at it in the morning when I can see what I'm doing. It might be a good thing if you could detail a man to keep an eye on it just in case someone tries to destroy the evidence by setting fire to it.'

'I'll do that.'

On the road the Inspector took charge and made arrangements quickly. The three prisoners, handcuffed together, were put in the back of the police van with two policemen. The other constable was to drive.

'Aren't you going with them?' Biggles asked the Inspector.

'No need. The station sergeant can deal with them till I get back. We still have another man to pick up.'

'And, I suspect, the most important one. It took a man with a brain to organize an escape scheme of this size. Let's press on, or we might be too late.'

They all got into Biggles' car; that is, Algy, Ginger and the Inspector. Biggles took the wheel and headed up the road, destination Hallstone Towers.

16

EXIT THE MASTER-MIND

BIGGLES drove past the broken pillars that marked the entrance of the drive leading to Hallstone Towers, and brought the car to a stop in the lay-by already used on more than one occasion. There they all got out and advanced on foot.

'This could be a tricky business,' remarked Biggles to the Inspector as they walked on. 'It will depend on how Trethallan behaves when you tell him he's under arrest. Incidentally, what are you going to charge him with?'

'Aiding and abetting an escaped convict, of course. That'll do to go on with. We've got Lewis as a witness.'

'What if he denies it and Lewis supports him?'

'I've got you for a witness. You saw them together in the house. So did your man who was taken to hospital.'

'It should be enough, although it's only our word against his should he try to brazen it out. We shall see. First we've got to catch him. He may have bolted.'

Reaching the drive they walked on to the house without any attempt at concealment. To Biggles' relief, and somewhat to his surprise, the Bentley still stood outside the front door. Moreover, the light was on in the usual room on the ground floor, the curtains still not quite meeting in the middle.

'Looks as if he's still here,' he observed. 'I thought it likely, having a car, he would have pulled out.'

'We've got his registration, so that wouldn't have done him much good. He wouldn't have got far. He probably realized that.'

'Wait here a minute while I see if he's in the room, and if so, what he's doing.' Biggles walked quietly to the lighted window. He took a quick peep and returned.

'Well?' queried the Inspector.

'He's in there.'

'What's he doing?'

'Smoking a cigar and having a whisky and soda.'

'Ah! He probably needs a drink after what's happened.'

They walked on to the door. The Inspector tried it. 'Not even locked,' he whispered. 'He must be pretty sure of himself. We'll go in and come on him before he has time to do anything.' He opened the door.

There was a light in the hall: a small paraffin lamp on a side table. The Inspector, being the only one in uniform, took the lead. A corridor led in the direction of the lighted room, revealed by a narrow strip of light at floor level. He stopped when he came to it, turned the handle, pushed the door open and, closely followed by the others, walked in.

The man they sought was sitting relaxed in an armchair, smoking a cigar with a drink at his elbow. He did not wait to be challenged. Rising to his feet he exclaimed wrathfully: 'What the hell do you mean by walking into my house as if it belonged to you?'

'Are you Sir Humphrey Trethallan?' asked the Inspector calmly.

'Yes, I am. What do you want, barging in on me at this hour?'

The Inspector, in the best official manner, remained unruffled. 'I'd be obliged, sir, if you'd come with me to Bodmin.'

'What the devil for?'

'I thought you might help me by answering some questions.'

'To Bodmin! Now! Questions! What about? Can't you ask them here?'

'If you prefer it that way. I have reason to believe this house has harboured a convict named Lewis, recently escaped from Dartmoor prison.'

'Are you out of your mind, man?' cried Trethallan, with a well-affected show of incredulity and indignation.

The Inspector went on imperturbably. 'I also have reason to think you were with Lewis on Bodmin Moor tonight for the purpose of helping him to get out of the country.'

'Get him out of the country?' Trethallan's voice rose high with simulated astonishment. 'I don't know what you're talking about. I've never heard of this man Lewis, much less seen him. Why in God's name should I help a crook to get anywhere?'

Biggles stepped forward, speaking. 'I'm Air Detective-Inspector Bigglesworth of Scotland Yard. I suggest you helped Lewis because you were paid to do it. You arranged for an aircraft to pick him up on the moor. The plane, the pilot, and Lewis, are under arrest.'

Trethallan laughed and finished his drink. 'That's a good one. How did you dream it up?'

'It's no use, Sir Humphrey,' said Biggles. 'It's no dream and you know it. I've been watching things here for some time. I've seen you, with Lewis, here, in this room.'

'Indeed. How did you manage that?'

'You were a bit careless with your curtains.'

Intuitively Trethallan's eyes went to the window. 'Yes, that *was* careless,' he agreed. 'I was always going to get a new pair but somehow I never got round to it.'

The Inspector said: 'Come along, sir. We're wasting time.'

Trethallan's manner suddenly changed. 'All right. You say you saw Lewis here. How are you going to prove it?' he sneered, looking at Biggles.

'You were seen counting the notes that were the proceeds of the robbery for which he was sent to Dartmoor. I believe I'm right in saying you took him in your car to fetch it from where he'd hidden it.'

'Prove it.'

'That shouldn't be too difficult,' Biggles said.

In dead silence, in a few strides he crossed the room to the fireplace. Taking hold of the carved head on the panelling on the left-hand side he pulled on it. It came out, revealing a cavity. Reaching inside he took out a bundle of bank-notes, held together by a strip of paper such as is used by banks. He tossed it on the table. 'How do you account for this?' he asked quietly. 'This is part of the money Lewis paid you for helping him. The numbers of the stolen notes are known.'

Here, actually, Biggles was taking a chance, because in fact he did not know for certain that the numbers of the notes were known. There had been no time to find out, but it could soon be checked. Trethallan wouldn't know, either.

Anyway, Trethallan must have believed this, for he abandoned bluffing. 'For God's sake! You *have* been busy,' he scoffed.

'Come along, sir,' said the Inspector again, a trifle impatiently.

'I'm not going anywhere,' Trethallan muttered. Moving like a cat, before anyone could stop him he had opened a drawer in the table and snatched out a revolver. 'Now what are you going to do about it?' he grated, glaring at Biggles.

Biggles shook his head sadly. 'It's no use. That isn't going to help you.'

'We'll see about that.'

'Look behind you.'

Trethallan snatched a quick glance over his shoulder and saw Algy, gun in hand, covering him. When he looked back at Biggles, he, too, held a gun.

'Put that gun down, Sir Humphrey,' advised Biggles. 'You haven't a chance.'

For a second Trethallan hesitated. A gleam of sardonic humour came into his eyes. 'Got it all nicely tied up, haven't you?' he said mockingly. 'Well, no one shall ever say I didn't know when I was beaten, or that I was a bad loser.' Then, before anyone could guess what he was going to do he had put the muzzle of the revolver in his mouth and pulled the trigger.

There was a muffled report, and he crumpled like a suit of clothes falling from a hook. A pale wreath of blue powder smoke drifted up.

For a moment nobody moved. The Inspector's face was white. 'My God! Who'd have thought he'd do that?'

Biggles shrugged. 'He was that sort of man. He must have known the game was up, and he preferred this way to going to prison.'

The Inspector walked to the body and bent over it. 'No use calling a doctor,' he said grimly. 'He's blown the back of his head off.' He looked at Biggles with an extraordinary expression on his face. 'It was you producing those notes that did it. How the devil did you know they were there?'

'That can wait. I'll tell you later. There are more in the drawer. With what Lewis had with him it should be the lot. Let's get this messy business cleared up.'

'I'll get the body to the mortuary,' said the Inspector. 'Where's the telephone? There must be one in the house somewhere.'

Ginger answered. 'It's in the hall. I saw it as we came in.'

The Inspector went out. He was soon back. 'That's fixed,' he stated. 'An ambulance is on its way here. I'll take care of this. There's no need for you fellows to stay if you don't want to. I can ride home in the ambulance.'

'That suits me,' replied Biggles. 'In that case we'll get along.

I'll see you at the station in the morning. I'd like a word with that pilot if you don't mind. At the same time I can tell you the whole story.'

'That's all right with me. I shall be interested to know how you got on to this.' The Inspector picked up the fatal gun.

'I'd be careful with that,' Biggles said.

'Any particular reason?'

'There's a chance that it may turn out to be the gun that fired the bullet that killed your Constable Harley. The ballistics experts should be able to tell us. Harley was on the moor the night he was murdered. It was partly that which brought us here.'

At this juncture the door was opened and an elderly woman came in. Seeing the body on the floor she threw up her hands, screamed and rushed out again.

'I'll attend to her,' the Inspector said.

'Who is it—his wife?'

'No. He wasn't married. We saw her when we came to search the house. She said she was his housekeeper.'

Biggles nodded. 'Okay. I'll get along for a spot of blanket drill.'

'What's that?'

'Bed,' answered Biggles, succinctly. 'I've lost a lot of beauty sleep lately. Come on, chaps.'

Leaving the Inspector there they walked to the car and were soon on their way to Bodmin. They travelled for the most part in silence, but on the main road Algy asked a question. 'What makes a man like Trethallan, born with a silver spoon in his mouth so to speak, make a complete mess of his life and then end it himself?'

Biggles answered: 'There must have been a flaw somewhere in his make-up. It's likely that when he was a young man he had too much money. That tends to make a fellow think he's smarter than he is. That wise King Solomon knew something when he said: "Vanity, vanity, all is vanity." But who are we to criticize? We all suffer from it, more or less.' He drove on.

Reaching the hotel and having parked the car, as they went in

Biggles said: 'There's one little job you can do for me, Ginger, before we hit the hay. Ring the Air Commodore and tell him not to worry. The bird is roosting on Bodmin Moor. You'll find me in the bar having a snack and a drink.'

When, some minutes later, Ginger joined him he reported: 'No use. I couldn't get him. I spoke to Mrs Raymond. She said she didn't expect her husband back for some time.'

'No matter. There's no great hurry. It'll do in the morning. You and Algy can have a lie-in, if you like. You must be tired. I shall be along early to see how Bertie's getting on.'

The following morning he was first down. Going through to the breakfast room, to his utter astonishment he found Air Commodore Raymond there, sipping coffee.

'Hello, sir. What are you doing here?' he asked, sitting next to him.

'I found I was able to get away, so I ran down, travelling overnight, to see how you were getting on. We shall soon have to do something.'

'There's nothing more to be done but the tidying up,' Biggles said. 'We rang you up last night to tell you that Trethallan had shot himself and the intruder was under arrest; but you weren't in.'

'Good heavens! I was on my way here. What happened?'

Over breakfast Biggles narrated the events of the previous night. 'How many crooks Trethallan has managed to get out of the country we may never know; but at the finish it was a case of once too often.'

'Why did he do it?'

'Money. What else? I imagine he was interested only in crooks who had a pile of swag tucked away. The underworld must have known about it. Lewis knew where to make for as soon as he broke gaol. He was carrying a load of notes when we picked him up. The police have the lot.'

'What are you going to do now?'

'First I'm going to the hospital to see Bertie. He took a nasty crack on the skull. Afterwards I shall go along to the police

station. I told the Inspector I'd be along early to help him get
things sorted out. After that I shall go to the moor to have a closer
look at the plane. I couldn't see much of it in the dark.'

'What make is it?'

'I don't know. Foreign job. Continental dashboard.'

'We shall have to find out where it was based.'

'Unless we can get the pilot to talk that will be difficult. It's a
marine aircraft—or rather, amphibious. Wheels through floats.
I haven't seen one of those for years. Thinking it over last night it
struck me that the machine may not be shore-based.'

'How do you mean?'

'It could have come from a ship. Kept below deck and put up
on the water by a crane when required, as they used to do in the
Navy before there were aircraft carriers.'

The Air Commodore thought for a moment. 'I think the best
thing would be to ask the Research Establishment to collect it.
They should be able to work out where it was built.'

'That suits me.' Biggles got up. 'Now, if you don't mind, sir,
I'll slip along and see Bertie.'

'I'll come with you,' said the Air Commodore.

There is not much more to be told. To inquiries at the hospital
they were given the usual answer: 'As well as could be expected.'
Bertie was sleeping comfortably and it would be better not to
disturb him.

They went on to the police station to learn that Lewis was
already on his way back to Dartmoor. Thoroughly disgruntled
he had refused to say anything. When told that Trethallan had
shot himself he had merely said: 'Serves the fool right. If he
hadn't made a mucker of it I wouldn't be here.'

The pilot of the aircraft was equally unco-operative. He sat in
his cell in sullen silence. Biggles told him it might be to his
advantage to talk; but he refused to open his mouth. He declined
to give his name and nationality. He carried no passport or any
other means of identification. All he had in his pocket was the
remains of a packet of American cigarettes, which can, of course,
be bought anywhere.

'He may talk when he's had more time to think things over,

and sees where he's landed himself,' said the Air Commodore after they had left the cell.

Biggles told the full story of his investigations to the Inspector. The Air Commodore, who did not know the details, listened with absorbed attention.

'What about this old mine?' asked the Inspector. 'Don't you want to go down it?'

'No, thank you,' replied Biggles. 'I'm nothing for mines, old or new. I'll leave that to you.'

It may as well be said here that nothing unexpected was found in the mine. From the remains of some food it had apparently been used simply as a place to wait for the plane. Short-wave radio equipment told its own story. As suspected, the aerial, which was in the old chimney stack, could be raised or lowered as occasion required. The passage used as an escape route was in fact an old ventilation shaft.

Biggles and his chief went on to the plane, still standing where it had been left in charge of a constable. They learned little from it. In view of what the Air Commodore had suggested about its disposal, they did not spend much time on it. 'We'll get a full report on it in due course from the Research people,' he said. 'Now I must be getting back to town. The Air Minister will be delighted to know there won't be any more night intrusions— not with this machine, anyway. Are you coming back with me?'

'If you don't mind, sir, I'll hang on here for a few days till Bertie's on his feet; then we can all come back together.'

'Do that,' agreed the Air Commodore. 'Which reminds me. Where are the rest of your party?'

'I told them they needn't hurry about getting up,' explained Biggles. 'We've put in quite a lot of overtime since we arrived in Cornwall.'

Thus ended the affair of the mysterious intruder, the plane that came by night to worry more than one Government department; although, to be sure, its purpose, while serious, proved to be less sinister than had been feared. Its arrest not only ended its criminal career, but, as Biggles had suspected from the outset, solved the mystery of the murdered constable: for the ballistic experts were able to prove that the bullet which had killed the policeman had been fired from the revolver that had at the finish ended the life of its owner. Just how that had come about could only be conjectured, for the man who had fired the fatal shot was beyond the reach of justice.